The Witches Trilogy

The Witches Trilogy

EQUAL RITES
WYRD SISTERS
WITCHES ABROAD

Terry Pratchett

VICTOR GOLLANCZ

LONDON

Equal Rites and *Wyrd Sisters* first published in 1987 and
1988 respectively by Victor Gollancz Ltd. in association with
Colin Smythe. *Witches Abroad* first published 1991 by
Victor Gollancz Ltd.

First published as one volume in Great Britain 1994
This edition published 1995
by Victor Gollancz Ltd.
An Imprint of Orion Books Ltd.
Orion House, 5 Upper St Martin's Lane, London WC2H 9EA

Reprinted 1999, 2000

A catalogue record for this book is available
from the British Library

ISBN 0 575 05896 X

Typeset in Great Britain
at The Spartan Press Ltd, Lymington, Hants
Printed in Finland by WS Bookwell

CONTENTS

EQUAL
RITES

Thanks to Neil Gaiman, who loaned
us the last surviving copy of the *Liber
Paginarum Fulvarum*, and a big hallo to all the
kids at the H. P. Lovecraft Holiday Fun Club.

I would like it to be clearly understood that this book is
not wacky. Only dumb redheads in Fifties' sitcoms
are wacky

No, it's not zany, either.

This is a story about magic and where it goes and perhaps more importantly where it comes from and why, although it doesn't pretend to answer all or any of these questions.

It may, however, help to explain why Gandalf never got married and why Merlin was a man. Because this is also a story about sex, although probably not in the athletic, tumbling, count-the-legs-and-divide-by-two sense unless the characters get totally beyond the author's control. They might.

However, it is primarily a story about a world. Here it comes now. Watch closely, the special effects are quite expensive.

A bass note sounds. It is a deep, vibrating chord that hints that the brass section may break in at any moment with a fanfare for the cosmos, because the scene is the blackness of deep space with a few stars glittering like the dandruff on the shoulders of God.

Then it comes into view overhead, bigger than the biggest, most unpleasantly-armed starcruiser in the imagination of a three-ring film-maker: a turtle, ten thousand miles long. It is Great A'Tuin, one of the rare astrochelonians from a universe where things are less as they are and more like people imagine them to be, and it carries on its meteor-pocked shell four giant elephants who bear on their enormous shoulders the great round wheel of the Discworld.

As the viewpoint swings around, the whole of the world can be seen by the light of its tiny orbiting sun. There are continents, archipelagos, seas, deserts, mountain ranges and even a tiny central ice cap. The inhabitants of this place, it is obvious, won't have any truck with global theories. Their world, bounded by an encircling ocean that falls forever into space in one long waterfall, is as round and flat as a geological pizza, although without the anchovies.

A world like that, which exists only because the gods enjoy a joke, must be a place where magic can survive. And sex too, of course.

☆   ☆   ☆

He came walking through the thunderstorm and you could tell he was a wizard, partly because of the long cloak and carven staff but mainly because the raindrops were stopping several feet from his head, and steaming.

It was good thunderstorm country, up here in the Ramtop Mountains, a country of jagged peaks, dense forests and little river valleys so deep the daylight had no sooner reached the bottom than it was time to leave again. Ragged wisps of cloud clung to the lesser peaks below the mountain trail along which the wizard slithered and slid. A few slot-eyed goats watched him with mild interest. It doesn't take a lot to interest goats.

Sometimes he would stop and throw his heavy staff into the air. It always came down pointing the same way and the wizard would sigh, pick it up, and continue his squelchy progress.

The storm walked around the hills on legs of lightning, shouting and grumbling.

The wizard disappeared around the bend in the track and the goats went back to their damp grazing.

Until something else caused them to look up. They stiffened, their eyes widening, their nostrils flaring.

This was strange, because there was nothing on the path. But the goats still watched it pass by until it was out of sight.

There was a village tucked in a narrow valley between steep woods. It wasn't a large village, and wouldn't have shown up on a map of the mountains. It barely showed up on a map of the village.

It was, in fact, one of those places that exist merely so that people can have come from them. The universe is littered with them: hidden villages, windswept little towns under wide skies, isolated cabins on chilly mountains, whose only mark on history is to be the incredibly ordinary place where something extraordinary started to happen. Often there is no more than a little plaque to reveal that, against all gynaecological probability, someone very famous was born halfway up a wall.

Mist curled between the houses as the wizard crossed a narrow bridge over the swollen stream and made his way to the village smithy, although the two facts had nothing to do with one another. The mist would have curled anyway: it was experienced mist and had got curling down to a fine art.

The smithy was fairly crowded, of course. A smithy is one place where you can depend on finding a good fire and someone to talk to. Several villagers were lounging in the warm shadows but, as the wizard approached, they sat up expectantly and tried to look intelligent, generally with indifferent success.

The smith didn't feel the need to be quite so subservient. He nodded at the wizard, but it was a greeting between equals, or at least between equals as far as the smith was concerned. After all, any halfway competent blacksmith has more than a nodding acquaintance with magic, or at least likes to think he has.

The wizard bowed. A white cat that had been sleeping by the furnace woke up and watched him carefully.

'What is the name of this place, sir?' said the wizard.

The blacksmith shrugged.

'Bad Ass,' he said.

'Bad – ?'

'Ass,' repeated the blacksmith, his tone defying anyone to make something of it.

The wizard considered this.

'A name with a story behind it,' he said at last, 'which were circumstances otherwise I would be pleased to hear. But I would like to speak to you, smith, about your son.'

'Which one?' said the smith, and the hangers-on sniggered. The wizard smiled.

'You have seven sons, do you not? And you yourself were an eighth son?'

The smith's face stiffened. He turned to the other villagers.

'All right, the rain's stopping,' he said. 'Piss off, the lot of you. Me and– ' he looked at the wizard with raised eyebrows.

'Drum Billet,' said the wizard.

'Me and Mr Billet have things to talk about.' He waved his hammer vaguely and, one after another, craning over their shoulders in case the wizard did anything interesting, the audience departed.

The smith drew a couple of stools from under a bench. He took a bottle out of a cupboard by the water tank and poured a couple of very small glasses of clear liquid.

The two men sat and watched the rain and the mist rolling over the bridge. Then the smith said: 'I know what son you mean. Old Granny is up with my wife now. Eighth son of an eighth son, of course. It did cross my mind but I never gave it much thought, to be honest. Well, well. A wizard in the family, eh?'

'You catch on very quickly,' said Billet. The white cat jumped down from its perch, sauntered across the floor and vaulted into the wizard's lap, where it curled up. His thin fingers stroked it absent-mindedly.

'Well, well,' said the smith again. 'A wizard in Bad Ass, eh?'

'Possibly, possibly,' said Billet. 'Of course, he'll have to go to university first. He may do very well, of course.'

The smith considered the idea from all angles, and decided he liked it a lot. A thought struck him.

'Hang on,' he said. 'I'm trying to remember what my father told me. A wizard who knows he's going to die can sort of pass on his sort of wizardness to a sort of successor, right?'

'I have never heard it put so succinctly, yes,' said the wizard.

'So you're going to sort of die?'

'Oh yes.' The cat purred as the fingers tickled it behind the ear.

The smith looked embarrassed. 'When?'

The wizard thought for a moment. 'In about six minutes' time.'

'Oh.'

'Don't worry,' said the wizard. 'I'm quite looking forward to it, to tell you the truth. I've heard it's quite painless.'

The blacksmith considered this. 'Who told you?' he said at last.

The wizard pretended not to hear him. He was watching the bridge, looking for tell-tale turbulence in the mist.

'Look,' said the smith. 'You'd better tell me how we go about bringing up a wizard, you see, because there isn't a wizard in these parts and– '

'It will all sort itself out,' said Billet pleasantly. 'The magic has guided me to you and the magic will take care of everything. It usually does. Did I hear a cry?'

The blacksmith looked at the ceiling. Above the splash of the rain he could make out the sound of a pair of new lungs at full bore.

The wizard smiled. 'Have him brought down here,' he said.

The cat sat up and looked interestedly at the forge's wide doorway. As the smith called excitedly up the stairs it jumped down and padded slowly across the floor, purring like a bandsaw.

A tall white-haired woman appeared at the bottom of the stairs, clutching a bundle in a blanket. The smith hurried her over to where the wizard sat.

'But– ' she began.

'This is very important,' said the smith importantly. 'What do we do now, sir?'

The wizard held up his staff. It was man-high and nearly as thick as his wrist, and covered with carvings that seemed to change as the smith looked at them, exactly as if they didn't want him to see what they were.

'The child must hold it,' said Drum Billet. The smith nodded, and fumbled in the blanket until he located a tiny pink hand. He guided it gently to the wood. It gripped it tightly.

'But– ' said the midwife.

'It's all right, Granny, I know what I'm about. She's a witch, sir, don't mind her. Right,' said the smith. 'Now what?'

The wizard was silent.

'What do we do n– ' the smith began, and stopped. He leaned down to look at the old wizard's face. Billet was smiling, but it was anyone's guess what the joke was.

The smith pushed the baby back into the arms of the frantic midwife. Then, as respectfully as possible, he unpried the thin, pale fingers from the staff.

It had a strange, greasy feel, like static electricity. The wood itself was almost black, but the carvings were slightly lighter, and hurt the eyes if you tried to make out precisely what they were supposed to be.

'Are you pleased with yourself?' said the midwife.

'Eh? Oh. Yes. As a matter of fact, yes. Why?'

She twitched aside a fold of the blanket. The smith looked down, and swallowed.

'No,' he whispered. 'He said– '

'And what would *he* know about it?' sneered Granny.

'But he said it would be a son!'

'Doesn't look like a son to me, laddie.'

The smith flopped down on his stool, his head in his hands.

'What have I done?' he moaned.

'You've given the world its first female wizard,' said the midwife. 'Whosa itsywitsy, den?'

'What?'

'I was talking to the *baby*.'

The white cat purred and arched its back as if it was rubbing up against the legs of an old friend. Which was odd, because there was no one there.

'I was foolish,' said a voice in tones no mortal could hear. 'I assumed the magic would know what it was doing.'

PERHAPS IT DOES.

'If only I could do something . . . '

THERE IS NO GOING BACK. THERE IS NO GOING BACK, said the deep, heavy voice like the closing of crypt doors.

The wisp of nothingness that was Drum Billet thought for a while.

'But she's going to have a lot of problems.'

THAT'S WHAT LIFE IS ALL ABOUT. SO I'M TOLD. I WOULDN'T KNOW, OF COURSE.

'What about reincarnation?'

Death hesitated.

YOU WOULDN'T LIKE IT, he said. TAKE IT FROM ME.

'I've heard that some people do it all the time.'

You've got to be trained to it. You've got to start off small and work up. You've no idea how horrible it is to be an ant.

'It's bad?'

You wouldn't believe it. And with your karma an ant is too much to expect.

The baby had been taken back to its mother and the smith sat disconsolately watching the rain.

Drum Billet scratched the cat behind its ears and thought about his life. It had been a long one, that was one of the advantages of being a wizard, and he'd done a lot of things he hadn't always felt good about. It was about time that . . .

I haven't got all day, you know, said Death, reproachfully.

The wizard looked down at the cat and realised for the first time how odd it looked now.

The living often don't appreciate how complicated the world looks when you are dead, because while death frees the mind from the straitjacket of three dimensions it also cuts it away from Time, which is only another dimension. So while the cat that rubbed up against his invisible legs was undoubtedly the same cat that he had seen a few minutes before, it was also quite clearly a tiny kitten and a fat, half-blind old moggy and every stage in between. All at once. Since it had started off small it looked like a white, cat-shaped carrot, a description that will have to do until people invent proper four-dimensional adjectives.

Death's skeletal hand tapped Billet gently on the shoulder.

Come away, my son.

'There's nothing I can do?'

Life is for the living. Anyway, you've given her your staff.

'Yes. There is that.'

The midwife's name was Granny Weatherwax. She was a witch. That was quite acceptable in the Ramtops, and no one had a bad word to say about witches. At least, not if he wanted to wake up in the morning the same shape as he went to bed.

The smith was still staring gloomily at the rain when she came back down the stairs and clapped a warty hand on his shoulder.

He looked up at her.

'What shall I do, Granny?' he said, unable to keep the pleading out of his voice.

'What have you done with the wizard?'

'I put him out in the fuel store. Was that right?'

'It'll do for now,' she said briskly. 'And now you must burn the staff.'

They both turned to stare at the heavy staff, which the smith had propped in the forge's darkest corner. It almost appeared to be looking back at them.

'But it's magical,' he whispered.

'Well?'

'Will it burn?'

'Never knew wood that didn't.'

'It doesn't seem right!'

Granny Weatherwax swung shut the big doors and turned to him angrily.

'Now you listen to me, Gordo Smith!' she said. 'Female wizards aren't right either! It's the wrong kind of magic for women, is wizard magic, it's all books and stars and jommetry. She'd never grasp it. Whoever heard of a female wizard?'

'There's witches,' said the smith uncertainly. 'And enchantresses too, I've heard.'

'Witches is a different thing altogether,' snapped Granny Weatherwax. 'It's magic out of the ground, not out of the sky, and men never could get the hang of it. As for enchantresses,' she added. 'They're no better than they should be. You take it from me, just burn the staff, bury the body and don't let on it ever happened.'

Smith nodded reluctantly, crossed over to the forge, and pumped the bellows until the sparks flew. He went back for the staff.

It wouldn't move.

'It won't move!'

Sweat stood out of his brow as he tugged at the wood. It remained uncooperatively immobile.

'Here, let me try,' said Granny, and reached past him. There was a snap and a smell of scorched tin.

Smith ran across the forge, whimpering slightly, to where Granny had landed upside down against the opposite wall.

'Are you all right?'

She opened two eyes like angry diamonds and said, 'I see. That's the way of it, is it?'

'The way of what?' said Smith, totally bewildered.

'Help me up, you fool. And fetch me a chopper.'

The tone of her voice suggested that it would be a very good idea not to disobey. Smith rummaged desperately among the junk at the back of the forge until he found an old double-headed axe.

'Right. Now take off your apron.'

'Why? What do you intend to do?' said the smith, who was beginning to lose his grip on events. Granny gave an exasperated sigh.

'It's leather, you idiot. I'm going to wrap it around the handle. It'll not catch me the same way twice!'

Smith struggled out of the heavy leather apron and handed it to her very gingerly. She wrapped it around the axe and made one or two passes in the air. Then, a spiderlike figure in the glow of the nearly incandescent furnace, she stalked across the room and with a grunt of triumph and effort brought the heavy blade sweeping down right in the centre of the staff.

There was a click. There was a noise like a partridge. There was a thud. There was silence.

Smith reached up very slowly, without moving his head, and touched the axe blade. It wasn't on the axe any more. It had buried itself in the door by his head, taking a tiny nick out of his ear.

Granny stood looking slightly blurred from hitting an absolutely immovable object, and stared at the stub of wood in her hands.

'Rrrrightttt,' she stuttered. 'Iiiinnn tthhatttt cccasseee–'

'No,' said Smith firmly, rubbing his ear. 'Whatever it is you're going to suggest, no. Leave it. I'll pile some stuff around it. No one'll notice. Leave it. It's just a stick.'

'*Just a stick?*'

'Have you got any better ideas? Ones that won't take my head off?'

She glared at the staff, which appeared not to notice.

'Not right now,' she admitted. 'But you just give me time–'

'All right, all right. Anyway, I've got things to do, wizards to bury, you know how it is.'

Smith took a spade from beside the back door and hesitated.

'Granny.'

'What?'

'Do you know how wizards like to be buried?'

'Yes!'

'Well, how?'

Granny Weatherwax paused at the bottom of the stairs.

'Reluctantly.'

Later, night fell gently as the last of the world's slow light flowed out of the valley, and a pale, rain-washed moon shone down in a night studded with stars. And in a shadowy orchard behind the forge there was the occasional clink of a spade or a muffled curse.

In the cradle upstairs the world's first female wizard dreamed of nothing much.

The white cat lay half-asleep on its private ledge near the furnace. The only sound in the warm dark forge was the crackle of the coals as they settled down under the ash.

The staff stood in the corner, where it wanted to be, wrapped in shadows that were slightly blacker than shadows normally are.

Time passed, which, basically, is its job.

There was a faint tinkle, and a swish of air. After a while the cat sat up and watched with interest.

Dawn came. Up here in the Ramtops dawn was always impressive, especially when a storm had cleared the air. The valley occupied by Bad Ass overlooked a panorama of lesser mountains and foothills, coloured purple and orange in the early morning light that flowed gently over them (because light travels at a dilatory pace in the Disc's vast magical field) and far off the great plains were still a puddle of shadows. Even further off the sea gave an occasional distant sparkle.

In fact, from here you could see right to the edge of the world.

That wasn't poetic imagery but plain fact, since the world was quite definitely flat and was, furthermore, known to be carried through space on the backs of four elephants that in turn stood on the shell of Great A'Tuin, the Great Sky Turtle.

Back down there in Bad Ass the village is waking up. The smith has just gone into the forge and found it tidier than it has been for the last hundred years, with all the tools back in their right places, the floor swept and a new fire laid in the furnace. He is sitting on the anvil, which has been moved right across the room, and is watching the staff and is trying to think.

Nothing much happened for seven years, except that one of the apple trees in the smithy orchard grew perceptibly taller than the others and was frequently climbed by a small girl with brown hair, a gap in her front teeth, and the sort of features that promised to become, if not beautiful, then at least attractively interesting.

She was named Eskarina, for no particular reason other than that her mother liked the sound of the word, and although Granny Weatherwax kept a careful watch on her she failed to spot any signs of magic whatsoever. It was true that the girl spent more time climbing trees and running around shouting than little girls normally did, but a girl with four older brothers still at home can be excused a lot of things. In fact, the witch began to relax and started to think the magic had not taken hold after all.

But magic has a habit of lying low, like a rake in the grass.

☆ ☆ ☆

Winter came round again, and it was a bad one. The clouds hung around the Ramtops like big fat sheep, filling the gulleys with snow and turning the forests into silent, gloomy caverns. The high passes were closed and the caravans wouldn't come again until spring. Bad Ass became a little island of heat and light.

Over breakfast Esk's mother said: 'I'm worried about Granny Weatherwax. She hasn't been around lately.'

Smith looked at her over his porridge spoon.

'I'm not complaining,' he said. 'She– '

'She's got a long nose,' said Esk.

Her parents glared at her.

'There's no call to make that kind of remark,' said her mother sternly.

'But father said she's always poking her– '

'Eskarina!'

'But he said– '

'I said– '

'Yes, but, he *did* say that she had– '

Smith reached down and slapped her. It wasn't very hard, and he regretted it instantly. The boys got the flat of his hand and occasionally the length of his belt whenever they deserved it. The trouble with his daughter, though, was not ordinary naughtiness but the infuriating way she had of relentlessly pursuing the thread of an argument long after she should have put it down. It always flustered him.

She burst into tears. Smith stood up, angry and embarrassed at himself, and stumped off to the forge.

There was a loud crack, and a thud.

They found him out cold on the floor. Afterwards *he* always maintained that he'd hit his head on the doorway. Which was odd, because he wasn't very tall and there had always been plenty of room before, but he was certain that whatever happened had nothing to do with the blur of movement from the forge's darkest corner.

Somehow the events set the seal on the day. It became a broken-crockery day, a day of people getting under each other's feet and being peevish. Esk's mother dropped a jug that had belonged to her grandmother and a whole box of apples in the loft turned out to be mouldy. In the forge the furnace went sullen and refused to draw. Jaims, the oldest son, slipped on the packed ice in the road and hurt his arm. The white cat, or possibly one of its descendants, since the cats led a private and complicated life of their own in the hayloft next to the forge, went and climbed up the chimney in the scullery and refused to come down. Even the sky pressed in like an old mattress, and the air felt stuffy, despite the snow.

Frayed nerves and boredom and bad temper made the air hum like thunderstorm weather.

'Right! That's it. That's just about enough!' shouted Esk's mother. 'Cern, you and Gulta and Esk can go and see how Granny is and– Where's Esk?'

The two youngest boys looked up from where they were half-heartedly fighting under the table.

'She went out to the orchard,' said Gulta. 'Again.'

'Go and fetch her in, then, and be off.'

'But it's cold!'

'It's going to snow again!'

'It's only a mile and the road is clear enough and who was so keen to be out in it when we had the first snowfall? Go on with you, and don't come back till you're in a better temper.'

They found Esk sitting in a fork of the big apple tree. The boys didn't like the tree much. For one thing, it was so covered in mistletoe that it looked green even in midwinter, its fruit was small and went from stomach-twisting sourness to wasp-filled rottenness overnight, and although it looked easy enough to climb it had a habit of breaking twigs and dislodging feet at inconvenient moments. Cern once swore that a branch had twisted just to spill him off. But it tolerated Esk, who used to go and sit in it if she was annoyed or fed up or just wanted to be by herself, and the boys sensed that every brother's right to gently torture his sister ended at the foot of its trunk. So they threw a snowball at her. It missed.

'We're going to see old Weatherwax.'

'But you don't have to come.'

'Because you'll just slow us down and probably cry anyway.'

Esk looked down at them solemnly. She didn't cry a lot, it never seemed to achieve much.

'If you don't want me to come then I'll come,' she said. This sort of thing passes for logic among siblings.

'Oh, we want you to come,' said Gulta quickly.

'Very pleased to hear it,' said Esk, dropping on to the packed snow.

They had a basket containing smoked sausages, preserved eggs and – because their mother was prudent as well as generous – a large jar of peach preserve that no one in the family liked very much. She still made it every year when the little wild peaches were ripe, anyway.

The people of Bad Ass had learned to live with the long winter snows and the roads out of the village were lined with boards to reduce drifting and, more important, stop travellers from straying. If they lived locally it wouldn't matter too much if they did, because an unsung genius on the village council several generations previously had come up with the idea of carving markers in every tenth tree in the forest around the village, out to a distance of nearly two miles. It had taken ages, and re-cutting markers was always a job for any man with spare time, but in winters where a blizzard could lose a man within yards of his home many a life had been saved by the pattern of notches found by probing fingers under the clinging snow.

It was snowing again when they left the road and started up the track where, in summer, the witch's house nestled in a riot of raspberry thickets and weird witch-growth.

'No footprints,' said Cern.

'Except for foxes,' said Gulta. 'They say she can turn herself into a fox. Or anything. A bird, even. Anything. That's how she always knows what's going on.'

They looked around cautiously. A scruffy crow was indeed watching them from a distant tree stump.

'They say there's a whole family over Crack Peak way that can turn themselves into wolves,' said Gulta, who wasn't one to leave a promising subject, 'because one night someone shot a wolf and next day their auntie was limping with an arrow wound in her leg, and . . . '

'I don't think people can turn themselves into animals,' said Esk, slowly.

'Oh yes, Miss Clever?'

'Granny is quite big. If she turned herself into a fox what would happen to all the bits that wouldn't fit?'

'She'd just magic them away,' said Cern.

'I don't think magic works like that,' said Esk. 'You can't just make things happen, there's a sort of – like a seesaw thing, if you push one end down, the other end goes up . . . ' Her voice trailed off.

They gave her a look.

'I can't see Granny on a seesaw,' said Gulta. Cern giggled.

'No, I mean every time something happens, something else has to happen too – I think,' said Esk uncertainly, picking her way around a deeper than usual snowdrift. 'Only in the . . . opposite direction.'

'That's silly,' said Gulta, 'because, look, you remember when that fair came last summer and there was a wizard with it and he made all those birds and things appear out of nothing? I mean it just happened, he just said these words and waved his hands, and it just happened. There weren't any seesaws.'

'There was a swing,' said Cern. 'And a thing where you had to throw things at things to win things.'

'And you didn't hit anything, Gul.'

'Nor did you, you said the things were stuck to the things so you couldn't knock them off, you said . . . '

Their conversation wandered away like a couple of puppies. Esk listened with half an ear. I know what I mean, she told herself. Magic's easy, you just find the place where everything is balanced and push. Anyone could do it. There's nothing magical about it. All the funny words and waving the hands is just . . . it's only for . . .

She stopped, surprised at herself. She knew what she meant. The idea was right up there in the front of her mind. But she didn't know how to say it in words, even to herself.

It was a horrible feeling to find things in your head and not know how they fitted. It . . .

'Come on, we'll be all day.'

She shook her head and hurried after her brothers.

The witch's cottage consisted of so many extensions and lean-tos that it was difficult to see what the original building had looked like, or even if there had ever been one. In the summer it was surrounded by dense beds of what Granny loosely called 'the Herbs' – strange plants, hairy or squat or twining, with curious flowers or vivid fruits or unpleasantly bulging pods. Only Granny knew what they were all for, and any wood-pigeon hungry enough to attack them generally emerged giggling to itself and bumping into things (or, sometimes, never emerged at all).

Now everything was deep under the snow. A forlorn windsock flapped against its pole. Granny didn't hold with flying but some of her friends still used broomsticks.

'It looks deserted,' said Cern.

'No smoke,' said Gulta.

The windows look like eyes, thought Esk, but kept it to herself.

'It's only Granny's house,' she said. 'There's nothing wrong.'

The cottage radiated emptiness. They could feel it. The windows *did* look like eyes, black and menacing against the snow. And no one in the Ramtops let their fire go out in the winter, as a matter of pride.

Esk wanted to say 'Let's go home,' but she knew that if she did the boys would run for it. Instead she said, 'Mother says there's a key on a nail in the privy,' and that was nearly as bad. Even an ordinary unknown privy held minor terrors like wasps' nests, large spiders, mysterious rustling things in the roof and, one very bad winter, a small hibernating bear that caused acute constipation in the family until it was persuaded to bed down in the haybarn. A witch's privy could contain *anything*.

'I'll go and look, shall I?' she added.

'If you like,' said Gulta airily, almost successfully concealing his relief.

In fact, when she managed to get the door open against the piled snow, it was neat and clean and contained nothing more sinister than an old almanack, or more precisely about half an old almanack, carefully hung on a nail. Granny had a philosophical objection to reading, but she'd be the last to say that books, especially books with nice thin pages, didn't have their uses.

The key shared a ledge by the door with a chrysalis and the stump of a candle. Esk took it gingerly, trying not to disturb the chrysalis, and hurried back to the boys.

It was no use trying the front door. Front doors in Bad Ass were used only by brides and corpses, and Granny had always avoided becoming either. Around the back the snow was piled in front of the door and no one had broken the ice on the water butt.

The light was starting to pour out of the sky by the time they dug through to the door and managed to persuade the key to turn.

Inside, the big kitchen was dark and chilly and smelled only of snow. It was *always* dark, but they were used to seeing a big fire in the wide chimney and smelling the thick fumes of whatever it was she was boiling up this time, which sometimes gave you a headache or made you see things.

They wandered around uncertainly, calling, until Esk decided they couldn't put off going upstairs any longer. The clonk of the thumb-latch on the door to the cramped staircase sounded a lot louder than it ought to .

Granny was on the bed, with her arms tightly folded across her chest. The tiny window had blown open. Fine snow had blown in across the floor and over the bed.

Esk stared at the patchwork quilt under the old woman, because there were times when a little detail could expand and fill the whole world. She barely heard Cern start to cry: she remembered her father, strangely enough, making the quilt two winters before when the snow was almost as bad and there wasn't much to do in the forge, and how he'd used all kinds of rags that had found their way to Bad Ass from every part of the world, like silk, dilemma leather, water cotton and tharga wool and, of course, since he wasn't much good at sewing either, the result was a rather strange lumpy thing more like a flat tortoise than a quilt, and her mother had generously decided to give it to Granny last Hogswatchnight, and . . .

'Is she dead?' asked Gulta, as if Esk was an expert in these things.

Esk stared up at Granny Weatherwax. The old woman's face looked thin and grey. Was that how dead people looked? Shouldn't her chest be going up and down?

Gulta pulled himself together.

'We ought to go and get someone and we ought to go now because it will get dark in a minute,' he said flatly. 'But Cern will stay here.'

His brother looked at him in horror.

'What for?' he said.

'Someone has got to stay with dead people,' said Gulta. 'Remember when Old Uncle Derghart died and Father had to go and sit up with all the candles and things all night? Otherwise something nasty comes and takes your soul off to . . . to somewhere,' he ended lamely. 'And then people come back and haunt you.'

Cern opened his mouth to start to cry again. Esk said hurriedly, 'I'll stay. I don't mind. It's only Granny.'

Gulta looked at her in relief.

'Light some candles or something,' he said. 'I think that's what you're supposed to do. And then– '

There was a scratching from the windowsill. A crow had landed, and stood there blinking suspiciously at them. Gulta shouted and threw his hat at it. It flew off with a reproachful caw and he shut the window.

'I've seen it around here before,' he said. 'I think Granny feeds it. Fed it,' he corrected himself. 'Anyway, we'll be back with people, we'll be hardly any time. Come on, Ce.'

They clattered down the dark stairs. Esk saw them out of the house and bolted the door behind them.

The sun was a red ball above the mountains, and there were already a few early stars out.

She wandered around the dark kitchen until she found a scrap of dip candle and a tinderbox. After a great deal of effort she managed to light the candle and stood it on the table, although it didn't really light the room, it simply peopled the darkness with shadows. Then she found Granny's rocking chair by the cold fireplace, and settled down to wait.

Time passed. Nothing happened.

Then there was a tapping at the window. Esk took up the candle stub and peered through the thick round panes.

A beady yellow eye blinked back at her.

The candle guttered, and went out.

She stood stock still, hardly breathing. The tapping started again, and then stopped. There was a short silence, and then the door-latch rattled.

Something nasty comes, the boys had said.

She felt her way back across the room until she nearly tripped over the rocking chair, and dragged it back and wedged it as best she could in front of the door. The latch gave a final clonk and went silent.

Esk waited, listening until the silence roared in her ears. Then something started to bang against the little window in the scullery, softly but insistently. After a while it stopped. A moment later it started again in the bedroom above her – a faint scrabbling noise, a claw kind of noise.

Esk felt that bravery was called for, but on a night like this bravery lasted only as long as a candle stayed alight. She felt her way back across the dark kitchen, eyes tightly shut, until she reached the door.

There was a thump from the fireplace as a big lump of soot fell down, and when she heard the desperate scratchings coming from the chimney she slipped the bolts, threw open the door and darted out into the night.

The cold struck like a knife. Frost had put a crust on the snow. She didn't care where she was going, but quiet terror gave her a burning determination to get there as fast as she could.

Inside the cottage the crow landed heavily in the fireplace, surrounded by soot and muttering irritably to itself. It hopped into the shadows, and a moment later there was the bang of the latch of the stairway door and the sound of fluttering on the stairs.

Esk reached up as high as she could and felt around the tree for the marker. This time she was lucky, but the pattern of dots and grooves told her she was over a mile from the village and had been running in the wrong direction.

There was a cheese-rind moon and a sprinkling of stars, small and bright and pitiless. The forest around her was a pattern of black shadows and pale snow and, she was aware, not all the shadows were standing still.

Everyone knew there were wolves in the mountains, because on some nights their howls echoed down from the high Tops, but they seldom came near the village – the modern wolves were the offspring of ancestors that had survived because they had learned that human meat had sharp edges.

But the weather was hard, and this pack was hungry enough to forget all about natural selection.

Esk remembered what all the children were told. Climb a tree. Light a fire. When all else fails, find a stick and at least hurt them. Never try to outrun them.

The tree behind her was a beech, smooth and unclimbable.

Esk watched a long shadow detach itself from a pool of darkness in front of her, and move a little closer. She knelt down, tired, frightened, unable to think, and scrabbled under the burning-cold snow for a stick.

Granny Weatherwax opened her eyes and stared at the ceiling, which was cracked and bulged like a tent.

She concentrated on remembering that she had arms, not wings, and didn't need to hop. It was always wise to lie down for a bit after a borrow, to let one's mind get used to one's body, but she knew she didn't have the time.

'Drat the child,' she muttered, and tried to fly on to the bedrail. The crow, who had been through all this dozens of times before and who considered, insofar as birds can consider anything, which is a very short distance indeed, that a steady diet of bacon rinds and choice kitchen scraps and a warm roost for the night was well worth the occasional inconvenience of letting Granny share its head, watched her with mild interest.

Granny found her boots and thumped down the stairs, sternly resisting the urge to glide. The door was wide open and there was already a drift of fine snow on the floor.

'Oh, bugger,' she said. She wondered if it was worth trying to find Esk's mind, but human minds were never so sharp and clear as animal minds and anyway the overmind of the forest itself made impromptu searching as hard as listening for a waterfall in a thunderstorm. But even without looking she could feel the packmind of the wolves, a sharp, rank feeling that filled the mouth with the taste of blood.

She could just make out the small footprints in the crust, half filled with fresh snow. Cursing and muttering, Granny Weatherwax pulled her shawl around her and set out.

The white cat awoke from its private ledge in the forge when it heard the sounds coming from the darkest corner. Smith had carefully shut the big doors behind him when he went off with the nearly-hysterical boys, and the cat watched with interest as a thin shadow prodded at the lock and tested the hinges.

The doors were oak, hardened by heat and time, but that didn't prevent them being blown right across the street.

Smith heard a sound in the sky as he hurried along the track. So did Granny. It was a determined whirring sound, like the flight of geese, and the snowclouds boiled and twisted as it passed.

The wolves heard it, too, as it spun low over the treetops and hurtled down into the clearing. But they heard it far too late.

Granny Weatherwax didn't have to follow the footprints now. She aimed herself for the distant flashes of weird light, the strange swishing and thumping, and the howls of pain and terror. A couple of wolves bolted past her with their ears flattened in grim determination to have it away on their paws no matter what stood in their way.

There was the crackle of breaking branches. Something big and heavy landed in a fir tree by Granny and crashed, whimpering into the snow. Another wolf passed her in a flat trajectory at about head height and bounced off a tree-trunk.

There was silence.

Granny pushed her way between the snow-covered branches.

She could see that the snow was flattened in a white circle. A few wolves lay at its edges, either dead or wisely deciding to make no move.

The staff stood upright in the snow and Granny got the feeling it was turning to face her as she walked carefully past it.

There was also a small heap in the centre of the circle, curled tightly up inside itself. Granny knelt down with some effort and reached out gently.

The staff moved. It was little more than a tremble, but her hand stopped just before it touched Esk's shoulder. Granny glared up at the wooden carvings, and dared it to move again.

The air thickened. Then the staff seemed to back away while not moving, while at the same time something quite indefinable made it absolutely clear to the old witch that as far as the staff was concerned this wasn't a defeat, it was merely a tactical consideration, and it wouldn't like her to think she had won in any way, because she hadn't.

Esk gave a shudder. Granny patted her vaguely.

'It's me, little one. It's only Granny.'

The hump didn't uncurl.

Granny bit her lip. She was never quite certain about children, thinking of them – when she thought about them at all – as coming somewhere between animals and people. She understood babies. You put milk in one end and kept the other end as clean as possible. Adults were even easier, because they did the feeding and cleaning themselves. But in between was a world of experience that she had never really enquired about. As far as she was aware, you just tried to stop them catching anything fatal and hoped that it would all turn out all right.

Granny, in fact, was at a loss, but she knew she had to do something.

'Didda nasty wolfie fwiten us, den?' she hazarded.

For quite the wrong reasons, this seemed to work. From the depths of the ball a muffled voice said: 'I *am* eight, you know.'

'People who are eight don't curl up in the middle of the snow,' said Granny, feeling her way through the intricacies of adult-child conversation.

The ball didn't answer.

'I've probably got some milk and biscuits at home,' Granny ventured.

There was no perceptible effect.

'Eskarina Smith, if you don't behave this minute I will give you such a smack!'

Esk poked her head out cautiously.

'There's no need to be like that,' she said.

When Smith reached the cottage Granny had just arrived, leading Esk by the hand. The boys peered around from behind him.

'Um,' said Smith, not quite aware of how to begin a conversation with someone who was supposed to be dead. 'They, um, told me you were – ill.' He turned and glared at his sons.

'I was just having a rest and I must have dozed off. I sleeps very sound.'

'Yes,' said Smith, uncertainly. 'Well. All's well, then. What's up with Esk?'

'She took a bit of a fright,' said Granny, squeezing the girl's hand. 'Shadows and whatnot. She needs a good warm. I was going to put her in my bed, she's a bit mazed, if that's all right with you.'

Smith wasn't absolutely sure that it was all right with him. But he was quite sure that his wife, like every other woman in the village, held Granny Weatherwax in solemn regard, even in awe, and that if he started to object he would rapidly get out of his depth.

'Fine, fine,' he said, 'if it's no trouble. I'll send along for her in the morning, shall I?'

'That's right,' said Granny. 'I'd invite you in, but there's me without a fire– '

'No, no, that's all right,' said Smith hurriedly. 'I've got my supper waiting. Drying up,' he added, looking down at Gulta, who opened his mouth to say something and wisely thought better of it.

When they had gone, with the sound of the two boys' protests ringing out among the trees, Granny opened the door, pushed Esk inside, and bolted it behind them. She took a couple of candles from her store above the dresser and lit them. Then she pulled some old but serviceable wool blankets, still smelling of anti-moth herbs, from an old chest, wrapped Esk in them and sat her in the rocking chair.

She got down on her knees, to an accompaniment of clicks and grunts, and started to lay the fire. It was a complicated business involving dry fungus punk, wood shavings, bits of split twig and much puffing and swearing.

Esk said: 'You don't have to do it like that, Granny.'

Granny stiffened, and looked at the fireback. It was a rather nice one Smith had cast for her, years ago, with an owl-and-bat motif. Currently, though, she wasn't interested in the design.

'Oh yes?' she said, her voice dead-level. 'You know of a better way, do you?'

'You could magic it alight.'

Granny paid attention to arranging bits of twig on the reluctant flames.

'How would I do that, pray?' she said, apparently addressing her remarks to the fireback.

'Er,' said Esk, 'I . . . I can't remember. But you must know anyway, don't you? Everyone knows you can do magic.'

'There's magic,' said Granny, 'and then again, there's magic. The important thing, my girl, is to know what magic is for and what it isn't for. And you can take it from me, it was never intended for lighting fires, you can be absolutely certain of that. If the Creator had meant us to use magic for lighting fires, then he wouldn't have given us – er, matches.'

'But could you light a fire with magic?' said Esk, as Granny slung an ancient black kettle on its hook. 'I mean, if you wanted to. If it was allowed.'

'Maybe,' said Granny, who couldn't: fire had no mind, it wasn't alive, and they were two of the three reasons.

'You could light it much better.'

'If a thing's worth doing, it's worth doing badly,' said Granny, fleeing into aphorisms, the last refuge of an adult under siege.

'Yes, but–'

'But me no buts.'

Granny rummaged in a dark wooden box on the dresser. She prided herself on her unrivalled knowledge of the properties of Ramtops herbage – none knew better than she the many uses of Earwort, Maiden's Wish and Love-Lies-Oozing – but there were times when she had to resort to her small stock of jealously traded and carefully hoarded medicines from Forn Parts (which as far as she was concerned was anywhere further than a day's journey) to achieve the desired effect.

She shredded some dry red leaves into a mug, topped it up with honey and hot water from the kettle, and pushed it into Esk's hands. Then she put a large round stone under the grate – later on, wrapped in a scrap of blanket, it would make a bedwarmer – and, with a stern injunction to the girl not to stir from the chair, went out into the scullery.

Esk drummed her heels on the chair legs and sipped the drink. It had a strange, peppery taste. She wondered what it was. She'd tasted Granny's brews before, of course, with a greater or lesser amount of honey in them depending on whether she thought you were making too much of a fuss, and Esk knew that she was famous throughout the mountains for special potions for illnesses that her mother – and some young women too, once in a while – just hinted at with raised eyebrows and lowered voices . . .

When Granny came back she was asleep. She didn't remember being put to bed, or Granny bolting the windows.

Granny Weatherwax went back downstairs and pulled her rocking chair closer to the fire.

There was something there, she told herself, lurking away in the child's mind. She didn't like to think about what it was, but she remembered what had happened to the wolves. And all that about lighting fires with magic. Wizards did that, it was one of the first things they learned.

Granny sighed. There was only one way to be sure, and she was getting rather old for this sort of thing.

She picked up the candle and went out through the scullery into the lean-to that housed her goats. They watched her without fear, each sitting in its pen like a furry blob, three mouths working rhythmically on the day's hay. The air smelled warm and slightly flatulent.

Up in the rafters was a small owl, one of a number of creatures who found that living with Granny was worth the occasional inconvenience. It came to her hand at a word, and she stroked its bullet head thoughtfully as she looked for somewhere comfortable to lie. A pile of hay it would have to be.

She blew out the candle and lay back, with the owl perched on her finger.

The goats chewed, burped and swallowed their way through their cosy night. They made the only sound in the building.

Granny's body stilled. The owl felt her enter its mind, and graciously made room. Granny knew she would regret this, Borrowing twice in one day would leave her good for nothing in the morning, and with a terrible desire to eat mice. Of course, when she was younger she thought nothing of it, running with the stags, hunting with the foxes, learning the strange dark ways of the moles, hardly spending a night in her own body. But it was getting harder now, especially coming back. Maybe the time would come when she couldn't get back, maybe the body back home would be so much dead flesh, and maybe that wouldn't be such a bad way of it, at that.

This was the sort of thing wizards could never know. If it occurred to them to enter a creature's mind they'd do it like a thief, not out of wickedness but because it simply wouldn't occur to them to do it any other way, the daft buggers. And what good would it do to take over an owl's body? You couldn't fly, you needed to spend a lifetime learning. But the gentle way was to ride in its mind, steering it as gently as a breeze stirs a leaf.

The owl stirred, fluttered up on to the little windowsill, and glided silently into the night.

The clouds had cleared and the thin moon made the mountains gleam. Granny peered out through owl eyes as she sped silently between the ranks of trees. This was the only way to travel, once a body had the way of it! She liked Borrowing birds best of all, using them to explore the high, hidden valleys where no one went, the secret lakes between black cliffs, the tiny walled fields on the scraps of flat ground, tucked on the sheer rock faces, that were the property of hidden and secretive beings. Once she had ridden with the geese that passed over the mountains every spring and autumn, and had got the shock of her life when she nearly went beyond range of returning.

The owl broke out of the forest and skimmed across the rooftops of the village, alighting in a shower of snow on the biggest apple tree in Smith's orchard. It was heavy with mistletoe.

She knew she was right as soon as her claws touched the bark. The tree resented her, she could feel it trying to push her away.

I'm not going, she thought.

In the silence of the night the tree said, *Bully me, then, just because I'm a tree. Typical woman.*

At least you're useful now, thought Granny. *Better a tree than a wizard, eh?*

It's not such a bad life, thought the tree. *Sun. Fresh air. Time to think. Bees, too, in the spring.*

There was something lascivious about the way the tree said 'bees' that quite put Granny, who had several hives, off the idea of honey. It was like being reminded that eggs were unborn chickens.

I've come about the girl, Esk, she hissed.

A promising child, thought the tree, *I'm watching her with interest. She likes apples, too.*

You beast, said Granny, shocked.

What did I say? Pardon me for not breathing, I'm sure.

Granny sidled closer to the trunk.

You must let her go, she thought. *The magic is starting to come through.*

Already? I'm impressed, said the tree.

It's the wrong sort of magic!, screeched Granny. *It's wizard magic, not women's magic! She doesn't know what it is yet, but it killed a dozen wolves tonight!*

Great! said the tree. Granny hooted with rage.

Great? Supposing she had been arguing with her brothers, and lost her temper, eh?

The tree shrugged. Snowflakes cascaded from its branches.

Then you must train her, it said.

Train? What do I know from training wizards!

Then send her to university.

She's female!, hooted Granny, bouncing up and down on her branch.

Well? Who says women can't be wizards?

Granny hesitated. The tree might as well have asked why fish couldn't be birds. She drew a deep breath, and started to speak. And stopped. She knew a cutting, incisive, withering and above all a *self-evident* answer existed. It was just that, to her extreme annoyance, she couldn't quite bring it to mind.

Women have never been wizards. It's against nature. You might as well say that witches can be men.

If you define a witch as one who worships the pancreative urge, that is, venerates the basic – the tree began, and continued for several minutes. Granny Weatherwax listened in impatient annoyance to phrases like *Mother Goddesses* and *primitive moon worship* and told herself that she was well aware of what being a witch was all about, it was about herbs and curses and flying around of nights and generally keeping on the right side of tradition, and it certainly didn't involve mixing with goddesses, mothers or otherwise, who apparently got up to some very questionable tricks. And when the tree started talking about *dancing naked* she tried not to listen, because although she was aware that somewhere under her complicated strata of vests and petticoats there was some skin, that didn't mean to say she approved of it.

The tree finished its monologue.

Granny waited until she was quite sure that it wasn't going to add anything, and said, *That's witchcraft, is it?*

Its theoretical basis, yes.

You wizards certainly get some funny ideas.

The tree said, *Not a wizard any more, just a tree.*

Granny ruffled her feathers.

Well, just you listen to me, Mr so-called Theoretical Basis Tree, if women were meant to be wizards they'd be able to grow long white beards and she is not going to be a wizard, is that quite clear, wizardry is not the way to use magic, do you hear, it's nothing but lights and fire and meddling with power and she'll be having no part of it and good night to you.

The owl swooped away from the branch. It was only because it would interfere with the flying that Granny wasn't shaking with rage. Wizards! They talked too much and pinned spells down in books like butterflies but, worst of all, they thought theirs was the only magic worth practising.

Granny was absolutely certain of one thing. Women had never been wizards, and they weren't about to start now.

She arrived back at the cottage in the pale shank of the night. Her body, at least, was rested after its slumber in the hay, and Granny had hoped to spend a few hours in the rocking chair, putting her thoughts in order. This was the time, when night wasn't quite over but day hadn't quite begun, when thoughts stood out bright and clear and without disguise. She . . .

The staff was leaning against the wall, by the dresser.

Granny stood quite still.

'I see,' she said at last. 'So that's the way of it, is it? In my own house, too?'

Moving very slowly, she walked over to the inglenook, threw a couple of split logs on to the embers of the fire, and pumped the bellows until the flames roared up the chimney.

When she was satisfied she turned, muttered a few precautionary protective spells under her breath, and grabbed the staff. It didn't resist; she nearly fell over. But now she had it in her hands, and felt the tingle of it, the distinctive thunderstorm crackle of the magic in it, and she laughed.

It was as simple as this, then. There was no fight in it now.

Calling down a curse upon wizards and all their works she raised the staff above her head and brought it down with a clang across the firedogs, over the hottest part of the fire.

Esk screamed. The sound bounced down through the bedroom floorboards and scythed through the dark cottage.

Granny was old and tired and not entirely clear about things after a long day, but to survive as a witch requires an ability to jump to very large conclusions and as she stared at the staff in the flames and heard the scream her hands were already reaching for the big black kettle. She upended it over the fire, dragged the staff out of the cloud of steam, and ran upstairs, dreading what she might see.

Esk was sitting up in the narrow bed, unsinged but shrieking. Granny took the child in her arms and tried to comfort her; she wasn't sure how one went about it, but a distracted patting on the back and vague reassuring noises seemed to work, and the screams became wails and, eventually, sobs. Here and there Granny could pick out words like 'fire' and 'hot', and her mouth set in a thin, bitter line.

Finally she settled the child down, tucked her in, and crept quietly down the stairs.

The staff was back against the wall. She was not surprised to see that the fire hadn't marked it at all.

Granny turned her rocking chair to face it, and sat down with her chin in her hand and an expression of grim determination.

Presently the chair began to rock, of its own accord. It was the only sound in a silence that thickened and spread and filled the room like a terrible dark fog.

Next morning, before Esk got up, Granny hid the staff in the thatch, well out of harm's way.

Esk ate her breakfast and drank a pint of goat's milk without the least sign of the events of the last twenty-four hours. It was the first time she had been inside Granny's cottage for more than a brief visit, and while the old woman washed the dishes and milked the goats she made the most of her implied licence to explore.

She found that life in the cottage wasn't entirely straightforward. There was the matter of the goats' names, for example.

'But they've got to have names!' she said. 'Everything's got a name.'

Granny looked at her around the pear-shaped flanks of the head nanny, while the milk squirted into the low pail.

'I daresay they've got names in Goat,' she said vaguely. 'What do they want names in Human for?'

'Well,' said Esk, and stopped. She thought for a bit. 'How do you make them do what you want, then?'

'They just do, and when they want me they holler.'

Esk gravely gave the head goat a wisp of hay. Granny watched her thoughtfully. Goats did have names for themselves, she well knew: there was 'goat who is my kid', 'goat who is my mother', 'goat who is herd leader', and half a dozen other names not least of which was 'goat who is this goat'. They had a complicated herd system and four stomachs and a digestive system that sounded very busy on still nights, and Granny had always felt that calling all this names like Buttercup was an insult to a noble animal.

'Esk?' she said, making up her mind.

'Yes?'

'What would you like to be when you grow up?'

Esk looked blank. 'Don't know.'

'Well,' said Granny, her hands still milking, 'what do you think you will do when you are grown up?'

'Don't know. Get married, I suppose.'

'Do you want to?'

Esk's lips started to shape themselves around the D, but she caught Granny's eye and stopped, and thought.

'All the grown ups I know are married,' she said at last, and thought some more. 'Except you,' she added, cautiously.

'That's true,' said Granny.

'Didn't you want to get married?'

It was Granny's turn to think.

'Never got around to it,' she said at last. 'Too many other things to do, you see.'

'Father says you're a witch,' said Esk, chancing her arm.

'I am that.'

Esk nodded. In the Ramtops witches were accorded a status similar to that which other cultures gave to nuns, or tax collectors, or cesspit cleaners. That is to say, they were respected, sometimes admired, generally applauded for doing a job which logically had to be done, but people never felt quite comfortable in the same room with them.

Granny said, 'Would you like to learn the witching?'

'Magic, you mean?' asked Esk, her eyes lighting up.

'Yes, magic. But not firework magic. Real magic.'

'Can you fly?'

'There's better things than flying.'

'And I can learn them?'

'If your parents say yes.'

Esk sighed. 'My father won't.'

'Then I shall have a word with him,' said Granny.

'Now you just listen to me, Gordo Smith!'

Smith backed away across his forge, hands half-raised to ward off the old woman's fury. She advanced on him one finger stabbing the air righteously.

'I brought you into the world, you stupid man, and you've got no more sense in you now than you had then– '

'But– ' Smith tried, dodging around the anvil.

'The magic's found her! Wizard magic! *Wrong* magic, do you understand? It was never intended for her!'

'Yes, but– '

'Have you any idea of what it can do?'

Smith sagged. 'No.'

Granny paused, and deflated a little.

'No,' she repeated, more softly. 'No, you wouldn't.'

She sat down on the anvil and tried to think calm thoughts.

'Look. Magic has a sort of – life of its own. That doesn't matter, because – anyway, you see, wizard magic– ' She looked up at his big, blank expression and tried again. 'Well, you know cider?'

Smith nodded. He felt he was on firmer ground here, but he wasn't certain of where it was going to lead.

'And then there's the licker. Applejack,' said the witch. The smith nodded. Everyone in Bad Ass made applejack in the winter, by leaving cider tubs outside overnight and taking out the ice until a tiny core of alcohol was left.

'Well, you can drink lots of cider and you just feel better and that's it, isn't it?'

The smith nodded again.

'But applejack, you drink that in little mugs and you don't drink a lot and you don't drink it often, because it goes right to your head?'

The smith nodded again and, aware that he wasn't making a major contribution to the dialogue, added, 'That's right.'

'That's the difference,' said Granny.

'The difference from what?'

Granny sighed. 'The difference between witch magic and wizard magic,' she said. 'And it's found her, and if she doesn't control it, then there are Those who will control her. Magic can be a sort of door, and there are unpleasant Things on the other side. Do you understand?'

The smith nodded. He didn't really understand, but he correctly surmised that if he revealed this fact Granny would start going into horrible details.

'She's strong in her mind and it might take a while,' said Granny. 'But sooner or later they'll challenge her.'

Smith picked up a hammer from his bench, looked at it as though he had never seen it before, and put it down again.

'But,' he said, 'if it's wizard magic she's got, learning witchery won't be any good, will it? You said they're different.'

'They're both magic. If you can't learn to ride an elephant, you can at least learn to ride a horse.'

'What's an elephant?'

'A kind of badger,' said Granny. She hadn't maintained forest-credibility for forty years by ever admitting ignorance.

The blacksmith sighed. He knew he was beaten. His wife had made it clear that she favoured the idea and, now that he came to think about it, there were some advantages. After all, Granny wouldn't last for ever, and being father to the area's only witch might not be too bad, at that.

'All right,' he said.

And so, as the winter turned and started the long, reluctant climb towards spring, Esk spent days at a time with Granny Weatherwax, learning witch craft.

It seemed to consist mainly of things to remember.

The lessons were quite practical. There was cleaning the kitchen table and Basic Herbalism. There was mucking out the goats and The Uses of Fungi. There was doing the washing and The Summoning of the Small Gods. And there was always tending the big copper still in the scullery and The Theory and Practice of Distillation. By the time the warm Rim winds were blowing, and the snow remained only as little streaks of slush on the Hub side of trees, Esk knew how to prepare a range of ointments, several medicinal brandies, a score of special infusions, and a number of mysterious potions that Granny said she might learn the use of in good time.

What she hadn't done was any magic at all.

'All in good time,' repeated Granny vaguely.

'But I'm supposed to be a witch!'

'You're not a witch yet. Name me three herbs good for the bowels.'

Esk put her hands behind her back, closed her eyes, and said: 'The flowering tops of Greater Peahane, the root pith of Old Man's Trousers, the stems of the Bloodwater Lily, the seedcases of– '

'All right. Where may water gherkins be found?'

'Peat bogs and stagnant pools, from the months of– '

'Good. You're learning.'

'But it's not magic!'

Granny sat down at the kitchen table.

'Most magic isn't,' she said. 'It's just knowing the right herbs, and learning to watch the weather, and finding out the ways of animals. And the ways of people, too.'

'That's all it is!' said Esk, horrified.

'*All? It's a pretty big all,*' said Granny, 'But no, it isn't *all*. There's other stuff.'

'Can't you teach me?'

'All in good time. There's no call to go showing yourself yet.'

'Showing myself? Who to?'

Granny's eyes darted towards the shadows in the corners of the room.

'Never you mind.'

Then even the last lingering tails of snow had gone and the spring gales roared around the mountains. The air in the forest began to smell of leaf mould and turpentine. A few early flowers braved the night frosts, and the bees started to fly.

'Now bees,' said Granny Weatherwax, 'is real magic.'

She carefully lifted the lid of the first hive.

'Your bees,' she went on, 'is your mead, your wax, your bee gum, your honey. A wonderful thing is your bee. Ruled by a queen, too,' she added, with a touch of approval.

'Don't they sting you?' said Esk, standing back a little. Bees boiled out of the comb and overflowed the rough wooden sides of the box.

'Hardly ever,' said Granny. 'You wanted magic. Watch.'

She put a hand into the struggling mass of insects and made a shrill, faint piping noise at the back of her throat. There was a movement in the mass, and a large bee, longer and fatter than the others, crawled on to her hand. A few workers followed it, stroking it and generally ministering to it.

'How did you do that?' said Esk.

'Ah,' said Granny. 'Wouldn't you like to know?'

'Yes. I would. That's why I asked, Granny,' said Esk, severely.

'Do you think I used magic?'

Esk looked down at the queen bee. She looked up at the witch.

'No,' she said. 'I think you just know a lot about bees.'

Granny grinned.

'Exactly correct. That's one form of magic, of course.'

'What, just knowing things?'

'Knowing things that other people *don't know*,' said Granny. She carefully dropped the queen back among her subjects and closed the lid of the hive.

'And I think it's time you learned a few secrets,' she added.

At last, thought Esk.

'But first, we must pay our respects to the Hive,' said Granny. She managed to sound the capital H.

Without thinking, Esk bobbed a curtsey.

Granny's hand clipped the back of her head.

'Bow, I told you,' she said, without rancour. 'Witches bow.' She demonstrated.

'But *why*?' complained Esk.

'Because witches have got to be different, and that's part of the secret,' said Granny.

They sat on a bleached bench in front of the rimward wall of the cottage. In front of them the Herbs were already a foot high, a sinister collection of pale green leaves.

'Right,' said Granny, settling herself down. 'You know the hat on the hook by the door? Go and fetch it.'

Esk obediently went inside and unhooked Granny's hat. It was tall, pointed and, of course, black.

Granny turned it over in her hands and regarded it carefully.

'Inside this hat,' she said solemnly, 'is one of the secrets of witchcraft. If you cannot tell me what it is, then I might as well teach you no more, because once you learn the secret of the hat there is no going back. Tell me what you know about the hat.'

'Can I hold it?'

'Be my guest.'

Esk peered inside the hat. There was some wire stiffening to give it a shape, and a couple of hatpins. That was all.

There was nothing particularly strange about it, except that no one in the village had one like it. But that didn't make it magical. Esk bit her lip; she had a vision of herself being sent home in disgrace.

It didn't feel strange, and there were no hidden pockets. It was just a typical witch's hat. Granny always wore it when she went into the village, but in the forest she just wore a leather hood.

She tried to recall the bits of lessons that Granny grudgingly doled out. It isn't what you know, it's what other people don't know. Magic can be something right in the wrong place, or something wrong in the right place. It can be–

Granny *always* wore it to the village. And the big black cloak, which certainly wasn't magical, because for most of the winter it had been a goat blanket and Granny washed it in the spring.

Esk began to feel the shape of the answer and she didn't like it much. It was like a lot of Granny's answers. Just a word trick. She just said things you knew all the time, but in a different way so they sounded important.

'I think I know,' she said at last.

'Out with it, then.'

'It's in sort of two parts.'

'Well?'

'It's a witch's hat because you wear it. But you're a witch because you wear the hat. Um.'

'So– ' prompted Granny.

'So people see you coming in the hat and the cloak and they know you're a witch and that's why your magic works?' said Esk.

'That's right,' said Granny. 'It's called headology.' She tapped her silver hair, which was drawn into a tight bun that could crack rocks.'

'But it's not real!' Esk protested. 'That's not magic, it's– it's– '

'Listen,' said Granny. 'If you give someone a bottle of red jollop for their wind it may work, right, but if you want it to work for sure then you let their mind *make* it work for them. Tell 'em it's moonbeams bottled in fairy wine or something. Mumble over it a bit. It's the same with cursing.'

'Cursing?' said Esk, weakly.

'Aye, cursing, my girl, and no need to look so shocked! You'll curse, when the need comes. When you're alone, and there's no help to hand, and–'

She hesitated and, uncomfortably aware of Esk's questioning eyes, finished lamely: ' – and people aren't showing respect. Make it loud, make it complicated, make it long, and make it up if you have to, but it'll work all right. Next day, when they hit their thumb or they fall off a ladder or their dog drops dead, they'll remember you. They'll behave better next time.'

'But it still doesn't seem like magic,' said Esk, scuffing the dust with her feet.

'I saved a man's life once,' said Granny. 'Special medicine, twice a day. Boiled water with a bit of berry juice in it. Told him I'd bought it from the dwarfs. That's the biggest part of doct'rin, really. Most people'll get over most things if they put their minds to it. You just have to give them an interest.'

She patted Esk's hand as nicely as possible. 'You're a bit young for this,' she said, 'but as you grow older you'll find most people don't set foot outside their own heads much. You too,' she added gnomically.

'I don't understand.'

'I'd be very surprised if you did,' said Granny briskly, 'but you can tell me five herbs suitable for dry coughs.'

Spring began to unfold in earnest. Granny started taking Esk on long walks that took all day, to hidden ponds or high on to the mountain scree to collect rare plants. Esk enjoyed that, high on the hills where the sun beat down strongly but the air was nevertheless freezing cold. Plants grew thickly and hugged the ground. From some of the highest peaks she could see all the way to the Rim Ocean that ran around the edge of the world; in the other direction the Ramtops marched into the distance, wrapped in eternal winter. They went all the way to the hub of the world where, it was generally agreed, the Gods lived on a ten-mile-high mountain of rock and ice.

'Gods are all right,' said Granny, as they ate their lunch and looked at the view. 'You don't bother gods, and gods don't come bothering you.'

'Do you know many gods?'

'I've seen the thundergods a few times,' said Granny, 'and Hoki, of course.'

'Hoki?'

Granny chewed a crustless sandwich. 'Oh, he's a nature god,' she said. 'Sometimes he manifests himself as an oak tree, or half a man and half a goat, but mainly I see him in his aspect as a bloody nuisance. You only find him in the deep woods, of course. He plays the flute. Very badly, if you must know.'

Esk lay on her stomach and looked out across the lands below while a few hardy, self-employed bumblebees patrolled the thyme clusters. The sun was warm on her back but, up here, there were still drifts of snow on the hubside of rocks.

'Tell me about the lands down there,' she said lazily.

Granny peered disapprovingly at ten thousand miles of landscape.

'They're just other places,' she said. 'Just like here, only different.'

'Are there cities and things?'

'I daresay.'

'Haven't you ever been to look?'

Granny sat back, gingerly arranging her skirt to expose several inches of respectable flannelette to the sun, and let the heat caress her old bones.

'No,' she said. 'There's quite enough troubles around here without going to look for them in forn parts.'

'I dreamed of a city once,' said Esk. 'It had hundreds of people in it, and there was this building with big gates, and they were magical gates—'

A sound like tearing cloth came from behind her. Granny had fallen asleep.

'Granny!'

'Mhnf?'

Esk thought for a moment. 'Are you having a good time?' she said artfully.

'Mnph.'

'You said you'd show me some real magic, all in good time,' said Esk, 'and this *is* a good time.'

'Mnph.'

Granny Weatherwax opened her eyes and looked straight up at the sky; it was darker up here, more purple than blue. She thought: why not? She's a quick learner. She knows more herblore than I do. At her age old Gammer Tumult had me Borrowing and Shifting and Sending all the hours of the day. Maybe I'm being too cautious.

'Just a bit?' pleaded Esk.

Granny turned it over in her mind. She couldn't think of any more excuses. I'm surely going to regret this, she told herself, displaying considerable foresight.

'All right,' she said shortly.

'Real magic?' said Esk. 'Not more herbs or headology?'

'Real magic, as you call it, yes.'

'A spell?'

'No. A Borrowing.'

Esk's face was a picture of expectation. She looked more alive, it seemed to Granny, than she had ever been before.

Granny looked over the valleys stretching out before them until she found what she was after. A grey eagle was circling lazily over a distant blue-hazed patch of forest. Its mind was currently at ease. It would do nicely.

She Called it gently, and it began to circle towards them.

'The first thing to remember about Borrowing is that you must be comfortable and somewhere safe,' she said, smoothing out the grass behind her. 'Bed's best.'

'But what *is* Borrowing?'

'Lie down and hold my hand. Do you see the eagle up there?'

Esk squinted into the dark, hot sky.

There were . . . *two doll figures on the grass below as she pivoted on the wind* . . .

She could feel the whip and wire of the air through her feathers. Because the eagle was not hunting, but simply enjoying the feel of the sun on its wings, the land below was a mere unimportant shape. But the air, the air was a complex, changing three-dimensional *thing*, an interlocked pattern of spirals and curves that stretched away into the distance, a switchback of currents built around thermal pillars. She . . .

. . . felt a gentle pressure restraining her.

'The next thing to remember,' said Granny's voice, very close, 'is not to upset the owner. If you let it know you're there it'll either fight you or panic, and you won't stand a chance either way. It's had a lifetime of being an eagle, and you haven't.'

Esk said nothing.

'You're not frightened, are you?' said Granny. 'It can take you that way the first time, and–'

'I'm not frightened,' said Esk, and 'How do I control it?'

'You don't. Not yet. Anyway, controlling a truly wild creature isn't easily learned. You have to – sort of *suggest* to it that it might feel inclined to do things. With a tame animal, of course, it's all different. But you can't make any creature do anything that is totally against its nature. Now try and find the eagle's mind.'

Esk could sense Granny as a diffuse silver cloud at the back of her own mind. After some searching she found the eagle. She almost missed it. Its mind was small, sharp and purple, like an arrowhead. It was concentrating entirely on flying, and took no notice of her.

'Good,' said Granny approvingly. 'We're not going to go far. If you want to make it turn, you must–'

'Yes, yes,' said Esk. She flexed her fingers, wherever they were, and the bird leaned against the air and turned.

'Very good,' said Granny, taken aback. 'How did you do that?'

'I – don't know. It just seemed obvious.'

'Hmph.' Granny gently tested the tiny eagle mind. It was still totally oblivious of its passengers. She was genuinely impressed, a very rare occurrence.

They floated over the mountain, while Esk excitedly explored the eagle's senses. Granny's voice droned through her consciousness, giving instructions and guidance and warnings. She listened with half an ear. It sounded far too complicated. Why couldn't she take over the eagle's mind? It wouldn't hurt it.

She could see how to do it, it was just a knack, like snapping your fingers – which in fact she had never managed to achieve – and then she'd be able to experience flying for real, not at second hand.

Then she could–

'Don't,' said Granny calmly. 'No good will come of it.'

'What?'

'Do you really think you're the first, my girl? Do you think we haven't all thought what a fine thing it would be, to take on another body and tread the wind or breathe the water? And do you really think it would be as easy as that?'

Esk glowered at her.

'No need to look like that,' said Granny. 'You'll thank me one day. Don't you start playing around before you know what you're about, eh? Before you get up to tricks you've got to learn what to do if things go wrong. Don't try to walk before you can run.'

'I can *feel* how to do it, Granny.'

'That's as maybe. It's harder than it seems, is Borrowing, although I'll grant you've got a knack. That's enough for today, bring us in over ourselves and I'll show you how to Return.'

The eagle beat the air over the two recumbent forms and Esk saw, in her mind's eye, two channels open for them. Granny's mindshape vanished.

Now–

Granny had been wrong. The eagle mind barely fought, and didn't have time to panic. Esk held it wrapped in her own mind. It writhed for an instant, and then melted into her.

Granny opened her eyes in time to see the bird give a hoarse cry of triumph, curve down low over the grass-grown scree, and skim away down the mountainside. For a moment it was a vanishing dot and then it had gone, leaving only another echoing shriek.

Granny looked down at Esk's silent form. The girl was light enough, but it was a long way home and the afternoon was dwindling.

'Drat,' she said, with no particular emphasis. She stood up, brushed herself down and, with a grunt of effort, hauled Esk's inert body over her shoulder.

High in the crystal sunset air above the mountains the eagle-Esk sought more height, drunk with the sheer vitality of flight.

On the way home Granny met a hungry bear. Granny's back was giving her gyp, and she was in no mood to be growled at. She muttered a few words under her breath and the bear, to its brief amazement, walked heavily into a tree and didn't regain consciousness for several hours.

When she reached the cottage Granny put Esk's body to bed and drew up the fire. She brought the goats in and milked them, and finished the chores of the evening.

She made sure all the windows were open and, when it began to grow dark, lit a lantern and put it on the windowsill.

Granny Weatherwax didn't sleep more than a few hours a night, as a rule, and woke again at midnight. The room hadn't changed, although the lantern had its own little solar system of very stupid moths.

When she woke again at dawn the candle had long burned down and Esk was still sleeping the shallow, unwakable sleep of the Borrower.

When she took the goats out to their paddock she looked intently at the sky.

Noon came and gradually the light drained out of another day. She paced the floor of the kitchen aimlessly. Occasionally she would throw herself into frantic bouts of housework; ancient crusts were unceremoniously dug out of the cracks in the flagstones, and the fireback was scraped free of the winter's soot and blackleaded to within an inch of its life. A nest of mice in the back of the dresser were kindly but firmly ejected into the goatshed.

Sunset came.

The light of the Discworld was old and slow and heavy. From the cottage door Granny watched as it drained off the mountains, flowing in golden rivers through the forest. Here and there it pooled in hollows until it faded and vanished.

She drummed her fingers sharply on the doorpost, humming a small and bitter little tune.

Dawn came, and the cottage was empty except for Esk's body, silent and unmoving on the bed.

But as the golden light flowed slowly across the Discworld like the first freshing of the tide over mudflats the eagle circled higher into the dome of heaven, beating the air down with slow and powerful wingbeats.

The whole of the world was spread out beneath Esk – all the continents, all the islands, all the rivers and especially the great ring of the Rim Ocean.

There was nothing else up here, not even sound.

Esk gloried in the feel of it, willing her flagging muscles into greater effort. But something was wrong. Her thoughts seemed to be chasing around beyond her control, and disappearing. Pain and exhilaration and weariness poured into her mind, but it was as if other things were spilling out at the same time. Memories dwindled away on the wind. As fast as she could latch on to a thought it evaporated, leaving nothing behind.

She was losing chunks of herself, and she couldn't remember what she was losing. She panicked, burrowing back to the things she was sure of . . .

I am Esk, and I have stolen the body of an eagle and *the feel of wind in feathers, the hunger, the search of the not-sky below* . . .

She tried again. I am Esk and *seeking the windpath, the pain of muscle, the cut of the air, the cold of it* . . .

I am Esk *high over air-damp-wet-white, above everything, the sky is thin . . .*

I am *I am.*

Granny was in the garden, among the beehives, the early morning wind whipping at her skirts. She went from hive to hive, tapping on their roofs. Then, in the thickets of borage and beebalm that she had planted around them, she stood with her arms outstretched in front of her and sang something in tones so high that no normal person could have heard them.

But a roar went up from the hives, and then the air was suddenly thick with the heavy, big-eyed, deep-voiced shapes of drone bees. They circled over her head, adding their own bass humming to her chant.

Then they were gone, soaring into the growing light over the clearing and streaming away over the trees.

It is well known – at least, it is well known to witches – that all colonies of bees are, as it were, just one part of the creature called the Swarm, in the same way that individual bees are component cells of the hivemind. Granny didn't mingle her thoughts with the bees very often, partly because insect minds were strange, alien things that tasted of tin, but mostly because she suspected that the Swarm was a good deal more intelligent than she was.

She knew that the drones would soon reach the wild bee colonies in the deep forest, and within hours every corner of the mountain meadows would be under very close scrutiny indeed. All she could do was wait.

At noon the drones returned, and Granny read in the sharp acid thoughts of the hivemind that there was no sign of Esk.

She went back into the cool of the cottage and sat down in the rocking chair, staring at the doorway.

She knew what the next step was. She hated the very idea of it. But she fetched a short ladder, climbed up creakily on to the roof, and pulled the staff from its hiding place in the thatch.

It was icy cold. It steamed.

'Above the snowline, then,' said Granny.

She climbed down, and rammed the staff into a flowerbed. She glared at it. She had a nasty feeling that it was glaring back.

'Don't think you've won, because you haven't,' she snapped. 'It's just that I haven't got the time to mess around. You must know where she is. I command you to take me to her!'

The staff regarded her woodenly.

'By– ' Granny paused, her invocations were a little rusty, ' – by stock and stone I order it!'

Activity, movement, liveliness – all these words would be completely inaccurate descriptions of the staff's response.

Granny scratched her chin. She remembered the little lesson all children get taught: what's the magic word?

'Please?' she suggested.

The staff trembled, rose a little way out of the ground, and turned in the air so that it hung invitingly at waist height.

Granny had heard that broomsticks were once again very much the fashion among younger witches, but she didn't hold with it. There was no way a body could look respectable while hurtling through the air aboard a household implement. Besides, it looked decidedly draughty.

But this was no time for respectability. Pausing only to snatch her hat from its hook behind the door she scrambled up on to the staff and perched as best she could, sidesaddle of course, and with her skirts firmly gripped between her knees.

'Right,' she said. 'Now wha-aaaaaaaaa–'

Across the forest animals broke and scattered as the shadow passed overhead, crying and cursing. Granny clung on with whitened knuckles, her thin legs kicking wildly as, high above the treetops, she learned important lessons about centres of gravity and air turbulence. The staff shot onwards, heedless of her yells.

By the time it had come out over the upland meadows she had come to terms with it somewhat, which meant that she could just about hang on with knees and hands provided she didn't mind being upside down. Her hat, at least, was useful, being aerodynamically shaped.

The staff plunged between black cliffs and along high bare valleys where, it was said, rivers of ice had once flowed in the days of the Ice Giants. The air became thin and sharp in the throat.

They came to an abrupt halt over a snowdrift. Granny fell off, and lay panting in the snow while she tried to remember why she was going through all this.

There was a bundle of feathers under an overhang a few feet away. As Granny approached it a head rose jerkily, and the eagle glared at her with fierce, frightened eyes. It tried to fly, and toppled over. When she reached out to touch it, it took a neat triangle of flesh out of her hand.

'I see,' said Granny quietly, to no one in particular. She looked around, and found a boulder of about the right size. She disappeared behind it for a few seconds, for the sake of respectability, and reappeared with a petticoat in her hand. The bird thrashed around, ruining several weeks of meticulous petit-point embroidery, but she managed to bundle it up and hold it so that she could avoid its sporadic lunges.

Granny turned to the staff, which was now upright in the snowdrift.
'I shall walk back,' she told it coldly.

It turned out that they were in a spur valley overlooking a drop of several
hundred feet on to sharp black rocks.

'Very well, then,' she conceded, 'but you're to fly slowly, d'you understand? And no going high.'

In fact, because she was slightly more experienced and perhaps because the
staff was taking more care, too, the ride back was almost sedate. Granny was
almost persuaded that, given time, she could come to merely dislike flying,
instead of loathing it. What it needed was some way of stopping yourself from
having to look at the ground.

The eagle sprawled on the rag rug in front of the empty hearth. It had drunk
some water, over which Granny had mumbled a few of the charms she
normally said to impress patients, but you never knew, there might be some
power in them, and it had also gulped a few strips of raw meat.

What it had not done was display the least sign of intelligence.

She wondered whether she had the right bird. She risked another pecking
and stared hard into its evil orange eyes, and tried to convince herself that way
down in their depths, almost beyond sight, was a strange little flicker.

She probed around inside its head. The eagle mind was still there right
enough, vivid and sharp, but there was something else. Mind, of course, has
no colour, but nevertheless the strands of the eagle's mind seemed to be
purple. Around them and tangled among them were faint strands of silver.

Esk had learned too late that mind shapes body, that Borrowing is one thing
but that the dream of truly taking on another form had its built-in penalty.

Granny sat and rocked. She was at a loss, she knew that. Unravelling the
tangled minds was beyond her power, beyond any power in the Ramtops,
beyond even–

There was no sound, but maybe there was a change in the texture of the air.
She looked up at the staff, which had been suffered to come back into the
cottage.

'No,' she said firmly.

Then she thought: whose benefit did I say that for? Mine? There's power
there, but it's not my kind of power.

There isn't any other kind around, though. And even now I may be too late.
I might never have been early enough.

She reached out again into the bird's head to calm its fears and dispel its
panic. It allowed her to pick it up and sat awkwardly on her wrist, its talons
gripping tight enough to draw blood.

Granny took the staff and made her way upstairs, to where Esk lay on the narrow bed in the low bedroom with its ancient contoured ceiling.

She made the bird perch on the bedrail and turned her attention to the staff. Once more the carvings shifted under her glare, never quite revealing their true form.

Granny was no stranger to the uses of power, but she knew she relied on gentle pressure subtly to steer the tide of things. She didn't put it like that, of course – she would have said that there was always a lever if you knew where to look. The power in the staff was harsh, fierce, the raw stuff of magic distilled out of the forces that powered the universe itself.

There would be a price. And Granny knew enough about wizardry to be certain that it would be a high one. But if you were worried about the price, then why were you in the shop?

She cleared her throat, and wondered what the hell she was supposed to do next. Perhaps if she–

The power hit her like a half-brick. She could feel it take her and lift her so that she was amazed to look down and see her feet still firmly on the floorboards. She tried to take a step forward and magical discharges crackled in the air around her. She reached out to steady herself against the wall and the ancient wooden beam under her hand stirred and started to sprout leaves. A cyclone of magic swirled around the room, picking up dust and briefly giving it some very disturbing shapes; the jug and basin on the washstand, with the particularly fetching rosebud pattern, broke into fragments. Under the bed the third member of the traditional china trio turned into something horrible and slunk away.

Granny opened her mouth to swear and thought better of it when her words blossomed out into rainbow-edged clouds.

She looked down at Esk and the eagle, which seemed oblivious to all this, and tried to concentrate. She let herself slide inside its head and again she could see the strands of mind, the silver threads bound so closely around the purple that they took on the same shape. But now she could see where the strands ended, and where a judicious tug or push would begin to unravel them. It was so obvious she heard herself laugh, and the sound curved away in shades of orange and red and vanished into the ceiling.

Time passed. Even with the power throbbing through her head it was a painfully hard task, like threading a needle by moonlight, but eventually she had a handful of silver. In the slow, heavy world in which she now appeared to be she took the hank and threw it slowly towards Esk. It became a cloud, swirled like a whirlpool, and vanished.

She was aware of a shrill chittering noise, and shadows on the edge of sight. Well, it happened to everyone sooner or later. They had come, drawn as always by a discharge of magic. You just had to learn to ignore them.

Granny woke with bright sunlight skewering into her eyes. She was slumped against the door, and her whole body felt as though it had toothache.

She reached out blindly with one hand, found the edge of the washstand and pulled herself into a sitting position. She was not really surprised to see that the jug and basin looked just the same as they had always done; in fact sheer curiosity overcame her aches and she gave a quick glance under the bed to check that, yes, things were as normal.

The eagle was still hunched on the bedpost. In the bed Esk was asleep, and Granny saw that it was a true sleep and not the stillness of a vacant body.

All she had to do now was hope that Esk wouldn't wake up with an irresistible urge to pounce on rabbits.

She carried the unresisting bird downstairs and let it free outside the back door. It flew heavily up into the nearest tree, where it settled to rest. It had a feeling it ought to have a grudge against somebody, but for the life of it, it couldn't remember why.

Esk opened her eyes and stared for a long time at the ceiling. Over the months she had grown familiar with every lump and crack of the plaster, which created a fantastic upside-down landscape that she had peopled with a private and complex civilisation.

Her mind thronged with dreams. She pulled an arm out from under the sheets and stared at it, wondering why it wasn't covered with feathers. It was all very puzzling.

She pushed the covers back, swung her legs to the edge of the bed, *spread her wings into the rush of the wind and glided out into the world* . . .

The thump on the bedroom floor brought Granny scurrying up the stairs, to take her in her arms and hold her tight as the terror hit her. She rocked back and forth on her heels, making meaningless soothing noises.

Esk looked up at her through a mask of horror.

'I could feel myself vanishing!'

'Yes, yes. Better now,' murmured Granny.

'You don't understand! I couldn't even remember my name!' Esk shrieked.

'But you can remember now.'

Esk hesitated, checking. 'Yes,' she said. 'Yes, of course. Now.'

'So no harm done.'

'But–'

Granny sighed. 'You have learned something,' she said, and thought it safe to insert a touch of sternness into her voice. 'They say a little knowledge is a dangerous thing, but it is not one half so bad as a lot of ignorance.'

'But what *happened*?'

'You thought that Borrowing wasn't enough. You thought it would be a fine thing to steal another's body. But you must know that a body is like – like a jelly mould. It sets a shape on its contents, d'you see? You can't have a girl's mind in an eagle's body. Not for long, at any rate.'

'I *became* an eagle?'

'Yes.'

'Not *me* at all?'

Granny thought for a while. She always had to pause when conversations with Esk led her beyond the reaches of a decent person's vocabulary.

'No,' she said at last, 'not in the way you mean. Just an eagle with maybe some strange dreams sometimes. Like when you dream you're flying, perhaps it would remember walking and talking.'

'Urgh.'

'But it's all over now,' said Granny, treating her to a thin smile. 'You're your true self again and the eagle has got its mind back. It's sitting in the big beech by the privy; I should like you to put out some food for it.'

Esk sat back on her heels, staring at a point past Granny's head.

'There were some strange things,' she said conversationally. Granny spun around.

'I meant, in a sort of dream I saw things,' said Esk. The old woman's shock was so visible that she hesitated, frightened that she had said something wrong.

'What kind of things?' said Granny flatly.

'Sort of big creatures, all sorts of shapes. Just sitting around.'

'Was it dark? I mean, these Things, were they in the dark?'

'There were stars, I think. Granny?'

Granny Weatherwax was staring at the wall.

'Granny?' Esk repeated.

'Mmph? Yes? Oh.' Granny shook herself. 'Yes. I see. Now I would like you to go downstairs and get the bacon that is in the pantry and put it out for the bird, do you understand? It would be a good idea to thank it, too. You never know.'

When Esk returned Granny was buttering bread. She pulled her stool up to the table, but the old woman waved the breadknife at her.

'First things first. Stand up. Face me.'

Esk did so, puzzled. Granny stuck the knife in the breadboard and shook her head.

'Drat it,' she said to the world at large. 'I don't know what way they have of it, there should be some kind of ceremony if I know wizards, they always have to complicate things . . . '

'What do you mean?'

Granny seemed to ignore her, but crossed to the dark corner by the dresser.

'Probably you should have one foot in a bucket of cold porridge and one glove on and all that kind of stuff,' she went on. 'I didn't want to do this, but They're forcing my hand.'

'What are you talking about, Granny?'

The old witch yanked the staff out of its shadow and waved it vaguely at Esk.

'Here. It's yours. Take it. I just hope this is the right thing to do.'

In fact the presentation of a staff to an apprentice wizard is usually a very impressive ceremony, especially if the staff has been inherited from an elder mage; by ancient lore there is a long and frightening ordeal involving masks and hoods and swords and fearful oaths about people's tongues being cut out and their entrails torn by wild birds and their ashes scattered to the eight winds and so on. After some hours of this sort of thing the apprentice can be admitted to the brotherhood of the Wise and Enlightened.

There is also a long speech. By sheer coincidence Granny got the essence of it in a nutshell.

Esk took the staff and peered at it.

'It's very nice,' she said uncertainly. 'The carvings are pretty. What's it for?'

'Sit down now. And listen properly for once. On the day you were born . . . '

' . . . and that's the shape of it.'

Esk looked hard at the staff, then at Granny.

'I've got to be a wizard?'

'Yes. No. I don't know.'

'That isn't really an answer, Granny,' Esk said reproachfully. 'Am I or amp't I?'

'Women can't be wizards,' said Granny bluntly. 'It's agin nature. You might as well have a female blacksmith.'

'Actually I've watched dad at work and I don't see why– '

'Look,' said Granny hurriedly, 'you can't have a female wizard any more than you can have a male witch, because– '

'I've heard of male witches,' said Esk meekly.

'Warlocks!'

'I think so.'

'I mean there's no male witches, only silly men,' said Granny hotly. 'If men were witches, they'd be wizards. It's all down to– ' she tapped her head ' – headology. How your mind works. Men's minds work different from ours, see. Their magic's all numbers and angles and edges and what the stars are doing, as if that really mattered. It's all power. It's all– ' Granny paused, and dredged up her favourite word to describe all she despised in wizardry, ' – jommetry.'

'That's all right, then,' said Esk, relieved. 'I'll stay here and learn witchery.'

'Ah,' said Granny gloomily, 'that's all very well for you to say. I don't think it will be as easy as that.'

'But *you* said that men can be wizards and women can be witches and it can't be the other way around.'

'That's right.'

'Well, then,' said Esk triumphantly, 'it's all solved, isn't it? I can't help but be a witch.'

Granny pointed to the staff. Esk shrugged.

'It's just an old stick.'

Granny shook her head. Esk blinked.

'No?'

'No.'

'And I can't be a witch?'

'I don't know what you can be. Hold the staff.'

'What?'

'Hold the staff. Now, I've laid the fire in the grate. Light it.'

'The tinderbox is– ' Esk began.

'You once told me there were better ways of lighting fires. Show me.'

Granny stood up. In the dimness of the kitchen she seemed to grow until she filled it with shifting, ragged shadows, shot with menace. Her eyes glared down at Esk.

'Show me,' she commanded, and her voice had ice in it.

'But– ' said Esk desperately, clutching the heavy staff to her and knocking her stool over in her haste to back away.

'*Show me.*'

With a scream Esk spun around. Fire flared from her fingertips and arced across the room. The kindling exploded with a force that hurled the furniture around the room and a ball of fierce green light spluttered on the hearth.

Changing patterns sped across it as it spun sizzling on the stones, which cracked and then flowed. The iron fireback resisted bravely for a few seconds before melting like wax; it made a final appearance as a red smear across the fireball and then vanished. A moment later the kettle went the same way.

Just when it seemed that the chimney would follow them the ancient hearthstone gave up, and with a final splutter the fireball sank from view.

The occasional crackle or puff of steam signalled its passage through the earth. Apart from that there was silence, the loud hissing silence that comes after an ear-splittering noise, and after the actinic glare the room seemed pitch dark.

Eventually Granny crawled out from behind the table and crept as closely as she dared to the hole, which was still surrounded by a crust of lava. She jerked back as another cloud of superheated steam mushroomed up.

'They say there's dwarf mines under the Ramtops,' she said inconsequentially. 'My, but them little buggers is in for a surprise.'

She prodded the little puddle of cooling iron where the kettle had been, and added, 'Shame about the fireback. It had owls on it, you know.'

She patted her singed hair gingerly with a shaking hand. 'I think this calls for a nice cup of, a nice cup of cold water.'

Esk sat looking in wonder at her hand.

'That was real magic,' she said at last, 'And I did it.'

'*One* type of real magic,' corrected Granny. 'Don't forget that. And you don't want to do that all the time, neither. If it's in you, you've got to learn to control it.'

'Can you teach me?'

'Me? No!'

'How can I learn if no one will teach me?'

'You've got to go where they can. Wizard school.'

'But you said– '

Granny paused in the act of filling a jug from the water bucket.

'Yes, yes,' she snapped. 'Never mind what I said, or common sense or anything. Sometimes you just have to go the way things take you, and I reckon you're going to wizard school one way or the other.'

Esk considered this.

'You mean it's my destiny?' she said at last.

Granny shrugged. 'Something like that. Probably. Who knows?'

That night, long after Esk had been sent to bed, Granny put on her hat, lit a fresh candle, cleared the table, and pulled a small wooden box from its secret hiding place in the dresser. It contained a bottle of ink, an elderly quill pen, and a few sheets of paper.

Granny was not entirely happy when faced with the world of letters. Her eyes protruded, her tongue stuck out, small beads of sweat formed on her forehead, but the pen scratched its way across the page to the accompaniment of the occasional quiet 'drat' or 'bugger the thing'.

The letter read as follows, although this version lacks the candle-wax, blots, crossings-out and damp patches of the original.

> *To ther Hed Wizzard, Unsene Universety, Greatings, I hop you ar well, I am sending to you won Escarrina Smith, shee hath thee maekings of wizzardery but whot may be ferther dun wyth hyr I knowe not shee is a gode worker and clene about hyr person allso skilled in diuerse arts of thee howse, I will send Monies wyth hyr May you liv longe and ende youre days in pese, And oblije, Esmerelder Weatherwaxe (Mss) Wytch.*

Granny held it up to the candlelight and considered it critically. It was a good letter. She had got 'diuerse' out of the *Almanack*, which she read every night. It was always predicting 'diuerse plagues' and 'diuerse ill-fortune'. Granny wasn't entirely sure what it meant, but it was a damn good word all the same.

She sealed it with candle-wax and put it on the dresser. She could leave it for the carrier to take when she went into the village tomorrow, to see about a new kettle.

Next morning Granny took some pains over her dress, selecting a black dress with a frog and bat motif, a big velvet cloak, or at least a cloak made of the sort of stuff velvet looks like after thirty years of heavy wear, and the pointed hat of office which was crucified with hatpins.

Their first call was to the stonemason, to order a replacement hearthstone. Then they called on the smith.

It was a long and stormy meeting. Esk wandered out into the orchard and climbed up to her old place in the apple tree while from the house came her father's shouts, her mother's wails and long silent pauses which meant that Granny Weatherwax was speaking softly in what Esk thought of as her 'just so' voice. The old woman had a flat, measured way of speaking sometimes. It was the kind of voice the Creator had probably used. Whether there was magic in it, or just headology, it ruled out any possibility of argument. It made it clear that whatever it was talking about was exactly how things should be.

The breeze shook the tree gently. Esk sat on a branch idly swinging her legs.

She thought about wizards. They didn't often come to Bad Ass, but there were a fair number of stories about them. They were wise, she recalled, and usually very old and they did powerful, complex and mysterious magics and almost all of them had beards. They were also, without exception, men.

She was on firmer ground with witches, because she'd trailed off with Granny to visit a couple of villages' witches further along the hills, and anyway witches figured largely in Ramtop folklore. Witches were cunning, she recalled, and usually very old, or at least they tried to look old, and they did slightly suspicious, homely and organic magics and some of them had beards. They were also, without exception, women.

There was some fundamental problem in all that which she couldn't quite resolve. Why wouldn't . . .

Cern and Gulta hurtled down the path and came to a pushing, shoving halt under the tree. They peered up at their sister with a mixture of fascination and scorn. Witches and wizards were objects of awe, but sisters weren't. Somehow, knowing your own sister was learning to be a witch sort of devalued the whole profession.

'You can't really do spells,' said Cern. 'Can you?'

'Course you can't,' said Gulta. 'What's this stick?'

Esk had left the staff leaning against the tree. Cern prodded it cautiously.

'I don't want you to touch it,' said Esk hurriedly. 'Please. It's mine.'

Cern normally had all the sensitivity of a ballbearing, but his hand stopped in mid-prod, much to his surprise.

'I didn't want to anyway,' he muttered to hide his confusion. 'It's only an old stick.'

'Is it true you can do spells?' asked Gulta. 'We heard Granny say you could.'

'We listened at the door,' added Cern.

'*You* said I couldn't,' said Esk, airily.

'Well, can you or can't you?' said Gulta, his face reddening.

'Perhaps.'

'You can't!'

Esk looked down at his face. She loved her brothers, when she reminded herself to, in a dutiful sort of way, although she generally remembered them as a collection of loud noises in trousers. But there was something awfully pig-like and unpleasant about the way Gulta was staring up at her, as though she had personally insulted him.

She felt her body start to tingle, and the world suddenly seemed very sharp and clear.

'I can,' she said.

Gulta looked from her to the staff, and his eyes narrowed. He kicked it viciously.

'Old stick!'

He looked, she thought, exactly like a small angry pig.

Cern's screams brought Granny and his parents first to the back door and then running down the cinder path.

Esk was perched in the fork of the apple tree, an expression of dreamy contemplation on her face. Cern was hiding behind the tree, his face a mere rim around a red, tonsil-vibrating bawl.

Gulta was sitting rather bewildered in a pile of clothing that no longer fitted him, wrinkling his snout.

Granny strode up to the tree until her hooked nose was level with Esk's.

'Turning people into pigs is *not allowed*,' she hissed. 'Even brothers.'

'I didn't do it, it just happened. Anyway, you must admit it's a better shape for him,' said Esk evenly.

'What's going on?' said Smith. 'Where's Gulta? What's this pig doing here?'

'This pig', said Granny Weatherwax, 'is your son.'

There was a sigh from Esk's mother as she collapsed gently backwards, but Smith was slightly less unprepared. He looked sharply from Gulta, who had managed to untangle himself from his clothing and was now rooting enthusiastically among the early windfalls, to his only daughter.

'She did this?'

'Yes. Or it was done through her,' said Granny, looking suspiciously at the staff.

'Oh.' Smith looked at his fifth son. He had to admit that the shape suited him. He reached out without looking and fetched the screaming Cern a thump on the back of his head.

'Can you turn him back again?' he asked. Granny spun around and glared the question at Esk, who shrugged.

'He didn't believe I could do magic,' she said calmly.

'Yes, well, I think you've made the point,' said Granny. 'And now you will turn him back, madam. This instant. Do you hear?'

'Don't want to. He was rude.'

'I *see*.'

Esk gazed down defiantly. Granny glared up sternly. Their wills clanged like cymbals and the air between them thickened. But Granny had spent a lifetime bending recalcitrant creatures to her bidding and, while Esk was a surprisingly strong opponent, it was obvious that she would give in before the end of the paragraph.

'Oh, all right,' she whined. 'I don't know why anyone would bother turning him into a pig when he was doing such a good job of it all by himself.'

She didn't know where the magic had come from, but she mentally faced that way and made a suggestion. Gulta reappeared, naked, with an apple in his mouth.

'Awts aughtning?' he said.

Granny spun around on Smith.

'Now will you believe me?' she snapped. 'Do you really think she's supposed to settle down here and forget all about magic? Can you imagine her poor husband if she marries?'

'But you always said it was impossible for women to be wizards,' said Smith. He was actually rather impressed. Old Granny Weatherwax had never been known to turn anyone into *anything*.

'Never mind that now,' said Granny, calming down a bit. 'She needs training. She needs to know how to control. For pity's sake put some clothes on that child.'

'Gulta, get dressed and stop grizzling,' said his father, and turned back to Granny.

'You said there was some sort of teaching place?' he hazarded.

'The Unseen University, yes. It's for training wizards.'

'And you know where it is?'

'Yes,' lied Granny, whose grasp of geography was slightly worse than her knowledge of sub-atomic physics.

Smith looked from her to his daughter, who was sulking.

'And they'll make a wizard of her?' he said.

Granny sighed.

'I don't know what they'll make of her,' she said.

And so it was that, a week later, Granny locked the cottage door and hung the key on its nail in the privy. The goats had been sent to stay with a sister witch further along the hills, who had also promised to keep an Eye on the cottage. Bad Ass would just have to manage without a witch for a while.

Granny was vaguely aware that you didn't find the Unseen University unless it wanted you to, and the only place to start looking was the town of Ohulan Cutash, a sprawl of a hundred or so houses about fifteen miles away. It was where you went to once or twice a year if you were a really cosmopolitan Bad Assian: Granny had only been once before in her entire life and hadn't approved of it at all. It had smelt all wrong, she'd got lost, and she distrusted city folk with their flashy ways.

They got a lift on the cart that came out periodically with metal for the smithy. It was gritty, but better than walking, especially since Granny had packed their few possessions in a large sack. She sat on it for safety.

Esk sat cradling the staff and watching the woods go by. When they were several miles outside the village she said, 'I thought you told me plants were different in forn parts.'

'So they are.'

'These trees look just the same.'

Granny regarded them disdainfully.

'Nothing like as good,' she said.

In fact she was already feeling slightly panicky. Her promise to accompany Esk to Unseen University had been made without thinking, and Granny, who picked up what little she knew of the rest of the Disc from rumour and the pages of her *Almanack*, was convinced that they were heading into earthquakes, tidal waves, plagues and massacres, many of them diuerse or even worse. But she was determined to see it through. A witch relied too much on words ever to go back on them.

She was wearing serviceable black, and concealed about her person were a number of hatpins and a breadknife. She had hidden their small store of money, grudgingly advanced by Smith, in the mysterious strata of her underwear. Her skirt pockets jingled with lucky charms, and a freshly forged horseshoe, always a potent preventative in time of trouble, weighed down her handbag. She felt about as ready as she ever would be to face the world.

The track wound down between the mountains. For once the sky was clear, the high Ramtops standing out crisp and white like the brides of the sky (with their trousseaux stuffed with thunderstorms) and the many little streams that bordered or crossed the path flowed sluggishly through strands of meadowsweet and go-faster-root.

By lunchtime they reached the suburb of Ohulan (it was too small to have more than one, which was just an inn and a handful of cottages belonging to people who couldn't stand the pressures of urban life) and a few minutes later the cart deposited them in the town's main, indeed its only, square.

It turned out to be market day.

Granny Weatherwax stood uncertainly on the cobbles, holding tightly to Esk's shoulder as the crowd swirled around them. She had heard that lewd things could happen to country women who were freshly arrived in big cities, and she gripped her handbag until her knuckles whitened. If any male stranger had happened to so much as nod at her it would have gone very hard indeed for him.

Esk's eyes were sparkling. The square was a jigsaw of noise and colour and smell. On one side of it were the temples of the Disc's more demanding deities, and weird perfumes drifted out to join with the reeks of commerce in a complex ragrug of fragrances. There were stalls filled with enticing curiosities that she itched to investigate.

Granny let the both of them drift with the crowd. The stalls were puzzling her as well. She peered among them, although never for one minute relaxing her vigilance against pickpockets, earthquakes and traffickers in the erotic, until she spied something vaguely familiar.

There was a small covered stall, black draped and musty, that had been wedged into a narrow space between two houses. Inconspicuous though it was, it nevertheless seemed to be doing a very busy trade. Its customers were mainly women, of all ages, although she did notice a few men. They all had one thing in common, though. No one approached it directly. They all sort of strolled almost past it, then suddenly ducked under its shady canopy. A moment later and they would be back again, hand just darting away from bag or pocket, competing for the world's Most Nonchalant Walk title so effectively that a watcher might actually doubt what he or she had just seen.

It was quite amazing that a stall so many people didn't know was there should be quite so popular.

'What's in there?' said Esk. 'What's everyone buying?'

'Medicines,' said Granny firmly.

'There must be a lot of very sick people in towns,' said Esk gravely.

Inside, the stall was a mass of velvet shadows and the herbal scent was thick enough to bottle. Granny poked a few bundles of dry leaves with an expert finger. Esk pulled away from her and tried to read the scrawled labels on the bottles in front of her. She was expert at most of Granny's preparations, but she didn't recognise anything here. The names were quite amusing, like Tiger Oil, Maiden's Prayer and Husband's Helper, and one or two of the stoppers smelled like Granny's scullery after she had done some of her secret distillations.

A shape moved in the stall's dim recesses and a brown wrinkled hand slid lightly on to hers.

'Can I assist you, missy?' said a cracked voice, in tones of syrup of figs. 'Is it your fortune you want telling, or is it your future you want changing, maybe?'

'She's with me,' snapped Granny, spinning around, 'and your eyes are betraying you, Hilta Goatfounder, if you can't tell her age.'

The shape in front of Esk bent forward.

'Esme Weatherwax?' it asked.

'The very same,' said Granny. 'Still selling thunder drops and penny wishes, Hilta? How goes it?'

'All the better for seeing you,' said the shape. 'What brings you down from the mountains, Esme? And this child – your assistant, perhaps?'

'What's it you're selling, please?' asked Esk. The shape laughed.

'Oh, things to stop things that shouldn't be and help things that should, love,' it said. 'Let me just close up, my dears, and I will be right with you.'

The shape bustled past Esk in a nasal kaleidoscope of fragrances and buttoned up the curtains at the front of the stall. Then the drapes at the back were thrown up, letting in the afternoon sunlight.

'Can't stand the dark and fug myself,' said Hilta Goatfounder, 'but the customers expect it. You know how it is.'

'Yes,' Esk nodded sagely. 'Headology.'

Hilta, a small fat woman wearing an enormous hat with fruit on it, glanced from her to Granny and grinned.

'That's the way of it,' she agreed. 'Will you take some tea?'

They sat on bales of unknown herbs in the private corner made by the stall between the angled walls of the houses, and drank something fragrant and green out of surprisingly delicate cups. Unlike Granny, who dressed like a very respectable raven, Hilta Goatfounder was all lace and shawls and colours and earrings and so many bangles that a mere movement of her arms sounded like a percussion section falling off a cliff. But Esk could see the likeness.

It was hard to describe. You couldn't imagine them curtseying to anyone.

'So,' said Granny, 'how goes the life?'

The other witch shrugged, causing the drummers to lose their grip again, just when they had nearly climbed back up.

'Like the hurried lover, it comes and goe– ' she began, and stopped at Granny's meaningful glance at Esk.

'Not bad, not bad,' she amended hurriedly. 'The council have tried to run me out once or twice, you know, but they all have wives and somehow it never quite happens. They say I'm not the right sort, but I say there'd be many a family in this town a good deal bigger and poorer if it wasn't for Madame Goatfounder's Pennyroyal Preventives. I know who comes into my shop, I do. I remember who buys buckeroo drops and ShoNuff Ointment, I do. Life isn't bad. And how is it up in your village with the funny name?'

'Bad Ass,' said Esk helpfully. She picked a small clay pot off the counter and sniffed at its contents.

'It is well enough,' conceded Granny. 'The handmaidens of nature are ever in demand.'

Esk sniffed again at the powder, which seemed to be pennyroyal with a base she couldn't quite identify, and carefully replaced the lid. While the two women exchanged gossip in a kind of feminine code, full of eye contact and unspoken adjectives, she examined the other exotic potions on display. Or

rather, not on display. In some strange way they appeared to be artfully
half-hidden, as if Hilta wasn't entirely keen to sell.

'I don't recognise any of these,' she said, half to herself. 'What do they
give to people?'

'Freedom,' said Hilta, who had good hearing. She turned back to Granny.
'How much have you taught her?'

'Not *that* much,' said Granny. 'There's power there, but what kind I'm
not sure. Wizard power, it might be.'

Hilta turned around very slowly and looked Esk up and down.

'Ah,' she said, 'that explains the staff. I wondered what the bees were
talking about. Well, well. Give me your hand, child.'

Esk held out her hand. Hilta's fingers were so heavy with rings it was like
dipping into a sack of walnuts.

Granny sat upright, radiating disapproval, as Hilta began to inspect Esk's
palm.

'I really don't think that is necessary,' she said sternly. 'Not between
us.'

'*You* do it, Granny,' said Esk, 'in the village. I've seen you. And teacups.
And cards.'

Granny shifted uneasily. 'Yes, well,' she said. 'It's all according. You just
hold their hand and people do their own fortune-telling. But there's no need
to go around *believing* it, we'd all be in trouble if we went around *believing*
everything.'

'The Powers That Be have many strange qualities, and puzzling and varied
are the ways in which they make their desires known in this circle of firelight
we call the physical world,' said Hilta solemnly. She winked at Esk.

'Well, really,' snapped Granny.

'No, straight up,' said Hilta. 'It's true.'

'Hmph.'

'I see you going upon a long journey,' said Hilta.

'Will I meet a tall dark stranger?' said Esk, examining her palm. 'Granny
always says that to women, she says– '

'No,' said Hilta, while Granny snorted. 'But it will be a very strange
journey. You'll go a long way while staying in the same place. And the
direction will be a strange one. It will be an exploration.'

'You can tell all that from my hand?'

'Well, mainly I'm just guessing,' said Hilta, sitting back and reaching for
the teapot (the lead drummer, who had climbed halfway back, fell on to the
toiling cymbalists). She looked carefully at Esk and added, 'A female wizard,
eh?'

'Granny is taking me to Unseen University,' said Esk.

Granny frowned. 'Not in so many words,' she admitted. 'I was hoping you could give me more explicit directions, you being more familiar with bricks and things.'

'They say it has many doors, but the ones in this world are in the city of Ankh-Morpork,' said Hilta. Granny looked blank. 'On the Circle Sea,' Hilta added. Granny's look of polite enquiry persisted. 'Five hundred miles away,' said Hilta.

'Oh,' said Granny.

She stood up and brushed an imaginary speck of dust off her dress.

'We'd better be going, then,' she added.

Hilta laughed. Esk quite liked the sound. Granny never laughed, she merely let the corners of her mouth turn up, but Hilta laughed like someone who had thought hard about Life and had seen the joke.

'Start tomorrow, anyway,' she said. 'I've got room at home, you can stay with me, and tomorrow you'll have the light.'

'We wouldn't want to presume,' said Granny.

'Nonsense. Why not have a look around while I pack up the stall?'

Ohulan was the market town for a wide sprawling countryside and the market day didn't end at sunset. Instead, torches flared at every booth and stall and light blared forth from the open doorways of the inns. Even the temples put out coloured lamps to attract nocturnal worshippers.

Hilta moved through the crowd like a slim snake through dry grass, her entire stall and stock reduced to a surprisingly small bundle on her back, and her jewellery rattling like a sackful of flamenco dancers. Granny stumped along behind her, her feet aching from the unaccustomed prodding of the cobbles.

And Esk got lost.

It took some effort, but she managed it. It involved ducking between two stalls and then scurrying down a side alley. Granny had warned her at length about the unspeakable things that lurked in cities, which showed that the old woman was lacking in a complete understanding of headology, since Esk was now determined to see one or two of them for herself.

In fact, since Ohulan was quite barbaric and uncivilised the only things that went on after dark to any degree were a little thievery, some amateurish trading in the courts of lust, and drinking until you fell over or started singing or both.

According to the standard poetic instructions one should move through a fair like the white swan at evening moves o'er the bay, but because of certain practical difficulties Esk settled for moving through the crowds like a small dodgem car, bumping from body to body with the tip of the staff waving a yard above her head. It caused some heads to turn, and not only because it had hit them; wizards occasionally passed through the town and it was the first time anyone had seen one four feet tall with long hair.

Anyone watching closely would have noticed strange things happening as she passed by.

There was, for example, the man with three upturned cups who was inviting a small crowd to explore with him the exciting world of chance and probability as it related to the position of a small dried pea. He was vaguely aware of a small figure watching him solemnly for a few moments, and then a sackful of peas cascaded out of every cup he picked up. Within seconds he was knee-deep in legumes. He was a lot deeper in trouble – he suddenly owed everyone a lot of money.

There was a small and wretched monkey that for years had shuffled vaguely at the end of a chain while its owner played something dreadful on a pipe-organ. It suddenly turned, narrowed its little red eyes, bit its keeper sharply in the leg, snapped its chain and had it away over the rooftops with the night's takings in a tin cup. History is silent about what they were spent on.

A boxful of marzipan ducks on a nearby stall came to life and whirred past the stallholder to land, quacking happily, in the river (where, by dawn, they had all melted: that's natural selection for you).

The stall itself sidled off down an alley and was never seen again.

Esk, in fact, moved through the fair more like an arsonist moves through a hayfield or a neutron bounces through a reactor, poets notwithstanding, and the hypothetical watcher could have detected her random passage by tracing the outbreaks of hysteria and violence. But, like all good catalysts, she wasn't actually involved in the processes she initiated, and by the time all the non-hypothetical potential watchers took their eyes off them she had been buffeted somewhere else.

She was also beginning to tire. While Granny Weatherwax approved of night on general principles, she certainly didn't hold with promiscuous candlelight – if she had any reading to do after dark she generally persuaded the owl to come and sit on the back of her chair, and read through its eyes. So Esk expected to go to bed around sunset, and that was long past.

There was a doorway ahead of her that looked friendly. Cheerful sounds were sliding out on the yellow light, and pooling on the cobbles. With the staff still radiating random magic like a demon lighthouse she headed for it, weary but determined.

The landlord of the Fiddler's Riddle considered himself to be a man of the world, and this was right, because he was too stupid to be really cruel, and too lazy to be really mean and although his body had been around quite a lot his mind had never gone further than the inside of his own head.

He wasn't used to being addressed by sticks. Especially when they spoke in a small piping voice, and asked for goat's milk.

Cautiously, aware that everyone in the inn was looking at him and grinning, he pulled himself across the bar top until he could see down. Esk stared up at him. Look 'em right in the eye, Granny had always said: focus your power on 'em, stare 'em out, no one can outstare a witch, 'cept a goat, of course.

The landlord, whose name was Skiller, found himself looking directly down at a small child who seemed to be squinting.

'What?' he said.

'Milk,' said the child, still focussing furiously. 'You get it out of goats. You know?'

Skiller sold only beer, which his customers claimed he got out of cats. No self-respecting goat would have endured the smell in the Fiddler's Riddle.

'We haven't got any,' he said. He looked hard at the staff and his eyebrows met conspiratorially over his nose.

'You could have a look,' said Esk.

Skiller eased himself back across the bar, partly to avoid the gaze, which was causing his eyes to water in sympathy, and partly because a horrible suspicion was congealing in his mind.

Even second-rate barmen tend to resonate with the beer they serve, and the vibrations coming from the big barrels behind him no longer had the twang of hop and head. They were broadcasting an altogether more lactic note.

He turned a tap experimentally, and watched a thin stream of milk curdle in the drip bucket.

The staff still poked up over the edge of the counter, like a periscope. He could swear that it was staring at him too.

'Don't waste it,' said a voice. 'You'll be grateful for it one day.'

It was the same tone of voice Granny used when Esk was less than enthusiastic about a plateful of nourishing sallet greens, boiled yellow until the last few vitamins gave in, but to Skiller's hypersensitive ears it wasn't an injunction but a prediction. He shivered. He didn't know where he would have to be to make him grateful for a drink of ancient beer and curdled milk. He'd rather be dead first.

Perhaps he *would* be dead first.

He very carefully wiped a nearly clean mug with his thumb and filled it from the tap. He was aware that a large number of his guests were quietly leaving. No one liked magic, especially in the hands of a woman. You never could tell what they might take it into their heads to do next.

'Your milk,' he said, adding, 'Miss.'

'I've got some money,' Esk said. Granny had always told her: always be ready to pay and you won't have to, people always like you to feel good about them, it's all headology.

'No, wouldn't dream of it,' said Skiller hastily. He leaned over the bar. 'If you could see, er, your way clear to turning the rest back, though? Not much call for milk in these parts.'

He sidled along a little way. Esk had leaned the staff against the bar while she drank her milk, and it was making him uncomfortable.

Esk looked at him over a moustache of cream.

'I didn't turn it into milk, I just knew it would be milk because I wanted milk,' she said. 'What did you think it was?'

'Er. Beer.'

Esk thought about this. She vaguely remembered trying beer once, and it had tasted sort of second-hand. But she could recall something which everyone in Bad Ass reckoned was much better than beer. It was one of Granny's most guarded recipes. It was good for you, because there was only fruit in it, plus lots of freezing and boiling and careful testing of little drops with a lighted flame.

Granny would put a very small spoonful in her milk if it was a really cold night. It had to be a wooden spoon, on account of what it did to metal.

She concentrated. She could picture the taste in her mind, and with the little skills that she was beginning to accept but couldn't understand she found she could take the taste apart into little coloured shapes . . .

Skiller's thin wife came out of their back room to see why it had all gone so quiet, and he waved her into shocked silence as Esk stood swaying very slightly with her eyes closed and her lips moving.

. . . little shapes that you didn't need went back into the great pool of shapes, and then you found the extra ones you needed and put them together, and then there was a sort of hook thing which meant that they would turn anything suitable into something just like them, and then . . .

Skiller turned very carefully and regarded the barrel behind him. The smell of the room had changed, he could feel the pure gold sweating gently out of that ancient woodwork.

With some care he took a small glass from his store under the counter and let a few splashes of the dark golden liquid escape from the tap. He looked at it thoughtfully in the lamplight, turned the glass around methodically, sniffed it a few times, and tossed its contents back in one swallow.

His face remained unchanged, although his eyes went moist and his throat wobbled somewhat. His wife and Esk watched him as a thin beading of sweat broke out on his forehead. The seconds passed, and he was obviously out to break some heroic record. There may have been steam curling out of his ears, but that could have been a rumour. His fingers drummed a strange tattoo on the bartop.

At last he swallowed, appeared to reach a decision, turned solemnly to Esk, and said, 'Hwarl,ish gnish saaarghs ishghs oorgsh?'

His brow wrinkled as he ran the sentence past his mind again and made a second attempt.

'Aargh argh shaah gok?'

He gave up.

'Bharrgsh nargh!'

His wife snorted and took the glass out of his unprotesting hand. She sniffed it. She looked at the barrels, all ten of them. She met his unsteady eye. In a private paradise for two they soundlessly calculated the selling price of six hundred gallons of triple-distilled white mountain peach brandy and ran out of numbers.

Mrs Skiller was quicker on the uptake than her husband. She bent down and smiled at Esk, who was too tired to squint back. It wasn't a particularly good smile, because Mrs Skiller didn't get much practice.

'How did you get here, little girl?' she said, in a voice that suggested gingerbread cottages and the slamming of big stove doors.

'I got lost from Granny.'

'And where's Granny now, dear?' Clang went the oven doors again; it was going to be a tough night for all wanderers in metaphorical forests.

'Just somewhere, I expect.'

'Would you like to go to sleep in a big feather bed, all nice and warm?'

Esk looked at her gratefully, even while vaguely realising that the woman had a face just like an eager ferret, and nodded.

You're right. It's going to take more than a passing woodchopper to sort *this* out.

Granny, meanwhile, was two streets away. She was also, by the standards of other people, lost. She would not see it like that. She knew where she was, it was just that everywhere else didn't.

It has already been mentioned that it is much harder to detect a human mind than, say, the mind of a fox. The human mind, seeing this as some kind of a slur, wants to know why. This is why.

Animal minds are simple, and therefore sharp. Animals never spend time dividing experience into little bits and speculating about all the bits they've missed. The whole panoply of the universe has been neatly expressed to them as things to (a) mate with, (b) eat, (c) run away from, and (d) rocks. This frees the mind from unnecessary thoughts and gives it a cutting edge where it matters. Your normal animal, in fact, never tries to walk and chew gum at the same time.

The average human, on the other hand, thinks about all sorts of things around the clock, on all sorts of levels, with interruptions from dozens of biological calendars and timepieces. There's thoughts about to be said, and private thoughts, and real thoughts, and thoughts about thoughts, and a whole gamut of subconscious thoughts. To a telepath the human head is a din. It is a railway terminus with all the Tannoys talking at once. It is a complete FM waveband – and some of those stations aren't reputable, they're outlawed pirates on forbidden seas who play late-night records with limbic lyrics.

Granny, trying to locate Esk by mind magic alone, was trying to find a straw in a haystack.

She was not succeeding, but enough blips of sense reached her through the heterodyne wails of a thousand brains all thinking at once to convince her that the world was, indeed, as silly as she had always believed it was.

She met Hilta at the corner of the street. She was carrying her broomstick, the better to conduct an aerial search (with great stealth, however; the men of Ohulan were right behind Stay Long Ointment but drew the line at flying women). She was distraught.

'Not so much as a hint of her,' said Granny.

'Have you been down to the river? She might have fallen in!'

'Then she'd have just fallen out again. Anyway, she can swim. I think she's hiding, drat her.'

'What are we going to do?'

Granny gave her a withering look. 'Hilta Goatfounder, I'm ashamed of you, acting like a cowin. Do I look worried?'

Hilta peered at her.

'You do. A bit. Your lips have gone all thin.'

'I'm just angry, that's all.'

'Gypsies always come here for the fair, they might have taken her.'

Granny was prepared to believe anything about city folk but here she was on firmer ground.

'Then they're a lot dafter than I'd give them credit for,' she snapped. 'Look, she's got the staff.'

'What good would that do?' said Hilta, who was close to tears.

'I don't think you've understood anything I've told you,' said Granny severely. 'All we need to do is go back to your place and wait.'

'What for?'

'The screams or the bangs or the fireballs or whatever,' Granny said vaguely.

'That's heartless!'

'Oh, I expect they've got it coming to them. Come on, you go on ahead and put the kettle on.'

Hilta gave her a mystified look, then climbed on her broom and rose slowly and erratically into the shadows among the chimneys. If broomsticks were cars, this one would be a split-window Morris Minor.

Granny watched her go, then stumped along the wet streets after her. She was determined that they wouldn't get her up in one of those things.

Esk lay in the big, fluffy and slightly damp sheets of the spare bed in the attic room of the Riddle. She was tired, but couldn't sleep. The bed was too chilly, for one thing. She wondered uneasily if she dared try to warm it up, but thought better of it. She couldn't seem to get the hang of fire spells, no matter how carefully she experimented. They either didn't work at all or worked only too well. The woods around the cottage were becoming treacherous with the holes left by disappearing fireballs; at least, if the wizardry thing didn't work then Granny said she'd have a fine future as a privy builder or well sinker.

She turned over and tried to ignore the bed's faint smell of mushrooms. Then she reached out in the darkness until her hand found the staff, propped against the bedhead. Mrs Skiller had been quite insistent about taking it downstairs, but Esk had hung on like grim death. It was the only thing in the world she was absolutely certain belonged to her.

The varnished surface with its strange carvings felt oddly comforting. Esk went to sleep, and dreamed bangles, and strange packages, and mountains. And distant stars above the mountains, and a cold desert where strange creatures lurched across the dry sand and stared at her through insect eyes . . .

There was a creak on the stairs. Then another. Then a silence, the sort of choking, furry silence made by someone standing as still as possible.

The door swung open. Skiller made a blacker shadow against the candlelight on the stairs, and there was a faintly whispered conversation before he tiptoed as silently as he could towards the bedhead. The staff slipped sideways as his first cautious grope dislodged it, but he caught it quickly and let his breath out very slowly.

So he hardly had enough left to scream with when the staff *moved* in his hands. He felt the scaliness, the coil and muscle of it . . .

Esk sat bolt upright in time to see Skiller roll backwards down the steep stairladder, still flailing desperately at something quite invisible that coiled around his arms. There was another scream from below as he landed on his wife.

The staff clattered to the floor and lay surrounded by a faint octarine glow.

Esk got out of the bed and padded across the floor. There was a terrible cursing; it sounded unhealthy. She peered around the door and looked down on the face of Mrs Skiller.

'Give me that staff!'

Esk reached down behind her and gripped the polished wood. 'No,' she said. 'It's mine.'

'It's not the right sort of thing for little girls,' snapped the barman's wife.

'It belongs to me,' said Esk, and quietly closed the door. She listened for a moment to the muttering from below and tried to think of what to do next. Turning the couple into something would probably only cause a fuss and, anyway, she wasn't quite certain how to do it.

The fact was the magic only really worked when she wasn't thinking about it. Her mind seemed to get in the way.

She padded across the room and pushed open the tiny window. The strange night-time smells of civilisation drifted in – the damp smell of streets, the fragrance of garden flowers, the distant hint of an overloaded privy. There were wet tiles outside.

As Skiller started back up the stairs she pushed the staff out on to the roof and crawled after it, steadying herself on the carvings above the window. The roof dipped down to an outhouse and she managed to stay at least vaguely upright as she half-slid, half-scrambled down the uneven tiles. A six-foot drop on to a stack of old barrels, a quick scramble down the slippery wood, and she was trotting easily across the inn yard.

As she kicked up the street mists she could hear the sounds of argument coming from the Riddle.

Skiller rushed past his wife and laid a hand on the tap of the nearest barrel. He paused, and then wrenched it open.

The smell of peach brandy filled the room, sharp as knives. He shut off the flow and relaxed.

'Afraid it would turn into something nasty?' asked his wife. He nodded.

'If you hadn't been so clumsy– ' she began.

'I tell you it bit me!'

'You could have been a wizard and we wouldn't have to bother with all this. Have you got no *ambition*?'

Skiller shook his head. 'I reckon it takes more than a staff to make a wizard,' he said. 'Anyway, I heard where it said wizards aren't allowed to get married, they're not even allowed to– ' He hesitated.

'To what? Allowed to what?'

Skiller writhed. 'Well. You know. Thing.'

'I'm sure I don't know what you're talking about,' said Mrs Skiller briskly.

'No, I suppose not.'

He followed her reluctantly out of the darkened bar-room. It seemed to him that perhaps wizards didn't have such a bad life, at that.

He was proved right when the following morning revealed that the ten barrels of peach brandy had, indeed, turned into something nasty.

Esk wandered aimlessly through the grey streets until she reached Ohulan's tiny river docks. Broad flat-bottomed barges bobbed gently against the wharves, and one or two of them curled wisps of smoke from friendly stovepipes. Esk clambered easily on to the nearest, and used the staff to lever up the oilcloth that covered most of it.

A warm smell, a mixture of lanolin and midden, drifted up. The barge was laden with wool.

It's silly to go to sleep on an unknown barge, not knowing what strange cliffs may be drifting past when you awake, not knowing that bargees traditionally get an early start (setting out before the sun is barely up), not knowing what new horizons might greet one on the morrow . . .

You know that. Esk didn't.

Esk awoke to the sound of someone whistling. She lay quite still, reeling the evening's events across her mind until she remembered why she was here, and then rolled over very carefully and raised the oilcloth a fraction.

Here she was, then. But 'here' had moved.

'This is what they call sailing, then,' she said, watching the far bank glide past. 'It doesn't seem very special.'

It didn't occur to her to start worrying. For the first eight years of her life the world had been a particularly boring place and now that it was becoming interesting Esk wasn't about to act ungrateful.

The distant whistler was joined by a barking dog. Esk lay back in the wool and reached out until she found the animal's mind, and Borrowed it gently. From its inefficient and disorganised brain she learned that there were at least four people on this barge, and many more on the others that were strung out in line with it on the river. Some of them seemed to be children.

She let the animal go and looked out at the scenery again for a long time – the barge was passing between high orange cliffs now, banded with so many colours of rock it looked as though some hungry God had made the all-time record club sandwich – and tried to avoid the next thought. But it persisted, arriving in her mind like the unexpected limbo dancer under the lavatory door of Life. Sooner or later she would have to go out. It wasn't her stomach that was pressing the point, but her bladder brooked no delay.

Perhaps if she–

The oilcloth over her head was pulled aside swiftly and a big bearded head beamed down at her.

'Well, well,' it said. 'What have we here, then? A stowaway, yesno?'

Esk gave it a stare. 'Yes,' she said. There seemed no sense in denying it. 'Could you help me out please?'

'Aren't you afraid I shall throw you to the – the pike?' said the head. It noticed her perplexed look. 'Big freshwater fish,' it added helpfully. Fast. Lot of teeth. Pike.'

The thought hadn't occurred to her at all. 'No,' she said truthfully. 'Why? Will you?'

'No. Not really. There's no need to be frightened.'

'I'm not.'

'Oh.' A brown arm appeared, attached to the head by the normal arrangements, and helped her out of her nest in the fleeces.

Esk stood on the deck of the barge and looked around. The sky was bluer than a biscuit barrel, fitting neatly over a broad valley through which the river ran as sluggishly as a planning inquiry.

Behind her the Ramtops still acted as a hitching rail for clouds, but they no longer dominated as they had done for as long as Esk had known them. Distance had eroded them.

'Where's this?' she said, sniffing the new smells of swamp and sedge.

'The Upper Valley of the River Ankh,' said her captor. 'What do you think of it?'

Esk looked up and down the river. It was already much wider than it had been at Ohulan.

'I don't know. There's certainly a lot of it. Is this your ship?'

'Boat,' he corrected. He was taller than her father, although not quite so old, and dressed like a gypsy. Most of his teeth had turned gold, but Esk decided it wasn't the time to ask why. He had the kind of real deep tan that rich people spend ages trying to achieve with expensive holidays and bits of tinfoil, when really all you need to do to obtain one is work your arse off in the open air every day. His brow crinkled.

'Yes, it's mine,' he said, determined to regain the initiative. 'And what are you doing on it, I would like to know? Running away from home, yesno? If you were a boy I'd say are you going to seek your fortune?'

'Can't girls seek their fortune?'

'I think they're supposed to seek a boy with a fortune,' said the man, and gave a 200-carat grin. He extended a brown hand, heavy with rings. 'Come and have some breakfast.'

'I'd actually like to use your privy,' she said. His mouth dropped open.

'This is a barge, yesno?'

'Yes?'

'That means there's only the river.' He patted her hand. 'Don't worry,' he added. 'It's quite used to it.'

Granny stood on the wharf, her boot tap-tap-tapping on the wood. The little man who was the nearest thing Ohulan had to a dockmaster was being treated to the full force of one of her stares, and was visibly wilting. Her expression wasn't perhaps as vicious as thumbscrews, but it did seem to suggest that thumbscrews were a real possibility.

'They left before dawn, you say,' she said.

'Yes-ss,' he said. 'Er. I didn't know they weren't supposed to.'

'Did you see a little girl on board?' Tap-tap went her boot.

'Um. No. I'm sorry.' He brightened. 'They were Zoons,' he said. 'If the child was with them she won't come to harm. You can always trust a Zoon, they say. Very keen on family life.'

Granny turned to Hilta, who was fluttering like a bewildered butterfly, and raised her eyebrows.

'Oh, yes,' Hilta trilled. 'The Zoons have a very good name.'

'Mmph,' said Granny. She turned on her heel and stumped back towards the centre of the town. The dockmaster sagged as though a coathanger had just been removed from his shirt.

Hilta's lodgings were over a herbalist's and behind a tannery, and offered splendid views of the rooftops of Ohuland. She liked it because it offered privacy, always appreciated by, as she put it, 'my more discerning clients who prefer to make their very special purchases in an atmosphere of calm where discretion is forever the watchword'.

Granny Weatherwax looked around the sitting room with barely concealed scorn. There were altogether too many tassels, bead curtains, astrological charts and black cats in the place. Granny couldn't abide cats. She sniffed.

'Is that the tannery?' she said accusingly.

'Incense,' said Hilta. She rallied bravely in the face of Granny's scorn. 'The customers appreciate it,' she said. 'It puts them in the right frame of mind. You know how it is.'

'I would have thought one could carry out a perfectly respectable business, Hilta, without resorting to *parlour* tricks,' said Granny, sitting down and beginning the long and tricky business of removing her hatpins.

'It's different in towns,' said Hilta. 'One has to move with the times.'

'I'm sure I don't know why. Is the kettle on?' Granny reached across the table and took the velvet cover off Hilta's crystal ball, a sphere of quartz as big as her head.

'Never could get the hang of this damn silicon stuff,' she said. 'A bowl of water with a drop of ink in it was good enough when I was a girl. Let's see, now . . . '

She peered into the dancing heart of the ball, trying to use it to focus her mind on the whereabouts of Esk. A crystal was a tricky thing to use at the best of times, and usually staring into it meant that the one thing the future could be guaranteed to hold was a severe migraine. Granny distrusted them, considering them to smack of wizardry; for two pins, it always seemed to her, the wretched thing would suck your mind out like a whelk from a shell.

'Damn thing's all sparkly,' she said, huffing on it and wiping it with her sleeve. Hilta peered over her shoulder.

'That's not sparkle, that means something,' she said slowly.

'What?'

'I'm not sure. Can I try? It's used to me.' Hilta pushed a cat off the other chair and leaned forward to peer into the glass depths.

'Mnph. Feel free,' said Granny, 'but you won't find– '

'Wait. Something's coming through.'

'Looks all sparkly from here,' Granny insisted. 'Little silver lights all floating around, like in them little snowstorm-in-a-bottle toys. Quite pretty, really.'

'Yes, but look beyond the flakes . . . '

Granny looked.

This was what she saw.

The viewpoint was very high up and a wide swathe of country lay below her, blue with distance, through which a broad river wriggled like a drunken snake. There were silver lights floating in the foreground but they were, in a manner of speaking, just a few flakes in the great storm of lights that turned in a great lazy spiral, like a geriatric tornado with a bad attack of snow, and funnelled down, down to the hazy landscape. By screwing up her eyes Granny could just make out some dots on the river.

Occasionally some sort of lighting would sparkle briefly inside the gently turning funnel of motes.

Granny blinked and looked up. The room seemed very dark.

'Odd sort of weather,' she said, because she couldn't really think of anything better. Even with her eyes shut the glittering motes still danced across her vision.

'I don't think it's weather,' said Hilta. 'I don't actually think people can see it, but the crystal shows it. I think it's magic, condensing out of the air.'

'Into the staff?'

'Yes. That's what a wizard's staff does. It sort of distils magic.'

Granny risked another glance at the crystal.

'Into Esk,' she said, carefully.

'Yes.'

'There looks like quite a lot of it.'

'Yes.'

Not for the first time, Granny wished she knew more about how wizards worked their magic. She had a vision of Esk filling up with magic, until every tissue and pore was bloated with the stuff. Then it would start leaking – slowly at first, arcing to ground in little bursts, but then building up to a great discharge of occult potentiality. It could do all kinds of damage.

'Drat,' she said. 'I never did like that staff.'

'At least she's heading towards the University place,' said Hilta. 'They'll know what to do.'

'That's as may be. How far downriver do you reckon they are?'

'Twenty miles or so. Those barges only go at walking pace. The Zoons aren't in any hurry.'

'Right.' Granny stood up, her jaw set defiantly. She reached for her hat and picked up her sack of possessions.

'Reckon I can walk faster than a barge,' she said. 'The river's all bendy but I can go in straight lines.'

'You're going to *walk* after her?' said Hilta, aghast. 'But there's forests and wild animals!'

'Good, I could do with getting back to civilisation. She needs me. That staff is taking over. I said it would, but did anyone listen?'

'Did they?' said Hilta, still trying to work out what Granny meant by getting back to civilisation.

'No,' said Granny coldly.

His name was Amschat B'hal Zoon. He lived on the raft with his three wives and three children. He was a Liar.

What always annoyed the enemies of the Zoon tribe was not simply their honesty, which was infuriatingly absolute, but their total directness of approach. The Zoons had never heard about a euphemism, and wouldn't understand what to do with it if they had one, except that they would certainly have called it 'a nice way of saying something nasty'.

Their rigid adherence to the truth was apparently not enjoined on them by a god, as is usually the case, but appeared to have a genetic base. The average Zoon could no more tell a lie than breathe underwater and, in fact, the very concept was enough to upset them considerably; telling a Lie meant no less than totally altering the universe.

This was something of a drawback to a trading race and so, over the millennia, the elders of the Zoon studied this strange power that everyone else had in such abundance and decided that they should possess it too.

Young men who showed faint signs of having such a talent were encouraged, on special ceremonial occasions, to bend the Truth ever further on a competitive basis. The first recorded Zoon proto-lie was: 'Actually my grandfather is quite tall,' but eventually they got the hang of it and the office of tribal Liar was instituted.

It must be understood that while the majority of Zoon cannot lie they have great respect for any Zoon who can say that the world is other than it is, and the Liar holds a position of considerable eminence. He represents his tribe in all his dealings with the outside world, which the average Zoon long ago gave up trying to understand. Zoon tribes are very proud of their Liars.

Other races get very annoyed about all this. They feel that the Zoon ought to have adopted more suitable titles, like 'diplomat' or 'public relations officer'. They feel they are poking fun at the whole thing.

'Is all that true?' said Esk suspiciously, looking around the barge's crowded cabin.

'No,' said Amschat firmly. His junior wife, who was cooking porridge over a tiny ornate stove, giggled. His three children watched Esk solemnly over the edge of the table.

'Don't you ever tell the truth?'

'Do you?' Amschat grinned his goldmine grin, but his eyes were not smiling. 'Why do I find you on my fleeces? Amschat is no kidnapper. There will be no people at home who will worry, yesno?'

'I expect Granny will come looking for me,' said Esk, 'but I don't think she will worry much. Just be angry, I expect. Anyway, I'm going to Ankh-Morpork. You can put me off the ship—'

'— boat—'

'— if you like. I don't mind about the pike.'

'I can't do that,' said Amschat.

'Was that a lie?'

'No! There is wild country around us, robbers and — things.'

Esk nodded brightly. 'That's settled, then,' she said. 'I don't mind sleeping in the fleeces. And I can pay my way. I can do–' She hesitated; her unfinished sentence hung like a little curl of crystal in the air while discretion made a successful bid for control of her tongue. ' – helpful things,' she finished lamely.

She was aware that Amschat was looking slightly sideways at his senior wife, who was sewing by the stove. By Zoon tradition she wore nothing but black. Granny would have thoroughly approved.

'What sort of helpful things?' he asked. 'Washing and sweeping, yesno?'

'If you like,' said Esk, 'or distillation using the bifold or triple alembic, the making of varnishes, glazes, creams, zuum-chats and punes, the rendering of waxes, the manufacture of candles, the proper selection of seeds, roots and cuttings, and most preparations from the Eighty Marvellous Herbs; I can spin, card, rett, flallow and weave on the hand, frame, harp and Noble looms and I can knit if people start the wool on for me, I can read soil and rock, do carpentry up to the three-way mortise and tenon, predict weather by means of beastsign and skyreck, make increase in bees, brew five types of mead, make dyes and mordants and pigments, including a fast blue, I can do most types of whitesmithing, mend boots, cure and fashion most leathers, and if you have any goats I can look after them. I like goats.'

Amschat looked at her thoughtfully. She felt she was expected to continue.

'Granny never likes to see people sitting around doing nothing,' she offered. 'She always says a girl who is good with her hands will never want for a living,' she added, by way of further explanation.

'Or a husband, I expect,' nodded Amschat, weakly.

'Actually, Granny had a lot to say about that–'

'I bet she did,' said Amschat. He looked at the senior wife, who nodded almost imperceptibly.

'Very well,' he said. 'If you can make yourself useful you can stay. And can you play a musical instrument?'

Esk returned his steady gaze, not batting an eyelid. 'Probably.'

And so Esk, with the minimum of difficulty and only a little regret, left the Ramtops and their weather and joined the Zoons on their great trading journey down the Ankh.

There were at least thirty barges with at least one sprawling Zoon family on each, and no two vessels appeared to be carrying the same cargo; most of them were strung together, and the Zoons simply hauled on the cable and stepped on to the next deck if they fancied a bit of socialising.

Esk set up home in the fleeces. It was warm, smelled slightly of Granny's cottage and, much more important, meant that she was undisturbed.

She was getting a bit worried about magic.

It was definitely getting out of control. She wasn't doing magic, it was just happening around her. And she sensed that people probably wouldn't be too happy if they knew.

It meant that if she washed up she had to clatter and splash at length to conceal the fact that the dishes were cleaning themselves. If she did some darning she had to do it on some private part of the deck to conceal the fact that the edges of the hole ravelled themselves together as if . . . as if by magic. Then she woke up on the second day of her voyage to find that several of the fleeces around the spot where she had hidden the staff had combed, carded and spun themselves into neat skeins during the night.

She put all thoughts of lighting fires out of her head.

There were compensations, though. Every sluggish turn of the great brown river brought new scenes. There were dark stretches hemmed in with deep forest, through which the barges travelled in the dead centre of the river with the men armed and the women below – except for Esk, who sat listening with interest to the snortings and sneezings that followed them through the bushes on the banks. There were stretches of farmland. There were several towns much larger than Ohulan. There were even some mountains, although they were old and flat and not young and frisky like her mountains. Not that she was homesick, exactly, but sometimes she felt like a boat herself, drifting on the edge of an infinite rope but always attached to an anchor.

The barges stopped at some of the towns. By tradition only the men went ashore, and only Amschat, wearing his ceremonial Lying hat, spoke to non-Zoons. Esk usually went with him. He tried hinting that she should obey the unwritten rules of Zoon life and stay afloat, but a hint was to Esk what a mosquito bite was to the average rhino because she was already learning that if you ignore the rules people will, half the time, quietly rewrite them so that they don't apply to you.

Anyway, it seemed to Amschat that when Esk was with him he always got a very good price. There was something about a small child squinting determinedly at them from behind his legs that made even market-hardened merchants hastily conclude their business.

In fact, it began to worry him. When a market broker in the walled town of Zemphis offered him a bag of ultramarines in exchange for a hundred fleeces a voice from the level of his pockets said: 'They're not ultramarines.'

'Listen to the child!' said the broker, grinning. Amschat solemnly held one of the stones to his eye.

'I am listening,' he said, 'and they do indeed look like ultramarines. They have the glit and shimmy.'

Esk shook her head. 'They're just spircles,' she said. She said it without thinking, and regretted it immediately as both men turned to stare at her.

Amschat turned the stone over in his palm. Putting the chameleon spircle stones into a box with some real gems so that they appeared to change their hue was a traditional trick, but these had the true inner blue fire. He looked up sharply at the broker. Amschat had been finely trained in the art of the Lie. He recognised the subtle signs, now that he came to think about it.

'There seems to be a doubt,' he said, 'but 'tis easily resolved, we need only take them to the assayer in Pine Street because the world knows that spircles will dissolve in hypactic fluid, yesno?'

The broker hesitated. Amschat had changed position slightly, and the set of his muscles suggested that any sudden movement on the broker's part would see him flat in the dust. And that damn child was squinting at him as though she could see through to the back of his mind. His nerve broke.

'I regret this unfortunate dispute,' he said. 'I had accepted the stones as ultramarines in good faith but rather than cause disharmony between us I will ask you to accept them as – as a gift, and for the fleeces may I offer this roseatte of the first sorting?'

He took a small red stone from a tiny velvet pouch. Amschat hardly looked at it but, without taking his eyes off the man, passed it down to Esk. She nodded.

When the merchant had hurried off Amschat took Esk's hand and half-dragged her to the assayer's stall, which was little more than a niche in the wall. The old man took the smallest of the blue stones, listened to Amschat's hurried explanation, poured out a saucerful of hypactic fluid and dropped the stone in. It frothed into nothingness.

'Very interesting,' he said. He took another stone in a tweezer and examined it under a glass.

'They are indeed spircles, but remarkably fine specimens in their own right,' he concluded. 'They are by no means worthless, and I for example would be prepared to offer you – is there something wrong with the little girl's eyes?'

Amschat nudged Esk, who stopped trying out another Look.

' – I would offer you, shall we say, two *zats* of silver?'

'Shall we say five?' said Amschat pleasantly.

'And I would like to keep one of the stones,' said Esk. The old man threw up his hands.

'But they are mere curios!' he said. 'Of value only to a collector!'

'A collector may yet sell them to an unsuspecting purchaser as finest roseattes or ultramarines,' said Amschat, 'especially if he was the only assayer in town.'

The assayer grumbled a bit at this, but at last they settled on three *zats* and one of the spircles on a thin silver chain for Esk.

When they were out of earshot Amschat handed her the tiny silver coins and said: 'These are yours. You have earned them. But– ' he hunkered down so that his eyes were on a level with hers, ' – you must tell me how you knew the stones were false.'

He looked worried, but Esk sensed that he wouldn't really like the truth. Magic made people uncomfortable. He wouldn't like it if she said simply: spircles are spircles and ultramarines are ultramarines, and though you may think they look the same that is because most people don't use their eyes in the right way. Nothing can entirely disguise its true nature.

Instead she said: 'The dwarfs mine spircles near the village where I was born, and you soon learn to see how they bend light in a funny way.'

Amschat looked into her eyes for some time. Then he shrugged.

'Okay,' he said. 'Fine. Well, I have some further business here. Why don't you buy yourself some new clothes, or something? I'd warn you against unscrupulous traders but, somehow, I don't know, I don't think you will have any trouble.'

Esk nodded. Amschat strode off through the market place. At the first corner he turned, looked at her thoughtfully, and then disappeared among the crowds.

Well, that's the end of sailing, Esk told herself. He's not quite sure but he's going to be watching me now and before I know what's happening the staff will be taken away and there'll be all sorts of trouble. Why does everyone get so upset about magic?

She gave a philosophical sigh and set about exploring the possibilities of the town.

There was the question of the staff, though. Esk had rammed it deep among the fleeces, which were not going to be unloaded yet. If she went back for it people would start asking questions, and she didn't know the answers.

She found a convenient alleyway and scuttled down it until a deep doorway gave her the privacy she required.

If going back was out of the question then only one thing remained. She held out a hand and closed her eyes.

She knew exactly what she wanted to do – it lay in front of her eyes. The staff mustn't come flying through the air, wrecking the barge and drawing attention to itself. All she wanted, she told herself, was for there to be a slight change in the way the world was organised. It shouldn't be a world where the staff was in the fleeces, it should be a world where it was in her hand. A tiny change, an infinitesimal alteration to the Way Things Were.

If Esk had been properly trained in wizardry she would have known that this was impossible. All wizards knew how to move things about, starting with protons and working upwards, but the important thing about moving something from A to Z, according to basic physics, was that at some point it should pass through the rest of the alphabet. The only way one could cause something to vanish at A and appear at Z would be to shuffle the whole of Reality sideways. The problems this would cause didn't bear thinking about.

Esk, of course, had not been trained, and it is well known that a vital ingredient of success is not knowing that what you're attempting can't be done. A person ignorant of the possibility of failure can be a halfbrick in the path of the bicycle of history.

As Esk tried to work out how to move the staff the ripples spread out in the magical ether, changing the Discworld in thousands of tiny ways. Most went entirely unnoticed. Perhaps a few grains of sand lay on their beaches in a slightly different position, or the occasional leaf hung on its tree in a marginally different way. But then the wavefront of probability struck the edge of Reality and rebounded like the slosh off the side of the pond which, meeting the laggard ripples coming the other way, caused small but important whirlpools in the very fabric of existence. You can have whirlpools in the fabric of existence, because it is a very strange fabric.

Esk was completely ignorant of all this, of course, but was quite satisfied when the staff dropped out of thin air into her hand.

It felt warm.

She looked at it for some time. She felt that she ought to do something about it; it was too big, too distinctive, too inconvenient. It attracted attention.

'If I'm taking you to Ankh-Morpork,' she said thoughtfully. 'You've got to go in disguise.'

A few late flickers of magic played around the staff, and then it went dark.

Eventually Esk solved the immediate problem by finding a stall in the main Zemphis marketplace that sold broomsticks, buying the largest, carrying it back to her doorway, removing the handle and ramming the staff deep into the birch twigs. It didn't seem right to treat a noble object in this way, and she silently apologised to it.

It made a difference, anyway. No one looked twice at a small girl carrying a broom.

She bought a spice pasty to eat while exploring (the stallholder carelessly shortchanged her, and only realised later that he had inexplicably handed over two silver pieces; also, rats mysteriously got in and ate all his stock during the night, and his grandmother was struck by lightning).

The town was smaller than Ohulan, and very different because it lay on the junction of three trade routes quite apart from the river itself. It was built around one enormous square which was a cross between a permanent exotic traffic jam and a tent village. Camels kicked mules, mules kicked horses, horses kicked camels and they all kicked humans; there was a riot of colours, a din of noise, a nasal orchestration of smells and the steady, heady sound of hundreds of people working hard at making money.

One reason for the bustle was that over large parts of the continent other people preferred to make money without working at all, and since the Disc had yet to develop a music recording industry they were forced to fall back on older, more traditional forms of banditry.

Strangely enough these often involved considerable effort. Rolling heavy rocks to the top of cliffs for a decent ambush, cutting down trees to block the road, and digging a pit lined with spikes while still keeping a wicked edge on a dagger probably involved a much greater expenditure of thoughts and muscle than more socially acceptable professions but, nevertheless, there were still people misguided enough to endure all this, plus long nights in uncomfortable surroundings, merely to get their hands on perfectly ordinary large boxes of jewels.

So a town like Zemphis was the place where caravans split, mingled and came together again, as dozens of merchants and travellers banded together for protection against the socially disadvantaged on the trails ahead. Esk, wandering unregarded amidst the bustle, learned all this by the simple method of finding someone who looked important and tugging on the hem of his coat.

This particular man was counting bales of tobacco and would have succeeded but for the interruption.

'What?'

'I said, what's happening here?'

The man meant to say: 'Push off and bother someone else.' He meant to give her a light cuff about the head. So he was astonished to find himself bending down and talking seriously to a small, grubby-faced child holding a large broomstick (which also, it seemed to him later, was in some indefinable way *paying attention*).

He explained about the caravans. The child nodded.

'People all get together to travel?'

'Precisely.'

'Where to?'

'All sorts of places. Sto Lat, Pseudopolis . . . Ankh-Morpork, of course . . .'

'But the river goes there,' said Esk, reasonably. 'Barges. The Zoons.'

'Ah, yes,' said the merchant, 'but they charge high prices and they can't carry everything and, anyway, no one trusts them much.'

'But they're very honest!'

'Huh, yes,' he said. 'But you know what they say: never trust an honest man.' He smiled knowingly.

'Who says that?'

'They do. You know. People,' he said, a certain uneasiness entering his voice.

'Oh,' said Esk. She thought about it. 'They must be very silly,' she said primly. 'Thank you, anyway.'

He watched her wander off and got back to his counting. A moment later there was another tug at his coat.

'Fiftysevenfiftysevenfiftysevenwell?' he said, trying not to lose his place.

'Sorry to bother you again,' said Esk, 'but those bale things . . . '

'What about them fiftysevenfiftysevenfiftyseven?'

'Well, are they supposed to have little white worm things in them?'

'Fiftysev– *What*?' The merchant lowered his slate and stared at Esk. 'What little worms?'

'Wriggly ones. White,' added Esk, helpfully. 'All sort of burrowing about in the middle of the bales.'

'You mean tobacco threadworm?' He looked wild-eyed at the stack of bales being unloaded by, now he came to think about it, a vendor with the nervous look of a midnight sprite who wants to get away before you find out what fairy gold turns into in the morning. 'But he told me these had been well stored and – how do you know, anyway?'

The child had disappeared among the crowds. The merchant looked hard at the spot where she had been. He looked hard at the vendor, who was grinning nervously. He looked hard at the sky. Then took his sampling knife out of his pocket, stared at it for a moment, appeared to reach a decision, and sidled towards the nearest bale.

Esk, meanwhile, had by random eavesdropping found the caravan being assembled for Ankh-Morpork. The trail boss was sitting at a table made up of a plank across two barrels.

He was busy.

He was talking to a wizard.

Seasoned travellers know that a party setting out to cross possibly hostile country should have a fair number of swords in it but should definitely have a wizard in case there is any need for magic arts and, even if these do not become necessary, for lighting fires. A wizard of the third rank or above does not expect to pay for the privilege of joining the party. Rather, he expects to be paid. Delicate negotiations were even now coming to a conclusion.

'Fair enough, Master Treatle, but what of the young man?' said the trail boss, one Adab Gander, an impressive figure in a trollhide jerkin, rakishly floppy hat and a leather kilt. 'He's no wizard, I can see.'

'He is in training,' said Treatle – a tall skinny wizard whose robes declared him to be a mage of the Ancient and Truly Original Brothers of the Silver Star, one of the eight orders of wizardry.

'Then no wizard he,' said Gander. 'I know the rules, and you're not a wizard unless you've got a staff. And he hasn't.'

'Even now he travels to the Unseen University for that small detail,' said Treatle loftily. Wizards parted with money slightly less readily than tigers parted with their teeth.

Gander looked at the lad in question. He had met a good many wizards in his time and considered himself a good judge and he had to admit that this boy looked like good wizard material. In other words, he was thin, gangling, pale from reading disturbing books in unhealthy rooms, and had watery eyes like two lightly poached eggs. It crossed Gander's mind that one must speculate in order to accumulate.

All he needs to get right to the top, he thought, is a bit of a handicap. Wizards are martyrs to things like asthma and flat feet, it somehow seems to give them their drive.

'What's your name, lad?' he said, as kindly as possible.

'Sssssssssssssss,' said the boy. His Adam's apple bobbed like a captive balloon. He turned to his companion, full of mute appeal.

'Simon,' said Treatle.

' – imon,' agreed Simon, thankfully.

'Can you cast fireballs or whirling spells, such as might be hurled against an enemy?'

Simon looked sideways at Treatle.

'Nnnnnnnnnn,' he ventured.

'My young friend follows higher magic than the mere hurling of sorceries,' said the wizard.

' – o,' said Simon.

Gander nodded.

'Well,' he said, 'maybe you will indeed be a wizard, lad. Maybe when you have your fine staff you'll consent to travel with me one time, yes? I will make an investment in you, yes?'

'Y–'

'Just nod,' said Gander, who was not naturally a cruel man.

Simon nodded gratefully. Treatle and Gander exchanged nods and then the wizard strode off, with his apprentice trailing behind under a weight of baggage.

Gander looked down at the list in front of him and carefully crossed out 'wizard'.

A small shadow fell across the page. He glanced up and gave an involuntary start.

'Well?' he said coldly.

'I want to go to Ankh-Morpork,' said Esk, 'please. I've got some money.'

'Go home to your mother, child.'

'No, really. I want to seek my fortune.'

Gander sighed. 'Why are you holding that broomstick?' he said.

Esk looked at it as though she had never seen it before.

'Everything's got to be somewhere,' she said.

'Just go home, my girl,' said Gander. 'I'm not taking any runaways to Ankh-Morpork. Strange things can happen to little girls in big cities.'

Esk brightened. 'What sort of strange things?'

'Look, I said go home, right? Now!'

He picked up his chalk and went on ticking off items on his slate, trying to ignore the steady gaze that seemed to be boring through the top of his head.

'I can be helpful,' said Esk, quietly.

Gander threw down the chalk and scratched his chin irritably.

'How old are you?' he said.

'Nine.'

'Well, Miss nine-years-old, I've got two hundred animals and a hundred people that want to go to Ankh, and half of them hate the other half, and I've not got enough people who can fight, and they say the roads are pretty bad and the bandits are getting really cheeky up in the Paps and the trolls are demanding a bigger bridge toll this year and there's weevils in the supplies and I keep getting these headaches and where, in all this, do I need you?'

'Oh,' said Esk. She looked around the crowded square. 'Which one of these roads goes to Ankh, then?'

'The one over there, with the gate.'

'Thank you,' she said gravely. 'Goodbye. I hope you don't have any more trouble and your head gets better.'

'Right,' said Gander uncertainly. He drummed his fingers on the tabletop as he watched Esk walk away in the direction of the Ankh road. A long, winding road. A road haunted by thieves and gnolls. A road that wheezed through high mountain passes and crawled, panting, over deserts.

'Oh bugger,' he said, under his breath. 'Hey! You!'

Granny Weatherwax was in trouble.

First of all, she decided, she should never have allowed Hilta to talk her into borrowing her broomstick. It was elderly, erratic, would fly only at night and even then couldn't manage a speed much above a trot.

Its lifting spells had worn so thin that it wouldn't even begin to operate until it was already moving at a fair lick. It was, in fact, the only broomstick ever to need bump-starting.

And it was while Granny Weatherwax, sweating and cursing, was running along a forest path holding the damn thing at shoulder height for the tenth time that she had found the bear trap.

The second problem was that a bear had found it first. In fact this hadn't been too much of a problem because Granny, already in a bad temper, hit it right between the eyes with the broomstick and it was now sitting as far away from her as it was possible to get in a pit, and trying to think happy thoughts.

It was not a very comfortable night and the morning wasn't much better for the party of hunters who, around dawn, peered over the edge of the pit.

'About time, too,' said Granny. 'Get me out.'

The startled heads withdrew and Granny could hear a hasty whispered conversation. They had seen the hat and broomstick.

Finally a bearded head reappeared, rather reluctantly, as if the body it was attached to was being pushed forward.

'Um,' it began, 'look, mother—'

'I'm not a mother,' snapped Granny. 'I'm certainly not your mother, if you ever had mothers, which I doubt. If I was your mother I'd have run away before you were born.'

'It's only a figure of speech,' said the head reproachfully.

'It's a damned insult is what it is!'

There was another whispered conversation.

'If I don't get out,' said Granny in ringing tones, 'there will be Trouble. Do you see my hat, eh? Do you see it?'

The head reappeared.

'That's the whole point, isn't it?' it said. 'I mean, what will there be if we let you out? It seems less risky all round if we just sort of fill the pit in. Nothing personal, you understand.'

Granny realised what it was that was bothering her about the head.

'Are you kneeling down?' she said accusingly. 'You're not, are you! You're dwarfs!'

Whisper, whisper.

'Well, what about it?' asked the head defiantly. 'Nothing wrong with that, is there? What have you got against dwarfs?'

'Do you know how to repair broomsticks?'

'Magic broomsticks?'

'Yes!'

Whisper, whisper.

'What if we do?'

'Well, we could come to some arrangement . . . '

The dwarf halls rang to the sound of hammers, although mainly for effect. Dwarfs found it hard to think without the sound of hammers, which they found soothing, so well-off dwarfs in the clerical professions paid goblins to hit small ceremonial anvils, just to maintain the correct dwarfish image.

The broomstick lay between two trestles. Granny Weatherwax sat on a rock outcrop while a dwarf half her height, wearing an apron that was a mass of pockets, walked around the broom and occasionally poked it.

Eventually he kicked the bristles and gave a long intake of breath, a sort of reverse whistle, which is the secret sign of craftsmen across the universe and means that something expensive is about to happen.

'Weellll,' he said. 'I could get the apprentices in to look at this, I could. It's an education in itself. And you say it actually managed to get airborne?'

'It flew like a bird,' said Granny.

The dwarf lit a pipe. 'I should very much like to see that bird,' he said reflectively. 'I should imagine it's quite something to watch, a bird like that.'

'Yes, but can you repair it?' said Granny. 'I'm in a hurry.'

The dwarf sat down, slowly and deliberately.

'As for *repair*,' he said, 'well, I don't know about *repair*. Rebuild, maybe. Of course, it's hard to get the bristles these days even if you can find people to do the proper binding, and the spells need– '

'I don't want it rebuilt, I just want it to work properly,' said Granny.

'It's an early model, you see,' the dwarf plugged on. 'Very tricky those early models. You can't get the wood– '

He was picked up bodily until his eyes were level with Granny's. Dwarfs, being magical in themselves as it were, are quite resistant to magic but her expression looked as though she was trying to weld his eyeballs to the back of his skull.

'Just repair it,' she hissed. 'Please?'

'What, make a bodge job?' said the dwarf, his pipe clattering to the floor.

'Yes.'

'Patch it up, you mean? Betray my training by doing half a job?'

'Yes,' said Granny. Her pupils were two little black holes.

'Oh,' said the dwarf. 'Right, then.'

☆　☆　☆

Gander the trail boss was a worried man.

They were three mornings out from Zemphis, making good time, and were climbing now towards the rocky pass through the mountains known as the Paps of Scilla (there were eight of them; Gander often wondered who Scilla had been, and whether he would have liked her).

A party of gnolls had crept up on them during the night. The nasty creatures, a variety of stone goblin, had slit the throat of a guard and must have been poised to slaughter the entire party. Only . . .

Only no one knew quite what had happened next. The screams had woken them up, and by the time people had puffed up the fires and Treatle the wizard had cast a blue radiance over the campsite the surviving gnolls were distant, spidery shadows, running as if all the legions of Hell were after them.

Judging by what had happened to their colleagues, they were probably right. Bits of gnolls hung from the nearby rocks, giving them a sort of jolly, festive air. Gander wasn't particularly sorry about that – gnolls liked to capture travellers and practise hospitality of the red-hot-knife-and-bludgeon kind – but he was nervous of being in the same area as Something that went through a dozen wiry and wickedly armed gnolls like a spoon through a lightly boiled egg but left no tracks.

In fact the ground was swept clean.

It had been a very long night, and the morning didn't seem to be an improvement. The only person more than half-awake was Esk, who had slept through the whole thing under one of the wagons and had complained only of odd dreams.

Still, it was a relief to get away from that macabre sight. Gander considered that gnolls didn't look any better inside than out. He hated their guts.

Esk sat on Treatle's wagon, talking to Simon who was steering inexpertly while the wizard caught up with some sleep behind them.

Simon did everything inexpertly. He was really good at it. He was one of those tall lads apparently made out of knees, thumbs and elbows. Watching him walk was a strain, you kept waiting for the strings to snap, and when he talked the spasm of agony on his face if he spotted an S or W looming ahead in the sentence made people instinctively say them for him. It was worth it for the grateful look which spread across his acned face like sunrise on the moon.

At the moment his eyes were streaming with hayfever.

'Did you want to be a wizard when you were a little boy?'

Simon shook his head. 'I just www–'

' – wanted – '

'– tto find out how things www–'

'– worked? –'

'Yes. Then someone in my village told the University and Master T-Treatle was sent to bring me. I shall be a www–'

'– wizard –'

'– one day. Master Treatle says I have an exceptional grasp of th-theory.' Simon's damp eyes misted over and an expression almost of bliss drifted across his ravaged face.

'He t-tells me they've got thousands of b-books in the library at Unseen University,' he said, in the voice of a man in love. 'More b-books than anyone could read in a lifetime.'

'I'm not sure I like books,' said Esk conversationally. 'How can paper know things? My granny says books are only good if the paper is thin.'

'No, that's not right,' said Simon urgently. 'Books are full of www–' he gulped air and gave her a pleading look.

'– words –' said Esk, after a moment's thought.

'– yes, and they can change th-things. Th-that's wuwuw, that wuwuw – whha–whha–'

'– what –'

'– I must f-find. I know it's th-there, somewhere in all the old books. They ssss–'

'– say –'

'there's no new spells but I know that it's there somewhere, hiding, the wwwwwuwu–'

'– words –'

'yes, that no wiwiwi–'

'– Wizard? –' said Esk, her face a frown of concentration.

'Yes, has ever found.' His eyes closed and he smiled a beatific smile and added, 'The Words that Will change the World.'

'What?'

'Eh?' said Simon, opening his eyes in time to stop the oxen wandering off the track.

'You said all those wubbleyous!'

'I did?'

'I heard you! Try again.'

Simon took a deep breath. 'The worworwor – the wuwuw–' he said. 'The wowowoo–' he continued.

'It's no good, it's gone,' he said. 'It happens sometimes, if I don't think about it. Master Treatle says I'm allergic to something.'

'Allergic to double-yous?'

'No, sisssisi–'

'– silly –' said Esk, generously.

'– there's sososo–'

'– something –'

' – in the air, p-pollen maybe, or g-grass dust. Master Treatle has tried to find the cause of it but no magic seems to h-help it.'

They were passing through a narrow pass of orange rock. Simon looked at it disconsolately.

'My granny taught me some hayfever cures,' Esk said. 'We could try those.'

Simon shook his head. It looked touch and go whether it would fall off.

'Tried everything,' he said. 'Fine wwiwwi– magician I'd make, eh, can't even sss– utter the wowo– name.'

'I could see where that would be a problem,' said Esk. She watched the scenery for a while, marshalling a train of thought.

'Is it, er, possible for a woman to be, you know, a wizard?' she said eventually.

Simon stared at her. She gave him a defiant look.

His throat strained. He was trying to find a sentence that didn't start with a W. In the end he was forced to make concessions.

'A curious idea,' he said. He thought some more, and started to laugh until Esk's expression warned him.

'Rather funny, really,' he added, but the laughter in his face faded and was replaced by a puzzled look. 'Never really th- thought about it, before.'

'Well? Can they?' You could have shaved with Esk's voice.

'Of course they can't. It is self-evident, child. Simon, return to your studies.'

Treatle pushed aside the curtain that led into the back of the wagon and climbed out on to the seat board.

The look of mild panic took up its familiar place in Simon's face. He gave Esk a pleading glance as Treatle took the reins from his hands, but she ignored him.

'Why not? What's so self-evident?'

Treatle turned and looked down at her. He hadn't really paid much attention before, she was simply just another figure around the campfires.

He was the Vice-Chancellor of Unseen University, and quite used to seeing vague scurrying figures getting on with essential but unimportant jobs like serving his meals and dusting his rooms. He was stupid, yes, in the particular way that very clever people can be stupid, and maybe he had all the tact of an avalanche and was as self-centred as a tornado, but it would never have occurred to him that children were important enough to be unkind to.

From long white hair to curly boots, Treatle was a wizard's wizard. He had the appropriate long bushy eyebrows, spangled robe and patriarchal beard that was only slightly spoiled by the yellow nicotine stains (wizards are celibate but, nevertheless, enjoy a good cigar).

'It will all become clear to you when you grow up,' he said. 'It's an amusing idea, of course, a nice play on words. A female wizard! You might as well invent a male witch!'

'Warlocks,' said Esk.

'Pardon me?'

'My granny says men can't be witches,' said Esk. 'She says if men tried to be witches they'd be wizards.'

'She sounds a very wise woman,' said Treatle.

'She says women should stick to what they're good at,' Esk went on.

'Very sensible of her.'

'She says if women were as good as men they'd be a lot better!'

Treatle laughed.

'She's a witch,' said Esk, and added in her mind: there, what do you think of that, Mr so-called cleverwizard?

'My dear young lady, am I supposed to be shocked? I happen to have a great respect for witches.'

Esk frowned. He wasn't supposed to say that.

'You have?'

'Yes indeed. I happen to believe that witchcraft is a fine career, for a woman. A very noble calling.'

'You do? I mean, it is?'

'Oh yes. Very useful in rural districts for, for people who are – having babies, and so forth. However, witches are not wizards. Witchcraft is Nature's way of allowing women access to the magical fluxes, but you must remember it is not *high* magic.'

'I see. Not high magic,' said Esk grimly.

'Oh, no. Witchcraft is very suitable for helping people through life, of course, but–'

'I expect women aren't really sensible enough to be wizards,' said Esk. 'I expect that's it, really.'

'I have nothing but the highest respect for women,' said Treatle, who hadn't noticed the fresh edge to Esk's tone. 'They are without parallel when, when–'

'For having babies and so forth?'

'There is that, yes,' the wizard conceded generously. 'But they can be a little unsettling at times. A little too excitable. High magic requires great clarity of thought, you see, and women's talents do not lie in that direction.

Their brains tend to overheat. I am sorry to say there is only one door into wizardry and that is the main gate at Unseen University and no woman has ever passed through it.'

'Tell me,' said Esk, 'what good is high magic, exactly?'

Treatle smiled at her.

'High magic, my child,' he said, 'can give us everything we want.'

'Oh.'

'So put all this wizard nonsense out of your head, all right?' Treatle gave her a benevolent smile. 'What is your name, child?'

'Eskarina.'

'And why do you go to Ankh, my dear?'

'I thought I might seek my fortune,' muttered Esk, 'but I think perhaps girls don't have fortunes to seek. Are you sure wizards give people what they want?'

'Of course. That is what high magic is for.'

'I see.'

The whole caravan was travelling only a little faster than walking pace. Esk jumped down, pulled the staff from its temporary hiding place among the bags and pails on the side of the wagon, and ran back along the line of carts and animals. Through her tears she caught a glimpse of Simon peering from the back of the wagon, an open book in his hands. He gave her a puzzled smile and started to say something, but she ran on and veered off the track.

Scrubby whinbushes scratched her legs as she scrambled up a clay bank and then she was running free across a barren plateau, hemmed in by the orange cliffs.

She didn't stop until she was good and lost but the anger still burned brightly. She had been angry before, but never like this; normally anger was like the red flame you got when the forge was first lit, all glow and sparks, but this anger was different – it had the bellows behind it, and had narrowed to the tiny blue-white flame that cuts iron.

It made her body tingle. She had to do something about it or burst.

Why was it that when she heard Granny ramble on about witchcraft she longed for the cutting magic of wizardry, but whenever she heard Treatle speak in his high-pitched voice she would fight to the death for witchcraft? She'd be both, or none at all. And the more they intended to stop her, the more she wanted it.

She'd be a witch and a wizard *too*. And she would *show* them.

Esk sat down under a low-spreading juniper bush at the foot of a steep, sheer cliff, her mind seething with plans and anger. She could sense doors being slammed before she had barely begun to open them. Treatle was right;

they wouldn't let her inside the University. Having a staff wasn't enough to be a wizard, there had to be training too, and no one was going to train her.

The midday sun beat down off the cliff and the air around Esk began to smell of bees and gin. She lay back, looking at the near-purple dome of the sky through the leaves and, eventually, she fell asleep.

One side-effect of using magic is that one tends to have realistic and disturbing dreams. There is a reason for this, but even thinking about it is enough to give a wizard nightmares.

The fact is that the minds of wizards can give thoughts a shape. Witches normally work with what actually exists in the world, but a wizard can, if he's good enough, put flesh on his imagination. This wouldn't cause any trouble if it wasn't for the fact that the little circle of candlelight loosely called 'the universe of time and space' is adrift in something much more unpleasant and unpredictable. Strange Things circle and grunt outside the flimsy stockades of normality; there are weird hootings and howlings in the deep crevices at the edge of Time. There are things so horrible that even the dark is afraid of them.

Most people don't know this and this is just as well because the world could not really operate if everyone stayed in bed with the blankets over their head, which is what would happen if people knew what horrors lay a shadow's width away.

The problem is people interested in magic and mysticism spend a lot of time loitering on the very edge of the light, as it were, which gets them noticed by the creatures from the Dungeon Dimensions who then try to use them in their indefatigable efforts to break into this particular Reality.

Most people can resist this, but the relentless probing by the Things is never stronger than when the subject is asleep.

Bel-Shamharoth, C'hulagen, the Insider – the hideous old dark gods of the Necrotelicomnicon, the book known to certain mad adepts by its true name of *Liber Paginarum Fulvarum*, are always ready to steal into a slumbering mind. The nightmares are often colourful and always unpleasant.

Esk had got used to them ever since that first dream after her first Borrowing, and familiarity had almost replaced terror. When she found herself sitting on a glittering, dusty plain under unexplained stars she knew it was time for another one.

'Drat,' she said. 'All right, come on then. Bring on the monsters. I just hope it isn't the one with his winkle on his face.'

But this time it seemed that the nightmare had changed. Esk looked around and saw, rearing up behind her, a tall black castle. Its turrets disappeared among the stars. Lights and fireworks and interesting music cascaded from its upper battlements. The huge double doors stood invitingly open. There seemed to be quite an amusing party going on in there.

She stood up, brushed the silver sand off her dress, and set off for the gates.

She had almost reached them when they slammed. They didn't appear to move; it was simply that in one instant they were lounging ajar, and the next they were tight shut with a clang that shook the horizons.

Esk reached out and touched them. They were black, and so cold that ice was beginning to form on them.

There was a movement behind her. She turned around and saw the staff, without its broomstick disguise, standing upright in the sand. Little worms of light crept around its polished wood and crept around the carvings no one could ever quite identify.

She picked it up and smashed it against the doors. There was a shower of octarine sparks, but the black metal was unscathed.

Esk's eyes narrowed. She held the staff at arm's length and concentrated until a thin line of fire leapt from the wood and burst against the gate. The ice flashed into steam but the darkness – she was sure now that it wasn't metal – absorbed the power without so much as glowing. She doubled the energy, letting the staff put all its stored magic into a beam that was now so bright that she had to shut her eyes (and could still see it as a brilliant line in her mind).

Then it winked out.

After a few seconds Esk ran forward and touched the doors gingerly. The coldness nearly froze her fingers off.

And from the battlements above she could hear the sound of sniggering. Laughter wouldn't have been so bad, especially an impressive demonic laugh with lots of echo, but this was just – sniggering.

It went on for a long time. It was one of the most unpleasant sounds Esk had ever heard.

She woke up shivering. It was long after midnight and the stars looked damp and chilly; the air was full of the busy silence of the night, which is created by hundreds of small furry things treading very carefully in the hope of finding dinner while avoiding being the main course.

A crescent moon was setting and a thin grey glow towards the rim of the world suggested that, against all probability, another day was on the cards.

Someone had wrapped Esk in a blanket.

'I know you're awake,' said the voice of Granny Weatherwax. 'You could make yourself useful and light a fire. There's damn all wood in these parts.'

Esk sat up, and clutched at the juniper bush. She felt light enough to float away.

'Fire?' she muttered.

'Yes. You know. Pointing the finger and whoosh,' said Granny sourly. She was sitting on a rock, trying to find a position that didn't upset her arthritis.

'I – I don't think I can.'

'You tell me?' said Granny cryptically.

The old witch leaned forward and put her hand on Esk's forehead; it was like being caressed by a sock full of warm dice.

'You're running a bit of a temperature,' she added. 'Too much hot sun and cold ground. That's forn parts for you.'

Esk let herself slump forward until her head lay in Granny's lap, with its familiar smells of camphor, mixed herbs and a trace of goat. Granny patted her in what she hoped was a soothing way.

After a while Esk said, in a low voice, 'They're not going to allow me into the University. A wizard told me, and I dreamed about it, and it was one of those true dreams. You know, like you told me, a maty-thing.'

'Metterfor,' said Granny calmly.

'One of them.'

'Did you think it would be easy?' asked Granny. 'Did you think you'd walk into their gates waving your staff? Here I am, I want to be a wizard, thank you very much?'

'He told me there's no women allowed in the University!'

'He's wrong.'

'No, I could tell he was telling the truth. You know, Granny, you can tell how–'

'Foolish child. All you could tell was that he thought he was telling the truth. The world isn't always as people see it.'

'I don't understand,' said Esk.

'You'll learn,' said Granny. 'Now tell me. This dream. They wouldn't let you into their university, right?'

'Yes, and they laughed!'

'And then you tried to burn down the doors?'

Esk turned her head in Granny's lap and opened a suspicious eye.

'How did you know?'

Granny smiled, but as a lizard would smile.

'I was miles away,' she said. 'I was bending my mind towards you, and suddenly you seemed to be everywhere. You shone out like a beacon, so you did. As for the fire – look around.'

In the half-light of dawn the plateau was a mass of baked clay. In front of Esk the cliff was glassy and must have flowed like tar under the onslaught; there were great gashes across it which had dripped molten rock and slag. When Esk listened she could hear the faint 'pink, pink' of cooling rock.

'Oh,' she said, 'did I do that?'

'So it would appear,' said Granny.

'But I was asleep! I was only dreaming!'

'It's the magic,' said Granny. 'It's trying to find a way out. The witch magic and the wizard magic are, I don't know, sort of feeding off each other. I think.'

Esk bit her lip.

'What can I do?' she asked. 'I dream of all sorts of things.'

'Well, for a start we're going straight to the University,' decided Granny. 'They must be used to apprentices not being able to control magic and having hot dreams, else the place would have burned down years ago.'

She glanced towards the Rim, and then down at the broomstick beside her.

We will pass over the running up and down, the tightening of the broomstick's bindings, the muttered curses against dwarfs, the brief moments of hope as the magic flickered fitfully, the horrible black feelings as it died, the tightening of the bindings again, the running again, the sudden catching of the spell, the scrambling aboard, the yelling, the takeoff . . .

Esk clung to Granny with one hand and held her staff in the other as they, frankly, pottered along a few hundred feet above the ground. A few birds flew alongside them, interested in this new flying tree.

'Bugger off!' screamed Granny, taking off her hat and flapping it.

'We're not going very fast, Granny,' said Esk meekly.

'We're going quite fast enough for me!'

Esk looked around. Behind them the Rim was a blaze of gold, barred with cloud.

'I think we ought to go lower, Granny,' she said urgently. 'You said the broomstick won't fly in sunlight.' She glanced down at the landscape below them. It looked sharp and inhospitable. It also looked expectant.

'I know what I'm doing, Miss,' snapped Granny, gripping the broomstick hard and trying to make herself as light as possible.

It has already been revealed that light on the Discworld travels slowly, the result of its passage through the Disc's vast and ancient magical field.

So dawn isn't the sudden affair that it is on other worlds. The new day doesn't erupt, it sort of sloshes gently across the sleeping landscape in the same way that the tide sneaks in across the beach, melting the sandcastles of the night. It tends to flow around mountains. If the trees are close together it comes out of woods cut to ribbons and sliced with shadows.

An observer on some suitable high point, let's say for the sake of argument a wisp of cirro-stratus on the edge of space, would remark on how lovingly the light spreads across the land, how it leaps forward on the plains and slows down when it encounters high ground, how beautifully it . . .

Actually, there are some kinds of observers who, faced with all this beauty, will whine that you can't have heavy light and certainly wouldn't be able to see it, even if you could. To which one can only reply, so how come you're standing on a cloud?

So much for cynicism. But down on the Disc itself the broomstick barrelled forward on the cusp of dawn, dropping ever backward in the shadow of night.

'Granny!'

Day burst upon them. Ahead of the broomstick the rocks seemed to flash into flame as the light washed over them. Granny felt the stick lurch and stared with horrified fascination at the little scudding shadow below them. It was getting closer.

'What will happen when we hit the ground?'

'That depends if I can find some soft rocks,' said Granny in a preoccupied voice.

'The broomstick's going to crash! Can't we do anything?'

'Well, I suppose we could get off.'

'Granny,' said Esk, in the exasperated and remarkably adult voice children use to berate their wayward elders. 'I don't think you quite understand. I don't want to hit the ground. It's never done anything to me.'

Granny was trying to think of a suitable spell and regretting that headology didn't work on rocks, and had she detected the diamond edge to Esk's tone perhaps she wouldn't have said: 'Tell the broomstick that, then.'

And they would indeed have crashed. But she remembered in time to grab her hat and brace herself. The broomstick gave a shudder, tilted–

– and the landscape blurred.

It was really quite a short trip but one that Granny knew she would always remember, generally around three o'clock in the morning after eating rich food. She would remember the rainbow colours that hummed in the rushing air, the horrible heavy feeling, the impression that something very big and heavy was sitting on the universe.

She would remember Esk's laughter. She would remember, despite her best efforts, the way the ground sped below them, whole mountain ranges flashing past with nasty zipping noises.

Most of all, she would remember *catching up* with the night.

It appeared ahead of her, a ragged line of darkness running ahead of the remorseless morning. She stared in horrified fascination as the line became a blot, a stain, a whole continent of blackness that raced towards them.

For an instant they were poised on the crest of the dawn as it broke in silent thunder on the land. No surfer ever rode such a wave, but the broomstick broke through the broil of light and shot smoothly through into the coolness beyond.

Granny let herself breathe out.

Darkness took some of the terror out of the flight. It also meant that if Esk lost interest the broomstick ought to be able to fly under its own rather rusty magic.

'.' Granny said, and cleared her bone-dry throat for a second try. 'Esk?'

'This is fun, isn't it? I wonder how I make it happen?'

'Yes, fun,' said Granny weakly. 'But can I fly the stick, please? I don't want us to go over the Edge. Please?'

'Is it true that there's a giant waterfall all around the edge of the world, and you can look down and see stars?' said Esk.

'Yes. Can we slow down now?'

'I'd like to see it.'

'No! I mean, no, not now.'

The broomstick slowed. The rainbow bubble around it vanished with an audible pop. Without a jolt, without so much as a shudder, Granny found herself flying at a respectable speed again.

Granny had built a solid reputation on always knowing the answer to everything. Getting her to admit ignorance, even to herself, was an astonishing achievement. But the worm of curiosity was chewing at the apple of her mind.

'How,' she said at last, 'did you do that?'

There was a thoughtful silence behind her. Then Esk said: 'I don't know. I just needed it, and it was in my head. Like when you remember something you've forgotten.'

'Yes, but *how*?'

'I – I don't know. I just had a picture of how I wanted things to be, and, and I, sort of – went into the picture.'

Granny stared into the night. She had never heard of magic like that, but it sounded awfully powerful and probably lethal. Went into the picture! Of course, all magic changed the world in some way, wizards thought there was no other use for it– they didn't truck with the idea of leaving the world as it was and changing the people – but this sounded more literal. It needed thinking about. On the ground.

For the first time in her life Granny wondered whether there might be
something important in all these books people were setting such store by
these days, although she was opposed to books on strict moral grounds,
since she had heard that many of them were written by dead people and
therefore it stood to reason reading them would be as bad as necromancy.
Among the many things in the infinitely varied universe with which
Granny did not hold was talking to dead people, who by all accounts had
enough troubles of their own.

But not, she was inclined to feel, as many as her. She looked down
bemusedly at the dark ground and wondered vaguely why the stars were
below her.

For a cardiac moment she wondered if they had indeed flown over the
edge, and then she realised that the thousands of little pinpoints below her
were too yellow, and flickered. Besides, whoever heard of stars arranged in
such a neat pattern?

'It's very pretty,' said Esk. 'Is it a city?'

Granny scanned the ground wildly. If it was a city, then it was too big.
But now she had time to think about it, it certainly smelled like a lot of
people.

The air around them reeked of incense and grain and spices and beer, but
mainly of the sort of smell that was caused by a high water-table,
thousands of people, and a robust approach to drainage.

She mentally shook herself. The day was hard on their heels. She looked
for an area where the torches were dim and widely spaced, reasoning that
this would mean a poor district and poor people did not object to witches,
and gently pointed the broom handle downwards.

She managed to get within five feet of the ground before dawn arrived
for the second time.

The gates were indeed big and black and looked as if they were made out
of solid darkness.

Granny and Esk stood among the crowds that thronged the square
outside the university and stared up at them. Finally Esk said: 'I can't see
how people get in.'

'Magic, I expect,' said Granny sourly. 'That's wizards for you. Anyone
else would have bought a doorknocker.'

She waved her broomstick in the direction of the tall doors.

'You've got to say some hocuspocus word to get in, I shouldn't wonder,'
she added.

They had been in Ankh-Morpork for three days and Granny was

beginning to enjoy herself, much to her surprise. She had found them lodgings in The Shades, an ancient part of the city whose inhabitants were largely nocturnal and never enquired about one another's business because curiosity not only killed the cat but threw it in the river with weights tied to its feet. The lodgings were on the top floor next to the well-guarded premises of a respectable dealer in stolen property because, as Granny had heard, good fences make good neighbours.

The Shades, in brief, were an abode of discredited gods and unlicensed thieves, ladies of the night and pedlars in exotic goods, alchemists of the mind and strolling mummers; in short, all the grease on civilisation's axle.

And yet, despite the fact that these people tend to appreciate the soft magics, there was a remarkable shortage of witches. Within hours the news of Granny's arrival had seeped through the quarter and a stream of people crept, sidled or strutted towards her door, seeking potions and charms and news of the future and various personal and specialised services that witches traditionally provide for those whose lives are a little clouded or full of stormy weather.

She was at first annoyed, and then embarrassed, and then flattered; her clients had money, which was useful, but they also paid in respect, and that was a rock-hard currency.

In short, Granny was even wondering about the possibility of acquiring slightly larger premises with a bit of garden and sending for her goats. The smell might be a problem, but the goats would just have to put up with it.

They had visited the sights of Ankh-Morpork, its crowded docks, its many bridges, its souks, its casbahs, its streets lined with nothing but temples. Granny had counted the temples with a thoughtful look in her eyes; gods were always demanding that their followers acted other than according to their true natures, and the human fallout this caused made plenty of work for witches.

The terrors of civilisation had so far failed to materialise, although a cutpurse had tried to make off with Granny's handbag. To the amazement of passers-by Granny called him back, and back he came, fighting his feet which had totally ceased to obey him. No one quite saw what happened to her eyes when she stared into his face or heard the words she whispered in his cowering ear, but he gave her back all her money plus quite a lot of money belonging to other people, and before she let him go had promised to have a shave, stand up straight, and be a better person for the rest of his life. By nightfall Granny's description was circulated to all the chapter houses of the Guild of Thieves, Cutpurses, Housebreakers and Allied

Trades*, with strict instructions to avoid her at all costs. Thieves, being largely creatures of the night themselves, know trouble when it stares them in the face.

Granny had also written two more letters to the University. There had been no reply.

'I liked the forest best,' said Esk.

'I dunno,' said Granny. 'This is a bit like the forest, really. Anyway, people certainly appreciate a witch here.'

'They're very friendly,' Esk conceded. 'You know the house down the street, where that fat lady lives with all those young ladies you said were her relatives?'

'Mrs Palm,' said Granny cautiously. 'Very respectable lady.'

'People come to visit them *all night long*. I watched. I'm surprised they get any sleep.'

'Um,' said Granny.

'It must be a trial for the poor woman with all those daughters to feed, too. I think people could be more considerate.'

'Well now,' said Granny, 'I'm not sure that–'

She was rescued by the arrival at the gates of the University of a large, brightly painted wagon. Its driver reined in the oxen a few feet from Granny and said: 'Excuse me, my good woman, but would you be so kind as to move, please?'

Granny stepped aside, affronted by this display of downright politeness and particularly upset at being thought of as anyone's good woman, and the driver saw Esk.

It was Treatle. He grinned like a worried snake.

'I say. It's the young lady who thinks women should be wizards, isn't it?'

'Yes,' said Esk, ignoring a sharp kick on the ankle from Granny.

'What fun. Come to join us, have you?'

'Yes,' said Esk, and then because something about Treatle's manner seemed to demand it, she added, 'sir. Only we can't get in.'

---

* A very respectable body which in fact represented the major law-enforcement agency in the city. The reason for this is as follows: the Guild was given an annual quota which represented a socially acceptable level of thefts, muggings and assassinations, and in return saw to it in very definite and final ways that unofficial crime was not only rapidly stamped out but knifed, garrotted, dismembered and left around the city in an assortment of paper bags as well. This was held to be a cheap and enlightened arrangement, except by those malcontents who *were* actually mugged or assassinated and refused to see it as their social duty, and it enabled the city's thieves to plan a decent career structure, entrance examinations and codes of conduct similar to those adopted by the city's other professions – which, the gap not being very wide in any case, they rapidly came to resemble.

'We?' said Treatle, and then glanced at Granny, 'Oh, yes, of course. This would be your aunt?'

'My granny. Only not really my granny, just sort of everyone's granny.'

Granny gave a stiff nod.

'Well, we cannot have this,' said Treatle, in a voice as hearty as a plum pudding. 'My word, no. Our first lady wizard left on the doorstep? That would be a disgrace. May I accompany you?'

Granny grasped Esk firmly by the shoulder.

'If it's all the same to you– ' she began. But Esk twisted out of her grip and ran towards the cart.

'You can really take me in?' she said, her eyes shining.

'Of course. I am sure the heads of the Orders will be most gratified to meet you. Most astonished and astounded,' he said, and gave a little laugh.

'Eskarina Smith– ' said Granny, and then stopped. She looked at Treatle.

'I don't know what is in your mind, Mr Wizard, but I don't like it,' she said. 'Esk, you know where we live. Be a fool if you must, but you might at least be your *own* fool.'

She turned on her heel and strode off across the square.

'What a remarkable woman,' said Treatle, vaguely. 'I see you still have your broomstick. Capital.'

He let go of the reins for a moment and made a complicated sign in the air with both hands.

The big doors swung back, revealing a wide courtyard surrounded by lawns. Behind them was a great rambling building, or buildings: it was hard to tell, because it didn't look so much as if it had been designed as that a lot of buttresses, arches, towers, bridges, domes, cupolas and so forth had huddled together for warmth.

'Is that it?' said Esk. 'It looks sort of – melted.'

'Yes, that's it,' said Treatle. 'Alma mater, gaudy armours eagle tour and so on. Of course, it's a lot bigger inside than out, like an iceberg or so I'm given to understand, I've never seen the things. Unseen University, only of course a lot of it is unseen. Just go in the back and fetch Simon, will you?'

Esk pushed aside the heavy curtains and peered into the back of the wagon. Simon was lying on a pile of rugs, reading a very large book and making notes on scraps of paper.

He looked up, and gave her a worried smile.

'Is that you?' he said.

'Yes,' said Esk, with conviction.

'We thought you'd left us. Everyone thought you were riding with everyone else and then wwwwhen we stopped– '

'I sort of caught up. I think Mr Treatle wants you to come and look at the University.'

'We're here?' he said, and gave her an odd look. '*You're* here?'

'Yes.'

'How?'

'Mr Treatle invited me in, he said everyone would be astounded to meet me.' Uncertainty flashed a fin in the depths of her eyes. 'Was he right?'

Simon looked down at his book, and dabbed at his running eyes with a red handkerchief.

'He has th-these little f-fancies,' he muttered, 'bbbut he's not a bad person.'

Bewildered, Esk looked down at the yellowed pages open in front of the boy. They were full of complicated red and black symbols which in some inexplicable way were as potent and unpleasant as a ticking parcel, but which nevertheless drew the eye in the same way that a really bad accident does. One felt that one would like to know their purpose, while at the same time suspecting that if you found out you would really prefer not to have done.

Simon saw her expression and hastily shut the book.

'Just some magic,' he mumbled. 'Something I'm wwwww–'

'– working –' said Esk, automatically.

'Thank you. On.'

'It must be quite interesting, reading books,' said Esk.

'Sort of. Can't you read, Esk?'

The astonishment in his voice stung her.

'I expect so,' she said defiantly. 'I've never tried.'

Esk wouldn't have known what a collective noun was if it had spat in her eye, but she knew there was a herd of goats and a coven of witches. She didn't know what you called a lot of wizards. An order of wizards? A conspiracy? A circle?

Whatever it was, it filled the University. Wizards strolled among the cloisters and sat on benches under the trees. Young wizards scuttled along pathways as bells rang, with their arms full of books or – in the case of senior students – with their books flapping through the air after them. The air had the greasy feel of magic and tasted of tin.

Esk walked along between Treatle and Simon and drank it all in. It wasn't just that there was magic in the air, but it was tamed and working, like a millrace. It was power, but it was harnessed.

Simon was as excited as she was, but it showed only because his eyes watered more and his stutter got worse. He kept stopping to point out the various colleges and research buildings.

One was quite low and brooding, with high narrow windows.

'T-hat's the l-l-library,' said Simon, his voice bursting with wonder and respect. 'Can I have a l-l-look?'

'Plenty of time for that later,' said Treatle. Simon gave the building a wistful look.

'All the b-books of magic ever written,' he whispered.

'Why are the windows barred?' said Esk.

Simon swallowed. 'Um, b-because b-books of m-magic aren't like other b-books, they lead a–'

'That's enough,' snapped Treatle. He looked down at Esk as if he had just noticed her, and frowned.

'Why are you here?'

'You invited me in,' said Esk.

'Me? Oh, yes. Of course. Sorry, mind wandering. The young lady who wants to be a wizard. Let us see, shall we?'

He led the way up a broad flight of steps to an impressive pair of doors. At least, they were designed to be impressive. The designer had invested deeply in heavy locks, curly hinges, brass studs and an intricately carved archway to make it absolutely clear to anyone entering that they were not very important people at all.

He was a wizard. He had forgotten the doorknocker.

Treatle rapped on the door with his staff. It hesitated for a while, and then slowly slid back its bolts and swung open.

The hall was full of wizards and boys. And boys' parents.

There are two ways of getting into Unseen University (in fact there are three, but at this time wizards hadn't realised it).

The first is to achieve some great work of magic, such as the recovery of an ancient and powerful relic or the invention of a totally new spell, but in these times it was seldom done. In the past there had been great wizards capable of forming whole new spells from the chaotic raw magic of the world, wizards from whom as it were all the spells of wizardry had flowed, but those days had gone; there were no more sourcerers.

So the more typical method was to be sponsored by a senior and respected wizard, after a suitable period of apprenticeship.

Competition was stiff for a University place and the honour and privileges an Unseen degree could bring. Many of the boys milling around the hall, and launching minor spells at each other, would fail and have to spend their lives as lowly *magicians*, mere magical technologists with defiant beards and leather patches on their elbows who congregated in small jealous groups at parties.

Not for them the coveted pointy hat with optional astrological symbols, or the impressive robes, or the staff of authority. But at least they could look down on *conjurers*, who tended to be jolly and fat and inclined to drop their aitches and drink beer and go around with sad thin women in spangly tights and really infuriate magicians by not realising how lowly they were and kept telling them jokes. Lowliest of all – apart from witches, of course – were thaumaturgists, who never got any schooling at all. A thaumaturgist could just about be trusted to wash out an alembic. Many spells required things like mould from a corpse dead of crushing, or the semen of a living tiger, or the root of a plant that gave an ultrasonic scream when it was uprooted. Who was sent to get them? Right.

It is a common error to refer to the lower magical ranks as hedge wizards. In fact hedge wizardry is a very honoured and specialised form of magic that attracts silent, thoughtful men of the druidical persuasion and topiaric inclinations. If you invited a hedge wizard to a party he would spend half the evening talking to your potted plant. And he would spend the other half listening.

Esk noticed that there were some women in the hall, because even young wizards had mothers and sisters. Whole families had turned up to bid the favoured sons farewell. There was a considerable blowing of noses, wiping of tears and the clink of coins as proud fathers tucked a little spending money into their offspring's hands.

Very senior wizards were perambulating among the crowds, talking to the sponsoring wizards and examining the prospective students.

Several of them pushed through the throng to meet Treatle, moving like gold-rimmed galleons under full sail. They bowed gravely to him and looked approvingly at Simon.

'This is young Simon, is it?' said the fattest of them, beaming at the boy. 'We've heard great reports of you, young man. Eh? What?'

'Simon, bow to Archchancellor Cutangle, Archmage of the Wizards of the Silver Star,' said Treatle. Simon bowed apprehensively.

Cutangle looked at him benevolently. 'We've heard great things about you, my boy,' he said. 'All this mountain air must be good for the brain, eh?'

He laughed. The wizards around him laughed. Treatle laughed. Which Esk thought was rather funny, because there wasn't anything particularly amusing happening.

'I ddddon't know, ssss– '

'From what we hear it must be the only thing you don't know, lad!' said Cutangle, his jowls waggling. There was another carefully timed bout of laughter.

Cutangle patted Simon on the shoulder.

'This is the scholarship boy,' he said. 'Quite astounding results, never seen better. Self-taught, too. Astonishing, what? Isn't that so, Treatle?'

'Superb, Archchancellor.'

Cutangle looked around at the watching wizards.

'Perhaps you could give us a sample,' he said. 'A little demonstration, perhaps?'

Simon looked at him in animal panic.

'A-actually I'm not very g-g-g– '

'Now, now,' said Cutangle, in what he probably really did think was an encouraging tone of voice. 'Do not be afraid. Take your time. When you are ready.'

Simon licked his dry lips and gave Treatle a look of mute appeal.

'Um,' he said, 'y-you s-s-s-s– ' He stopped and swallowed hard. 'The f-f-f-f– '

His eyes bulged. The tears streamed from his eyes, and his shoulders heaved.

Treatle patted him reassuringly on the back.

'Hayfever,' he explained. 'Don't seem to be able to cure it. Tried everything.'

Simon swallowed, and nodded. He waved Treatle away with his long white hands and closed his eyes.

For a few seconds nothing happened. He stood with his lips moving soundlessly, and then silence spread out from him like candlelight. Ripples of noiselessness washed across the crowds in the hall, striking the walls with all the force of a blown kiss and then curling back in waves. People watched their companions mouthing silently and then went red with effort when their own laughter was as audible as a gnat's squeak.

Tiny motes of light winked into existence around his head. They whirled and spiralled in a complex three-dimensional dance, and then formed a shape.

In fact it seemed to Esk that the shape had been there all the time, waiting for her eyes to see it, in the same way that a perfectly innocent cloud can suddenly become, without changing in any way, a whale or a ship or a face.

The shape around Simon's head was the world.

That was quite clear, although the glitter and rush of the little lights blurred some of the detail. But there was Great A'Tuin the sky turtle, with the four Elephants on its back, and on them the Disc itself. There was the sparkle of the great waterfall around the edge of the world, and there at the very hub a tiny needle of rock that was the great mountain Cori Celesti, where the gods lived.

The image expanded and homed in on the Circle Sea and then on Ankh itself, the little lights flowing away from Simon and winking out of existence a few feet from his head. Now they showed the city from the air, rushing towards the watchers. There was the University itself, growing larger. There was the Great Hall–

– there were the people, watching silent and open-mouthed, and Simon himself, outlined in specks of silver light. And a tiny sparkling image in the air around him, and *that* image contained an image and another and another–

There was a feeling that the universe had been turned inside out in all dimensions at once. It was a bloated, swollen sensation. It sounded as though the whole world had said 'gloop'.

The walls faded. So did the floor. The paintings of former great mages, all scrolls and beards and slightly constipated frowns, vanished. The tiles underfoot, a rather nice black and white pattern, evaporated – to be replaced by fine sand, grey as moonlight and cold as ice. Strange and unexpected stars glittered overhead; on the horizon were low hills, eroded not by wind or rain in this weatherless place but by the soft sandpaper of Time itself.

No one else seemed to have noticed. No one else, in fact, seemed alive. Esk was surrounded by people as still and silent as statues.

And they weren't alone. There were other – Things – behind them, and more were appearing all the time. They had no shape, or rather they seemed to be taking their shapes at random from a variety of creatures; they gave the impression that they had heard about arms and legs and jaws and claws and organs but didn't really know how they all fitted together. Or didn't care. Or were so hungry they hadn't bothered to find out.

They made a sound like a swarm of flies.

They were the creatures out of her dreams, come to feed on magic. She knew they weren't interested in her now, except in the nature of an after-dinner mint. Their whole concentration was focused on Simon, who was totally unaware of their presence.

Esk kicked him smartly on the ankle.

The cold desert vanished. The real world rushed back. Simon opened his eyes, smiled faintly, and gently fell backwards into Esk's arms.

A buzz went up from the wizards, and several of them started to clap. No one seemed to have noticed anything odd, apart from the silver lights.

Cutangle shook himself, and raised a hand to quell the crowd.

'Quite – astonishing,' he said to Treatle. 'You say he worked it out all by himself?'

'Indeed, lord.'

'No one helped him at all?'

'There was no one to help him,' said Treatle. 'He was just wandering from village to village, doing small spells. But only if people paid him in books or paper.'

Cutangle nodded. 'It was no illusion,' he said, 'yet he didn't use his hands. What was he saying to himself? Do you know?'

'He says it's just words to make his mind work properly,' said Treatle, and shrugged. 'I can't understand half of what he says and that's a fact. He says he's having to invent words because there aren't any for the things he's doing.'

Cutangle glanced sideways at his fellow mages. They nodded.

'It will be an honour to admit him to the University,' he said. 'Perhaps you would tell him so when he wakes up.'

He felt a tugging at his robe, and looked down.

'Excuse me,' said Esk.

'Hallo, young lady,' said Cutangle, in a sugarmouse voice. 'Have you come to see your brother enter the University?'

'He's not my brother,' said Esk. There were times when the world had seemed to be full of brothers, but this wasn't one of them.

'Are you important?' she said.

Cutangle looked at his colleagues, and beamed. There were fashions in wizardry, just like anything else; sometimes wizards were thin and gaunt and talked to animals (the animals didn't listen, but it's the thought that counts) while at other times they tended towards the dark and saturnine, with little black pointed beards. Currently Aldermanic was In. Cutangle swelled with modesty.

'Quite important,' he said. 'One does one's best in the service of one's fellow man. Yes. Quite important, I would say.'

'I want to be a wizard,' said Esk.

The lesser wizards behind Cutangle stared at her as if she was a new and interesting kind of beetle. Cutangle's face went red and his eyes bulged. He looked down at Esk and seemed to be holding his breath. Then he started to laugh. It started somewhere down in his extensive stomach regions and worked its way up, echoing from rib to rib and causing minor wizardquakes across his chest until it burst forth in a series of strangled snorts. It was quite fascinating to watch, that laugh. It had a personality all of its own.

But he stopped when he saw Esk's stare. If the laugh was a music-hall clown then Esk's determined squint was a whitewash bucket on a fast trajectory.

'A wizard?' he said. '*You* want to be a wizard?'

'Yes,' said Esk, pushing the dazed Simon into Treatle's reluctant arms. 'I'm the eighth son of an eighth son. I mean daughter.'

The wizards around her were looking at one another and whispering. Esk tried to ignore them.

'What did she say?'

'Is she serious?'

'I always think children are so delightful at that age, don't you?'

'You're the eighth son of an eighth daughter?' said Cutangle. 'Really?'

'The other way around, only not exactly,' said Esk, defiantly.

Cutangle dabbed his eyes with a handkerchief.

'This is quite fascinating,' he said. 'I don't think I've ever heard of something quite like this before. Eh?'

He looked around at his growing audience. The people at the back couldn't see Esk and were craning to check if some interesting magic was going on. Cutangle was at a loss.

'Well, now,' he said. 'You want to be a wizard?'

'I keep telling everyone but no one seems to listen,' said Esk.

'How old are you, little girl?'

'Nearly nine.'

'And you want to be a wizard when you grow up.'

'I want to be a wizard *now*,' said Esk firmly. 'This *is* the right place, isn't it?'

Cutangle looked at Treatle and winked.

'I saw that,' said Esk.

'I don't think there's ever been a lady wizard before,' said Cutangle. 'I rather think it might be against the lore. Wouldn't you rather be a witch? I understand it's a fine career for girls.'

A minor wizard behind him started to laugh. Esk gave him a look.

'Being a witch is quite good,' she conceded. 'But I think wizards have more fun. What do you think?'

'I think you are a very singular little girl,' said Cutangle.

'What does that mean?'

'It means there's only one of you,' said Treatle.

'That's right,' said Esk, 'and I still want to be a wizard.'

Words failed Cutangle. 'Well, you can't,' he said. 'The very idea!'

He drew himself up to his full width and turned away. Something tugged at his robe.

'Why not?' said a voice.

He turned.

'Because,' he said, slowly and deliberately, 'because . . . the whole idea is completely laughable, that's why. And it's absolutely against the lore!'

'But I can do wizard magic!' said Esk, the faintest suggestion of a tremble in her voice.

Cutangle bent down until his face was level with hers.

'No you can't,' he hissed. 'Because you are not a wizard. Women aren't wizards, do I make myself clear?'

'Watch,' said Esk.

She extended her right hand with the fingers spread and sighted along it until she spotted the statue of Malich the Wise, the founder of the University. Instinctively the wizards between her and it edged out of the way, and then felt rather silly.

'I mean it,' she said.

'Go away, little girl,' said Cutangle.

'Right,' said Esk. She squinted hard at the statue and concentrated . . .

The great doors of Unseen University are made of octiron, a metal so unstable that it can only exist in a universe saturated with raw magic. They are impregnable to all force save magic: no fire, no battering ram, no army can breach them.

Which is why most ordinary visitors to the University use the back door, which is made of perfectly normal wood and doesn't go around terrorising people, or even stand still terrorising people. It had a proper knocker and everything.

Granny examined the doorposts carefully and gave a grunt of satisfaction when she spotted what she was looking for. She hadn't doubted that it *would* be there, cunningly concealed by the natural grain of the wood.

She grasped the knocker, which was shaped like a dragon's head, and rapped smartly, three times. After a while the door was opened by a young woman with her mouth full of clothes-pegs.

'Ot oo oo ont?' she enquired.

Granny bowed, giving the girl a chance to take in the pointy black hat with the batwing hatpins. It had an impressive effect: she blushed and, peering out into the quiet alley-way, hurriedly motioned Granny inside.

There was a big mossy courtyard on the other side of the wall, crisscrossed with washing lines. Granny had the chance to become one of the very few women to learn what it really is that wizards wear under their robes, but modestly averted her eyes and followed the girl across the flagstones and down a wide flight of steps.

They led into a long, high tunnel lined with archways and, currently, full of steam. Granny caught sight of long lines of washtubs in the big rooms off to the sides; the air had the warm fat smell of ironing. A gaggle of girls carrying washbaskets pushed past her and hurried up the steps – then stopped, halfway up, and turned slowly to look at her.

Granny set her shoulders back and tried to look as mysterious as possible.

Her guide, who still hadn't got rid of her clothes-pegs, led her down a side-passage into a room that was a maze of shelves piled with laundry. In the very centre of the maze, sitting at a table, was a very fat woman with a ginger wig. She had been writing in a very large laundry book – it was still open in front of her – but was currently inspecting a large stained vest.

'Have you tried bleaching?' she asked.

'Yes, m'm,' said the maid beside her.

'What about tincture of myrryt?'

'Yes, m'm. It just turned it blue, m'm.'

'Well, it's a new one on me,' said the laundry woman. 'And Ay've seen brimstone and soot and dragon blood and demon blood and Aye don't know what else.' She turned the vest over and read the nametape carefully sewn inside. 'Hmm. Granpone the White. He's going to be Granpone the Grey if he doesn't take better care of his laundry. Aye tell you, girl, a white magician is just a black magician with a good housekeeper. Take it– '

She caught sight of Granny, and stopped.

'Ee ocked hat hee oor,' said Granny's guide, dropping a hurried curtsey. 'Oo ed hat– '

'Yes, yes, thank you, Ksandra, you may go,' said the fat woman. She stood up and beamed at Granny, and with an almost perceptible click wound her voice up several social classes.

'Pray hexcuse us,' she said. 'You find us hall at sixes and sevens, it being washing day and heverything. His this a courtesy call or may I make so bold as to ask– ' she lowered her voice– 'His there a message from the Hother Sade?'

Granny looked blank, but only a fraction of a second. The witchmarks on the doorpost had said that the housekeeper welcomed witches and was particularly anxious for news of her four husbands; she was also in random pursuit of a fifth, hence the ginger wig and, if Granny's ears weren't deceiving her, the creak of enough whalebone to infuriate an entire ecology movement. Gullible and foolish, the signs had said. Granny withheld judgement, because city witches didn't seem that bright themselves.

The housekeeper must have mistaken her expression.

'Don't be afraid,' she said. 'May staff have distinct instructions to welcome witches, although of course *they upstairs* don't approve. No doubt you would like a cup of tea and something to eat?'

Granny bowed solemnly.

'And Aye will see if we can't find a nice bundle of old clothes for you, too,' the housekeeper beamed.

'Old clothes? Oh. Yes. Thank you, m'm.'

The housekeeper swept forward with a sound like an elderly tea clipper in a gale, and beckoned Granny to follow her.

'Aye'll have the tea brought to my flat. Tea with a lot of tea-leaves.'

Granny stumped along after her. Old clothes? Did this fat woman really mean it? The nerve! Of course, if they were good quality . . .

There seemed to be a whole world under the University. It was a maze of cellars, coldrooms, stillrooms, kitchens and sculleries, and every inhabitant was either carrying something, pumping something, pushing something or just standing around and shouting. Granny caught glimpses of rooms full of ice, and others glowing with the heat from red-hot cooking stoves, wall-sized. Bakeries smelled of new bread and taprooms smelled of old beer. Everything smelled of sweat and woodsmoke.

The housekeeper led her up an old spiral staircase and unlocked the door with one of the large number of keys that hung from her belt.

The room inside was pink and frilly. There were frills on things that no one in their right mind would frill. It was like being inside candyfloss.

'Very nice,' said Granny. And, because she felt it was expected of her, 'Tasteful.' She looked around for something unfrilly to sit on, and gave up.

'Whatever am Aye thinking of?' the housekeeper trilled. 'Aye'm Mrs Whitlow but I expect you know, of course. And Aye have the honour to be addressing–'

'Eh? Oh, Granny Weatherwax,' said Granny. The frills were getting to her. They gave pink a bad name.

'Ay'm psychic myself, of course,' said Mrs Whitlow.

Granny had nothing against fortune-telling provided it was done badly by people with no talent for it. It was a different matter if people who ought to know better did it, though. She considered that the future was a frail enough thing at best, and if people looked at it hard they changed it. Granny had some quite complex theories about space and time and why they shouldn't be tinkered with, but fortunately good fortune-tellers were rare and anyway people preferred bad fortune-tellers, who could be relied upon for the correct dose of uplift and optimism.

Granny knew all about bad fortune-telling. It was harder than the real thing. You needed a good imagination.

She couldn't help wondering if Mrs Whitlow was a born witch who somehow missed her training. She was certainly laying siege to the future. There was a crystal ball under a sort of pink frilly tea cosy, and several sets of divinatory cards, and a pink velvet bag of rune stones, and one of those little tables on wheels that no prudent witch would touch with a ten-foot broomstick, and – Granny wasn't sure on this point – either some special dried monkey turds from a llamassary or some dried llama turds from a monastery, which apparently could be thrown in such a way as to reveal the sum total of knowledge and wisdom in the universe. It was all rather sad.

'Or there's the tea-leaves, of course,' said Mrs Whitlow, indicating the big brown pot on the table between them. 'Aye know witches often prefer them, but they always seem so, well, *common* to me. No offence meant.'

There probably wasn't any offence meant, at that, thought Granny. Mrs Whitlow was giving her the sort of look generally used by puppies when they're not sure what to expect next, and are beginning to worry that it may be the rolled-up newspaper.

She picked up Mrs Whitlow's cup and had started to peer into it when she caught the disappointed expression that floated across the housekeeper's face like a shadow across a snowfield. Then she remembered what she was doing, and turned the cup widdershins three times, made a few vague passes over it and mumbled a charm (which she normally used to cure mastitis in elderly goats, but never mind). This display of obvious magical talent seemed to cheer up Mrs Whitlow no end.

Granny wasn't normally very good at tea-leaves, but she squinted at the sugar-encrusted mess at the bottom of the cup and let her mind wander. What she really needed now was a handy rat or even a cockroach that happened to be somewhere near Esk, so that she could Borrow its mind.

What Granny actually found was that the University had a mind of its own.

It is well known that stone can think, because the whole of electronics is based on that fact, but in some universes men spend ages looking for other intelligences in the sky without once looking under their feet. That is because they've got the time-span all wrong. From stone's point of view the universe is hardly created and mountain ranges are bouncing up and down like organ-stops while continents zip backwards and forwards in general high spirits, crashing into each other from the sheer joy of momentum and getting their rocks off. It is going to be quite some time before stone notices its disfiguring little skin disease and starts to scratch, which is just as well.

The rocks from which Unseen University was built, however, have been absorbing magic for several thousand years and all that random power has had to go somewhere.

The University has, in fact, developed a personality.

Granny could sense it like a big and quite friendly animal, just waiting to roll over on its roof and have its floor scratched. It was paying no attention to her, however. It was watching Esk.

Granny found the child by following the threads of the University's attention and watched in fascination as the scenes unfolded in the Great Hall . . .

'– in there?'

The voice came from a long way away.

'Mmph?'

'Aye said, what do you see in there?' repeated Mrs Whitlow.

'Eh?'

'Aye *said*, what do– '

'Oh.' Granny reeled her mind in, quite confused. The trouble with *Borrowing* another mind was, you always felt out of place when you got back to your own body, and Granny was the first person ever to read the mind of a building. Now she was feeling big and gritty and full of passages.

'Are you all right?'

Granny nodded, and opened her windows. She extended her east and west wings and tried to concentrate on the tiny cup held in her pillars.

Fortunately Mrs Whitlow put her plaster complexion and stony silence down to occult powers at work, while Granny found that a brief exposure to the vast silicon memory of the University had quite stimulated her imagination.

In a voice like a draughty corridor, which made the housekeeper very impressed, she wove a future full of keen young men fighting for Mrs Whitlow's ample favours. She also spoke very quickly, because what she had seen in the Great Hall made her anxious to go around to the main gates again.

'There is another thing,' she added.

'Yes? Yes?'

'I see you hiring a new servant – you do hire the servants here, don't you? Right – and this one is a young girl, very economical, very good worker, can turn her hand to anything.'

'What about her, then?' said Mrs Whitlow, already savouring Granny's surprisingly graphic descriptions of her future and drunk with curiosity.

'The spirits are a little unclear on this point,' said Granny. 'But it is very important that you hire her.'

'No problem there,' said Mrs Whitlow, 'can't keep servants here, you know, not for long. It's all the magic. It *leaks* down here, you know. Especially from the library, where they keep all them magical books. Two of the top floor maids walked out yesterday, actually, they said they were fed up going to bed not knowing what shape they would wake up in the morning. The senior wizards turn them back, you know. But it's not the same.'

'Yes, well, the spirits say this young lady won't be any trouble as far as that is concerned,' said Granny grimly.

'If she can sweep and scrub she's welcome, Aye'm sure,' said Mrs Whitlow, looking puzzled.

'She even brings her own broom. According to the spirits, that is.'

'How very helpful. When is this young lady going to arrive?'

'Oh, soon, soon – that's what the spirits say.'

A faint suspicion clouded the housekeeper's face. 'This isn't the sort of thing spirits normally say. Where do they say that, exactly?'

'Here,' said Granny. 'Look, the little cluster of tea-leaves between the sugar and this crack here. Am I right?'

Their eyes met. Mrs Whitlow might have had her weaknesses but she was quite tough enough to rule the below-stairs world of the University. However, Granny could outstare a snake; after a few seconds the housekeeper's eyes began to water.

'Yes, Aye expect you are,' she said meekly, and fished a handkerchief from the recesses of her bosom.

'Well then,' said Granny, sitting back and replacing the teacup in its saucer.

'There are plenty of opportunities here for a young woman willing to work hard,' said Mrs Whitlow. 'Aye myself started as a maid, you know.'

'We all do,' said Granny vaguely. 'And now I must be going.' She stood up and reached for her hat.

'But–'

'Must hurry. Urgent appointment,' said Granny over her shoulder as she hurried down the steps.

'There's a bundle of old clothes–'

Granny paused, her instincts battling for mastery.

'Any black velvet?'

'Yes, and some silk.'

Granny wasn't sure she approved of silk, she'd heard it came out of a caterpillar's bottom, but black velvet had a powerful attraction. Loyalty won.

'Put it on one side, I may call again,' she shouted, and ran down the corridor.

Cooks and scullery maids darted for cover as the old woman pounded along the slippery flagstones, leapt up the stairs to the courtyard and skidded out into the lane, her shawl flying out behind her and her boots striking sparks from the cobbles. Once out into the open she hitched up her skirts and broke into a full gallop, turning the corner into the main square in a screeching two-boot drift that left a long white scratch across the stones.

She was just in time to see Esk come running through the gates, in tears.

☆   ☆   ☆

'The magic just wouldn't work! I could feel it there but it just wouldn't come out!'

'Perhaps you were trying too hard,' said Granny. 'Magic's like fishing. jumping around and splashing never caught any fish, you have to bide quiet and let it happen natural.'

'And then everyone laughed at me! Someone even gave me a sweet!'

'You got some profit out of the day, then,' said Granny.

'Granny!' said Esk accusingly.

'Well, what did you expect?' she asked. 'At least they only laughed at you. Laughter don't hurt. You walked up to chief wizard and showed off in front of everyone and only got laughed at? You're doing well, you are. Have you eaten the sweet?'

Esk scowled. 'Yes.'

'What kind was it?'

'Toffee.'

'Can't abide toffee.'

'Huh,' said Esk, 'I suppose you want me to get peppermint next time?'

'Don't you sarky me, young-fellow-me-lass. Nothing wrong with peppermint. Pass me that bowl.'

Another advantage of city life, Granny had discovered, was glassware. Some of her more complicated potions required aparatus which either had to be bought from the dwarfs at extortionate rates or, if ordered from the nearest human glassblower, arrived in straw and, usually, pieces. She had tried blowing her own and the effort always made her cough, which produced some very funny results. But the city's thriving alchemy profession meant that there were whole shops full of glass for the buying, and a witch could always arrange bargain prices.

She watched carefully as yellow steam surged along a twisty maze of tubing and eventually condensed as one large, sticky droplet. She caught it neatly on the end of a glass spoon and very carefully tipped it into a tiny glass phial.

Esk watched her through her tears.

'What's that?' she asked.

'It's a neveryoumind,' said Granny, sealing the phial's cork with wax.

'A medicine?'

'In a manner of speaking.' Granny pulled her writing set towards her and selected a pen. Her tongue stuck out of the corner of her mouth as she very carefully wrote out a label, with much scratching and pausing to work out the spellings.

'Who's it for?'

'Mrs Herapath, the glassblower's wife.'

Esk blew her nose. 'He's the one who doesn't blow much glass, isn't he?'

Granny looked at her over the top of the desk.

'How do you mean?'

'When she was talking to you yesterday she called him Old Mister Once A Fortnight.'

'Mmph,' said Granny. She carefully finished the sentence: 'Dylewt in won pint warter and won droppe in hys tee and be shure to wear loose clowthing allso that no vysitors exspected.'

One day, she told herself, I'm going to have to have that talk with her.

The child seemed curiously dense. She had already assisted at enough births and taken the goats to old Nanny Annaple's billy without drawing any obvious conclusions. Granny wasn't quite certain what she should do about it, but the time never seemed appropriate to bring up the subject. She wondered whether, in her heart of hearts, she was too embarrassed; she felt like a farrier who could shoe horses, cure them, rear them and judge them, but had only the sketchiest idea about how one rode them.

She pasted the label on to the phial and wrapped it carefully in plain paper. Now.

'There is another way into the University,' she said, looking sidelong at Esk, who was making a disgruntled job of mashing herbs in a mortar. 'A witches' way.'

Esk looked up. Granny treated herself to a thin smile and started work on another label; writing labels was always the hard part of magic, as far as she was concerned.

'But I don't expect you'd be interested,' she went on. 'It's not very glamorous.'

'They laughed at me,' Esk mumbled.

'Yes. You said. So you won't be wanting to try again, then. I *quite* understand.'

There was silence broken only by the scratching of Granny's pen. Eventually Esk said: 'This way– '

'Mmph?'

'It'll get me into the University?'

'Of course,' said Granny haughtily. 'I said I'd find a way, didn't I? A very good way, too. You won't have to bother with lessons, you can go all over the place, no one will notice you – you'll be invisible really – and, well, you can really clean up. But of course, after all that laughing, you won't be interested. Will you?'

☆   ☆   ☆

'Pray have another cup of tea, Mrs Weatherwax?' said Mrs Whitlow.

'Mistress,' said Granny.

'Pardon?'

'It's Mistress Weatherwax,' said Granny. 'Three sugars, please.'

Mrs Whitlow pushed the bowl towards her. Much as she looked forward to Granny's visits it came expensive in sugar. Sugar lumps never seemed to last long around Granny.

'Very bad for the figure,' she said. 'And the teeth, so Aye hear.'

'I never had a figure to speak of and my teeth take care of themselves,' said Granny. It was true, more's the pity. Granny suffered from robustly healthy teeth, which she considered a big drawback in a witch. She really envied Nanny Annaple, the witch over the mountain, who managed to lose all her teeth by the time she was twenty and had real crone-credibility. It meant you ate a lot of soup, but you also got a lot of respect. And then there was warts. Without any effort Nanny managed to get a face like a sockful of marbles, while Granny had tried every reputable wart-causer and failed to raise even the obligatory nose wart. Some witches had all the luck.

'Mmph?' she said, aware of Mrs Whitlow's fluting.

'Aye said,' said Mrs Whitlow, 'that young Eskarina is a real treasure. *Quate* the little find. She keeps the floors spotless, *spotless*. No task too big. Aye said to her yesterday, Aye said, that broom of yours might as well have a life of its own, and do you know what she said?'

'I couldn't even venture a guess,' said Granny, weakly.

'She said the dust was afraid of it! Can you imagine?'

'Yes,' said Granny.

Mrs Whitlow pushed her teacup towards her and gave her an embarrassed smile.

Granny sighed inwardly and squinted into the none-too-clean depths of the future. She was definitely beginning to run out of imagination.

The broom whisked down the corridor raising a great cloud of dust which, if you looked hard at it, seemed somehow to be sucked back into the broomstick. If you looked even harder you'd see that the broom handle had strange markings on it, which were not so much carved as clinging and somehow changed shape as you watched.

But no one looked.

Esk sat at one of the high deep windows and stared out over the city. She was feeling angrier than usual, so the broom attacked the dust with unusual vigour. Spiders ran desperate eight-legged dashes for safety as ancestral cobwebs disappeared into the void. In the walls mice clung to each other, legs braced against the inside of their holes. Woodworm scrabbled in the ceiling beams as they were drawn, inexorably, backwards down their tunnels.

'"You can really clean up",' said Esk. 'Huh!'

There were some good points, she had to admit. The food was simple but there was plenty of it, and she had a room to herself somewhere in the roof and it was quite luxurious because here she could lie in until five a.m., which to Granny's way of thinking was practically noon. The work certainly wasn't hard. She just started sweeping until the staff realised what was expected of it, and then she could amuse herself until it was finished. If anyone came the staff would immediately lean itself nonchalantly against a wall.

But she wasn't learning any wizardry. She could wander into empty classrooms and look at the diagrams chalked on the board, and on the floor too in the more advanced classes, but the shapes were meaningless. And unpleasant.

They reminded Esk of the pictures in Simon's book. They looked alive.

She gazed out across the rooftops of Ankh-Morpork and reasoned like this: writing was only the words that people said, squeezed between layers of paper until they were fossilised (fossils were well-known on the Discworld, great spiralled shells and badly constructed creatures that were left over from the time when the Creator hadn't really decided what He wanted to make and was, as it were, just idly messing around with the Pleistocene). And the words people said were just shadows of real things. *But* some things were too big to be really trapped in words, and even the words were too powerful to be completely tamed by writing.

So it followed that some writing was actually trying to become *things*. Esk's thoughts became confused things at this point, but she was certain that the really magic words were the ones that pulsed angrily, trying to escape and become real.

They didn't look very nice.

But then she remembered the previous day.

It had been rather odd. The University classrooms were designed on the funnel principle, with tiers of seats – polished by the bottoms of the Disc's greatest mages – looking precipitously down into a central area where there was a workbench, a couple of blackboards and enough floor space for a decent-sized instructional octogram. There was a lot of dead space under the tiers and Esk had found it a quite useful observation post, peering around between the apprentice wizards' pointy boots at the instructor. It was very restful, with the droning of the lecturers drifting over her as gently as the buzzing of the slightly zonked bees in Granny's special herb garden. There never seemed to be any practical magic, it always seemed to be just words. Wizards seemed to like words.

But yesterday had been different. Esk had been sitting in the dusty gloom, trying to do even some very simple magic, when she heard the door open and boots clump across the floor. That was surprising in itself. Esk knew the timetable, and the Second Year students who normally occupied this room were down for Beginners' Dematerialisation with Jeophal the Spry in the gym. (Students of magic had little use for physical exercise; the gym was a large room lined with lead and rowan wood, where neophytes could work out at High magic without seriously unbalancing the universe, although not always without seriously unbalancing themselves. Magic had no mercy on the ham-fisted. Some clumsy students were lucky enough to walk out, others were removed in bottles.)

Esk peeped between the slats. These weren't students, they were wizards. Quite high ones, to judge by their robes. And there was no mistaking the figure that climbed on to the lecturer's dais like a badly strung puppet, bumping heavily into the lectern and absent-mindedly apologising to it. It was Simon. No one else had eyes like two raw eggs in warm water and a nose bright red from blowing. For Simon, the pollen count always went to infinity.

It occurred to Esk that, minus his general allergy to the whole of Creation and with a decent haircut and a few lessons in deportment, the boy could look quite handsome. It was an unusual thought, and she squirrelled it away for future consideration.

When the wizards had settled down, Simon began to talk. He read from notes, and every time he stuttered over a word the wizards, as one man, without being able to stop themselves, chorused it for him.

After a while a stick of chalk rose from the lectern and started to write on the blackboard behind him. Esk had picked up enough about wizard magic to know that this was an astounding achievement – Simon had been at the University for a couple of weeks, and most students hadn't mastered Light Levitation by the end of their second year.

The little white stub skittered and squeaked across the blackness to the accompaniment of Simon's voice. Even allowing for the stutter, he was not a very good speaker. He dropped notes. He corrected himself. He ummed and ahhed. And as far as Esk was concerned he wasn't saying anything very much. Phrases filtered down to her hiding place. 'Basic fabric of the universe' was one, and she didn't understand what that was, unless he meant denim, or maybe flannelette. 'Mutability of the possibility matrix' she couldn't guess at all.

Sometimes he seemed to be saying that nothing existed unless people thought it did, and the world was really only there at all because people kept on imagining it. But then he seemed to be saying that there was lots of worlds, all nearly the same and all sort of occupying the same place but all separated by the thickness of a shadow, so that everything that ever could happen would have somewhere to happen *in*.

(Esk could get to grips with this. She had half-suspected it ever since she cleaned out the senior wizards' lavatory, or rather while the staff got on with the job while Esk examined the urinals and, with the assistance of some half-remembered details of her brothers in the tin bath in front of the fire at home, formulated her unofficial General Theory of comparative anatomy. The senior wizards' lavatory was a magical place, with real running water and interesting tiles and, most importantly, two big silver mirrors fixed to opposite walls so that someone looking into one could see themselves repeated again and again until the image was too small to see. It was Esk's first introduction to the idea of infinity. More to the point, she had a suspicion that one of the mirror Esks, right on the edge of sight, was waving at her.)

There was something disturbing about the phrases Simon used. Half the time he seemed to be saying that the world was about as real as a soap bubble, or a dream.

The chalk shrieked its way across the board behind him. Sometimes Simon had to stop and explain symbols to the wizards, who seemed to Esk to be getting excited at some very silly sentences. Then the chalk would start again, curving across the darkness like a comet, trailing its dust behind it.

The light was fading out of the sky outside. As the room grew more gloomy the chalked words glowed and the blackboard appeared to Esk to be not so much dark as simply not there at all, but just a square hole cut out of the world.

Simon talked on, about the world being made up of tiny things whose presence could only be determined by the fact that they were not there, little spinning balls of nothingness that magic could shunt together to make stars and butterflies and diamonds. Everything was made up of emptiness.

The funny thing was, he seemed to find this fascinating.

Esk was only aware that the walls of the room grew as thin and insubstantial as smoke, as if the emptiness in them was expanding to swallow whatever it was that defined them as walls, and instead there was nothing but the familiar cold, empty, glittering plain with its distant worn hills, and the creatures that stood as still as statues, looking down.

There were a lot more of them now. They seemed for all the world to be clustering like moths around a light.

One important difference was that a moth's face, even close up, was as friendly as a bunny rabbit's compared to the things watching Simon.

Then a servant came in to light the lamps and the creatures vanished, turning into perfectly harmless shadows that lurked in the corners of the room.

At some time in the recent past someone had decided to brighten the ancient corridors of the University by painting them, having some vague notion that Learning Should Be Fun. It hadn't worked. It's a fact known throughout the universes that no matter how carefully the colours are chosen, institutional décor ends up as either vomit green, unmentionable brown, nicotine yellow or surgical appliance pink. By some little-understood process of sympathetic resonance, corridors painted in those colours *always smell slightly of boiled cabbage* – even if no cabbage is ever cooked in the vicinity.

Somewhere in the corridors a bell rang. Esk dropped lightly from her windowsill, grabbed the staff and started to sweep industriously as doors were flung open and the corridors filled with students. They streamed past her on two sides, like water around a rock. For a few minutes there was utter confusion. Then doors slammed, a few laggard feet pattered away in the distance, and Esk was by herself again.

Not for the first time, Esk wished that the staff could talk. The other servants were friendly enough, but you couldn't *talk* to them. Not about magic, anyway.

She was also coming to the conclusion that she ought to learn to read. This reading business seemed to be the key to wizard magic, which was all about words. Wizards seemed to think that names were the same as things, and that if you changed the name, you changed the thing. At least, it seemed to be something like that . . .

Reading. That meant the library. Simon had said there were thousands of books in it, and amongst all those words there were bound to be one or two she could read. Esk put the staff over her shoulder and set off resolutely for Mrs Whitlow's office.

She was nearly there when a wall said 'Psst!' When Esk stared at it it turned out to be Granny. It wasn't that Granny could make herself invisible, it was just that she had this talent for being able to fade into the foreground so that she wasn't noticed.

'How are you getting on, then?' asked Granny. 'How's the magic coming along?'

'What are you doing here, Granny?' said Esk.

'Been to tell Mrs Whitlow her fortune,' said Granny, holding up a large bundle of old clothes with some satisfaction. Her smile faded under Esk's stern gaze.

'Well, things are different in the city,' she said. 'City people are always worried about the future, it comes from eating unnatural food. Anyway,' she added, suddenly realising that she was whining, 'why shouldn't I tell fortunes?'

'*You* always said Hilta was playing on the foolishness of her sex,' said Esk. '*You* said that them as tell fortunes should be ashamed of themselves, and anyway, you don't need old clothes.'

'Waste not, want not,' said Granny primly. She had spent her entire life on the old-clothes standard and wasn't about to let temporary prosperity dislodge her: 'Are you getting enough to eat?'

'Yes,' said Esk. 'Granny, about this wizard magic, it's all words– '

'Always said it was,' said Granny.

'No, I mean– ' Esk began, but Granny waved a hand irritably.

'Can't be bothered with this at the moment,' she said. 'I've got some big orders to fill by tonight, if it goes on like this I'm going to have to train someone up. Can't you come and see me when you get an afternoon off, or whatever it is they give you?'

'Train someone up?' said Esk, horrified. 'You mean as a witch?'

'No,' said Granny. 'I mean, perhaps.'

'But what about me?'

'Well, you're going your own way,' said Granny. 'Wherever that is.'

'Mmph,' said Esk. Granny stared at her.

'I'll be off, then,' she said at last. She turned and strode off towards the kitchen entrance. As she did so her cloak swirled out, and Esk saw that it was now lined with red. A dark, winy red, but red nevertheless. On Granny, who had never been known to wear any visible clothing that was other than a serviceable black, it was quite shocking.

'The library?' said Mrs Whitlow. 'Aye don't think anyone cleans the library!' She looked genuinely puzzled.

'Why?' said Esk. 'Doesn't it get dusty?'

'Well,' said Mrs Whitlow. She thought for a while. 'Aye suppose it must do, since you come to mention it. Aye never really thought about it.'

'You see, I've cleaned everywhere else,' said Esk, sweetly.

'Yes,' said Mrs Whitlow, 'you have, haven't you.'

'Well, then.'

'It's just that we've never – done it before,' said Mrs Whitlow, 'but for the life of me, Aye can't think why.'

'Well, then,' said Esk.

☆   ☆   ☆

'Ook?' said the Head Librarian, and backed away from Esk. But she had heard about him and had come prepared. She offerd him a banana.

The orang-utan reached out slowly and then snatched it with a grin of triumph.

There may be universes where librarianship is considered a peaceful sort of occupation, and where the risks are limited to large volumes falling off the shelves on to one's head, but the keeper of a *magic* library is no job for the unwary. Spells have power, and merely writing them down and shoving them between covers doesn't do anything to reduce it. The stuff leaks. Books tend to react with one another, creating randomised magic with a mind of its own. Books of magic are usually chained to their shelves, but not to prevent them being stolen . . .

One such accident had turned the librarian into an ape, since when he had resisted all attempts to turn him back, explaining in sign language that life as an orang-utan was considerably better than life as a human being, because all the big philosophical questions resolved themselves into wondering where the next banana was coming from. Anyway, long arms and prehensile feet were ideal for dealing with high shelves.

Esk gave him the whole bunch of bananas and scurried away amongst the books before he could object.

Esk had never seen more than one book at a time and so the library was, for all she knew, just like any other library. True, it was a bit odd the way the floor seemed to become the wall in the distance, and there was something strange about the way the shelves played tricks on the eyes and seemed to twist through rather more dimensions than the normal three, and it was quite surprising to look up and see shelves on the ceiling, with the occasional student wandering unconcernedly among them.

The truth was that the presence of so much magic distorted the space around it. Down in the stacks the very denim, or possibly flannelette, of the universe was tortured into very peculiar shapes. The millions of trapped words, unable to escape, bent reality around them.

It seemed logical to Esk that among all these books should be one that told you how to read all the others. She wasn't sure how to find it, but deep in her soul she felt it would probably have pictures of cheerful rabbits and happy kittens on the cover.

The library certainly wasn't silent. There was the occasional zip and sizzle of a magical discharge, and an octarine spark would flash from shelf to shelf. Chains clinked, faintly. And, of course, there was the faint rustle of thousands of pages in their leather-bound prisons.

Esk made sure no one was paying her any attention and pulled at the nearest volume. It sprang open in her hands, and she saw gloomily that there were the same unpleasant types of diagram that she had noticed in Simon's book. The writing was entirely unfamiliar, and she was glad about that – it would be horrible to know what all those letters, which seemed to be made up of ugly creatures doing complicated things to each other, actually meant. She forced the cover shut, even though the words seemed to be desperately pushing back. There was a drawing of a creature on the front; it looked suspiciously like one of the things from the cold desert. It certainly didn't look like a happy kitten.

'Hallo! Esk, isn't it? H-how d-did you get h-here?'

It was Simon, standing there with a book under each arm. Esk blushed.

'Granny won't tell me,' she said. 'I think it's something to do with men and women.'

Simon looked at her blankly. Then he grinned. Esk thought about the question a second time.

'I work here. I sweep up.' She waved the staff in explanation.

'In *here*?'

Esk stared at him. She felt alone, and lost, and more than a little betrayed. Everyone seemed to be busy living their own lives, except her. She would spend the rest of *her* life cleaning up after wizards. It wasn't fair, and she'd had enough.

'Actually I don't. Actually I'm learning to read so I can be a wizard.'

The boy regarded her through his damp eyes for some seconds. Then he gently took the book out of Esk's hands and read its title.

'*Demonylogie Malyfycorum of Henchanse thee Unsatysfactory*. How did you think you could learn to r-read this?'

'Um,' said Esk. 'Well, you just keep trying until you can, don't you? Like milking, or knitting, or . . . ' Her voice faded away.

'I don't know about that. These books can be a bit, well, aggressive. If you d-don't be careful they start reading *you*.'

'What do you mean?'

'T-they ssss– '

' – say – ' said Esk, automatically.

' – that there was once a wwww– '

' – wizard – '

' – who started to r-read the *Necrotelecomnicon* and let his m-mind wwwwww– '

' – wander – '

' – and next morning they f-found all his clothes on the chair and h-his hat on t-top of them and the b-book had– '

Esk put her fingers in her ears, but not too hard in case she missed anything.

'I don't want to know about it if it's horrid.'

' – had *a lot more pages.*'

Esk took her fingers out of her ears. 'Was there anything on the pages?'

Simon nodded solemnly. 'Yes. On every sssingle one of th-them there www– '

'No,' said Esk. 'I don't even want to imagine it. I thought reading was more peaceful than that, I mean, Granny read her *Almanack* every day and nothing ever happened to her.'

'I d-daresay ordinary tame www– '

' – words – '

' – are all right,' Simon conceded, magnanimously.

'Are you absolutely certain?' said Esk.

'It's just that words can have power,' said Simon, slotting the book firmly back on its shelf, where it rattled its chains at him. 'And they do say the p-pen is mightier than the sss– '

' – sword,' said Esk. 'All right, but which would you rather be hit with?'

'Um, I d-don't think it's any use m-me t-telling you you shouldn't be in here, is it?' said the young wizard.

Esk gave this due consideration. 'No,' she said, 'I don't think it is.'

'I could send for the p-porters and have you t-taken away.'

'Yes, but you won't.'

'I just d-don't www– '

' – want – '

' – you to get hurt, you see. I r-really don't. This can b-be a ddddangerou– '

Esk caught a faint swirling in the air above his head. For a moment she saw them, the great grey shapes from the cold place. Watching. And in the calm of the Library, when the weight of magic was wearing the Universe particularly thin, they had decided to Act.

Around her the muted rustling of the books rose to a desperate riffling of pages. Some of the more powerful books managed to jerk out of their shelves and swung, flapping madly, from the end of their chains. A huge grimoire plunged from its eyrie on the topmost shelf – tearing itself free of its chain in the process – and flopped away like a frightened chicken, scattering its pages behind it.

A magical wind blew away Esk's headscarf and her hair streamed out behind her. She saw Simon trying to steady himself against a bookshelf as books exploded around him. The air was thick and tasted of tin. It buzzed.

'They're trying to get in!' she screamed.

Simon's tortured face turned to her. A fear-crazed incunable hit him heavily in the small of the back and knocked him to the heaving floor before it bounced high over the shelves. Esk ducked as a flock of thesauri wheeled past, towing their shelf behind them, and scuttled on hands and knees towards him.

'That's what's making the books so frightened!' she shrieked in his ear. 'Can't you *see* them up there?'

Simon mutely shook his head. A book burst its bindings over them, showering them in pages.

Horror can steal into the mind via all the senses. There's the sound of the little meaningful chuckle in the locked dark room, the sight of half a caterpillar in your forkful of salad, the curious smell from the lodger's bedroom, the taste of slug in the cauliflower cheese. Touch doesn't normally get a look-in.

But something happened to the floor under Esk's hands. She looked down, her face a rictus of horror, because the dusty floorboards suddenly felt gritty. And dry. And very, very cold.

There was fine silver sand between her fingers.

She grabbed the staff and, sheltering her eyes against the wind, waved it at the towering figures above her. It would have been nice to report that a searing flash of pure white fire cleansed the greasy air. It failed to materialise . . .

The staff twisted like a snake in her hand and caught Simon a crack on the side of the head.

The grey Things wavered and vanished.

Reality returned, and tried to pretend that it had never left. Silence settled like thick velvet, wave after wave of it. A heavy, echoing silence. A few books dropped heavily out of the air, feeling silly.

The floor under Esk's feet was undoubtedly wooden. She kicked it hard to make sure.

There was blood on the floor, and Simon lay very quietly in the centre of it. Esk stared down at him, and then up at the still air, and then at the staff. It looked smug.

She was aware of distant voices and hurrying feet.

A hand like a fine leather glove slipped gently into hers and a voice behind said, 'Ook,' very softly. She turned, and found herself staring down into the gentle, inner-tube face of the librarian. He put his finger to his lips in an unmistakable gesture and tugged gently at her hand.

'I've killed him!' she whispered.

The librarian shook his head, and tugged insistently.

'Ook,' he explained. 'Ook.'

He dragged her reluctantly down a side alley-way in the maze of ancient shelving a few seconds before a party of senior wizards, drawn by the noise, rounded the corner.

'The books have been fighting again . . . '

'Oh, no! It'll take ages to capture all the spells again, you know they go and find places to hide . . . '

'Who's that on the floor?'

There was a pause.

'He's knocked out. A shelf caught him by the looks of it.'

'Who is he?'

'That new lad. You know, the one they say has got a whole head full of brains?'

'If that shelf had been a bit closer we'd be able to see if they were right.'

'You two, get him along to the infirmary. The rest of you better get these books rounded up. Where's the damn librarian? He ought to know better than to let a Critical Mass build up.'

Esk glanced sideways at the orang-utan, who waggled his eyebrows at her. He pulled a dusty volume of gardening spells out of the shelves beside him, extracted a soft brown banana from the recess behind it, and ate it with the quiet relish of one who knows that whatever the problems are, they belong firmly to human beings.

She looked the other way, at the staff in her hand, and her lips went thin. She knew her grip hadn't slipped. The staff had *lunged* at Simon, with murder in its heartwood.

The boy lay on a hard bed in a narrow room, a cold towel folded across his forehead. Treatle and Cutangle watched him carefully.

'How long has it been?' said Cutangle.

Treatle shrugged. 'Three days.'

'And he hasn't come round once?'

'No.'

Cutangle sat down heavily on the edge of the bed, and pinched the bridge of his nose wearily. Simon had never looked particularly healthy, but now his face had a horrible sunken look.

'A brilliant mind, that one,' he said. 'His explanation of the fundamental principles of magic and matter – quite astounding.'

Treatle nodded.

'The way he just absorbs knowledge,' said Cutangle: 'I've been a working wizard all my life, and somehow I never really understood magic until he explained it. So clear. So, well, *obvious*.'

'Everyone says that,' said Treatle gloomily. 'They say it's like having a hoodwink pulled off and seeing the daylight for the first time.'

'That's exactly it,' said Cutangle. 'He's sourcerer material, sure enough. You were right to bring him here.'

There was a thoughtful pause.

'Only–' said Treatle.

'Only what?' asked Cutangle.

'Only *what* was it you understood?' said Treatle. 'That's what's bothering me. I mean, can you explain it?'

'How do you mean, explain?' Cutangle looked worried.

'What he keeps talking about,' said Treatle, a hint of desperation in his voice. 'Oh, it's the genuine stuff, I know. But what exactly *is* it?'

Cutangle looked at him, his mouth open. Eventually he said, 'Oh, that's easy. Magic fills the universe, you see, and every time the universe changes, no, I mean every time magic is invoked, the universe changes, only in every direction at once, d'you see, and–' he moved his hands uncertainly, trying to recognise a spark of comprehension in Treatle's face. 'To put it another way, any piece of matter, like an orange or the world or, or–'

'– a crocodile?' suggested Treatle.

'Yes, a crocodile, or – whatever, is basically shaped like a carrot.'

'I don't remember that bit,' said Treatle.

'I'm sure that's what he said,' said Cutangle. He was starting to sweat.

'No, I remember the bit where he seemed to suggest that if you went far enough in any direction you would see the back of your head,' Treatle insisted.

'You're sure he didn't mean someone else's head?'

Treatle thought for a bit.

'No, I'm pretty sure he said the back of your own head,' he said. 'I think he said he could prove it.'

They considered this in silence.

Finally Cutangle spoke, very slowly and carefully.

'I look at it like this,' he said. 'Before I heard him talk, I was like everyone else. You know what I mean? I was confused and uncertain about all the little details of life. But now,' he brightened up, 'while I'm still confused and uncertain it's on a much higher plane, d'you see, and at least I know I'm bewildered about the really fundamental and important facts of the universe.'

Treatle nodded. 'I hadn't looked at it like that,' he said, 'but you're absolutely right. He's really pushed back the boundaries of ignorance. There's so much about the universe we don't know.'

They both savoured the strange warm glow of being much more ignorant than ordinary people, who were ignorant of only ordinary things.

Then Treatle said: 'I just hope he's all right. He's over the fever but he just doesn't seem to want to wake up.'

A couple of servants came in with a bowl of water and fresh towels. One

of them carried a rather tatty broomstick. As they began to change the
sweat-soaked sheets under the boy the two wizards left, still discussing the
vast vistas of unknowingness that Simon's genius had revealed to the world.

Granny waited until their footsteps had died away and took off her
headscarf.

'Damn thing,' she said. 'Esk, go and listen at the door.' She removed the
towel from Simon's head and felt his temperature.

'It was very good of you to come,' said Esk. 'And you so busy with your
work, and everything.'

'Mmmph.' Granny pursed her lips. She pulled up Simon's eyelids and
sought his pulse. She laid an ear on his xylophone chest and listened to his
heart. She sat for some time quite motionless, probing around inside his
head.

She frowned.

'Is he all right?' said Esk anxiously.

Granny looked at the stone walls.

'Drat this place,' she said. 'It's no place for sick people.'

'Yes, but is he all right?'

'What?' Granny was startled out of her thoughts. 'Oh. Yes. Probably.
Wherever he is.'

Esk stared at her, and then at Simon's body.

'Nobody's home,' said Granny, simply.

'What do you mean?'

'Listen to the child,' said Granny. 'You'd think I taught her nothing. I
mean his mind's Wandering. He's gone Out of his Head.'

She looked at Simon's body with something verging on admiration.

'Quite surprisin', really,' she added. 'I never yet met a wizard who could
Borrow.'

She turned to Esk, whose mouth was a horrified O.

'I remember when I was a girl, Old Nanny Annaple went Wanderin'. Got
too wrapped up with being a vixen, as I recall. Took us days to find her. And
then there was you, too. I never would have found you if it wasn't for that
staff thing, and – what have you done with it, girl?'

'It hit him,' Esk muttered. 'It tried to kill him. I threw it in the river.'

'Not a nice thing to do to it after it saved you,' said Granny.

'It saved me by hitting him?'

'Didn't you realise? He was callin' to – them Things.'

'That's not true!'

Granny stared into Esk's defiant eyes and the thought came to her mind:
I've lost her. Three years of work down the privy. She couldn't be a wizard
but she might have been a witch.

'Why isn't it true, Miss Clever?' she said.

'He wouldn't do something like that!' Esk was near to tears. 'I heard him speak, he's – well, he's not evil, he's a brilliant person, he nearly understands how everything works, he's–'

'I expect he's a very nice boy,' said Granny sourly. 'I never said he was a black wizard, did I?'

'They're horrible Things!' Esk sobbed. 'He wouldn't call out to them, he wants everything that they're not, and you're a wicked old–'

The slap rang like a bell. Esk staggered back, white with shock. Granny stood with her hand upraised, trembling.

She'd struck Esk once before – the blow a baby gets to introduce it to the world and give it a rough idea of what to expect from life. But that had been the last time. In three years under the same roof there had been cause enough, when milk had been left to boil over or the goats had been carelessly left without water, but a sharp word or a sharper silence had done more than force ever could and left no bruises.

She grabbed Esk firmly by the shoulders and stared into her eyes.

'Listen to me,' she said urgently. 'Didn't I always say to you that if you use magic you should go through the world like a knife goes through water? Didn't I say that?'

Esk, mesmerised like a cornered rabbit, nodded.

'And you thought that was just old Granny's way, didn't you? But the fact is that if you use magic you draw attention to yourself. From Them. They watch the world all the time. Ordinary minds are just vague to them, they hardly bother with them, but a mind with magic in it shines out, you see, it's a beacon to them. It's not darkness that calls Them, it's light, light that creates the shadows!'

'But – but – why are They interested? What do They w-want?'

'Life and shape,' said Granny.

She sagged, and let go of Esk.

'They're pathetic, really,' she said. 'They've got no life or shape them-selves but what they can steal. They could no more survive in this world than a fish could live in a fire, but that doesn't stop Them trying. And they're just bright enough to hate us because we're alive.'

Esk shivered. She remembered the gritty feel of the cold sand.

'What are They? I always thought they were just a sort – a sort of demon?'

'Nah. No one really knows. They're just the Things from the Dungeon Dimensions outside the universe, that's all. Shadow creatures.'

She turned back to the prone form of Simon.

'You wouldn't have any idea where he is, would you?' she said, looking shrewdly at Esk. 'Not gone off flying with the seagulls, has he?'

Esk shook her head.

'No,' said Granny, 'I didn't think so. They've got him, haven't they.'

It wasn't a question. Esk nodded, her face a mask of misery.

'It's not your fault,' said Granny. 'His mind gave Them an opening, and when he was knocked out they took it back with them. Only . . . '

She drummed her fingers on the edge of the bed, and appeared to reach a decision.

'Who's the most important wizard around here?' she demanded.

'Um, Lord Cutangle,' said Esk. 'He's the Archchancellor. He was one of the ones who was in here.'

'The fat one, or the one like a streak of vinegar?'

Esk dragged her mind from the image of Simon on the cold desert and found herself saying: 'He's an Eighth Level wizard and a 33° mage, actually.'

'You mean he's bent?' said Granny. 'All this hanging around wizards has made you take them seriously, my girl. They all call themselves the Lord High this and the Imperial That, it's all part of the game. Even magicians do it, you'd think they'd be more sensible at least, but no, they call around saying they're the Amazing-Bonko-and-Doris. Anyway, where is this High Rumtiddlypo?'

'They'll be at dinner in the Great Hall,' said Esk. 'Can he bring Simon back, then?'

'That's the difficult part,' said Granny. 'I daresay we could all get *something* back easily enough, walking and talking just like anyone. Whether it would be Simon is quite another sack of ferrets.'

She stood up. 'Let's find this Great Hall, then. No time to waste.'

'Um, women aren't allowed in,' said Esk.

Granny stopped in the doorway. Her shoulders rose. She turned around very slowly.

'*What* did you say?' she said. 'Did these old ears deceive me, and don't say they did because they didn't.'

'Sorry,' said Esk. 'Force of habit.'

'I can see you've been getting ideas below your station,' said Granny coldly. 'Go and find someone to watch over the lad, and let's see what's so great about this hall that I mustn't set foot in it.'

And thus it was that while the entire faculty of Unseen University were dining in the venerable hall the doors were flung back with a dramatic effect that was rather spoiled when one of them rebounded off a waiter and caught Granny a crack on the shin. Instead of the defiant strides she had intended to make across the chequered floor she was forced to half-hop, half-limp. But she hoped that she hopped with dignity.

Esk hurried along behind her, acutely aware of the hundreds of eyes that were turned towards them.

The roar of conversation and the clatter of cutlery faded away. A couple of chairs were knocked over. At the far end of the hall she could see the most senior wizards at their high table, which in fact bobbed a few feet off the floor. They were staring.

A medium-grade wizard – Esk recognised him as a lecturer in Applied Astrology – rushed towards them, waving his hands.

'Nononono,' he shouted. 'Wrong door. You must go away.'

'Don't mind me,' said Granny calmly, pushing past him.

'Nonono, it's against the lore, you must go away *now*. Ladies are not allowed in here!'

'I'm not a lady, I'm a witch,' said Granny. She turned to Esk. 'Is he very important?'

'I don't think so,' said Esk.

'Right.' Granny turned to the lecturer: 'Go and find me an important wizard, please. Quickly.'

Esk tapped her on the back. A couple of wizards with a rather greater presence of mind had nipped smartly out of the door behind them, and now several college porters were advancing threateningly up the hall, to the cheers and catcalls of the students. Esk had never much liked the porters, who lived a private life in their lodge, but now she felt a pang of sympathy for them.

Two of them reached out hairy hands and grabbed Granny's shoulders. Her arm disappeared behind her back and there was a brief flurry of movement that ended with the men hopping away, clutching bits of themselves and swearing.

'Hatpin,' said Granny. She grabbed Esk with her free hand and swept towards the high table, glaring at anyone who so much as looked as if they were going to get in her way. The younger students, who knew free entertainment when they saw it, stamped and cheered and banged their plates on the long tables. The high table settled on the tiles with a thump and the senior wizards hurriedly lined up behind Cutangle as he tried to summon up his reserves of dignity. His efforts didn't really work; it is very hard to look dignified with a napkin tucked into one's collar.

He raised his hands for silence, and the hall waited expectantly as Granny and Esk approached him. Granny was looking interestedly at the ancient paintings and statues of bygone mages.

'Who are them buggers?' she said out of the corner of her mouth.

'They used to be chief wizards,' whispered Esk.

'They look constipated. I never met a wizard who was regular,' said Granny.

'They're a nuisance to dust, that's all I know,' said Esk.

Cutangle stood with legs planted wide apart, arms akimbo and stomach giving an impression of a beginners' ski slope, the whole of him therefore adopting a pose usually associated with Henry VIII but with an option on Henry IX and X as well.

'*Well*?' he said. 'What is the meaning of this *outrage*?'

'Is he important?' said Granny to Esk.

'*I*, madam, am the Archchancellor! And I happen to run this University! And you, madam, are trespassing in very dangerous territory indeed! I warn you that – *stop looking at me like that*!'

Cutangle staggered backwards, his hands raised to ward off Granny's gaze. The wizards behind him scattered, turning over tables in their haste to avoid the stare.

Granny's eyes had changed.

Esk had never seen them like this before. They were perfectly silver, like little round mirrors, reflecting all they saw. Cutangle was a vanishingly small dot in their depths, his mouth open, his tiny matchstick arms waving in desperation.

The Archchancellor backed into a pillar, and the shock made him recover. He shook his head irritably, cupped a hand and sent a stream of white fire streaking towards the witch.

Without dropping her iridescent stare Granny raised a hand and deflected the flames towards the roof. There was an explosion and a shower of tile fragments.

Her eyes widened.

Cutangle vanished. Where he had been standing a huge snake coiled, poised to strike.

Granny vanished. Where she had been standing was a large wicker basket.

The snake became a giant reptile from the mists of time.

The basket became the snow wind of the Ice Giants, coating the struggling monster with ice.

The reptile became a sabre-toothed tiger, crouched to spring.

The gale became a bubbling tar pit.

The tiger managed to become an eagle, stooping.

The tar pits became a tufted hood.

Then the images began to flicker as shape replaced shape. Stroboscope shadows danced around the hall. A magical wind sprang up, thick and greasy, striking octarine sparks from beards and fingers. In the middle of it all Esk, peering through streaming eyes, could just make out the two figures of Granny and Cutangle, glossy statues in the midst of the hurtling images.

She was also aware of something else, a high-pitched sound almost beyond hearing.

She had heard it before, on the cold plain – a busy chittering noise, a beehive noise, an anthill sound . . .

'They're coming!' she screamed about the din. 'They're coming *now*!'

She scrambled out from behind the table where she had taken refuge from the magical duel and tried to reach Granny. A gust of raw magic lifted her off her feet and bowled her into a chair.

The buzzing was louder now, so that the air roared like a three-week corpse on a summer's day. Esk made another attempt to reach Granny and recoiled when green fire roared along her arm and singed her hair.

She looked around wildly for the other wizards, but those who had fled from the effects of the magic were cowering behind overturned furniture while the occult storm raged over their heads.

Esk ran down the length of the hall and out into the dark corridor. Shadows curled around her as she hurried, sobbing, up the steps and along the buzzing corridors towards Simon's narrow room.

Something would try to enter the body, Granny had said. Something that would walk and talk like Simon, but would be something else . . .

A cluster of students were hovering anxiously outside the door. They turned pale faces towards Esk as she darted towards them, and were sufficiently shaken to draw back nervously in the face of her determined progress.

'Something's in there,' said one of them.

'We can't open the door!'

They looked at her expectantly. Then one of them said: 'You wouldn't have a pass key, by any chance?'

Esk grabbed the doorhandle and turned it. It moved slightly, but then spun back with such force it nearly took the skin off her hands. The chittering inside rose to a crescendo and there was another noise, too, like leather flapping.

'You're wizards!' she screamed. 'Bloody well wizz!'

'We haven't done telekinesis yet,' said one of them.

'I was ill when we did Firethrowing–'

'Actually, I'm not very good at Dematerialisation–'

Esk went to the door, and then stopped with one foot in the air. She remembered Granny talking about how even buildings had a mind, if they were old enough. The University was very old.

She stepped carefully to one side and ran her hands over the ancient stones. It had to be done carefully, so as not to frighten it – and now she could feel the mind in the stones, slow and simple, but still mind. It pulsed around her; she could feel the little sparkles deep in the rock.

Something was hooting behind the door.

The three students watched in astonishment as Esk stood rock still with her hands and forehead pressed against the wall.

She was almost there. She could feel the weight of herself, the ponderousness of her body, the distant memories of the dawn of time when rock was molten and free. For the first time in her life she knew what it was like to have balconies.

She moved gently through the building-mind, refining her impressions, looking as fast as she dared for *this* corridor, this door.

She stretched out one arm, very carefully. The students watched as she uncurled one finger, very slowly.

The door hinges began to creak.

There was a moment of tension and then the nails sprang from the hinges and clattered into the wall behind her. The planks began to bend as the door still tried to force itself open against the strength of – whatever was holding it shut.

The wood *billowed*.

Beams of blue light lanced out into the corridor, moving and dancing as indistinct shapes shuffled through the blinding brilliance inside the room. The light was misty and actinic, the sort of light to make Steven Spielberg reach for his copyright lawyer.

Esk's hair leapt from her head so that she looked like an ambulant dandelion. Little firesnakes of magic crackled across her skin as she stepped through the doorway.

The students outside watched in horror as she disappeared into the light.

It vanished in a silent explosion.

When they eventually found enough courage to look inside the room, they saw nothing there but the sleeping body of Simon. And Esk, silent and cold on the floor, breathing very slowly. And the floor was covered with a fine layer of silver sand.

Esk floated through the mists of the world, noticing with a curious impersonal feeling the precise way in which she passed through solid matter.

There were others with her. She could hear their chittering.

Fury rose like bile. She turned and set out after the noise, fighting the seductive forces that kept telling her how nice it would be just to relax her grip on her mind and sink into a warm sea of nothingness. Being angry, that was the thing. She knew it was most important to stay really angry.

The Discworld fell away, and lay below her as it did on the day she had been an eagle. But this time the Circle Sea was below her – it certainly was circular, as if God had run out of ideas – and beyond it lay the arms of the continent, and the long chain of the Ramtops marching all the way to the Hub. There were other continents she had never heard of, and tiny island chains.

As her point of view changed, the Rim came into sight. It was night time and, since the Disc's orbiting sun was below the world, it lit up the long waterfall that girdled the Edge.

It also lit up Great A'Tuin the World Turtle. Esk had often wondered if the Turtle was really a myth. It seemed a lot of trouble to go to just to move a world. But there It was, almost as big as the Disc it carried, frosted with stardust and pocked with meteor craters.

Its head passed in front of her and she looked directly into an eye big enough to float all the fleets in the world. She had heard it said that if you could look far enough into the direction that Great A'Tuin was staring, you would see the end of the universe. Maybe it was just the set of Its beak, but Great A'Tuin looked vaguely hopeful, even optimistic. Perhaps the end of everything wasn't as bad as all that.

Dreamlike, she reached out and tried to Borrow the biggest mind in the universe.

She stopped herself just in time, like a child with a toy toboggan who expected a little gentle slope and suddenly looks out on the magnificent mountains, snow-covered, stretching into the icefields of infinity. No one would ever Borrow that mind, it would be like trying to drink all the sea. The thoughts that moved through it were as big and as slow as glaciers.

Beyond the Disc were the stars, and there was something wrong with them. They were swirling like snowflakes. Every now and again they would settle down and look as immobile as they always did, and then they'd suddenly take it into their heads to dance.

Real stars shouldn't do that, Esk decided. Which meant she wasn't looking at real stars. Which meant she wasn't exactly in a real place. But a chittering close at hand reminded her that she could almost certainly really die if she once lost track of those noises. She turned and pursued the sounds through the stellar snowstorm.

And the stars jumped, and settled, jumped, and settled . . .

As she swooped upward Esk tried to concentrate on everyday things, because if she let her mind dwell on precisely what it was she was following then she knew she would turn back, and she wasn't sure she knew the way. She tried to remember the eighteen herbs that cured ear-ache, which kept her occupied for a while because she could never recall the last four.

A star swooped past, and then was violently jerked away; it was about twenty feet across.

When she ran out of herbs she started on the diseases of goats, which took quite a long time because goats can catch a lot of things that cows can catch plus a lot of things that sheep can catch plus a complete range of horrible ailments of their very own. When she had finished listing wooden udder, ear wilt and the octarine garget she tried to recall the complex code of dots and lines that they used to cut in the trees around Bad Ass, so that lost villagers could find their way home on snowy nights.

She was only as far as dot dot dot dash dot dash (Hub-by-Turnwise, one mile from the village) when the universe around her vanished with a faint pop. She fell forward, hit something hard and gritty and rolled to a halt.

The grittiness was sand. Fine, dry, *cold* sand. You could tell that even if you dug down several feet it would be just as cold and just as dry.

Esk lay with her face in it for a moment, summoning the courage to look up. She could just see, a few feet away from her, the hem of someone's dress. Something's dress, she corrected herself. Unless it was a wing. It *could* be a wing, a particularly tatty and leathery one.

Her eyes followed it up until she found a face, higher than a house, outlined against the starry sky. Its owner was obviously trying to look nightmarish, but had tried too hard. The basic appearance was that of a chicken that had been dead for about two months, but the unpleasant effect was rather spoiled by warthog tusks, moth antennae, wolf ears and a unicorn spike. The whole thing had a self-assembled look, as if the owner had heard about anatomy but couldn't quite get to grips with the idea.

It was staring, but not at her. Something behind her occupied all its interest. Esk turned her head very slowly.

Simon was sitting cross-legged in the centre of a circle of Things. There were hundreds of them, as still and silent as statues, watching him with reptilian patience.

There was something small and angular held in his cupped hands. It gave off a fuzzy blue light that made his face look strange.

Other shapes lay on the ground beside him, each in its little soft glow. They were the regular sort of shapes that Granny dismissed airily as jommetry – cubes, many-sided diamonds, cones, even a globe. Each one was transparent and inside was . . .

Esk edged closer. No one was taking any notice of her.

Inside a crystal sphere that had been tossed aside on to the sand floated a blue-green ball, crisscrossed with tiny white cloud patterns and what could almost have been continents if anyone was silly enough to try to live on a ball. It might have been a sort of model, except something about its glow told Esk that it was quite real and probably very big and not – in every sense – totally inside the sphere.

She put it down very gently and sidled over to a ten-sided block in which floated a much more acceptable world. It was properly disc-shaped, but instead of the Rimfall there was a wall of ice and instead of the Hub there was a gigantic tree, so big that its roots merged into mountain ranges.

A prism beside it held another slowly turning disc, surrounded by little stars. But there were no ice walls around this one, just a red-gold thread that turned out on closer inspection to be a snake – a snake big enough to encircle a world. For reasons best known to itself it was biting its own tail.

Esk turned the prism over and over curiously, noticing how the little disc inside stayed resolutely upright.

Simon giggled softly. Esk replaced the snake-disc and peered carefully over his shoulder.

He was holding a small glass pyramid. There were stars in it, and occasionally he would give it a little shake so that the stars swirled up like snow in the wind, and then settled back in their places. Then he would giggle.

And beyond the stars . . .

It was the Discworld. A Great A'Tuin no bigger than a small saucer toiled along under a world that looked like the work of an obsessive jeweller.

Jiggle, swirl. Jiggle, swirl, giggle. There were already hairline cracks in the glass.

Esk looked at Simon's blank eyes and then up into the hungry faces of the nearest Things, and then she reached across and pulled the pyramid out of his hands and turned and ran.

The Things didn't stir as she scurried towards them, bent almost double, with the pyramid clasped tightly to her chest. But suddenly her feet were no longer running over the sand and she was being lifted into the frigid air, and a Thing with a face like a drowned rabbit turned slowly towards her and extended a talon.

You're not really here, Esk told herself. It's only a sort of dream, what Granny calls an annaloggy. You can't really be hurt, it's all imagination. There's absolutely no harm that can come to you, it's all really inside your mind.

I wonder if *it* knows that?

The talon picked her out of the air and the rabbit face split like a banana skin. There was no mouth, just a dark hole, as if the Thing was itself an opening to an even worse dimension, a place by comparison with which freezing sand and moonless moonlight would be a jolly afternoon at the seaside.

Esk held the Disc-pyramid and flailed with her free hand at the claw around her. It had no effect. The darkness loomed over her, a gateway to total oblivion.

She kicked it as hard as she could.

Which was not, given the circumstances, very hard. But where her foot struck there was an explosion of white sparks and a pop – which would have been a much more satisfying bang if the thin air here didn't suck the sound away.

The Thing screeched like a chainsaw encountering, deep inside an unsuspecting sapling, a lurking and long-forgotten nail. The others around it set up a sympathetic buzzing.

Esk kicked again and the Thing shrieked and dropped her to the sand. She was bright enough to roll, with the tiny world hugged protectively to her, because even in a dream a broken ankle can be painful.

The Thing lurched uncertainly above her. Esk's eyes narrowed. She put the world down very carefully, hit the Thing very hard around the point where its shins would be, if there were shins under that cloak, and picked up the world again in one neat movement.

The creature howled, bent double, and then toppled slowly, like a sackful of coathangers. When it hit the ground it collapsed into a mass of disjointed limbs; the head rolled away and rocked to a standstill.

Is that all? thought Esk. They can hardly walk, even! When you hit them they just fall over?

The nearest Things chittered and tried to back away as she marched determinedly towards them, but since their bodies seemed to be held together more or less by wishful thinking they weren't very good at it. She hit one, which had a face like a small family of squid, and it deflated into a pile of twitching bones and bits of fur and odd ends of tentacle, very much like a Greek meal. Another was slightly more successful and had begun to shamble uncertainly away before Esk caught it a crack on one of its five shins.

It flailed desperately as it fell and brought down another two.

By then the others had managed to lurch out of her way and stood watching from a distance.

Esk took a few steps towards the nearest one. It tried to move away, and fell over.

They may have been ugly. They may have been evil. But when it came to poetry in motion, the Things had all the grace and co-ordination of a deck-chair.

Esk glared at them, and took a look at the Disc in its glass pyramid. All the excitement didn't seem to have disturbed it a bit.

She'd been able to get *out*, if this indeed was *out* and if the Disc could be said to be *in*. But how was one supposed to get back?

Somebody laughed. It was the sort of laugh–

Basically, it was p'ch'zarni'chiwkov. This epiglottis-throttling word is seldom used on the Disc except by highly paid stunt linguists and, of course, the tiny tribe of the K'turni, who invented it. It has no direct synonym, although the Cumhoolie word 'squernt' ('the feeling upon finding that the previous occupant of the privy has used all the paper') begins to approach it in general depth of feeling. The closest translation is as follows:

> the nasty little sound of a sword being unsheathed right behind one at just the point when one thought one had disposed of one's enemies

– although K'turni speakers say that this does not convey the cold sweating, heart-stopping, gut-freezing sense of the original.

It was that kind of laugh.

Esk turned around slowly. Simon drifted towards her across the sand, with his hands cupped in front of him. His eyes were tight shut.

'Did you really think it would be as easy as that?' he said. Or something said; it didn't sound like Simon's voice, but like dozens of voices speaking at once.

'Simon?' she said, uncertainly.

'He is of no further use to us,' said the Thing with Simon's shape. 'He has shown us the way, child. Now give us our property.'

Esk backed away.

'I don't think it belongs to you,' she said, 'whoever you are.'

The face in front of her opened its eyes. There was nothing there but blackness – not a colour, just holes into some other space.

'We could say that if you gave it to us we would be merciful. We could say we would let you go from here in your own shape. But there wouldn't really be much point in us saying that, would there?'

'I wouldn't believe you,' said Esk.

'Well, then.'

The Simon-thing grinned.

'You're only putting off the inevitable,' it said.

'Suits me.'

'We could take it anyway.'

'Take it, then. But I don't think you can. You can't take anything unless it's given to you, can you?'

They circled round.

'You'll give it to us,' said the Simon-thing.

Some of the other Things were approaching now, striding back across the desert with horrible jerky motions.

'You'll get tired,' it continued. 'We can wait. We're very good at waiting.'

It made a feint to the left, but Esk swung around to face it.

'That doesn't matter,' she said. 'I'm only dreaming this, and you can't get hurt in dreams.'

The Thing paused, and looked at her with its empty eyes.

'Have you got a word in your world, I think it's called "psychosomatic"?'

'Never heard of it,' snapped Esk.

'It means you *can* get hurt in your dreams. And what is so interesting is that if you die in your dreams you stay here. That would be niiiiice.'

Esk glanced sideways at the distant mountains, sprawled on the chilly horizon like melted mud pies. There were no trees, not even any rocks. Just sand and cold stars and–

She felt the movement rather than heard it and turned with the pyramid held between her hands like a club. It hit the Simon-thing in mid-leap with a satisfying thump, but as soon as it hit the ground it somersaulted forward and bounced upright with unpleasant ease. But it had heard her gasp and had seen the brief pain in her eyes. It paused.

'Ah, that hurt you, did it not? You don't like to see another one suffer, yes? Not this one, it seems.'

It turned and beckoned, and two of the tall Things lurched over to it and gripped it firmly by the arms.

Its eyes changed. The darkness faded, and then Simon's own eyes looked out of his face. He stared up at the Things on either side of him and struggled briefly, but one had several pairs of tentacles wrapped around his wrist and the other was holding his arm in the world's largest lobster claw.

Then he saw Esk, and his eyes fell to the little glass pyramid.

'Run away!' he hissed. 'Take it away from here! Don't let them get it!' He grimaced as the claw tightened on his arm.

'Is this a trick?' said Esk. 'Who are you really?'

'Don't you recognise me?' he said wretchedly. 'What are you doing in my dream?'

'If this is a dream then I'd like to wake up, please,' said Esk.

'Listen. You must run away now, do you understand? Don't stand there with your mouth open.'

GIVE IT TO US, said a cold voice inside Esk's head.

Esk looked down at the glass pyramid with its unconcerned little world and stared up at Simon, her mouth an O of puzzlement.

'But what *is* it?'

'Look hard at it!'

Esk peered through the glass. If she squinted it seemed that the little Disc was granular, as if it was made up of millions of tiny specks. If she looked hard at the specks–

'It's just numbers!' she said. 'The whole world – it's all made up of numbers . . . '

'It's not the world, it's an idea of the world,' said Simon. 'I created it for them. They can't get through to us, do you see, but ideas have got a shape here. Ideas are real!'

GIVE IT TO US.

'But ideas can't hurt anyone!'

'I turned things into numbers to understand them, but they just want to control,' Simon said bitterly. 'They burrowed into my numbers like– '

He screamed.

GIVE IT TO US OR WE WILL TAKE HIM TO BITS.

Esk looked up at the nearest nightmare face.

'How do I know I can trust you?' she said.

YOU CAN'T TRUST US. BUT YOU HAVE NO CHOICE.

Esk looked at the ring of faces that not even a necrophile could love, faces put together from a fishmonger's midden, faces picked randomly from things that lurked in deep ocean holes and haunted caves, faces that were not human enough to gloat or leer but had all the menace of a suspiciously v-shaped ripple near an incautious bather.

She couldn't trust them. But she had no choice.

Something else was happening, in a place as far away as the thickness of a shadow.

The student wizards had run back to the Great Hall, where Cutangle and Granny Weatherwax were still locked in the magical equivalent of Indian arm wrestling. The flagstones under Granny were half-melted and cracked and the table behind Cutangle had taken root and already bore a rich crop of acorns.

One of the students had earned several awards for bravery by daring to tug at Cutangle's cloak . . .

And now they were crowded into the narrow room, looking at the two bodies.

Cutangle summoned doctors of the body and doctors of the mind, and the room buzzed with magic as they got to work.

Granny tapped him on the shoulder.

'A word in your ear, young man,' she said.

'Hardly young, madam,' sighed Cutangle, 'hardly young.' He felt drained. It had been decades since he'd duelled in magic, although it was common enough among students. He had a nasty feeling that Granny would have won eventually. Fighting her was like swatting a fly on your own nose. He couldn't think what had come over him to try it.

Granny led him out into the passage and around the corner to a window-seat. She sat down, leaning her broomstick against the wall. Rain drummed heavily on the roofs outside, and a few zigzags of lightning indicated a storm of Ramtop proportions approaching the city.

'That was quite an impressive display,' she said: 'You nearly won once or twice there.'

'Oh,' said Cutangle, brightening up. 'Do you really think so?'

Granny nodded.

Cutangle patted at various bits of his robe until he located a tarry bag of tobacco and a roll of paper. His hands shook as he fumbled a few shreds of second-hand pipeweed into a skinny homemade. He ran the wretched thing across his tongue, and barely moistened it. Then a dim remembrance of propriety welled up in the back of his mind.

'Um,' he said. 'Do you mind if I smoke?'

Granny shrugged. Cutangle struck a match on the wall and tried desperately to navigate the flame and the cigarette into approximately the same position. Granny gently took the match from his trembling hand and lit it for him.

Cutangle sucked on the tobacco, had a ritual cough and settled back, the glowing end of the rollup the only light in the dim corridor.

'They've gone Wandering,' said Granny at last.

'I know,' said Cutangle.

'Your wizards won't be able to get them back.'

'I know that, too.'

'They might get *something* back, though.'

'I wish you hadn't said that.'

There was a pause while they contemplated what might come back, inhabiting living bodies, acting almost like the original inhabitants.

'It's probably my fault– ' they said in unison, and stopped in astonishment.

'You first, madam,' said Cutangle.

'Them cigaretty things,' asked Granny, 'are they good for the nerves?'

Cutangle opened his mouth to point out very courteously that tobacco was a habit reserved for wizards, but thought better of it. He extended the tobacco pouch towards Granny.

She told him about Esk's birth, and the coming of the old wizard, and the staff, and Esk's forays into magic. By the time she had finished she had succeeded in rolling a tight, thin cylinder that burned with a small blue flame and made her eyes water.

'I don't know that shaky nerves wouldn't be better,' she wheezed.

Cutangle wasn't listening.

'This is quite astonishing,' he said. 'You say the child didn't suffer in any way?'

'Not that I noticed,' said Granny. 'The staff seemed – well, on her side, if you know what I mean.'

'And where is this staff now?'

'She said she threw it in the river . . . '

The old wizard and the elderly witch stared at each other, their faces illuminated by a flare of lightning outside.

Cutangle shook his head. 'The river's flooding,' he said. 'It's a million-to-one chance.'

Granny smiled grimly. It was the sort of smile that wolves ran away from. Granny grasped her broomstick purposefully.

'Million-to-one chances,' she said, 'crop up nine times out of ten.'

There are storms that are frankly theatrical, all sheet lightning and metallic thunder rolls. There are storms that are tropical and sultry, and incline to hot winds and fireballs. But this was a storm of the Circle Sea plains, and its main ambition was to hit the ground with as much rain as possible. It was the kind of storm that suggests that the whole sky has swallowed a diuretic. The thunder and lightning hung around in the background, supplying a sort of chorus, but the rain was the star of the show. It tap-danced across the land.

The grounds of the University stretched right down to the river. By day they were a neat formal pattern of gravel paths and hedges, but in the middle of a wet wild night the hedges seemed to have moved and the paths had simply gone off somewhere to stay dry.

A weak wyrdlight shone inefficiently among the dripping leaves. But most of the rain found its way through anyway.

'Can you use one of them wizard fireballs?'

'Have a heart, madam.'

'Are you sure she would have come this way?'

'There's a sort of jetty thing down here somewhere, unless I'm lost.'

There was the sound of a heavy body blundering wetly into a bush, and then a splash.

'I've found the river, anyway.'

Granny Weatherwax peered through the soaking darkness. She could hear a roaring and could dimly make out the white crests of floodwater. There was also the distinctive river smell of the Ankh, which suggested that several armies had used it first as a urinal and then as a sepulchre.

Cutangle splashed dejectedly towards her.

'This is foolishness,' he said, 'meaning no offence, madam. But it'll be out to sea on this flood. And I'll die of cold.'

'You can't get any wetter than you are now. Anyway, you walk wrong for rain.'

'I beg your pardon?'

'You go all hunched up, you fight it, that's not the way. You should – well, move between the drops.' And, indeed, Granny seemed to be merely damp.

'I'll bear that in mind. Come on, madam. It's me for a roaring fire and a glass of something hot and wicked.'

Granny sighed. 'I don't know. Somehow I expected to see it sticking out of the mud, or something. Not just all this water.'

Cutangle patted her gently on the shoulder.

'There may be something else we can do– ' he began, and was interrupted by a zip of lightning and another roll of thunder.

'I said maybe there's something–' he began again.

'What was that I saw?' demanded Granny.

'What was what?' said Cutangle, bewildered.

'Give me some light!'

The wizard sighed wetly, and extended a hand. A bolt of golden fire shot out across the foaming water and hissed into oblivion.

'There!' said Granny triumphantly.

'It's just a boat,' said Cutangle. 'The boys use them in the summer– '

He waded after Granny's determined figure as fast as he could.

'You can't be thinking of taking it out on a night like this,' he said. 'It's madness!'

Granny slithered along the wet planking of the jetty, which was already nearly under water.

'You don't know anything about boats!' Cutangle protested.

'I shall have to learn quickly, then,' replied Granny calmly.

'But I haven't been in a boat since I was a boy!'

'I wasn't actually asking you to come. Does the pointy bit go in front?'

Cutangle moaned.

'This is all very creditable,' he said, 'but perhaps we can wait till morning?'

A flash of lightning illuminated Granny's face.

'Perhaps not,' Cutangle conceded. He lumbered along the jetty and pulled the little rowing boat towards him. Getting in was a matter of luck but he managed it eventually, fumbling with the painter in the darkness.

The boat swung out into the flood and was carried away, spinning slowly.

Granny clung to the seat as it rocked in the turbulent waters, and looked expectantly at Cutangle through the murk.

'Well?' she said.

'Well what?' said Cutangle.

'You said you knew all about boats.'

'No. I said *you* didn't.'

'Oh.'

They hung on as the boat wallowed heavily, miraculously righted itself, and was carried backwards downstream.

'When you said you hadn't been in a boat since you were a boy . . . ' Granny began.

'I was two years old, I think.'

The boat caught on a whirlpool, spun around, and shot off across the flow.

'I had you down as the sort of boy who was in and out of boats all day long.'

'I was born up in the mountains. I get seasick on damp grass, if you must know,' said Cutangle.

The boat banged heavily against a submerged tree-trunk, and a wavelet lapped the prow.

'I know a spell against drowning,' he added miserably.

'I'm glad about that.'

'Only you have to say it while you're standing on dry land.'

'Take your boots off.' Granny commanded.

'What?'

'Take your boots off, man!'

Cutangle shifted uneasily on his bench.

'What have you in mind?' he said.

'The water is supposed to be *outside* the boat, I know that much!' Granny pointed to the dark tide sloshing around the bilges: 'Fill your boots with water and tip it over the side!'

Cutangle nodded. He felt that the last couple of hours had somehow carried him along without him actually touching the sides, and for a moment he nursed the strangely consoling feeling that his life was totally beyond his control and whatever happened no one could blame him. Filling his boots with water while adrift on a flooded river at midnight with what he could only describe as a *woman* seemed about as logical as anything could be in the circumstances.

A fine figure of a woman, said a neglected voice at the back of his mind. There was something about the way she used the tattered broomstick to scull the boat across the choppy water that troubled long-forgotten bits of Cutangle's subconscious.

Not that he could be certain about the fine figure, of course, what with the rain and the wind and Granny's habit of wearing her entire wardrobe in one go. Cutangle cleared his throat uncertainly. Metaphorically a fine figure, he decided.

'Um, look,' he said. 'This is all very creditable, but consider the facts, I mean, the rate of drift and so forth, you see? It could be miles out on the ocean by now. It might never come to shore again. It might even go over the Rimfall.'

Granny, who had been staring out across the water, turned around.

'Can't you think of anything else at all helpful that we could be doing?' she demanded.

Cutangle baled for a few moments.

'No,' he said.

'Have you ever heard of anyone coming Back?'

'No.'

'Then it's worth a try, isn't it?'

'I never liked the ocean,' said Cutangle. 'It ought to be paved over. There's dreadful things in it, down in the deep bits. Ghastly sea monsters. Or so they say.'

'Keep baling, my lad, or you'll be able to see if they're right.'

The storm rolled backwards and forwards overhead. It was lost here on the flat river plains; it belonged in the high Ramtops, where they knew how to appreciate a good storm. It grumbled around, looking for even a moderately high hill to throw lightning at.

The rain settled down to the gentle patter of rain that is quite capable of keeping it up for days. A sea fog also rolled in to assist it.

'If we had some oars we could row, if we knew where we were going,' said Cutangle. Granny didn't answer.

He heaved a few more bootfuls of water over the side, and it occurred to him that the gold braiding on his robe would probably never be the same again. It would be nice to think it might matter, one day.

'I don't suppose you *do* know which way the Hub is, by any chance?' he ventured. 'Just making conversation.'

'Look for the mossy side of trees,' said Granny without turning her head.

'Ah,' said Cutangle, and nodded.

He peered down gloomily at the oily waters, and wondered which particular oily waters they were. Judging by the salty smell they were out in the bay now.

What really terrified him about the sea was that the only thing between him and the horrible things that lived at the bottom of it was water. Of course, he knew that logically the only thing that separated him from, say, the man-eating tigers in the jungles of Klatch was mere distance, but that wasn't the same thing at all. Tigers didn't rise up out of the chilly depths, mouths full of needle teeth . . .

He shivered.

'Can't you feel it?' asked Granny. 'You can taste it in the air. Magic! It's leaking out from something.'

'It's not actually water soluble,' said Cutangle. He smacked his lips once or twice. There was indeed a tinny taste to the fog, he had to admit, and a faint greasiness to the air.

'You're a wizard,' said Granny, severely. 'Can't you call it up or something?'

'The question has never arisen,' said Cutangle. 'Wizards never throw their staffs away.'

'It's around here somewhere,' snapped Granny. 'Help me look for it, man!'

Cutangle groaned. It had been a busy night, and before he tried any more magic he really needed twelve hours' sleep, several good meals, and a quiet afternoon in front of a big fire. He was getting too old, that was the trouble. But he closed his eyes and concentrated.

There was magic around, all right. There are some places where magic naturally accumulates. It builds up around deposits of the transmundane metal octiron, in the wood of certain trees, in isolated lakes, it sleets through the world and those skilled in such things can catch it and store it. There was a store of magic in the area.

'It's potent,' he said. 'Very potent.' He raised his hands to his temples.

'It's getting bloody cold,' said Granny. The insistent rain had turned to snow.

There was a sudden change in the world. The boat stopped, not with a jar, but as if the sea had suddenly decided to become solid. Granny looked over the side.

The sea had become solid. The sound of the waves was coming from a long way away and getting further away all the time.

She leaned over the side of the boat and tapped on the water.

'Ice,' she said. The boat was motionless in an ocean of ice. It creaked ominously.

Cutangle nodded slowly.

'It makes sense,' he said. 'If they are . . . where we think they are, then it's very cold. As cold as the night between the stars, it is said. So the staff feels it too.'

'Right,' said Granny, and stepped out of the boat. 'All we have to do is find the middle of the ice and there's the staff, right?'

'I knew you were going to say that. Can I at least put my boots on?'

They wandered across the frozen waves, with Cutangle stopping occasionally to try and sense the exact location of the staff. His robes were freezing on him. His teeth chattered.

'Aren't you cold?' he said to Granny, whose dress fairly crackled as she walked.

'I'm cold,' she conceded, 'I just ain't shivering.'

'We used to have winters like this when I was a lad,' said Cutangle, blowing on his fingers. 'It doesn't snow in Ankh, hardly.'

'Really,' said Granny, peering ahead through the freezing fog.

'There was snow on the tops of the mountains all year round, I recall. Oh, you don't get temperatures like you did when I was a boy.'

'At least, until now,' he added, stamping his feet on the ice. It creaked menacingly, reminding him that it was all that lay between him and the bottom of the sea. He stamped again, as softly as possible.

'What mountains were these?' asked Granny.

'Oh, the Ramtops. Up towards the Hub, in fact. Place called Brass Neck.'

Granny's lips moved. 'Cutangle, Cutangle,' she said softly. 'Any relation to old Acktur Cutangle? Used to live in a big old house under Leaping Mountain, had a lot of sons.'

'My father. How on disc d'you know that?'

'I was raised up there,' said Granny, resisting the temptation merely to smile knowingly. 'Next valley. Bad Ass. I remember your mother. Nice woman, kept brown and white chickens, I used to go up there to buy eggs for me mam. That was before I was called to witching, of course.'

'I don't remember you,' said Cutangle. 'Of course, it was a long time ago. There was always a lot of children around our house.' He sighed. 'I suppose it's possible I pulled your hair once. It was the sort of thing I used to do.'

'Maybe. I remember a fat little boy. Rather unpleasant.'

'That might have been me. I seem to recall a rather bossy girl, but it was a long time ago. A long time ago.'

'I didn't have white hair in those days,' said Granny.

'Everything was a different colour in those days.'

'That's true.'

'It didn't rain so much in the summer time.'

'The sunsets were redder.'

'There were more old people. The world was full of them,' said the wizard.

'Yes, I know. And now it's full of young people. Funny, really. I mean, you'd expect it to be the other way round.'

'They even had a better kind of air. It was easier to breathe,' said Cutangle.

They stamped on through the swirling snow, considering the curious ways of time and Nature.

'Ever been home again?' said Granny.

Cutangle shrugged. 'When my father died. It's odd, I've never said this to anyone, but – well, there were my brothers, because I am an eighth son of course, and they had children and even grandchildren, and not one of them can hardly write his name. I could have bought the whole village. And they treated me like a king, but – I mean, I've been to places and seen things that would curdle their minds, I've faced down creatures wilder than their nightmares, I know secrets that are known to a very few–'

'You felt left out,' said Granny. 'There's nothing strange in that. It happens to all of us. It was our choice.'

'Wizards should never go home,' said Cutangle.

'I don't think they *can* go home,' agreed Granny. 'You can't cross the same river twice, I always say.'

Cutangle gave this some thought.

'I think you're wrong there,' he said. 'I must have crossed the same river, oh, thousands of times.'

'Ah, but it wasn't the same river.'

'It wasn't?'

'No.'

Cutangle shrugged. 'It looked like the same bloody river.'

'No need to take that tone,' said Granny. 'I don't see why I should listen to that sort of language from a wizard who can't even answer letters!'

Cutangle was silent for a moment, except for the castanet chatter of his teeth.

'Oh,' he said. 'Oh, I see. They were from you, were they?'

'That's right. I signed them on the bottom. It's supposed to be a sort of clue, isn't it?'

'All right, all right. I just thought they were a joke, that's all,' said Cutangle sullenly.

'A joke?'

'We don't get many applications from women. We don't get *any*.'

'I wondered why I didn't get a reply,' said Granny.

'I threw them away, if you must know.'

'You could at least have – *there it is*!'

'Where? Where? Oh, there.'

The fog parted and they now saw it clearly – a fountain of snowflakes, an ornamental pillar of frozen air. And below it . . .

The staff wasn't locked in ice, but lay peacefully in a seething pool of water.

One of the unusual aspects of a magical universe is the existence of opposites. It has already been remarked that darkness isn't the opposite of light, it is simply the absence of light. In the same way absolute zero is merely the absence of heat. If you want to know what *real* cold is, the cold so intense that water can't even freeze but anti-boils, look no further than this pool.

They looked in silence for some seconds, their bickering forgotten. Then Cutangle said slowly: 'If you stick your hand in that, your fingers'll snap like carrots.'

'Do you think you can lift it out by magic?' said Granny.

Cutangle started to pat his pockets and eventually produced his rollup bag. With expert fingers he shredded the remains of a few dogends into a fresh paper and licked it into shape, without taking his eyes off the staff.

'No,' he said, 'but I'll try anyway.'

He looked longingly at the cigarette and then poked it behind his ear. He extended his hands, fingers splayed, and his lips moved soundlessly as he mumbled a few words of power.

The staff spun in its pool and then rose gently away from the ice, where it immediately became the centre of a cocoon of frozen air. Cutangle groaned with the effort – direct levitation is the hardest of the practical magics, because of the ever-present danger of the well-known principles of action and reaction, which means that a wizard attempting to lift a heavy item by mind power alone faces the prospect of ending up with his brains in his boots.

'Can you stand it upright?' said Granny.

With great delicacy the staff turned slowly in the air until it hung in front of Granny a few inches above the ice. Frost glittered on its carvings, but it seemed to Cutangle – through the red haze of migraine that hovered in front of his eyes – to be watching him. *Resentfully*.

Granny adjusted her hat and straightened up purposefully.

'*Right*,' she said. Cutangle swayed. The tone of voice cut through him like a diamond saw. He could dimly remember being scolded by his mother when he was small; well, this was that voice, only refined and concentrated and edged with little bits of carborundum, a tone of command that would have a corpse standing to attention and could probably have marched it halfway across its cemetery before it remembered it was dead.

Granny stood in front of the hovering staff, almost melting its icy covering by the sheer anger in her gaze.

'This is your idea of proper behaviour, is it? Lying around on the sea while people die? Oh, very well done!'

She stomped around in a semi-circle. To Cutangle's bewilderment, the staff turned to follow her.

'So you were thrown away,' snapped Granny. 'So what? She's hardly more than a child, and children throw us all away sooner or later. Is this loyal service? Have you no shame, lying around sulking when you could be of some use at last?'

She leaned forward, her hooked nose a few inches from the staff. Cutangle was almost certain that the staff tried to lean backwards out of her way.

'Shall I tell you what happens to wicked staffs?' she hissed. 'If Esk is lost to the world, shall I tell you what I will do to you? You were saved from the fire once, because you could pass on the hurt to her. Next time it won't be the fire.'

Her voice sank to a whiplash whisper.

'First it'll be the spokeshave. And then the sandpaper, and the auger, and the whittling knife–'

'I say, steady on,' said Cutangle, his eyes watering.

' – and what's left I'll stake out in the woods for the fungus and the woodlice and the beetles. It could take *years*.'

The carvings writhed. Most of them had moved around the back, out of Granny's gaze.

'Now,' she said. 'I'll tell you what I'm going to do. I'm going to pick you up and we are all going back to the University, aren't we? Otherwise it's blunt saw time.'

She rolled up her sleeves and extended a hand.

'Wizard,' she said, 'I shall want you to release it.'

Cutangle nodded miserably.

'When I say now, now! *Now!*'

Cutangle opened his eyes again.

Granny was standing with her left arm extended full length in front of her, her hand clamped around the staff.

The ice was exploding off it, in gouts of steam.

'Right,' finished Granny, 'and if this happens again I shall be *very* angry, do I make myself clear?'

Cutangle lowered his hands and hurried towards her.

'Are you hurt?'

She shook her head. 'It's like holding a hot icicle,' she said. 'Come on, we haven't got time to stand around chatting.'

'How are we going to get back?'

'Oh, show some backbone, man, for goodness sake. We'll fly.'

Granny waved her broomstick. The Archchancellor looked at it doubtfully.

'On that?'

'Of course. Don't wizards fly on their staffs?'

'It's rather undignified.'

'If I can put up with that, so can you.'

'Yes, but is it safe?'

Granny gave him a withering look.

'Do you mean in the absolute sense?' she asked. 'Or, say, compared with staying behind on a melting ice floe?'

'This is the first time I have ever ridden on a broomstick,' said Cutangle.

'Really.'

'I thought you just had to get on them and they flew,' said the wizard. 'I didn't know you had to do all that running up and down and shouting at them.'

'It's a knack,' said Granny.

'I thought they went faster,' Cutangle continued, 'and, to be frank, higher.'

'What do you mean, higher?' asked Granny, trying to compensate for the wizard's weight on the pillion as they turned back upriver. Like pillion passengers since the dawn of time, he persisted in leaning the wrong way.

'Well, more sort of *above* the trees,' said Cutangle, ducking as a dripping branch swept his hat away.

'There's nothing wrong with this broomstick that you losing a few stone wouldn't cure,' snapped Granny. 'Or would you rather get off and walk?'

'Apart from the fact that half the time my feet are touching the ground anyway,' said Cutangle. 'I wouldn't want to embarrass you. If someone had asked me to list all the perils of flying, you know, it would never have occurred to me to include having one's legs whipped to death by tall bracken.'

'Are you smoking?' said Granny, staring grimly ahead. 'Something's burning.'

'It was just to calm my nerves what with all this headlong plunging through the air, madam.'

'Well, put it out this minute. And hold on.'

The broomstick lurched upwards and increased its speed to that of a geriatric jogger.

'Mr Wizard.'

'Hallo?'

'When I said hold on–'

'Yes?'

'I didn't mean there.'

There was a pause.

'Oh. Yes. I see. I'm terribly sorry.'

'That's all right.'

'My memory isn't what it was . . . I assure you . . . no offence meant.'

'None taken.'

They flew in silence for a moment.

'Nevertheless,' said Granny thoughtfully, 'I think that, on the whole, I would prefer you to move your hands.'

Rain gushed across the leads of Unseen University and poured into the gutters where ravens' nests, abandoned since the summer, floated like very badly built boats. The water gurgled along ancient, crusted pipes. It found its way under tiles and said hallo to the spiders under the eaves. It leapt from gables and formed secret lakes high amongst the spires.

Whole ecologies lived in the endless rooftops of the University, which by comparison made Gormenghast look like a toolshed on a railway allotment; birds sang in tiny jungles grown from apple pips and weed seeds, little frogs swam in the upper gutters, and a colony of ants were busily inventing an interesting and complex civilisation.

One thing the water couldn't do was gurgle out of the ornamental gargoyles ranged around the roofs. This was because the gargoyles wandered off and sheltered in the attics at the first sign of rain. They held that just because you were ugly it didn't mean you were stupid.

It rained streams. It rained rivers. It rained seas. But mainly it rained through the roof of the Great Hall, where the duel between Granny and Cutangle had left a very large hole, and Treatle felt that it was somehow raining on him personally.

He stood on a table organising the teams of students who were taking down the paintings and ancient tapestries before they got soaked. It had to be a table, because the floor was already several inches deep in water.

Not rainwater, unfortunately. This was water with real personality, the kind of distinctive character water gets after a long journey through silty countryside. It had the thick texture of authentic Ankh water – too stiff to drink, too runny to plough.

The river had burst its banks and a million little watercourses were flowing backwards, bursting in through the cellars and playing peekaboo under the flagstones. There was the occasional distant boom as some forgotten magic in a drowned dungeon shorted out and surrendered up its power; Treatle wasn't at all keen on some of the unpleasant bubblings and hissings that were escaping to the surface.

He thought again how nice it would be to be the sort of wizard who lived in a little cave somewhere and collected herbs and thought significant thoughts and knew what the owls were saying. But probably the cave would be damp and the herbs would be poisonous and Treatle could never be sure, when all was said and done, exactly what thoughts were really significant.

He got down awkwardly and paddled through the dark swirling waters. Well, he had done his best. He'd tried to organise the senior wizards into repairing the roof by magic, but there was a general argument over the spells that could be used and a consensus that this was in any case work for artisans.

That's wizards for you, he thought gloomily as he waded between the dripping arches, always probing the infinite but never noticing the definite, especially in the matter of household chores. We never had this trouble before that woman came.

He squelched up the steps, lit by a particularly impressive flash of lightning. He had a cold certainty that while of course no one could possibly blame him for all this, everybody would. He seized the hem of his robe and wrung it out wretchedly, then he reached for his tobacco pouch.

It was a nice green waterproof one. That meant that all the rain that had got into it couldn't get out again. It was indescribable.

He found his little clip of papers. They were fused into one lump, like the legendary pound note found in the back pockets of trousers after they have been washed, spun, dried and ironed.

'Bugger,' he said, with feeling.

'I say! Treatle!'

Treatle looked around. He had been the last to leave the hall, where even now some of the benches were beginning to float. Whirlpools and patches of bubble marked the spots where magic was leaking from the cellars, but there was no one to be seen.

Unless, of course, one of the statues had spoken. They had been too heavy to move, and Treatle remembered telling the students that a thorough wash would probably do them good.

He looked at their stern faces and regretted it. The statues of very powerful dead mages were sometimes more lifelike than statues had any right to be. Maybe he should have kept his voice down.

'Yes?' he ventured, acutely aware of the stony stares.

'Up here, you fool!'

He looked up. The broomstick descended heavily through the rain in a series of swoops and jerks. About five feet above the water it lost its few remaining aerial pretensions, and flopped noisily into a whirlpool.

'Don't stand there, idiot!'

Treatle peered nervously into the gloom.

'I've got to stand somewhere,' he said.

'I mean give us a hand!' snapped Cutangle, rising from the wavelets like a fat and angry Venus. 'The lady first, of course.'

He turned to Granny, who was fishing around in the water.

'I've lost my hat,' she said.

Cutangle sighed. 'Does that really matter at a time like this?'

'A witch has got to have a hat, otherwise who's to know?' said Granny. She made a grab as something dark and sodden drifted by, cackled triumphantly, tipped out the water and rammed the hat on her head. It had lost its stiffening and flopped rather rakishly over one eye.

'Right,' she said, in a tone of voice that suggested the whole universe had just better watch out.

There was another brilliant flash of lightning, which shows that even the weather gods have a well-developed sense of theatre.

'It rather suits you,' said Cutangle.

'Excuse me,' said Treatle, 'but isn't she the w–'

'Never mind that,' said Cutangle, taking Granny's hand and helping her up the steps. He flourished the staff.

'But it's against the lore to allow w–'

He stopped and stared as Granny reached out and touched the damp wall by the door. Cutangle tapped him on the chest.

'Show me where it's written down,' said Cutangle.

'They're in the Library,' Granny interrupted.

'It was the only dry place,' said Treatle, 'but–'

'This building is frightened of thunderstorms,' said Granny. 'It could do with comforting.'

'But the lore–' repeated Treatle desperately.

Granny was already striding down the passage, with Cutangle hopping along behind. He turned.

'You heard the lady,' he said.

Treatle watched them go, with his mouth hanging open. When their footsteps had died away in the distance he stood silently for a moment, thinking about life and where his could have gone wrong.

However, he wasn't going to be accused of disobedience.

Very carefully, without knowing exactly why, he reached out and gave the wall a friendly pat.

'There, there,' he said.

Strangely enough, he felt a lot better.

It occurred to Cutangle that he ought to lead the way in his own premises, but Granny in a hurry was no match for a near-terminal nicotine addict and he kept up only by a sort of crabwise leaping.

'It's this way,' he said, splashing through the puddles.

'I know. The building told me.'

'Yes, I was meaning to ask about that,' said Cutangle, 'because you see it's never said anything to me and I've lived here for years.'

'Have you ever listened to it?'

'Not exactly listened, no,' Cutangle conceded. 'Not as such.'

'Well, then,' said Granny, edging past a waterfall where the kitchen steps used to be (Mrs Whitlow's washing would never be the same again). 'I think it's up here and along the passage, isn't it?'

She swept past a trio of astonished wizards, who were surprised by her and completely startled by her hat.

Cutangle panted after her and caught her arm at the doors to the Library.

'Look,' he said desperately. 'No offence, Miss – um, Mistress– '

'I think Esmerelda will suffice now. What with us having shared a broomstick and everything.'

'Can I go in front? It *is* my Library,' he begged.

Granny turned around, her face a mask of surprise. Then she smiled.

'Of course. I'm so sorry.'

'For the look of the thing, you see,' said Cutangle apologetically. He pushed the door open.

The Library was full of wizards, who care about their books in the same way that ants care about their eggs and in time of difficulty carry them around in much the same way. The water was getting in even here, and turning up in rather odd places because of the Library's strange gravitational effects. All the lower shelves had been cleared and relays of wizards and students were piling the volumes on every available table and dry shelf. The air was full of the sound of angry rustling pages, which almost drowned out the distant fury of the storm.

This was obviously upsetting the librarian, who was scurrying from wizard to wizard, tugging ineffectually at their robes and shouting 'ook'.

He spotted Cutangle and knuckled rapidly towards him. Granny had never seen an orang-utan before, but wasn't about to admit it, and remained quite calm in the face of a small pot-bellied man with extremely long arms and a size 12 skin on a size 8 body.

'Ook,' it explained, '*ooook*.'

'I expect so,' said Cutangle shortly, and grabbed the nearest wizard, who was tottering under the weight of a dozen grimoires. The man stared at him as if he was a ghost, looked sideways at Granny, and dropped the books on the floor. The librarian winced.

'Archchancellor?' gasped the wizard, 'you're alive? I mean – we heard you'd been spirited away by– ' he looked at Granny again, '– I mean, we thought – Treatle told us–'

'*Oook,*' said the librarian, shooing some pages back between their covers.

'Where are young Simon and the girl? What have you done with them?' Granny demanded.

'They – we put them over here,' said the wizard, backing away. 'Um– '

'Show us,' said Cutangle. 'And stop stuttering, man, you'd think you'd never seen a woman before.'

The wizard swallowed hard and nodded vigorously.

'Certainly. And – I mean – please follow me – um – '

'You weren't going to say anything about the lore, were you?' asked Cutangle.

'Um – no, Archchancellor.'

'Good.'

They followed hard on his trodden-down heels as he scurried between the toiling wizards, most of whom stopped working to stare as Granny strode past.

'This is getting embarrassing,' said Cutangle, out of the corner of his mouth. 'I shall have to declare you an honorary wizard.'

Granny stared straight ahead and her lips hardly moved.

'You do,' she hissed, 'and I will declare you an honorary witch.'

Cutangle's mouth snapped shut.

Esk and Simon were lying on a table in one of the side reading-rooms, with half a dozen wizards watching over them. They drew back nervously as the trio approached, with the librarian swinging along behind.

'I've been thinking,' said Cutangle. 'Surely it would be better to give the staff to Simon? He *is* a wizard, and– '

'Over my dead body,' said Granny. 'Yours, too. They're getting their power through him, do you want to give them more?'

Cutangle sighed. He had been admiring the staff, it was one of the best he had seen.

'Very well. You're right, of course.'

He leaned down and laid the staff on Esk's sleeping form, and then stood back dramatically.

Nothing happened.

One of the wizards coughed nervously.

Nothing continued to happen.

The carvings on the staff appeared to be grinning.

'It's not working,' said Cutangle, 'is it?'

'Ook.'

'Give it time,' said Granny.

They gave it time. Outside the storm strode around the sky, trying to lift the lids off houses.

Granny sat down on a pile of books and rubbed her eyes. Cutangle's hands strayed towards his tobacco pocket. The wizard with the nervous cough was helped out of the room by a colleague.

'Ook,' said the librarian.

'I know!' said Granny, so that Cutangle's half-rolled homemade shot out of his nerveless fingers in a shower of tobacco.

'What?'

'It's not finished!'

'What?'

'She can't use the staff, of course,' said Granny, standing up.

'But you said she swept the floors with it and it protects her and– ' Cutangle began.

'Nonono,' said Granny. 'That means the staff uses itself or it uses her, but she's never been able to use *it*, d'you see?'

Cutangle stared at the two quiet bodies. 'She should be able to use it. It's a proper wizard's staff.'

'Oh,' said Granny. 'So she's a proper wizard, is she?'

Cutangle hesitated.

'Well, of course not. You can't ask us to declare her a wizard. Where's the precedent?'

'The what?' asked Granny, sharply.

'It's never happened before.'

'Lots of things have never happened before. We're only born once.'

Cutangle gave her a look of mute appeal. 'But it's against the l– '

He began to say 'lore', but the word mumbled into silence.

'Where does it say it?' said Granny triumphantly. 'Where does it say women can't be wizards?'

The following thoughts sped through Cutangle's mind:

. . . It doesn't say it anywhere, it says it everywhere.

. . . But young Simon seemed to say that everywhere is so much like nowhere that you can't really tell the difference.

. . . Do I want to be remembered as the first Archchancellor to allow women into the University? Still . . . I'd be remembered, that's for sure.

. . . She really is a rather impressive woman when she stands in that sort of way.

. . . That staff has got ideas of its own.

. . . There's a sort of sense to it.

. . . I would be laughed at.

. . . It might not work.

. . . It might work.

☆   ☆   ☆

She couldn't trust them. But she had no choice.

Esk stared at the terrible faces peering down at her, and the lanky bodies mercifully cloaked.

Her hands tingled.

In the shadow-world, ideas are real. The thought seemed to travel up her arms.

It was a buoyant sort of thought, a thought full of fizz. She laughed, and moved her hands apart, and the staff sparkled in her hands like solid electricity.

The Things started to chitter nervously and one or two at the back started to lurch away. Simon fell forward as his captors hastily let go, and he landed on his hands and knees in the sand.

'Use it!' he shouted. 'That's it! They're frightened!'

Esk gave him a smile, and continued to examine the staff. For the first time she could see what the carvings actually were.

Simon snatched up the pyramid of the world and ran towards her.

'Come on!' he said. 'They hate it!'

'Pardon?' said Esk.

'Use the staff,' said Simon urgently, and reached out for it. 'Hey! It bit me!'

'Sorry,' said Esk. 'What were we talking about?' She looked up and regarded the keening Things as it were for the first time. 'Oh, *those*. They only exist inside our heads. If we didn't believe in them, they wouldn't exist at all.'

Simon looked around at them.

'I can't honestly say I believe you,' he said.

'I think we should go home now,' said Esk. 'People will be worrying.'

She moved her hands together and the staff vanished, although for a moment her hands glowed as though they were cupped around a candle.

The Things howled. A few of them fell over.

'The important thing about magic is how you don't use it,' said Esk, taking Simon's arm.

He stared at the crumbling figures around him, and grinned foolishly.

'You *don't* use it?' he queried.

'Oh, yes,' said Esk, as they walked towards the Things. 'Try it yourself.'

She extended her hands, brought the staff out of the air, and offered it to him. He went to take it, then drew back his hand.

'Uh, no,' he said, 'I don't think it likes me much.'

'I think it's all right if I give it to you. It can't really argue with that,' said Esk.

'Where does it *go*?'

'It just becomes an idea of itself, I think.'

He reached out his hand again and closed his fingers around the shining wood.

'*Right*,' he said, and raised it in the classical revengeful wizard's pose. 'I'll show them!'

'No, wrong.'

'What do you mean, wrong? I've got the power!'

'They're sort of – reflections of us,' said Esk. 'You can't beat your reflections, they'll always be as strong as you are. That's why they draw nearer to you when you start using magic. And they don't get tired. They feed off magic, so you can't beat them with magic. No, the thing is . . . well, not not using magic because you can't, that's no use at all. But not using magic because you *can*, that really upsets them. They hate the idea. If people stopped using magic they'd die.'

The Things ahead of them fell over each other in their haste to back away.

Simon looked at the staff, then at Esk, then at the Things, then back at the staff.

'This needs a lot of thinking about,' he said uncertainly. 'I'd really like to work this out.'

'I expect you'll do it very well.'

'Because you're saying that the real power is when you go right through magic and out the other side.'

'It works, though, doesn't it?'

They were alone on the cold plain now. The Things were distant stick figures.

'I wonder if this is what they mean by sourcery?' said Simon.

'I don't know. It might be.'

'I'd really like to work this out,' said Simon again, turning the staff over and over in his hands. 'We could set up some experiments, you know, into deliberately not using magic. We could carefully not draw an octogram on the floor, and we could deliberately not call up all sorts of things, and – it makes me sweat just to think about it!'

'I'd like to think about how to get home,' said Esk, looking down at the pyramid.

'Well, that is supposed to be *my* idea of the world. I should be able to find a way. How do you do this thing with the hands?'

He moved his hands together. The staff slid between them, the light glowing through his fingers for a moment, and then vanished. He grinned. 'Right. Now all we have to do is look for the University . . . '

✩   ✩   ✩

Cutangle lit his third rollup from the stub of the second. This last cigarette owed a lot to the creative powers of nervous energy, and looked like a camel with the legs cut off.

He had already watched the staff lift itself gently from Esk and land on Simon.

Now it had floated up into the air again.

Other wizards had crowded into the room. The librarian was sitting under the table.

'If only we had some idea what is going on,' said Cutangle. 'It's the suspense I can't stand.'

'Think positively, man,' snapped Granny. 'And put out that bloody cigarette, I can't imagine anyone wanting to come back to a room that smells like a fireplace.'

As one man the assembled college of wizards turned their faces towards Cutangle, expectantly.

He took the smouldering mess out of his mouth and, with a glare that none of the assembled wizards cared to meet, trod it underfoot.

'Probably time I gave it up anyway,' he said. 'That goes for the rest of you, too. Worse than an ashpit in this place, sometimes.'

Then he saw the staff. It was–

The only way Cutangle could describe the effect was that it seemed to be going very fast while staying in exactly the same place.

Streamers of gas flared away from it and vanished, if they were gas. It blazed like a comet designed by an inept special-effects man. Coloured sparks leapt out and disappeared somewhere.

It was also changing colour, starting with a dull red and then climbing through the spectrum until it was a painful violet. Snakes of white fire coruscated along its length.

(There should be a word for words that sound like things would sound like if they made a noise, he thought. The word 'glisten' does indeed gleam oilily, and if there was ever a word that sounded exactly the way sparks look as they creep across burned paper, or the way the lights of cities would creep across the world if the whole of human civilisation was crammed into one night, then you couldn't do better than 'coruscate'.)

He knew what would happen next.

'Look out,' he whispered. 'It's going to go– '

In total silence, in the kind of silence in fact that sucks in sounds and stifles them, the staff flashed into pure octarine along the whole of its length.

The eighth colour, produced by light falling through a strong magical field, blazed out through bodies and bookshelves and walls. Other colours blurred and ran together, as though the light was a glass of gin poured over the watercolour painting of the world. The clouds over the University glowed, twisted into fascinating and unexpected shapes, and streamed upwards.

An observer above the Disc would have seen a little patch of land near the Circle Sea sparkle like a jewel for several seconds, then wink out.

The silence of the room was broken by a wooden clatter as the staff dropped out of the air and bounced on the table.

Someone said 'Ook', very faintly.

Cutangle eventually remembered how to use his hands and raised them to where he hoped his eyes would be. Everything had gone black.

'Is – anyone else there?' he said.

'Gods, you don't know how glad I am to hear you say that,' said another voice. The silence was suddenly full of babble.

'Are we still where we were?'

'I don't know. Where were we?'

'Here, I think.'

'Can you reach out?'

'Not unless I am quite certain about what I'm going to touch, my good man,' said the unmistakable voice of Granny Weatherwax.

'Everyone try and reach out,' said Cutangle, and choked down a scream as a hand like a warm leather glove closed around his ankle. There was a satisfied little 'ook', which managed to convey relief, comfort and the sheer joy of touching a fellow human being or, in this case, anthropoid.

There was a scratch and then a blessed flare of red light as a wizard on the far side of the room lit a cigarette.

'Who did that?'

'Sorry, Archchancellor, force of habit.'

'Smoke all you like, that man.'

'Thank you, Archchancellor.'

'I think I can see the outline of the door now,' said another voice.

'Granny?'

'Yes, I can definitely see– '

'*Esk?*'

'I'm here, Granny.'

'Can I smoke too, sir?'

'Is the boy with you?'

'Yes.'

'Ook.'

'I'm here.'

'What's happening?'

'*Everyone stop talking!*'

Ordinary light, slow and easy on the eye, sidled back into the Library.

Esk sat up, dislodging the staff. It rolled under the table. She felt something slip over her eyes, and reached up for it.

'Just a moment,' said Granny, darting forward. She gripped the girl's shoulders and peered into her eyes.

'Welcome back,' she said, and kissed her.

Esk reached up and patted something hard on her head. She lifted it down to examine it.

It was a pointed hat, slightly smaller than Granny's, but bright blue with a couple of silver stars painted on it.

'A wizard hat?' she said.

Cutangle stepped forward.

'Ah, yes,' he said, and cleared his throat: 'You see, we thought – it seemed – anyway, when we considered it– '

'You're a wizard,' said Granny, simply. 'The Archchancellor changed the lore. Quite a simple ceremony, really.'

'There's the staff somewhere about here,' said Cutangle. 'I saw it fall down – oh.'

He stood up with the staff in his hand, and showed it to Granny.

'I thought it had carvings on,' he said. 'This looks just like a stick.' And that was a fact. The staff looked as menacing and potent as a piece of kindling.

Esk turned the hat around in her hands, in the manner of one who, opening the proverbial brightly wrapped package, finds bath salts.

'It's very nice,' she said uncertainly.

'Is that all you can say?' said Granny.

'It's pointed, too.' Somehow being a wizard didn't feel any different from not being a wizard.

Simon leaned over.

'Remember,' he said, 'you've got to have *been* a wizard. Then you can start looking on the other side. Like you said.'

Their eyes met, and they grinned.

Granny stared at Cutangle. He shrugged.

'Search me,' he said. 'What's happened to your stutter, boy?'

'Seems to have gone, sir,' said Simon brightly. 'Must have left it behind, somewhere.'

The river was still brown and swollen but at least it resembled a river again.

It was unnaturally hot for late autumn, and across the whole of the lower part of Ankh-Morpork the steam rose from thousands of carpets and blankets put out to dry. The streets were filled with silt, which on the whole was an improvement – Ankh-Morpork's impressive civic collection of dead dogs had been washed out to sea.

The steam also rose from the flagstones of the Archchancellor's personal verandah, and from the teapot on the table.

Granny lay back in an ancient cane chair and let the unseasonal warmth creep around her ankles. She idly watched a team of city ants, who had lived under the flagstones of the University for so long that the high levels of background magic had permanently altered their genes, anthandling a damp sugar lump down from the bowl on to a tiny trolley. Another group was erecting a matchstick gantry at the edge of the table.

Granny may or may not have been interested to learn that one of the ants was Drum Billet, who had finally decided to give Life another chance.

'They say,' she said, 'that if you can find an ant on Hogswatch Day it will be very mild for the rest of the winter.'

'Who says that?' said Cutangle.

'Generally people who are wrong,' said Granny. 'I makes a note in my *Almanack*, see. I checks. Most things most people believe are wrong.'

'Like "red sky at night, the city's alight",' said Cutangle. 'And you can't teach an old dog new tricks.'

'I don't think that's what old dogs are for,' said Granny. The sugar lump had reached the gantry now, and a couple of ants were attaching it to a microscopic block and tackle.

'I can't understand half the things Simon says,' said Cutangle, 'although some of the students get very excited about it.'

'I understand what Esk says all right, I just don't believe it,' said Granny. 'Except the bit about wizards needing a heart.'

'She said that witches need a head, too,' said Cutangle. 'Would you like a scone? A bit damp, I'm afraid.'

'She told me that if magic gives people what they want, then not using magic can give them what they need,' said Granny, her hand hovering over the plate.

'So Simon tells me. I don't understand it myself, magic's for using, not storing up. Go on, spoil yourself.'

'Magic beyond magic,' snorted Granny. She took the scone and spread jam on it. After a pause she spread cream on it too.

The sugar lump crashed to the flagstones and was immediately surrounded by another team of ants, ready to harness it to a long line of red ants enslaved from the kitchen garden.

Cutangle shifted uneasily in his seat, which creaked.

'Esmerelda,' he began, 'I've been meaning to ask– '

'No,' said Granny.

'Actually I was going to say that we think we might allow a few more girls into the University. On an experimental basis. Once we get the plumbing sorted out,' said Cutangle.

'That's up to you, of course.'

'And, and, it seemed to me that since we seem destined to become a co-educational establishment, as it were, it seemed to me, that is– '

'Well?'

'If you might see your way clear to becoming, that is, whether you would accept a Chair.'

He sat back. The sugar lump passed under his chair on matchstick rollers, the squeaking of the slavedriver ants just at the edge of hearing.

'Hmm,' said Granny, 'I don't see why not. I've always wanted one of those big wicker ones, you know, with the sort of sunshade bit on the top. If that's not too much trouble.'

'That isn't exactly what I meant,' said Cutangle, adding quickly, 'although I'm sure that could be arranged. No, I mean, would you come and lecture the students? Once in a while?'

'What on?'

Cutangle groped for a subject.

'Herbs?' he hazarded. 'We're not very good on herbs here. And headology. Esk told me a lot about headology. It sounds fascinating.'

The sugar lump disappeared through a crack in a nearby wall with a final jerk. Cutangle nodded towards it.

'They're very heavy on the sugar,' he said, 'but we haven't got the heart to do anything about it.'

Granny frowned, and then nodded across the haze over the city to the distant glitter of the snow on the Ramtops.

'It's a long way,' she said. 'I can't be keeping on going backwards and forwards at my time of life.'

'We could buy you a much better broomstick,' said Cutangle. 'One you don't have to bump start. And you, you could have a flat here. And all the old clothes you can carry,' he added, using the secret weapon. He had wisely invested in some conversation with Mrs Whitlow.

'Mmph,' said Granny. 'Silk?'

'Black *and* red,' said Cutangle. An image of Granny in black and red silk trotted across his mind, and he bit heavily into his scone.

'And maybe we can bring some students out to your cottage in the summer,' Cutangle went on, 'for extra-mural studies.'

'Who's Extra Muriel?'

'I mean, there's lots they can learn, I'm sure.'

Granny considered this. Certainly the privy needed a good seeing-to before the weather got too warm, and the goat shed was ripe for the mucking-out by spring. Digging over the Herb bed was a chore, too. The bedroom ceiling was a disgrace, and some of the tiles needed fixing.

'Practical things?' she said, thoughtfully.

'Absolutely,' said Cutangle.

'Mmph. Well, I'll think about it,' said Granny, dimly aware that one should never go too far on a first date.

'Perhaps you would care to dine with me this evening and let me know?' said Cutangle, his eyes agleam.

'What's to eat?'

'Cold meat and potatoes.' Mrs Whitlow had done her work well.

There was.

Esk and Simon went on to develop a whole new type of magic that no one could exactly understand but which nevertheless everyone considered very worthwhile and somehow comforting.

Perhaps more importantly, the ants used all the sugar lumps they could steal to build a small sugar pyramid in one of the hollow walls, in which, with great ceremony, they entombed the mummified body of a dead queen. On the wall of one tiny hidden chamber they inscribed, in insect hieroglyphs, the true secret of longevity.

They got it absolutely right and it would probably have important implications for the universe if it hadn't, next time the University flooded, been completely washed away.

WYRD
SISTERS

(Starring Three Witches, also kings, daggers,
crowns, storms, dwarfs, cats, ghosts, spectres,
apes, bandits, demons, forests, heirs, jesters,
tortures, trolls, turntables,
general rejoicing and divers alarums.)

The wind howled. Lightning stabbed at the earth erratically, like an inefficient assassin. Thunder rolled back and forth aross the dark, rain-lashed hills.

The night was as black as the inside of a cat. It was the kind of night, you could believe, on which gods moved men as though they were pawns on the chessboard of fate. In the middle of this elemental storm a fire gleamed among the dripping furze bushes like the madness in a weasel's eye. It illuminated three hunched figures. As the cauldron bubbled an eldritch voice shrieked: 'When shall we three meet again?'

There was a pause.

Finally another voice said, in far more ordinary tones: 'Well, I can do next Tuesday.'

Through the fathomless deeps of space swims the star turtle Great A'Tuin, bearing on its back the four giant elephants who carry on their shoulders the mass of the Discworld. A tiny sun and moon spin around them, on a complicated orbit to induce seasons, so probably nowhere else in the multiverse is it sometimes necessary for an elephant to cock a leg to allow the sun to go past.

Exactly why this should be may never be known. Possibly the Creator of the universe got bored with all the usual business of axial inclination, albedos and rotational velocities, and decided to have a bit of fun for once.

It would be a pretty good bet that the gods of a world like this probably do not play chess and indeed this is the case. In fact no gods anywhere play chess. They haven't got the imagination. Gods prefer simple, vicious games, where you Do Not Achieve Transcendence but Go Straight To Oblivion; a key to the understanding of all religion is that a god's idea of amusement is Snakes and Ladders with greased rungs.

Magic glues the Discworld together – magic generated by the turning of the world itself, magic wound like silk out of the underlying structure of existence to suture the wounds of reality.

A lot of it ends up in the Ramtop Mountains, which stretch from the frozen lands near the Hub all the way, via a lengthy archipelago, to the warm seas which flow endlessly into space over the Rim.

Raw magic crackles invisibly from peak to peak and earths itself in the mountains. It is the Ramtops that supply the world with most of its witches and wizards. In the Ramtops the leaves on the trees move even when there is no breeze. Rocks go for a stroll of an evening.

Even the land, at times, seems alive . . .

At times, so does the sky.

The storm was really giving it everything it had. This was its big chance. It had spent years hanging around the provinces, putting in some useful work as a squall, building up experience, making contacts, occasionally leaping out on unsuspecting shepherds or blasting quite small oak trees. Now an opening in the weather had given it an opportunity to strut its hour, and it was building up its role in the hope of being spotted by one of the big climates.

It was a *good* storm. There was quite effective projection and passion there, and critics agreed that if it would only learn to control its thunder it would be, in years to come, a storm to watch.

The woods roared their applause and were full of mists and flying leaves.

On nights such as these the gods, as has already been pointed out, play games other than chess with the fates of mortals and the thrones of kings. It is important to remember that they always cheat, right up to the end . . .

And a coach came hurtling along the rough forest track, jerking violently as the wheels bounced off tree roots. The driver lashed at the team, the desperate crack of his whip providing a rather neat counterpoint to the crash of the tempest overhead.

Behind – only a little way behind, and getting closer – were three hooded riders.

On nights such as this, evil deeds are done. And good deeds, of course. But mostly evil, on the whole.

On nights such as this, witches are abroad.

Well, not actually *abroad*. They don't like the food and you can't trust the water and the shamans always hog the deckchairs. But there was a full moon breasting the ragged clouds and the rushing air was full of whispers and the very broad hint of magic.

In their clearing above the forest the witches spoke thus:

'I'm babysitting on Tuesday,' said the one with no hat but a thatch of white curls so thick she might have been wearing a helmet. 'For our Jason's youngest. I can manage Friday. Hurry up with the tea, luv. I'm that parched.'

The junior member of the trio gave a sigh, and ladled some boiling water out of the cauldron into the teapot.

The third witch patted her hand in a kindly fashion.

'You said it quite well,' she said. 'Just a bit more work on the screeching. Ain't that right, Nanny Ogg?'

'Very useful screeching, I thought,' said Nanny Ogg hurriedly. 'And I can see Goodie Whemper, maysherestinpeace, gave you a lot of help with the squint.'

'It's a good squint,' said Granny Weatherwax.

The junior witch, whose name was Magrat Garlick, relaxed considerably, She held Granny Weatherwax in awe. It was known throughout the Ramtop Mountains that Mss Weatherwax did not approve of anything very much. If she said it was a good squint, then Magrat's eyes were probably staring up her own nostrils.

Unlike wizards, who like nothing better than a complicated hierarchy, witches don't go in much for the structured approach to career progression. It's up to each individual witch to take on a girl to hand the area over to when she dies. Witches are not by nature gregarious, at least with other witches, and they certainly don't have leaders.

Granny Weatherwax was the most highly regarded of the leaders they didn't have.

Magrat's hands shook slightly as they made the tea. Of course, it was all very gratifying, but it was a bit nerve-racking to start one's working life as village witch between Granny and, on the other side of the forest, Nanny Ogg. It'd been her idea to form a local coven. She felt it was more, well, occult. To her amazement the other two had agreed or, at least, hadn't disagreed much.

'An oven?' Nanny Ogg had said. 'What'd we want to join an oven for?'

'She means a coven, Gytha,' Granny Weatherwax had explained. 'You know, like in the old days. A meeting.'

'A knees up?' said Nanny Ogg hopefully.

'No dancing,' Granny had warned. 'I don't hold with dancing. Or singing or getting over-excited or all that messing about with ointments and similar.'

'Does you good to get out,' said Nanny happily.

Magrat had been disappointed about the dancing, and was relieved that she hadn't ventured one or two other ideas that had been on her mind. She

fumbled in the packet she had brought with her. It was her first sabbat, and
she was determined to do it right.

'Would anyone care for a scone?' she said.

Granny looked hard at hers before she bit. Magrat had baked bat designs
on it. They had little eyes made of currants.

The coach crashed through the trees at the forest edge, ran on two wheels for
a few seconds as it hit a stone, righted itself against all the laws of balance,
and rumbled on. But it was going slower now. The slope was dragging at it.

The coachman, standing upright in the manner of a charioteer, pushed his
hair out of his eyes and peered through the murk. No one lived up here, in
the lap of the Ramtops themselves, but there was a light ahead. By all that
was merciful, there was a light there.

An arrow buried itself in the coach roof behind him.

Meanwhile, King Verence, monarch of Lancre, was making a discovery.

Like most people – most people, at any rate, below the age of sixty or so –
Verence hadn't exercised his mind much about what happened to you when
you died. Like most people since the dawn of time, he assumed it all
somehow worked out all right in the end.

And, like most people since the dawn of time, he was now dead.

He was in fact lying at the bottom of one of his own stairways in Lancre
Castle, with a dagger in his back.

He sat up, and was surprised to find that while someone he was certainly
inclined to think of as himself was sitting up, something very much like his
body remained lying on the floor.

It was a pretty good body, incidentally, now he came to see it from
outside for the first time. He had always been quite attached to it although,
he had to admit, this did not now seem to be the case.

It was big and well-muscled. He'd looked after it. He'd allowed it a
moustache and long-flowing locks. He'd seen it got plenty of healthy
outdoor exercise and lots of red meat. Now, just when a body would have
been useful, it had let him down. Or out.

On top of that, he had to come to terms with the tall, thin figure standing
beside him. Most of it was hidden in a hooded black robe, but the one arm
which extended from the folds to grip a large scythe was made of bone.

When one is dead, there are things one instinctively recognises.

HALLO.

Verence drew himself up to his full height, or what would have been his full height if that part of him to which the word 'height' could have been applied was not lying stiff on the floor and facing a future in which only the word 'depth' could be appropriate.

'I *am* a king, mark you,' he said.

Was, your Majesty.

'What?' Verence barked.

I said was. It's called the past tense. You'll soon get used to it.

The tall figure tapped its calcareous fingers on the scythe's handle. It was obviously upset about something.

If it came to that, Verence thought, so am I. But the various broad hints available in his present circumstances were breaking through even the mad brave stupidity that made up most of his character, and it was dawning on him that whatever kingdom he might currently be in, he wasn't king of it.

'Are you Death, fellow?' he ventured.

I have many names.

'Which one are you using at present?' said Verence, with a shade more deference. There were people milling around them; in fact, quite a few people were milling *through* them, like ghosts.

'Oh, so it was Felmet,' the king added vaguely, looking at the figure lurking with obscene delight at the top of the stairs. 'My father said I should never let him get behind me. Why don't I feel angry?'

Glands, said Death shortly. Adrenalin and so forth. And emotions. You don't have them. All you have now is thought.

The tall figure appeared to reach a decision.

This is very irregular, he went on, apparently to himself. However, who am I to argue?

'Who indeed.'

What?

'I said, who indeed.'

Shut up.

Death stood with his skull on one side, as though listening to some inner voice. As his hood fell away the late king noticed that Death resembled a polished skeleton in every way but one. His eye sockets glowed sky blue. Verence wasn't frightened, however; not simply because it is difficult to be in fear of anything when the bits you need to be frightened *with* are curdling several yards away, but because he had never really been frightened of anything in his life, and wasn't going to start now. This was partly because he didn't have the imagination, but he was also one of those rare individuals who are totally focused in time.

Most people aren't. They live their lives as a sort of temporal blur around the point where their body actually is – anticipating the future, or holding on to the past. They're usually so busy thinking about what happens next that the only time they ever find out what is happening now is when they come to look back on it. Most people are like this. They learn how to fear because they can actually tell, down at the subconscious level, what is going to happen next. It's already happening to them.

But Verence had always lived only for the present. Until now, anyway.

Death sighed.

I SUPPOSE NO ONE MENTIONED ANYTHING TO YOU? he hazarded.

'Say again?'

NO PREMONITIONS? STRANGE DREAMS? MAD OLD SOOTHSAYERS SHOUTING THINGS AT YOU IN THE STREET?

'About what? Dying?'

NO, I SUPPOSE NOT. IT WOULD BE TOO MUCH TO EXPECT, said Death sourly. THEY LEAVE IT ALL TO ME.

'Who do?' said Verence, mystified.

FATE. DESTINY. ALL THE REST OF THEM. Death laid a hand on the king's shoulder. THE FACT IS, I'M AFRAID, YOU'RE DUE TO BECOME A GHOST.

'Oh.' He looked down at his . . . body, which seemed solid enough. Then someone walked through him.

DON'T LET IT UPSET YOU.

Verence watched his own stiff corpse being carried reverentially from the hall.

'I'll try,' he said.

GOOD MAN.

'I don't think I will be up to all that business with the white sheets and chains, though,' he said. 'Do I have to walk around moaning and screaming?'

Death shrugged. DO YOU WANT TO? he said.

'No.'

THEN I SHOULDN'T BOTHER, IF I WERE YOU. Death pulled an hour-glass from the recesses of his dark robe and inspected it closely.

AND NOW I REALLY MUST BE GOING, he said. He turned on his heel, put his scythe over his shoulder and started to walk out of the hall through the wall.

'I say? Just hold on there!' shouted Verence, running after him.

Death didn't look back. Verence followed him through the wall; it was like walking through fog.

'Is that all?' he demanded. 'I mean, how long will I be a ghost? *Why* am I a ghost? You can't just leave me like this.' He halted and raised an imperious, slightly transparent finger. 'Stop! I command you!'

Death shook his head gloomily, and stepped through the next wall. The king hurried after him with as much dignity as he could still muster, and found Death fiddling with the girths of a large white horse standing on the battlements. It was wearing a nosebag.

'You can't leave me like this!' he repeated, in the face of the evidence.

Death turned to him.

I CAN, he said. YOU'RE UNDEAD, YOU SEE. GHOSTS INHABIT A WORLD BETWEEN THE LIVING AND THE DEAD. IT'S NOT MY RESPONSIBILITY. He patted the king on the shoulder. DON'T WORRY, he said, IT WON'T BE FOR EVER.

'Good.'

IT MAY *SEEM* LIKE FOR EVER.

'How long will it really be?'

UNTIL YOU HAVE FULFILLED YOUR DESTINY, I ASSUME.

'And how will I know what my destiny is?' said the king, desperately.

CAN'T HELP THERE. I'M SORRY.

'Well, how can I find out?'

THESE THINGS GENERALLY BECOME APPARENT, I UNDERSTAND, said Death, and swung himself into the saddle.

'And until then I have to haunt this place.' King Verence stared around at the draughty battlements. 'All alone, I suppose. Won't anyone be able to see me?'

OH, THE PSYCHICALLY INCLINED. CLOSE RELATIVES. AND CATS, OF COURSE.

'I hate cats.'

Death's face became a little stiffer, if that were possible. The blue glow in his eye sockets flickered red for an instant.

I SEE, he said. The tone suggested that death was too good for cat haters. YOU LIKE GREAT BIG DOGS, I IMAGINE.

'As a matter of fact, I do.' The king stared gloomily at the dawn. His dogs. He'd really miss his dogs. And it looked like such a good hunting day.

He wondered if ghosts hunted. Almost certainly not, he imagined. Or ate, or drank either for that matter, and that was really depressing. He liked a big noisy banquet and had quaffed* many a pint of good ale. And bad ale, come to that. He'd never been able to tell the difference till the following morning, usually.

He kicked despondently at a stone, and noted gloomily that his foot went right through it. No hunting, drinking, carousing, no wassailing, no hawking . . . It was dawning on him that the pleasures of the flesh were pretty sparse without the flesh. Suddenly life wasn't worth living. The fact that he wasn't living it didn't cheer him up at all.

---

* Quaffing is like drinking, but you spill more.

SOME PEOPLE *LIKE* TO BE GHOSTS, said Death.

'Hmm?' said Verence, gloomily.

IT'S NOT SUCH A WRENCH, I ASSUME. THEY CAN SEE HOW THEIR DESCEND-
ANTS GET ON. SORRY? IS SOMETHING THE MATTER?

But Verence had vanished into the wall.

DON'T MIND ME, WILL YOU, said Death peevishly. He looked around him
with a gaze that could see through time and space and the souls of men, and
noted a landslide in distant Klatch, a hurricane in Howondaland, a plague in
Hergen.

BUSY, BUSY, he muttered, and spurred his horse into the sky.

Verence ran through the walls of his own castle. His feet barely touched
the ground – in fact, the unevenness of the floor meant that at times they
didn't touch the ground at all.

As a king he was used to treating servants as if they were not there, and
running through them as a ghost was almost the same. The only difference
was that they didn't stand aside.

Verence reached the nursery, saw the broken door, the trailed sheets . . .

Heard the hoofbeats. He reached the window, saw his own horse go full
tilt through the open gateway in the shafts of the coach. A few seconds later
three horsemen followed it. The sound of hooves echoed for a moment on
the cobbles and died away.

The king thumped the sill, his fist going several inches into the stone.

Then he pushed his way out into the air, disdaining to notice the drop, and
half flew, half ran down across the courtyard and into the stables.

It took him a mere twenty seconds to learn that, to the great many things a
ghost cannot do, should be added the mounting of a horse. He did succeed
in getting into the saddle, or at least in straddling the air just above it, but
when the horse finally bolted, terrified beyond belief by the mysterious
things happening behind its ears, Verence was left sitting astride five feet of
fresh air.

He tried to run, and got about as far as the gateway before the air around
him thickened to the consistency of tar.

'You can't,' said a sad, old voice behind him. 'You have to stay where you
were killed. That's what haunting means. Take it from me. I know.'

Granny Weatherwax paused with a second scone halfway to her mouth.

'Something comes,' she said.

'Can you tell by the pricking of your thumbs?' said Magrat earnestly.
Magrat had learned a lot about witchcraft from books.

'The pricking of my ears,' said Granny. She raised her eyebrows at Nanny

Ogg. Old Goodie Whemper had been an excellent witch in her way, but far too *fanciful*. Too many flowers and romantic notions and such.

The occasional flash of lightning showed the moorland stretching down to the forest, but the rain on the warm summer earth had filled the air with mist wraiths.

'Hoofbeats?' said Nanny Ogg. 'No one would come up here this time of night.'

Magrat peered around timidly. Here and there on the moor were huge standing stones, their origins lost in time, which were said to lead mobile and private lives of their own. She shivered.

'What's to be afraid of?' she managed.

'Us,' said Granny Weatherwax, smugly.

The hoofbeats neared, slowed. And then the coach rattled between the furze bushes, its horses hanging in their harnesses. The driver leapt down, ran around to the door, pulled a large bundle from inside and dashed towards the trio.

He was halfway aross the damp peat when he stopped and stared at Granny Weatherwax with a look of horror.

'It's all right,' she whispered, and the whisper cut through the grumbling of the storm as clearly as a bell.

She took a few steps forward and a convenient lightning flash allowed her to look directly into the man's eyes. They had the peculiarity of focus that told those who had the Know that he was no longer looking at anything in this world.

With a final jerking movement he thrust the bundle into Granny's arms and toppled forward, the feathers of a crossbow bolt sticking out of his back.

Three figures moved into the firelight. Granny looked up into another pair of eyes, which were as chilly as the slopes of Hell.

Their owner threw his crossbow aside. There was a glimpse of chain mail under his sodden cloak as he drew his sword.

He didn't flourish it. The eyes that didn't leave Granny's face weren't the eyes of one who bothers about flourishing things. They were the eyes of one who knows exactly what swords are for. He reached out his hand.

'You will give it to me,' he said.

Granny twitched aside the blanket in her arms and looked down at a small face, wrapped in sleep.

She looked up.

'No,' she said, on general principles.

The soldier glanced from her to Magrat and Nanny Ogg, who were as still as the standing stones of the moor.

'You are witches?' he said.

Granny nodded. Lightning skewered down from the sky and a bush a hundred yards away blossomed into fire. The two soldiers behind the man muttered something, but he smiled and raised a mailed hand.

'Does the skin of witches turn aside steel?' he said.

'Not that I'm aware,' said Granny, levelly. 'You could give it a try.'

One of the soldiers stepped forward and touched the man's arm gingerly.

'Sir, with respect, sir, it's not a good idea – '

'Be silent.'

'But it's terrible bad luck to – '

'Must I ask you again?'

'Sir,' said the man. His eyes caught Granny's for a moment, and reflected hopeless terror.

The leader grinned at Granny, who hadn't moved a muscle.

'Your peasant magic is for fools, mother of the night. I can strike you down where you stand.'

'Then strike, man,' said Granny, looking over his shoulder. 'If your heart tells you, strike as hard as you dare.'

The man raised his sword. Lightning speared down again and split a stone a few yards away, filling the air with smoke and the stink of burnt silicon.

'Missed,' he said smugly, and Granny saw his muscles tense as he prepared to bring the sword down.

A look of extreme puzzlement crossed his face. He tilted his head sideways and opened his mouth, as if trying to come to terms with a new idea. His sword dropped out of his hand and landed point downwards in the peat. Then he gave a sigh and folded up, very gently, collapsing in a heap at Granny's feet.

She gave him a gentle prod with her toe. 'Perhaps you weren't aware of what I was aiming at,' she whispered. 'Mother of the night, indeed!'

The soldier who had tried to restrain the man stared in horror at the bloody dagger in his hand, and backed away.

'I-I-I couldn't let. He shouldn't of. It's – it's not right to,' he stuttered.

'Are you from around these parts, young man?' said Granny.

He dropped to his knees. 'Mad Wolf, ma'am,' he said. He stared back at the fallen captain. 'They'll kill me now!' he wailed.

'But you did what you thought was right,' said Granny.

'I didn't become a soldier for this. Not to go round killing people.'

'Exactly right. If I was you, I'd become a sailor,' said Granny thoughtfully. 'Yes, a nautical career. I should start as soon as possible. Now, in fact. Run off, man. Run off to sea where there are no tracks. You will have a long and successful life, I promise.' She looked thoughtful for a moment, and added, 'At least, longer than it's likely to be if you hang around here.'

He pulled himself upward, gave her a look compounded of gratitude and awe, and ran off into the mist.

'And now perhaps someone will tell us what this is all about?' said Granny, turning to the third man.

To where the third man had been.

There was the distant drumming of hooves on the turf, and then silence.

Nanny Ogg hobbled forward.

'I could catch him,' she said. 'What do you think?'

Granny shook her head. She sat down on a rock and looked at the child in her arms. It was a boy, no more than two years old, and quite naked under the blanket. She rocked him vaguely and stared at nothing.

Nanny Ogg examined the two corpses with the air of one for whom laying-out holds no fears.

'Perhaps they were bandits,' said Magrat tremulously.

Nanny shook her head.

'A strange thing,' she said. 'They both wear this same badge. Two bears on a black and gold shield. Anyone know what that means?'

'It's the badge of King Verence,' said Magrat.

'Who's he?' said Granny Weatherwax.

'He rules this country,' said Magrat.

'Oh. That king,' said Granny, as if the matter was hardly worth noting.

'Soldiers fighting one another. Doesn't make sense,' said Nanny Ogg. 'Magrat, you have a look in the coach.'

The youngest witch poked around inside the bodywork and came back with a sack. She upended it, and something thudded on to the turf.

The storm had rumbled off to the other side of the mountain now, and the watery moon shed a thin gruel of light over the damp moorland. It also gleamed off what was, without any doubt, an extremely important crown.

'It's a crown,' said Magrat. 'It's got all spiky bits on it.'

'Oh, dear,' said Granny.

The child gurgled in its sleep. Granny Weatherwax didn't hold with looking at the future, but now she could feel the future looking at her.

She didn't like its expression at all.

King Verence was looking at the past, and had formed pretty much the same view.

'You can see me?' he said.

'Oh, yes. Quite clearly, in fact,' said the newcomer.

Verence's brows knotted. Being a ghost seemed to require considerably more mental effort than being alive; he'd managed quite well for forty years without having to think more than once or twice a day, and now he was doing it all the time.

'Ah,' he said. 'You're a ghost, too.'

'Well spotted.'

'It was the head under your arm,' said Verence, pleased with himself. 'That gave me a clue.'

'Does it bother you? I can put it back on if it bothers you,' said the old ghost helpfully. He extended his free hand. 'Pleased to meet you. I'm Champot, King of Lancre.'

'Verence. Likewise.' He peered down at the old king's features, and added, 'Don't seem to recall seeing your picture in the Long Gallery . . .'

'Oh, all that was after my time,' said Champot dismissively.

'How long have you been here, then?'

Champot reached down and rubbed his nose. 'About a thousand years,' he said, his voice tinged with pride. 'Man and ghost.'

'A thousand years!'

'I built this place, in fact. Just got it nicely decorated when my nephew cut my head off while I was asleep. I can't tell you how much that upset me.'

'But . . . a thousand years . . .' Verence repeated, weakly.

Champot took his arm. 'It's not that bad,' he confided, as he led the unresisting king across the courtyard. 'Better than being alive, in many ways.'

'They must be bloody strange ways, then!' snapped Verence. 'I *liked* being alive!'

Champot grinned reassuringly. 'You'll soon get used to it,' he said.

'I don't want to get used to it!'

'You've got a strong morphogenic field,' said Champot. 'I can tell. I look for these things. Yes. Very strong, I should say.'

'What's that?'

'I was never very good with words, you know,' said Champot. 'I always found it easier to hit people with something. But I gather it all boils down to how alive you were. When you were alive, I mean. Something called – ' he paused – 'animal vitality. Yes, that was it. Animal vitality. The more you had, the more you stay yourself, as it were, if you're a ghost. I expect you were one hundred per cent alive, when you were alive,' he added.

Despite himself, Verence felt flattered. 'I tried to keep myself busy,' he said. They had strolled through the wall into the Great Hall, which was now empty. The sight of the trestle tables triggered an automatic reaction in the king.

'How do we go about getting breakfast?' he said.

Champot's head looked surprised.

'We don't,' he said. 'We're ghosts.'

'But I'm hungry!'

'You're not, you know. It's just your imagination.'

There was a clattering from the kitchens. The cooks were already up and, in the absence of any other instructions, were preparing the castle's normal breakfast menu. Familiar smells were wafting up from the dark archway that led to the kitchens.

Verence sniffed.

'Sausages,' he said dreamily. 'Bacon. Eggs. Smoked fish.' He stared at Champot. 'Black pudding,' he whispered.

'You haven't actually got a stomach,' the old ghost pointed out. 'It's all in the mind. Just force of habit. You just *think* you're hungry.'

'I *think* I'm ravenous.'

'Yes, but you can't actually touch anything, you see,' Champot explained gently. 'Nothing at all.'

Verence lowered himself gently on to a bench, so that he did not drift through it, and sank his head in his hands. He'd heard that death could be bad. He just hadn't realised how bad.

He wanted revenge. He wanted to get out of this suddenly horrible castle, to find his son. But he was even more terrified to find that what he really wanted, right now, was a plate of kidneys.

A damp dawn flooded across the landscape, scaled the battlements of Lancre Castle, stormed the keep and finally made it through the casement of the solar.

Duke Felmet stared gloomily at the dripping forest. There was such a lot of it. It wasn't, he decided, that he had anything against trees as such, it was just that the sight of so much of them was terribly depressing. He kept wanting to count them.

'Indeed, my love,' he said.

The duke put those who met him in mind of some sort of lizard, possibly the type that lives on volcanic islands, moves once a day, has a vestigial third eye and blinks on a monthly basis. He considered himself to be a civilised man more suited to the dry air and bright sun of a properly organised climate.

On the other hand, he mused, it might be nice to be a tree. Trees didn't have ears, he was pretty sure of this. And they seemed to manage without the blessed state of matrimony. A male oak tree – he'd have to look this up – a male oak tree just shed its pollen on the breeze and all the business with the acorns, unless it was oak apples, no, he was pretty sure it was acorns, took place somewhere else . . .

'Yes, my precious,' he said.

Yes, trees had got it all worked out. Duke Felmet glared at the forest roof. Selfish bastards.

'Certainly, my dear,' he said.

'What?' said the duchess.

The duke hesitated, desperately trying to replay the monologue of the last five minutes. There had been something about him being half a man, and . . . infirm on purpose? And he was sure there had been a complaint about the coldness of the castle. Yes, that was probably it. Well, those wretched trees could do a decent day's work for once.

'I'll have some cut down and brought in directly, my cherished,' he said.

Lady Felmet was momentarily speechless. This was by way of being a calendar event. She was a large and impressive woman, who gave people confronting her for the first time the impression that they were seeing a galleon under full sail; the effect was heightened by her unfortunate belief that red velvet rather suited her. However, it didn't set off her complexion. It matched it.

The duke often mused on his good luck in marrying her. If it wasn't for the engine of her ambition he'd be just another local lord, with nothing much to do but hunt, drink and exercise his droit de seigneur.* Instead, he was now just a step away from the throne, and might soon be monarch of all he surveyed.

Provided that all he surveyed was trees.

He sighed.

'Cut *what* down?' said Lady Felmet, icily.

'Oh, the trees,' said the duke.

'What have trees got to do with it?'

'Well . . . there are such a *lot* of them,' said the duke, with feeling.

'Don't change the subject!'

'Sorry, my sweet.'

'What I *said* was, how could you have been so stupid as to let them get away? I told you that servant was far too loyal. You can't trust someone like that.'

'No, my love.'

'You didn't by any chance consider sending someone after them, I suppose?'

'Bentzen, my dear. And a couple of guards.'

'Oh.' The duchess paused. Bentzen, as captain of the duke's personal

---

* Whatever that was. He'd never found anyone prepared to explain it to him. But it was definitely something a feudal lord ought to have and, he was pretty sure, it needed regular exercise. He imagined it was some kind of large hairy dog. He was definitely going to get one, and damn well exercise it.

bodyguard, was as efficient a killer as a psychotic mongoose. He would have been her choice. It annoyed her to be temporarily deprived of a chance to fault her husband, but she rallied quite well.

'He wouldn't have needed to go out at all, if only you'd listened to me. But you never do.'

'Do what, my passion?'

The duke yawned. It had been a long night. There had been a thunderstorm of quite unnecessarily dramatic proportions, and then there had been all that messy business with the knives.

It has already been mentioned that Duke Felmet was one step away from the throne. The step in question was at the top of the flight leading to the Great Hall, down which King Verence had tumbled in the dark only to land, against all the laws of probability, on his own dagger.

It had, however, been declared by his own physician to be a case of natural causes. Bentzen had gone to see the man and explained that falling down a flight of steps with a dagger in your back was a disease caused by unwise opening of the mouth.

In fact it had already been caught by several members of the king's own bodyguard who had been a little bit hard of hearing. There had been a minor epidemic.

The duke shuddered. There were details about last night that were both hazy and horrible.

He tried to reassure himself that all the unpleasantness was over now, and he had a kingdom. It wasn't much of one, apparently being mainly trees, but it was a kingdom and it had a crown.

If only they could find it.

Lancre Castle was built on an outcrop of rock by an architect who had heard about Gormenghast but hadn't got the budget. He'd done his best, though, with a tiny confection of cut-price turrets, bargain basements, buttresses, crenellations, gargoyles, towers, courtyards, keeps and dungeons; in fact, just about everything a castle needs except maybe reasonable foundations and the kind of mortar that doesn't wash away in a light shower.

The castle leaned vertiginously over the racing white water of the Lancre river, which boomed darkly a thousand feet below. Every now and again a few bits fell in.

Small as it was, though, the castle contained a thousand places to hide a crown.

The duchess swept out to find someone else to berate, and left Lord Felmet looking gloomily at the landscape. It started to rain.

It was on this cue that there came a thunderous knocking at the castle

door. It seriously disturbed the castle porter, who was playing Cripple
Mister Onion with the castle cook and the castle's Fool in the warmth of the
kitchen.

He growled and stood up. 'There is a knocking without,' he said.

'Without what?' said the Fool.

'Without the door, idiot.'

The Fool gave him a worried look. 'A knocking without a door?' he said
suspiciously. 'This isn't some kind of Zen, is it?'

When the porter had grumbled off in the direction of the gatehouse the
cook pushed another farthing into the kitty and looked sharply over his
cards at the Fool.

'What's a Zen?' he said.

The Fool's bells tinkled as he sorted through his cards. Without thinking,
he said: 'Oh, a sub-sect of the Turnwise Klatch philosophical system of
Sumtin, noted for its simple austerity and the offer of personal tranquillity
and wholeness achieved through meditation and breathing techniques; an
interesting aspect is the asking of apparently nonsensical questions in order
to widen the doors of perception.'

'How's that again?' said the cook suspiciously. He was on edge. When he'd
taken the breakfast up to the Great Hall he'd kept getting the feeling that
something was trying to take the tray out of his hands. And as if that wasn't
bad enough, this new duke had sent him back for . . . He shuddered. Oatmeal!
And a runny boiled egg! The cook was too old for this sort of thing. He was
set in his ways. He was a cook in the real feudal tradition. If it didn't have an
apple in its mouth and you couldn't roast it, he didn't want to serve it.

The Fool hesitated with a card in his hand, suppressed his panic and
thought quickly.

'I'faith, nuncle,' he squeaked. 'thou't more full of questions than a
martlebury is of mizzensails.'

The cook relaxed.

'Well, okay,' he said, not entirely satisfied. The Fool lost the next three
hands, just to be on the safe side.

The porter, meanwhile, unfastened the hatch in the wicket gate and peered
out.

'Who dost knock without?' he growled.

The soldier, drenched and terrified though he was, hesitated.

'Without? Without what?' he said.

'If you're going to bugger about, you can bloody well stay without all
day,' said the porter calmly.

'No! I must see the duke upon the instant!' shouted the guard. 'Witches
are abroad!'

The porter was about to come back with, 'Good time of year for it', or 'Wish I was, too', but stopped when he saw the man's face. It wasn't the face of a man who would enter into the spirit of the thing. It was the look of someone who had seen things a decent man shouldn't wot of . . .

'Witches?' said Lord Felmet.

'Witches!' said the duchess.

In the draughty corridors, a voice as faint as the wind in distant keyholes said, with a note of hope, 'Witches!'

The psychically inclined . . .

'It's meddling, that's what it is,' said Granny Weatherwax. 'And no good will come of it.'

'It's very *romantic*,' said Magrat breathily, and heaved a sigh.

'Goochy goo,' said Nanny Ogg.

'Anyway,' said Magrat. 'You killed that horrid man!'

'I never did. I just encouraged . . . things to take their course.' Granny Weatherwax frowned. 'He didn't have no respect. Once people lose their respect, it means trouble.'

'Izzy wizzy wazzy, den.'

'That other man brought him out here to save him!' shouted Magrat. 'He wanted us to keep him safe! It's obvious! It's destiny!'

'Oh, *obvious*,' said Granny. 'I'll grant you it's *obvious*. Trouble is, just because things are obvious doesn't mean they're true.'

She weighed the crown in her hands. It felt very heavy, in a way that went beyond mere pounds and ounces.

'Yes, but the point is – ' Magrat began.

'The point is,' said Granny, 'that people are going to come looking. Serious people. Serious looking. Pull-down-the-walls and burn-off-the-thatch looking. And – '

'Howsa boy, den?'

' – *And*, Gytha, I'm sure we'll all be a *lot* happier if you'd stop gurgling like that!' Granny snapped. She could feel her nerves coming on. Her nerves always played up when she was unsure about things. Besides, they had retired to Magrat's cottage, and the decor was getting to her, because Magrat believed in Nature's wisdom and elves and the healing power of colours and the cycle of the seasons and a lot of other things Granny Weatherwax didn't have any truck with.

'You're not after telling me how to look after a child,' snapped Nanny Ogg mildly. 'And me with fifteen of my own?'

'I'm just saying that we ought to think about it,' said Granny.

The other two watched her for some time.

'Well?' said Magrat.

Granny's fingers drummed on the edge of the crown. She frowned.

'First, we've got to take him away from here,' she said, and held up a hand. 'No, Gytha, I'm sure your cottage is ideal and everything, but it's not safe. He's got to be somewhere away from here, a long way away, where no one knows who he is. And then there's this.' She tossed the crown from hand to hand.

'Oh, that's easy,' said Magrat. 'I mean, you just hide it under a stone or something. That's easy. Much easier than babies.'

'It ain't,' said Granny. 'The reason being, the country's full of babies and they all look the same, but I don't reckon there's many crowns. They have this way of being found, anyway. They kind of call out to people's minds. If you bunged it under a stone up here, in a week's time it'd get itself discovered by accident. You mark my words.'

'It's true, is that,' said Nanny Ogg, earnestly. 'How many times have you thrown a magic ring into the deepest depths of the ocean and then, when you get home and have a nice bit of turbot for your tea, there it is?'

They considered this in silence.

'Never,' said Granny irritably. 'And nor have you. Anyway, he might want it back. If it's rightfully his, that is. Kings set a lot of store by crowns. Really, Gytha, sometimes you say the most – '

'I'll just make some tea, shall I?' said Magrat brightly, and disappeared into the scullery.

The two elderly witches sat on either side of the table in polite and prickly silence. Finally Nanny Ogg said, 'She done it up nice, hasn't she? Flowers and everything. What are them things on the walls?'

'Sigils,' said Granny sourly. 'Or some such.'

'Fancy,' said Nanny Ogg, politely. 'And all them robes and wands and things, too.'

'*Modern*,' said Granny Weatherwax, with a sniff. 'When I was a gel, we had a lump of wax and a couple of pins and had to be content. We had to make our *own* enchantment in them days.'

'Ah, well, we've all passed a lot of water since then,' said Nanny Ogg sagely. She gave the baby a comforting jiggle.

Granny Weatherwax sniffed. Nanny Ogg had been married three times and ruled a tribe of children and grandchildren all over the kingdom. Certainly, it was not actually *forbidden* for witches to get married. Granny had to concede that, but reluctantly. Very reluctantly. She sniffed again, disapprovingly; this was a mistake.

'What's that smell?' she snapped.

'Ah,' said Nanny Ogg, carefully repositioning the baby. 'I expect I'll just go and see if Magrat has any clean rags, shall I?'

And now Granny was left alone. She felt embarrassed, as one always does when left alone in someone else's room, and fought the urge to get up and inspect the books on the shelf over the sideboard or examine the mantelpiece for dust. She turned the crown round and round in her hands. Again, it gave the impression of being bigger and heavier than it actually was.

She caught sight of the mirror over the mantelpiece and looked down at the crown. It was tempting. It was practically begging her to try it for size. Well, and why not? She made sure that the others weren't around and then, in one movement, whipped off her hat and placed the crown on her head.

It seemed to fit. Granny drew herself up proudly, and waved a hand imperiously in the general direction of the hearth.

'Jolly well do this,' she said. She beckoned arrogantly at the grandfather clock. 'Chop his head off, what ho,' she commanded. She smiled grimly.

And froze as she heard the screams, and the thunder of horses, and the deadly whisper of arrows and the damp, solid sound of spears in flesh. Charge after charge echoed across her skull. Sword met shield, or sword, or bone – relentlessly. Years streamed across her mind in the space of a second. There were times when she lay among the dead, or hanging from the branch of a tree; but always there were hands that would pick her up again, and place her on a velvet cushion.

Granny very carefully lifted the crown off her head – it was an effort, it didn't like it much – and laid it on the table.

'So that's being a king for you, is it?' she said softly. 'I wonder why they all want the job?'

'Do you take sugar?' said Magrat, behind her.

'You'd have to be a born fool to be a king,' said Granny.

'Sorry?'

Granny turned. 'Didn't see you come in,' she said. 'What was it you said?'

'Sugar in your tea?'

'Three spoons,' said Granny promptly. It was one of the few sorrows of Granny Weatherwax's life that, despite all her efforts, she'd arrived at the peak of her career with a complexion like a rosy apple and all her teeth. No amount of charms could persuade a wart to take root on her handsome if slightly equine features, and vast intakes of sugar only served to give her boundless energy. A wizard she'd consulted had explained it was on account

of her having a metabolism, which at least allowed her to feel vaguely
superior to Nanny Ogg, who she suspected had never even seen one.

Magrat dutifully dug out three heaped ones. It would be nice, she thought
wistfully, if someone could say 'thank you' occasionally.

She became aware that the crown was staring at her.

'You can feel it, can you?' said Granny. 'I said, didn't I? Crowns call out!'

'It's horrible.'

'No, no. It's just being what it is. It can't help it.'

'But it's magic!'

'It's just being what it is,' Granny repeated.

'It's trying to get me to try it on,' said Magrat, her hand hovering.

'It does that, yes.'

'But I shall be strong,' said Magrat.

'So I should think,' said Granny, her expression suddenly curiously
wooden. 'What's Gytha doing?'

'She's giving the baby a wash in the sink,' said Magrat vaguely. 'How can
we hide something like this? What'd happen if we buried it really deeply
somewhere?'

'A badger'd dig it up,' said Granny wearily. 'Or someone'd go prospect-
ing for gold or something. Or a tree'd tangle its roots around it and then be
blown over in a storm, and then someone'd pick it up and put it on – '

'Unless they were as strong-minded as us,' Magrat pointed out.

'Unless that, of course,' said Granny, staring at her fingernails. 'Though
the thing with crowns is, it isn't the putting them on that's the problem, it's
the taking them off.'

Magrat picked it up and turned it over in her hands.

'It's not as though it even looks much like a crown,' she said.

'You've seen a lot, I expect,' said Granny. 'You'd be an expert on them,
naturally.'

'Seen a fair few. They've got a lot more jewels on them, and cloth bits in
the middle,' said Magrat defiantly. 'This is just a thin little thing – '

'Magrat Garlick!'

'I have. When I was being trained up by Goodie Whemper – '

' – maysherestinpeace – '

' – maysherestinpeace, she used to take me over to Razorback or into
Lancre whenever the strolling players were in town. She was very keen on
the theatre. They've got more crowns than you can shake a stick at although,
mind – ' she paused – 'Goodie did say they're made of tin and paper and
stuff. And just glass for the jewels. But they look more realler than this one.
Do you think that's strange?'

'Things that try to look like things often do look more like things than things. Well-known fact,' said Granny. 'But I don't hold with encouraging it. What do they stroll about playing, then, in these crowns?'

'You don't know about the theatre?' said Magrat.

Granny Weatherwax, who never declared her ignorance of anything, didn't hesitate. 'Oh, yes,' she said. 'It's one of *them* style of things, then, is it?'

'Goodie Whemper said it held a mirror up to life,' said Magrat. 'She said it always cheered her up.'

'I expect it would,' said Granny, striking out. 'Played properly, at any rate. Good people, are they, these theatre players?'

'I think so.'

'And they stroll around the country, you say?' said Granny thoughtfully, looking towards the scullery door.

'All over the place. There's a troupe in Lancre now, I heard. I haven't been because, you know.' Magrat looked down. ''Tis not right, a woman going into such places by herself.'

Granny nodded. She thoroughly approved of such sentiments so long as there was, of course, no suggestion that they applied to her.

She drummed her fingers on Magrat's tablecloth.

'Right,' she said. 'And why not? Go and tell Gytha to wrap the baby up well. It's a long time since I heard a theatre played properly.'

Magrat was entranced, as usual. The theatre was no more than some lengths of painted sacking, a plank stage laid over a few barrels, and half a dozen benches set out in the village square. But at the same time it had also managed to become The Castle, Another Part of the Castle, The Same Part A Little Later, The Battlefield and now it was A Road Outside the City. The afternoon would have been perfect if it wasn't for Granny Weatherwax.

After several piercing glares at the three-man orchestra to see if she could work out which instrument the theatre was, the old witch had finally paid attention to the stage, and it was beginning to become apparent to Magrat that there were certain fundamental aspects of the theatre that Granny had not yet grasped.

She was currently bouncing up and down on her stool with rage.

'He's killed him,' she hissed. 'Why isn't anyone doing anything about it? He's killed him! And right up there in front of everyone!'

Magrat held on desperately to her colleague's arm as she struggled to get to her feet.

'It's all right,' she whispered. 'He's not dead!'

'Are you calling me a liar, my girl?' snapped Granny. 'I saw it all!'

'Look, Granny it's not really real, d'you see?'

Granny Weatherwax subsided a little, but still grumbled under her breath. She was beginning to feel that things were trying to make a fool of her.

Up on the stage a man in a sheet was giving a spirited monologue. Granny listened intently for some minutes, and then nudged Magrat in the ribs.

'What's he on about now?' she demanded.

'He's saying how sorry he was that the other man's dead,' said Magrat, and in an attempt to change the subject added hurriedly, 'There's a lot of crowns, isn't there?'

Granny was not to be distracted. 'What'd he go and kill him for, then?' she said.

'Well, it's a bit complicated – ' said Magrat, weakly.

'It's shameful!' snapped Granny. 'And the poor dead thing still lying there!'

Magrat gave an imploring look to Nanny Ogg, who was masticating an apple and studying the stage with the glare of a research scientist.

'I *reckon*,' she said slowly, 'I reckon it's all just pretendin'. Look, he's still breathing.'

The rest of the audience, who by now had already decided that this commentary was part of the play, stared as one man at the corpse. It blushed.

'And look at his boots, too,' said Nanny critically. 'A real king'd be ashamed of boots like that.'

The corpse tried to shuffle its feet behind a cardboard bush.

Granny, feeling in some obscure way that they had scored a minor triumph over the purveyors of untruth and artifice, helped herself to an apple from the bag and began to take a fresh interest. Magrat's nerves started to unknot, and she began to settle down to enjoy the play. But not, as it turned out, for very long. Her willing suspension of disbelief was interrupted by a voice saying:

'What's this bit?'

Magrat sighed. 'Well,' she hazarded, '*he* thinks that *he* is the prince, but *he's* really the other king's daughter, dressed up as a man.'

Granny subjected the actor to a a a long analytical stare.

'He *is* a man,' she said. 'In a straw wig. Making his voice squeaky.'

Magrat shuddered. She knew a little about the conventions of the theatre. She had been dreading this bit. Granny Weatherwax had Views.

'Yes, but,' she said wretchedly. 'it's the Theatre, see. All the women are played by men.'

'Why?'

'They don't allow no women on the stage,' said Magrat in a small voice. She shut her eyes.

In fact, there was no outburst from the seat on her left. She risked a quick glance.

Granny was quietly chewing the same bit of apple over and over again, her eyes never leaving the action.

'Don't make a fuss, Esme,' said Nanny, who also knew about Granny's Views. 'This is a good bit. I reckon I'm getting the hang of it.'

Someone tapped Granny on the shoulder and a voice said, 'Madam, will you kindly remove your hat?'

Granny turned around very slowly on her stool, as though propelled by hidden motors, and subjected the interrupter to a hundred kilowatt diamond-blue stare. The man wilted under it and sagged back on to his stool, her face following him all the way down.

'No,' she said.

He considered the options. 'All right,' he said.

Granny turned back and nodded to the actors, who had paused to watch her.

'I don't know what you're staring at,' she growled. 'Get on with it.'

Nanny Ogg passed her another bag.

'Have a humbug,' she said.

Silence again filled the makeshift theatre except for the hesitant voices of the actors, who kept glancing at the bristling figure of Granny Weatherwax, and the sucking sounds of a couple of boiled humbugs being relentlessly churned from cheek to cheek.

Then Granny said, in a piercing voice that made one actor drop his wooden sword, 'There's a man over on the side there whispering to them!'

'He's a prompter,' said Magrat. 'He tells them what to say.'

'Don't they know?'

'I think they're forgetting,' said Magrat sourly. 'For some reason.'

Granny nudged Nanny Ogg.

'What's going on now?' she said. 'Why're all them kings and people up there?'

'It's a banquet, see,' said Nanny Ogg authoritatively. 'Because of the dead king, him in the boots, as was, only now if you look, you'll see he's pretending to be a soldier, and everyone's making speeches about how good he was and wondering who killed him.'

'Are they?' said Granny, grimly. She cast her eyes along the cast, looking for the murderer.

She was making up her mind.

Then she stood up.

Her black shawl billowed around her like the wings of an avenging angel, come to rid the world of all that was foolishness and pretence and artifice and sham. She seemed somehow a lot bigger than normal. She pointed an angry finger at the guilty party.

'He done it!' she shouted triumphantly. 'We all *seed* 'im! He done it with a dagger!'

The audience filed out, contented. It had been a good play on the whole, they decided, although not very easy to follow. But it had been a jolly good laugh when all the kings had run off, and the woman in black had jumped up and did all the shouting. That alone had been well worth the ha'penny admission.

The three witches sat alone on the edge of the stage.

'I wonder how they get all them kings and lords to come here and do this?' said Granny, totally unabashed. 'I'd have thought they'd been too busy. Ruling and similar.'

'No,' said Magrat, wearily. 'I still don't think you quite understand.'

'Well, I'm going to get to the bottom of it,' snapped Granny. She got back on to the stage and pulled aside the sacking curtains.

'You!' she shouted. 'You're dead!'

The luckless former corpse, who was eating a ham sandwich to calm his nerves, fell backwards off his stool.

Granny kicked a bush. Her boot went right through it.

'See?' she said to the world in general in a strangely satisfied voice. 'Nothing's real! It's all just paint, and sticks and paper at the back.'

'May I assist you, good ladies?'

It was a rich and wonderful voice, with every diphthong gliding beautifully into place. It was a golden brown voice. If the Creator of the multiverse had a voice, it was a voice such as this. If it had a drawback, it was that it wasn't a voice you could use, for example, for ordering coal. Coal ordered by this voice would become diamonds.

It apparently belonged to a large fat man who had been badly savaged by a moustache. Pink veins made a map of quite a large city on his cheeks; his nose could have hidden successfully in a bowl of strawberries. He wore a ragged jerkin and holey tights with an aplomb that nearly convinced you that his velvet-and-vermine robes were in the wash just at the moment. In one hand he held a towel, with which he had clearly been removing the make-up that still greased his features.

'I know you,' said Granny. 'You done the murder.' She looked sideways at Magrat, and admitted, grudgingly, 'Leastways, it looked like it.'

'*So* glad. It is always a pleasure to meet a true connoisseur. Olwyn Vitoller, *at* your service. Manager of this band of vagabonds,' said the man and, removing his moth-eaten hat, he treated her to a low bow. It was less an obeisance than an exercise in advanced topology.

The hat swerved and jerked through a series of complex arcs, ending up at the end of an arm which was now pointing in the direction of the sky. One of his legs, meanwhile, had wandered off behind him. The rest of his body sagged politely until his head was level with Granny's knees.

'Yes, well,' said Granny. She felt that her clothes had grown a bit larger and much hotter.

'I thought you was very good, too,' said Nanny Ogg. 'The way you shouted all them words so graciously. I could tell you was a king.'

'I hope we didn't upset things,' said Magrat.

'My dear lady,' said Vitoller. 'Could I begin to tell you how gratifying it is for a mere mummer to learn that his audience has seen behind the mere shell of greasepaint to the spirit beneath?'

'I expect you could,' said Granny. 'I expect you could say anything, Mr Vitoller.'

He replaced his hat and their eyes met in the long calculating stare of one professional weighing up another. Vitoller broke first, and tried to pretend he hadn't been competing.

'And now,' he said, 'to what do I owe this visit from three such charming ladies?'

In fact he'd won. Granny's mouth fell open. She would not have described herself as anything much above 'handsome, considering'. Nanny, on the other hand, was as gummy as a baby and had a face like a small dried raisin. The best you could say for Magrat was that she was decently plain and well-scrubbed and as flat-chested as an ironing board with a couple of peas on it, even if her head was too well stuffed with fancies. Granny could feel something, some sort of magic at work. But not the kind she was used to.

It was Vitoller's voice. By the mere process of articulation it transformed everything it talked about.

Look at the two of them, she told herself, primping away like a couple of ninnies. Granny stopped her hand in the process of patting her own iron-hard bun, and cleared her throat meaningfully.

'We'd like to talk to you, Mr Vitoller.' She indicated the actors, who were dismantling the set and staying well out of her way, and added in a conspiratorial whisper, 'Somewhere private.'

'Dear lady, but of a certain,' he said. 'Currently I have lodgings in yonder esteemed watering hole.'

The witches looked around. Eventually Magrat risked, 'You mean in the pub?'

☆   ☆   ☆

It was cold and draughty in the Great Hall of Lancre Castle, and the new chamberlain's bladder wasn't getting any younger. He stood and squirmed under the gaze of Lady Felmet.

'Oh, yes,' he said. 'We've got them all right. Lots.'

'And people don't *do* anything about them?' said the duchess.

The chamberlain blinked. 'I'm sorry?' he said.

'People tolerate them?'

'Oh, indeed,' said the chamberlain happily. 'It's considered good luck to have a witch living in your village. My word, yes.'

'Why?'

The chamberlain hesitated. The last time he had resorted to a witch it had been because certain rectal problems had turned the privy into a daily torture chamber, and the jar of ointment she had prepared had turned the world into a nicer place.

'They smooth out life's little humps and bumps,' he said.

'Where I come from, we don't allow witches,' said the duchess sternly. 'And we don't propose to allow them here. You will furnish us with their addresses.'

'Addresses, ladyship?'

'Where they live. I trust your tax gatherers know where to find them?'

'Ah,' said the chamberlain, miserably.

The duke leaned forward on his throne.

'I trust,' he said, 'that they do pay taxes?'

'Not exactly *pay* taxes, my lord,' said the chamberlain.

There was silence. Finally the duke prompted. 'Go on, man.'

'Well, it's more that they *don't* pay, you see. We never felt, that is, the old king didn't think . . . Well, they just don't.'

The duke laid a hand on his wife's arm.

'I see,' he said coldly. 'Very well. You may go.'

The chamberlain gave him a brief nod of relief and scuttled crabwise from the hall.

'Well!' said the duchess.

'Indeed.'

'That was how your family used to run a kingdom, was it? You had a positive *duty* to kill your cousin. It was clearly in the interests of the species,' said the duchess. 'The weak don't deserve to survive.'

The duke shivered. She would keep on reminding him. He didn't, on the whole, object to killing people, or at least ordering them to be killed and then watching it happen. But killing a kinsman rather stuck in the throat or – he recalled – the liver.

'Quite so,' he managed. 'Of course, there would appear to be many witches, and it might be difficult to find the three that were on the moor.'

'That doesn't matter.'

'Of course not.'

'Put matters in hand.'

'Yes, my love.'

Matters in hand. He'd put matters in hand all right. If he closed his eyes he could see the body tumbling down the steps. Had there been a hiss of shocked breath, down in the darkness of the hall? He'd been certain they were alone. Matters in hand! He'd tried to wash the blood off his hand. If he could wash the blood off, he told himself, it wouldn't have happened. He'd scrubbed and scrubbed. Scrubbed till he screamed.

Granny wasn't at home in public houses. She sat stiffly to attention behind her port-and-lemon, as if it were a shield against the lures of the world.

Nanny Ogg, on the other hand, was enthusiastically downing her third drink and, Granny thought sourly, was well along that path which would probably end up with her usual dancing on the table, showing her petticoats and singing 'The Hedgehog Can Never be Buggered at All'.

The table was covered with copper coins. Vitoller and his wife sat at either end, counting. It was something of a race.

Granny considered Mrs Vitoller as she snatched farthings from under her husband's fingers. She was an intelligent-looking woman, who appeared to treat her husband much as a sheepdog treats a favourite lamb. The complexities of the marital relationship were known to Granny only from a distance, in the same way that an astronomer can view the surface of a remote and alien world, but it had already occurred to her that a wife to Vitoller would have to be a very special woman with bottomless reserves of patience and organisational ability and nimble fingers.

'Mrs Vitoller,' she said eventually, 'may I make so bold as to ask if your union has been blessed with fruit?'

The couple looked blank.

'She means – ' Nanny Ogg began.

'No, I see,' said Mrs Vitoller, quietly. 'No. We had a little girl once.'

A small cloud hung over the table. For a second or two Vitoller looked merely human-sized, and much older. He stared at the small pile of cash in front of him.

'Only, you see, there is this child,' said Granny, indicating the baby in Nanny Ogg's arms. 'And he needs a home.'

The Vitollers stared. Then the man sighed.

'It is no life for a child,' he said. 'Always moving. Always a new town. And no room for schooling. They say that's very important these days.' But his eyes didn't look away.

Mrs Vitoller said, 'Why does he need a home?'

'He hasn't got one,' said Granny. 'At least, not one where he would be welcome.'

The silence continued. Then Mrs Vitoller said, 'And you, who ask this, you are by way of being his – ?'

'Godmothers,' said Nanny Ogg promptly. Granny was slightly taken aback. It never would have occurred to her.

Vitoller played abstractly with the coins in front of him. His wife reached out across the table and touched his hand, and there was a moment of unspoken communion. Granny looked away. She had grown expert at reading faces, but there were times when she preferred not to.

'Money is, alas, tight – ' Vitoller began.

'But it will stretch,' said his wife firmly.

'Yes. I think it will. We should be happy to take care of him.'

Granny nodded, and fished in the deepest recesses of her cloak. At last she produced a small leather bag, which she tipped out on to the table. There was a lot of silver, and even a few tiny gold coins.

'This should take care of – ' she groped – 'nappies and suchlike. Clothes and things. Whatever.'

'A hundred times over, I should think,' said Vitoller weakly. 'Why didn't you mention this before?'

'If I'd had to buy you, you wouldn't be worth the price.'

'But you don't know anything about us!' said Mrs Vitoller.

'We don't, do we?' said Granny, calmly. 'Naturally we'd like to hear how he gets along. You could send us letters and suchlike. But it would not be a good idea to talk about all this after you've left, do you see? For the sake of the child.'

Mrs Vitoller looked at the two old women.

'There's something else here, isn't there?' she said. 'Something big behind all this?'

Granny hesitated, and then nodded.

'But it would do us no good at all to know it?'

Another nod.

Granny stood up as several actors came in, breaking the spell. Actors had a habit of filling all the space around them.

'I have other things to see to,' she said. 'Please excuse me.'

'What's his name?' said Vitoller.

'Tom,' said Granny, hardly hesitating.

'John,' said Nanny. The two witches exchanged glances. Granny won.

'Tom John,' she said firmly, and swept out.

She met a breathless Magrat outside the door.

'I found a box,' she said. 'It had all the crowns and things in. So I put it in, like you said, right underneath everything.'

'Good,' said Granny.

'Our crown looked really tatty compared to the others!'

'It just goes to show, doesn't it,' said Granny. 'Did anyone see you?'

'No, everyone was too busy, but – ' Magrat hesitated, and blushed.

'Out with it, girl.'

'Just after that a man came up and pinched my bottom.' Magrat went a deep crimson and slapped her hand over her mouth.

'Did he?' said Granny. 'And then what?'

'And then, and then – '

'Yes?'

'He said, he said – '

'What did he say?'

'He said, "Hello, my lovely, what are you doing tonight?"'

Granny ruminated on this for a while and then said, 'Old Goodie Whemper, she didn't get out and about much, did she?'

'It was her leg, you know,' said Magrat.

'But she taught you all the midwifery and everything?'

'Oh, yes, *that*,' said Magrat. 'I done lots.'

'But – ' Granny hesitated, groping her way across unfamiliar territory – 'she never talked about what you might call the *previous*.'

'Sorry?'

'You know,' said Granny, with an edge of desperation in her voice. 'Men and such.'

Magrat looked as if she was about to panic. 'What about them?'

Granny Weatherwax had done many unusual things in her time, and it took a lot to make her refuse a challenge. But this time she gave in.

'I think,' she said helplessly, 'that it might be a good idea if you have a quiet word with Nanny Ogg one of these days. Fairly soon.'

There was a cackle of laughter from the window behind them, a chink of glasses, and a thin voice raised in song:

' – with a giraffe, If you stand on a stool. But the hedgehog – '

Granny stopped listening. 'Only not just now,' she added.

The troupe got under way a few hours before sunset, their four carts lurching off down the road that led towards the Sto plains and the big cities.

Lancre had a town rule that all mummers, mountebanks and other potential criminals were outside the gates by sundown; it didn't offend anyone really because the town had no walls to speak of, and no one much minded if people nipped back in again after dark. It was the look of the thing that counted.

The witches watched from Magrat's cottage, using Nanny Ogg's ancient green crystal ball.

'It's about time you learned how to get sound on this thing,' Granny muttered. She gave it a nudge, filling the image with ripples.

'It was very strange,' said Magrat. 'In those carts. The things they had! Paper trees, and all kinds of costumes, and – ' she waved her hands – 'there was this great big picture of forn parts, with all temples and things, all rolled up. It was beautiful.'

Granny grunted.

'I thought it was amazing the way all those people became kings and things, didn't you? It was like magic.'

'Magrat Garlick, what are you saying? It was just paint and paper. Anyone could see that.'

Magrat opened her mouth to speak, ran the ensuing argument through her head, and shut it again.

'Where's Nanny?' she said.

'She's lying out on the lawn,' said Granny. 'She felt a bit poorly.' And from outside came the sound of Nanny Ogg being poorly at the top of her voice.

Magrat sighed.

'You know,' she said, 'if we *are* his godmothers, we ought to have given him three gifts. It's traditional.'

'What are you talking about, girl?'

'Three good witches are supposed to give the baby three gifts. You know, like good looks, wisdom and happiness.' Magrat pressed on defiantly. 'That's how it used to be done in the old days.'

'Oh, you mean gingerbread cottages and all that,' said Granny dismissively. 'Spinning wheels and pumpkins and pricking your finger on rose thorns and similar. I could never be having with all that.'

She polished the ball reflectively.

'Yes, but – ' Magrat said. Granny glanced up at her. That was Magrat for you. Head full of pumpkins. Everyone's fairy godmother, for two pins. But a good soul, underneath it all. Kind to small furry animals. The sort of person who worried about baby birds falling out of nests.

'Look, if it makes you any happier,' she muttered, surprised at herself. She waved her hands vaguely over the image of the departing cars. 'What's it to be – wealth, beauty?'

'Well, money isn't everything, and if he takes after his father he'll be handsome enough,' Magrat said, suddenly serious. 'Wisdom, do you think?'

'That's something he'll have to learn for himself,' said Granny.

'Perfect eyesight? A good singing voice?' From the lawn outside came Nanny Ogg's cracked but enthusiastic voice telling the night sky that A Wizard's Staff Has A Knob On The End.

'Not important,' said Granny loudly. 'You've got to think headology, see? Not muck about with all this beauty and wealth business. That's not important.'

She turned back to the ball and gestured half-heartedly. 'You'd better go and get Nanny, then, seeing as there should be three of us.'

Nanny was helped in, eventually, and had to have things explained to her.

'Three gifts, eh?' she said. 'Haven't done one of them things since I was a gel, it takes me back – what're you doing?'

Magrat was bustling around the room, lighting candles.

'Oh, we've got to create the right magical ambience,' she explained. Granny shrugged, but said nothing, even in the face of the extreme provocation. All witches did their magic in their own way, and this was Magrat's house.

'What're we going to give him, then?' said Nanny.

'We was just discussing it,' said Granny.

'I know what he'll want,' said Nanny. She made a suggestion, which was received in frozen silence.

'I don't see what use *that* would be,' said Magrat, eventually. 'Wouldn't it be rather uncomfortable?'

'He'll thank us when he grows up, you mark my words,' said Nanny. 'My first husband, he always said – '

'Something a bit less physical is generally the style of things,' interrupted Granny, glaring at Nanny Ogg. 'There's no need to go and spoil everything, Gytha. Why do you always have to – '

'Well, at least I can say that I – ' Nanny began.

Both voices faded to a mutter. There was a long edgy silence.

'I think,' said Magrat, with brittle brightness, 'that perhaps it would be a good idea if we all go back to our little cottages and do it in our own way. You know. Separately. It's been a long day and we're all rather tired.'

'Good idea,' said Granny firmly, and stood up. 'Come, Nanny Ogg,' she snapped. 'It's been a long day and we're all rather tired.'

Magrat heard them bickering as they wandered down the path.

She sat rather sadly amidst the coloured candles, holding a small bottle of extremely thaumaturgical incense that she had ordered from a magical supplies emporium in faraway Ankh-Morpork. She had been rather looking

forward to trying it. Sometimes, she thought, it would be nice if people
could be a bit kinder . . .

She stared at the ball.

Well, she could make a start.

'He will make friends easily,' she whispered. It wasn't much, she knew,
but it was something she'd never been able to get the hang of.

Nanny Ogg, sitting alone in her kitchen with her huge tomcat curled up
on her lap, poured herself a nightcap and through the haze tried to
remember the words of verse seventeen of the Hedgehog song. There was
something about goats, she recalled, but the details eluded her. Time abraded
memory.

She toasted the invisible presence.

'A bloody good memory is what he ought to have,' she said. 'He'll always
remember the words.'

And Granny Weatherwax, striding home alone through the midnight
forest, wrapped her shawl around her and considered. It had been a long
day, and a trying one. The theatre had been the worst part. All people
pretending to be other people, things happening that weren't real, bits of
countryside you could put your foot through . . . Granny liked to know
where she stood, and she wasn't certain she stood for that sort of thing. The
world seemed to be changing all the time.

It didn't use to change so much. It was bewildering.

She walked quickly through the darkness with the frank stride of someone
who was at least certain that the forest, on this damp and windy night,
contained strange and terrible things and she was it.

'Let him be whoever he thinks he is,' she said. 'That's all anybody could
hope for in this world.'

Like most people, witches *are* unfocused in time. The difference is that
they dimly realise it, and make use of it. They cherish the past because part
of them is still living there, and they can see the shadows the future casts
before it.

Granny could feel the shape of the future, and it had knives in it.

It began at five the next morning. Four men rode through the woods near
Granny's cottage, tethered the horses out of earshot, and crept very
cautiously through the mists.

The sergeant in charge was not happy in his work. He was a Ramtops
man, and wasn't at all certain how you went about arresting a witch. He was
pretty certain, though, that the witch wouldn't like the idea. He didn't like
the idea of a witch not liking the idea.

The men were Ramtoppers as well. They were following him very closely, ready to duck behind him at the first sign of anything more unexpected than a tree.

Granny's cottage was a fungoid shape in the mist. Her unruly herb garden seemed to move, even in the still air. It contained plants seen nowhere else in the mountains, their roots and seeds traded across five thousand miles of the Discworld, and the sergeant could swear that one or two blooms turned towards him. He shuddered.

'What now, sarge?'

'We – we spread out,' he said. 'Yes. We spread out. That's what we do.'

They moved carefully through the bracken. The sergeant crouched behind a handy log, and said, 'Right. Very good. You've got the general idea. Now let's spread out again, and this time we spread out separately.'

The men grumbled a bit, but disappeared into the mist. The sergeant gave them a few minutes to take up positions, then said, 'Right. Now we – '

He paused.

He wondered whether he dared shout, and decided against it.

He stood up. He removed his helmet, to show respect, and sidled through the damp grass to the back door. He knocked, very gently.

After a wait of several seconds he clamped his helmet back on his head, said, 'No one in. Blast,' and started to stride away.

The door opened. It opened very slowly, and with the maximum amount of creak. Simple neglect wouldn't have caused that depth of groan; you'd need careful work with hot water over a period of weeks. The sergeant stopped, and then turned round very slowly while contriving to move as few muscles as possible.

He had mixed feelings about the fact that there was nothing in the doorway. In his experience, doors didn't just open themselves.

He cleared his throat nervously.

Granny Weatherwax, right by his ear, said, 'That's a nasty cough you've got there. You did right in coming to me.'

The sergeant looked up at her with an expression of mad gratitude. He said, 'Argle.'

'She did *what*?' said the duke.

The sergeant stared fixedly at an area a few inches to the right of the duke's chair.

'She give me a cup of tea, sir,' he said.

'And what about your men?'

'She give them one too, sir.'

The duke rose from his chair and put his arm around the sergeant's rusting chain-mail shoulders. He was in a bad mood. He had spent half the night washing his hands. He kept thinking that something was whispering in his ear. His breakfast oatmeal had been served up too salty and roasted with an apple in it, and the cook had hysterics in the kitchen. You could tell the duke was extremely annoyed. He was polite. The duke was the kind of man who becomes more and more agreeable as his temper drains away, until the point is reached where the words 'Thank you so much' have the cutting edge of a guillotine.

'Sergeant,' he said, walking the man slowly across the floor.

'Sir?'

'I'm not sure I made your orders clear, sergeant,' said the duke, in snake tones.

'Sir?'

'I mean, it is possible I may have confused you. I meant to say "Bring me a witch, in chains if necessary", but perhaps what I *really* said was "Go and have a cup of tea". Was this in fact the case?'

The sergeant wrinkled his forehead. Sarcasm had not hitherto entered his life. His experience of people being annoyed with him generally involved shouting and occasional bits of wood.

'No, sir,' he said.

'I wonder why, then, you did not in fact do this thing that I asked?'

'Sir?'

'I expect she said some magic words, did she? I've heard about witches,' said the duke, who had spent the night before reading, until his bandaged hands shook too much, some of the more excitable works on the subject.* 'I imagine she offered you visions of unearthly delight? Did she show you – ' the duke shuddered – 'dark fascinations and forbidden raptures, the like of which mortal men should not even think of, and demonic secrets that took you to the depths of man's desires?'

The duke sat down and fanned himself with his handkerchief.

'Are you all right, sir?' said the sergeant.

'What? Oh, perfectly, perfectly.'

'Only you've gone all red.'

'Don't change the subject, man,' snapped the duke, pulling himself together a bit. 'Admit it – she offered you hedonistic and licentious pleasures known only to those who dabble in the carnal arts, didn't she?'

The sergeant stood to attention and stared straight ahead.

---

* Written by wizards, who are celibate and get some pretty funny ideas around four o'clock in the morning.

'No, sir,' he said, in the manner of one speaking the truth come what may. 'She offered me a bun.'

'A bun?'

'Yes, sir. It had currants in it.'

Felmet sat absolutely still while he fought for internal peace. Finally, all he could manage was, 'And what did your men do about this?'

'They had a bun too, sir. All except young Roger, who isn't allowed fruit, sir, on account of his trouble.'

The duke sagged back on the window seat and put his hand over his eyes. I was born to rule down on the plains, he thought, where it's all flat and there isn't all this weather and everything and there are people who don't appear to be made of dough. He's going to tell me what this Roger had.

'He had a biscuit, sir.'

The duke stared out at the trees. He was angry. He was extremely angry. But twenty years of marriage to Lady Felmet had taught him not simply to control his emotions but to control his instincts as well, and not so much as the twitching of a muscle indicated the workings of his mind. Besides, arising out of the black depths of his head was an emotion that, hitherto, he had little time for. Curiosity was flashing a fin.

The duke had managed quite well for fifty years without finding a use for curiosity. It was not a trait much encouraged in aristocrats. He had found certainty was a much better bet. However, it occurred to him that for once curiosity might have its uses.

The sergeant was standing in the middle of the floor with the stolid air of one who is awaiting a word of command, and who is quite prepared so to wait until continental drift budges him from his post. He had been in the undemanding service of the kings of Lancre for many years, and it showed. His body was standing to attention. Despite all his efforts his stomach stood at ease.

The duke's gaze fell on the Fool, who was sitting on his stool by the throne. The hunched figure looked up, embarrassed, and gave his bells a half-hearted shake.

The duke reached a decision. The way to progress, he'd found, was to find weak spots. He tried to shut away the thought that these included such things as the king's kidneys at the top of a dark stairway, and concentrated on the matter in hand.

. . . hand. He'd scrubbed and scrubbed, but it seemed to have no effect. Eventually he'd gone down to the dungeons and borrowed one of the torturer's wire brushes, and scrubbed and scrubbed with that, too. That had no effect, either. It made it worse. The harder he scrubbed, the more blood there was. He was afraid he might go mad . . .

He wrestled the thought to the back of his mind. Weak spots. That was it. The Fool looked all weak spot.

'You may go, sergeant.'

'Sir,' said the sergeant, and marched out stiffly.

'Fool?'

'Marry, sir – ' said the Fool nervously, and gave his hated mandolin a quick strum.

The duke sat down on the throne.

'I am already extremely married,' he said. 'Advise me, my Fool.'

'I' faith, nuncle – ' said the Fool.

'Nor am I thy nuncle. I feel sure I would have remembered,' said Lord Felmet, leaning down until the prow of his nose was a few inches from the Fool's stricken face. 'If you preface your next remark with nuncle, i' faith or marry, it will go hard with you.'

The Fool moved his lips silently, and then said, 'How do you feel about Prithee?'

The duke knew when to allow some slack. 'Prithee I can live with,' he said. 'So can you. But no capering.' He grinned encouragingly. 'How long have you been a Fool, boy?'

'Prithee, sirrah – '

'The sirrah,' said the duke, holding up a hand, 'on the whole, I think not.'

'Prithee, sirra – sir,' said the Fool, and swallowed nervously. 'All my life, sir. Seventeen years under the bladder, man and boy. And my father before me. And my nuncle at the same time as him. And my grandad before them. And his – '

'Your whole family have been Fools?'

'Family tradition, sir,' said the Fool. 'Prithee, I mean.'

The duke smiled again, and the Fool was too worried to notice how many teeth it contained.

'You come from these parts, don't you?' said the duke.

'Ma – Yes, sir.'

'So you would know all about the native beliefs and so on?'

'I suppose so, sir. Prithee.'

'Good. Where do you sleep, my Fool?'

'In the stables, sir.'

'From now on you may sleep in the corridor outside my room,' said the duke beneficently.

'Gosh!'

'And now,' said the duke, his voice dripping across the Fool like treacle over pudding, 'tell me about witches . . .'

☆   ☆   ☆

That night the Fool slept on good royal flagstones in the whistling corridor above the Great Hall instead of the warm stuffy straw of the stables.

'This is foolish,' he told himself. 'Marry, but is it foolish *enough*?'

He dozed off fitfully, into some sort of dream where a vague figure kept trying to attract his attention, and was only dimly aware of the voices of Lord and Lady Felmet on the other side of the door.

'It's certainly a lot less draughty,' said the duchess grudgingly.

The duke sat back in the armchair and smiled at his wife.

'Well?' she demanded. 'Where are the witches?'

'The chamberlain would appear to be right, beloved. The witches seem to have the local people in thrall. The sergeant of the guard came back empty-handed.' Handed . . . he came down heavily on that importunate thought.

'You must have him executed,' she said promptly. 'To make an example to the others.'

'A course of action, my dear, which ultimately results in us ordering the last soldier to cut his own throat as an example to himself. By the way,' he added mildly, 'there would appear to be somewhat fewer servants around the place. You know I would not normally interfere – '

'Then don't,' she snapped. 'Housekeeping is under my control. I cannot abide *slackness*.'

'I'm sure you know best, but – '

'What of these witches? Will you stand idly by and let trouble seed for the future? Will you let these witches defy you? What of the crown?'

The duke shrugged. 'No doubt it ended in the river,' he said.

'And the child? He was *given* to the witches. Do they do human sacrifice?'

'It would appear not,' said the duke. The duchess looked vaguely disappointed.

'These witches,' said the duke. 'Apparently, they seem to cast a spell on people.'

'Well, obviously – '

'Not like a magic spell. They seem to be respected. They do medicine and so on. It's rather strange. The mountain people seem to be afraid of them and proud of them at the same time. It might be a little difficult to move against them.'

'I could come to believe,' said the duchess darkly, 'that they have cast a glamour over you as well.'

In fact the duke *was* intrigued. Power was always darkly fascinating, which was why he had married the duchess in the first place. He stared fixedly at the fire.

'In fact,' said the duchess, who recognised the malign smile, 'you like it, don't you? The thought of the danger. I remember when we were married; all the business with the knotted rope – '

She snapped her fingers in front of the duke's glazed eyes. He sat up.

'Not at all!' he shouted.

'Then what will you do?'

'Wait.'

'*Wait*?'

'Wait, and consider. Patience is a virtue.'

The duke sat back. The smile he smiled could have spent a million years sitting on a rock. And then, just below one eye, he started to twitch.

Blood was oozing between the bandages on his hand.

Once again the full moon rode the clouds.

Granny Weatherwax milked and fed the goats, banked the fire, put a cloth over the mirror and pulled her broomstick out from behind the door. She went out, locked the back door behind her, and hung the key on its nail in the privy.

This was quite sufficient. Only once, in the entire history of witchery in the Ramtops, had a thief broken into a witch's cottage. The witch concerned visited the most terrible punishment on him.*

Granny sat on the broom and muttered a few words, but without much conviction. After a further couple of tries she got off, fiddled with the binding, and had another go. There was a suspicion of glitter from one end of the stick, which quickly died away.

'Drat,' she said, under her breath.

She looked around carefully, in case anyone was watching. In fact it was only a hunting badger who, hearing the thumping of running feet, poked its head out from the bushes and saw Granny hurtling down the path with the broomstick held stiff-armed beside her. At last the magic caught, and she managed to vault clumsily on to it before it trundled into the night sky as gracefully as a duck with one wing missing.

From above the tree came a muffled curse against all dwarfish mechanics.

Most witches preferred to live in isolated cottages with the traditional curly chimneys and weed-grown thatch. Granny Weatherwax approved of this; it was no good being a witch unless you let people *know*.

---

* She did nothing, although sometimes when she saw him in the village she'd smile in a faint, puzzled way. After three weeks of this the suspense was too much for him and he took his own life; in fact he took it all the way across the continent, where he became a reformed character and never went home again.

Nanny Ogg didn't care much about what people knew and even less for what they thought, and lived in a new, knick-knack crammed cottage in the middle of Lancre town itself and at the heart of her own private empire. Various daughters and daughters-in-law came in to cook and clean on a sort of rota. Every flat surface was stuffed with ornaments brought back by far-travelling members of the family. Sons and grandsons kept the logpile stacked, the roof shingled, the chimney swept; the drinks cupboard was always full, the pouch by her rocking chair always stuffed with tobacco. Above the hearth was a huge pokerwork sign saying 'Mother'. No tyrant in the whole history of the world had ever achieved a domination so complete.

Nanny Ogg also kept a cat, a huge one-eyed grey tom called Greebo who divided his time between sleeping, eating and fathering the most enormous incestuous feline tribe. He opened his eye like a yellow window into Hell when he heard Granny's broomstick land awkwardly on the back lawn. With the instinct of his kind he recognised Granny as an inveterate cat-hater and oozed gently under a chair.

Magrat was already seated primly by the fire.

It is one of the few unbendable rules of magic that its practitioners cannot change their own appearance for any length of time. Their bodies develop a kind of morphic inertia and gradually return to their original shape. But Magrat tried. Every morning her hair was long, thick, and blond, but by the evening it had always returned to its normal worried frizz. To ameliorate the effect she had tried to plait violets and cowslips in it. The result was not all she had hoped. It gave the impression that a window box had fallen on her head.

'Good evening,' said Granny.

'Well met by moonlight,' said Magrat politely. 'Merry meet. A star shines on – '

'Wotcha,' said Nanny Ogg. Magrat winced.

Granny sat down and started removing the hatpins that nailed her tall hat to her bun. Finally the sight of Magrat dawned on her.

'Magrat!'

The young witch jumped, and clamped her knuckly hands to the virtuous frontage of her gown.

'Yes?' she quavered.

'What have you got on your lap?'

'It's my familiar,' she said defensively.

'What happened to that toad you had?'

'It wandered off,' muttered Magrat. 'Anyway, it wasn't very good.'

Granny sighed. Magrat's desperate search for a reliable familiar had been going on for some time, and despite the love and attention she lavished on them they all seemed to have some terrible flaw, such as a tendency to bite, get trodden on or, in extreme cases, metamorphose.

'That makes fifteen this year,' said Granny. 'Not counting the horse. What's this one?'

'It's a rock,' chuckled Nanny Ogg.

'Well, at least it should last,' said Granny.

The rock extended a head and gave her a look of mild amusement.

'It's a tortoyse,' said Magrat. 'I bought it down in Sheepridge market. It's incredibly old and knows many secrets, the man said.'

'I know that man,' said Granny. 'He's the one who sells goldfish that tarnish after a day or two.'

'Anyway, I shall call him Lightfoot,' said Magrat, her voice warm with defiance. 'I can if I want.'

'Yes, yes, all right, I'm sure,' said Granny. 'Anyway, how goes it, sisters? It is two months since last we met.'

'It should be every new moon,' said Magrat sternly. 'Regular.'

'It was our Grame's youngest's wedding,' said Nanny Ogg. 'Couldn't miss it.'

'And I was up all night with a sick goat,' said Granny Weatherwax promptly.

'Yes, well,' said Magrat doubtfully. She rummaged in her bag. 'Anyway, if we're going to start, we'd better light the candles.'

The senior witches exchanged a resigned glance.

'But we got this lovely new lamp our Tracie sent me,' said Nanny Ogg innocently. 'And I was going to poke up the fire a bit.'

'I have *ex*cellent night vision, Magrat,' said Granny sternly. 'And you've been reading them funny books. Grimmers.'

'Grimoires – '

'You ain't going to draw on the floor again, neither,' warned Nanny Ogg. 'It took our Dreen days to clean up all those wossnames last time – '

'Runes,' said Magrat. There was a look of pleading in her eyes. 'Look, just one candle?'

'All right,' said Nanny Ogg, relenting a bit. 'If it makes you feel any better. Just the one, mind. And a decent white one. Nothing fancy.'

Magrat sighed. It probably wasn't a good idea to bring out the rest of the contents of her bag.

'We ought to get a few more here,' she said sadly. 'It's not right, a coven of three.'

'I didn't know we was still a coven. No one told me we was still a coven,' sniffed Granny Weatherwax. 'Anyway, there's no one else this side of the mountain, excepting old Gammer Dismass, and she doesn't get out these days.'

'But a lot of young girls in my village . . .' said Magrat. 'You know. They could be keen.'

'That's not how we do it, as well you know,' said Granny disapprovingly. 'People don't go and find witchcraft, it comes and finds them.'

'Yes, yes,' said Magrat. 'Sorry.'

'Right,' said Granny, slightly mollified. She'd never mastered the talent for apologising, but she appreciated it in other people.

'What about this new duke, then,' said Nanny, to lighten the atmosphere.

Granny sat back. 'He had some houses burned down in Bad Ass,' she said. 'Because of taxes.'

'How horrible,' said Magrat.

'Old King Verence used to do that,' said Nanny. 'Terrible temper he had.'

'*He* used to let people out first, though,' said Granny.

'Oh yes,' said Nanny, who was a staunch royalist. 'He could be very gracious like that. He'd pay for them to be rebuilt, as often as not. If he remembered.'

'And every Hogswatchnight, a side of venison. Regular,' said Granny wistfully.

'Oh, yes. Very respectful to witches, he was,' added Nanny Ogg. 'When he was out hunting people, if he met me in the woods, it was always off with his helmet and "I hopes I finds you well, Mistress Ogg" and next day he'd send his butler down with a couple of bottles of something. He was a proper king.'

'Hunting people isn't really right, though,' said Magrat.

'Well, no,' Granny Weatherwax conceded. 'But it was only if they'd done something bad. He said they enjoyed it really. And he used to let them go if they gave him a good run.'

'And then there was that great hairy thing of his,' said Nanny Ogg.

There was a perceptible change in the atmosphere. It became warmer, darker, filled at the corners with the shadows of unspoken conspiracy.

'Ah,' said Granny Weatherwax distantly. 'His droit de seigneur.'

'Needed a lot of exercise,' said Nanny Ogg, staring at the fire.

'But next day he'd send his housekeeper round with a bag of silver and a hamper of stuff for the wedding,' said Granny. 'Many a couple got a proper start in life thanks to that.'

'Ah,' agreed Nanny. 'One or two individuals, too.'

'Every inch a king,' said Granny.

'What are you talking about?' said Magrat suspiciously. 'Did he keep pets?'

The two witches surfaced from whatever deeper current they had been swimming in. Granny Weatherwax shrugged.

'I must say,' Magrat went on, in severe tones, 'if you think so much of the old king, you don't seem very worried about him being killed. I mean, it was a pretty suspicious accident.'

'That's kings for you,' said Granny. 'They come and go, good and bad. His father poisoned the king we had before.'

'That was old Thargum,' said Nanny Ogg. 'Had a big red beard, I recall. He was very gracious too, you know.'

'Only now no one must say Felmet killed the king,' said Magrat.

'What?' said Granny.

'He had some people executed in Lancre the other day for saying it,' Magrat went on. 'Spreading malicious lies, he said. He said anyone saying different will see the inside of his dungeons, only not for long. He said Verence died of natural causes.'

'Well, being assassinated *is* natural causes for a king,' said Granny. 'I don't see why he's so sheepish about it. When old Thargum was killed they stuck his head on a pole, had a big bonfire and everyone in the palace got drunk for a week.'

'I remember,' said Nanny. 'They carried his head all round the villages to show he was dead. Very convincing, I thought. Specially for him. He was grinning. I think it was the way he would have liked to go.'

'I think we might have to keep an eye on this one, though,' said Granny. 'I think he might be a bit clever. That's not a good thing, in a king. And I don't think he knows how to show respect.'

'A man came to see me last week to ask if I wanted to pay any taxes,' said Magrat. 'I told him no.'

'He came to see me, too,' said Nanny Ogg. 'But our Jason and our Wane went out and told him we didn't want to join.'

'Small man, bald, black cloak?' said Granny thoughtfully.

'Yes,' said the other two.

'He was hanging about in my raspberry bushes,' said Granny. 'Only, when I went out to see what he wanted, he ran away.'

'Actually, I gave him tuppence,' said Magrat. 'He said he was going to be tortured, you see, if he didn't get witches to pay their taxes . . .'

Lord Felmet looked carefully at the two coins in his lap.

Then he looked at his tax gatherer.

'Well?' he said.

The tax gatherer cleared his throat. 'Well, sir, you see. I explained about the need to employ a standing army, ekcetra, and they said why, and I said because of bandits, ekcetra, and they said bandits never bothered them.'

'And civil works?'

'Ah. Yes. Well, I pointed out the need to build and maintain bridges, ekcetra.'

'And?'

'They said they didn't use them.'

'Ah,' said the duke knowledgeably. 'They can't cross running water.'

'Not sure about that, sir. I think witches cross anything they like.'

'Did they say anything else?' said the duke.

The tax gatherer twisted the hem of his robe distractedly.

'Well, sir. I mentioned how taxes help to maintain the King's Peace, sir . . .'

'And?'

'They said the king should maintain his own peace, sir. And then they gave me a look.'

'What sort of look?'

The duke sat with his thin face cupped in one hand. He was fascinated.

'It's sort of hard to describe,' said the taxman. He tried to avoid Lord Felmet's gaze, which was giving him the distinct impression that the tiled floor was fleeing away in all directions and had already covered several acres. Lord Felmet's fascination was to him what a pin is to a Purple Emperor.

'Try,' the duke invited.

The taxman blushed.

'Well,' he said. 'It . . . wasn't nice.'

Which demonstrates that the tax gatherer was much better at figures than words. What he would have said, if embarrassment, fear, poor memory and a complete lack of any kind of imagination hadn't conspired against it, was:

'When I was a little boy, and staying with my aunt, and she had told me not to touch the cream, ekcetra, and she had put it on a high shelf in the pantry, and I got a stool and went after it when she was out anyway, and she'd come back and I didn't know, and I couldn't reach the bowl properly and it smashed on the floor, and she opened the door and glared at me: it was that look. But the worst thing was, they *knew* it.'

'Not nice,' said the duke.

'No, sir.'

The duke drummed his fingers of his left hand on the arm of his throne. The tax gatherer coughed again.

'You're – you're not going to force me to go back, are you?' he said.

'Um?' said the duke. He waved a hand irritably. 'No, no,' he said. 'Not at all. Just call in at the torturer on your way out. See when he can fit you in.'

The taxman gave him a look of gratitude, and bobbed a bow.

'Yes, sir. At once, sir. Thank you, sir. You're very – '

'Yes, yes,' said Lord Felmet, absently. 'You may go.'

The duke was left alone in the vastness of the hall. It was raining again. Every once in a while a piece of plaster smashed down on the tiles, and there was a crunching from the walls as they settled still further. The air smelled of old cellars.

Gods, he hated this kingdom.

It was so small, only forty miles long and maybe ten miles wide, and nearly all of it was cruel mountains with ice-green slopes and knife-edge crests, or dense huddled forests. A kingdom like that shouldn't be any trouble.

What he couldn't quite fathom was this feeling that it had *depth*. It seemed to contain far too much geography.

He rose and paced the floor to the balcony, with its unrivalled view of trees. It struck him that the trees were also looking back at him.

He could feel the resentment. But that was odd, because the people themselves hadn't objected. They didn't seem to object to anything very much. Verence had been popular enough, in his way. There'd been quite a turnout for the funeral; he recalled the lines of solemn faces. Not stupid faces. By no means stupid. Just preoccupied, as though what kings did wasn't really very important.

He found that almost as annoying as trees. A jolly good riot, now, that would have been more – more appropriate. One could have ridden out and hanged people, there would have been the creative tension so essential to the proper development of the state. Back down on the plains, if you kicked people they kicked back. Up here, when you kicked people they moved away and just waited patiently for your leg to fall off. How could a king go down in history ruling a people like that? You couldn't oppress them any more than you could oppress a mattress.

He had raised taxes and burned a few villages on general principles, just to show everyone who they were dealing with. It didn't seem to have any effect.

And then there were these witches. They haunted him.

'Fool!'

The Fool, who had been having a quiet doze behind the throne, awoke in terror.

'Yes!'

'Come hither, Fool.'

The Fool jingled miserably across the floor.

'Tell me, Fool, does it always rain here?'

'Marry, nuncle – '

'Just answer the question,' said Lord Felmet, with iron patience.

'Sometimes it stops, sir. To make room for the snow. And sometimes we get some right squand'ring orgulous fogs,' said the Fool.

'Orgulous?' said the duke, absently.

The Fool couldn't stop himself. His horrified ears heard his mouth blurt out: 'Thick, my lord. From the Latatian *orgulum*, a soup or broth.'

But the duke wasn't listening. Listening to the prattle of underlings was not, in his experience, particularly worthwhile.

'I am bored, Fool.'

'Let me entertain you, my lord, with many a merry quip and lightsome jest.'

'Try me.'

The Fool licked his dry lips. He hadn't actually expected this. King Verence had been happy enough just to give him a kick, or throw a bottle at his head. A *real* king.

'I'm waiting. Make me laugh.'

The Fool took the plunge.

'Why, sirrah,' he quavered, 'why may a caudled fillhorse be deemed the brother to a hiren candle in the night?'

The duke frowned. The Fool felt it better not to wait.

'Withal, because the candle may be greased, yet a fillhorse be without a fat argier,' he said and, because it was part of the joke, patted Lord Felmet lightly with his balloon on a stick and twanged his mandolin.

The duke's index finger tapped an abrupt tattoo on the arm of the throne.

'Yes?' he said. 'And then what happened?'

'That, er, was by way of being the whole thing,' said the Fool, and added, 'My grandad thought it was one of his best.'

'I daresay he told it differently,' said the duke. He stood up. 'Summon my huntsmen. I think I shall ride out on the chase. And you can come too.'

'My lord, I cannot ride!'

For the first time that morning Lord Felmet smiled.

'Capital!' he said. 'We will give you a horse that can't be ridden. Ha. Ha.'

He looked down at his bandages. And afterwards, he told himself, I'll get the armourer to send me up a file.

A year went past. The days followed one another patiently. Right back at the beginning of the multiverse they had tried all passing at the same time, and it hadn't worked.

Tomjon sat under Hwel's rickety table, watching his father as he walked up and down between the lattys, waving one arm and talking. Vitoller always waved his arms when he spoke; if you tied his hands behind his back he would be dumb.

'All right,' he was saying, 'how about *The King's Brides*?'

'Last year,' said the voice of Hwel.

'All right, then. We'll give them *Mallo, the Tyrant of Klatch*,' said Vitoller, and his larynx smoothly changed gear as his voice became a great rolling thing that could rattle the windows across the width of the average town square. '"In blood I came, And by blood rule, That none will dare assay these walls of blood – "'

'We did it the year before,' said Hwel calmly. 'Anyway, people are fed up with kings. They want a bit of a chuckle.'

'They are not fed up with *my* kings,' said Vitoller. 'My dear boy, people do not come to the theatre to laugh, they come to Experience, to Learn, to Wonder – '

'To laugh,' said Hwel, flatly. 'Have a look at this one.'

Tomjon heard the rustle of paper and the creak of wickerwork as Vitoller lowered his weight on to a prop basket.

'*A Wizard of Sorts*,' Vitoller read. '*Or, Please Yourself*.'

Hwel stretched his legs under the table and dislodged Tomjon. He hauled the boy out by one ear.

'What's this?' said Vitoller. 'Wizards? Demons? Imps? Merchants?'

'I'm rather pleased with Act II, Scene IV,' said Hwel, propelling the toddler towards the props box. 'Comic Washing Up with Two Servants.'

'Any death-bed scenes?' said Vitoller hopefully.

'No–o,' said Hwel. 'But I can do you a humorous monologue in Act III.'

'A humorous monologue!'

'All right, there's room for a soliloquy in the last act,' said Hwel hurriedly. 'I'll write one tonight, no problem.'

'And a stabbing,' said Vitoller, getting to his feet. 'A foul murder. That always goes down well.'

He strode away to organise the setting up of the stage.

Hwel sighed, and picked up his quill. Somewhere behind the sacking walls was the town of Hangdog, which had somehow allowed itself to be built in a hollow perched in the nearly sheer walls of a canyon. There was plenty of flat ground in the Ramtops. The problem was that nearly all of it was vertical.

Hwel didn't like the Ramtops, which was odd because it was traditional dwarf country and he was a dwarf. But he'd been banished from his tribe years ago, not only because of his claustrophobia but also because he had a tendency to daydream. It was felt by the local dwarf king that this is not a valuable talent for someone who is supposed to swing a pickaxe without forgetting what he is supposed to hit with it, and so Hwel had been given a very small bag of gold, the tribe's heartfelt best wishes, and a firm goodbye.

It had happened that Vitoller's strolling players had been passing through at the time, and the dwarf had ventured one small copper coin on a performance of *The Dragon of the Plains.* He had watched it without a muscle moving in his face, gone back to his lodgings, and in the morning had knocked on Vitoller's latty with the first draft of *King Under the Mountain.* It wasn't in fact very good, but Vitoller had been perceptive enough to see that inside the hairy bullet head was an imagination big enough to bestride the world and so, when the strolling players strolled off, one of them was running to keep up . . .

Particles of raw inspiration sleet through the universe all the time. Every once in a while one of them hits a receptive mind, which then invents DNA or the flute sonata form or a way of making light bulbs wear out in half the time. But most of them miss. Most people go through their lives without being hit by even one.

Some people are even more unfortunate. They get them *all.*

Such a one was Hwel. Enough inspirations to equip a complete history of the performing arts poured continuously into a small heavy skull designed by evolution to do nothing more spectacular than be remarkably resistant to axe blows.

He licked his quill and looked bashfully around the camp. No one was watching. He carefully lifted up the *Wizard* and revealed another stack of paper.

It wasn't another potboiler. Every page was stained with sweat and the words themselves scrawled across the manuscript on a trellis of blots and crossings-out and tiny scribbled insertions. Hwel stared at it for a moment, alone in a world that consisted of him, the next blank page and the shouting, clamouring voices that haunted his dreams.

He began to write.

Free of Hwel's never-too-stringent attention, Tomjon pushed open the lid of the props hamper and, in the methodical way of the very young, began to unpack the crowns.

The dwarf stuck out his tongue as he piloted the errant quill across the ink-speckled page. He'd found room for the star-crossed lovers, the comic gravediggers and the hunchback king. It was the cats and the roller skates that were currently giving him trouble . . .

A gurgle made him look up.

'For goodness sake, lad,' he said. 'It hardly fits. Put it back.'

☆   ☆   ☆

The Disc rolled into winter.

Winter in the Ramtops could not honestly be described as a magical frosty wonderland, each twig laced with confections of brittle ice. Winter in the Ramptops didn't mess about; it was a gateway straight through to the primeval coldness that lived before the creation of the world. Winter in the Ramtops was several yards of snow, the forests a mere collection of shadowy green tunnels under the drifts. Winter meant the coming of the lazy wind, which couldn't be bothered to blow around people and blew right through them instead. The idea that Winter could actually be enjoyable would never have occurred to Ramtop people, who had eighteen different words for snow.*

The ghost of King Verence prowled the battlements, bereft and hungry, and stared out across his beloved forests and waited his chance.

It was a winter of portents. Comets sparkled against the chilled skies at night. Clouds shaped mightily like whales and dragons drifted over the land by day. In the village of Razorback a cat gave birth to a two-headed kitten, but since Greebo, by dint of considerable effort, was every male ancestor for the last thirty generations this probably wasn't all that portentous.

However, in Bad Ass a cockerel laid an egg and had to put up with some very embarrassing personal questions. In Lancre town a man swore he'd met a man who had actually seen with his own eyes a tree get up and walk. There was a short sharp shower of shrimps. There were odd lights in the sky. Geese walked backwards. Above all of this flared the great curtains of cold fire that were the Aurora Coriolis, the Hublights, whose frosty tints illuminated and coloured the midnight snows.

There was nothing the least unusual about any of this. The Ramtops, which as it were lay across the Disc's vast magical standing wave like an iron bar dropped innocently across a pair of subway rails, were so saturated with magic that it was constantly discharging itself into the environment. People would wake up in the middle of the night, mutter, 'Oh, it's just another bloody portent', and go back to sleep.

Hogswatchnight came round, marking the start of another year. And, with alarming suddenness, nothing happened.

The skies were clear, the snow deep and crisped like icing sugar.

The freezing forests were silent and smelled of tin. The only things that fell from the sky were the occasional fresh showers of snow.

A man walked across the moors from Razorback to Lancre town without seeing a single marshlight, headless dog, strolling tree, ghostly coach or

---

* All of them, unfortunately, unprintable.

comet, and had to be taken in by a tavern and given a drink to unsteady his nerves.

The stoicism of the Ramtoppers, developed over the years as a sovereign resistance to the thaumaturgical chaos, found itself unable to cope with the sudden change. It was like a noise which isn't heard until it stops.

Granny Weatherwax heard it now as she lay snug under a pile of quilts in her freezing bedroom. Hogswatchnight is, traditionally, the one night of the Disc's long year when witches are expected to stay at home, and she'd had an early night in the company of a bag of apples and a stone hotwater bottle. But something had awoken her from her doze.

An ordinary person would have crept downstairs, possibly armed with a poker. Granny simply hugged her knees and let her mind wander.

It hadn't been in the house. She could feel the small, fast minds of mice, and the fuzzy minds of her goats as they lay in their cozy flatulence in the outhouse. A hunting owl was a sudden dagger of alertness as it glided over the rooftops.

Granny concentrated harder, until her mind was full of the tiny chittering of the insects in the thatch and the woodworm in the beams. Nothing of interest there.

She snuggled down and let herself drift out into the forest, which was silent except for the occasional muffled thump as snow slid off a tree. Even in midwinter the forest was full of life, usually dozing in burrows or hibernating in the middle of trees.

All as usual. She spread herself further, to the high moors and secret passes where the wolves ran silently over the frozen crust; she touched their minds, sharp as knives. Higher still, and there was nothing in the snowfields but packs of vermine.*

Everything was as it should be, with the exception that nothing was right. There was something – yes, there was something *alive* out there, something young and ancient and . . .

Granny turned over the feeling in her mind. Yes. That was it. Something forlorn. Something lost. And . . .

Feelings were never simple, Granny knew. Strip them away and there were others underneath . . .

Something that, if it didn't stop feeling lost and forlorn very soon, was going to get *angry*.

And still she couldn't find it. She could feel the tiny minds of chrysalises down under the frozen leafmould. She could sense the earthworms, which

---

* The vermine is a small black and white furry creature, much famed for its pelt. It is a more careful relative of the lemming; it only throws itself over small pebbles.

had migrated below the frost line. She could even sense a few people, who were hardest of all – human minds were thinking so many thoughts all at the same time that they were nearly impossible to locate; it was like trying to nail fog to the wall.

Nothing there. Nothing there. The feeling was all around her, and there was nothing to cause it. She'd gone down about as far as she could, to the smallest creature in the kingdom, and there was nothing there.

Granny Weatherwax sat up in bed, lit a candle and reached for an apple. She glared at her bedroom wall.

She didn't like being beaten. There was something out there, something drinking in magic, something growing, something that seemed so alive it was all around the house, and she couldn't find it.

She reduced the apple to its core and placed it carefully in the tray of the candlestick. Then she blew out the candle.

The cold velvet of night slid back into the room.

Granny had one last try. Perhaps she was looking in the wrong way . . .

A moment later she was lying on the floor with the pillow clasped around her head.

And to think she had expected it to be *small* . . .

Lancre Castle shook. It wasn't a violent shaking, but it didn't need to be, the construction of the castle being such that it swayed slightly even in a gentle breeze. A small turret toppled slowly into the depths of the misty canyon.

The Fool lay on his flagstones and shivered in his sleep. He appreciated the honour, if it was an honour, but sleeping in the corridor always made him dream of the Fools' Guild, behind whose severe grey walls he had trembled his way through seven years of terrible tuition. The flagstones were slightly softer than the beds there, though.

A few feet away a suit of armour jingled gently. Its pike vibrated in its mailed glove until, swishing through the night air like a swooping bat, it slid down and shattered the flagstone by the Fool's ear.

The Fool sat up and realised that he was still shivering. So was the floor.

In Lord Felmet's room the shaking sent cascades of dust down from the ancient four-poster. He awoke from a dream that a great beast was tramping around the castle, and decided with horror that it might be true.

A portrait of some long-dead king fell off the wall. The duke screamed.

The Fool stumbled in, trying to keep his balance on a floor that was now heaving like the sea, and the duke staggered out of bed and grabbed the little man by his jerkin.

'What's happening?' he hissed. 'Is it an earthquake?'

'We don't have them in these parts, my lord,' said the Fool, and was knocked aside as a chaise-longue drifted slowly across the carpet.

The duke dashed to the window, and looked out at the forests in the moonlight. The white-capped trees shook in the still night air.

A slab of plaster crashed on to the floor. Lord Felmet spun around and this time his grip lifted the Fool a foot off the floor.

Among the very many luxuries the duke had dispensed with in his life was that of ignorance. He liked to feel he knew what was going on. The glorious uncertainties of existence held no attraction for him.

'It's the witches, isn't it?' he growled, his left cheek beginning to twitch like a landed fish. 'They're out there, aren't they? They're putting an Influence on the castle, aren't they?'

'Marry, nuncle – ' the Fool began.

'They run this country, don't they?'

'No, my lord, they've never – '

'*Who asked you?*'

The Fool was trembling with fear in perfect anti-phase to the castle, so that he was the only thing that now appeared to be standing perfectly still.

'Er, you did, my lord,' he quavered.

'Are you arguing with me?'

'No, my lord!'

'I thought so. You're in league with them, I suppose?'

'My lord!' said the Fool, really shocked.

'You're all in league, you people!' the duke snarled. 'The whole bunch of you! You're nothing but a pack of ringleaders!'

He flung the Fool aside and thrust the tall windows open, striding out into the freezing night air. He glared out over the sleeping kingdom.

'Do you all hear me?' he screamed. 'I am the king!'

The shaking stopped, catching the duke off-balance. He steadied himself quickly and brushed the plaster dust off his nightshirt.

'Right, then,' he said.

But this was worse. Now the forest was listening. The words he spoke vanished into a great vacuum of silence.

There was something out there. He could feel it. It was strong enough to shake the castle, and now it was watching him, listening to him.

The duke backed away, very carefully, fumbling behind him for the window catch. He stepped carefully into the room, shut the windows and hurriedly pulled the curtains across.

'I am the king,' he repeated, quietly. He looked at the Fool, who felt that something was expected of him.

The man is my lord and master, he thought. I have eaten his salt, or whatever all that business was. They told me at Guild school that a Fool should be faithful to his master until the very end, after all others have deserted him. Good or bad doesn't come into it. Every leader needs his Fool. There is only loyalty. That's the whole thing. Even if he is clearly three-parts bonkers, I'm his Fool until one of us dies.

To his horror he realised the duke was weeping.

The Fool fumbled in his sleeve and produced a rather soiled red and yellow handkerchief embroidered with bells. The duke took it with an expression of pathetic gratitude and blew his nose. Then he held it away from him and gazed at it with demented suspicion.

'Is this a dagger I see before me?' he mumbled.

'Um. No, my lord. It's my handkerchief, you see. You can sort of tell the difference if you look closely. It doesn't have as many sharp edges.'

'*Good* fool,' said the duke, vaguely.

Totally mad, the Fool thought. Several bricks short of a bundle. So far round the twist you could use him to open wine bottles.

'Kneel beside me, my Fool.'

The Fool did so. The duke laid a soiled bandage on his shoulder.

'Are you loyal, Fool?' he said. 'Are you trustworthy?'

'I swore to follow my lord until death,' said the Fool hoarsely.

The duke pressed his mad face close to the Fool, who looked up into a pair of bloodshot eyes.

'I didn't want to do it,' he hissed conspiratorially. 'They made me do it. I didn't want – '

The door swung open. The duchess filled the doorway. In fact, she was nearly the same shape.

'Leonal!' she barked.

The Fool was fascinated by what happened to the duke's eyes. The mad red flame vanished, was sucked backwards, and was replaced by the hard blue stare he had come to recognise. It didn't mean, he realised, that the duke was any less mad. Even the coldness of his sanity was madness in a way. The duke had a mind that ticked like a clock and, like a clock, it regularly went cuckoo.

Lord Felmet looked up calmly.

'Yes, my dear?'

'What is the meaning of all this?' she demanded.

'Witches, I suspect,' said Lord Felmet.

'I really don't think – ' the Fool began. Lady's Felmet's glare didn't merely silence him, it almost nailed him to the wall.

'That is clearly apparent,' she said. 'You are an idiot.'

'A Fool, my lady.'

'As well,' she added, and turned back to her husband.

'So,' she said, smiling grimly. 'Still they defy you?'

The duke shrugged. 'How should I fight magic?' he said.

'With words,' said the Fool, without thinking, and was instantly sorry. They were both staring at him.

'What?' said the duchess.

The Fool dropped his mandolin in his embarrassment.

'In – in the Guild,' said the Fool, 'we learned that words can be more powerful even than magic.'

'Clown!' said the duke. 'Words are just words. Brief syllables. Sticks and stones may break my bones – ' he paused, savouring the thought – 'but words can never hurt me.'

'My lord, there are such words that can,' said the Fool. 'Liar! Usurper! Murderer!'

The duke jerked back and gripped the arms of the throne, wincing.

'Such words have no truth,' said the Fool, hurriedly. 'But they can spread like fire underground, breaking out to burn – '

'It's true! It's true!' screamed the duke. 'I hear them, all the time!' He leaned forward. 'It's the witches!' he hissed.

'Then, then, then they can be fought with other words,' said the Fool. 'Words can fight even witches.'

'What words?' said the duchess, thoughtfully.

The Fool shrugged. 'Crone. Evil eye. Stupid old woman.'

The duchess raised one thick eyebrow.

'You are not entirely an idiot, are you?' she said. 'You refer to rumour.'

'Just so, my lady.' The Fool rolled his eyes. What had he got himself into?

'It's the witches,' whispered the duke, to no one in particular. 'We must tell the world about the witches. They're evil. They make it come back, the blood. Even sandpaper doesn't work.'

There was another tremor as Granny Weatherwax hurried along the narrow, frozen pathways in the forest. A lump of snow slipped off a tree branch and poured over her hat.

This wasn't right, she knew. Never mind about the – whatever it was – but it was unheard of for a witch to go out on Hogswatchnight. It was against all tradition. No one knew why, but that wasn't the point.

She came out on to the moorland and pounded across the brittle heather, which had been scoured of snow by the wind. There was a crescent moon near the horizon, and its pale glow lit up the mountains that towered over her. It was a different world up there, and one even a witch would rarely venture into; it was a landscape left over from the frosty birth of the world, all green ice and knife-edge ridges and deep, secret valleys. It was a landscape never intended for human beings – not hostile, any more than a brick or a cloud is hostile, but terribly, terribly uncaring.

Except that, this time, it was watching her. A mind quite unlike any other she had ever encountered was giving her a great deal of its attention. She glared up at the icy slopes, half expecting to see a mountainous shadow move against the stars.

'Who are you?' she shouted. 'What do you want?'

Her voice bounced and echoed among the rocks. There was a distant boom of an avalanche, high among the peaks.

On the crest of the moor, where in the summer partridges lurked among the bushes like small whirring idiots, was a standing stone. It stood roughly where the witches' territories met, although the boundaries were never formally marked out.

The stone was about the same height as a tall man, and made of a bluish tinted rock. It was considered intensely magical because, although there was only one of it, *no one had ever been able to count it*; if it saw anyone looking at it speculatively, it shuffled behind them. It was the most self-effacing monolith ever discovered.

It was also one of the numerous discharge points for the magic that accumulated in the Ramtops. The ground around it for several yards was bare of snow, and steamed gently.

The stone began to edge away, and watched her suspiciously from behind a tree.

She waited for ten minutes until Magrat came hurrying up the path from Mad Stoat, a village whose good-natured inhabitants were getting used to ear massage and flower-based homeopathic remedies for everything short of actual decapitation.* She was out of breath, and wore only a shawl over a nightdress that, if Magrat had anything to reveal, would have been very revealing.

'You felt it too?' she said.

Granny nodded. 'Where's Gytha?' she said.

They looked down the path that led to Lancre town, a huddle of lights in the snowy gloom.

☆ ☆ ☆

---

* They worked. Witches' remedies generally did, regardless of the actual form of delivery.

There was a party going on. Light poured out into the street. A line of people were winding in and out of Nanny Ogg's house, from inside which came occasional shrieks of laughter and the sounds of breaking glass and children grizzling. It was clear that family life was being experienced to its limits in that house.

The two witches stood uncertainly in the street.

'Do you think we should go in?' said Magrat diffidently. 'It's not as though we were invited. And we haven't brought a bottle.'

'Sounds to me as if there's a deal too many bottles in there already,' said Granny Weatherwax disapprovingly. A man staggered out of the doorway, burped, bumped into Granny, said, 'Happy Hogswatchnight, missus,' glanced up at her face and sobered up instantly.

'*Mss*,' snapped Granny.

'I am most frightfully sorry – ' he began.

Granny swept imperiously past him. 'Come, Magrat,' she commanded.

The din inside hovered around the pain threshold. Nanny Ogg got around the Hogswatchnight tradition by inviting the whole village in, and the air in the room was already beyond the reach of pollution controls. Granny navigated through the press of bodies by the sound of a cracked voice explaining to the world at large that, compared to an unbelievable variety of other animals, the hedgehog was quite fortunate.

Nanny Ogg was sitting in a chair by the fire with a quart mug in one hand, and was conducting the reprise with a cigar. She grinned when she saw Granny's face.

'What ho, my old boiler,' she screeched above the din. 'See you turned up, then. Have a drink. Have two. Wotcher, Magrat. Pull up a chair and call the cat a bastard.'

Greebo, who was curled up in the inglenook and watching the festivities with one slit yellow eye, flicked his tail once or twice.

Granny sat down stiffly, a ramrod figure of decency.

'We're not staying,' she said, glaring at Magrat, who was tentatively reaching out towards a bowl of peanuts. 'I can see you're busy. We just wondered whether you might have noticed – anything. Tonight. A little while ago.'

Nanny Ogg wrinkled her forehead.

'Our Darron's eldest was sick,' she said. 'Been at his dad's beer.'

'Unless he was *extremely* ill,' said Granny, 'I doubt if it was what I was referring to.' She made a complex occult sign in the air, which Nanny totally ignored.

'Someone tried to dance on the table,' she said. 'Fell into our Reet's pumpkin dip. We had a good laugh.'

Granny waggled her eyebrows and placed a meaningful finger alongside her nose.

'I was alluding to things of a *different* nature,' she hinted darkly.

Nanny Ogg peered at her.

'Something wrong with your eye, Esme?' she hazarded.

Granny Weatherwax sighed.

'Extremely worry developments of a magical tendency are even now afoot,' she said loudly.

The room went quiet. Everyone stared at the witches, except for Darron's eldest, who took advantage of the opportunity to continue his alcoholic experiments. Then, swiftly as they had fled, several dozen conversations hurriedly got back into gear.

'It might be a good idea if we can go and talk somewhere more private,' said Granny, as the comforting hubbub streamed over them again.

They ended up in the washhouse, where Granny tried to give an account of the mind she had encountered.

'It's out there somewhere, in the mountains and the high forests,' she said. 'And it is very big.'

'I thought it was looking for someone,' said Magrat. 'It put me in mind of a large dog. You know, lost. Puzzled.'

Granny thought about this. Now she came to think of it . . .

'Yes,' she said. 'Something like that. A *big* dog.'

'Worried,' said Magrat.

'Searching,' said Granny.

'And getting angry,' said Magrat.

'Yes,' said Granny, staring fixedly at Nanny.

'Could be a troll,' said Nanny Ogg. 'I left the best part of a pint in there, you know,' she added reproachfully.

'I know what a troll's mind feels like, Gytha,' said Granny. She didn't snap the words out. In fact it was the quiet way she said them that made Nanny hesitate.

'They say there's really big trolls up towards the Hub,' said Nanny slowly. 'And ice giants, and big hairy wossnames that live above the snowline. But you don't mean anything like that, do you?'

'No.'

'Oh.'

Magrat shivered. She told herself that a witch had absolute control over her own body, and the goosepimples under her thin nightdress were just a figment of her own imagination. The trouble was, she had an excellent imagination.

Nanny Ogg sighed.

'We'd better have a look, then,' she said, and took the lid off the copper.

Nanny Ogg never used her washhouse, since all her washing was done by the daughters-in-law, a tribe of grey-faced, subdued women whose names she never bothered to remember. It had become, therefore, a storage place for dried-up old bulbs, burnt-out cauldrons and fermenting jars of wasp jam. No fire had been lit under the copper for ten years. Its bricks were crumbling, and rare ferns grew around the firebox. The water under the lid was inky black and, according to rumour, bottomless; the Ogg grandchildren were encouraged to believe that monsters from the dawn of time dwelt in its depths, since Nanny believed that a bit of thrilling and pointless terror was an essential ingredient of the magic of childhood.

In summer she used it as a beer cooler.

'It'll have to do. I think perhaps we should join hands,' she said. 'And you, Magrat, make sure the door's shut.'

'What are you going to try?' said Granny. Since they were on Nanny's territory, the choice was entirely up to her.

'I always say you can't go wrong with a good Invocation,' said Nanny. 'Haven't done one for years.'

Granny Weatherwax frowned. Magrat said, 'Oh, but you can't. Not here. You need a cauldron, and a magic sword. And an octogram. And spices, and all sorts of stuff.'

Granny and Nanny exchanged glances.

'It's not her fault,' said Granny. 'It's all them grimmers she was bought.' She turned to Magrat.

'You don't need none of that,' she said. 'You need headology.' She looked around the ancient washroom.

'You just use whatever you've got,' she said.

She picked up the bleached copper stick, and weighed it thoughtfully in her hand.

'*We conjure and abjure thee by means of this –* ' Granny hardly paused – 'sharp and terrible copper stick.'

The waters in the boiler rippled gently.

'*See how we scatter –* ' Magrat sighed – 'rather old washing soda and some extremely hard soap flakes in thy honour. Really, Nanny, I don't think – '

'Silence! Now you, Gytha.'

'*And I invoke and bind thee* with the balding scrubbing brush of Art and the washboard of Protection,' said Nanny, waving it. The wringer attachment fell off.

'Honesty is all very well,' whispered Magrat, wretchedly, 'but somehow it isn't the same.'

'You listen to me, my girl,' said Granny. 'Demons don't care about the outward shape of things. It's what *you* think that matters. Get on with it.'

Magrat tried to imagine that the bleached and ancient bar of lye soap was the rarest of scented whatever, ungulants or whatever they were, from distant Klatch. It was an effort. The gods alone knew what kind of demon would respond to a summoning like this.

Granny was also a little uneasy. She didn't much care for demons in any case, and all this business with incantations and implements whiffed of wizardry. It was pandering to the things, making them feel important. Demons ought to come when they were called.

But protocol dictated that the host witch had the choice, and Nanny quite liked demons, who were male, or apparently so.

At this point Granny was alternately cajoling and threatening the nether world with two feet of bleached wood. She was impressed at her own daring.

The waters seethed a little, because very still and then, with a sudden movement and a little popping noise, moulded up into a head. Magrat dropped her soap.

It was a good-looking head, maybe a little cruel around the eyes and beaky about the nose, but nevertheless handsome in a hard kind of way. There was nothing surprising about this; since the demon was only extending an image of itself into this reality, it might as well make a good job of it. It turned slowly, a gleaming black statue in the fitful moonlight.

'*Well?*' it said.

'Who're you?' said Granny, bluntly.

The head revolved to face her.

'*My name is unpronounceable in your tongue, woman,*' it said.

'I'll be the judge of that,' warned Granny, and added, 'Don't you call me woman.'

'*Very well. My name is WxrtHltl-jwlpklz,*' said the demon smugly.

'Where were you when the vowels were handed out? Behind the door?' said Nanny Ogg.

'Well, Mr – ' Granny hesitated only fractionally – 'WxrtHltl-jwlpklz, I expect you're wondering why we called you here tonight.'

'*You're not supposed to say that,*' said the demon. '*You're supposed to say – *'

'Shut up. We have the sword of Art and the octogram of Protection, I warn you.'

'*Please yourself. They look like a washboard and a copper stick to me,*' sneered the demon.

Granny glanced sideways. The corner of the washroom was stacked with kindling wood, with a big heavy sawhorse in front of it. She stared fixedly at the demon and, without looking, brought the stick down hard across the thick timber.

The dead silence that followed was broken only by the two perfectly sliced halves of the sawhorse teetering backwards and forwards and folding slowly into the heap of kindling.

The demon's face remained impassive.

'*You are allowed three questions,*' it said.

'Is there something strange at large in the kingdom?' said Granny.

It appeared to think about it.

'And no lying,' said Magrat earnestly. 'Otherwise it'll be the scrubbing brush for you.'

'*You mean stranger than usual?*'

'Get on with it,' said Nanny. 'My feet are freezing out here.'

'*No. There is nothing strange.*'

'But we felt it – ' Magrat began.

'Hold on, hold on,' said Granny. Her lips moved soundlessly. Demons were like genies or philosophy professors – if you didn't word things *exactly* right, they delighted in giving you absolutely accurate and completely misleading answers.

'Is there something in the kingdom that wasn't there before?' she hazarded.

'*No.*'

Tradition said that there could only be three questions. Granny tried to formulate one that couldn't be deliberately misunderstood. Then she decided that this was playing the wrong kind of game.

'What the hell's going on?' she said carefully. 'And no mucking about trying to wriggle out of it, otherwise I'll boil you.'

The demon appeared to hesitate. This was obviously a new approach.

'Magrat, just kick that kindling over here, will you?' said Granny.

'*I protest at this treatment,*' said the demon, its voice tinged with uncertainty.

'Yes, well, we haven't got time to bandy legs with you all night,' said Granny. 'These word games might be all right for wizards, but we've got other fish to fry.'

'Or boil,' said Nanny.

'*Look,*' said the demon, and now there was a whine of terror in its voice. '*We're not supposed to volunteer information just like that. There are rules, you know.*'

'There's some old oil in the can on the shelf, Magrat,' said Nanny.

'*If I simply tell you –* ' the demon began.

'Yes?' said Granny, encouragingly.

'*You won't let on, will you?*' it implored.

'Not a word,' promised Granny.

'Lips are sealed,' said Magrat.

'*There is nothing new in the kingdom,*' said the demon, '*but the land has woken up.*'

'What do you mean?' said Granny.

'*It's unhappy. It wants a king that cares for it.*'

'How – ' Magrat began, but Granny waved her into silence.

'You don't mean people, do you?' she said. The glistening head shook. 'No, I didn't think so.'

'What – ' Nanny began. Granny put a finger to her lips.

She turned and walked to the washhouse's window, a dusty spiderweb graveyard of faded butterfly wings and last summer's bluebottles. A faint glow beyond the frosted panes suggested that, against all reason, a new day would soon dawn.

'Can you tell us why?' she said, without turning round. She'd felt the mind of a whole country . . .

She was rather impressed.

'*I'm just a demon. What do I know? Only what is, not the why and how of it.*'

'I see.'

'*May I go now?*'

'Um?'

'*Please?*'

Granny jerked upright again.

'Oh. Yes. Run along,' she said distractedly. 'Thank you.'

The head didn't move. It hung around, like a hotel porter who has just carried fifteen suitcases up ten flights of stairs, shown everyone where the bathroom is, plumped up the pillows, and feels he has adjusted all the curtains he is going to adjust.

'*You wouldn't mind banishing me, would you?*' said the demon, when no one seemed to be taking the hint.

'What?' said Granny, who was thinking again.

'*Only I'd feel better for being properly banished. "Run along" lacks that certain something,*' said the head.

'Oh. Well, if it gives you any pleasure. Magrat!'

'Yes?' said Magrat, startled.

Granny tossed the copper stick to her.

'Do the honours, will you?' she said.

Magrat caught the stick by what she hoped Granny was imagining as the handle, and smiled.

'Certainly. Right. Okay. Um. Begone, foul fiend, unto the blackest pit – '

The head smiled contentedly as the words rolled over it. This was more like it.

It melted back into the waters of the copper like candlewax under a flame. Its last contemptuous comment, almost lost in the swirl, was '*Run aaaalonggg . . .*'

Granny went home alone as the cold pink light of dawn glided across the snow, and let herself into her cottage.

The goats were uneasy in their outhouse. The starlings muttered and rattled their false teeth under the roof. The mice were squeaking behind the kitchen dresser.

She made a pot of tea, conscious that every sound in the kitchen seemed slightly louder than it ought to be. When she dropped the spoon into the sink it sounded like a bell being hit with a hammer.

She always felt uncomfortable after getting involved in organised magic or, as she would put it, out of sorts with herself. She found herself wandering around the place looking for things to do, and then forgetting them when they were half-complete. She paced back and forth across the cold flagstones.

It is at times like this that the mind finds the oddest jobs to do in order to avoid its primary purpose, i.e., thinking about things. If anyone had been watching they would have been amazed at the sheer dedication with which Granny tackled such tasks as cleaning the teapot stand, rooting ancient nuts out of the fruit bowl on the dresser, and levering fossilised bread crusts out of the cracks in the flagstones with the back of a teaspoon.

Animals had minds. People had minds, although human minds were vague foggy things. Even insects had minds, little pointy bits of light in the darkness of non-mind.

Granny considered herself something of an expert on minds. She was pretty certain things like countries didn't have minds.

They weren't even *alive*, for goodness sake. A country was, well, was –

Hold on. Hold on . . . A thought stole gently into Granny's mind and sheepishly tried to attract her attention.

There was a way in which those brooding forests could have a mind. Granny sat up, a piece of antique loaf in her hand, and gazed speculatively at the fireplace. Her mind's eye looked through it, out at the snow-filled aisles of trees. Yes. It had never occurred to her before. Of course, it'd be a mind made up of all the other little minds inside it; plant minds, bird minds, bear minds, even the great slow minds of the trees themselves . . .

She sat down in her rocking chair, which started to rock all by itself.

She'd often thought of the forest as a sprawling creature, but only metterforically, as a wizard would put it; drowsy and purring with bumblebees in the summer, roaring and raging in autumn gales, curled in on itself and sleeping in the winter. It occurred to her that in addition to being a collection of other things, the forest was a thing in itself. Alive, only not alive in the way that, say, a shrew was alive.

And *much slower*.

That would have to be important. How fast did a forest's heart beat? Once a year, maybe. Yes, that sounded about right. Out there the forest was waiting for the brighter sun and longer days that would pump a million gallons of sap several hundred feet into the sky in one great systolic thump too big and loud to be heard.

And it was at about this point that Granny bit her lip.

She'd just thought the word 'systolic', and it certainly wasn't in her vocabulary.

Somebody was inside her head with her.

Some thing.

Had she just thought all those thoughts, or had they been thought *through* her?

She glared at the floor, trying to keep her ideas to herself. But her mind was being watched as easily as if her head was made of glass.

Granny Weatherwax got to her feet and opened the curtains.

And they were out there on what – in warmer months – was the lawn. And every single one of them was staring at her.

After a few minutes Granny's front door opened. This was an event in its own right; like most Ramtoppers Granny lived her life via the back door. There were only three times in your life when it was proper to come through the front door, and you were carried every time.

It opened with considerable difficulty, in a series of painful jerks and thumps. A few flakes of paint fell on to the snowdrift in front of the door, which sagged inward. Finally, when it was about halfway open, the door wedged.

Granny sidled awkwardly through the gap and out on to the hitherto undisturbed snow.

She had put her pointed hat on, and the long black cloak which she wore when she wanted anyone who saw her to be absolutely clear that she was a witch.

There was an elderly kitchen chair half buried in snow. In summer it was a handy place to sit and do whatever hand chores were necessary, while keeping one eye on the track. Granny hauled it out, brushed the snow off the seat, and sat down firmly with her knees apart and her arms folded defiantly. She stuck out her chin.

The sun was well up but the light on this Hogswatchday was still pink and slanting. It glowed on the great cloud of steam that hung over the assembled creatures. They hadn't moved, although every now and again one of them would stamp a hoof or scratch itself.

Granny looked up at a flicker of movement. She hadn't noticed before, but every tree around her garden was so heavy with birds that it looked as though a strange brown and black spring had come early.

Occupying the patch where the herbs grew in summer were the wolves, sitting or lolling with their tongues hanging out. A contingent of bears was crouched behind them, with a platoon of deer beside them. Occupying the metterforical stalls was a rabble of rabbits, weasels, vermine, badgers, foxes and miscellaneous creatures who, despite the fact that they live their entire lives in a bloody atmosphere of hunter and hunted, killing or being killed by claw, talon and tooth, are generally referred to as woodland folk.

They rested together on the snow, their normal culinary relationships entirely forgotten, trying to outstare her.

Two things were immediately apparent to Granny. One was that this seemed to represent a pretty accurate cross-section of the forest life.

The other she couldn't help saying aloud.

'I don't know what this spell is,' she said. 'But I'll tell you this for nothing – when it wears off, some of you little buggers had better get moving.'

None of them stirred. There was no sound except for an elderly badger relieving itself with an embarrassed expression.

'Look,' said Granny. 'What can I do about it? It's not good you coming to me. He's the new lord. This is his kingdom. I can't go meddling. It's not *right* to go meddling, on account of I can't interfere with people ruling. It has to sort itself out, good or bad. Fundamental rule of magic, is that. You can't go round ruling people with spells, because you'd have to use more and more spells all the time.' She sat back, grateful that long-standing tradition didn't allow the Crafty and the Wise to rule. She remembered what it had felt like to wear the crown, even for a few seconds.

No, things like crowns had a troublesome effect on clever folk; it was best to leave all the reigning to the kind of people whose eyebrows met in the middle when they tried to think. In a funny sort of way, they were much better at it.

She added, 'People have to sort it out for themselves. Well-known fact.'

She felt that one of the larger stags was giving her a particularly doubting look.

'Yes, well, so he killed the old king,' she conceded. 'That's nature's way, ain't it? Your lot know all about this. Survival of the wossname. You wouldn't know what an heir was, unless you thought it was a sort of rabbit.'

She drummed her fingers on her knees.

'Anyway, the old king wasn't much of a friend to you, was he? All that hunting, and such.'

Three hundred pairs of dark eyes bored in at her.

'It's no good you all looking at me,' she tried. 'I can't go around mucking about with kings just because you don't like them. Where would it all end? It's not as if he's done me any harm.'

She tried to avoid the gaze of a particularly cross-eyed stoat.

'All right, so it's selfish,' she said. 'That's what bein' a witch is all about. Good day to you.'

She stamped inside, and tried to slam the door. It stuck once or twice, which rather spoiled the effect.

Once inside she drew the curtains and sat down in the rocking chair and rocked fiercely.

'That's the whole point,' she said. 'I can't go around meddling. That's the whole point.'

The lattys lurched slowly over the rutted roads, towards yet another little city whose name the company couldn't quite remember and would instantly forget. The winter sun hung low over the damp, misty cabbage fields of the Sto Plains, and the foggy silence magnified the creaking of the wheels.

Hwel sat with his stubby legs dangling over the backboard of the last latty.

He'd done his best. Vitoller had left the education of Tomjon in his hands; 'You're better at all that business,' he'd said, adding with his usual tact, 'Besides, you're more his height.'

But it wasn't working.

'Apple,' he repeated, waving the fruit in the air.

Tomjon grinned at him. He was nearly three years old, and hadn't said a word anyone could understand. Hwel was harbouring dark suspicions about the witches.

'But he seems bright enough,' said Mrs Vitoller, who was travelling inside the latty and darning the chain mail. 'He knows what things are. He does what he's told. I just wish you'd speak,' she said softly, patting the boy on the cheek.

Hwel gave the apple to Tomjon, who accepted it gravely.

'I reckon them witches did you a bad turn, missus,' said the dwarf. 'You know. Changelings and whatnot. There used to be a lot of that sort of thing. My great-great-grandmother said it was done to us, once. The fairies swapped a human and a dwarf. We never realised until he started banging his head on things, they say – '

> 'They say this fruit be like unto the world
> So sweet. Or like, say I, the heart of man
> So red without and yet within, unclue'd,
> We find the worm, the rot, the flaw.
> However glows his bloom the bite
> Proves many a man be rotten at the core.'

The two of them swivelled around to stare at Tomjon, who nodded to them and proceeded to eat the apple.

'That was the Worm speech from *The Tyrant*,' whispered Hwel. His normal grasp of the language temporarily deserted him. 'Bloody hell,' he said.

'But he sounded just like – '

'I'm going to get Vitoller,' said Hwel, and dropped off the tailboard and ran through the frozen puddles to the front of the convoy, where the actor-manager was whistling tunelessly and, yes, strolling.

'What ho, *b'zugda-hiara**,*' he said cheerfully.

'You've got to come at once! He's talking!'

'Talking?'

Hwel jumped up and down. 'He's *quoting*!' he shouted. 'You've got to come! He sounds just like – '

'Me?' said Vitoller, a few minutes later, after they had pulled the lattys into a grove of leafless trees by the roadside. 'Do I sound like that?'

'Yes,' chorused the company.

Young Willikins, who specialised in female roles, prodded Tomjon gently as he stood on an upturned barrel in the middle of the clearing.

'Here, boy, do you know my speech from *Please Yourself*?' he said.

Tomjon nodded. ' "He is not dead, I say, who lies beneath the stone. For if Death could but hear – " '

They listened in awed silence as the endless mists rolled across the dripping fields and the red ball of the sun floated down the sky. When the boy had finished hot tears were streaming down Hwel's face.

'By all the gods,' he said, when Tomjon had finished, 'I must have been on damn good form when I wrote that.' He blew his nose noisily.

---

* A killing insult in Dwarfish, but here used as a term of endearment. It means 'lawn ornament'.

'Do I sound like that?' said Willikins, his face pale.

Vitoller patted him gently on the shoulder.

'If you sounded like that, my bonny,' he said, 'you wouldn't be standing arse-deep in slush in the middle of these forsaken fields, with nothing but liberated cabbage for thy tea.'

He clapped his hands.

'No more, no more,' he said, his breath making puffs of steam in the freezing air. 'Backs to it, everybody. We must be outside the walls of Sto Lat by sunset.'

As the grumbling actors awoke from the spell and wandered back to the shafts of the lattys Vitoller beckoned to the dwarf and put his arm around his shoulders, or rather around the top of his head.

'Well?' he said. 'You people know all about magic, or so it is said. What do you make of it?'

'He spends all his time around the stage, master. It's only natural that he should pick things up,' said Hwel vaguely.

Vitoller leaned down.

'Do you believe that?'

'I believe I heard a voice that took my doggerel and shaped it and fired it back through my ears and straight into my heart,' said Hwel simply. 'I believe I heard a voice that got behind the crude shape of the words and said the things I had meant them to say, but had not the skill to achieve. Who knows where such things come from?'

He stared impassively into Vitoller's red face. 'He may have inherited it from his father,' he said.

'But – '

'And who knows what witches may achieve?' said the dwarf.

Vitoller felt his wife's hand pushed into his. As he stood up, bewildered and angry, she kissed him on the back of the neck.

'Don't torture yourself,' she said. 'Isn't it all for the best? Your son has declaimed his first word.

Spring came, and ex-King Verence still wasn't taking being dead lying down. He prowled the castle relentlessly, seeking for a way in which its ancient stones would release their grip on him.

He was also trying to keep out of the way of the other ghosts.

Champot was all right, if a bit tiresome. But Verence had backed away at the first sight of the Twins, toddling hand in hand along the midnight corridors, their tiny ghosts a memorial to a deed darker even than the usual run of regicidal unpleasantness.

And then there was the Troglodyte Wanderer, a rather faded monkeyman in a furry loincloth who apparently happened to haunt the castle merely because it had been built on his burial mound. For no obvious reason a chariot with a screaming woman in it occasionally rumbled through the laundry room. As for the kitchen . . .

One day he'd given in, despite everything old Champot had said, and had followed the smells of cooking into the big, hot, high domed cavern that served the castle as kitchen and abattoir. Funny thing, that. He'd never been down there since his childhood. Somehow kings and kitchens didn't go well together.

It was *full* of ghosts.

But they weren't human. They weren't even proto-human.

They were stags. They were bullocks. They were rabbits, and pheasants, and partridges, and sheep, and pigs. There were even some round blobby things that looked unpleasantly like the ghosts of oysters. They were packed so tightly that in fact they emerged and mingled, turning the kitchen into a silent, jostling nightmare of teeth and fur and horns, half-seen and misty. Several noticed him, and there was a weird blarting of noises that sounded far-off, tinny and unpleasantly out of register. Through them all the cook and his assistants wandered quite unconcernedly, making vegetarian sausages.

Verence had stared for half a minute and then fled, wishing that he still had a real stomach so that he could stick his fingers down his throat for forty years and bring up everything he'd eaten.

He'd sought solace in the stables, where his beloved hunting dogs had whined and scratched at the door and had generally been very ill-at-ease at his sensed but unseen presence.

Now he haunted – and how he hated the word – the Long Gallery, where paintings of long-dead kings looked down at him from the dusty shadows. He would have felt a lot more kindly towards them if he hadn't met a number of them gibbering in various parts of the premises.

Verence had decided that he had two aims in death. One was to get out of the castle and find his son, and the other was to get his revenge on the duke. But not by killing him, he'd decided, even if he could find a way, because an eternity in that giggling idiot's company would lend a new terror to death.

He sat under a painting of Queen Bemery (670–722), whose rather stern good looks he would have felt a whole lot happier about if he hadn't seen her earlier that morning walking through the wall.

Verence tried to avoid walking through walls. A man had his dignity.

He became aware that he was being watched.

He turned his head.

There was a cat sitting in the doorway, subjecting him to a slow blink. It was a mottled grey and extremely fat . . .

No. It was extremely *big*. It was covered with so much scar tissue that it looked like a fist with fur on it. Its ears were a couple of perforated stubs, its one eye a yellow slit of easy-going malevolence, its tail a twitching series of question marks as it stared at him.

Greebo had heard that Lady Felmet had a small white female cat and had strolled up to pay his respects.

Verence had never seen an animal with so much built-in villainy. He didn't resist as it waddled across the floor and tried to rub itself against his legs, purring like a waterfall.

'Well, well,' said the king, vaguely. He reached down and made an effort to scratch it behind the two ragged bits on top of its head. It was a relief to find someone else besides another ghost who could see him, and Greebo, he couldn't help feeling, was a distinctly unusual cat. Most of the castle cats were either pampered pets or flat-eared kitchen and stable habitués who generally resembled the very rodents they lived on. This cat, on the other hand, was its own animal. All cats give that impression, of course, but instead of the mindless animal self-absorption that passes for secret wisdom in the creatures, Greebo radiated genuine intelligence. He also radiated a smell that would have knocked over a wall and caused sinus trouble in a dead fox.

Only one type of person kept a cat like this.

The king tried to hunker down, and found he was sinking slightly into the floor. He pulled himself together and drifted upwards. Once a man allowed himself to go native in the ethereal world there would be no hope for him, he felt.

Only close relatives and the psychically inclined, Death had said. There weren't many of either in the castle. The duke qualified under the first heading, but his relentless self-interest made him about as psychically useful as a carrot. As for the rest, only the cook and the Fool seemed to qualify, but the cook spent a lot of his time weeping in the pantry because he wasn't being allowed to roast anything more bloody than a parsnip and the Fool was already such a bundle of nerves that Verence had given up his attempts to get through.

A witch, now. If a witch wasn't psychically inclined, then he, King Verence, was a puff of wind. He had to get a witch into the castle. And then . . .

He'd got a plan. In fact, it was more than that; it was a Plan. He spent months over it. He hadn't got anything else to do, except think. Death had been right about that. All that ghosts had were thoughts, and although thoughts in general had always been alien to the king the absence of anybody to distract him with its assorted humours had actually given him the chance to savour the joys of cerebration. He'd never had a Plan before, or at least one that went much further than 'Let's find something and kill it'. And here, sitting in front of him washing itself, was the key.

'Here, pussy,' he ventured. Greebo gave him a penetrating yellow stare.

'Cat,' the king amended hastily, and backed away, beckoning. For a moment it seemed that the cat wouldn't follow and then, to his relief, Greebo stood up, yawned, and padded towards him. Greebo didn't often see ghosts, and was vaguely interested in this tall, bearded man with the see-through body.

The king led him along a dusty side corridor and towards a lumber room crammed with crumbling tapestries and portraits of long-dead kings. Greebo examined it critically, and then sat down in the middle of the dusty floor, looking at the king expectantly.

'There's plenty of mice and things in here, d'you see,' said Verence. 'And the rain blows in through the broken window. Plus there's all these tapestries to sleep on.'

'Sorry,' the king added, and turned to the door.

This was what he had been working on all these months. When he was alive he had always taken a lot of care of his body, and since being dead he had taken care to preserve its shape. It was too easy to let yourself go and become all fuzzy around the edges; there were ghosts in the castle who were mere pale blobs. But Verence had wielded iron self-control and exercised – well, had thought hard about exercise – and fairly bulged with spectral muscles. Months of pumping ectoplasm had left him in better shape than he had ever been, apart from being dead.

Then he'd started out small, with dust motes. The first one had nearly killed him*, but he'd persevered and progressed to sand grains, then whole dried peas; he still didn't dare venture into the kitchens, but he had amused himself by oversalting Felmet's food a pinch at a time until he pulled himself together and told himself that poisoning wasn't honourable, even against vermin.

Now he leaned all his weight on the door, and with every microgramme of his being forced himself to become as heavy as possible. The sweat of auto-suggestion dripped off his nose and vanished before it hit the floor. Greebo watched with interest as ghostly muscles moved on the king's arms like footballs mating.

The door began to move, creaked, then accelerated and hit the doorway with a thump. The latch clicked into place.

* In a manner of speaking.

It bloody well had to work now, Verence told himself. He'd never be able to lift the latch by himself. But a witch would certainly come looking for her cat – wouldn't she?

In the hills beyond the castle the Fool lay on his stomach and stared into the depths of a little lake. A couple of trout stared back at him.

Somewhere on the Disc, reason told him, there must be someone more miserable than he was. He wondered who it was.

He hadn't asked to be a Fool, but it wouldn't have mattered if he had, because he couldn't recall anyone in his family ever listening to anything he said after Dad ran away.

Certainly not Grandad. His earliest memory was of Grandad standing over him making him repeat the jokes by rote, and hammering home every punchline with his belt; it was thick leather, and the fact that it had bells on didn't improve things much.

Grandad was credited with seven official new jokes. He'd won the honorary cap and bells of the Grand Prix des Idiots Blithering at Ankh-Morpork four years in a row, which no one else had ever done, and presumably that made him the funniest man who ever lived. He had worked hard at it, you had to give him that.

The Fool recalled with a shudder how, at the age of six, he'd timidly approached the old man after supper with a joke he'd made up. It was about a duck.

It had earned him the biggest thrashing of his life, which even then must have presented the old joker with a bit of a challenge.

'You will learn, my lad – ' he recalled, with every sentence punctuated by jingling cracks – 'that there is nothing more serious than jesting. From now on you will never – ' the old man paused to change hands – 'never, never, ever utter a joke that has not been approved by the Guild. Who are you to decide what is amusing? Marry, let the untutored giggle at unskilled banter; it is the laughter of the ignorant. Never. Never. Never let me catch you joculating again.'

After that he'd gone back to learning the three hundred and eighty-three Guild-approved jokes, which was bad enough, and the glossary, which was a lot bigger and much worse.

And then he'd been sent to Ankh, and there, in the bare, severe rooms, he'd found there were books other than the great heavy brass-bound *Monster Fun Book*. There was a whole circular world out there, full of weird places and people doing interesting things, like . . .

Singing. He could hear singing.

He raised his head cautiously, and jumped at the tinkle of the bells on his cap. He gripped the hated things hurriedly.

The singing went on. The Fool peeped cautiously through the drift of meadowsweet that was providing him with perfect concealment.

The singing wasn't particularly good. The only word the singer appeared to know was 'la', but she was making it work hard. The general tune gave the impression that the singer believed that people were supposed to sing 'lalala' in certain circumstances, and was determined to do what the world expected of her.

The Fool risked raising his head a little further, and saw Magrat for the first time.

She had stopped dancing rather self-consciously through the narrow meadow and was trying to plait some daisies in her hair, without much success.

The Fool held his breath. On long nights on the hard flagstones he had dreamed of women like her. Although, if he really thought about it, not much like her; they were better endowed around the chest, their noses weren't so red and pointed, and their hair tended to flow more. But the Fool's libido was bright enough to tell the difference between the impossible and the conceivably attainable, and hurriedly cut in some filter circuits.

Magrat was picking flowers and talking to them. The Fool strained to hear.

'Here's Woolly Fellwort,' she said. 'And Treacle Wormseed, which is for inflammation of the ears . . .'

Even Nanny Ogg, who took a fairly cheerful view of the world, would have been hard put to say anything complimentary about Magrat's voice. But it fell on the Fool's ears like blossom.

'. . . and Five-leaved False Mandrake, sovereign against fluxes of the bladder. Ah, and here's Old Man's Frogbit. That's for constipation.'

The Fool stood up sheepishly, in a carillon of jingles. To Magrat it was as if the meadow, hitherto supporting nothing more hazardous than clouds of pale blue butterflies and a few self-employed bumblebees, had sprouted a large red-and-yellow demon.

It was opening and shutting its mouth. It had three menacing horns.

An urgent voice at the back of her mind said: You should run away now, like a timid gazelle; this is the accepted action in these circumstances.

Common sense intervened. In her most optimistic moments Magrat would not have compared herself to a gazelle, timid or otherwise. Besides, it added, the basic snag about running away like a timid gazelle was that in all probability she would easily outdistance him.

'Er,' said the apparition.

Uncommon sense, which, despite Granny Weatherwax's general belief that Magrat was several sticks short of a bundle, she still had in sufficiency, pointed out that few demons tinkled pathetically and appeared to be quite so breathless.

'Hallo,' she said.

The Fool's mind was also working hard. He was beginning to panic.

Magrat shunned the traditional pointed hat, as worn by the older witches, but she still held to one of the most fundamental rules of witchcraft. It's not much use being a witch unless you look like one. In her case this meant lots of silver jewellery with octograms, bats, spiders, dragons and other symbols of everyday mysticism; Magrat would have painted her fingernails black, except that she didn't think she would be able to face Granny's withering scorn.

It was dawning on the Fool that he had surprised a witch.

'Whoops,' he said, and turned to run for it.

'Don't – ' Magrat began, but the Fool was already pounding down the forest path that led back to the castle.

Magrat stood and stared at the wilting posy in her hands. She ran her fingers through her hair and a shower of wilted petals fell out.

She felt that an important moment had been allowed to slip out of her grasp as fast as a greased pig in a narrow passageway.

She felt an overpowering urge to curse. She knew a great many curses. Goodie Whemper had been really imaginative in that department; even the creatures of the forest used to go past her cottage at a dead run.

She couldn't find a single one that fully expressed her feelings.

'Oh, bugger,' she said.

It was a full moon again that night, and most unusually all three witches arrived at the standing stone early; it was so embarrassed by this that it went and hid in some gorse bushes.

'Greebo hasn't been home for two days,' said Nanny Ogg, as soon as she arrived. 'It's not like him. I can't find him anywhere.'

'Cats can look after themselves,' said Granny Weatherwax. 'Countries can't. I have intelligence to report. Light the fire, Magrat.'

'Mmm?'

'I said, light the fire, Magrat.'

'Mmm? Oh. Yes.'

The two old women watched her drift vaguely across the moorland, tugging absently at dried-up whin clumps. Magrat seemed to have her mind on something.

'Doesn't seem to be her normal self,' said Nanny Ogg.

'Yes. Could be an improvement,' said Granny shortly, and sat down on a rock. 'She should of got it lit before we arrived. It's her job.'

'She means well,' said Nanny Ogg, studying Magrat's back reflectively.

'I used to mean well when I was a girl, but that didn't stop the sharp end of Goodie Filter's tongue. Youngest witch serves her time, you know how it is. We had it tougher, too. Look at her. Doesn't even wear the pointy hat. How's anyone going to *know*?'

'You got something on *your* mind, Esme?' said Nanny.

Granny nodded gloomily.

'Had a visit yesterday,' she said.

'Me too.'

Despite her worries, Granny was slightly annoyed at this. 'Who from?' she said.

'The mayor of Lancre and a bunch of burghers. They're not happy about the king. They want a king they can trust.'

'I wouldn't trust any king a burgher could trust,' said Granny.

'Yes, but it's not good for anyone, all this taxing and killing folk. That new sergeant they've got is a keen man when it comes to setting fire to cottages, too. Old Verence used to do it too, mind, but . . . well . . .'

'I know, I know. It was more personal,' said Granny. 'You felt he *meant* it. People like to feel they're valued.'

'This Felmet hates the kingdom,' Nanny went on. 'They all say it. They say when they go to talk to him he just stares at them and giggles and rubs his hand and twitches a bit.'

Granny scratched her chin. 'The old king used to shout at them and kick them out of the castle, mind. He used to say he didn't have no time for shopkeepers and such,' she added, with a note of personal approval.

'But he was always very gracious about it,' said Nanny Ogg. 'And he – '

'The kingdom is worried,' said Granny.

'Yes, I already said.'

'I didn't mean the people, I meant the kingdom.'

Granny explained. Nanny interrupted a few times with brief questions. It didn't occur to her to doubt anything she heard. Granny Weatherwax never made things up.

At the end of it she said, 'Well.'

'My feelings exactly.'

'Fancy that.'

'Quite so.'

'And what did the animals do then?'

'Went away. *It* had brought them there, it let them go.'

'No one et anyone else?'

'Not where I saw.'

'Funny thing.'

'Right enough.'

Nanny Ogg stared at the setting sun.

'I don't reckon a lot of kingdoms do that sort of thing,' she said. 'You saw the theatre. Kings and such are killing one another the whole time. Their kingdoms just make the best of it. How come this one takes offence all of a sudden?'

'It's been here a long time,' said Granny.

'So's everywhere,' said Nanny, and added, with the air of a lifetime student. 'Everywhere's been where it is ever since it was first put there. It's called geography.'

'That's just about land,' said Granny. 'It's not the same as a kingdom. A kingdom is made up of all sorts of things. Ideas. Loyalties. Memories. It all sort of exists together. And then all these things create some kind of life. Not a body kind of life, more like a living idea. Made up of everything that's alive and what they're thinking. And what the people *before* them thought.'

Magrat reappeared and began to lay the fire with the air of one in a trance.

'I can see you've been thinking about this a lot,' said Nanny, speaking very slowly and carefully. 'And this kingdom wants a better king, is that it?'

'No! That is yes. Look – ' she leaned forward – 'it doesn't have the same kind of likes and dislikes as people, right?'

Nanny Ogg leaned back. 'Well, it wouldn't, would it,' she ventured.

'It doesn't care if people are good or bad. I don't think it could even *tell*, any more than you could tell if an ant was a good ant. But it expects the king to care for it.'

'Yes, but,' said Nanny wretchedly. She was becoming a bit afraid of the gleam in Granny's eye. 'Lots of people have killed each other to become king of Lancre. They've done all kinds of murder.'

'Don't matter! Don't matter!' said Granny, waving her arms. She started counting on her fingers. 'For why,' she said. 'One, kings go round killing each other because it's all part of destiny and such and doesn't count as murder, and two, they killed for the kingdom. That's the important bit. But this new man just wants the power. He hates the kingdom.'

'It's a bit like a dog, really,' said Magrat. Granny looked at her with her mouth open to frame some suitable retort, and then her face softened.

'Very much like,' she said. 'A dog doesn't care if its master's good or bad, just so long as it likes the dog.'

'Well, then,' said Nanny. 'No one and nothing likes Felmet. What are we going to do about it?'

'Nothing. You know we can't meddle.'

'You saved that baby,' said Nanny.

'That's not meddling!'

'Have it your own way,' said Nanny. 'But maybe one day he'll come back. Destiny again. And you said we should hide the crown. It'll all come back, mark my words. Hurry up with that tea, Magrat.'

'What are you going to do about the burghers?' said Granny.

'I told them they'll have to sort it out themselves. Once we use magic, I said, it'd never stop. You know that.'

'Right,' said Granny, but there was a hint of wistfulness in her voice.

'I'll tell you this, though,' said Nanny. 'They didn't like it much. They was muttering when they left.'

Magrat blurted out. 'You know the Fool, who lives up at the castle?'

'Little man with runny eyes?' said Nanny, relieved that the conversation had returned to more normal matters.

'Not that little,' said Magrat. 'What's his name, do you happen to know?'

'He's just called Fool,' said Granny. 'No job for a man, that. Running around with bells on.'

'His mother was a Beldame, from over Blackglass way,' said Nanny Ogg, whose knowledge of the genealogy of Lancre was legendary. 'Bit of a beauty when she was younger. Broke many a heart, she did. Bit of a scandal there, I did hear. Granny's right, though. At the end of the day, a Fool's a Fool.'

'Why d'you want to know, Magrat?' said Granny Weatherwax.

'Oh . . . one of the girls in the village was asking me,' said Magrat, crimson to the ears.

Nanny cleared her throat, and grinned at Granny Weatherwax, who sniffed aloofly.

'It's a steady job,' said Nanny. 'I'll grant you that.'

'Huh,' said Granny. 'A man who tinkles all day. No kind of a husband for anyone, I'd say.'

'You – she'd always know where he was,' said Nanny, who was enjoying this. 'You'd just have to listen.'

'Never trust a man with horns on his hat,' said Granny flatly.

Magrat stood up and pulled herself together, giving the impression that some bits had to come quite a long way.

'You're a pair of silly old women,' she said quietly. 'And I'm going home.'

She marched off down the path to her village without another word.

The old witches stared at one another.

'Well!' said Nanny.

'It's all these books they read today,' said Granny. 'It overheats the brain. You haven't been putting ideas in her head, have you?'

'What do you mean?'

'You *know* what I mean.'

Nanny stood up. 'I certainly don't see why a girl should have to be single her whole life just because you think it's the right thing,' she said. 'Anyway, if people didn't have children, where would we be?'

'None of your girls is a witch,' said Granny, also standing up.

'They *could* have been,' said Nanny defensively.

'Yes, if you'd let them work it out for themselves, instead of encouragin' them to throw themselves at men.'

'They're good-lookin'. You can't stand in the way of human nature. You'd know that if you'd ever – '

'If I'd ever what?' said Granny Weatherwax, quietly.

They stared at one another in shocked silence. They could both feel it, the tension creeping into their bodies from the ground itself, the hot, aching feeling that they'd started something they must finish, no matter what.

'I knew you when you were a gel,' said Nanny sullenly. 'Stuck-up, you were.'

'At least I spent most of the time upright,' said Granny. 'Disgustin', that was. Everyone thought so.'

'How would you know?' snapped Nanny.

'You were the talk of the whole village,' said Granny.

'And you were, too! They called you the Ice Maiden. Never knew that, did you?' sneered Nanny.

'I wouldn't sully my lips by sayin' what they called you,' shouted Granny.

'Oh yes?' shrieked Nanny. 'Well, let me tell you, my good woman – '

'Don't you dare talk to me in that tone of voice! I'm not anyone's good woman – '

'*Right!*'

There was another silence while they stared at one another, nose to nose, but this silence was a whole quantum level of animosity higher than the last one; you could have roasted a turkey in the heat of this silence. There was no more shouting. Things had got far too bad for shouting. Now the voices came in low and full of menace.

'I should have known better than to listen to Magrat,' growled Granny. 'This coven business is ridiculous. It attracts entirely the wrong sort of people.'

'I'm very glad we had this little talk,' hissed Nanny Ogg. 'Cleared the air.'

She looked down.

'*And* you're in my territory, madam.'

'*Madam!*'

Thunder rolled in the distance. The permanent Lancre storm, after a trip through the foothills, had drifted back towards the mountains for a one-night stand. The last rays of sunset shone livid through the clouds, and fat drops of water began to thud on the witches' pointed hats.

'I really don't have time for all this,' snapped Granny, trembling. 'I have far more important things to do.'

'And me,' said Nanny.

'Good night to you.'

'And you.'

They turned their backs on one another and strode away into the downpour.

The midnight rain drummed on Magrat's curtained windows as she thumbed her way purposefully through Goodie Whemper's books of what, for want of any better word, could be called natural magic.

The old woman had been a great collector of such things and, most unusually, had written them down; witches didn't normally have much use for literacy. But book after book was filled with tiny, meticulous handwriting detailing the results of patient experiments in applied magic. Goodie Whemper had, in fact, been a research witch.*

Magrat was looking up love spells. Every time she shut her eyes she saw a red-and-yellow figure on the darkness inside. Something had to be done about it.

She shut the book with a snap and looked at her notes. First, she had to find out his name. The old peel-the-apple trick should do that. You just peeled an apple, getting one length of peel, and threw the peel behind you; it'd land in the shape of his name. Millions of girls had tried it and had inevitably been disappointed, unless the loved one was called Scscs. That was because they hadn't used an unripe Sunset Wonder picked three minutes before noon on the first frosty day in the autumn and peeled left-handedly using a silver knife with a blade less than half an inch wide; Goodie had done a lot of experimenting and was quite explicit on the subject. Magrat always kept a few by for emergencies, and this probably was one.

* Someone had to do it. It's all very well calling for eye of newt, but do you mean Common, Spotted or Great Crested? Which eye, anyway? Will tapioca do just as well? If we substitute egg white will the spell a) work b) fail or c) melt the bottom out of the cauldron? Goodie Whemper's curiosity about such things was huge and insatiable†.

† Nearly insatiable. It was probably satiated in her last flight to test whether a broomstick could survive having its bristles pulled out one by one in mid-air. According to the small black raven she had trained as a flight recorder, the answer was almost certainly no.

She took a deep breath, and threw the peel over her shoulder.

She turned slowly.

I'm a witch, she told herself. This is just another spell. There's nothing to be frightened of. Get a grip of yourself, girl. *Woman*.

She looked down, and bit the back of her hand out of nervousness and embarrassment.

'Who'd have thought it?' she said aloud.

It had worked.

She turned back to her notes, her heart fluttering. What was next? Ah, yes – gathering fern seed in a silk handkerchief at dawn. Goodie Whemper's tiny handwriting went on for two pages of detailed botanical instructions which, if carefully followed, resulted in the kind of love potion that had to be kept in a tightly stoppered jar at the bottom of a bucket of iced water.

Magrat pulled open her back door. The thunder had passed, but now the first grey light of the new day was drowned in a steady drizzle. But it still qualified as dawn, and Magrat was determined.

Brambles tugging at her dress, her hair plastered against her head by the rain, she set out into the dripping forest.

The trees shook, even without a breeze.

Nanny Ogg was also out early. She hadn't been able to get any sleep anyway, and besides, she was worried about Greebo. Greebo was one of her few blind spots. While intellectually she would concede that he was indeed a fat, cunning, evil-smelling multiple rapist, she nevertheless instinctively pictured him as the small fluffy kitten he had been decades before. The fact that he had once chased a female wolf up a tree and seriously surprised a she-bear who had been innocently digging for roots didn't stop her worrying that something bad might happen to him. It was generally considered by everyone else in the kingdom that the only thing that might slow Greebo down was a direct meteorite strike.

Now she was using a bit of elementary magic to follow his trail, although anyone with a sense of smell could have managed it. It had led her through the damp streets and to the open gates of the castle.

She gave the guards a nod as she went through. It didn't occur to either of them to stop her because witches, like beekeepers and big gorillas, went where they liked. In any case, an elderly lady banging a bowl with a spoon was probably not the spearhead of an invasion force.

Life as a castle guard in Lancre was extremely boring. One of them, leaning on his spear as Nanny went past, wished there could be some excitement in his job. He will shortly learn the error of his ways. The other guard pulled himself together, and saluted.

'Mornin', Mum.'

'Mornin', our Shawn,' said Nanny, and set off across the inner courtyard.

Like all witches Nanny Ogg had an aversion to front doors. She went around the back and entered the keep via the kitchens. A couple of maids curtsied to her. So did the head housekeeper, whom Nanny Ogg vaguely recognised as a daughter-in-law, although she couldn't remember her name.

And so it was that when Lord Felmet came out of his bedroom he saw, coming along the passage towards him, a witch. There was no doubt about it. From the tip of her pointed hat to her boots, she was a witch. And she was coming for him.

Magrat slid helplessly down a bank. She was soaked to the skin and covered in mud. Somehow, she thought bitterly, when you read these spells you always think of it being a fine sunny morning in late spring. And she had forgotten to check what bloody kind of bloody fern it bloody was.

A tree tipped a load of raindrops on to her. Magrat pushed her sodden hair out of her eyes and sat down heavily on a fallen log, from which grew great clusters of pale and embarrassing fungus.

It had seemed such a lovely idea. She'd had great hopes of the coven. She was sure it wasn't right to be a witch alone, you could get funny ideas. She'd dreamed of wise discussions of natural energies while a huge moon hung in the sky, and then possibly they'd try a few of the old dances described in some of Goodie Whemper's books. Not actually *naked*, or skyclad as it was rather delightfully called, because Magrat had no illusions about the shape of her own body and the older witches seemed solid across the hems, and anyway that wasn't absolutely necessary. The books said that the old-time witches had sometimes danced in their shifts. Magrat had wondered about how you danced in shifts. Perhaps there wasn't room for them all to dance at once, she'd thought.

What she hadn't expected was a couple of crotchety old women who were barely civil at the best of times and simply didn't enter into the spirit of things. Oh, they'd been kind to the baby, in their own way, but she couldn't help feeling that if a witch was kind to someone it was entirely for deeply selfish reasons.

And when they did magic, they made it look as ordinary as housekeeping. They didn't wear any occult jewellery. Magrat was a great believer in occult jewellery.

It was all going wrong. And she was going home.

She stood up, wrapped her damp dress around her, and set off through the misty woods . . .

. . . and heard the running feet. Someone was coming through them at high speed, without caring who heard him, and over the top of the sound of breaking twigs was a curious dull jingling. Magrat sidled behind a dripping holly bush and peered cautiously through the leaves.

It was Shawn, the youngest of Nanny Ogg's sons, and the metal noise was caused by his suit of chain mail, which was several sizes too big for him. Lancre is a poor kingdom, and over the centuries the chain mail of the palace guards has had to be handed down from one generation to another, often on the end of a long stick. This one made him look like a bullet-proof bloodhound.

She stepped out in front of him.

'Is that you, Mss Magrat?' said Shawn, raising the flap of mail that covered his eyes. 'It's mam!'

'What's happened to her?'

'*He's* locked her up! Said she was coming to poison him! And I can't get down to the dungeons to see because there's all new guards! They say she's been put in chains – ' Shawn frowned – 'and that means something horrible's going to happen. You know what she's like when she loses her temper. We'll never hear the last of it, miz.'

'Where were you going?' demanded Magrat.

'To fetch our Jason and our Wane and our Darron and our – '

'Wait a moment.'

'Oh, Mss Magrat, suppose they try to torture her? You know what a tongue she's got on her when she gets angry – '

'I'm thinking,' said Magrat.

'He's put his own bodyguards on the gates and everything – '

'Look, just shut up a minute, will you, Shawn?'

'When our Jason finds out, he's going to give the duke a real seeing-to, miz. He says it's about time someone did.'

Nanny Ogg's Jason was a young man with the build and, Magrat had always thought, the brains of a herd of oxen. Thick-skinned though he was, she doubted whether he could survive a hail of arrows.

'Don't tell him yet,' she said thoughtfully. 'There could be another way . . .'

'I'll go and find Granny Weatherwax, shall I, miz?' said Shawn, hopping from one leg to another. '*She'll* know what to do, she's a witch.'

Magrat stood absolutely still. She had thought she was angry before, but now she was furious. She was wet and cold and hungry and this *person* –

once upon a time, she heard herself thinking, she would have burst into tears at this point.

'Oops,' said Shawn. 'Um. I didn't mean. Whoops. Um . . .' He backed away.

'If you happen to see Granny Weatherwax,' said Magrat slowly, in tones that should have etched her words into glass, 'you can tell her that I will sort it all out. Now go away before I turn you into a frog. You look like one anyway.'

She turned, hitched up her skirts, and ran like hell towards her cottage.

Lord Felmet was one of nature's gloaters. He was good at it.

'Quite comfortable, are we?' he said.

Nanny Ogg considered this. 'Apart from these stocks, you mean?'

'I am impervious to your foul blandishments,' said the duke. 'I scorn your devious wiles. You are to be tortured, I'll have you know.'

This didn't appear to have the required effect. Nanny was staring around the dungeon with the vaguely interested gaze of a sightseer.

'And then you will be burned,' said the duchess.

'Okay,' said Nanny.

'*Okay?*'

'Well, it's bloody freezing down here. What's that big wardrobe thing with the spikes?'

The duke was trembling. 'Aha,' he said. 'Now you realise, eh? That, my dear lady, is an Iron Maiden. It's the latest thing. Well may you – '

'Can I have a go in it?'

'Your pleas fall on deaf . . .' The duke's voice trailed off. His twitch started up.

The duchess leaned forward until her big red face was inches away from Nanny's nose.

'This insouciance gives you pleasure,' she hissed, 'but soon you will laugh on the other side of your face!'

'It's only got this side,' said Nanny.

The duchess fingered a tray of implements lovingly. 'We shall see,' she said, picking up a pair of pliers.

'And you need not think any others of your people will come to your aid,' said the duke, who was sweating despite the chill. 'We alone hold the keys to this dungeon. Ha ha. You will be an example to all those who have been spreading malicious rumours about me. Do not protest your innocence! I hear the voices all the time, lying . . .'

The duchess gripped him ferociously by the arm. 'Enough,' she rasped. 'Come, Leonal. We will let her reflect on her fate for a while.'

'. . . the faces . . . wicked lies . . . I wasn't there, and anyway he fell . . . my porridge, all salty . . .' murmured the duke, swaying.

The door slammed behind them. There was a click of locks and a thudding of bolts.

Nanny was left alone in the gloom. A flickering torch high on the wall only made the surrounding darkness more forbidding. Strange metal shapes, designed for no more exalted purpose than the destruct-testing of the human body, cast unpleasant shadows. Nanny Ogg stirred in her chains.

'All right,' she said. 'I can see you. Who are you?'

King Verence stepped forward.

'I saw you making faces behind him,' said Nanny Ogg. 'All I could do to keep a straight face myself.'

'I wasn't making faces, woman, I was scowling.'

Nanny squinted. ''Ere, I know you,' she said. 'You're dead.'

'I prefer the term "passed over",' said the king.

'I'd bow*,' said Nanny. 'Only there's all these chains and things. You haven't seen a cat around here, have you?'

'Yes. He's in a room upstairs, asleep.'

Nanny appeared to relax. 'That's all right, then,' she said. 'I was beginning to worry.' She stared around the dungeon again. 'What's that big bed thing over there?'

'The rack,' said the king, and explained its use. Nanny Ogg nodded.

'What a busy little mind he's got,' she said.

'I fear, madam, that I may be responsible for your present predicament,' said Verence, sitting down on or at least just above a handy anvil. 'I wished to attract a witch.'

'I suppose you're no good at locks?'

'I fear they would be beyond my capabilities as yet . . . but surely – ' the ghost of the king waved a hand in a vague gesture which encompassed the dungeon, Nanny and her manacles – 'to a witch all this is just so much – '

'Solid iron,' said Nanny. 'You might be able to walk through it, but I can't.'

'I didn't realise,' said Verence. 'I thought witches could do magic.'

'Young man,' said Nanny, 'you will oblige me by shutting up.'

'Madam! I am a king!'

'You are also dead, so I wouldn't aspire to hold any opinions if I was you. Now just be quiet and wait, like a good boy.'

---

* Witches never curtsey.

Against all his instincts, the king found himself obeying. There was no gainsaying that tone of voice. It spoke to him across the years, from his days in the nursery. Its echoes told him that if he didn't eat it all up he would be sent straight to bed.

Nanny Ogg stirred in her chains. She hoped they would turn up soon.

'Er,' said the king uneasily. 'I feel I owe you an explanation . . .'

'Thank you,' said Granny Weatherwax, and because Shawn seemed to be expecting it, added, 'You've been a good boy.'

'Yes'm,' said Shawn. 'M'm?'

'Was there something else?'

Shawn twisted the end of his chain-mail vest out of embarrassment. 'It's not true what everyone's been saying about our mam, is it, m'm,' he said. 'She doesn't go round putting evil curses on folk. Except for Daviss the butcher. And old Cakebreak, after he kicked her cat. But they wasn't what you'd call real curses, was they, m'm?'

'You can stop calling me m'm.'

'Yes, m'm.'

'They've been saying that, have they?'

'Yes, m'm.'

'Well, your mam does upset people sometimes.'

Shawn hopped from one leg to another.

'Yes, m'm, but they says terrible things about you, m'm, savin' your presence, m'm.'

Granny stiffened.

'What things?'

'Don't like to say, m'm.'

'*What things?*'

Shawn considered his next move. There weren't many choices.

'A lot of things what aren't true, m'm,' he said, establishing his credentials as early as possible. 'All sorts of things. Like, old Verence was a bad king and you helped him on the throne, and you caused that bad winter the other year, and old Norbut's cow dint give no milk after you looked at it. Lot of lies, m'm,' he added, loyally.

'Right,' said Granny.

She shut the door in his panting face, stood in thought for a moment, and retired to her rocking chair.

Eventually she said, once more, 'Right.'

A little later she added, 'She's a daft old besom, but we can't have people going round doing things to witches. Once you've lost your respect, you ain't got a thing. I don't remember looking at old Norbut's cow. Who's old Norbut?'

She stood up, took her pointed hat from its hook behind the door and, glaring into the mirror, skewered it in place with a number of ferocious hatpins. They slid on one by one by one, as unstoppable as the wrath of God.

She vanished into the outhouse for a moment and came back with her witch's cloak, which served as a blanket for sick goats when not otherwise employed.

Once upon a time it had been black velvet; now it was just black. It was carefully and slowly fastened by a tarnished silver brooch.

No samurai, no questing knight, was ever dressed with as much ceremony.

Finally Granny drew herself up, surveyed her dark reflection in the glass, gave a thin little smile of approval, and left via the back door.

The air of menace was only slightly dispelled by the sound of her running up and down outside, trying to get her broomstick started.

Magrat was also regarding herself in the mirror.

She'd dug out a startlingly green dress that was designed to be both revealing and clinging, and would have been if Magrat had anything to display or cling to, so she'd shoved a couple of rolled-up stockings down the front in an effort to make good the more obvious deficiencies. She had also tried a spell on her hair, but it was naturally magic-resistant and already the natural shape was beginning to assert itself (a dandelion clock at about 2pm).

Magrat had also tried make-up. This wasn't an unqualified success. She didn't have much practice. She was beginning to wonder if she'd overdone the eyeshadow.

Her neck, fingers and arms between them carried enough silverware to make a full-sized dinner service, and over everything she had thrown a black cloak lined with red silk.

In a certain light and from a carefully chosen angle, Magrat was not unattractive. Whether any of these preparations did anything for her is debatable, but they did mean that a thin veneer of confidence overlaid her trembling heart.

She drew herself up and turned this way and that. The clusters of amulets, magical jewellery and occult bangles on various parts of her body jingled together; any enemy wouldn't only have to be blind to fail to notice that a witch was approaching, he'd have to be deaf as well.

She turned to her worktable and examined what she rather self-consciously, and never in Granny's hearing, called her Tools of the Craft. There was the white-handled knife, used in the preparation of magical ingredients. There was the black-handled knife, used in the magical workings themselves; Magrat had carved so many runes into its handle it was in constant danger of falling in half. They were undoubtedly powerful, but . . .

Magrat shook her head regretfully, went over to the kitchen dresser and took out the breadknife. Something told her that at times like these a good sharp breadknife was probably the best friend a girl could have.

'I spy, with my little eye,' said Nanny Ogg, 'something beginning with P.'

The ghost of the king stared wearily around the dungeons.

'Pliers,' he suggested.

'No.'

'Pilliwinks?'

'That's a pretty name. What is it?'

'It's a kind of thumbscrew. Look,' said the king.

'It's not that,' said Nanny.

'Choke-pear?' he said desperately.

'That's a C, and anyway I don't know what it is,' said Nanny Ogg. The king obligingly indicated it on the tray, and explained its use.

'Definitely not,' said Nanny.

'Smouldering Boot of Punishment?' said the king.

'You're a bit too good at these names,' said Nanny sharply. 'You sure you didn't use them when you were alive?'

'Absolutely, Nanny,' said the ghost.

'Boys that tell lies go to a bad place,' warned Nanny.

'Lady Felmet had most of them installed herself, it's the truth,' said the king desperately; he felt his position to be precarious enough without having any bad places to worry about.

Nanny sniffed. 'Right, then,' she said, slightly mollified. 'It was "pinchers".'

'But pinchers is just another name for pl–' the king began, and stopped himself in time. During his adult life he'd been afraid of no man, beast or combination of the two, but Nanny's voice brought back old memories of schoolroom and nursery, of life under strict orders given by stern ladies in long skirts, and nursery food – mostly grey and brown – which seemed indigestible at the time but now appeared a distant ambrosia.

'That's five to me,' said Nanny happily.

'They'll be back soon,' said the king. 'Are you sure you'll be all right?'

'If I'm not, precisely how much help can you be?' said Nanny.

There was the sound of bolts sliding back.

*   *   *

There was already a crowd outside the castle as Granny's broomstick wobbled uncertainly towards the ground. They went quiet as she strode forward, and parted to let her pass. She had a basket of apples under her arm.

'There's a witch in the dungeons,' someone whispered to Granny. 'And foul tortures, they say!'

'Nonsense,' said Granny. 'It couldn't be. I expect Nanny Ogg has just gone to advise the king, or something.'

'They say Jason Ogg's gone to fetch his brothers,' said a stallholder, in awe.

'I really advise you all to return home,' said Granny Weatherwax. 'There has probably been a misunderstanding. Everyone knows a witch cannot be held against her will.'

'It's gone too far this time,' said a peasant. 'All this burning and taxing and now this. I blame you witches. It's got to stop. I know my rights.'

'What rights are they?' said Granny.

'Dunnage, cowhage-in-ordinary, badinage, leftovers, scrommidge, clary and spunt,' said the peasant promptly. 'And acornage, every other year, and the right to keep two-thirds of a goat on the common. Until he set fire to it. It was a bloody good goat, too.'

'A man could go far, knowing his rights like you do,' said Granny. 'But right now he should go home.'

She turned and looked at the gates. There were two extremely apprehensive guards on duty. She walked up to them, and fixed one of them with a look.

'I am a harmless old seller of apples,' she said, in a voice more appropriate for the opening of hostilities in a middle-range war. 'Pray let me past, dearie.' The last word had knives in it.

'No one must enter the castle,' said one of the guards. 'Orders of the duke.'

Granny shrugged. The apple-seller gambit had never worked more than once in the entire history of witchcraft, as far as she knew, but it was traditional.

'I know you, Champett Poldy,' she said. 'I recall I laid out your grandad and I brought you into the world.' She glanced at the crowd, who had regathered a little way off, and turned back to the guard, whose face was already a mask of terror. She leaned a little closer, and said, 'I gave you your first good hiding in this valley of tears and by all the gods if you cross me now I will give you your last.'

There was a soft metallic noise as the spear fell out of the man's fearful fingers. Granny reached and gave the trembling man a reassuring pat on the shoulder.

'But don't worry about it,' she added. 'Have an apple.'

She made to step forward, and a second spear barred her way. She looked up with interest.

The other guard was not a Ramtopper, but a city-bred mercenary brought up to swell the ranks depleted in recent years. His face was a patchwork of scar tissue. Several of the scars rearranged themselves into what was possibly a sneer.

'So that's witches' magic, is it?' said the guard. 'Pretty poor stuff. Maybe it frightens these country idiots, woman, but it doesn't frighten me.'

'I imagine it takes a lot to frighten a big strong lad like you,' said Granny, reaching up to her hat.

'And don't you try to put the wind up me, neither.' The guard stared straight ahead, and rocked gently on the balls of his feet. 'Old ladies like you, twisting people around. It shouldn't be stood for, like they say.'

'Just as you like,' said Granny, pushing the spear aside.

'Listen, I *said* – ' the guard began, and grabbed Granny's shoulder. Her hand moved so quickly it hardly seemed to move at all, but suddenly he was clutching at his arm and moaning.

Granny replaced the hatpin in her hat and ran for it.

'We will begin,' said the duchess, leering, 'with the Showing of the Implements.'

'Seen 'em,' said Nanny. 'Leastways, all the ones beginning with P, S, I, T and W.'

'Then let us see how long you can keep that light conversational tone. Light the brazier, Felmet,' snapped the duchess.

'Light the brazier, Fool,' said the duke.

The Fool moved slowly. He hadn't expected any of this. Torturing people hadn't been on his mental agenda. Hurting old ladies in cold blood wasn't his cup of tea, and actually hurting witches in blood of any temperature whatsoever failed to be an entire twelve-court banquet. Words, he'd said. All this probably came under the heading of sticks and stones.

'I don't like doing this,' he murmured under his breath.

'Fine,' said Nanny Ogg, whose hearing was superb. 'I'll remember that you didn't like it.'

'What's that?' said the duke sharply.

'Nothing,' said Nanny. 'Is this going to take long? I haven't had breakfast.'

The Fool lit a match. There was the faintest disturbance in the air beside him, and it went out. He swore, and tried another. This time his shaking hands managed to get it as far as the brazier before it, too, flared and darkened.

'Hurry up, man!' said the duchess, laying out a tray of tools.

'Doesn't seem to want to light –' muttered the Fool, as another match became a fluttering streak of flame and then went out.

The duke snatched the box from his trembling fingers and caught him across the cheek with a handful of rings.

'Can no orders of mine be obeyed?' he screamed. 'Infirm of purpose! Weak! Give me the box!'

The Fool backed away. Someone he couldn't see was whispering things he couldn't quite make out in his ear.

'Go outside,' hissed the duke, 'and see that we are not disturbed!'

The Fool tripped over the bottom step, turned and, with a last imploring look at Nanny, scampered through the door. He capered a little bit, out of force of habit.

'The fire isn't completely necessary,' said the Duchess. 'It merely assists. Now, woman, will you confess?'

'What to?' said Nanny.

'It's common knowledge. Treason. Malicious witchcraft. Harbouring the king's enemies. Theft of the crown –'

A tinkling noise made them look down. A blood-stained dagger had fallen off the bench, as though someone had tried to pick it up but just couldn't get the strength together. Nanny heard the king's ghost swear under its breath, or what would have been its breath.

' – and spreading false rumours,' finished the duchess.

' – salt in my food –' said the duke, nervously, staring at the bandages on his hand. He kept getting the feeling that there was a fourth person in the dungeon.

'If you *do* confess,' said the duchess, 'You will merely be burned at the stake. And, please, no humorous remarks.'

'What false rumours?'

The duke closed his eyes, but the visions were still there. 'Concerning the accidental death of the late King Verence,' he whispered hoarsely. The air swirled again.

Nanny sat with her head cocked to one side, as though listening to a voice only she could hear. Except that the duke was certain that he could hear something too, not exactly a voice, something like a distant sighing of the wind.

'Oh, I don't know nothing false,' she said. 'I know you stabbed him, and *you* gave him the dagger. It was at the top of the stairs.' She paused, head cocked, nodded, and added, 'Just by the suit of armour with the pike, and *you* said, "If it's to be done, it's better if it's done quickly", or something, and then you snatched the king's own dagger, the very same what is now lying on the floor, out of his belt and –'

'You lie! There were no witnesses. We made . . . there was nothing to witness! I heard someone in the dark, but there was no one there! There couldn't have been anyone seeing anything!' screamed the duke. His wife scowled at him.

'Do shut up, Leonal,' she said. 'I think within these four walls we can dispense with that sort of thing.'

'Who told her? Did you tell her?'

'And calm down. No one told her. She's a witch, for goodness sake, they find out about these things. Second glance, or something.'

'Sight,' said Nanny.

'Which you will not possess much longer, my good woman, unless you tell us who else knows and indeed, assist us on a number of other matters,' said the duchess grimly. 'And you will do so, believe me. I am skilled in these things.'

Nanny glanced around the dungeon. It was beginning to get crowded. King Verence was bursting with such angry vitality that he was very nearly apparent, and was furiously trying to get a grip on a knife. But there were others behind – wavering, broken shapes, not exactly ghosts but memories, implanted in the very substances of the walls themselves by sheer pain and terror.

'My own dagger! The bastards! They killed me with my own dagger,' said the ghost of King Verence silently, raising his transparent arms and imploring the netherworld in general to witness this ultimate humiliation. 'Give me strength . . .'

'Yes,' said Nanny. 'It's worth a try.'

'And now we will commence,' said the duchess.

'What?' said the guard.

'I SAID,' said Magrat, 'I've come to sell my lovely apples. Don't you listen?'

'There's not a sale on, is there?' The guard was extremely nervous since his colleague had been taken off to the infirmary. He hadn't taken the job in order to deal with this sort of thing.

It dawned on him.

'You're not a witch, are you?' he said, fumbling awkwardly with his pike.

'Of course not. Do I look like one?'

The guard looked at her occult bangles, her lined cloak, her trembling hands and her face. Her face was particularly worrying. Magrat had used a lot of powder to make her face pale and interesting. It combined with the lavishly applied mascara to give the guard the impression that he was looking at two flies that had crashed into a sugar bowl. He found his fingers wanted to make a sign to ward off the evil eyeshadow.

'Right,' he said uncertainly. His mind was grinding through the problem. She was a witch. Just lately there'd been a lot of gossip about witches being bad for your health. He'd been told not to let witches pass, but no one had said anything about apple sellers. Apple sellers were not a problem. It was witches that were the problem. She'd said she was an apple seller and he wasn't about to doubt a witch's word.

Feeling happy with this application of logic, he stood to one side and gave an expansive wave.

'Pass, apple seller,' he said.

'Thank you,' said Magrat sweetly. 'Would you like an apple?'

'No, thanks. I haven't finished the one the other witch gave me.' His eyes rolled. 'Not a witch. Not a witch, an apple seller. An apple seller. She ought to know.'

'How long ago was this?'

'Just a few minutes . . .'

Granny Weatherwax was not lost. She wasn't the kind of person who ever became lost. It was just that, at the moment, while she knew exactly where SHE was, she didn't know the position of anywhere else. Currently she had arrived in the kitchens again, precipitating a breakdown in the cook, who was trying to roast some celery. The fact that several people had tried to buy apples from her wasn't improving her temper.

Magrat found her way to the Great Hall, empty and deserted at this time of day except for a couple of guards who were playing dice. They wore the tabards of Felmet's own personal bodyguard, and stopped their game as soon as she appeared.

'Well, well,' said one, leering. 'Come to keep us company, have you, my pretty.*'

'I was looking for the dungeons,' said Magrat, to whom the words 'sexual harassment' were a mere collection of syllables.

'Just fancy,' said one of the guards, winking at the other. 'I reckon we can help you there.' They got up and stood either side of her; she was aware of two chins you could strike matches on and an overpowering smell of stale beer. Frantic signals from outlying portions of her mind began to break down her iron-hard conviction that bad things only happened to bad people.

They escorted her down several flights of steps into a maze of dank, arched passageways as she sought hurriedly for some polite way of disengaging herself.

---

* No one knows why men say things like this. Any minute now he is probably going to say he likes a girl with spirit.

'I should warn you,' she said, 'I am not, as I may appear, a simple apple seller.'

'Fancy that.'

'I am, in fact, a witch.'

This did not make the impression she had hoped. The guards exchanged glances.

'Fair enough,' said one. 'I've always wondered what it was like to kiss a witch. Around here they do say you gets turned into a frog.'

The other guard nudged him. 'I reckon, then,' he said, in the slow, ripe tones of one who thinks that what he is about to say next is going to be incredibly funny, 'you kissed one years ago.'

The brief guffaw was suddenly interrupted when Magrat was flung against the wall and treated to a close up view of the guard's nostrils.

'Now listen to me, sweetheart,' he said. 'You ain't the first witch we've had down here, if witch you be, but you could be lucky and walk out again. If you are nice to us, d'you see?'

There was a shrill, short scream from somewhere nearby.

'That, you see,' said the guard, 'was a witch having it the hard way. You could do us all a favour, see? Lucky you met us, really.'

His questing hand stopped its wandering. 'What's this?' he said to Magrat's pale face. 'A knife? A knife? I reckon we've got to take that very seriously, don't you, Hron?'

'You got to tie her hands and gag her,' said Hron hurriedly. 'They can't do no magic if they can't speak or wave their hands about . . .'

'You can take your hands off her!'

All three stared down the passage at the Fool. He was jingling with rage.

'Let her go this minute!' he shouted. 'Or I'll report you!'

'Oh, you'll report us, will you?' said Hron. 'And will anyone listen to you, you earwax-coloured little twerp?'

'This is a witch we have here,' said the other guard. 'So you can go and tinkle somewhere else.' He turned back to Magrat. 'I like a girl with spirit,' he said, incorrectly as it turned out.

The Fool advanced with the bravery of the terminally angry.

'I told you to let her go,' he repeated.

Hron drew his sword and winked at his companion.

Magrat struck. It was an unplanned, instinctive blow, its stopping power considerably enhanced by the weight of rings and bangles; her arm whirred around in an arc that connected with her captor's jaw and spun him twice before he folded up in a heap with a quiet little sigh, and incidentally with several symbols of occult significance embossed on his cheek.

Hron gaped at him, and then looked at Magrat. He raised his sword at about the same moment that the Fool cannoned into him, and the two men went down in a struggling heap. Like most small men the Fool relied on the initial mad rush to secure an advantage and was at a loss for a follow-through, and it would probably have gone hard with him if Hron hadn't suddenly become aware that a breadknife was pressed to his neck.

'Let go of him,' said Magrat, pushing her hair out of her eyes.

He stiffened. 'You're wondering whether I really would cut your throat,' panted Magrat. 'I don't know either. Think of the fun we could have together, finding out.'

She reached down with her other hand and hauled the Fool to his feet by his collar.

'Where did that scream come from?' she said, without taking her eyes off the guard.

'It was down this way. They've got her in the torture dungeon and I don't like it, it's going too far, and I couldn't get in and I came to look for someone – '

'Well, you've found me,' said Magrat.

'You,' she said to Hron, 'will stay here. Or run away, for all I care. But you won't follow us.'

He nodded, and stared after them as they hurried down the passage. 'The door's locked,' said the Fool. 'There's all sorts of noises, but the door's locked.'

'Well, it's a dungeon, isn't it?'

'They're not supposed to lock from the inside!'

It was, indeed, unbudgeable. Silence came from the other side – a busy, thick silence that crawled through the cracks and spilled out into the passage, a kind of silence that is worse than screams.

The Fool hopped from one foot to the other as Magrat explored the door's rough surface.

'Are you really a witch?' he said. 'They said you were a witch, are you really? You don't look like a witch, you look very . . . that is . . .' he blushed. 'Not like a, you know, crone at all, but absolutely beautiful . . .' His voice trailed into silence . . .

I am totally in control of the situation, Magrat told herself. I never thought I would be, but I am thinking absolutely clearly.

And she realised, in an absolutely clear way, that her padding had slipped down to her waist, her head felt as though a family of unhygienic birds had been nesting in it, and her eyeshadow had not so much run as sprinted. Her dress was torn in several places, her legs were scratched, her arms were bruised, and for some reason she felt on top of the world.

'I think you'd better stand back, Verence,' she said. 'I'm not sure how this is going to work.'

There was a sharp intake of breath.

'How did you know my name?'

Magrat sized up the door. The oak was old, centuries old, but she could sense just a little sap under a surface varnished by the years into something that was nearly as tough as a stone. Normally what she had in mind would require a day's planning and a bagful of exotic ingredients. At least, so she'd always believed. Now she was prepared to doubt it. If you could conjure demons out of washtubs, you could do anything.

She became aware that the Fool had spoken.

'Oh, I expect I heard it somewhere,' she said vaguely.

'I shouldn't think so, I never use it,' said the Fool. 'I mean, it's not a popular name with the duke. It was me mam, you see. They like to name you after kings, I suppose. My grandad said I had no business having a name like that and he said I shouldn't go around – '

Magrat nodded. She was looking around the dank tunnel with a professional's eye.

It wasn't a promising place. The old oak planks had been down here in the darkness all these years, away from the clock of the seasons . . .

On the other hand . . . Granny had said that somehow all trees were one tree, or something like that. Magrat thought she understood it, although she didn't know exactly what it meant. And it was springtime up there. The ghost of life that still lived in the wood must know that. Or if it had forgotten, it must be told.

She put her palms flat on the door again and shut her eyes, tried to think her way out through the stone, out of the castle, and into the thin, black soil of the mountains, into the air, into the sunlight . . .

The Fool was merely aware that Magrat was standing very still. Then her hair stood out from her head, gently, and there was a smell of leafmould.

And then, without warning, the hammer that can drive a marshmallow-soft toadstool through six inches of solid pavement or an eel across a thousand miles of hostile ocean to a particular pond in an upland field, struck up through her and into the door.

She stepped back carefully, her mind stunned, fighting against a desperate urge to bury her toes into the rock and put forth leaves. The Fool caught her, and the shock nearly knocked him over.

Magrat sagged against the faintly jingling body, and felt triumphant. She had done it! And with no artificial aids! If only the others could have seen this . . .

'Don't go near it,' she mumbled. 'I think I gave it rather . . . a lot.' The

Fool was still holding her toastrack body in his arms and was too overcome to utter a word, but she still got a reply.

'I reckon you did,' said Granny Weatherwax, stepping out of the shadows. 'I never would have thought of it myself.'

Magrat peered at her.

'You've been here all the time?'

'Just a few minutes.' Granny glanced at the door. 'Good technique,' she said. 'but it's old wood. Been in a fire, too, I reckon. Lots of iron nails and stuff in there. Can't see it working, I'd have tried the stones if it was me, but – '

She was interrupted by a soft 'pop'.

There was another, and then a whole series of them together, like a shower of meringues.

Behind her, very gently, the door was breaking into leaf.

Granny stared at it for a few seconds, and then met Magrat's terrified gaze.

'Run!' she yelled.

They grabbed the Fool and scurried into the shelter of a convenient buttress.

The door gave a warning creak. Several of its planks twisted in vegetable agony and there was a shower of rock splinters when nails were expelled like thorns from a wound, ricocheting off the stonework. The Fool ducked as part of the lock whirred over his head and smashed into the opposite wall.

The lower parts of the planks extended questing white roots, which slithered across the damp stone to the nearest crack and began to auger in. Knotholes bulged, burst and thrust out branches which hit the stones of the doorway and tumbled them aside. And all the time there was a low groan, the sound of the cells of the wood trying to contain the surge of raw life pounding through them.

'If it had been *me*,' said Granny Weatherwax, as part of the ceiling caved in further along the passage, 'I wouldn't have done it like that. Not that I'm objecting, mind you,' she said, as Magrat opened her mouth. 'It's a reasonable job. I think you might have overdone it a bit, that's all.'

'Excuse me,' said the Fool.

'I can't do rocks,' said Magrat.

'Well, no, rocks is an acquired taste – '

'Excuse me.'

The two witches stared at him, and he backed away.

'Weren't you supposed to be rescuing someone?' he said.

'Oh,' said Granny. 'Yes. Come on, Magrat. We'd better see what she's been getting up to.'

'There were screams,' said the Fool, who couldn't help feeling they weren't taking things seriously enough.

'I daresay,' said Granny, pushing him aside and stepping over a writhing taproot. 'If anyone locked *me* in a dungeon, there'd be screams.'

There was a lot of dust inside the dungeon, and by the nimbus of light around its one torch Magrat could dimly make out two figures cowering in the furthest corner. Most of the furniture had been overturned and scattered across the floor; it didn't look as though any of it had been designed to be the last word in comfort. Nanny Ogg was sitting quite calmly in what appeared to be a sort of stocks.

'Took your time,' she observed. 'Let me out of this, will you? I'm getting cramp.'

And there was the dagger.

It spun gently in the middle of the room, glinting when the turning blade caught the light.

'My own dagger!' said the ghost of the king, in a voice only the witches could hear. 'All this time and I never knew it! My own dagger! They bloody well did me in with my own bloody knife!'

He took another step towards the royal couple, waving the dagger. A faint gurgle escaped from the lips of the duke, glad to be out of there.

'He's doing well, isn't he,' said Nanny, as Magrat helped her out of her prison.

'Isn't that the old king? Can they see him?'

'Shouldn't think so.'

King Verence staggered slightly under the weight. He was too old for such poltergeist activity; you had to be an adolescent for this . . .

'Let me just get a grip on this thing,' he said. 'Oh, damn . . .'

The knife dropped from the ghost's tenuous grasp and clattered to the floor. Granny Weatherwax stepped forward smartly and put her foot on it.

'The dead shouldn't kill the living,' she said. 'It could be a dangerous wossname, precedent. We'd all be outnumbered, for one thing.'

The duchess surfaced from her terror first. There had been knives swooping through the air and exploding doors, and now these women were defying her in her own dungeons. She couldn't be sure how she was supposed to react to the supernatural items, but she had very firm ideas about how she should tackle the last one.

Her mouth opened like the gateway to a red hell. 'Guards!' she yelled, and spotted the Fool hovering near the door. 'Fool! Fetch the guards!'

'They're busy. We were just leaving,' said Granny. 'Which one of you is the duke?'

Felmet stared pink-eyed up at her from his half-crouch in the corner.

A thin dribble of saliva escaped from the corner of his mouth, and he giggled.

Granny looked closer. In the centre of those streaming eyes something else looked back at her.

'I'm going to give you no cause,' she said quietly. 'But it would be better for you if you left this country. Abdicate, or whatever.'

'In favour of whom?' said the duchess icily. 'A witch?'

'I won't,' said the duke.

'What did you say?'

The duke pulled himself upright, brushed some of the dust off his clothes, and looked Granny full in the face. The coldness in the centre of his eyes was larger.

'I said I won't,' he said. 'Do you think a bit of simple conjuring would frighten me? I am the king by right of conquest, and you cannot change it. It is as simple as that, witch.'

He moved closer.

Granny stared at him. She hadn't faced anything like this before. The man was clearly mad, but at the heart of his madness was a dreadful cold sanity, a core of pure interstellar ice in the centre of the furnace. She'd thought him weak under a thin shell of strength, but it went a lot further than that. Somewhere deep inside his mind, somewhere beyond the event horizon of rationality, the sheer pressure of insanity had hammered his madness into something harder than diamond.

'If you defeat me by magic, magic will rule,' said the duke. 'And you can't do it. And any king raised with your help would be under your power. Hag-ridden, I might say. That which magic rules, magic destroys. It would destroy you, too. You know it. Ha. Ha.'

Granny's knuckles whitened as he moved closer.

'You could strike me down,' he said. 'And perhaps you could find someone to replace me. But he would have to be a fool indeed, because he would know he was under your evil eye, and if he mispleased you, why, his life would be instantly forfeit. You could protest all you wished, but he'd know he ruled with your permission. And that would make him no king at all. Is this not true?'

Granny looked away. The other witches hung back, ready to duck.

'I *said*, is this not true?'

'Yes,' said Granny. 'It is true . . .'

'Yes.'

'. . . but there is one who could defeat you,' said Granny slowly.

'The child? Let him come when he is grown. A young man with a sword, seeking his destiny.' The duke sneered. 'Very romantic. But I have many years to prepare. Let him try.'

Beside him King Verence's fist smashed through the air and quite failed to connect.

The duke leaned closer until his nose was an inch from Granny's face.

'Get back to your cauldrons, wyrd sisters,' he said softly.

Granny Weatherwax stalked through the passages of Lancre Castle like a large, angry bat, the duke's laughter echoing around her head.

'You could give him boils or something,' said Nanny Ogg. 'Haemorrhoids are good. That's allowed. It won't stop him from ruling, it just means he'll have to rule standing up. Always good for a laugh, that. Or piles.'

Granny Weatherwax said nothing. If fury were heat, her hat would have caught fire.

'Mind you, that'd probably make him worse,' said Nanny, running to keep up. 'Same with toothache.' She gave a sideways glance at Granny's twitching features.

'You needn't fret,' she said. 'They didn't do anything much. But thanks, anyway.'

'I ain't worried about you, Gytha Ogg,' snapped Granny. 'I only come along 'cos Magrat was fretting. What I say is, if a witch can't look after herself, she's got no business calling herself a witch.'

'Magrat done well with the woodwork, I thought.'

Even in the grip of her sullen fury, Granny Weatherwax spared a nod.

'She's coming along,' she said. She looked up and down the corridor, and then leaned closer to Nanny Ogg's ear.

'I ain't going to give him the pleasure of saying it,' she said, 'but he's got us beaten.'

'Well, I don't know,' said Nanny. 'Our Jason and a few sharp lads could soon – '

'You saw some of his guards. These aren't the old sort. These are a tough kind.'

'We could give the boys just a bit of help – '

'It wouldn't work. People have to sort this sort of thing out for themselves.'

'If you say so, Esme,' said Nanny meekly.

'I do. Magic's there to be ruled, not for ruling.'

Nanny nodded and then, remembering a promise, reached down and picked up a fragment of stone from the rubble on the tunnel floor.

'I thought you'd forgotten,' said the ghost of the king, by her ear.

Further down the passage the Fool was capering after Magrat.

'Can I see you again?' he said.

'Well . . . I don't know,' said Magrat, her heart singing a smug song.

'How about tonight?' said the Fool.

'Oh, no,' said Magrat. 'I'm very busy tonight.' She had intended to curl up with a hot milk drink and Goodie Whemper's notebooks on experimental astrology, but instinct told her that any suitor should have an uphill struggle put in front of him, just to make him keener.

'Tomorrow night, then?' the Fool persisted.

'I think I should be washing my hair.'

'I could get Friday night free.'

'We do a lot of work at night, you see – '

'The afternoon, then.'

Magrat hesitated. Perhaps instinct had got it wrong. 'Well – ' she said.

'About two o'clock. In the meadow by the pond, all right?'

'Well – '

'See you there, then. All right?' said the Fool desperately.

'Fool!' The duchess's voice echoed along the passage, and a look of terror crossed his face.

'I've got to go,' he said. 'The meadow, okay? I'll wear something so you recognise me. All right?'

'All right,' echoed Magrat, hypnotised by the sheer pressure of his persistence. She turned and ran after the other witches.

There was pandemonium outside the castle. The crowd that had been there at Granny's arrival had grown considerably, and had flowed in through the now unguarded gateway and lapped around the keep. Civil disobedience was new to Lancre, but its inhabitants had already mastered some of its more elementary manifestations, viz, the jerking of rakes and sickles in the air with simple up-and-down motions accompanied by grimaces and cries of 'Gerrh!', although a few citizens, who hadn't quite grasped the idea, were waving flags and cheering. Advanced students were already eyeing the more combustible buildings inside the walls. Several sellers of hot meat pies and sausages in a bun had appeared from nowhere* and were doing a brisk trade. Pretty soon someone was going to throw something.

The three witches stood at the top of the steps that led to the keep's main door and surveyed the sea of faces.

'There's our Jason,' said Nanny happily. 'And Wane and Darron and Kev and Trev and Nev – '

---

* They always do, everywhere. No one sees them arrive. The logical explanation is that the franchise includes the stall, the paper hat and a small gas-powered time machine.

'I will remember their faces,' said Lord Felmet, emerging between them and putting a hand on their shoulders. 'And do you see my archers, on the walls?'

'I see 'em,' said Granny grimly.

'Then smile and wave,' said the duke. 'So that the people may know that all is well. After all, have you not been to see me today on matters of state?'

He leaned closer to Granny.

'Yes, there are a hundred things you could do,' he said. 'But the ending would always be the same.' He drew back. 'I'm not an unreasonable man, I hope,' he added, in cheerful tones. 'Perhaps, if you persuade the people to be calm, I may be prevailed upon to moderate my rule somewhat. I make no promises, of course.'

Granny said nothing.

'Smile and wave,' commanded the duke.

Granny raised one hand in a vague motion and produced a brief rictus that had nothing whatsoever to do with humour. Then she scowled and nudged Nanny Ogg, who was waving and mugging like a maniac.

'No need to get carried away,' she hissed.

'But there's our Reet and our Sharleen and their babbies,' said Nanny. 'Coo-eee!'

'Will you shut up, you daft old besom!' snapped Granny. 'And pull yourself together!'

'Jolly good, well done,' said the duke. He raised his hands, or at least his hand. The other still ached. He'd tried the grater again last night, but it hadn't worked.

'People of Lancre,' he cried, 'do not be afeared! I am your friend. I will protect you from the witches! They have agreed to leave you in peace!'

Granny stared at him as he spoke. 'He's one of these here maniac depressives,' she said. 'Up and down like a wossname. Kill you one minute and ask you how you're feeling the next.'

She became aware that he was looking at her expectantly.

'What?'

'I said, I'll now call upon the respected Granny Weatherwax to say a few words, ha ha,' he said.

'You said that, did you?'

'Yes!'

'You've gone a long way too far,' said Granny.

'I have, haven't I!' The duke giggled.

Granny turned to the expectant crowd, which went silent.

'Go home,' she said.

There was a further long silence.

'Is that all?' said the duke.

'Yes.'

'What about pledges of eternal allegiance?'

'What about them? Gytha, will you stop waving at people!'

'Sorry.'

'And now we are going to go, too,' said Granny.

'But we were getting on so well,' said the duke.

'Come, Gytha,' said Granny icily. 'And where's Magrat got to?'

Magrat looked up guiltily. She had been deep in conversation with the Fool, although it was the kind of conversation where both parties spend a lot of time looking at their feet and picking at their fingernails. Ninety per cent of true love is acute, ear-burning embarrassment.

'We're leaving,' said Granny.

'Friday afternoon, remember,' hissed the Fool.

'Well, if I can,' said Magrat.

Nanny Ogg leered.

And so Granny Weatherwax swept down the steps and through the crowds, with the other two running behind her. Several of the grinning guards caught her eye and wished they hadn't, but here and there, among the watching crowd, was a barely suppressed snigger. She hurtled through the gateway, across the drawbridge and through the town. Granny walking fast could beat most other people at a run.

Behind them the duke, who had crested the latest manic peak on the switchback of his madness and was coasting speedily towards the water-splash of despair, laughed.

'Ha ha.'

Granny didn't stop until she was outside the town and under the welcoming eaves of the forest. She turned off the road and flumped down on a log, her face in her hands.

The other two approached her carefully. Magrat patted her on the back.

'Don't despair,' she said. 'You handled it very well, we thought.'

'I ain't despairing, I'm thinking,' said Granny. 'Go away.'

Nanny Ogg raised her eyebrows at Magrat in a warning fashion. They backed off to a suitable distance although, with Granny in her present mood, the next universe might not be far enough, and sat down on a moss-grown stone.

'Are you all right?' said Magrat. 'They didn't do anything, did they?'

'Never laid a finger on me,' said Nanny. She sniffed. 'They're not your real royalty,' she added. 'Old King Gruneweld, for one, he wouldn't have wasted time waving things around and menacing people. It'd've been bang, needles right under the fingernails from the word go, and no messing. None of this evil laughter stuff. He was a *real* king. Very gracious.'

'He was threatening to burn you.'

'Oh, I wouldn't of stood for it. I see you've got a follower,' said Nanny.

'Sorry?' said Magrat.

'The young fellow with the bells,' said Nanny. 'And the face like a spaniel what's just been kicked.'

'Oh, him.' Magrat blushed hotly under her pale makeup. 'Really, he's just this man. He just follows me around.'

'Can be difficult, can that,' said Nanny sagely.

'Besides, he's so small. And he *capers* all over the place,' said Magrat.

'Looked at him carefully, have you?' said the old witch.

'Pardon?'

'You haven't, have you. I thought not. He's a very clever man, that Fool. He ought to have been one of them actor men.'

'What do you mean?'

'Next time you have a look at him like a witch, not like a woman,' said Nanny, and gave Magrat a conspiratorial nudge. 'Good bit of work with the door back there,' she added. 'Coming on well, you are. I hope you told him about Greebo.'

'He said he'd let him out directly, Nanny.'

There was a snort from Granny Weatherwax.

'Did you hear the sniggering in the crowd?' she said. 'Someone sniggered!'

Nanny Ogg sat down beside her.

'And a couple of them pointed,' she said. 'I know.'

'It's not to be borne!'

Magrat sat down on the other end of the log.

'There's other witches,' she said. 'There's lot of witches further up the Ramtops. Maybe they can help.'

The other two looked at her in pained surprise.

'I don't think we need go *that* far,' sniffed Granny. '*Asking* for *help*.'

'Very bad practice,' nodded Nanny Ogg.

'But you asked a demon to help you,' said Magrat.

'No, we didn't,' said Granny.

'Right. We didn't.'

'We ordered it to assist.'

''S right.'

Granny Weatherwax stretched out her legs and looked at her boots. They were good strong boots, with hobnails and crescent-shaped scads; you couldn't believe a cobbler had made them, someone had laid down a sole and *built* up from there.

'I mean, there's that witch over Skund way,' she said. 'Sister Whosis, wossname, her son went off to be a sailor – you know, Gytha, her who sniffs and puts them antimassacres on the backs of chairs soon as you sits down – '

'Grodley,' said Nanny Ogg. 'Sticks her little finger out when she drinks her tea and drops her Haitches all the time.'

'Yes. Hwell. I haven't hlowered myself to talk to her hever since that business with the gibbet, you recall. I daresay she'd just love to come snooping haround here, running her fingers over heverything and sniffing, telling us how to do things. Oh, yes. *Help.* We'd all be in a fine to-do if we went around helping all the time.'

'Yes, and over Skund way the trees talk to you and walk around of night,' said Nanny. 'Without even asking permission. Very poor organisation.'

'Not really good organisation, like we've got here?' said Magrat.

Granny stood up purposefully.

'I'm going home,' she said.

There are thousands of good reasons why magic doesn't rule the world. They're called witches and wizards, Magrat reflected, as she followed the other two back to the road.

It was probably some wonderful organisation on the part of Nature to protect itself. It saw to it that everyone with any magical talent was about as ready to co-operate as a she-bear with toothache, so all that dangerous power was safely dissipated as random bickering and rivalry. There were differences in style, of course. Wizards assassinated each other in draughty corridors, witches just cut one another dead in the street. And they were all as self-centred as a spinning top. Even when they help other people, she thought, they're secretly doing it for themselves. Honestly, they're just like big children.

Except for me, she thought smugly.

'She's very upset, isn't she,' said Magrat to Nanny Ogg.

'Ah, well,' said Nanny. 'There's the problem, see. The more you get used to magic, the more you don't want to use it. The more it gets in your way. I expect, when you were just starting out, you learned a few spells from Goodie Whemper, maysherestinpeace, and you used them all the time, didn't you?'

'Well, yes. Everyone does.'

'Well-known fact,' agreed Nanny. 'But when you get along in the Craft, you learn that the hardest magic is the sort you don't use at all.'

Magrat considered the proposition cautiously. 'This isn't some kind of Zen, is it?' she said.

'Dunno. Never seen one.'

'When we were in the dungeons, Granny said something about trying the rocks. That sounded like pretty hard magic.'

'Well, Goodie wasn't much into rocks,' said Nanny. 'It's not really hard. You just prod their memories. You know, of the old days. When they were hot and runny.'

She hesitated, and her hand flew to her pocket. She gripped the lump of castle stone and relaxed.

'Thought I'd forgotten it, for a minute there,' she said, lifting it out. 'You can come out now.'

He was barely visible in the brightness of day, a mere shimmer in the air under the trees. King Verence blinked. He wasn't used to daylight.

'Esme,' said Nanny. 'There's someone to see you.'

Granny turned slowly and squinted at the ghost.

'I saw you in the dungeon, didn't I?' she said. 'Who're you?'

'Verence, King of Lancre,' said the ghost, and bowed. 'Do I have the honour of addressing Granny Weatherwax, doyenne of witches?'

It has already been pointed out that just because Verence came from a long line of kings didn't mean that he was basically stupid, and a year without the distractions of the flesh had done wonders as well. Granny Weatherwax considered herself totally unsusceptible to buttering up, but the king was expertly applying the equivalent of the dairy surplus of quite a large country. Bowing was a particularly good touch.

A muscle twitched at the corner of Granny's mouth. She gave a stiff little bow in return, because she wasn't quite sure what 'doyenne' meant.

'I'm her,' she conceded.

'You can get up now,' she added, regally.

King Verence remained kneeling, about two inches above the actual ground.

'I crave a boon,' he said urgently.

'Here, how did you get out of the castle?' said Granny.

'The esteemed Nanny Ogg assisted me,' said the king. 'I reasoned, if I am anchored to the stones of Lancre, then I can also go where the stones go. I am afraid I indulged in a little trickery to arrange matters. Currently I am haunting her apron.'

'Not the first, either,' said Granny, automatically.

'Esme!'

'And I beg you, Granny Weatherwax, to restore my son to the throne.'

'Restore?'

'You know what I mean. He is in good health?'

Granny nodded. 'The last time we Looked at him, he was eating an apple,' she said.

'It is his destiny to be King of Lancre!'

'Yes, well. Destiny is tricky, you know,' said Granny.

'You will not help?'

Granny looked wretched. 'It's meddling, you see,' she said. 'It always goes wrong if you meddle in politics. Like, once you start, you can't stop. Fundamental rule of magic, is that. You can't go around messing with fundamental rules.'

'You're not going to help?'

'Well . . . naturally, one day, when your lad is a bit older . . .'

'Where is he now?' said the king, coldly.

The witches avoided one another's faces.

'We saw him safe out of the country, you see,' said Granny awkwardly.

'Very good family,' Nanny Ogg put in quickly.

'What kind of people?' said the king. 'Not commoners, I trust?'

'Absolutely not,' said Granny with considerable firmness as a vision of Vitoller floated across her imagination. 'Not common at all. Very uncommon. Er.'

Her eyes implored Magrat for help.

'They were Thespians,' said Magrat firmly, her voice radiating such approval that the king found himself nodding automatically.

'Oh,' he said. 'Good.'

'Were they?' whispered Nanny Ogg. 'They didn't look it.'

'Don't show your ignorance, Gytha Ogg,' sniffed Granny. She turned back to the ghost of the king. 'Sorry about that, your majesty. It's just her showing off. She don't even know where Thespia *is*.'

'Wherever it is, I hope that they know how to school a man in the arts of war,' said Verence. 'I know Felmet. In ten years he'll be dug in here like a toad in a stone.'

The king looked from witch to witch. 'What kind of kingdom will he have to come back to? I fear what the kingdom is becoming, even now. Will you watch it change, over the years, become shoddy and mean?' The king's ghost faded.

His voice hung in the air, faint as a breeze.

'Remember, good sisters,' he said, 'the land and the king are one.'

And he vanished.

The embarrassed silence was broken by Magrat blowing her nose.

'One what?' said Nanny Ogg.

'We've got to do something,' said Magrat, her voice choked with emotion. 'Rules or no rules!'

'It's very vexing,' said Granny, quietly.

'Yes, but what are you going to do?' she said.

'Reflect on things,' said Granny. 'Think about it all.'

'You've been thinking about it for a year,' Magrat said.

'One what? Are one what?' said Nanny Ogg.

'It's no good just reacting,' said Granny. 'You've got to – '

A cart came bouncing and rumbling along the track from Lancre. Granny ignored it.

' – give these things careful consideration.'

'You don't know what to do, do you?' said Magrat.

'Nonsense. I – '

'There's a cart coming, Granny.'

Granny Weatherwax shrugged. 'What you youngsters don't realise – ' she began.

Witches never bothered with elementary road safety. Such traffic as there was on the roads of Lancre either went around them or, if this was not possible, waited until they moved out of the way. Granny Weatherwax had grown up knowing this for a fact; the only reason she didn't die knowing that it wasn't was that Magrat, with rather better reflexes, dragged her into the ditch.

It was an interesting ditch. There were jiggling corkscrew things in it which were direct descendants of things which had been in the primordial soup of creation. Anyone who thought that ditchwater was dull could have spent an instructive half-hour in that ditch with a powerful microscope. It also had nettles in it, and now it had Granny Weatherwax.

She struggled up through the weeds, incoherent with rage, and rose from the ditch like Venus Anadyomene, only older and with more duckweed.

'T-t-t,' she said, pointing a shaking finger at the disappearing cart.

'It was young Nesheley from over Inkcap way,' said Nanny Ogg, from a nearby bush. 'His family were always a bit wild. Of course, his mother was a Whipple.'

'He ran us down!' said Granny.

'You could have got out of the way,' said Magrat.

'*Get out of the way?*' said Granny. 'We're witches! People get out of *our* way!' She squelched on to the track, her finger still pointing at the distant cart. 'By Hoki, I'll make him wish he'd never been born – '

'He was quite a big baby, I recall,' said the bush. 'His mother had a terrible time.'

'It's never happened to me before, ever,' said Granny, still twanging like a bowstring. 'I'll teach him to run us down as though, as though, as though we was ordinary people!'

'He already knows,' said Magrat. 'Just help me get Nanny out of this bush, will you?'

'I'll turn his – '

'People haven't got any respect any more, that's what it is,' said Nanny, as

Magrat helped her with the thorns. 'It's all due to the king being one, I expect.'

'We're witches!' screamed Granny, turning her face towards the sky and shaking her fists.

'Yes, yes,' said Magrat. 'The harmonious balance of the universe and everything. I think Nanny's a bit tired.'

'What've I been doing all this time?' said Granny, with a rhetorical flourish that would have made even Vitoller gasp.

'Not a lot,' said Magrat.

'Laughed at! Laughed at! On my own roads! In my own country!' screamed Granny. 'That just about does it! I'm not taking ten more years of this! I'm not taking another *day* of it!'

The trees around her began to sway and the dust from the road sprang up into writhing shapes that tried to swirl out of her way. Granny Weatherwax extended one long arm and at the end of it unfolded one long finger and from the tip of its curving nail there was a brief flare of octarine fire.

Half a mile down the track all four wheels fell off the cart at once.

'Lock up a witch, would he?' Granny shouted at the trees.

Nanny struggled to her feet.

'We'd better grab her,' she whispered to Magrat. The two of them leapt at Granny and forced her arms down to her sides.

'I'll bloody well show him what a witch could do!' she yelled.

'Yes, yes, very good, very *good*,' said Nanny. 'Only perhaps not just now and not just like this, eh?'

'Wyrd sisters, indeed!' Granny yelled. 'I'll make his – '

'Hold her a minute, Magrat,' said Nanny Ogg, and rolled up her sleeve.

'It can be like this with the highly trained ones,' she said, and brought her palm round in a slap that lifted both witches off their feet. On such a flat, final note the universe might have ended.

At the conclusion of the breathless silence which followed Granny Weatherwax said, 'Thank you.'

She adjusted her dress with some show of dignity, and added, 'But I meant it. We'll meet tonight at the stone and do what must be done. Ahem.'

She reset the pins in her hat and set off unsteadily in the direction of her cottage.

'Whatever happened to the rule about not meddling in politics?' said Magrat, watching her retreating back.

Nanny Ogg massaged some life back into her fingers.

'By Hoki, that woman's got a jaw like an anvil,' she said. 'What was that?'

'I said, what about this rule about not meddling?' said Magrat.

'Ah,' said Nanny. She took the girl's arm. 'The thing is,' she explained, 'as you progress in the Craft, you'll learn there is another rule. Esme's obeyed it all her life.'

'And what's that?'

'When you break rules, break 'em good and hard,' said Nanny, and grinned a set of gums that were more menacing than teeth.

The duke smiled out over the forest.

'It works,' he said. 'The people mutter against the witches. How do you do it, Fool?'

'Jokes, nuncle. And gossip. People are halfway ready to believe it anyway. Everyone respects the witches. The point is that no one actually likes them very much.'

Friday afternoon, he thought. I'll have to get some flowers. And my best suit, the one with the silver bells. Oh gosh.

'This is very pleasing. If it goes on like this, Fool, you shall have a knighthood.'

This was no.302, and the Fool knew better than to let a feed line go hungry. 'Marry, nuncle,' he said wearily, ignoring the spasm of pain that crawled across the duke's face, 'if'n I had a Knighthood (Night Hood), why, it would keep my ears Warm in Bedde; i'faith, if many a Knight is a Fool, why, should a – '

'Yes, yes, all right,' snapped Lord Felmet. In fact he was feeling much better already. His porridge hadn't been oversalted this evening, and there was a decently empty feel about the castle. There were no more voices on the cusp of hearing.

He sat down on the throne. It felt really comfortable for the first time.

The duchess sat beside him, her chin on her hand, watching the Fool intently. This bothered him. He thought he knew where he stood with the duke, it was just a matter of hanging on until his madness curved back to the cheerful stage, but the duchess genuinely frightened him.

'It seems that words are extremely powerful,' she said.

'Indeed, lady.'

'You must have made a lengthy study.'

The Fool nodded. The power of words had sustained him through the hell of the Guild. Wizards and witches used words as if they were tools to get things done, but the Fool reckoned that words were things in their own right.

'Words can change the world,' he said.

Her eyes narrowed.

'So you have said before. I remain unconvinced. Strong men change the world,' she said. 'Strong men and their deeds. Words are just like marzipan on a cake. Of course you think words are important. You are weak, you have nothing else.'

'Your ladyship is wrong.'

The duchess's fat hand drummed impatiently on the arm of her throne.

'You had better,' she said, 'be able to substantiate that comment.'

'Lady, the duke wishes to chop down the forests, is this not so?'

'The trees talk about me,' whispered Lord Felmet. 'I hear them whisper when I go riding. They tell lies about me!'

The duchess and the Fool exchanged glances.

'But,' the Fool continued, 'this policy has met with fanatical opposition.'

'What?'

'People don't like it.'

The duchess exploded. 'What does that matter?' she roared. 'We rule! They will do what we say or they will be pitilessly executed!'

The Fool bobbed and capered and waved his hands in a conciliatory fashion.

'But, my love, we will run out of people,' murmured the duke.

'No need, no need!' said the Fool desperately. 'You don't have to do that at all! What you do is, you – ' he paused for a moment, his lips moving quickly – 'you embark upon a far-reaching and ambitious plan to expand the agricultural industry, provide long-term employment in the sawmills, open new land for development, and reduce the scope for banditry.'

This time the duke looked baffled. 'How will I do that?' he said.

'Chop down the forests.'

'But you said – '

'Shut up, Felmet,' said the duchess. She subjected the Fool to another long, thoughtful stare.

'Exactly how,' she said, eventually, 'does one go about knocking over the houses of people one does not like?'

'Urban clearance,' said the Fool.

'I was thinking of burning them down.'

'*Hygienic* urban clearance,' the Fool added promptly.

'And sowing the ground with salt.'

'Marry, I suspect that is hygienic urban clearance and a programme of environmental improvements. It might be a good idea to plant a few trees as well.'

'No more trees!' shouted Felmet.

'Oh, it's all right. They won't survive. The important thing is to have planted them.'

'But I also want us to raise taxes,' said the duchess.

'Why, nuncle – '

'And I am not your nuncle.'

'N'aunt?' said the Fool.

'No.'

'Why . . . prithee . . . you need to finance your ambitious programme for the country.'

'Sorry?' said the duke, who was getting lost again.

'He means that chopping down trees costs money,' said the duchess. She smiled at the Fool. It was the first time he had ever seen her look at him as if he was other than a disgusting little cockroach. There was still a large element of cockroach in her glance, but it said: good little cockroach, you have learned a trick.

'Intriguing,' she said. 'But can your words change the past?'

The Fool considered this.

'More easily, I think,' he said. 'Because the past is what people remember, and memories are words. Who knows how a king behaved a thousand years ago? There is only recollection, and stories. And plays, of course.'

'Ah, yes. I saw a play once,' said Felmet. 'Bunch of funny fellows in tights. A lot of shouting. The people liked it.'

'You tell me history is what people are told?' said the duchess.

The Fool looked around the throne room and found King Gruneberry the Good (906–967).

'*Was* he?' he said, pointing. 'Who knows, now? What was he good *at*? But he will be Gruneberry the Good until the end of the world.'

The duke was leaning forward in his throne, his eyes gleaming.

'I want to be a *good* ruler,' he said. 'I want people to like me. I would like people to remember me fondly.'

'Let us assume,' said the duchess, 'that there were other matters, subject to controversy. Matters of historical record that had . . . been clouded.'

'I didn't do it, you know,' said the duke, quickly. 'He slipped and fell. That was it. Slipped and fell. I wasn't even there. He attacked me. It was self-defence. That's it. He slipped and fell on his own dagger in self-defence.' His voice fell to a mumble. 'I have no recollection of it at this time,' he murmured. He rubbed his dagger hand, although the word was becoming inappropriate.

'Be quiet, husband,' snapped the duchess. 'I know you didn't do it. I wasn't there with you, you may recall. It was I who didn't hand you the dagger.' The duke shuddered again.

'And now, Fool,' said Lady Felmet. 'I was saying, I believe, that perhaps there are matters that should be *properly recorded*.'

'Marry, that you were not there at the time?' said the Fool, brightly.

It is true that words have power, and one of the things they are able to do is get out of someone's mouth before the speaker has the chance to stop them. If words were sweet little lambs, then the Fool watched them bound cheerfully away into the flamethrower of the duchess's glare.

'Not *where*?' she said.

'Anywhere,' said the Fool hastily.

'Stupid man! Everyone is somewhere.'

'I mean, you were everywhere but at the top of the stairs,' said the Fool.

'Which stairs?'

'Any stairs,' said the Fool, who was beginning to sweat. 'I distinctly remember not seeing you!'

The duchess eyed him for a while.

'So long as you remember it,' she said. The duchess rubbed her chin, which made an audible rasping noise.

'Reality is only weak words, you say. Therefore, words are reality. But how can words become history?'

'It was a very good play, the play that I saw,' said Felmet dreamily. 'There were fights, and no one really died. Some very good speeches, I thought.'

There was another sandpapery sound from the duchess.

'Fool?' she said.

'Lady?'

'Can you write a play? A play that will go around the world, a play that will be remembered long after rumour has died?'

'No, lady. It is a special talent.'

'But can you find someone who has it?'

'There are such people, lady.'

'Find one,' murmured the duke. 'Find the best. Find the best. The truth will out. Find one.'

The storm was resting. It didn't want to be, but it was. It had spent a fortnight understudying a famous anticyclone over the Circle Sea, turning up every day, hanging around in the cold front, grateful for a chance to uproot the occasional tree or whirl a farmhouse to any available emerald city of its choice. But the big break in the weather had never come.

It consoled itself with the thought that even the really great storms of the past – the Great Gale of 1789, for example, or Hurricane Zelda and Her Amazing Raining Frogs – had gone through this sort of thing at some stage in their career. It was just part of the great tradition of the weather.

Besides, it had had a good stretch in the equivalent of pantomime down on the plains, bringing seasonal snow and terminal frostbite to millions. It just had to be philosophical about being back up here now with nothing much to do except wave the heather about. If weather was people, this storm would be filling in time wearing a cardboard hat in a hamburger hell.

Currently it was observing three figures moving slowly over the moor, converging with some determination on a bare patch where the standing stone stood, or usually stood, though just at the moment it wasn't visible.

It recognised them as old friends and connoisseurs, and conjured up a brief unseasonal roll of thunder as a form of greeting. This was totally ignored.

'The bloody stone's gone,' said Granny Weatherwax. 'However many there is of it.'

Her face was pale. It might also have been drawn; if so, then it was by a very neurotic artist. She looked as though she meant business. Bad business.

'Light the fire, Magrat,' she added automatically.

'I daresay we'll all feel better for a cup of tea,' said Nanny Ogg, mouthing the words like a mantra. She fumbled in the recesses of her shawl. 'With something in it,' she added, producing a small bottle of applejack.

'Alcohol is a deceiver and tarnishes the soul,' said Magrat virtuously.

'I never touch the stuff,' said Granny Weatherwax. 'We should keep a clear head, Gytha.'

'Just a drop in your tea isn't drinking,' said Nanny. 'It's medicine. It's a chilly old wind up here, sisters.'

'Very well,' said Granny. 'But just a drop.'

They drank in silence. Eventually Granny said, 'Well, Magrat. You know all about the coven business. We might as well do it right. What do we do next?'

Magrat hesitated. She wasn't up to suggesting dancing naked.

'There's a song,' she said. 'In praise of the full moon.'

'It ain't full,' Granny pointed out. 'It's wossname. Bulging.'

'Gibbous,' said Nanny obligingly.

'I think it's in praise of full moons in general,' Magrat hazarded. 'And then we have to raise our consciousness. It really ought to be full moon for that, I'm afraid. Moons are very important.'

Granny gave her a long, calculating look.

'That's modern witchcraft for you, is it?' she said.

'It's part of it, Granny. There's a lot more.'

Granny Weatherwax sighed. 'Each to her own, I suppose. I'm blowed if I'll let a ball of shiny rock tell *me* what to do.'

'Yes, bugger all that,' said Nanny. 'Let's curse somebody.'

☆   ☆   ☆

The Fool crept cautiously along the night-time corridors. He wasn't taking any chances either. Magrat had given him a graphic account of Greebo's general disposition, and the Fool had borrowed a couple of gloves and a sort of metal wimple from the castle's store of hereditary chain mail.

He reached the lumber room, lifted the latch cautiously, pushed the door and then flung himself against the wall.

The corridor became slightly darker as the more intense darkness inside the room spilled out and mingled with the rather lighter darkness already there.

Apart from that, nothing. The number of spitting, enraged balls of murderous fur pouring through the door was zero. The Fool relaxed, and slipped inside.

Greebo dropped on his head.

It had been a long day. The room did not offer the kind of full life that Greebo had come to expect and demand. The only point of interest had been the discovery, around mid-morning, of a colony of mice who had spent generations eating their way through a priceless tapestry history of Lancre and had just got as far as King Murune (709–745), who met a terrible fate*, when they did, too. He had sharpened his claws on a bust of Lancre's only royal vampire, Queen Grimnir the Impaler (1514–1553, 1553–1557, 1557–1562, 1562–1567 and 1568–1573). He had performed his morning ablutions on a portrait of an unknown monarch, which was beginning to dissolve. Now he was bored, and also angry.

He raked his claws across the place where the Fool's ears should have been, and was rewarded with nothing more than a metallic scraping noise.

'Who's a good boy, den?' said the Fool. 'Wowsa wowsa whoosh.'

This intrigued Greebo. The only other person who had ever spoken to him like this was Nanny Ogg; everyone else addressed him as 'Yarrgeroffoutofityahbarstard'. He leaned down very carefully, intrigued by the new experience.

From the Fool's point of view an upside-down cat face lowered itself slowly into his field of vision, wearing an expression of evil-eyed interest.

'Does oo want to go home, den?' said the Fool hopefully. 'Look, Mr Door is *open*.'

Greebo increased his grip. He had found a friend.

The Fool shrugged, very carefully, turned, and walked back into the passage. He made his way down through the hall, out into the courtyard,

---

* Involving a red-hot poker, a privy, ten pounds of live eels, a three mile stretch of frozen river, a butt of wine, a couple of tulip bulbs, a number of poisoned eardrops, an oyster and a large man with a mallet. King Murune didn't make friends easily.

around the side of the guardroom and out through the main gate, nodding – carefully – to the guards.

'Man just went past with a cat on his head,' one of them remarked, after a minute or two's reflection.

'See who it was?'

'The Fool, I think.'

There was a thoughtful pause. The second guard shifted his grip on his halberd.

'It's a rotten job,' he said. 'But I suppose someone's got to do it.'

'We ain't going to curse anyone,' said Granny firmly. 'It hardly ever works if they don't know you've done it.'

'What you do is, you send him a doll of himself with pins in.'

'No, Gytha.'

'All you have to do is get hold of some of his toenails,' Nanny persisted, enthusiastically.

'No.'

'Or some of his hair or anything. I've got some pins.'

'*No.*'

'Cursing people is morally unsound and extremely bad for your karma,' said Magrat.

'Well, I'm going to curse him anyway,' said Nanny. 'Under my breath, like. I could of caught my death in that dungeon for all he cared.'

'We ain't going to curse him,' said Granny. 'We're going to replace him. What did you do with the old king?'

'I left the rock on the kitchen table,' said Nanny. 'I couldn't stand it any more.'

'I don't see why,' said Magrat. 'He seemed very pleasant. For a ghost.'

'Oh, *he* was all right. It was the others,' said Nanny.

'Others?'

'"Pray carry a stone out of the palace so's I can haunt it, good mother," he says,' said Nanny Ogg. '"It's bloody boring in here, Mistress Ogg, excuse my Klatchian," he said, so of course I did. I reckon they was all listening. Ho yes, they all thinks, all aboard, time for a bit of a holiday. I've nothing against ghosts. Especially royal ghosts,' she added loyally. 'But my cottage isn't the place for them. I mean, there's some woman in a chariot yelling her head off in the washhouse. I ask you. And there's a couple of little kiddies in the pantry, and men without heads all over the place, and someone screaming under the sink, and there's this little hairy man wandering around looking lost and everything. It's not right.'

'Just so long as he's not here,' said Granny. 'We don't want any men around.'

'He's a ghost, not a man,' said Magrat.

'We don't have to go into details,' Granny said icily.

'But you can't put the old king back on the throne,' said Magrat. 'Ghosts can't rule. You'd never get the crown to stay on. It'd drop through.'

'We're going to replace him with his son,' said Granny. 'Proper succession.'

'Oh, we've been through all that,' said Nanny dismissively. 'In about fifteen years time, perhaps, but – '

'Tonight,' said Granny.

'A child on the throne? He wouldn't last five minutes.'

'Not a child,' said Granny quietly. 'A grown man. Remember Aliss Demurrage?'

There was silence. Then Nanny Ogg sat back.

'Bloody hell,' she whispered. 'You ain't going to try that, are you?'

'I mean to have a go.'

'Bloody hell,' said Nanny again, very quietly, and added. 'You've been thinking about this, have you?'

'Yes.'

'See here, Esme. I mean, Black Aliss was one of the best. I mean, you're very good at, well, headology and thinking and that. I mean, Black Aliss, well, she just upped and went at it.'

'You saying I couldn't do it, are you?'

'Excuse me,' said Magrat.

'No. No. Of course not,' said Nanny, ignoring her.

'Right.'

'Only . . . well, she was a, you know, a hoyden of witches, like the king said.'

'Doyenne,' said Granny, who had looked it up. 'Not hoyden.'

'Excuse me,' said Magrat, louder this time. 'Who was Black Aliss? And,' she added quickly, 'none of this exchanging meaningful glances and talking over my head. There's three witches in this coven, remember?'

'She was before your time,' said Nanny Ogg. 'Before mine, really. She lived over Skund way. Very powerful witch.'

'If you listen to rumour,' said Granny.

'She turned a pumpkin into a royal coach once,' said Nanny.

'Showy,' said Granny Weatherwax. 'That's no help to anyone, turning up at a ball smelling like a pie. And that business with the glass slipper. Dangerous, to my mind.'

'But the biggest thing she ever did,' said Nanny, ignoring the interruption, 'was to send a whole palace to sleep for a hundred years until . . .' She hesitated. 'Can't remember. Was there rose bushes involved, or was it spinning wheels in that one? I think some princess had to finger . . . no, there was a prince. That was it.'

'Finger a prince?' said Magrat, uneasily.

'No . . . he had to kiss her. Very romantic, Black Aliss was. There was always a bit of romance in her spells. She liked nothing better than Girl meets Frog.'

'Why did they call her Black Aliss?'

'Fingernails,' said Granny.

'And teeth,' said Nanny Ogg. 'She had a sweet tooth. Lived in a real gingerbread cottage. Couple of kids shoved her in her own oven at the end. Shocking.'

'And you're going to send the castle to sleep?' said Magrat.

'She never sent the castle to sleep,' said Granny. 'That's just an old wives' tale,' she added, glaring at Nanny. 'She just stirred up time a little. It's not as hard as people think. Everyone does it all the time. It's like rubber, is time. You can stretch it to suit yourself.'

Magrat was about to say, that's not right, time is time, every second lasts a second, that's what it's for, that's its *job* . . .

And then she recalled weeks that had flown past and afternoons that had lasted for ever. Some minutes had lasted hours, some hours had gone past so quickly she hadn't been aware they'd gone past at all . . .

'But that's just people's perception,' she said. 'Isn't it?'

'Oh, yes,' said Granny, 'of course it is. It all is. What difference does that make?'

'A hundred years'd be over-egging it, mind,' said Nanny.

'I reckon fifteen'd be a nice round number,' said Granny. 'That means the lad will be eighteen at the finish. We just do the spell, go and fetch him, he can manifest his destiny, and everything will be nice and neat.'

Magrat didn't comment on this, because it had occurred to her that destinies sounded easy enough when you talked about them but were never very bankable where real human beings were concerned. But Nanny Ogg sat back and tipped another generous measure of apple brandy in her tea.

'Could work out nice,' she said. 'A bit of peace and quiet for fifteen years. If I recall the spell, after you say it you have to fly around the castle before cock crow.'

'I wasn't thinking about that,' said Granny. 'It wouldn't be right. Felmet would still be king all that time. The kingdom would still get sick. No, what I was thinking of doing was moving the whole kingdom.'

She beamed at them.

'The whole of Lancre?' said Nanny.

'Yes.'

'Fifteen years into the future?'

'Yes.'

Nanny looked at Granny's broomstick. It was a well-made thing, built to last, apart from the occasional starting problem. But there were limits.

'You'll never do it,' she said. 'Not around the whole kingdom in that. That's all the way up to Powderknife and down to Drumlin's Fell. You just couldn't carry enough magic.'

'I've thought of that,' said Granny.

She beamed again. It was terrifying.

She explained the plan. It was dreadful.

A minute later the moor was deserted, as the witches hurried to their tasks. It was silent for a while, apart from the squeak of bats and the occasional rustle of the wind in the heather.

Then there was a bubbling from the nearby peat bog. Very slowly, crowned with a thicket of sphagnum moss, the standing stone surfaced and peered around the landscape with an air of deep distrust.

Greebo was really enjoying this. At first he thought his new friend was taking him to Magrat's cottage, but for some reason he'd wandered off the path in the dark and was taking a stroll in the forest. In one of the more interesting bits, Greebo had always felt. It was a hummocky area, rich in hidden potholes and small, intense swamps, full of mist even in fine weather. Greebo often came up here on the offchance that a wolf was lying up for the day.

'I thought cats could find their own way home,' the Fool muttered.

He cursed himself under his breath. It would have been easy to take this wretched creature back to Nanny Ogg's house, which was only a few streets away, almost in the shadow of the castle. But then he'd had the idea of delivering it to Magrat. It would impress her, he thought. Witches were very keen on cats. And then she'd be bound to ask him in, for a cup of tea or something . . .

He put his foot in another water-filled hole. Something wriggled underneath it. The Fool groaned, and stepped back on to a tumescent mushroom.

'Look, cat,' he said. 'You've got to come down, right? And then you can find your way home and I'll follow you. Cats are good at seeing in the dark and finding their own way home,' he added hopefully.

He reached up. Greebo sank his claws into his arm as a friendly warning, and found to his surprise that this had no effect on chain mail.

'There's a good cat,' said the Fool, and lowered him to the ground. 'Go on, find your way home. Any home will do.'

Greebo's grin gradually faded, until there was nothing left but the cat. This was nearly as spooky as the opposite way round.

He stretched and yawned to hide his embarrassment. Being called a good cat in the middle of one of his favourite stalking grounds wasn't going to do anything for his prowl-credibility. He disappeared into the under-growth.

The Fool peered into the gloom. It dawned on him that while he liked forests, he liked them at one remove, as it were; it was nice to know that they were there, but the forests of the mind were not quite the same as real forests that, for example, you got lost in. They had more mighty oaks and fewer brambles. They also tended to be viewed in daylight, and the trees didn't have malevolent faces and long scratchy branches. The trees of the imagina-tion were proud giants of the forest. Most of the trees here appeared to be vegetable gnomes, mere trellises for fungi and ivy.

The Fool was vaguely aware that you could tell which direction the Hub lay by seeing which side of the trees the moss grew on. A quick inspection of the nearby trunks indicated that, in defiance of all normal geography, the Hub lay everywhere.

Greebo had vanished.

The Fool sighed, removed his chain-mail protection, and tinkled gently through the night in search of high ground. High ground seemed a good idea. The ground he was on at the moment appeared to be trembling. He was sure it shouldn't do that.

Magrat hovered on her broomstick several hundred feet above the Turnwise borders of Lancre, looking down on a sea of mist through which the occasional treetop poked like a seaweed-covered rock at high tide. A bulging moon floated above her, probably gibbous again. Even a decent thin crescent would have been better, she felt. More appropriate.

She shivered and wondered where Granny Weatherwax was at this moment.

The old witch's broomstick was known and feared throughout the skies of Lancre. Granny had been introduced to flying quite late in life, and after some initial suspicion had taken to it like a bluebottle to an ancient fish-head. A problem, however, was that Granny saw every flight simply as a straight line from A to B and was unable to get alongside the idea that other users of the air might have any rights whatsoever; the flight migration patterns of an entire continent had been changed because of that simple fact.

High-speed evolution among local birds had developed a generation that
flew on their backs, so that they could keep a watchful eye on the skies.

Granny's implicit belief that everything should get out of her way
extended to other witches, very tall trees and, on occasion, mountains.

Granny had also browbeaten the dwarfs who lived under the mountains
and in fear of their lives into speeding the thing up. Many an egg had been
laid in mid-air by unsuspecting fowls who had suddenly glimpsed Granny
bearing down on them, scowling over the top of the broomstick.

'Oh dear,' thought Magrat. 'I hope she hasn't happened to someone.'

A midnight breeze turned her gently around in the air, like an unsup-
ported weathercock. She shivered and squinted at the moonlit mountains,
the high Ramtops, whose freezing crags and ice-green chasms acknowledged
no king or cartographer. Only on the Rimward side was Lancre open to the
world; the rest of its borders looked as jagged as a wolf's mouth and far
more impassable. From up here it was possible to see the whole kingdom . . .

There was a ripping noise in the sky above her, a blast of wind that spun
her around again, and a Doppler-distorted cry of, 'Stop dreaming, girl!'

She gripped the bristles with her knees and urged the stick upwards.

It took several minutes to catch up with Granny, who was lying almost
full length along her broomstick to reduce wind resistance. Dark treetops
roared far below them as Magrat came alongside. Granny turned to her,
holding her hat on with one hand.

'Not before time,' she snapped. 'I don't reckon this one's got more'n a few
minutes flight left. Come on, get a move on.'

She reached out a hand. So did Magrat. Unsteadily, the broomsticks
bucking and dipping in one another's slipstream, they touched fingertips.

Magrat's arm tingled as the power flowed up it.* Granny's broomstick
jerked forward.

'Leave me a bit,' shouted Magrat. 'I've got to get down!'

'Shouldn't be difficult,' screamed Granny, above the noise of the wind.

'I mean get down safely!'

'You're a witch, ain't you? By the way, did you bring the cocoa? I'm
freezing up here!'

Magrat nodded desperately, and with her spare hand passed up a straw
bag.

'Right,' said Granny. 'Well done. See you at Lancre Bridge.'

She uncurled her fingers.

Magrat whirled away in the buffeting wind, clinging tightly to a
broomstick which now, she feared, had about as much buoyancy as a bit of

---

* Possibly the first ever attempt at the in-flight refuelling of a broomstick.

firewood. It certainly wasn't capable of sustaining a full-grown woman against the beckoning fingers of gravity.

As she plunged down towards the forest roof in a long shallow dive she reflected that there was possibly something complimentary in the way Granny Weatherwax resolutely refused to consider other people's problems. It implied that, in her considerable opinion, they were quite capable of sorting them out by themselves.

Some kind of Change spell was probably in order.

Magrat concentrated.

Well, that seemed to work.

Nothing in the sight of mortal man had in fact changed. What Magrat had achieved was a mere adjustment of the mental processes, from a bewildered and slightly frightened woman gliding inexorably towards the inhospitable ground to a clear-headed, optimistic and positive-thinking woman who had really got it together, and was taking full responsibility for her own life and in general knew where she was coming from although, unfortunately, where she was *heading* had not changed in any way. But she felt a lot better about it.

She dug her heels in and forced the broomstick to yield the last dregs of its power in a brief burst, sending it skimming erratically a few feet from the trees. As it sagged again and started to plough a furrow among the midnight leaves she tensed herself, prayed to whatever gods of the forest might be listening that she would land on something soft, and let go.

There are three thousand known major gods on the Disc, and research theologians discover more every week. Apart from the minor gods of rock, tree and water, there are two that haunt the Ramtops – Hoki, half a man, half a goat, and entirely a bad practical joker, who was banished from Dunmanifestin for pulling the old exploding mistletoe joke on Blind Io, chief of all the gods; and also Herne the Hunted, the terrified and apprehensive deity of all small furry creatures whose destiny it is to end their lives as a brief, crunchy squeak . . .

Either could have been candidates for the small miracle which then occurred, for – in a forest full of cold rocks, jagged stumps and thorn bushes – Magrat landed on something soft.

Granny, meanwhile, was accelerating towards the mountains on the second leg of the journey. She consumed the regrettably tepid cocoa and, with proper environmental consideration, dropped the bottle as she passed over an upland lake.

It turned out that Magrat's idea of sustaining food was two rounds of egg and cress sandwiches with the crusts cut off and, Granny noticed before the wind whipped it away, a small piece of parsley placed with consideration and care on top of each one. Granny regarded them for some time. Then she ate them.

A chasm loomed, still choked with winter snow. Like a tiny spark in the darkness, a dot of light against the hugeness of the Ramtops, Granny tackled the maze of the mountains.

Back in the forest, Magrat sat up and absent-mindedly pulled a twig from her hair. A few yards away the broomstick dropped through the trees, showering leaves.

A groan and a small, half-hearted tinkle caused her to peer into the gloom. An indistinct figure was on its hands and knees, searching for something.

'Did I land on you?' said Magrat.

'Someone did,' said the Fool.

They crawled nearer to one another.

'You?'

'You!'

'What are you doing here?'

'Marry, I was walking along the ground,' said the Fool. 'A lot of people do, you know. I mean, I know it's been done before. It's not original. It probably lacks imagination but, well, it's always been good enough for me.'

'Did I hurt you?'

'I think I've got one or two bells that won't be the same again.' The Fool scrabbled through the leaf mould, and finally located his hated hat. It clonked.

'Totally crushed, i'faith,' he said, putting it on anyway. He seemed to feel better for that, and went on, 'Rain, yes, hail, yes, even lumps of rock. Fish and small frogs, okay. Women, no, up till now. Is it going to happen again?'

'You've got a bloody hard head,' said Magrat, pulling herself to her feet.

'Modesty forbids me to comment,' said the Fool, and then remembered himself and added, quickly, 'Prithee.'

They stared at one another again, their minds racing.

Magrat thought: Nanny said look at him properly. I'm looking at him. He just looks the same. A sad thin little man in a ridiculous jester's outfit, he's practically a hunchback.

Then, in the same way that a few random bulges in a cloud can suddenly become a galleon or a whale in the eye of the beholder, Magrat realised that the Fool was not a little man. He was at least of average height, but he *made* himself small, by hunching his shoulders, bandying his legs and walking in a half-crouch that made him appear as though he was capering on the spot.

I wonder what else Gytha Ogg noticed? she thought, intrigued.

He rubbed his arm and gave her a lopsided grin.

'I suppose you haven't got any idea where we are?' he said.

'Witches never get lost,' said Magrat firmly. 'Although they can become temporarily mislaid. Lancre's over *that* way, I think. I've got to find a hill, if you'll excuse me.'

'To see where you are?'

'To see when, I think. There's a lot of magic going on tonight.'

'Is there? Then I think I'll accompany you,' the Fool added chivalrously, after peering cautiously into the tree-haunted gloom that apparently lay between him and his flagstones. 'I wouldn't want anything to happen to you.'

Granny lay low over the broomstick as it plunged through the trackless chasms of the mountains, leaning from side to side in the hope that this might have some effect on the steering which seemed, strangely, to be getting worse. Falling snow behind her was shipped and spiralled into odd shapes by the wind of her passage. Rearing waves of crusted snow, poised all winter over the glacial valleys, trembled and then began the long, silent fall. Her flight was punctuated by the occasional boom of an avalanche.

She looked down at a landscape of sudden death and jagged beauty, and knew it was looking back at her, as a dozing man may watch a mosquito. She wondered if it realised what she was doing. She wondered if it'd make her fall any softer, and mentally scolded herself for such softness. No, the land wasn't like that. It didn't bargain. The land gave hard, and took hard. A dog always bit deepest on the veterinary hand.

And then she was through, vaulting so low over the last peak that one of her boots filled with snow, and barrelling down towards the lowlands.

The mist, never far away in the mountains, was back again, but this time it was making a fight of it and had become a thick, silver sea in front of her. She groaned.

Somewhere in the middle of it Nanny Ogg floated, taking the occasional pull from a hip flask as a preventative against the chill.

And thus it was that Granny, her hat and iron-grey hair dripping with moisture, her boots shedding lumps of ice, heard the distant and muffled sound of a voice enthusiastically explaining to the invisible sky that the hedgehog had less to worry about than just about any other mammal. Like a hawk that has spotted something small and fluffy in the grass, like a wandering interstellar flu germ that has just seen a nice blue planet drifting by, Granny turned the stick and plunged down through the choking billows.

'Come on!' she screamed, drunk with speed and exhilaration, and the sound from five hundred feet overhead put a passing wolf severely off its supper. 'This minute, Gytha Ogg!'

Nanny Ogg caught her hand with considerable reluctance and the pair of broomsticks swept up again and into the clear, starlit sky.

The Disc, as always, gave the impression that the Creator has designed it specifically to be looked at from above. Streamers of cloud in white and silver stretched away to the rim, stirred into thousand-mile swirls by the turning of the world. Behind the speeding brooms the sullen roof of the fog was dragged up into a curling tunnel of white vapour, so that the watching gods – and they were certainly watching – could see the terrible flight as a furrow in the sky.

A thousand feet and rising fast into the frosty air, the two witches were bickering again.

'It was a bloody stupid idea,' moaned Nanny. 'I never liked heights.'

'Did you bring something to drink?'

'Certainly. You said.'

'Well?'

'I drank it, didn't I,' said Nanny. 'Sitting around up there at my age. Our Jason would have a fit.'

Granny gritted her teeth. 'Well, let's have the power,' she said. 'I'm running out of up. Amazing how – '

Granny's voice ended in a scream as, without any warning at all, her broomstick pinwheeled sharply across the clouds and dropped from sight.

The Fool and Magrat sat on a log on a small outcrop that looked out across the forest. The lights of Lancre town were in fact not very far away, but neither of them had suggested leaving.

The air between them crackled with unspoken thoughts and wild surmisings.

'You've been a Fool long?' said Magrat, politely. She blushed in the darkness. In that atmosphere it sounded the most impolite of questions.

'All my life,' said the Fool bitterly. 'I cut my teeth on a set of bells.'

'I suppose it gets handed on, from father to son?' said Magrat.

'I never saw much of my father. He went off to be Fool for the Lords of Quirm when I was small,' said the Fool. 'Had a row with my grandad. He comes back from time to time, to see my mam.'

'That's terrible.'

There was a sad jingle as the Fool shrugged. He vaguely recalled his father as a short, friendly little man, with eyes like a couple of oysters. Doing something as brave as standing up to the old boy must have been quite outside his nature. The sound of two suits of bells shaken in anger still haunted his memory, which was full enough of bad scenes as it was.

'Still,' said Magrat, her voice higher than usual and with a vibrato of uncertainty, 'it must be a happy life. Making people laugh, I mean.'

When there was no reply she turned to look at the man. His face was like stone. In a low voice, talking as though she was not there, the Fool spoke.

He spoke of the Guild of Fools and Joculators in Ankh-Morpork.

Most visitors mistook it at first sight for the offices of the Guild of Assassins, which in fact was the rather pleasant, airy collection of buildings next door (the Assassins always had plenty of money); sometimes the young Fools, slaving at their rote in rooms that were always freezing, even in high summer, heard the young Assassins at play over the wall and envied them, even though, of course, the number of piping voices grew noticeably fewer towards the end of term (the Assassins also believed in competitive examination).

In fact all sorts of sounds managed to breach the high grim windowless walls, and from keen questioning of servants the younger Fools picked up a vision of the city beyond. There were taverns out there, and parks. There was a whole bustling world, in which the students and apprentices of the various Guilds and Colleges took a full ripe part, either by playing tricks on it, running through it shouting, or throwing parts of it up. There was laughter which paid no attention to the Five Cadences or Twelve Inflections. And – although the students debated this news in the dormitories at night – there was apparently unauthorised humour, delivered freestyle, with no reference to the *Monster Fun Book* or the Council or anyone.

Out there, beyond the stained stonework, people were telling jokes without reference to the Lords of Misrule.

It was a sobering thought. Well, not a sobering thought in actual fact, because alcohol wasn't allowed in the Guild. But if it was, it would have been.

There was nowhere more sober than the Guild.

The Fool spoke bitterly of the huge, red-faced Brother Prankster, of evenings learning the Merry Jests, or long mornings in the freezing gymnasium learning the Eighteen Pratfalls and the accepted trajectory for a custard pie. And juggling. Juggling! Brother Jape, a man with a soul like cold boiled string, taught juggling. It wasn't that the Fool was bad at juggling that reduced him to incoherent fury. Fools were *expected* to be bad at juggling, especially if juggling inherently funny items like custard pies, flaming torches or extremely sharp cleavers. What had Brother Jape laying about him in red-hot, clanging rage was the fact that the Fool was bad at juggling *because he wasn't any good at it.*

'Didn't you want to be anything else?' said Magrat.

'What else is there?' said the Fool. 'I haven't seen anything else I could be.'

Student Fools were allowed out, in the last year of training, but under a fearsome set of restrictions. Capering miserably through the streets he'd seen wizards for the first time, moving like dignified carnival floats. He'd seen the surviving assassins, foppish, giggling young men in black silk, as sharp as knives underneath; he'd seen priests, their fantastic costumes only slightly marred by the long rubber sacrificial aprons they wore for major services. Every trade and profession had its costume, he saw, and he realised for the first time that the uniform he was wearing had been carefully and meticulously designed for no other purpose than making its wearer look a complete and utter pillock.

Even so, he'd persevered. He'd spent his whole life persevering.

He persevered precisely because he had absolutely no talent, and because grandfather would have flayed him alive if he didn't. He memorised the authorised jokes until his head rang, and got up even earlier in the morning to juggle until his elbows creaked. He had perfected his grasp of the comic vocabulary until only the very senior Lords could understand him. He'd capered and clowned with an impenetrable grim determination and he'd graduated top of his year and been awarded the Bladder of Honour. He'd dropped it down the privy when he came home.

Magrat was silent.

The Fool said, 'How did you get to be a witch?'

'Um?'

'I mean, did you go to a school or something?'

'Oh. No. Goodie Whemper just walked down to the village one day, got all us girls lined up, and chose me. You don't choose the Craft, you see. It chooses you.'

'Yes, but when do you actually become a witch?'

'When the other witches treat you as one, I suppose.' Magrat sighed. 'If they ever do,' she added. 'I thought they would after I did that spell in the corridor. It was pretty good, after all.'

'Marry, t'was a rite of passage,' said the Fool, unable to stop himself. Magrat gave him a blank look. He coughed.

'The other witches being those two old ladies?' he said, relapsing into his usual gloom.

'Yes.'

'Very strong characters, I imagine.'

'Very,' said Magrat, with feeling.

'I wonder if they ever met my grandad,' said the Fool.

Magrat looked at her feet.

'They're quite nice really,' she said. 'It's just that, well, when you're a witch you don't think about other people. I mean, you *think* about them, but you don't actually think about their feelings, if you see what I mean. At least, not unless you think about it.' She looked at her feet again.

'You're not like that,' said the Fool.

'Look, I wish you'd stop working for the duke,' said Magrat desperately. 'You know what he's like. Torturing people and setting fire to their cottages and everything.'

'But I'm his Fool,' said the Fool. 'A Fool has to be loyal to his master. Right up until he dies. I'm afraid it's tradition. Tradition is very important.'

'But you don't even like being a Fool!'

'I hate it. But that's got nothing to do with it. If I've got to be a Fool, I'll do it properly.'

'That's really stupid,' said Magrat.

'Foolish, I'd prefer.'

The Fool had been edging along the log. 'If I kiss you,' he added carefully, 'do I turn into a frog?'

Magrat looked down at her feet again. They shuffled themselves under her dress, embarrassed at all this attention.

She could sense the shades of Gytha Ogg and Esme Weatherwax on either side of her. Granny's spectre glared at her. *A witch is master of every situation*, it said.

Mistress, said the vision of Nanny Ogg, and made a brief gesture involving much grinning and waving of forearms.

'We shall have to see,' she said.

It was destined to be the most impressive kiss in the history of foreplay.

Time, as Granny Weatherwax had pointed out, is a subjective experience. The Fool's years in the Guild had been an eternity whereas the hours with Magrat on the hilltop passed like a couple of minutes. And, high above Lancre, a double handful of seconds extended like taffy into hours of screaming terror.

'Ice!' screamed Granny. 'It's iced up!'

Nanny Ogg came alongside, trying vainly to match courses with the tumbling, bucking broomstick. Octarine fire crackled over the frozen bristles, shorting them out at random. She leaned over and snatched a handful of Granny's skirt.

'I told you it was daft!' she shouted. 'You went all through all that wet mist and then up into the cold air, you daft besom!'

'You let go of my skirt, Gytha Ogg!'

'Come on, grab hold o'mine. You're on fire at the back there!'

They shot through the bottom of the cloud bank and screamed in unison as the shrub-covered ground emerged from nowhere and aimed itself directly at them.

And *went past*.

Nanny looked down a black perspective at the bottom of which a boil of white water was dimly visible. They had flown over the edge of Lancre Gorge.

Blue smoke was pouring out of Granny's broomstick but she hung on, determined, and forced it around.

'What the hell you doing?' roared Nanny.

'I can follow the river,' Granny Weatherwax screamed, above the crackle of flames. 'Don't you worry!'

'You come aboard, d'you hear? It's all over, you can't do it . . .'

There was a small explosion behind Granny and several handfuls of burning bristles broke off and whirled away into the booming depths of the gorge. Her stick jerked sideways and Nanny grabbed her around the shoulders as a bout of fire snapped another binding.

The blazing broomstick shot from between her legs, twisted in the air, and went straight upwards, trailing sparks and making a noise like a wet finger dragged around the top of a wineglass.

This left Nanny flying upside down, supporting Granny Weatherwax at arm's length. They stared into one another's face and screamed.

'I can't pull you up!'

'Well, I can't climb up, can I? Act your age, Gytha!'

Nanny considered this. Then she let go.

Three marriages and an adventurous girlhood had left Nanny Ogg with thigh muscles that could crack coconuts, and the G-forces sucked at her as she forced the speeding stick down and around in a tight loop.

Ahead of her she made out Granny Weatherwax dropping like a stone, one hand clutching her hat, the other trying to prevent gravity from seeing up her skirts. She urged the stick forwards until it creaked, snatched the falling witch around the waist, fought the plunging stick back up to level flight, and sagged.

The subsequent silence was broken by Granny Weatherwax saying, 'Don't you ever do that again, Gytha Ogg.'

'I promise.'

'Now turn us around. We're heading for Lancre Bridge, remember?'

Nanny obediently turned the broomstick, brushing the canyon walls as she did so.

'It's still miles to go,' she said.

'I mean to do it,' said Granny. 'There's plenty of night left.'

'Not enough, I'm thinking.'

'A witch doesn't know the meaning of the word "failure", Gytha.'

They shot up into the clear air again. The horizon was a line of golden light as the slow dawn of the Disc sped across the land, bulldozing the suburbs of the night.

'Esme?' said Nanny Ogg, after a while.

'What?'

'It means "lack of success".'

They flew in chilly silence for several seconds.

'I was speaking wossname. Figuratively,' said Granny.

'Oh. Well. You should of said.'

The line of light was bigger, brighter. For the first time a flicker of doubt invaded Granny Weatherwax's mind, puzzled to find itself in such unfamiliar surroundings.

'I wonder how many cockerels there are in Lancre?' she said quietly.

'Was that one of them wossname questions?'

'I was just wondering.'

Nanny Ogg sat back. There were thirty-two of crowing age, she knew. She knew because she'd worked it out last night – *tonight* – and had given Jason his instructions. She had fifteen grown-up children and innumerable grandchildren and great-grandchildren, and they'd had most of the evening to get into position. It should be enough.

'Did you hear that?' said Granny. 'Over Razorback way?'

Nanny looked innocently across the misty landscape. Sound travelled very clearly in these early hours.

'What?' she said.

'Sort of an "urk" noise?'

'No.'

Granny spun around.

'Over there,' she said. 'I definitely heard it this time. Something like "cock-a-doo-arrgh".'

'Can't say I did, Esme,' said Nanny, smiling at the sky. 'Lancre Bridge up ahead.'

'And over there! Right down there! It was a definite squawk!'

'Dawn chorus, Esme, I expect. Look, only half a mile to go.'

Granny glared at the back of her colleague's head.

'There's something going on here,' she said.

'Search me, Esme.'

'Your shoulders are shaking!'

'Lost my shawl back there. I'm a bit chilly. Look, we're nearly there.'

Granny glared ahead, her mind a maze of suspicions. She was going to get to the bottom of this. When she had time.

The damp logs of Lancre's main link to the outside world drifted gently underneath them. From the chicken farm half a mile away came a chorus of strangled squawks and a thud.

'And that? What was that, then?' demanded Granny.

'Fowl pest. Careful, I'm bringing us down.'

'Are you laughing at me?'

'Just pleased for you, Esme. You'll go down in history for this, you know.'

They drifted between the timbers of the bridge. Granny Weatherwax alighted cautiously on the greasy planking and adjusted her dress.

'Yes. Well,' she added, nonchalantly.

'Better than Black Aliss, everyone'll say,' Nanny Ogg went on.

'Some people will say anything,' said Granny. She peered over the parapet at the foaming torrent far below, and then up at the distant outcrop on which stood Lancre Castle.

'Do you think they will?' she added, nonchalantly.

'Mark my words.'

'Hmm.'

'But you've got to complete the spell, mind.'

Granny Weatherwax nodded. She turned to face the dawn, raised her arms, and completed the spell.

It is almost impossible to convey the sudden passage of fifteen years and two months in words.

It's a lot easier in pictures, when you just use a calendar with lots of pages blowing off, or a clock with the hands moving faster and faster until they blur, or trees bursting into blossom and fruiting in a matter of seconds . . .

Well, *you* know. Or the sun becomes a fiery streak across the sky, and days and nights flicker past jerkily like a bad zoetrope, and the fashions visible in the clothes shop across the road whip on and off faster than a lunchtime stripper with five pubs to do.

There are any amount of ways, but they won't be required because, in fact, none of this happened.

The sun *did* jerk sideways a bit, and it seemed that the trees on the rimward side of the gorge were rather taller, and Nanny couldn't shake off the sensation that someone had just sat down heavily on her, squashed her flat, and then opened her out again.

This was because the kingdom did not, in so many words, move through time in the normal flickering sky, high-speed photography sense of the word. It moved around it, which is much cleaner, considerably easier to achieve, and saves all that travelling around trying to find a laboratory opposite a dress shop that will keep the same dummy in the window for sixty years, which has traditionally been the most time-consuming and expensive bit of the whole business.

The kiss lasted more than fifteen years.

Not even frogs can manage that.

The Fool drew back, his eyes glazed, his expression one of puzzlement.

'Did you feel the world move?' he said.

Magrat peered over his shoulder at the forest.

'I think she's done it,' she said.

'Done what?'

Magrat hesitated. 'Oh. Nothing. Nothing much, really.'

'Shall we have another try? I don't think we got it quite right that time.'

Magrat nodded.

This time it lasted only fifteen seconds. It seemed longer.

A tremor ran through the castle, shaking the breakfast tray from which the Duke Felmet, much to his relief, was eating porridge that wasn't too salty.

It was felt by the ghosts that now filled Nanny Ogg's cottage like a rugby team in a telephone box.

It spread to every henhouse in the kingdom, and a number of hands relaxed their grip. And thirty-two purple-faced cockerels took a deep breath and crowed like maniacs, but they were too late, too late . . .

'I still reckon you were up to something,' said Granny Weatherwax.

'Have another cup of tea,' said Nanny pleasantly.

'You won't go and put any drink in it, will you,' Granny said flatly. 'It was the drink what did it last night. I would never have put myself forward like that. It's shameful.'

'Black Aliss never done anything like it,' said Nanny, encouragingly. 'I mean, it was a hundred years, all right, but it was only one castle she moved. I reckon anyone could do a castle.'

Granny's frown puckered at the edge.

'And she let all weeds grow over it,' she observed primly.

'Right enough.'

'Very well done,' said King Verence, eagerly. 'We all thought it was superb. Being in the ethereal plane, of course, we were in a position to observe closely.'

'Very good, your graciousness,' said Nanny Ogg. She turned and observed the crowding ghosts behind him, who hadn't been granted the privilege of sitting at, or partly through, the kitchen table.

'But you lot can bugger off back to the outhouse,' she said. 'The cheek! Except the kiddies, they can stay,' she added. 'Poor little mites.'

'I am afraid it feels so good to be out of the castle,' said the king.

Granny Weatherwax yawned.

'Anyway,' she said, 'we've got to find the boy now. That's the next step.'

'We shall look for him directly after lunch.'

'Lunch?'

'It's chicken,' said Nanny. 'And you're tired. Besides, making a decent search will take a long time.'

'He'll be in Ankh-Morpork,' said Granny. 'Mark my words. Everyone ends up there. We'll start with Ankh-Morpork. You don't have to search for people when destiny is involved, you just wait for them in Ankh-Morpork.'

Nanny brightened up. 'Our Karen got married to an innkeeper from there,' she said. 'I haven't seen the baby yet. We could get free board and everything.'

'We needn't actually go. The whole point is that he should come *here*. There's something about that city,' said Granny. 'It's like a drain.'

'It's five hundred miles away!' said Magrat. 'You'll be away for ages!'

'I can't help it,' said the Fool. 'The duke's given me special instructions. He trusts me.'

'Huh! To hire more soldiers, I expect?'

'No. Nothing like that. Not as bad as that.' The Fool hesitated. He'd introduced Felmet to the world of words. Surely that was better than hitting people with swords? Wouldn't that buy time? Wouldn't it be best for everybody, in the circumstances?

'But you don't have to go! You don't *want* to go!'

'That doesn't have much to do with it. I promised to be loyal to him – '

'Yes, yes, until you're dead. But you don't even *believe* that! You were telling me how much you hated the whole Guild and everything!'

'Well, yes. But I still have to do it. I gave my word.'

Magrat came close to stamping her foot, but didn't sink so low.

'Just when we were getting to know one another!' she shouted. 'You're pathetic!'

The Fool's eyes narrowed. 'I'd only be pathetic if I broke my word,' he said. 'But I may be incredibly ill-advised. I'm sorry. I'll be back in a few weeks, anyway.'

'Don't you understand I'm asking you not to listen to him?'

'I said I'm sorry. I couldn't see you again before I go, could I?'

'I shall be washing my hair,' said Magrat stiffly.

'When?'

'Whenever!'

☆   ☆   ☆

Hwel pinched the bridge of his nose and squinted wearily at the wax-spattered paper.

The play wasn't going at all well.

He'd sorted out the falling chandelier, and found a place for a villain who wore a mask to conceal his disfigurement, and he'd rewritten one of the funny bits to allow for the fact that the hero had been born in a handbag. It was the clowns who were giving him trouble again. They kept changing every time he thought about them. He preferred them in twos, that was traditional, but now there seemed to be a third one, and he was blowed if he could think of any funny lines for him.

His quill moved scratchily over the latest sheet of paper, trying to catch the voices that had streamed through his dreaming mind and had seemed so funny at the time.

His tongue began to stick out of the corner of his mouth. He was sweating.

This iss My Little Study, he wrote. *Hey, with a Little Study youe could goe a Long Way. And I wishe youed start now. Iffe You can't leave yn a Cab then leave yn a Huff. Iff thates too soone, thenn leave yn a minute and a Huff. Say, have you Gott a Pensil? A crayon?* –

Hwel stared at this in horror. On the page it looked nonsensical, ridiculous. And yet, and yet, in the throned auditorium of his mind . . .

He dipped the quill in the inkpot, and chased the echoes further.

Seconde Clown: Atsa right, Boss.

Third Clowne: [businesse with bladder on stick] Honk. Honk.

Hwel gave up. Yes, it was funny, he knew it was funny, he'd heard the laughter in his dreams. But it wasn't right. Not yet. Maybe never. It was like the other idea about the two clowns, one fat, one thin . . . *Thys ys amain Dainty Messe youe have got me into, Stanleigh* . . . He had laughed until his chest ached, and the rest of the company had looked at him in astonishment. But in his dreams it was hilarious.

He laid down the pen and rubbed his eyes. It must be nearly midnight, and the habit of a lifetime told him to spare the candles although, for a fact, they could afford all the candles they could eat now, whatever Vitoller might say.

Hour gongs were being struck all across the city and nightwatchmen were proclaiming that it was indeed midnight and also that, in the face of all the evidence, all was well. Many of them got as far as the end of the sentence before being mugged.

Hwell pushed open the shutters and looked out at Ankh-Morpork.

It would be tempting to say the twin city was at its best this time of year, but that wouldn't be entirely correct. It was at its most *typical*.

The river Ankh, the cloaca of half a continent, was already pretty wide and silt laden when it reached the city's outskirts. By the time it left it didn't so much flow as exude. Owing to the accretion of the mud of centuries the bed of the river was in fact higher than some of the low-lying areas and now, with the snow melt swelling the flow, many of the low-rent districts on the Morpork side were flooded, if you can use that word for a liquid you could pick up in a net. This sort of thing happened every year and would have caused havoc with the drains and sewage systems, so it is just as well that the city didn't have very many. Its inhabitants merely kept a punt handy in the back yard and, periodically, built another storey on the house.

It was reckoned to be very healthy there. Very few germs were able to survive.

Hwel looked across a sort of misty sea in which buildings clustered like a sandcastle competition at high tide. Flares and lighted windows made pleasing patterns on the iridescent surface, but there was one glare of light, much closer to hand, which particularly occupied his attention.

On a patch of slightly higher ground by the river, bought by Vitoller for a ruinous sum, a new building was rising. It was growing even by night, like a mushroom – Hwel could see the cressets burning all along the scaffolding as the hired craftsmen and even some of the players themselves refused to let the mere shade of the sky interrupt their labours.

New buildings were rare in Morpork, but this was even a new *type* of building.

The *Dysk*.

Vitoller had been aghast at the idea at first, but young Tomjon had kept at him. And everyone knew that once the lad had got the feel of it he could persuade water to flow uphill.

'But we've *always* moved around, laddie,' said Vitoller, in the desperate voice of one who knows that, at the end of it all, he's going to lose the argument. 'I can't go around settling down at my time of life.'

'It's not doing you any good,' said Tomjon firmly. 'All these cold nights and frosty mornings. You're not getting any younger. We should stay put somewhere, and let people come to us. And they will, too. You know the crowds we're getting now. Hwel's plays are famous.'

'It's not my plays,' Hwel had said. 'It's the players.'

'I can't see me sitting by a fire in a stuffy room and sleeping on feather beds and all that nonsense,' said Vitoller, but he'd seen the look on his wife's face and had given in.

And then there had been the theatre itself. Making water run uphill was a parlour trick compared to getting the cash out of Vitoller but, it was a fact, they had been doing well these days. Ever since Tomjon had been big enough to wear a ruff and say two words without his voice cracking.

Hwel and Vitoller had watched the first few beams of the wooden framework go up.

'It's against nature,' Vitoller had complained, leaning on his stick. 'Capturing the spirit of the theatre, putting it in a cage. It'll kill it.'

'Oh, I don't know,' said Hwel diffidently. Tomjon had laid his plans well, he'd devoted an entire evening to Hwel before even broaching the subject to his father, and now the dwarf's mind was on fire with the possibilities of backdrops and scenery changes and wings and flies and magnificent engines that could lower gods from the heavens and trapdoors that could raise demons from hell. Hwel was no more capable of objecting to the new theatre than a monkey was of resenting a banana plantation.

'Damn thing hasn't even got a name,' Vitoller had said. 'I should call it the *Golde Mine*, because that's what it's costing me. Where's the money going to come from, that's what I'd like to know.'

In fact they'd tried a lot of names, none of which suited Tomjon.

'It's got to be a name that means everything,' he said. 'Because there's everything inside it. The whole world on the stage, do you see?'

And Hwel had said, knowing as he said it that what he was saying was exactly right, 'The Disc.'

And now the Dysk was nearly done, and still he hadn't written the new play.

He shut the window and wandered back to his desk, picked up the quill, and pulled another sheet of paper towards him. A thought struck him. The whole world *was* a stage, to the gods . . .

Presently he began to write.

All the Disc it is but an Theater, he wrote, *Ane alle men and wymmen are but Players*. He made the mistake of pausing, and another inspiration sleeted down, sending his train of thought off along an entirely new track.

He looked at what he had written and added: *Except Those who selle popcorn*.

After a while he crossed this out, and tried: *Like unto thee Staje of a Theater ys the World, whereon alle Persons strut as Players*.

This seemed a bit better.

He thought for a bit, and continued conscientiously: *Sometimes they walke on. Sometimes they walke off*.

He seemed to be losing it. Time, time, what he needed was an infinity . . .

There was a muffled cry and a thump from the next room. Hwel dropped the quill and pushed open the door cautiously.

The boy was sitting up in bed, white-faced. He relaxed when Hwel came in.

'Hwel?'

'What's up, lad? Nightmares?'

'Gods, it was terrible! I saw them again! I really thought for a minute that – '

Hwel, who was absent-mindedly picking up the clothes that Tomjon had strewn around the room, paused in his work. He was keen on dreams. That was when the ideas came.

'That what?' he said.

'It was like . . . I mean, I was sort of *inside* something, like a bowl, and there were these three terrible faces peering in at me.'

'Aye?'

'Yes, and then they all said "All hail . . ." and then they started arguing about my name, and then they said, "Anyway, who shall be king hereafter." And then one of them said "Here after what?" and one of the other two said, "Just hereafter, girl, it's what you're supposed to say in these circumstances, you might try and make an effort", and then they all peered closer, and one of the others said, "He looks a bit peaky, I reckon it's all that foreign food" and then the youngest one said, "Nanny, I've told you already, there's no such place as Thespia", and then they bickered a bit, and one of the old ones said "He can't hear us, can he? He's tossing and turning a bit" and the other one said, "You know I've never been able to get sound on this thing, Esme" and then they bickered some more, and it went cloudy, and then . . . I woke up . . .' he finished lamely. 'It was horrible, because every time they came close to the bowl it sort of magnified everything, so all you could see was eyes and nostrils.'

Hwel hoisted himself on to the edge of the narrow bed.

'Funny old things, dreams,' he said.

'Not much funny about that one.'

'No, but I mean, last night, I had this dream about a little bandy-legged man walking down a road,' said Hwel. 'He had a little black hat on, and he walked as though his boots were full of water.'

Tomjon nodded politely.

'Yes?' he said. 'And – ?'

Well, that was it. And nothing. He had this little cane which he twirled and, you know, it was incredibly . . .'

The dwarf's voice trailed off. Tomjon's face had that familiar expression of polite and slightly condescending puzzlement that Hwel had come to know and dread.

'Anyway, it was very amusing,' he said, half to himself. But he knew he'd never convince the rest of the company. If it didn't have a custard pie in it somewhere, they said, it wasn't funny.

Tomjon swung his legs out of bed and reached for his britches.

'I'm not going back to sleep,' he said. 'What's the time?'

'It's after midnight,' said Hwel. 'And you know what your father said about going to bed late.

'I'm not,' said Tomjon, pulling on his boots. 'I'm getting up early. Getting up early is very healthy. And now I'm going out for a very healthy drink. You can come too,' he added, 'to keep an eye on me.'

Hwel gave him a doubting look.

'You also know what your father says about going out drinking,' he said.

'Yes. He said he used to do it all the time when he was a lad. He said he'd think nothing of quaffing ale all night and coming home at 5 a.m., smashing windows. He said he was a bit of a roister-doister, not like these white-livered people today who can't hold their drink.' Tomjon adjusted his doublet in front of the mirror, and added. 'You know, Hwel, I reckon responsible behaviour is something to get when you grow older. Like varicose veins.'

Hwel sighed. Tomjon's memory for ill-judged remarks was legendary.

'All right,' he said. 'Just the one, though. Somewhere decent.'

'I promise.' Tomjon adjusted his hat. It had a feather in it.

'By the way,' he said, 'exactly how does one quaff?'

'I think it means you spill most of it,' said Hwel.

If the water of the river Ankh was rather thicker and more full of personality than ordinary river water, so the air in the Mended Drum was more crowded than normal air. It was like dry fog.

Tomjon and Hwel watched it spilling out into the street. The door burst open and a man came through backwards, not actually touching the ground until he hit the wall on the opposite side of the street.

An enormous troll, employed by the owners to keep a measure of order in the place, came out dragging two more limp bodies which he deposited on the cobbles, kicking them once or twice in soft places.

'I reckon they're roistering in there, don't you?' said Tomjon.

'It looks like it,' said Hwel. He shivered. He hated taverns. People always put their drinks down on his head.

They scurried in quickly while the troll was holding one unconscious drinker up by one leg and banging his head on the cobbles in a search for concealed valuables.

Drinking in the Drum has been likened to diving in a swamp, except that in a swamp the alligators don't pick your pockets first. Two hundred eyes watched the pair as they pushed their way through the crowd to the bar, a hundred mouths paused in the act of drinking, cursing or pleading, and ninety-nine brows crinkled with the effort of working out whether the newcomers fell into category A, people to be frightened of or B, people to frighten.

Tomjon walked through the crowd as though it was his property and, with the impetuosity of youth, rapped on the bar. Impetuosity was not a survival trait in the Mended Drum.

'Two pints of your finest ale, landlord,' he said, in tones so carefully judged that the barman was astonished to find himself obediently filling the first mug before the echoes had died away.

Hwel looked up. There was an extremely big man on his right, wearing the outside of several large bulls and more chains than necessary to moor a warship. A face that looked like a building site with hair on it glared down at him.

'Bloody hell,' it said. 'It's a bloody lawn ornament.'

Hwel went cold. Cosmopolitan as they were, the people of Morpork had a breezy, no-nonsense approach to the non-human races, i.e., hit them over the head with a brick and throw them in the river. This did not apply to trolls, naturally, because it is very difficult to be racially prejudiced against creatures seven feet tall who can bite through walls, at least for very long. But people three feet high were absolutely *designed* to be discriminated against.

The giant prodded Hwel on the top of his head.

'Where's your fishing rod, lawn ornament,' he said.

The barman pushed the mugs across the puddled counter.

'Here you are,' he said, leering. 'One pint. And one half pint.'

Tomjon opened his mouth to speak, but Hwel nudged him sharply in the knee. Put up with it, put up with it, slip out as soon as possible, it was the only way . . .

'Where's your little pointy hat, then?' said the bearded man.

The room had gone quiet. This looked like being cabaret time.

'I *said*, where's your pointy hat, dopey?'

The barman got a grip of the blackthorn stick with nails in which lived under the counter, just in case, and said, 'Er – '

'I was talking to the lawn ornament here.'

The man took the dregs of his own drink and poured them carefully over the silent dwarf's head.

'I ain't drinking here again,' he muttered, when even this failed to have any effect. 'It's bad enough they let monkeys drink here, but pygmies – '

Now the silence in the bar took on a whole new intensity in which the sound of a stool being slowly pushed back was like the creak of doom. All

eyes swivelled to the other end of the room, where sat the one drinker in the
Mended Drum who came into category C.

What Tomjon had thought was an old sack hunched over the bar was
extending arms and – other arms, except that they were its legs. A sad,
rubbery face turned towards the speaker, its expression as melancholy as the
mists of evolution. Its funny lips curled back. There was absolutely nothing
funny about its teeth.

'Er,' said the barman again, his voice frightening even him in that terrible
simian silence. 'I don't think you meant that, did you? Not about monkeys,
eh? You didn't really, did you?'

'What the hell's that?' hissed Tomjon.

'I think it's an orang-utan,' said Hwel. 'An ape.'

'A monkey's a monkey,' said the bearded man, at which several of the
Drum's more percipient customers started to edge for the door. 'I mean, so
what? But these bloody lawn ornaments – '

Hwel's fist struck out at groin height.

Dwarfs have a reputation as fearsome fighters. Any race of three-foot tall
people who favour axes and go into battle as into a championship tree-felling
competition soon get talked about. But years of wielding a pen instead of a
hammer had relieved Hwel's punches of some of their stopping power, and
it could have been the end of him when the big man yelled and drew his
sword if a pair of delicate, leathery hands hadn't instantly jerked the thing
from his grip and, with only a small amount of effort, bent it double.*

When the giant growled, and turned around, an arm like a couple of
broom handles strung together with elastic and covered with red fur
unfolded itself in a complicated motion and smacked him across the jaw so
hard that he rose several inches in the air and landed on a table.

By the time that the table had slid into another table and overturned a
couple of benches there was enough impetus to start the night's overdue
brawl, especially since the big man had a few friends with him. Since no one
felt like attacking the ape, who had dreamily pulled a bottle from the shelf
and smashed the bottom off on the counter, they hit whoever happened to

---

* An explanation may be needed at this point. The Librarian of the magic library at
Unseen University, the Disc's premier college of wizardry, had been turned into an
orang-utan some years previously by a magical accident in that accident-prone academy,
and since then had strenuously resisted all well-meaning efforts to turn him back. For one
thing, longer arms and prehensile toes made getting around the higher shelves a whole lot
easier, and being an ape meant you didn't have to bother with all this *angst* business. He
had also been rather pleased to find that his new body, although looking deceptively like a
rubber sack full of water, gave him three times the strength and twice the reach of his old
one.

be nearest, on general principles. This is absolutely correct etiquette for a
tavern brawl.

Hwel walked under a table and dragged Tomjon, who was watching all
this with interest, after him.

'So this is roistering. I always wondered.'

'I think perhaps it would be a good idea to leave,' said the dwarf firmly.
'Before there's, you know, any trouble.'

There was a thump as someone landed on the table above them, and a
tinkle of broken glass.

'Is it real roistering, do you suppose, or merely rollicking?' said Tomjon,
grinning.

'It's going to be bloody murder in a minute, my lad!'

Tomjon nodded, and crawled back out into the fray. Hwel heard him
thump on the bar counter with something and call for silence.

Hwel put his arms over his head in panic.

'I didn't mean – ' he began.

In fact calling for silence was a sufficiently rare event in the middle of a
tavern brawl that silence was what Tomjon got. And silence was what he
filled.

Hwel started as the boy's voice rang out, full of confidence and absolutely
first-class projection.

'*Brothers! And yet may I call all men brother, for on this night –* '

The dwarf craned up to see Tomjon standing on a chair, one hand raised in
the prescribed declamatory fashion. Around him men were frozen in the act
of giving one another a right seeing-to, their faces turned to his.

Down at tabletop height Hwel's lips moved in perfect synchronisation
with the words as Tomjon went through the familiar speech. He risked
another look.

The fighters straightened up, pulled themselves together, adjusted the
hang of their tunics, glanced apologetically at one another. Many of them
were in fact standing to attention.

Even Hwel felt a fizz in his blood, and he'd written those words. He'd
slaved half a night over them, years ago, when Vitoller had declared that they
needed another five minutes in Act III of *The King of Ankh*.

'Scribble us something with a bit of spirit it in,' he'd said. 'A bit of zip and
sizzle, y'know. Something to summon up the blood and put a bit of
backbone in our friends in the ha'penny seats. And just long enough to give
us time to change the set.'

He'd been a bit ashamed of that play at the time. The famous Battle of
Morpork, he strongly suspected, had consisted of about two thousand men
lost in a swamp on a cold, wet day, hacking one another into oblivion with

rusty swords. What would the last King of Ankh have said to a pack of ragged men who knew they were outnumbered, outflanked and outgeneralled? Something with bite, something with edge, something like a drink of brandy to a dying man; no logic, no explanation, just words that would reach right down through a tired man's brain and pull him to his feet by his testicles.

Now he was seeing its effect.

He began to think the walls had fallen away, and there was a cold mist blowing over the marshes, its choking silence broken only by the impatient cries of the carrion birds . . .

And this voice.

And he'd written the words, they were *his*, no half-crazed king had ever really spoken like this. And he'd written all this to fill in a gap so that a castle made of painted sacking stretched over a frame could be shoved behind a curtain, and this voice was taking the coal dust of his words and filling the room with diamonds.

I *made* these words, Hwel thought. But they don't belong to me. They belong to him.

Look at those people. Not a patriotic thought among them, but if Tomjon asked them, this bunch of drunkards would storm the Patrician's palace tonight. And they'd probably succeed.

I just hope his mouth never falls into the wrong hands . . .

As the last syllables died away, their white-hot echoes searing across every mind in the room, Hwel shook himself and crawled out of hiding and jabbed Tomjon on the knee.

'Come away now, you fool,' he hissed. 'Before it wears off.'

He grasped the boy firmly by the arm, handed a couple of complimentary tickets to the stunned barman, and hurried up the steps. He didn't stop until they were a street away.

'I thought I was doing rather well there,' said Tomjon.

'A good deal too well, I reckon.'

The boy rubbed his hands together. 'Right. Where shall we go next?'

'*Next*?'

'Tonight is young!'

'No, *tonight* is dead. It's *today* that's young,' said the dwarf hurriedly.

'Well, I'm not going home yet. Isn't there somewhere a bit more friendly? We haven't actually drunk anything.'

Hwel sighed.

'A troll tavern,' said Tomjon. 'I've heard about them. There's some down in the Shades.* I'd like to see a troll tavern.'

---

* The Shades is an ancient part of Ankh-Morpork considered considerably more unpleasant and disreputable than the rest of the city. This always amazes visitors.

'They're for trolls only, boy. Molten lava to drink and rock music and cheese 'n chutney flavoured pebbles.'

'What about dwarf bars?'

'You'd hate it,' said Hwel, fervently. 'Besides, you'd run out of headroom.'

'Low dives, are they?'

'Look at it like this – how long do you think you could sing about gold?'

' "It's yellow and it goes chink and you can buy things with it," ' said Tomjon experimentally, as they strolled through the crowds on the Plaza of Broken Moons. 'Four seconds, I think.'

'Right. Five hours of it gets a bit repetitive.' Hwel kicked a pebble gloomily. He'd investigated a few dwarf bars last time they were in town, and hadn't approved. For some reason his fellow expatriates, who at home did nothing more objectionable than mine a bit of iron ore and hunt small creatures, felt impelled, once in the big city, to wear chain-mail underwear, go around with axes in their belts, and call themselves names like Timkin Rumbleguts. And no one could beat a city dwarf when it came to quaffing. Sometimes they missed their mouths altogether.

'Anyway,' he added, 'you'd get thrown out for being too creative. The actual words are, "Gold, gold, gold, gold, gold, gold".'

'Is there a chorus?'

' "Gold, gold, gold, gold, gold",' said Hwel.

'You left out a "gold" there.'

'I think it's because I wasn't cut out to be a dwarf.'

'Cut *down*, lawn ornament,' said Tomjon.

There was a little hiss of indrawn breath.

'Sorry,' said Tomjon hurriedly. 'It's just that father – '

'I've known your father for a long time,' said Hwel. 'Through thick and thin, and there was a damn sight more thin than thick. Since before you were bor– ' He hesitated. 'Times were hard in those days,' he mumbled. 'So what I'm saying is . . . well, some things you earn.'

'Yes. I'm sorry.'

'You see, just – ' Hwel paused at the mouth of a dark alley. 'Did you hear something?' he said.

They squinted into the alley, once again revealing themselves as newcomers to the city. Morporkians don't look down dark alleys when they hear strange noises. If they see four struggling figures their first instinct is not to rush to anyone's assistance, or at least not to rush to the assistance of the one who appears to be losing and on the wrong end of someone else's boot. Nor do they shout 'Oi!'. Above all, they don't look surprised when the assailants, instead of guiltily running off, flourish a small piece of cardboard in front of them.

'What's this?' said Tomjon.

'It's a clown!' said Hwel. 'They've mugged a clown!'

'"Theft Licence"?' said Tomjon, holding the card up to the light.

'That's right,' said the leader of the three. 'Only don't expect us to do you too, 'cos we're on our way home.'

''S right,' said one of the assistants. 'It's the thingy, the quota.'

'But you were kicking him!'

'Worl, not a lot. Not what you'd call actual kicking.'

'More foot nudging, sort of thing,' said the third thief.

'Fair's fair. He bloody well went and fetched Ron here a right thump, didn't he.'

'Yeah. Some people have no idea.'

'Why, you heartless – ' Hwel began, but Tomjon laid a cautioning hand on his head.

The boy turned the card over. The obverse read:

J. H. 'Flannelfoot' Boggis and Nephews
Bespoke Thieves
'The Old Firm'
(Estblshd AM 1789)
All type Theft carried out Professionly and
with Disgression
Houses cleared. 24-hr service. No job too small.
LET US QUOTE YOU FOR OUR FAMILY RATE

'It seems to be in order,' he said reluctantly.

Hwel paused in the act of helping the dazed victim to his feet.

'In order?' he shouted. 'To rob someone?'

'We'll give him a chitty, of course,' said Boggis. 'Lucky we found him first, really. Some of these newcomers in the business, they've got no idea.'*

---

* Ankh-Morpork's enviable system of licensed criminals owes much to the current Patrician, Lord Vetinari. He reasoned that the only way to police a city of a million inhabitants was to recognise the various gangs and robber guilds, give them professional status, invite the leaders to large dinners, allow an acceptable level of street crime *and then make the guild leaders responsible for enforcing it*, on pain of being stripped of their new civic honours along with large areas of their skins. It worked. Criminals, it turned out, made a very good police force; unauthorised robbers soon found, for example, that instead of a night in the cells they could now expect an eternity at the bottom of the river.

However, there was the problem of apportioning the crime statistics, and so there arose a complex system of annual budgeting, chits and allowances to see that a) the members could make a reasonable living and b) no citizen was robbed or assaulted more than an agreed number of times. Many foresighted citizens in fact arranged to get an acceptable minimum of theft, assault, etc, over at the beginning of the financial year, often in the privacy and comfort of their own homes, and thus be able to walk the streets quite safely for the rest of the year. It all ticked over extremely peacefully and efficiently, demonstrating once again that compared to the Patrician of Ankh, Machiavelli could not have run a whelk stall.

'Cowboys,' agreed a nephew.

'How much did you steal?' said Tomjon.

Boggis opened the clown's purse, which was stuck in his belt. Then he went pale.

'Oh, bleeding hell,' he said. The Nephews clustered around.

'We're for it, sort of thing.'

'Second time this year, uncle.'

Boggis glared at the victim.

'Well, how was I to know? I wasn't to know, was I? I mean, look at him, how much would *you* expect him to have on him? Couple of coppers, right? I mean, we'd never have done for him, only it was on our way home. You try and do someone a favour, this is what happens.'

'How much has he got, then?' said Tomjon.

'There must be a hundred silver dollars in here,' moaned Boggis, waving a purse. 'I mean, that's not my league. That's not my class. I can't handle that sort of money. You've got to be in the Guild of Lawyers or something to steal that much. It's way over my quota, is that.'

'Give it back then,' said Tomjon.

'But I done him a receipt!'

'They've all got, you know, numbers on,' explained the younger of the nephews. 'The Guild checks up, sort of . . .'

Hwel grabbed Tomjon's hand.

'Will you excuse us a moment?' he said to the frantic thief, and dragged Tomjon to the other side of the alley.

'Okay,' he said. 'Who's gone mad? Them? Me? You?'

Tomjon explained.

'It's legal?'

'Up to a certain point. Fascinating, isn't it? Man in a pub told me about it, sort of thing.'

'But he's stolen *too much*?'

'So it appears. I gather the Guild is very strict about it.'

There was a groan from the victim hanging between them. He tinkled gently.

'Look after him,' said Tomjon. 'I'll sort this out.'

He went back to the thieves, who were looking very worried.

'My client feels,' he said, 'that the situation could be resolved if you give the money back.'

'Ye-es,' said Boggis, approaching the idea as if it was a brand new theory of cosmic creation. 'But it's the receipt, see, we have to fill it up, time and place, signed and everything . . .'

'My client feels that possibly you could rob him of, let us say, five copper pieces,' said Tomjon, smoothly.

' – I bloody don't! – ' shouted the Fool, who was coming round.

'That represents two copper pieces as the going rate, plus expenses of three copper pieces for time, call-out fees – '

'Wear and tear on cosh,' said Boggis.

'Exactly.'

'Very fair. Very fair.' Boggis looked over Tomjon's head at the Fool, who was now completely conscious and very angry. 'Very fair,' he said loudly. 'Statesmanlike. Much obliged, I'm sure.' He looked down at Tomjon. 'And anything for yourself, sir?' he added. 'Just say the word. We've got a special on GBH this season. Practically painless, you'll barely feel a thing.'

'Hardly breaks the skin,' said the older nephew. 'Plus you get choice of limb.'

'I believe I am well served in that area,' said Tomjon smoothly.

'Oh. Well. Right you are then. No problem.'

'Which merely leaves,' continued Tomjon, as the thieves started to walk away, 'the question of legal fees.'

The gentle greyness at the stump of the night flowed across Ankh-Morpork. Tomjon and Hwel sat on either side of the table in their lodgings, counting.

'Three silver dollars and eighteen copper pieces in profit, I make it,' said Tomjon.

'That was amazing,' said the Fool. 'I mean, the way they volunteered to go home and get some more money as well, after you gave them that speech about the rights of man.'

He dabbed some more ointment on his head.

'And the youngest one started to cry,' he added. 'Amazing.'

'It wears off,' said Hwel.

'You're a dwarf, aren't you?'

Hwel didn't feel he could deny this.

'I can tell you're a Fool,' he said.

'Yes. It's the bells, isn't it?' said the Fool wearily, rubbing his ribs.

'Yes, and the bells.' Tomjon grimaced and kicked Hwel under the table.

'Well, I'm very grateful,' said the Fool. He stood up, and winced. 'I'd really like to show my gratitude,' he added. 'Is there a tavern open around here?'

Tomjon joined him at the window, and pointed down the length of the street.

'See all those tavern signs?' he said.

'Yes. Gosh. There's hundreds.'

'Right. See the one at the end, with the blue and white sign?'

'Yes. I think so.'

'Well, as far as I know, that's the only one around here that's ever closed.'

'Then pray allow me to treat you to a drink. It's the least I can do,' said the Fool nervously. 'And I'm sure the little fellow would like something to quaff.'

Hwel gripped the edge of the table and opened his mouth to roar.

And stopped.

He stared at the two figures. His mouth stayed open.

It closed again with a snap.

'Something the matter?' said Tomjon.

Hwel looked away. It had been a long night. 'Trick of the light,' he muttered. 'And I could do with a drink,' he added. 'A bloody good quaff.'

In fact, he thought, why fight it? 'I'll even put up with the singing,' he said.

'Was' the nex' wor'?'

''S gold. I think.'

'Ah.'

Hwel looked unsteadily into his mug. Drunkenness had this to be said for it, it stopped the flow of inspirations.

'And you left out the "gold",' he said.

'Where?' said Tomjon. He was wearing the Fool's hat.

Hwel considered this. 'I reckon,' he said, concentrating, 'it was between the "gold" and the "gold". An' I reckon,' he peered again into the mug. It was empty, a horrifying sight. 'I reckon,' he tried again, and finally gave up, and substituted, 'I reckon I could do with another drink.'

'My shout this time,' said the Fool. 'Hahaha. My squeak. Hahaha.' He tried to stand up, and banged his head.

In the gloom of the bar a dozen axes were gripped more firmly. The part of Hwel that was sober, and was horrified to see the rest of him being drunk, urged him to wave his hand at the beetling brows glaring at them through the gloom.

''S all right,' he said, to the bar at large. 'He don't mean it, he ver' funny wossname, idiot. Fool. Ver' funny Fool, all the way from wassisplace.'

'Lancre,' said the Fool, and sat down heavily on the bar.

''S right. Long way away from wossname, sounds like foot disease. Don't know how to behave. Don't know many dwarfs.'

'Hahaha,' said the Fool, clutching his head. 'Bit *short* of them where I come from.'

Someone tapped Hwel on the shoulder. He turned and looked into a craggy, hairy face under an iron helmet. The dwarf in question was tossing a throwing axe up and down in a meaningful way.

'You ought to tell your friend to be a bit less funny,' he suggested. 'Otherwise he will be amusing the demons in Hell!'

Hwel squinted at him through the alcoholic haze.

'Who're you?' he said.

'Grabpot Thundergust,' said the dwarf, striking his chain-mailed torso. 'And I say – '

Hwel peered closer.

'Here, I know you,' he said. 'You got a cosmetics mill down Hobfast Street. I bought a lot of greasepaint off you last week – '

A look of panic crossed Thundergust's face. He leaned forward in panic. 'Shutup, shutup,' he whispered.

'That's right, it said the Halls of Elven Perfume and Rouge Co.,' said Hwel happily.

'Ver' good stuff,' said Tomjon, who was trying to stop himself from sliding off the tiny bench. 'Especially your No. 19, Corpse Green, my father swears it's the best. First class.'

The dwarf hefted his axe uneasily. 'Well, er,' he said. 'Oh. But. Yes. Well, thank you. Only the finest ingredients, mark you.'

'Chop them up with that, do you?' said Hwel innocently, pointing to the axe. 'Or is it your night off?'

Thundergust's brows beetled again like a cockroach convention.

'Here, you're not with the theatre?'

'Tha's us,' said Tomjon. 'Strolling players.' He corrected himself. 'Standing-still players now. Haha. Slidin'-down players now.'

The dwarf dropped his axe and sat down on the bench, his face suddenly softened with enthusiasm.

'I went last week,' he said. 'Bloody good, it was. There was this girl and this fellow, but she was married to this old man, and there was this other fellow, and they said he'd died, and she pined away and took poison, but then it turned out this man was the other man really, only he couldn't tell her on account of – ' Thundergust stopped, and blew his nose. 'Everyone died in the end,' he said. 'Very tragic. I cried all the way home, I don't mind telling you. She was so pale.'

'No. 19 and a layer of powder,' said Tomjon cheerfully. 'Plus a bit of brown eyeshadow.'

'Eh?'

'And a couple of hankies in the vest,' he added.

'What's he saying?' said the dwarf to the company at, for want of a better word, large.

Hwel smiled into his tankard.

'Give 'em a bit of Gretalina's soliloquy, boy,' he said.

'Right.'

Tomjon stood up, hit his head, sat down and then knelt on the floor as a compromise. He clasped his hands to what would have been, but for a few chance chromosomes, his bosom.

'*You lie who call it Summer . . .*' he began.

The assembled dwarfs listened in silence for several minutes. One of them dropped his axe, and was noisily hushed by the rest of them.

'*. . . and melting snow. Farewell.*' Tomjon finished. 'Drinks phial, collapses behind battlements, down ladder, out of dress and into tabard for Comic Guard No. 2, wait one, entrance left. *What ho, good –* '

'That's about enough,' said Hwel quietly.

Several of the dwarfs were crying into their helmets. There was a chorus of blown noses.

Thundergust dabbed at his eyes with a chain-mail handkerchief.

'That was the most saddest thing I've ever heard,' he said. He glared at Tomjon. 'Hang on,' he said, as realisation dawned. 'He's a man. I bloody fell in love with that girl on stage.' He nudged Hwel. 'He's not a bit of an elf, is he?'

'Absolutely human,' said Hwel. 'I know his father.'

Once again he stared hard at the Fool, who was watching them with his mouth open, and looked back at Tomjon.

Nah, he thought. Coincidence.

''S acting,' he said. 'A good actor can be anything, right?'

He could feel the Fool's eye boring into the back of his short neck.

'Yes, but dressing up as women, it's a bit – ' said Thundergust doubtfully.

Tomjon slipped off his shoes and knelt down on them, bringing his face level with the dwarf's. He gave him a calculating stare for a few seconds, and then adjusted his features.

And there were two Thundergusts. True, one of them was kneeling and had apparently been shaved.

'What ho, what ho,' said Tomjon in the dwarf's voice.

This was by way of being a hilarious gag to the rest of the dwarfs, who had an uncomplicated sense of humour. As they gathered round the pair Hwel felt a gentle touch on the shoulder.

'You two are with a theatre?' said the Fool, now almost sober.

''S right.'

'Then I've come five hundred miles to find you.'

It was, as Hwel would have noted in his stage directions, Later the Same Day. The sounds of hammering as the Dysk theatre rose from its cradle of scaffolding thumped through Hwel's head and out the other side.

He could remember the drinking, he was certain. And the dwarfs bought lots more rounds when Tomjon did his impersonations. Then they had all gone to another bar Thundergust knew, and then they'd gone to a Klatchian takeaway, and after that it was just a blur . . .

He wasn't very good at quaffing. Too much of the drink actually landed in his mouth.

Judging by the taste in it, some incontinent creature of the night had also scored a direct hit.

'Can you do it?' said Vitoller.

Hwel smacked his lips to get rid of the taste.

'I expect,' said Tomjon. 'It sounded interesting, the way he told it. Wicked king ruling with the help of evil witches. Storms. Ghastly forests. True Heir to Throne in Life-and-Death Struggle. Flash of Dagger. Screams, alarums. Evil king dies. Good triumphs. Bells ring out.'

'Showers of rose petals could be arranged,' said Vitoller. 'I know a man who can get them at practically cost.'

They both looked at Hwel, who was drumming his fingers on his stool. All three found their attention drawn to the bag of silver the Fool had given Hwel. Even by itself it represented enough money to complete the Dysk. And there had been talk of more to follow. Patronage, that was the thing.

'You'll do it then, will you?' said Vitoller.

'It's got a certain something,' Hwel conceded. 'But . . . I don't know . . .'

'I'm not trying to pressure you,' said Vitoller. All three pairs of eyes swivelled back to the money bag.

'It seems a bit fishy,' Tomjon conceded. 'I mean, the Fool is decent enough. But the way he tells it . . . it's very odd. His mouth says the words, and his eyes say something else. And I got the impression he'd much rather we believed his eyes.'

'On the other hand,' said Vitoller hurriedly, 'what harm could it do? The pay's the thing.'

Hwel raised his head.

'What?' he said muzzily.

'I said, the play's the thing,' said Vitoller.

There was silence again, except for the drumming of Hwel's fingertips. The bag of silver seemed to have grown larger. In fact, it seemed to fill the room.

'The thing is – ' Vitoller began, unnecessarily loud.

'The way I see it – ' Hwel began.

They both stopped.

'After you. Sorry.'

'It wasn't important. Go ahead.'

'I was going to say, we could afford to build the Dysk anyway,' said Hwel.

'Just the shell and the stage,' said Vitoller. 'But not all the other things. Not the trapdoor mechanism, or the machine for lowering gods out of heaven. Or the big turntable, or the wind fans.'

'We used to manage without all that stuff,' said Hwel. 'Remember the old days? All we had was a few planks and a bit of painted sacking. But we had a lot of spirit. If we wanted wind we had to make it ourself.' He drummed his fingers for a while. 'Of course,' he added quietly, 'we should be able to afford a wave machine. A small one. I've got this idea about this ship wrecked on an island, where there's this – '

'Sorry.' Vitoller shook his head.

'But we've had some huge audiences!' said Tomjon.

'Sure, lad. Sure. But they pay in ha'pennies. The artificers want silver. If we wanted to be rich men – people,' he corrected hurriedly, 'we should have been born carpenters.' Vitoller shifted uneasily. 'I already owe Chrystophrase the Troll more than I should.'

The other two stared.

'He's the one that has people's limbs torn off!' said Tomjon.

'How much do you owe him?' said Hwel.

'It's all right,' said Vitoller hurriedly, 'I'm keeping up the interest payments. More or less.'

'Yes, but how much does he want?'

'An arm and a leg.'

The dwarf and boy stared at him in horror. 'How could you have been so – '

'I did it for you two! Tomjon deserves a better stage, he doesn't want to go ruining his health sleeping in lattys and never knowing a home, and you, my man, you need somewhere settled, with all the proper things you ought to have, like trapdoors and . . . wave machines and so forth. You talked me into it, and I thought, they're right. It's no life out on the road, giving two performances a day to a bunch of farmers and going round with a hat afterwards, what sort of future is that? I thought, we've got to get a place somewhere, with comfortable seats for the gentry, people who don't throw potatoes at the stage. I said, blow the cost. I just wanted you to – '

'All right, all right!' shouted Hwel. 'I'll write it!'

'I'll act it,' said Tomjon.

'I'm not forcing you mind,' said Vitoller. 'It's your own choice.'

Hwel frowned at the table. There were, he had to admit, some nice touches. Three witches was good. Two wouldn't be enough, four would be too many. They could be meddling with the destinies of mankind, and everything. Lots of smoke and green light. You could do a lot with three witches. It was surprising no one had thought of it before.

'So we can tell this Fool that we'll do it, can we?' said Vitoller, his hand on the bag of silver.

And of course you couldn't go wrong with a good storm. And there was the ghost routine that Vitoller had cut out of *Please Yourself*, saying they couldn't afford the muslin. And perhaps he could put Death in, too. Young Dafe would make a damn good Death, with white make-up and platform soles . . .

'How far away did he say he'd come from?' he said.

'The Ramtops,' said the playmaster. 'Some little kingdom no one has ever heard of. Sounds like a chest infection.'

'It'd take months to get there.'

'I'd like to go, anyway,' said Tomjon. 'That's where I was born.'

Vitoller looked at the ceiling. Hwel looked at the floor. Anything was better, just at that moment, than looking at each other's face.

'That's what you said,' said the boy. 'When you did a tour of the mountains, you said.'

'Yes, but I can't remember where,' said Vitoller. 'All those little mountain towns looked the same to me. We spent more time pushing the lattys across rivers and dragging them up hills than we ever did on the stage.'

'I could take some of the younger lads and we could make a summer of it,' said Tomjon. 'Put on all the old favourites. And we could still be back by Soulcake Day. You could stay here and see to the theatre, and we could be back for a Grand Opening.' He grinned at his father. 'It'd be good for them,' he said slyly. 'You always said some of the young lads don't know what a real acting life is like.'

'Hwel's still got to write the play,' Vitoller pointed out.

Hwel was silent. He was staring at nothing at all. After a while one hand fumbled in his doublet and brought out a sheaf of paper, and then disappeared in the direction of his belt and produced a small corked ink pot and a bundle of quills.

They watched as, without once looking at them, the dwarf smoothed out the paper, opened the ink pot, dipped a quill, held it poised like a hawk waiting for its prey, and then began to write.

Vitoller nodded at Tomjon.

Walking as quietly as they could, they left the room.

Around mid-afternoon they took up a tray of food and a bundle of paper.

The tray was still there at teatime. The paper had gone.

A few hours later a passing member of the company reported hearing a yell of 'It can't work! It's back to front!' and the sound of something being thrown across the room.

Around supper Vitoller heard a shouted request for more candles and fresh quills.

Tomjon tried to get an early night, but sleep was murdered by the sound of creativity from the next room. There were mutterings about balconies, and whether the world really needed wave machines. The rest was silence, except for the insistent scratching of quills.

Eventually, Tomjon dreamed.

'*Now. Have we got everything this time?*'

'*Yes, Granny.*'

'*Light the fire, Magrat.*'

'*Yes, Granny.*'

'*Right. Let's see now –* '

'*I wrote it all down, Granny.*'

'*I can read, my girl, thank you very much. Now, what's this. "Round about the cauldron go, In the poisoned entrails throw . . ." What are these supposed to be?*'

'*Our Jason slaughtered a pig yesterday, Esme.*'

'*These look like perfectly good chitterlin's to me, Gytha. There's a couple of decent meals in them, if I'm any judge.*'

'*Please, Granny.*'

'*There's plenty of starvin' people in Klatch who wouldn't turn up their nose at 'em, that's all I'm saying . . . All right, all right. "Whole grain wheat and lentils too, In the cauldron seethe and stew"? What happened to the toad?*'

'*Please, Granny. You're slowing it down. You know Goodie was against all unnecessary cruelty. Vegetable protein is a perfectly acceptable substitute.*'

'*That means no newt or fenny snake either, I suppose?*'

'*No, Granny.*'

'*Or tiger's chaudron?*'

'*Here.*'

'*What the hell's this, excuse my Klatchian?*'

'*It's a tiger's chaudron. Our Wane bought it off a merchant from forn parts.*'

'*You sure?*'

'*Our Wane asked special, Esme.*'

'*Looks like any other chaudron to me. Oh, well. "Double, hubble, stubble trouble, Fire burn and cauldron bub–" WHY isn't the cauldron bubbling, Magrat?*'

Tomjon awoke, shivering. The room was dark. Outside a few stars pierced the mists of the city, and there was the occasional whistle of burglars and footpads as they went about their strictly lawful occasions.

There was silence from the next room, but he could see the light of a candle under the door.

He went back to bed.

Across the turgid river the Fool had also awakened. He was staying in the Fools' Guild, not out of choice but because the duke hadn't given him any money for anything else, and getting to sleep had been difficult in any case. The chilly walls had brought back too many memories. Besides, if he listened hard he could hear the muted sobs and occasional whimpers from the students' dormitories, as they contemplated with horror the life that lay ahead of them.

He punched the rock-hard pillow, and sank into a fitful sleep. Perchance to dream.

'Slab and grue, yes. But it doesn't say how slab and grue.'

'Goodie Whemper recommended testing a bit in a cup of cold water, like toffee.'

'How inconvenient that we didn't think to bring one, Magrat.'

'I think we should be getting on, Esme. The night's nearly gone.'

'Just don't blame me if it doesn't work properly, that's all. Lessee . . . "Baboon hair and . . ." Who's got the baboon hair? Oh, thank you, Gytha, though it looks more like cat hair to me, but never mind. "Baboon hair and mandrake root", and if that's real mandrake I'm very surprised, "carrot juice and tongue of boot", I see, a little humour, I suppose . . .'

'Please hurry!'

'All right, all right. "Owl hoot and glow-worm glimmer. Boil – and then allow to simmer."'

'You know, Esme, this doesn't taste half bad.'

'You're not supposed to drink it, you daft doyenne!'

Tomjon sat bolt upright in bed. That was them again, the same faces, the bickering voices, distorted by time and space.

Even after he looked out of the window, where fresh daylight was streaming through the city, he could still hear the voices grumbling into the distance, like old thunder, fading away . . .

'I for one didn't believe it about the tongue of boot.'

'It's still very runny. Do you think we should put some cornflour into it?'

'It won't matter. Either he's on his way, or he isn't . . .'

He got up and doused his face in the washbasin.

Silence rolled in swathes from Hwel's room. Tomjon slipped on his clothes and pushed open the door.

It looked as though it had snowed indoors, great heavy flakes that had drifted into odd corners of the room. Hwel sat at his low table in the middle of the floor, his head pillowed on a pile of paper, snoring.

Tomjon tiptoed across the room and picked up a discarded ball of paper at random. He smoothed it out and read:

> KING: Now, I'm just going to put the crown on this bush here, and you will tell me if anyone tries to take it, won't you?
> GROUNDLINGS: Yes!
> KING: Now if I could just find my horsey . . .
> *(1st assassin pops up behind rock.)*
> AUDIENCE: Behind you!
> *(1st assassin disappears)*
> KING: You're trying to play tricks on old Kingy, you naughty . . .

There was a lot of crossing out, and a large blot. Tomjon threw it aside and selected another ball at random.

> KING: Is this a ~~duck knife~~ dagger I see ~~behind beside in front of~~ before me, its ~~beak~~ handle pointing at ~~me~~ my hand?
> 1ST MURDERER: I'faith, it is not so. ~~Oh, no it isn't!~~
> 2ND MURDERER: Thou speakest truth, sire. ~~Oh, yes it is!~~

Judging by the creases in the paper, this one had been thrown at the wall particularly hard. Hwel had once explained to Tomjon his theory about inspirations, and by the look of it a whole shower had fallen last night.

Fascinated by this insight into the creative processes, however, Tomjon tried a third discarded attempt:

> QUEEN: Faith, there is a sound without! Mayhap it is my husband returning! Quick, into the garderobe, and wait not upon the order of your going!
> MURDERER: Marry, but your maid still has my pantoufles!
> MAID *(opening door)*: The Archbishop, your majesty.
> PRIEST *(under bed)*: Bless my soul!
> *(Divers alarums)*

Tomjon wondered vaguely what divers alarums, which Hwel always included somewhere in the stage directions, actually were. Hwel always refused to say. Perhaps they referred to dangerous depths, or lack of air pressure.

He sidled towards the table and, with great care, pulled the sheaf of paper from under the sleeping dwarf's head, lowering it gently on to a cushion.

The top sheet read:

~~Verence~~ ~~Felmet~~ ~~Small~~ ~~God's~~ ~~Eve~~ A Night Of ~~Knives~~ ~~Daggers~~ Kings, by, Hwel of Vitoller's Men. A ~~Comedy~~ Tragedy in ~~Eight~~ ~~Five~~ ~~Six~~ ~~Three~~ Nine Acts.

Characters: Felmet, A Good King.
Verence, A Bad King.
Wethewacs, Ane Evil Witch
Hogg, Ane Likewise Evil Witch
Magerat, Ane Sirene . . .

Tomjon flicked over the page.

Scene: ~~A~~ ~~Drawing~~ ~~Room~~ ~~Ship~~ ~~at~~ ~~See~~ ~~Street~~ ~~in~~ ~~Pseudopolis~~ Blasted Moor. Enter Three Witches . . .

The boy read for a while and then turned to the last page.

Gentles, leave us dance and sing, and wish good health unto the king (Exeunt all, singing falala, etc. Shower of rose petals. Ringing of bells. Gods descend from heaven, demons rise from hell, much ado with turntable, etc.) The End.

Hwel snored.

In his dreams gods rose and fell, ships moved with cunning and art across canvas oceans, pictures jumped and ran together and became flickering images; men flew on wires, flew without wires, great ships of illusion fought against one another in imaginary skies, seas opened, ladies were sawn in half, a thousand special-effects men giggled and gibbered. Through it all he ran with his arms open in desperation, knowing that none of this really existed or ever would exist and all he *really* had was a few square yards of planking, some canvas and some paint on which to trap the beckoning images that invaded his head.

Only in our dreams are we free. The rest of the time we need wages.

'It's a good play,' said Vitoller, 'apart from the ghost.'

'The ghost stays,' said Hwel sullenly.

'But people always jeer and throw things. Anyway, you know how hard it is to get all the chalk dust out of the clothes.'

'The ghost stays. It's a dramatic necessity.'

'You *said* it was a dramatic necessity in the last play.'

'Well, it was.'

'And in *Please Yourself*, and in *A Wizard of Ankh*, and all the rest of them.'

'I like ghosts.'

They stood to one side and watched the dwarf artificers assembling the wave machine. It consisted of half a dozen long spindles, covered in complex canvas spirals painted in shades of blue and green and white, and stretching the complete width of the stage. An arrangement of cogs and endless belts led to a treadmill in the wings. When the spirals were all turning at once people with weak stomachs had to look away.

'Sea battles,' breathed Hwel. 'Shipwrecks. Tritons. Pirates!'

'Squeaky bearings, laddie,' groaned Vitoller, shifting his weight on his stick. 'Maintenance expenses. Overtime.'

'It does look extremely . . . intricate,' Hwel admitted. 'Who designed it?'

'A daft old chap in the Street of Cunning Artificers,' said Vitoller. 'Leonard of Quirm. He's a painter really. He just does this sort of thing for a hobby. I happened to hear that he's been working on this for months. I just snapped it up quick when he couldn't get it to fly.'

They watched the mock waves turn.

'You're bent on going?' said Vitoller, at last.

'Yes. Tomjon's still a bit wild. He needs an older head around the place.'

'I'll miss you, laddie. I don't mind telling you. You've been like a son to me. How old are you, exactly? I never did know.'

'A hundred and two.'

Vitoller nodded gloomily. He was sixty, and his arthritis was playing him up.

'You've been like a father to me, then,' he said.

'It evens out in the end,' said Hwel diffidently. 'Half the height, twice the age. You could say that on the overall average we live about the same length of time as humans.'

The playmaster sighed. 'Well, I don't know what I will do without you and Tomjon around, and that's a fact.'

'It's only for the summer, and a lot of the lads are staying. In fact it's mainly the apprentices that are going. You said yourself it'd be good experience.'

Vitoller looked wretched and, in the chilly air of the half-finished theatre, a good deal smaller than usual, like a balloon two weeks after the party. He prodded some wood shavings distractedly with his stick.

'We grow old, Master Hwel. At least,' he corrected himself, 'I grow old and you grow older. We have heard the gongs at midnight.'

'Aye. You don't want him to go, do you?'

'I was all for it at first. You know. Then I thought, there's destiny afoot.

Just when things are going well, there's always bloody destiny. I mean, that's where he came from. Somewhere up in the mountains. Now fate is calling him back. I shan't see him again.'

'It's only for the summer – '

Vitoller held up a hand. 'Don't interrupt. I'd got the right dramatic flow there.'

'Sorry.'

Flick, flick, went the stick on the wood shavings, knocking them into the air.

'I mean, you know he's not my flesh and blood.'

'He's your son, though,' said Hwel. 'This hereditary business isn't all it's cracked up to be.'

'It's fine of you to say that.'

'I mean it. Look at me. I wasn't supposed to be writing plays. Dwarfs aren't even supposed to be able to *read*. I shouldn't worry too much about destiny, if I was you. I was destined to be a miner. Destiny gets it wrong half the time.'

'But you said he looks like the Fool person. I can't see it myself, mark you.'

'The light's got to be right.'

'Could be some destiny at work there.'

Hwel shrugged. Destiny was funny stuff, he knew. You couldn't trust it. Often you couldn't even see it. Just when you knew you had it cornered, it turned out to be something else – coincidence, maybe, or providence. You barred the door against it, and it was standing behind you. Then just when you thought you had it nailed down it walked away with the hammer.

He used destiny a lot. As a tool for his plays it was even better than a ghost. There was nothing like a bit of destiny to get the old plot rolling. But it was a mistake to think you could spot the shape of it. And as for thinking it could be controlled . . .

Granny Weatherwax squinted irritably into Nanny Ogg's crystal ball. It wasn't a particularly good one, being a greenish glass fishing float brought back from forn seaside parts by one of her sons. It distorted everything including, she suspected, the truth.

'He's definitely on his way,' she said, at last. 'In a cart.'

'A fiery white charger would have been favourite,' said Nanny Ogg. 'You know. Caparisoned, and that.'

'Has he got a magic sword?' said Magrat, craning to see.

Granny Weatherwax sat back.

'You're a disgrace, the pair of you,' she said. 'I don't know – magic chargers, fiery swords. Ogling away like couple of milkmaids.'

'A magic sword *is* important,' said Magrat. 'You've got to have one. We could make him one,' she added wistfully. 'Out of thunderbolt iron. I've got a spell for that. You take some thunderbolt iron,' she said uncertainly, 'and then you make a sword out of it.'

'I can't be having with that old stuff,' said Granny. 'You can wait days for the damn things to hit and then they nearly take your arm off.'

'And a strawberry birthmark,' said Nanny Ogg, ignoring the interruption.

The other two looked at her expectantly.

'A strawberry birthmark,' she repeated. 'It's one of those things you've got to have if you're a prince coming to claim your kingdom. That's so's everyone will know. O'course, I don't know how they know it's *strawberry*.'

'Can't abide strawberries,' said Granny vaguely, quizzing the crystal again.

In its cracked green depths, smelling of bygone lobsters, a minute Tomjon kissed his parents, shook hands or hugged the rest of the company, and climbed aboard the leading latty.

It must of worked, she told herself. Else he wouldn't be coming here, would he? All those others must be his trusty band of good companions. After all, common sense, he's got to come five hundred miles across difficult country, anything could happen.

I daresay the armour and swords is in the carts.

She detected a twinge of doubt, and set out to quell it instantly. There isn't any other reason for him to come, stands to reason. We got the spell exactly right. Except for the ingredients. And most of the poetry. And it probably wasn't the right time. And Gytha took most of it home for the cat, which couldn't of been proper.

But he's on his way. What can't speak, can't lie.

'Best put the cloth over it when you've done, Esme,' said Nanny. 'I always get worried someone'll peer in at me when I'm having my bath.'

'He's on his way,' said Granny, the satisfaction in her voice so strong you could have ground corn with it. She dropped the black velvet bag over the ball.

'It's a long road,' said Nanny. 'There's many a slip twixt dress and drawers. There could be bandits.'

'We shall watch over him,' said Granny.

'That's not right. If he's going to be king he ought to be able to fight his own battles,' said Magrat.

'We don't want him to go wasting his strength,' said Nanny primly. 'We want him good and fresh for when he gets here.'

'And then, I hope, we shall leave him to fight his battles in his own way,' said Magrat.

Granny clapped her hands together in a businesslike fashion.

'Quite right,' she said. 'Provided he looks like winning.'

They had been meeting at Nanny Ogg's cottage. Magrat made an excuse to tarry after Granny left, around dawn, allegedly to help Nanny with tidying up.

'Whatever happened to not meddling?' she said.

'What do you mean?'

'You know, Nanny.'

'It's not proper meddling,' said Nanny awkwardly. 'Just helping matters along.'

'Surely you can't really think that!'

Nanny sat down and fidgeted with a cushion.

'Well, see, all this not meddling business is fine in the normal course of things,' she said. 'Not meddling is easy when you don't have to. And then I've got the family to think about. Our Jason's been in a couple of fights because of what people have been saying. Our Shawn was thrown out of the army. The way I see it, when we get the new king in, he should owe us a few favours. It's only fair.'

'But only last week you were saying – ' Magrat stopped, shocked at this display of pragmatism.

'A week is a long time in magic,' said Nanny. 'Fifteen years, for one thing. Anyway, Esme is determined and I'm in no mood to stop her.'

'So what you're saying,' said Magrat, icily, 'is that this "not meddling" thing is like taking a vow not to swim. You'll absolutely never break it unless of course you happen to find yourself in the water?'

'Better than drowning,' Nanny said.

She reached up to the mantelpiece and took down a clay pipe that was like a small tar pit. She lit it with a spill from the remains of the fire, while Greebo watched her carefully from his cushion.

Magrat idly lifted the hood from the ball and glared at it.

'I think,' she said, 'that I will never really understand about witchcraft. Just when I think I've got a grip on it, it changes.'

'We're all just people.' Nanny blew a cloud of blue smoke at the chimney. 'Everyone's just people.'

'Can I borrow the crystal?' said Magrat suddenly.

'Feel free,' said Nanny. She grinned at Magrat's back. 'Had a row with your young man?' she said.

'I really don't know what you're talking about.'

'Haven't see him around for weeks.'

'Oh, the duke sent him to – ' Magrat stopped, and went on – 'sent him away for something or other. Not that it bothers me at all, either way.'

'So I see. Take the ball, by all means.'

Magrat was glad to get back home. No one was about on the moors at night anyway, but over the couple of months things had definitely been getting worse. On top of the general suspicion of witches, it was dawning on the few people in Lancre who had dealings with the outside world that a) either more things had been happening than they had heard about before or b) time was out of joint. It wasn't easy to prove*, but the few traders who came along the mountain tracks after the winter seemed to be rather older than they should have been. Unexplained happenings were always more or less expected in the Ramtops because of the high magical potential, but several years disappearing overnight was a bit of a first.

She locked the door, fastened the shutters, and carefully laid the green glass globe on the kitchen table.

She concentrated . . .

The Fool dozed under the tarpaulins of a river barge, heading up the Ankh at a steady two miles an hour. It wasn't an exciting method of transport but it got you there eventually.

He looked safe enough, but he was tossing and turning in his sleep.

Magrat wondered what it was like, spending your whole life doing something you didn't want to do. Like being dead, she considered, only worse, the reason being, you were alive to suffer it.

She considered the Fool to be weak, badly led and sorely in need of some backbone. And she was longing for him to get back, so she could look forward to never seeing him again.

☆   ☆   ☆

* Because of the way time was recorded among the various states, kingdoms and cities. After all, when over an area of a hundred square miles the same year is variously the Year of the Small Bat, the Anticipated Monkey, the Hunting Cloud, Fat Cows, Three Bright Stallions and at least nine numbers recorded the time since† assorted kings, prophets, and strange events were either crowned, born or happened, and each year has a different number of months, and some of them don't have weeks, and one of them refused to accept the day as a measure of time, the only thing possible to be sure of is that good sex doesn't last long enough.‡

† The calendar of the Theocracy of Muntab counts *down*, not up. No one knows why, but it might not be a good idea to hang around and find out.

‡ Except for the Zabingo tribe of the Great Nef, of course.

It was a long, hot summer.

They didn't rush things. There was a lot of country between Ankh-Morpork and the Ramtops. It was, Hwel had to admit, fun. It wasn't a word dwarfs were generally at home with.

Please Yourself went over well. It always did. The apprentices excelled themselves. They forgot lines, and played jokes; in Sto Lat the whole third act of *Gretalina and Mellias* was performed against the backdrop for the second act of *The Mage Wars*, but no one seemed to notice that the greatest love scene in history was played on a set depicting a tidal wave sweeping across a continent. That was possibly because Tomjon was playing Gretalina. The effect was so disconcertingly riveting that Hwel made him swap roles for the next house, if you could apply the term to a barn hired for the day, and the effect still had more rivets than a suit of plate armour, including the helmet, and even though Gretalina in this case was now young Wimsloe, who was a bit simple and tended to stutter and whose spots might eventually clear up.

The following day, in some nameless village in the middle of an endless sea of cabbages, he let Tomjon play Old Miskin in *Please Yourself*, a role that Vitoller always excelled in. You couldn't let anyone play it who was under the age of forty, not unless you wanted an Old Miskin with a cushion up his jerkin and greasepaint wrinkles.

Hwel didn't consider himself old. His father had still been digging three tons of ore a day at the age of two hundred.

Now he felt old. He watched Tomjon hobble off the stage, and for a fleeting instant knew what it was to be a fat old man, pickled in wine, fighting old wars that no one cared about any more, hanging grimly on to the precipice of late middle-age for fear of dropping off into antiquity, but only with one hand, because with the other he was raising two fingers at Death. Of course, he'd known that when he wrote the part. But he hadn't *known* it.

The same magic didn't seem to infuse the new play. They tried it a few times, just to see how it went. The audience watched attentively, and went home. They didn't even bother to throw anything. It wasn't that they thought it was bad. They didn't think it was anything.

But all the right ingredients were there, weren't they? Tradition was full of people giving evil rulers a well-justified seeing to. Witches were always a draw. The apparition of Death was particularly good, with some lovely lines. Mix them all together . . . and they seemed to cancel out, become a mere humdrum way of filling the stage for a couple of hours.

Late at night, when the cast was asleep, Hwel would sit up in one of the carts and feverishly rewrite. He rearranged scenes, cut lines, *added* lines, introduced a clown, included another fight, and tuned up the special effects. It didn't seem to have any effect. The play was like some marvellous intricate painting, a feast of impressions close to, a mere blur from a distance.

When the inspirations were sleeting fast he even tried changing the style. In the morning the early risers grew accustomed to finding discarded experiments decorating the grass around the carts, like extremely literate mushrooms.

Tomjon kept one of the strangest:

> 1st Witche: He's late.
>
> *(Pause)*
>
> 2nd Witche: He said he would come.
>
> *(Pause)*
>
> 3rd Witche: He said he would come but he hasn't. This is my last newt. I saved it for him. And he hasn't come.
>
> *(Pause)*

'I think,' said Tomjon, later, 'you ought to slow down a bit. You've done what was ordered. No one said it had to *sparkle*.'

'It could, you know. If I could just get it right.'

'You're absolutely sure about the ghost, are you?' said Tomjon. The way he threw the line away made it clear that he wasn't.

'There's nothing wrong with the ghost,' snapped Hwel. 'The scene with the ghost is the best I've done.'

'I was just wondering if this is the right play for it, that's all.'

'The ghost stays. Now let's get on, boy.'

Two days later, with the Ramtops a blue and white wall that was beginning to dominate the Hubward horizon, the company was attacked. There wasn't much drama; they had just manhandled the lattys across a ford and were resting in the shade of a grove of trees, which suddenly fruited robbers.

Hwel looked along the line of half a dozen stained and rusty blades. Their owners seemed slightly uncertain about what to do next.

'We've got a receipt somewhere – ' he began.

Tomjon nudged him. 'These don't look like Guild thieves,' he hissed. 'They definitely look freelance to me.'

It would be nice to say that the leader of the robbers was a black-bearded, swaggering brute, with a red headscarf and one gold earring and a chin you could clean pots with. Actually it would be practically compulsory. And, in fact, this was so. Hwel thought the wooden leg was overdoing it, but the man had obviously studied the role.

'Well now,' said the bandit chief. 'What have we here, and do they have any money?'

'We're actors,' said Tomjon.

'That ought to answer both questions,' said Hwel.

'And none of your repartee,' said the bandit. 'I've been to the city, I have. I know repartee when I see it and – ' he half turned to his followers, raising an eyebrow to indicate that the next remark was going to be witty – 'if you're not careful I can make a few *cutting* remarks of my own.'

There was dead silence behind him until he made an impatient gesture with his cutlass.

'All right,' he said, against a chorus of uncertain laughter. 'We'll just take any loose change, valuables, food and clothing you might be having.'

'Could I say something?' said Tomjon.

The company backed away from him. Hwel smiled at his own feet.

'You're going to beg for mercy, are you?' said the bandit.

'That's right.'

Hwel thrust his hands deep into his pockets and looked up at the sky, whistling under his breath and trying not to break into a maniac grin. He was aware that the other actors were also looking expectantly at Tomjon.

He's going to give them the mercy speech from *The Troll's Tale*, he thought . . .

'The point I'd just like to make is that – ' said Tomjon, and his stance changed subtly, his voice became deeper, his right hand flung out dramatically – ' "The worth of man lies not in feats of arms, Or the fiery hunger o' the ravening – " '

It's going to be like when that man tried to rob us back in Sto Lat, Hwel thought. If they end up giving us their swords, what the hell can we do with them? And it's so embarrassing when they start crying.

It was at this moment that the world around him took a green tint and he thought he could make out, right on the cusp of hearing, other voices.

'*There's men with swords, Granny!*'

' – rend with glowing blades the marvel of the world – ' Tomjon said, and the voices at the edge of imagination said, '*No king of mine is going to beg anything off anyone. Give me that milk jug, Magrat.*'

' – the heart of compassion, the kiss – '

'*That was a present from my aunt.*'

' – this jewel of jewels, this crown of crowns.'

There was silence. One or two of the bandits were weeping silently into their hands.

Their chief said, 'Is that it?'

For the first time in his life Tomjon looked nonplussed.

'Well, yes,' he said. 'Er. Would you like me to repeat it?'

'It was a good speech,' the bandit conceded. 'But I don't see what it's got to do with me. I'm a practical man. Hand over your valuables.'

His sword came up until it was level with Tomjon's throat.

'And all the rest of you shouldn't be standing there like idiots,' he added. 'Come on. Or the boy gets it.'

Wimsloe the apprentice raised a cautious hand.

'What?' said the bandit.

'A-are you s-sure you listened carefully, sir?'

'I won't tell you again! Either I hear the clink of coins, or you hear a gurgle!'

In fact what they all heard was a whistling noise, high in the air, and the crash as a milk jug, its sides frosted with the ice of altitude, dropped out of the sky on to the spike atop the chief's helmet.

The remaining bandits took one look at the results, and fled.

The actors stared down at the recumbent bandit. Hwel prodded a lump of frozen milk with his boot.

'Well, well,' he said weakly.

'He didn't take any notice!' whispered Tomjon.

'A born critic,' said the dwarf. It was a blue and white jug. Funny how little details stood out at a time like this. It had been smashed several times in the past, he could see, because the pieces had been carefully glued together again. Someone had really loved that jug.

'What we're dealing with here,' he said, rallying some shreds of logic, 'is a freak whirlwind. Obviously.'

'But milk jugs don't just drop out of the sky,' said Tomjon, demonstrating the astonishing human art of denying the obvious.

'I don't know about that. I've heard of fish and frogs and rocks,' said Hwel. 'There's nothing against crockery.' He began to rally. 'It's just one of these uncommon phenomenons. They happen all the time in this part of the world, there's nothing unusual about it.'

They got back on to the carts and rode on in unaccustomed silence. Young Wimsloe collected every bit of jug he could find and stored them carefully in the props box, and spent the rest of the day watching the sky, hoping for a sugar basin.

The lattys toiled up the dusty slopes of the Ramtops, mere motes in the foggy glass of the crystal.

'Are they all right?' said Magrat.

'They're wandering all over the place,' said Granny. 'They may be good at the acting, but they've got something to learn about the travelling.'

'It was a nice jug,' said Magrat. 'You can't get them like that any more. I mean, if you'd have said what was on your mind, there was a flatiron on the shelf.'

'There's more to life than milk jugs.'

'It had a daisy pattern round the top.'

Granny ignored her.

'I think,' she said, 'it's time we had a look at this new king. Close up.' She cackled.

'You cackled, Granny,' said Magrat darkly.

'I did not! It was,' Granny fumbled for a word, 'a chuckle.'

'I bet Black Aliss used to cackle.'

'You want to watch out you don't end up the same way as she did,' said Nanny, from her seat by the fire. 'She went a bit funny at the finish, you know. Poisoned apples and suchlike.'

'Just because I might have chuckled a . . . a bit roughly,' sniffed Granny. She felt that she was being unduly defensive. 'Anyway, there's nothing wrong with cackling. In moderation.'

'I think,' said Tomjon, 'that we're lost.'

Hwel looked at the baking purple moorland around them, which stretched up to the towering spires of the Ramtops themselves. Even in the height of summer there were pennants of snow flying from the highest peaks. It was a landscape of describable beauty.

Bees were busy, or at least endeavouring to look and sound busy, in the thyme by the trackside. Cloud shadows flickered over the alpine meadows. There was the kind of big, empty silence made by an environment that not only doesn't have any people in it, but doesn't need them either.

Or signposts.

'We were lost ten miles ago,' said Hwel. 'There's got to be a new word for what we are now.'

'You said the mountains were honeycombed with dwarf mines,' said Tomjon. 'You said a dwarf could tell wherever he was in the mountains.'

'*Underground*, I said. It's all a matter of strata and rock formations. Not on the surface. All the landscape gets in the way.'

'We could dig you a hole,' said Tomjon.

But it was a nice day and, as the road meandered through clumps of hemlock and pine, outposts of the forest, it was pleasant enough to let the mules go at their own pace. The road, Hwel felt, had to go somewhere.

This geographical fiction has been the death of many people. Roads don't necessarily have to go anywhere, they just have to have somewhere to start.

'We *are* lost, aren't we?' said Tomjon, after a while.

'Certainly not.'

'Where are we, then?'

'The mountains. Perfectly clear on any atlas.'

'We ought to stop and ask someone.'

Tomjon gazed around at the rolling countryside. Somewhere a lonely curlew howled, or possibly it was a badger – Hwel was a little hazy about rural matters, at least those that took place higher than about the limestone layer. There wasn't another human being within miles.

'Who did you have in mind?' he said sarcastically.

'That old woman in the funny hat,' said Tomjon, pointing. 'I've been watching her. She keeps ducking down behind a bush when she thinks I've seen her.'

Hwel turned and looked down at a bramble bush, which wobbled.

'Ho there, good mother,' he said.

The bush sprouted an indignant head.

'Whose mother?'

Hwel hesitated. 'Just a figure of speech, Mrs . . . Miss . . .'

'Mistress,' snapped Granny Weatherwax. 'And I'm a poor old woman gathering wood,' she added defiantly.

She cleared her throat. 'Lawks,' she went on. 'You did give me a fright, young master. My poor old heart.'

There was silence from the carts. Then Tomjon said, 'I'm sorry?'

'What?' said Granny.

'Your poor old heart what?'

'What about my poor old heart?' said Granny, who wasn't used to acting like an old woman and had a very limited repertoire in this area. But it's traditional that young heirs seeking their destiny get help from mysterious old women gathering wood, and she wasn't about to buck tradition.

'It's just that you mentioned it,' said Hwel.

'Well, it isn't important. Lawks. I expect you're looking for Lancre,' said Granny testily, in a hurry to get to the point.

'Well, yes,' said Tomjon. 'All day.'

'You've come too far,' said Granny. 'Go back about two miles, and take the track on the right, past the stand of pines.'

Wimsloe tugged at Tomjon's shirt.

'When you m-meet a m-mysterious old lady in the road,' he said, 'you've got to offer to s-share your lunch. Or help her across the r-river.'

'You have?'

'It's t-terribly b-bad luck not to.'

Tomjon gave Granny a polite smile.

'Would you care to share our lunch, good mo– old wo– ma'am?'

Granny looked doubtful.

'What is it?'

'Salt pork.'

She shook her head. 'Thanks all the same,' she said graciously. 'But it gives me wind.'

She turned on her heel and set off through the bushes.

'We could help you across the river if you like,' shouted Tomjon after her.

'What river?' said Hwel. 'We're on the moor, there can't be a river in miles.'

'Y-you've got to get them on y-your side,' said Wimsloe. 'Then t-they help you.'

'Perhaps we should have asked her to wait while we went and looked for one,' said Hwel sourly.

They found the turning. It led into a forest crisscrossed with as many tracks as a marshalling yard, the sort of forest where the back of your head tells you the trees are turning around to watch you as you go past and the sky seems to be very high up and a long way off. Despite the heat of the day a dank, impenetrable gloom hovered among the tree-trunks, which crowded up to the track as if intending to obliterate it completely.

They were soon lost again, and decided that being lost somewhere where you didn't know where you were was even worse than being lost in the open.

'She could have given more explicit instructions,' said Hwel.

'Like ask at the next crone,' said Tomjon. 'Look over there.'

He stood up in the seat.

'Ho there, old . . . good . . .' he hazarded.

Magrat pushed back her shawl.

'Just a humble wood gatherer,' she snapped. She held up a twig for proof. Several hours waiting with nothing but trees to talk to hadn't improved her temper.

Wimsloe nudged Tomjon, who nodded and fixed his face in an in-gratiating smile.

'Would you care to share our lunch, old . . . good wo . . . miss?' he said. 'It's only salt pork, I'm afraid.'

'Meat is extremely bad for the digestive system,' said Magrat. 'If you could see inside your colon you'd be horrified.'

'I think I would,' muttered Hwel.

'Did you know that an adult male carries up to five pounds of undigested red meat in his intestines at all times?' said Magrat, whose informative lectures on nutrition had been known to cause whole families to hide in the cellar until she went away. 'Whereas pine kernels and sunflower seeds – '

'There aren't any rivers around that you need helping over, are there,' said Tomjon desperately.

'Don't be silly,' said Magrat. 'I'm just a humble wood gatherer, lawks, collecting a few sticks and mayhap directing lost travellers on the road to Lancre.'

'Ah,' said Hwel, 'I thought we'd get to that.'

'You fork left up ahead and turn right at the big stone with the crack in it, you can't miss it,' said Magrat.

'Fine,' growled Hwel. 'Well, we won't keep you. I'm sure you've got a lot of wood to collect and so forth.'

He whistled the mules into a plod again, grumbling to himself.

When, an hour later, the track ran out among a landscape of house-sized boulders, Hwel laid down the reins carefully and folded his arms. Tomjon stared at him.

'What do you think you're doing?' he said.

'Waiting,' said the dwarf grimly.

'It'll be getting dark soon.'

'We won't be here long,' said Hwel.

Eventually Nanny Ogg gave up and came out from behind her rock.

'It's salt pork, understand,' said Hwel sharply. 'Take it or leave it, okay? Now – which way's Lancre?'

'Keep on, left at the ravine, then you pick up the track that leads to a bridge, you can't miss it,' said Nanny promptly.

Hwel grabbed the reins. 'You forgot about the lawks.'

'Bugger. Sorry. Lawks.'

'And you're a humble old wood gatherer, I expect,' Hwel went on.

'Spot on, lad,' said Nanny cheerfully. 'Just about to make a start, as a matter of fact.'

Tomjon nudged the dwarf.

'You forgot about the river,' he said. Hwel glared at him.

'Oh yes,' he muttered, 'and can you wait here while we go and find a river.'

'To help you across,' said Tomjon carefully.

Nanny Ogg gave him a bright smile. 'There's a perfectly good bridge,' she said. 'But I wouldn't say no to a lift. Move over.'

To Hwel's irritation Nanny Ogg hitched up her skirts and scrambled on to the board, inserting herself between Tomjon and the dwarf and then twisting like an oyster knife until she occupied half the seat.

'You mentioned salt pork,' she said. 'There wouldn't be any mustard, would there?'

'No,' said Hwel sullenly.

'Can't abide salt pork without condiments,' said Nanny conversationally. 'But pass it over, anyway.' Wimsloe wordlessly handed over the basket holding the troupe's supper. Nanny lifted the lid and gave it a critical assessment.

'That cheese in there is a bit off,' she said. 'It needs eating up quick. What's in the leather bottle?'

'Beer,' said Tomjon, a fraction of a second before Hwel had the presence of mind to say, 'Water.'

'Pretty weak stuff,' said Nanny, eventually. She fumbled in her apron pocket for her tobacco pouch.

'Has anyone got a light?' she enquired.

A couple of actors produced bundles of matches. Nanny nodded, and put the pouch away.

'Good,' she said. 'Now, has anyone got any tobacco?'

Half an hour later the lattys rattled over the Lancre bridge, across some of the outlying farmlands, and through the forests that made up most of the kingdom.

'This is it?' said Tomjon.

'Well, not all of it,' said Nanny, who had been expecting rather more enthusiasm. 'There's lots more of it behind the mountains over there. But this is the flat bit.'

'You call this flat?'

'Flattish,' Nanny conceded. 'But the air's good. That's the palace up there, offering outstanding views of the surrounding countryside.'

'You mean forests.'

'You'll like it here,' said Nanny encouragingly.

'It's a bit small.'

Nanny thought about this. She'd spent nearly all her life inside the boundaries of Lancre. It had always seemed about the right size to her.

'Bijou,' she said. 'Handy for everywhere.'

'Everywhere, *where*?'

Nanny gave up. 'Everywhere close,' she said.

Hwel said nothing. The air *was* good, rolling down the unclimbable slopes of the Ramtops like a sinus wash, tinted with turpentine from the high forests. They passed through a gateway into what was, up here, probably called a town; the cosmopolitan he had become decided that, down on the plains, it would just about have qualified as an open space.

'There's an inn,' said Tomjon doubtfully.

Hwel followed his gaze. 'Yes,' he said, eventually. 'Yes, it probably is.'

'When are we going to do the play?'

'I don't know. I think we just send up to the castle and say we're here.' Hwel scratched his chin. 'Fool said the king or whoever would want to see the script.'

Tomjon looked around Lancre town. It seemed peaceful enough. It didn't look like the kind of place likely to turn actors out at nightfall. It needed the population.

'This is the capital city of the kingdom,' said Nanny Ogg. 'Well-designed streets, you'll notice.'

'Streets?' said Tomjon.

'Street,' corrected Nanny. 'Also houses in quite good repair, stone's throw from river – '

'Throw?'

'Drop,' Nanny conceded. 'Neat middens, look, and extensive – '

'Madam, we've come to entertain the town, not buy it,' said Hwel.

Nanny Ogg looked sidelong at Tomjon.

'Just wanted you to see how attractive it is,' she said.

'Your civic pride does you credit,' said Hwel. 'And now, please, leave the cart. I'm sure you've got some wood to gather. Lawks.'

'Much obliged for the snack,' said Nanny, climbing down.

'Meals,' corrected Hwel.

Tomjon nudged him. 'You ought to be more polite,' he said. 'You never know.' He turned to Nanny. 'Thank you, good – oh, she's gone.'

'They've come to do a theatre,' said Nanny.

Granny Weatherwax carried on shelling beans in the sun, much to Nanny's annoyance.

'Well? Aren't you going to say something? I've been finding out things,' she said. 'Picking up information. Not sitting around making soup – '

'Stew.'

'I reckon it's very important,' sniffed Nanny.

'What kind of a theatre?'

'They didn't say. Something for the duke, I think.'

'What's he want a theatre for?'

'They didn't say that, either.'

'It's probably all a trick to get in the castle,' Granny said knowingly. 'Very clever idea. Did you see anything in the carts?'

'Boxes and bundles and such.'

'They'll be full of armour and weapons, depend upon it.'

Nanny Ogg looked doubtful.

'They didn't look very much like soldiers to me. They were awfully young and spotty.'

'Clever. I expect in the middle of the play the king will manifest his destiny, right where everyone can see him. Good plan.'

'That's another thing,' said Nanny, picking up a beanpod and chewing it. 'He doesn't seem to like the place much.'

'Of course he does. It's in his blood.'

'I brought him the pretty way. He didn't seem very impressed.'

Granny hesitated.

'He was probably suspicious of you,' she concluded. 'He was probably too overcome to speak, really.'

She put down the bowl of beans and looked thoughtfully at the trees.

'Have you got any family still working up at the castle?' she said.

'Shirl and Daff help out in the kitchens since the cook went off his head.'

'Good. I'll have a word with Magrat. I think we should see this theatre.'

'Perfect,' said the duke.

'Thank you,' said Hwel.

'You've got it exactly spot on about that dreadful accident,' said the duke. 'You might almost have been there. Ha. Ha.'

'You weren't were you?' said Lady Felmet, leaning forward and glaring at the dwarf.

'I just used my imagination,' said Hwel hurriedly. The duchess glared at him, suggesting that his imagination could consider itself lucky it wasn't being dragged off to the courtyard to explain itself to four angry wild horses and a length of chain.

'Exactly right,' said the duke, leafing one-handedly through the pages. 'This is exactly, exactly, exactly how it was.'

'*Will have been*,' snapped the duchess.

The duke turned another page.

'You're in this too,' he said. 'Amazing. It's word for word how I'm going to remember it. I see you've got Death in it, too.'

'Always popular,' said Hwel. 'People expect it.'

'How soon can you act it?'

'Stage it,' corrected Hwel, and added. 'We've tried it out. As soon as you like.' And then we can get away from here, he said to himself, away from your eyes like two raw eggs and this female mountain in the red dress and this castle which seems to act like a magnet for the wind. This is not going to go down as one of my best plays, I know that much.

'How much did we say we were going to pay you?' said the duchess.

'I think you mentioned another hundred silver pieces,' said Hwel.

'Worth every penny,' said the duke.

Hwel left hurriedly, before the duchess could start to bargain. But he felt he'd gladly pay something to be out of this place. Bijou, he thought. Gods, how could anyone like a kingdom like this?

The Fool waited in the meadow with the lake. He stared wistfully at the sky and wondered where the hell Magrat was. This was, she said, *their* place; the fact that a few dozen cows also shared it at the moment didn't appear to make any difference.

She turned up in a green dress and a filthy temper.

'What's all this about a play?' she said.

The Fool sagged on to a willow log.

'Aren't you glad to see me?' he said.

'Well, yes. Of course. Now, this play . . .'

'My lord wants something to convince people that he is the rightful King of Lancre. Himself mostly, I think.'

'Is that why you went to the city?'

'Yes.'

'It's disgusting!'

The Fool sat calmly. 'You would prefer the duchess's approach?' he said. 'She just thinks they ought to kill everyone. She's good at that sort of thing. And then there'd be fighting, and everything. Lots of people would die anyway. This way might be easier.'

'Oh, where's your spunk, man?'

'Pardon?'

'Don't you want to die nobly for a just cause?'

'I'd much rather live quietly for one. It's all right for you witches, you can do what you like, but I'm circumscribed,' said the Fool.

Magrat sat down beside him. *Find out all about this play*, Granny had ordered. *Go and talk to that jingling friend of yours*. She'd replied, *He's very loyal. He might not tell me anything*. And Granny had said, *This is no time for half measures. If you have to, seduct him*..

'When's this play going to be, then?' she said, moving closer.

'Marry, I'm sure I'm not allowed to tell you,' said the Fool. 'The duke said to me, he said, don't tell the witches that it's tomorrow night.'

'I shouldn't then,' agreed Magrat.

'At eight o'clock.'

'I see.'

'But meet for sherry beforehand at seven-thirty, i'faith.'

'I expect you shouldn't tell me who *is* invited, either,' said Magrat.

'That's right. Most of the dignitaries of Lancre. You understand I'm not telling you this.'

'That's right,' said Magrat.

'But I think you have a right to know what it is you're not being told.'

'Good point. Is there still that little gate around the back, that leads to the kitchens?'

'The one that is often left unguarded?'

'Yes.'

'Oh, we hardly ever guard it these days.'

'Do you think there might be someone guarding it around eight o'clock tomorrow?'

'Well, *I* might be there.'

'Good.'

The Fool pushed away the wet nose of an inquisitive cow.

'The duke will be expecting you,' he added.

'You said he said we weren't to know.'

'He said I mustn't tell you. But he also said, "They'll come anyway, I hope they do." Strange, really. He seemed in a very good mood when he said it. Um. Can I see you after the show?'

'Is that all he said?'

'Oh, there was something about showing witches their future. I didn't understand it. I really would like to see you after the show, you know. I bought – '

'I think I might be washing my hair,' said Magrat vaguely. 'Excuse me, I really ought to be going.'

'Yes, but I brought you this pres– ' said the Fool vaguely, watching her departing figure.

He sagged as she disappeared between the trees, and looked down at the necklace wound tightly between his nervous fingers. It was, he had to admit, terribly tasteless, but it was the sort of thing she liked, all silver and skulls. It had cost him too much.

A cow, misled by his horns, stuck its tongue in his ear.

It was true, the Fool thought. Witches *did* do unpleasant things to people, sometimes.

Tomorrow night came, and the witches went by a roundabout route to the castle, with considerable reluctance.

'If he wants us to be here, I don't want to go,' said Granny. 'He's got some plan. He's using headology on us.'

'There's something up,' said Magrat. 'He had his men set fire to three cottages in our village last night. He always does that when he's in a good mood. That new sergeant is a quick man with the matches, too.'

'Our Daff said she saw them actors practisin' this morning,' said Nanny Ogg, who was carrying a bag of walnuts and a leather bottle from which rose a rich, sharp smell. 'She said it was all shouting and stabbing and then wondering who done it and long bits with people muttering to themselves in loud voices.'

'Actors,' said Granny, witheringly. 'As if the world weren't full of enough history without inventing more.'

'They shout so loud, too,' said Nanny. 'You can hardly hear yourself talk.' She was also carrying, deep in her apron pocket, a lump of haunted castle rock. The king was getting in free.

Granny nodded. But, she thought, it was going to be worth it. She hadn't got the faintest idea what Tomjon had in mind, but her inbuilt sense of drama assured her that the boy would be bound to do something important. She wondered if he would leap off the stage and stab the duke to death, and realised that she was hoping like hell that he would.

'All hail wossname,' she said under her breath, 'who shall be king here, after.'

'Let's get a move on,' said Nanny. 'All the sherry'll be gone.'

The Fool was waiting despondently inside the little wicket gate. His face brightened when he saw Magrat, and then froze in an expression of polite surprise when he saw the other two.

'There's not going to be any trouble, is there?' he said. 'I don't want there to be any trouble. Please.'

'I'm sure I don't know what you mean,' said Granny regally, sweeping past.

'Wotcha, jinglebells,' said Nanny, elbowing the man in the ribs. 'I hope you haven't been keeping our girl here up late o'nights!'

'Nanny!' said Magrat, shocked. The Fool gave the terrified, ingratiating rictus of young men everywhere when confronted by importunate elderly women commenting on their intimately personal lives.

The older witches brushed past. The Fool grabbed Magrat's hand.

'I know where we can get a good view,' he said.

She hesitated.

'It's all right,' said the Fool urgently. 'You'll be perfectly safe with me.'

'Yes. I will, won't I,' said Magrat, trying to look around him to see where the others had gone.

'They're staging the play outside, in the big courtyard. We'll get a lovely view from one of the gate towers, and no one else will be there. I put some wine up there for us, and everything.'

When she still looked half-reluctant he added, 'And there's a cistern of water and a fireplace that the guards use sometimes. In case you want to wash your hair.'

The castle was full of people standing around in that polite, sheepish way affected by people who see each other all day and are now seeing each other again in unusual social circumstances, like an office party. The witches passed quite unremarked among them and found seats in the rows of benches in the main courtyard, set up before a hastily assembled stage.

Nanny Ogg waved her bag of walnuts at Granny.

'Want one?' she said.

An alderman of Lancre shuffled past her and pointed politely to the seat on her left.

'Is anyone sitting here?' he said.

'Yes,' said Nanny.

The alderman looked distractedly at the rest of the benches, which were filling up fast, and then down at the clearly empty space in front of him. He hitched up his robes with a determined expression.

'I think that since the play is commencing to start, your friends must find a seat elsewhere, when they arrive,' he said, and sat down.

Within seconds his face went white. His teeth began to chatter. He clutched at his stomach and groaned.*

'I *told* you,' said Nanny, as he lurched away. 'What's the good of asking if you're not going to listen?' She leaned towards the empty seat. 'Walnut?'

'No, thank you,' said King Verence, waving a spectral hand. 'They go right through me, you know.'

'*Pray, gentles all, list to our tale . . .*'

'What's this?' hissed Granny. 'Who's the fellow in the tights?'

'He's the Prologue,' said Nanny. 'You have to have him at the beginning so everyone knows what the play's about.'

'Can't understand a word of it,' muttered Granny. 'What's a gentle, anyway?'

'Type of maggot,' said Nanny.

'That's nice, isn't it? "Hallo maggots, welcome to the show." Puts people in a nice frame of mind, doesn't it?'

There was a chorus of 'sshs'.

---

* The observant will realise that this was because the king was already seated there. It was not because the man had used the phrase 'commence to start' in cold blood. But it ought to have been.

'These walnuts are damn tough,' said Nanny, spitting one out into her hand. 'I'm going to have to take my shoe off to this one.'

Granny subsided into unaccustomed, troubled silence, and tried to listen to the prologue. The theatre worried her. It had a magic of its own, one that didn't belong to her, one that wasn't in her control. It changed the world, and said things were otherwise than they were. And it was worse than that. It was magic that didn't belong to magical people. It was commanded by ordinary people, who didn't know the rules. They altered the world because it sounded better.

The duke and duchess were sitting on their thrones right in front of the stage. As Granny glared at them the duke half turned, and she saw his smile.

I want the world the way it is, she thought. I want the past the way it was. The past used to be a lot better than it is now.

And the band struck up.

Hwel peered around a pillar and signalled to Wimsloe and Brattsley, who hobbled out into the glare of the torches.

OLD MAN (an Elder): *'What hath befell the land?'*

OLD WOMAN (a Crone): *' 'Tis a terror – '*

The dwarf watched them for a few seconds from the wings, his lips moving soundlessly. Then he scuttled back to the guardroom where the rest of the cast were still in the last hasty stages of dressing. He uttered the stage manager's traditional scream of rage.

'C'mon,' he ordered. 'Soldiers of the king, at the double! And the witches – *where are the blasted witches?'*

Three junior apprentices presented themselves.

'I've lost my wart!'

'The cauldron's all full of yuk!'

'There's something living in this wig!'

'Calm down, calm down,' screamed Hwel. 'It'll all be all right on the night!'

'This is the night, Hwel!'

Hwel snatched a handful of putty from the make-up table and slammed on a wart like a orange. The offending straw wig was rammed on its owner's head, livestock and all, and the cauldron was very briefly inspected and pronounced full of just the right sort of yuk, nothing wrong with yuk like that.

On stage a guard dropped his shield, bent to pick it up, and dropped his spear. Hwel rolled his eyes and offered up a silent prayer to any gods that might be watching.

It was already going wrong. The earlier rehearsals had their little teething troubles, it was true, but Hwel had known one or two monumental horrors in his time and this one was shaping up to be the worst. The company was more jittery than a potful of lobsters. Out of the corner of his ear he heard the on-stage dialogue falter, and scurried to the wings.

' – avenge the terror of thy father's death – ' he hissed, and hurried back to the trembling witches. He groaned. Divers alarums. This lot were supposed to be terrorising a kingdom. He had about a minute before the cue.

'Right!' he said, pulling himself together. 'Now, what are you? You're evil hags, right?'

'Yes, Hwel,' they said meekly.

'Tell me what you are,' he commanded.

'We're evil hags, Hwel.'

'Louder!'

'We're Evil Hags!'

Hwel stalked the length of the quaking line, then turned abruptly on his heel. 'And what are you going to do?'

The 2nd Witche scratched his crawling wig.

'We're going to curse people?' he ventured. 'It says in the script – '

'I–can't–HEAR–you!'

'We're going to curse people!' they chorused, springing to attention and staring straight ahead to avoid his gaze.

Hwel stumped back along the line.

'What are you?'

'We're hags, Hwel!'

'What kind of hags?'

'We're black and midnight hags!' they yelled, getting into the spirit.

'What kind of black and midnight hags?'

'*Evil* black and midnight hags!'

'Are you scheming?'

'Yeah!'

'Are you secret?'

'*Yeah!*'

Hwel drew himself to his full height, such as it was.

'What–are–you?' he screamed.

'We're scheming evil secret black and midnight hags!'

'Right!' He pointed a vibrating finger towards the stage and lowered his voice and, at that moment, a dramatic inspiration dived through the atmosphere and slammed into his creative node, causing him to say, 'Now I want you to get out there and give 'em hell. Not for me. Not for the goddam captain.' He shifted the butt of an imaginary cigar from one side of his mouth to the other, and pushed back a non-existent tin helmet, and rasped, 'But for Corporal Walkowski and his little dawg.'

They stared at him in disbelief.

On cue, someone shook a sheet of tin and broke the spell.

Hwel rolled his eyes. He'd grown up in the mountains, where thunderstorms stalked from peak to peak on legs of lightning. He remembered thunderstorms that left mountains a different shape and flattened whole forests. Somehow, a sheet of tin wasn't the same, no matter how enthusiastically it was shaken.

Just once, he thought, just once. Let me get it right just once.

He opened his eyes and glared at the witches.

'What are you hanging around here for?' he yelled. 'Get out there and *curse* them!'

He watched them scamper on to the stage, and then Tomjon tapped him on the head.

'Hwel, there's no crown.'

'Hmm?' said the dwarf, his mind wrestling with ways of building thunder-and-lightning machines.

'There's no crown, Hwel. I've got to wear a crown.'

'Of course there's a crown. The big one with the red glass, very impressive, we used it in that place with the big square – '

'I think we left it there.'

There was another tinny roll of thunder but, even so, the part of Hwel that was living the play heard a faltering voice on stage. He darted to the wings.

' – I have smother'd many a babe – ' he hissed, and sprinted back.

'Well, just find another one, then,' he said vaguely. 'In the props box. You're the Evil King, you've got to have a crown. Get on with it, lad, you're on in a few minutes. Improvise.'

Tomjon wandered back to the box. He'd grown up among crowns, big golden crowns made of wood and plaster, studded with finest glass. He'd cut his teeth on the hatbrims of Authority. But most of them had been left in the Dysk now. He pulled out collapsible daggers and skulls and vases, the strata of the years and, right at the bottom, his fingers closed on something thin and crown shaped, which no one had ever wanted to wear because it looked so uncrownly.

It would be nice to say it tingled under his hand. Perhaps it did.

Granny was sitting as still as a statue, and almost as cold. The horror of realisation was stealing over her.

'That's us,' she said. 'Round that silly cauldron. That's meant to be us, Gytha.'

Nanny Ogg paused with a walnut halfway to her gums. She listened to the words.

'I never shipwrecked anybody!' she said. 'They just said they shipwreck people! I never did!'

Up in the tower Magrat elbowed the Fool in the ribs.

'Green blusher,' she said, staring at the 3rd Witche. 'I don't look like that. I don't, do I?'

'Absolutely not,' said the Fool.

'And that hair!'

The Fool peered through the crenellations like an over-eager gargoyle.

'It looks like straw,' he said. 'Not very clean, either.'

He hesitated, picking at the lichened stonework with his fingers. Before he'd left the city he'd asked Hwel for a few suitable words to say to a young lady, and he had been memorising them on the way home. It was now or never.

'I'd iike to know if I could compare you to a summer's day. Because – well, June 12th was quite nice, and . . . Oh. You've gone . . .'

King Verence gripped the edge of his seat; his fingers went through it. Tomjon had strutted on to the stage.

'That's him, isn't it? That's my son?'

The uncracked walnut fell from Nanny Ogg's fingers and rolled on to the floor. She nodded.

Verence turned a haggard, transparent face towards her.

'But what is he doing? What is he saying?'

Nanny shook her head. The king listened with his mouth open as Tomjon, lurching crabwise across the stage, launched into his major speech.

'I think he's meant to be you,' said Nanny, distantly.

'But I never walked like that! Why's he got a hump on his back? What's happened to his leg?' He listened some more, and added, in horrified tones, 'And I certainly never did *that!* Or that. Why is he saying I did that?'

The look he gave Nanny was full of pleading. She shrugged.

The king reached up, lifted off his spectral crown, and examined it.

'And it's my crown he's wearing! Look, this is it! And he's saying I did all those – ' He paused for a minute, to listen to the latest couplet, and added, 'All right. Maybe I did *that*. So I set fire to a few cottages. But everyone does that. It's good for the building industry, anyway.'

He put the ghostly crown back on his head.

'Why's he saying all this about me?' he pleaded.

'It's art,' said Nanny. 'It wossname, holds a mirror up to life.'

Granny turned slowly in her seat to look at the audience. They were staring at the performance, their faces rapt. The words washed over them in the breathless air. This was real. This was more real even than reality. This was history. It might not be true, but that had nothing to do with it.

Granny had never had much time for words. They were so insubstantial. Now she wished that she had found the time. Words were indeed insubstantial. They were as soft as water, but they were also as powerful as water and now they were rushing over the audience, eroding the levees of veracity, and carrying away the past.

That's us down there, she thought. Everyone knows who we really are, but the things down there are what they'll remember – three gibbering old baggages in pointy hats. All we've ever done, all we've ever been, won't exist any more.

She looked at the ghost of the king. Well, he'd been no worse than any other king. Oh, he might burn down the odd cottage every now and again, in a sort of absent-minded way, but only when he was really angry about something, and he could give it up any time he liked. Where he wounded the world, he left the kind of wounds that healed.

Whoever wrote this Theatre knew about the uses of magic. Even I believe what's happening, and I know there's no truth in it.

This is Art holding a Mirror up to Life. That's why everything is exactly the wrong way round.

We've lost. There is nothing we can do against this without becoming exactly what we aren't.

Nanny Ogg gave her a violent nudge in the ribs.

'Did you hear that?' she said. 'One of 'em said we put babbies in the cauldron! They've done a slander on me! I'm not sitting here and have 'em say we put babbies in a cauldron!'

Granny grabbed her shawl as she tried to stand up.

'Don't do anything!' she hissed. 'It'll make things worse.'

' "Ditch-delivered by a drabe", they said. That'll be young Millie Hipwood, who didn't dare tell her mum and then went out gathering firewood. I was up all night with that one,' Nanny muttered. 'Fine girl she produced. It's a slander! What's a drabe?' she added.

'Words,' said Granny, half to herself. 'That's all that's left. Words.'

'And now there's a man with a trumpet come on. What's he going to do? Oh. End of Act One,' said Nanny.

The words won't be forgotten, thought Granny. They've got a power to them. They're damn good words, as words go.

There was yet another rattle of thunder, which ended with the kind of crash made, for example, by a sheet of tin escaping from someone's hands and hitting the wall.

In the world outside the stage the heat pressed down like a pillow, squeezing the very life out of the air. Granny saw a footman bend down to the duke's ear. No, he won't stop the play. Of course he won't. He wants it to run its course.

The duke must have felt the heat of her gaze on the back of his neck. He turned, focused on her, and gave her a strange little smile. Then he nudged his wife. They both laughed.

Granny Weatherwax was often angry. She considered it one of her strong points. Genuine anger was one of the world's great creative forces. But you had to learn how to control it. That didn't mean you let it trickle away. It meant you dammed it, carefully, let it develop a working head, let it drown whole valleys of the mind and then, just when the whole structure was about to collapse, opened a tiny pipeline at the base and let the iron-hard stream of wrath power the turbines of revenge.

She felt the land below her, even through several feet of foundations, flagstones, one thickness of leather and two thicknesses of sock. She felt it waiting.

She heard the king say, 'My own flesh and blood? Why has he done this to me? I'm going to confront him!'

She gently took Nanny Ogg's hand.

'Come, Gytha,' she said.

Lord Felmet sat back in his throne and beamed madly at the world, which was looking good right at the moment. Things were working out better than he had dared to hope. He could feel the past melting behind him, like ice in the spring thaw.

On an impulse he called the footman back.

'Call the captain of the guard,' he said, 'and tell him to find the witches and arrest them.'

The duchess snorted.

'Remember what happened last time, foolish man?'

'We left two of them loose,' said the duke. 'This time . . . all three. The tide of public feeling is on our side. That sort of thing affects witches, depend upon it.'

The duchess cracked her knuckles to indicate her view of public opinion.

'You must admit, my treasure, that the experiment seems to be working.'

'It would appear so.'

'Very well. Don't just stand there, man. Before the play ends, tell him. Those witches are to be under lock and key.'

Death adjusted his cardboard skull in front of the mirror, twitched his cowl into a suitable shape, stood back and considered the general effect. It was going to be his first speaking part. He wanted to get it right.

'Cower now, Brief Mortals,' he said. 'For I am Death, 'Gainst Whom No . . . no . . . no . . . Hwel, 'gainst whom no?'

'Oh, good grief, Dafe. " 'Gainst whom no lock will hold nor fasten'd portal bar", I really don't see why you have difficulty with . . . not that way up, you idiots!' Hwel strode off through the backstage mêlée in pursuit of a pair of importunate scene shifters.

'Right,' said Death, to no one in particular. He turned back to the mirror.

''Gainst Whom No . . . Tumpty-Tum . . . nor Tumpty-Tumpty bar,' he said, uncertainly, and flourished his scythe. The end fell off.

'Do you think I'm fearsome enough?' he said, as he tried to fix it on again.

Tomjon, who was sitting on his hump and trying to drink some tea, gave him an encouraging nod.

'No problem, my friend,' he said. 'Compared to a visit from you, even Death himself would hold no fears. But you could try a bit more hollowness.'

'How d'you mean?'

Tomjon put down his cup. Shadows seemed to move across his face; his eyes sank, his lips drew back from his teeth, his skin stretched and paled.

'I HAVE COME TO GET YOU, YOU TERRIBLE ACTOR,' he intoned, each syllable falling into place like a coffin lid. His features sprang back into shape.

'Like that,' he said.

Dafe, who had flattened himself against the wall, relaxed a bit and gave a nervous giggle.

'Gods, I don't know how you do it,' he said. 'Honestly, I'll never be as good as you.'

'There really isn't anything to it. Now run along, Hwel's fit to be tied as it is.'

Dafe gave him a look of gratitude and ran off to help with the scene shifting.

Tomjon sipped his tea uneasily, the backstage noises whirring around him like so much fog. He was worried.

Hwel had said that everything about the play was fine, except for the play itself. And Tomjon kept thinking that the play itself was trying to force itself into a different shape. His mind had been hearing other words, just too faint for hearing. It was almost like eavesdropping on a conversation. He'd had to shout more to drown out the buzzing in his head.

This wasn't right. Once a play was written it was, well, written. It shouldn't come alive and start twisting itself around.

No wonder everyone needed prompting all the time. The play was writhing under their hands, trying to change itself.

Ye gods, he'd be glad to get out of this spooky castle, and away from this mad duke. He glanced around, decided that it would be some time before the next act was called, and wandered aimlessly in search of fresher air.

A door yielded to his touch and he stepped out on to the battlements. He pushed it shut behind him, cutting off the sounds of the stage and replacing them by a velvet hush. There was a livid sunset imprisoned behind bars of cloud, but the air was as still as a mill pond and as hot as a furnace. In the forest below some night bird screamed.

He walked to the other end of the battlements and peered down into the sheer depths of the gorge. Far beneath, the Lancre boiled in its eternal mists.

He turned, and walked into a draught of such icy coldness that he gasped.

Unusual breezes plucked at his clothing. There was a strange muttering in his ear, as though someone was trying to talk to him but couldn't get the speed right. He stood rigid for a moment, getting his breath, and then fled for the door.

'But we're *not* witches!'

'Why do you look like them, then? Tie their hands, lads.'

'Yes, excuse me, but we're not *really* witches!'

The captain of the guard looked from face to face. His gaze took in the pointy hats, the disordered hair smelling of damp haystacks, the sickly green complexions and the herd of warts. Guard captain for the duke wasn't a job that offered long-term prospects for those who used initiative. Three witches had been called for, and these seemed to fit the bill.

The captain never went to the theatre. When he was on the rack of adolescence he'd been badly frightened by a Punch and Judy show, and since then had taken pains to avoid any organised entertainment and had kept away from anywhere where crocodiles could conceivably be expected. He'd spent the last hour enjoying a quiet drink in the guardroom.

'I said tie their hands, didn't I?' he snapped.

'Shall we gag them as well, cap'n?'

'But if you'd just *listen*, we're with the theatre – '

'Yes,' said the captain, shuddering. 'Gag them.'

'Please . . .'

The captain leaned down and stared at three pairs of frightened eyes. He was trembling.

'That,' he said, 'is the last time *you*'ll eat anyone's sausage.'

He was aware that now the soldiers were giving him odd looks as well. He coughed and pulled himself together.

'Very well then, my theatrical witches,' he said. 'You've done your show, and now it's time for your applause.' He nodded to his men.

'Clap them in chains,' he said.

Three other witches sat in the gloom behind the stage, staring vacantly into the darkness. Granny Weatherwax had picked up a copy of the script, which she peered at from time to time, as if seeking ideas.

'"Divers alarums and excursions",' she read, uncertainly.

'That means lots of terrible happenings,' said Magrat. 'You always put that in plays.'

'Alarums and what?' said Nanny Ogg, who hadn't been listening.

'Excursions,' said Magrat patiently.

'Oh.' Nanny Ogg brightened a bit. 'The seaside would be nice,' she said.

'Do shut up, Gytha,' said Granny Weatherwax. 'They're not for you. They're only for divers, like it says. Probably so they can recover from all them alarums.'

'We can't let this happen,' said Magrat, quickly and loudly. 'If this gets about, witches'll always be old hags with green blusher.'

'And meddlin' in the affairs of kings,' said Nanny. 'Which we never do, as is well known.'

'It's not the meddlin' I object to,' said Granny Weatherwax, her chin on her hand. 'It's the *evil* meddling.'

'And the unkindness to animals,' muttered Magrat. 'All that stuff about eye of dog and ear of toad. *No one* uses that kind of stuff.'

Granny Weatherwax and Nanny Ogg carefully avoided one another's faces.

'Drabe!' said Nanny Ogg bitterly.

'Witches just aren't like that,' said Magrat. 'We live in harmony with the great cycles of Nature, and do no harm to anyone, and it's wicked of them to say we don't. We ought to fill their bones with hot lead.'

The other two looked at her with a certain amount of surprised admiration. She blushed, although not greenly, and looked at her knees.

'Goodie Whemper did a recipe,' she confessed. 'It's quite easy. What you do is, you get some lead, and you – '

'I don't think that would be appropriate,' said Granny carefully, after a certain amount of internal struggle. 'It could give people the wrong idea.'

'But not for long,' said Nanny wistfully.

'No, we can't be having with that sort of thing,' said Granny, a little more firmly this time. 'We'd never hear the last of it.'

'Why don't we just change the words?' said Magrat. 'When they come back on stage we could just put the 'fluence on so they forget what they're saying, and give them some new words.'

'I suppose you're an expert at theatre words?' said Granny sarcastically. 'They'd have to be the proper sort, otherwise people would suspect.'

'Shouldn't be too difficult,' said Nanny Ogg dismissively. 'I've been studyin' it. You go tumpty-tumpty-tumpty.'

Granny gave this some consideration.

'There's more to it than that, I believe,' she said. 'Some of those speeches were very good. I couldn't understand hardly any of it.'

'There's no trick to it at all,' Nanny Ogg insisted. 'Anyway, half of them are forgetting their lines as it is. It'll be easy.'

'We could put words in their mouths?' said Magrat.

Nanny Ogg nodded. 'I don't know about *new* words,' she said. 'But we can make them forget these words.'

They both looked at Granny Weatherwax. She shrugged.

'I suppose it's worth a try,' she conceded.

'Witches as yet unborn will thank us for it,' said Magrat ardently.

'Oh, good,' said Granny.

'At last! What are you three playing at? We've been looking for you everywhere!'

The witches turned to see an irate dwarf trying to loom over them.

'Us?' said Magrat. 'But we're not in – '

'Oh yes you are, remember, we put it in last week. Act Two, Downstage, around the cauldron. You haven't got to say anything. You're symbolising occult forces at work. Just be as wicked as you can. Come on, there's good lads. You've done well so far.'

Hwel slapped Magrat on the bottom. 'Good complexion you've got there, Wilph,' he said encouragingly. 'But for goodness' sake use a bit more padding, you're still the wrong shape. Fine warts there, Billem. I must say,' he added, standing back, 'you look as nasty a bunch of hags as a body might hope to clap eyes on. Well done. Shame about the wigs. Now run along. Curtain up in one minute. Break a leg.'

He gave Magrat another ringing slap on her rump, slightly hurting his hand, and hurried off to shout at someone else.

None of the witches dared to speak. Magrat and Nanny Ogg found themselves instinctively turning towards Granny.

She sniffed. She looked up. She looked around. She looked at the brightly lit stage behind her. She brought her hands together with a clap that echoed around the castle, and then rubbed them together.

'Useful,' she said grimly. 'Let's do the show right here.'

Nanny squinted sullenly after Hwel. 'Break your own leg,' she muttered.

Hwel stood in the wings and gave the signal for the curtains. And for the thunder.

It didn't come.

'Thunder!' he hissed, in a voice heard by half the audience. 'Get on with it!'

A voice from behind the nearest pillar wailed, 'I went and bent the thunder, Hwel! It just goes clonk-clonk!'

Hwel stood silent for a moment, counting. The company watched him, awestruck but not, unfortunately, thunderstruck.

At last he raised his fists to the open sky and said, 'I wanted a storm! Just a storm. Not even a big storm. Any storm. Now I want to make myself absolutely CLEAR! I have had ENOUGH! I want thunder right NOW!'

The stab of lightning that answered him turned the multi-hued shadows of the castle into blinding white and searing black. It was followed by a roll of thunder, on cue.

It was the loudest noise Hwel had ever heard. It seemed to start inside his head and work its way outwards.

It went on and on, shaking every stone in the castle. Dust rained down. A distant turret broke away with balletic slowness and, tumbling end over end, dropped gently into the hungry depths of the gorge.

When it finished it left a silence that rang like a bell.

Hwel looked up at the sky. Great black clouds were blowing across the castle, blotting out the stars.

The storm was back.

It had spent ages learning its craft. It had spent years lurking in distant valleys. It had practised for hours in front of a glacier. It had studied the great storms of the past. It had honed its art to perfection. And now, tonight, with what it could see was clearly an appreciative audience waiting for it, it was going to take them by, well . . . tempest.

Hwel smiled. Perhaps the gods *did* listen, after all. He wished he'd asked for a really good wind machine as well.

He gestured frantically at Tomjon.

'Get on with it!'

The boy nodded, and launched into his main speech.

'*And now our domination is complete –* '

Behind him on the stage the witches bent over the cauldron.

'It's just tin, this one,' hissed Nanny. 'And it's full of all yuk.'

'And the fire is just red paper,' whispered Magrat. 'It looked so real from up there, it's just red paper! Look, you can poke it – '

'Never mind,' said Granny. 'Just look busy, and wait until I say.'

As the Evil King and the Good Duke began the exchange that was going to lead to the exciting Duel Scene they became uncomfortably aware of activity behind them, and occasional chuckles from the audience. After a totally inappropriate burst of laughter Tomjon risked a sideways glance.

One of the witches was taking their fire to bits. Another one was trying to clean the cauldron. The third was sitting with her arms folded, glaring at him.

'*The very soil crys out at tyranny* – ' said Wimsloe, and then caught the expression on Tomjon's face and followed his gaze. His voice trailed into silence.

'"And calls me forth for vengeance",' prompted Tomjon helpfully.

'B-but – ' whispered Wimsloe, trying to point surreptitiously with his dagger.

'I wouldn't be seen dead with a cauldron like this,' said Nanny Ogg, in a whisper loud enough to carry to the back of the courtyard. 'Two days' work with a scourer and a bucket of sand, is this.'

'"And calls me forth for vengeance"!' hissed Tomjon. Out of the tail of his eye he saw Hwel in the wings, frozen in an attitude of incoherent rage.

'How do they make it flicker?' said Magrat.

'Be quiet, you two,' said Granny. 'You're upsetting people.' She raised her hat to Wimsloe. 'Go ahead, young man. Don't mind us.'

'Wha?' said Wimsloe.

'Aha, it calls you forth for vengeance, does it?' said Tomjon, in desperation. 'And the heavens cry revenge, too, I expect.'

On cue, the storm produced a thunderbolt that blew the top off another tower . . .

The duke crouched in his seat, his face a panorama of fear. He extended what had once been a finger.

'There they are,' he breathed. 'That's them. What are they doing in my play? Who said they could be in my play?'

The duchess, who was less inclined to deal in rhetorical questions, beckoned to the nearest guard.

On stage Tomjon was sweating under the load of the script. Wimsloe was incoherent. Now Gumridge, who was playing the part of the Good Duchess in a wig of flax, had lost the thread as well.

'Aha, thou callst me an evil king, though thou whisperest it so none save I may hear it,' Tomjon croaked. 'And thou hast *summoned the guard*, possibly by some most secret signal, owing nought to artifice of lips or tongue.'

A guard came on crabwise, still stumbling from Hwel's shove. He stared at Granny Weatherwax.

'Hwel says what the hell's going on?' he hissed.

'What was that?' said Tomjon. 'Did I hear you say *I come, my lady*?'

'Get these people off, he says!'

Tomjon advanced to the front of the stage.

'Thou babblest, man. See how I dodge thy tortoise spear. I *said*, see how I dodge thy tortoise spear. Thy spear, man. You're holding it in thy bloody hand, for goodness' sake.'

The guard gave him a desperate, frozen grin.

Tomjon hesitated. Three other actors around him were staring fixedly at the witches. Looming up in front of him with all the inevitability of a tax demand was a sword fight during which, it was beginning to appear, he would have to parry his own wild thrusts and stab himself to death.

He turned to the three witches. His mouth opened.

For the first time in his life his awesome memory let him down. He could think of nothing to say.

Granny Weatherwax stood up. She advanced to the edge of the stage. The audience held its breath. She held up a hand.

'Ghosts of the mind and all device away, I bid the Truth to have – ' she hesitated – 'its tumpty-tumpty day.'

Tomjon felt the chill engulf him. The others, too, jolted into life.

Up from out of the depths of their blank minds new words rushed, words red with blood and revenge, words that had echoed among the castle's stones, words stored in silicon, words that would have themselves heard, words that gripped their mouths so tightly that an attempt not to say them would result in a broken jaw.

'Do you fear him now?' said Gumridge. 'And he so mazed with drink? Take his dagger, husband – you are a blade's width from the kingdom.'

'I dare not,' Wimsloe said, trying to look in astonishment at his own lips.

'Who will know?' Gumridge waved a hand towards the audience. He'd never act so well again. 'See, there is only eyeless night. Take the dagger now, take the kingdom tomorrow. Have a stab at it, man.'

Wimsloe's hand shook.

'I have it, wife,' he said. 'Is this a dagger I see before me?'

'Of course it's a bloody dagger. Come on, do it now. The weak deserve no mercy. We'll say he fell down the stairs.'

'But people will suspect!'

'Are there no dungeons? Are there no pilliwinks? Possession is nine parts of the law, husband, when what you possess is a knife.'

Wimsloe drew his arm back.

'I cannot! He has been kindness itself to me!'

'And you can be Death itself to him . . .'

Dafe could hear the voices a long way off. He adjusted his mask, checked the deathliness of his appearance in the mirror, and peered at the script in the empty backstage gloom.

'Cower Now, Brief Mortals,' he said. 'I Am Death, 'Gainst Who – 'Gainst Who – '

WHOM.

'Oh, thanks,' said the boy distractedly. ''Gainst Whom No Lock May Hold – '

WILL HOLD.

'*Will* Hold Nor Fasten'd Portal Bar, Here To – to – to'

HERE TO TAKE MY TALLY ON THIS NIGHT OF KINGS.

Dafe sagged.

'You're so much better at it,' he moaned. 'You've got the right voice and you can remember the words.' He turned around. 'It's only three lines and Hwel will . . . have . . . my . . . guts . . . for.'

He froze. His eyes widened and became two saucers of fear as Death snapped his fingers in front of the boy's rigid face.

FORGET, he commanded, and turned and stalked silently towards the wings.

His eyeless skull took in the line of costumes, the waxy debris of the make-up table. His empty nostrils snuffed up the mixed smells, of mothballs, grease and sweat.

There was something here, he thought, that nearly belonged to the gods. Humans had built a world inside the world, which reflected it in pretty much the same way as a drop of water reflects the landscape. And yet . . . and yet . . .

Inside this little world they had taken pains to put all the things you might think they would want to escape from – hatred, fear, tyranny, and so forth. Death was intrigued. They thought they wanted to be taken out of themselves, and every art humans dreamt up took them further *in*. He was fascinated.

He was here for a very particular and precise purpose. There was a soul to be claimed. There was no time for inconsequentialities. But what was time, after all?

His feet did an involuntary little clicking dance across the stones. Alone, in the grey shadows, Death tapdanced.

– THE NEXT NIGHT IN YOUR DRESSING ROOM THEY HANG A STAR –

He pulled himself together, adjusted his scythe, and waited silently for his cue.

He'd never missed one yet.

He was going to get out there and slay them.

'And you can be Death itself to him. Now!'

Death entered, his feet clicking across the stage.

COWER NOW, BRIEF MORTALS, he said, FOR I AM DEATH, 'GAINST WHOM NO . . . NO . . . 'GAINST WHOM . . .

He hesitated. He hesitated, for the very first time in the eternity of his existence.

For although the Death of the Discworld was used to dealing with people by the million, at the same time every death was intimate and personal.

Death was seldom seen except by those of an occult persuasion and his clients themselves. The reason that no one else saw him was that the human brain is clever enough to edit sights too horrible for it to cope with, but the problem here was that several hundred people were in fact *expecting* to see Death at this point, and were therefore seeing him.

Death turned slowly and stared back at hundreds of watching eyes.

Even in the grip of the truth Tomjon recognised a fellow actor in distress, and fought for mastery of his lips.

' ". . . lock will hold . . ." ' he whispered, through teeth fixed in a grimace.

Death gave him a manic grin of stagefright.

WHAT? he whispered, in a voice like an anvil being hit with a small lead hammer.

' ". . . lock will hold, nor fasten'd portal . . .", ' said Tomjon encouragingly.

. . . LOCK WILL HOLD NOR FASTEN'D PORTAL . . . UH . . . repeated Death desperately, watching his lips.

' ". . . bar! . . ." '

BAR.

'No, I cannot do it!' said Wimsloe. 'I will be seen! Down there in the hall, someone watches!'

'There is no one!'

'I feel the stare!'

'Dithering idiot! Must I put it in for you? See, his foot is upon the top stair!'

Wimsloe's face contorted with fear and uncertainty. He drew back his hand.

'No!'

The scream came from the audience. The duke was half-risen from his seat, his tortured knuckles at his mouth. As they watched he lurched forward between the shocked people.

'No! I did not do it! It was not like that! You cannot say it was like that! You were not there!' He stared at the upturned faces around him, and sagged.

'Nor was I,' he giggled. 'I was asleep at the time, you know. I remember it quite well. There was blood on the counterpane, there was blood on the floor, I could not wash off the blood, but these are not proper subjects for the inquiry. I cannot allow the discussion of national security. It was just a dream, and when I awoke, he'd be alive tomorrow. And tomorrow it wouldn't have happened because it was not done. And tomorrow you can say I did not know. And tomorrow you can say I had no recollection. What a noise he made in falling! Enough to wake the dead . . . who would have thought he had so much blood in him? . . .' By now he had climbed on to the stage, and grinned brightly at the assembled company.

'I hope that sorts it all out,' he said. 'Ha. Ha.'

In the silence that followed Tomjon opened his mouth to utter something suitable, something soothing, and found that there was nothing he could say.

But another personality stepped into him, took over his lips, and spoke thusly:

'With my own bloody dagger, you bastard! I know it was you! I saw you at the top of the stairs, sucking your thumb! I'd kill you now, except for the thought of having to spend eternity listening to your whining. I, Verence, formerly King of – '

'What testimony is this?' said the duchess. She stood in front of the stage, with half a dozen soldiers beside her.

'These are just slanders,' she added. 'And treason to boot. The rantings of mad players.'

'I was bloody King of Lancre!' shouted Tomjon.

'In which case you are the alleged victim,' said the duchess calmly. 'And unable to speak for the prosecution. It is against all precedent.'

Tomjon's body turned towards Death.

'You were there! You saw it all!'

I SUSPECT I WOULD NOT BE CONSIDERED AN APPROPRIATE WITNESS.

'Therefore there is no proof, and where there is no proof there is no crime,' said the duchess. She motioned the soldiers forward.

'So much for your experiment,' she said to her husband. 'I think my way is better.'

She looked around the stage, and found the witches.

'Arrest them,' she said.

'No,' said the Fool, stepping out of the wings.

'*What* did you say?'

'I saw it all,' said the Fool, simply. 'I was in the Great Hall that night. You killed the king, my lord.'

'I did not!' screamed the duke. 'You were not there! I did not see you there! I *order* you not to be there!'

'You did not dare say this before,' said Lady Felmet.

'Yes, lady. But I must say it now.'

The duke focused unsteadily on him.

'You swore loyalty unto death, my Fool,' he hissed.

'Yes, my lord. I'm sorry.'

'You're *dead*.'

The duke snatched a dagger from Wimsloe's unresisting hand, darted forward, and plunged it to the hilt into the Fool's heart. Magrat screamed.

The Fool rocked back and forth unsteadily.

'Thank goodness that's over,' he said, as Magrat pushed her way through the actors and clasped him to what could charitably be called her bosom. It struck the Fool that he had never looked a bosom squarely in the face, at least since he was a baby, and it was particularly cruel of the world to save the experience until after he was dead.

He gently moved one of Magrat's arms and pulled the despicable horned cowl from his head, and tossed it as far as possible. He didn't have to be a Fool any more or, he realised, bother about vows or anything. What with bosoms as well, death seemed to be an improvement.

'I didn't do it,' said the duke.

No pain, thought the Fool. Funny, that. On the other hand, you obviously can't feel pain when you are dead. It would be wasted.

'You all saw that I didn't do it,' said the duke.

Death gave the Fool a puzzled look. Then he reached into the recesses of his robes and pulled out an hourglass. It had bells on it. He gave it a gentle shake, which make them tinkle.

'I gave no orders that any such thing should be done,' said the duke calmly. His voice came from a long way off, from wherever his mind was now. The company stared at him wordlessly. It wasn't possible to hate someone like this, only to feel acutely embarrassed about being anywhere near him. Even the Fool felt embarrassed, and he was dead.

Death tapped the hourglass, and then peered at it to see if it had gone wrong.

'You are all lying,' said the duke, in tranquil tones. 'Telling lies is naughty.'

He stabbed several of the nearest actors in a dreamy, gentle way, and then held up the blade.

'You see?' he said. 'No blood! It wasn't me.' He looked up at the duchess, towering over him now like a red tsunami over a small fishing village.

'It was her,' he said. 'She did it.'

He stabbed her once or twice, on general principles, and then stabbed himself and let the dagger drop from his fingers.

After a few seconds reflection he said, in a voice far nearer the worlds of sanity, 'You can't get me now.'

He turned to Death. 'Will there be a comet?' he said. 'There must be a comet when a prince dies. I'll go and see, shall I?'

He wandered away. The audience broke into applause.

'You've got to admit he was real royalty,' said Nanny Ogg, eventually. 'It only goes to show, royalty goes eccentric far better than the likes of you and me.'

Death held the hourglass to his skull, his face radiating puzzlement.

Granny Weatherwax picked up the fallen dagger and tested the blade with her finger. It slid into the handle quite easily, with a faint squeaking noise.

She passed it to Nanny.

'There's your magic sword,' she said.

Magrat looked at it, and then back at the Fool.

'Are you dead or not?' she said.

'I must be,' said the Fool, his voice slightly muffled. 'I think I'm in paradise.'

'No, look, I'm serious.'

'I don't know. But I'd like to breathe.'

'Then you must be alive.'

'Everyone's alive,' said Granny. 'It's a trick dagger. Actors probably can't be trusted with real ones.'

'After all, they can't even keep a cauldron clean,' said Nanny.

'Whether everyone is alive or not is a matter for me,' said the duchess. 'As ruler it is my pleasure to decide. Clearly my husband has lost his wits.' She turned to her soldiers. 'And I decree – '

'Now!' hissed King Verence in Granny's ear. 'Now!'

Granny Weatherwax drew herself up.

'Be silent, woman!' she said. 'The true King of Lancre stands before you!'

She clapped Tomjon on the shoulder.

'What, him?'

'Who, me?'

'Ridiculous,' said the duchess. 'He's a mummer, of sorts.'

'She's right, miss,' said Tomjon, on the edge of panic. 'My father runs a theatre, not a kingdom.'

'He is the true king. We can prove it,' said Granny.

'Oh, no,' said the duchess. 'We're not having that. There's no mysterious returned heirs in this kingdom. Guards – take him.'

Granny Weatherwax held up a hand. The soldiers lurched from foot to foot, uncertainly.

'She's a witch, isn't she?' said one of them, tentatively.

'Certainly,' said the duchess.

The guards shifted uneasily.

'We seen where they turn people into newts,' said one.

'And then shipwreck them.'

'Yeah, and alarum the divers.'

'Yeah.'

'We ought to talk about this. We ought to get extra for witches.'

'She could do anything to us, look. She could be a drabe, even.'

'Don't be foolish,' said the duchess. 'Witches don't do that sort of thing. They're just stories to frighten people.'

The guard shook his head.

'It looked pretty convincing to me.'

'Of course it did, it was *meant* – ' the duchess began. She sighed, and snatched a spear out of the guard's hand.

'I'll show you the power of these witches,' she said, and hurled it at Granny's face.

Granny moved her hand across at snakebite speed and caught the spear just behind the head.

'So,' she said, 'and it comes to this, does it?'

'You don't frighten me, wyrd sisters,' said the duchess.

Granny stared her in the eye for a few seconds. She gave a grunt of surprise.

'You're right,' she said. 'We really don't, do we . . .'

'Do you think I haven't studied you? Your witchcraft is all artifice and illusion, to amaze weak minds. It holds no fears for me. Do your worst.'

Granny studied her for a while.

'My worst?' she said eventually. Magrat and Nanny Ogg shuffled gently out of her way.

The duchess laughed.

'You're clever,' she said. 'I'll grant you that much. And quick. Come on, hag. Bring on your toads and demons, I'll . . .'

She stopped, her mouth opening and shutting a bit without any words emerging. Her lips drew back in a rictus of terror, her eyes looked beyond Granny, beyond the world, towards something else. One knuckled hand flew to her mouth and she made a little whimpering noise. She froze, like a rabbit that has just seen a stoat and knows, without any doubt, that it is the last stoat that it will ever see.

'What have you done to her?' said Magrat, the first to dare to speak. Granny smirked.

'Headology,' said Granny, and smirked. 'You don't need any Black Aliss magic for it.'

'Yes, but what have you *done*?'

'No one becomes like she is without building walls inside their head,' she said. 'I've just knocked them down. Every scream. Every plea. Every pang of guilt. Every twinge of conscience. All at once. There's a little trick to it.'

She gave Magrat a condescending smile. 'I'll show you one day, if you like.'

Magrat thought about it. 'It's horrible,' she said.

'Nonsense,' Granny smiled terribly. 'Everyone wants to know their true self. Now, she does.'

'Sometimes you have to be kind to be cruel,' said Nanny Ogg approvingly.

'I think it's probably the worst thing that could happen to anyone,' said Magrat, as the duchess swayed backwards and forwards.

'For goodness' sake use your imagination, girl,' said Granny. 'There are far worse things. Needles under the fingernails, for one. Stuff with pliers.'

'Red-hot knives up the jacksie,' said Nanny Ogg. 'Handle first, too, so you cut your fingers trying to pull them out – '

'This is simply the worst that I can do,' said Granny Weatherwax primly. 'It's all right and proper, too. A witch should act like that, you know. There's no need for any dramatic stuff. Most magic goes on in the head. It's headology. Now, if you'd – '

A noise like a gas leak escaped from the duchess's lips. Her head jerked back suddenly. She opened her eyes, blinked, and focused on Granny. Sheer hatred suffused her features.

'Guards!' she said. 'I told you to take them!'

Granny's jaw sagged. 'What?' she said. 'But – but I showed you your true self . . .'

'I'm supposed to be upset by that, am I?' As the soldiers sheepishly grabbed Granny's arms the duchess pressed her face close to Granny's, her tremendous eyebrows a V of triumphant hatred. 'I'm supposed to grovel on the floor, is that it? Well, old woman, I've seen exactly what I am, do you understand, and I'm proud of it! I'd do it all again, only hotter and longer! I enjoyed it, and I did it because I wanted to!'

She thumped the vast expanse of her chest.

'You gawping idiots!' she said. 'You're so *weak*. You really think that people are basically decent underneath, don't you?'

The crowd on the stage backed away from the sheer force of her exultation.

'Well, I've looked underneath,' said the duchess. 'I know what drives people. It's fear. Sheer, deep-down fear. There's not one of you who doesn't fear me, I can make you widdle your drawers out of terror, and now I'm going to take – '

At this point Nanny Ogg hit her on the back of the head with the cauldron.

'She does go on, doesn't she?' she said conversationally, as the duchess collapsed. 'She was a bit eccentric, if you ask me.'

There was a long, embarrassed silence.

Granny Weatherwax coughed. Then she treated the soldiers holding her to a bright, friendly smile, and pointed to the mound that was now the duchess.

'Take her away and put her in a cell somewhere,' she commanded. The men snapped to attention, grabbed the duchess by her arms, and pulled her upright with considerable difficulty.

'Gently, mind,' said Granny.

She rubbed her hands together and turned to Tomjon, who was watching her with his mouth open.

'Depend on it,' she hissed. 'Here and now, my lad, you don't have a choice. You're the King of Lancre.'

'But I don't know how to be a king!'

'We all seed you! You had it down just right, including the shouting.'

'That's just acting.'

'Act, then. Being a king is, is – ' Granny hesitated, and snapped her fingers at Magrat. 'What do you call them things, there's always a hundred of them in anything?'

Magrat looked bewildered. 'Do you mean per cents?' she said.

'Them,' agreed Granny. 'Most of the per cents in being a king is acting, if you ask me. You ought to be good at it.'

Tomjon looked for help into the wings, where Hwel should have been. The dwarf was in fact there, but he wasn't paying much attention. He had the script in front of him, and was rewriting furiously.

BUT I ASSURE YOU, YOU ARE NOT DEAD. TAKE IT FROM ME.

The duke giggled. He had found a sheet from somewhere and had draped it over himself, and was sidling along some of the castle's more deserted corridors. Sometimes he would go 'whoo-oo' in a low voice.

This worried Death. He was used to people claiming that they were *not* dead, because death always came as a shock, and a lot of people had some trouble getting over it. But people claiming that they were dead with every breath in their body was a new and unsettling experience.

'I shall jump out on people,' said the duke dreamily. 'I shall rattle my bones all night, I shall perch on the roof and foretell a death in the house – '

THAT'S BANSHEES.

'I shall if I want,' said the duke, with a trace of earlier determination. 'And I shall float through walls, and knock on tables, and drip ectoplasm on anyone I don't like. Ha. Ha.'

IT WON'T WORK. LIVING PEOPLE AREN'T ALLOWED TO BE GHOSTS. I'M SORRY.

The duke made an unsuccessful attempt to float through a wall, gave up, and opened a door out on to a crumbling section of the battlements. The storm had died away a bit, and a thin rind of moon lurked behind the clouds like a ticket tout for eternity.

Death stalked through the wall behind him.

'Well, then,' said the duke, 'if I'm *not* dead, why are you here?'

WAITING.

'Wait for ever, bone face!' said the duke triumphantly. 'I shall hover in the twilight world, I shall find some chains to shake, I shall – '

He stepped backwards, lost his balance, landed heavily on the wall, and slid. For a moment the remnant of his right hand scrabbled ineffectually at the stonework, and then it vanished.

Death is obviously potentially everywhere at the same time, and in one sense it is no more true to say that he was on the battlements, picking vaguely at non-existent particles of glowing metal on the edge of his scythe blade, than that he was waist-deep in the foaming, rock-toothed waters in the depths of Lancre gorge, his calcareous gaze sweeping downwards and stopping abruptly at a point where the torrent ran a few treacherous inches off a bed of angular pebbles.

After a while the duke sat up, transparent in the phosphorescent waves.

'I shall haunt their corridors,' he said, 'and whisper under the doors on still nights.' His voice grew fainter, almost lost in the ceaseless roar of the river. 'I shall make basket chairs creak most alarmingly, just you wait and see.'

Death grinned at him.

NOW YOU'RE TALKING.

It started to rain.

☆   ☆   ☆

Ramtop rain has a curiously penetrative quality which makes ordinary rain seem almost arid. It poured in torrents over the castle roofs, and somehow seemed to go right through the tiles and fill the Great Hall with a warm, uncomfortable moistness.*

The hall was crowded with half the population of Lancre. Outside, the rushing of the rain even drowned out the distant roar of the river. It soaked the stage. The colours ran and mingled in the painted backdrop, and one of the curtains sagged away from its rail and flapped sadly into a puddle.

Inside, Granny Weatherwax finished speaking.

'You forgot about the crown,' whispered Nanny Ogg.

'Ah,' said Granny. 'Yes, the crown. It's on his head, d'you see. We hid it among the crowns when the actors left, the reason being, no one would look for it there. See how it fits him so perfectly.'

It was a tribute to Granny's extraordinary powers of persuasion that everyone did see how perfectly it fitted Tomjon. In fact the only one who didn't was Tomjon himself, who was aware that it was only his ears that were stopping it becoming a necklace.

'Imagine the sensation when he put it on for the first time,' she went on. 'I expect there was an eldritch tingling sensation.'

'Actually, it felt rather – ' Tomjon began, but no one was listening to him. He shrugged and leaned over to Hwel, who was still scribbling busily.

'Does eldritch mean uncomfortable?' he hissed.

The dwarf looked at him with unfocused eyes.

'What?'

'I said, does eldritch mean uncomfortable?'

'Eh? Oh. No. No, I shouldn't think so.'

'What *does* it mean, then?'

'Dunno. Oblong, I think.' Hwel's glance returned to his scrawl as though magnetised. 'Can you remember what he said after all those tomorrows? I didn't catch the bit after that . . .'

'And there wasn't any need for you to tell everyone I was – adopted,' said Tomjon.

'That's how it was, you see,' said the dwarf vaguely. 'Best to be honest about these things. Now then, did he actually stab her, or just accuse her?'

'I don't want to be a king!' Tomjon whispered hoarsely. 'Everyone says I take after dad!'

'Funny thing, all this taking after people,' said the dwarf vaguely. 'I mean, if I took after *my* dad, I'd be a hundred feet underground digging rocks, whereas – ' His voice died away. He stared at the nib of his pen as though it held an incredible fascination.

* Like Bognor.

'Whereas what?'

'Eh?'

'Aren't you even *listening*?'

'I knew it was wrong when I wrote it. I knew it was the wrong way round . . . What? Oh, yes. Be a king. It's a good job. It seems there's a lot of competition, at any rate. I'm very happy for you. Once you're a king, you can do anything you want.'

Tomjon looked at the faces of the Lancre worthies around the table. They had a keen, calculating look, like the audience at the fatstock show. They were weighing him up. It crept upon him in a cold and clammy way that once he was king, he could do anything he wanted. Provided that what he wanted to do was be king.

'You could build your own theatre,' said Hwel, his eyes lighting up for a moment. 'With as many trapdoors as you wanted, and magnificent costumes. You could act in a new play every night. I mean, it would make the Dysk look like a shed.'

'Who would come to see me?' said Tomjon, sagging in his seat.

'Everyone.'

'What, every night?'

'You could order them to,' said Hwel, without looking up.

I knew he was going to say that, Tomjon thought. He can't really mean it, he added charitably. He's got his play. He doesn't really exist in this world, not right now at the moment.

He took off the crown and turned it over and over in his hands. There wasn't much metal in it, but it felt heavy. He wondered how heavy it would get if you wore it all the time.

At the head of the table was an empty chair containing, he had been assured, the ghost of his real father. It would have been nice to report that he had experienced anything more, when being introduced to it, than an icy sensation and a buzzing in the ears.

'I suppose I could help father pay off on the Dysk,' he said.

'That would be nice, yes,' said Hwel.

He spun the crown in his fingers and listened glumly to the talk flowing back and forth over his head.

'Fifteen years?' said the Mayor of Lancre.

'We had to,' said Granny Weatherwax.

'I thought the baker was a bit early last week.'

'No, no,' said the witch impatiently. 'It doesn't work like that. No one's lost anything.'

'According to my figuring,' said the man who doubled as Lancre's beadle, town clerk and gravedigger, 'we've all lost fifteen years.'

'No, we've all gained them,' said the mayor. 'It stands to reason. Time's like this sort of wiggly road, see, but we took a short cut across the fields.'

'Not at all,' said the clerk, sliding a sheet of paper across the table. 'Look here . . .'

Tomjon let the waters of debate close over him again.

Everyone wanted him to be king. No one thought twice about what he wanted. His views didn't count.

Yes, that was it. No one wanted *him* to be king, not precisely *him*. He just happened to be convenient.

Gold does not tarnish, at least physically, but Tomjon felt that the thin band of metal in his hands had an unpleasant depth to its lustre. It had sat on too many troubled heads. If you held it to your ear, you could hear the screams.

He became aware of someone else looking at him, their gaze playing across his face like a blowlamp on a lolly. He looked up.

It was the third witch, the young . . . the youngest one, with the intense expression and the hedgerow hairstyle. Sitting next to old Fool as though she owned a controlling interest.

It wasn't his face she was examining. It was his features. Her eyeballs were tracking him from nape to nose like a pair of calipers. He gave her a little brave smile, which she ignored. Just like everyone else, he thought.

Only the Fool noticed him, and returned the smile with an apologetic grin and a tiny conspiratorial wave of the fingers that said: 'What are we doing here, two sensible people like us?' The woman was looking at him again, turning her head this way and that and narrowing her eyes. She kept glancing at the Fool and back to Tomjon. Then she turned to the oldest witch, the only person in the entire, hot, damp room who seemed to have acquired a mug of beer, and whispered in her ear.

The two started a spirited, whispered conversation. It was, thought Tomjon, a particularly feminine way of talking. It normally took place on doorsteps, with all the participants standing with their arms folded and, if anyone was so ungracious as to walk past, they'd stop abruptly and watch them in silence until they were safely out of earshot.

He became aware that Granny Weatherwax had stopped talking, and that the entire hall was staring at him expectantly.

'Hallo?' he said.

'It might be a good idea to hold the coronation tomorrow,' said Granny. 'It's not good for a kingdom to be without a ruler. It doesn't like it.'

She stood up, pushed back her chair, and came and took Tomjon's hand. He followed her unprotestingly across the flagstones and up the steps to the throne, where she put her hands on his shoulders and pressed him gently down on to the threadbare red plush cushions.

There was a scraping of benches and chairs. He looked around in panic.

'What's happening now?' he said.

'Don't worry,' said Granny firmly. 'Everyone wants to come and swear loyalty to you. You just nod graciously and ask everyone what they do and if they enjoy it. Oh, and you'd better give them the crown back.'

Tomjon removed it quickly.

'Why?' he said.

'They want to present it to you.'

'But I've already got it!' said Tomjon desperately.

Granny gave a patient sigh.

'Only in the wossname, real sense,' she said. 'This is more ceremonial.'

'You mean unreal?'

'Yes,' said Granny. 'But much more important.'

Tomjon gripped the arms of the throne.

'Fetch me Hwel,' he said.

'No, you must do it like that. It's precedent, you see, first you meet the – '

'I *said*, fetch me the dwarf. Didn't you hear me, woman?' This time Tomjon got the spin and pitch of his voice just right, but Granny rallied magnificently.

'I don't think you quite realise who you are talking to, young man,' she said.

Tomjon half rose in his seat. He had played a great many kings, and most of them weren't the kind of kings who shook hands graciously and asked people whether they enjoyed their work. They were far more the type of kings who got people to charge into battle at five o'clock on a freezing morning *and still managed to persuade them that this was better than being in bed.* He summoned them all, and treated Granny Weatherwax to a blast of royal hauteur, pride and arrogance.

'We thought we were talking to a *subject*,' he said. 'Now do as we say!'

Granny's face was immobile for several seconds as she worked out what to do next. Then she smiled to herself, said lightly, 'As you wish,' and went and dislodged Hwel, who was still writing.

The dwarf gave a stiff bow.

'None of that,' snapped Tomjon. 'What do I do next?'

'I don't know. Do you want me to write an acceptance speech?'

'I told you. I don't want to be king!'

'Could be a problem with an acceptance speech, then,' the dwarf agreed. 'Have you really thought about this? Being king is a great role.'

'But it's the only one you get to play!'

'Hmm. Well, just tell them "no", then.'

'Just like that? Will it work?'

'It's got to be worth a try.'

A group of Lancre dignitaries were approaching with the crown on a cushion. They wore expressions of constipated respect coupled with just a hint of self-satisfaction. They carried the crown as if it was a Present for a Good Boy.

The Mayor of Lancre coughed behind his hand.

'A proper coronation will take some time to arrange,' he began, 'but we would like – '

'No,' said Tomjon.

The mayor hesitated. 'Pardon?' he said.

'I won't accept it.'

The mayor hesitated again. His lips moved and his eyes glazed slightly. He felt that he had got lost somewhere, and decided it would be best to start again.

'A proper coronation will take – ' he ventured.

'It won't,' said Tomjon. 'I will not be king.'

The mayor was mouthing like a carp.

'Hwel?' said Tomjon desperately. 'You're good with words.'

'The problem we've got here,' said the dwarf, 'is that "no" is apparently not among the options when you are offered a crown. I think he could cope with "maybe".'

Tomjon stood up, and grabbed the crown. He held it above his head like a tambourine.

'Listen to me, all of you,' he said. 'I thank you for your offer, it's a great honour. But I can't accept it. I've worn more crowns than you can count, and the only kingdom I know how to rule has got curtains in front of it. I'm sorry.'

Dead silence greeted this. They did not appear to have been the right words.

'Another problem,' said Hwel conversationally, 'is that you don't actually have a choice. You *are* the king, you see. It's a job you are lined up for when you're born.'

'I'd be no good at it!'

'That doesn't matter. A king isn't something you're good at, it's something you are.'

'You can't leave me here! There's nothing but forests!'

Tomjon felt the suffocating cold sensation again, and the slow buzzing in his ears. For a moment he thought he saw, faint as a mist, a tall sad man in front of him, stretching out a hand in supplication.

'I'm sorry,' he whispered. 'I really am.'

Through the fading shape he saw the witches, watching him intently.

Beside him Hwel said, 'The only chance you'd have is if there was another heir. You don't remember any brothers and sisters, do you?'

'I don't remember anyone! Hwel, I – '

There was another ferocious argument among the witches. And then Magrat was striding, striding across the hall, moving like a tidal wave, moving like a rush of blood to the head, shaking off Granny Weatherwax's restraining hand, bearing down on the throne like a piston, and dragging the Fool behind her.

'I say?'

'Er. Hallo*ee*!'

'Er, I say, excuse me, can anyone hear us?'

The castle up above was full of hubbub and general rejoicing, and there was no one to hear the polite and frantic voices that echoed along the dungeon passages, getting politer and more frantic with each passing hour.

'Um, I say? Excuse me? Billem's got this terrible *thing* about rats, if you don't mind. Cooeee!'

Let the camera of the mind's eye pan slowly back along the dim, ancient corridors, taking in the dripping fungi, the rusting chains, the damp, the shadows . . .

'Can anyone hear us? Look, it's really too much. There's been some laughable mistake, look, the wigs come right off . . .'

Let the plaintive echoes dwindle among the cobwebbed corners and rodent-haunted tunnels, until they're no more than a reedy whisper on the cusp of hearing.

'*I say? I say, excuse me, help?*'

Someone is bound to come down here again one of these days.

Some time afterwards Magrat asked Hwel if he believed in long engagements. The dwarf paused in the task of loading up the latty.*

'About a week, maximum,' he said at last. 'With matinees, of course.'

A month went past. The early damp-earth odours of autumn drifted over the velvety-dark moors, where the watery starlight was echoed by one spark of a fire.

---

* At least, of supervising the loading. Actual physical assistance was a little difficult because he had, the day before, slipped on something and broken his leg.

The standing stone was back in its normal place, but still poised to run if any auditors came into view.

The witches sat in careful silence. This was not going to rate among the hundred most exciting coven meetings of all time. If Mussorgsky had seen them, the night on the bare mountain would have been over by teatime.

Then Granny Weatherwax said, 'It was a good banquet, I thought.'

'I was nearly sick,' said Nanny Ogg ṗroudly. 'And my Shirl helped out in the kitchen and brought me home some scraps.'

'I heard,' said Granny coldly. 'Half a pig and three bottles of fizzy wine went missing, they say.'

'It's nice that some people think of the old folk,' said Nanny Ogg, completely unabashed. 'I got a coronation mug, too.' She produced it. 'It says "Viva Verence II Rex". Fancy him being called Rex. I can't say it's a good likeness, mind you. I don't recall him having a handle sticking out of his ear.'

There was another long, terribly polite pause. Then Granny said, 'We were a bit surprised you weren't there, Magrat.'

'We thought you'd be up at the top of the table, kind of thing,' said Nanny. 'We thought you'd have moved in up there.'

Magrat stared fixedly at her feet.

'I wasn't invited,' she said meekly.

'Well, I don't know about *invited*,' said Granny. 'We weren't *invited*. People don't have to invite witches, they just know we'll turn up if we want to. They soon find room for us,' she added, with some satisfaction.

'You see, he's been very busy,' said Magrat to her feet. 'Sorting everything out, you know. He's very clever, you know. Underneath.'

'Very sober lad,' said Nanny.

'Anyway, it's full moon,' said Magrat quickly. 'You've got to go to coven meetings at full moon, no matter what other pressing engagements there may be.'

'Have y– ?' Nanny Ogg began, but Granny nudged her sharply in the ribs.

'It's a very good thing he's paying so much attention to getting the kingdom working again,' said Granny, soothingly. 'It shows proper consideration. I daresay he'll get around to everything, sooner or later. It's very demanding, being a king.'

'Yes,' said Magrat, her voice barely audible.

The silence that followed was almost solid. It was broken by Nanny, in a voice as bright and brittle as ice.

'Well, I brought a bottle of that fizzy wine with me,' she said. 'In case he'd . . . in case . . . in case we felt like a drink,' she rallied, and waved it at the other two.

'I don't want any,' said Magrat sullenly.

'You drink up, girl,' said Granny Weatherwax. 'It's a chilly night. It'd be good for your chest.'

She squinted at Magrat as the moon drifted out from behind its cloud.

'Here,' she said. 'Your hair looks a bit grubby. It looks as though you haven't washed it for a month.'

Magrat burst into tears.

The same moon shone down on the otherwise unremarkable town of Rham Nitz, some ninety miles from Lancre.

Tomjon left the stage to thunderous applause at the concluding act of *The Troll of Ankh*. A hundred people would go home tonight wondering whether trolls were really as bad as they had hitherto thought although, of course, this wouldn't actually stop them disliking them in any way whatsoever.

Hwel patted him on the back as he sat down at the make-up table and started scraping off the thick grey sludge that was intended to make him look like a walking rock.

'Well done,' he said. 'The love scene – just right. And when you turned around and roared at the wizard I shouldn't think there was a dry seat in the house.'

'I know.'

Hwel rubbed his hands together.

'We can afford a tavern tonight,' he said. 'So if we just – '

'We'll sleep in the carts,' said Tomjon firmly, squinting at himself in the shard of mirror.

'But you know how much the Fo – the king gave us! It could be feather beds all the way home!'

'It's straw mattresses and a good profit for us,' said Tomjon. 'And that'll buy you gods from heaven and demons from hell and the wind and the waves and more trapdoors than you can count, my lawn ornament.'

Hwel's hand rested on Tomjon's shoulder for a moment. Then he said, 'You're right, boss.'

'Certainly I am. How's the play going?'

'Hmm? What play?' said Hwel, innocently.

Tomjon carefully removed a plaster brow ridge.

'You know,' he said. 'That one. The Lancre King.'

'Oh. Coming along. Coming along, you know. I'll get it right one of these days.' Hwel changed the subject with speed. 'You know, we could work our way down to the river and take a boat home. That would be nice, wouldn't it?'

'But we could work our way home overland and pick up some more cash. That would be better, wouldn't it?' Tomjon grinned. 'We took one hundred and three pence tonight; I counted heads during the Judgement speech. That's nearly one silver piece after expenses.'

'You're your father's son, and no mistake,' said Hwel.

Tomjon sat back and looked at himself in the mirror.

'Yes,' he said, 'I thought I had better be.'

Magrat didn't like cats and hated the idea of mousetraps. She'd always felt that it should be possible to come to some sort of arrangement with creatures like mice so that all available food was rationed in the best interest of all parties. This was a very humanitarian outlook, which is to say that it was not a view shared by mice, and therefore her moonlit kitchen was alive.

When there was a knocking at the door the entire floor appeared to rush towards the walls.

After a few seconds the knocking came again.

There was another pause. Then the knocking rattled the door on its hinges, and a voice cried, 'Open in the name of the king!'

A second voice said, in hurt tones, 'You don't have to shout like that. Why did you shout like that? I didn't order you to shout like that. It's enough to frighten anybody, shouting like that.'

'Sorry, sire! It goes with the job, sire!'

'Just knock again. A bit more gently, please.'

The knocking might have been a bit softer. Magrat's apron dropped off its hook on the back of the door.

'Are you sure I can't do it myself?'

'It's not done, sire, kings knocking at humble cottage doors. Best leave it to me. OPEN IN THE – '

'Sergeant!'

'Sorry, sire. Forgot myself.'

'Try the latch.'

There was the sound of someone being extremely hesitant.

'Don't like the sound of that, sire,' said the invisible sergeant. 'Could be dangerous. If you want my advice, sire, I'd set fire to the thatch.'

'Set fire?'

'Yessire. We always do that if they don't answer the door. Brings them out a treat.'

'I don't think that would be appropriate, sergeant. I think I'll try the latch, if it's all the same to you.'

'Breaks my heart to see you do it, sire.'

'Well, I'm sorry.'

'You could at least let me buff it up for you.'

'No!'

'Well, couldn't I just set fire to the privy – ?'

'Absolutely not!'

'That chicken house over there looks as if it would go up like – '

'*Sergeant!*'

'Sire!'

'Go back to the castle!'

'What, and leave you all alone, sire?'

'This is a matter of extreme delicacy, sergeant. I am sure you are a man of sterling qualities, but there are times when even a king needs to be alone. It concerns a young woman, you understand.'

'Ah. Point taken, sire.'

'Thank you. Help me dismount, please.'

'Sorry about all that, sire. Tactless of me.'

'Don't mention it.'

'If you need any help getting her alight – '

'*Please* go back to the castle, sergeant.'

'Yes, sire. If you're sure, sire. Thank you, sire.'

'Sergeant?'

'Yes, sire?'

'I shall need someone to take my cap and bells back to the Fools' Guild in Ankh-Morpork now I'm leaving. It seems to me you're the ideal man.'

'Thank you, sire. Much obliged.'

'It's your, ah, burning desire to be of service.'

'Yes, sire?'

'Make sure they put you up in one of the guest rooms.'

'Yes, sire. Thank you, sire.'

There was the sound of a horse trotting away. A few seconds later the latch clonked and the Fool crept in.

It takes considerable courage to enter a witch's kitchen in the dark, but probably no more than it takes to wear a purple shirt with velvet sleeves and scalloped edges. It had this in its favour, though. There were no bells on it.

He had brought a bottle of sparkling wine and a bouquet of flowers, both of which had gone flat during the journey. He laid them on the table, and sat down by the embers of the fire.

He rubbed his eyes. It had been a long day. He wasn't, he felt, a good king, but he'd had a lifetime of working hard at being something he wasn't cut out to be, and he was persevering. As far as he could see, none of his predecessors had tried at all. So much to do, so much to repair, so much to organise . . .

On top of it all there was the problem with the duchess. Somehow he'd felt moved to put her in a decent cell in an airy tower. She was a widow, after all. He felt he ought to be kind to widows. But being kind to the duchess didn't seem to achieve much, she didn't understand it, she thought it was just weakness. He was dreadfully afraid that he might have to have her head cut off.

No, being a king was no laughing matter. He brightened up at the thought. There was that to be said about it.

And, after a while, he fell asleep.

The duchess was not asleep. She was currently halfway down the castle wall on a rope of knotted sheets, having spent the previous day gradually chipping away the mortar around the bars of her window although, in truth, you could hack your way out of the average Lancre Castle wall with a piece of cheese. The fool! He'd given her cutlery, and plenty of bedclothes! That was how these people reacted. They let their fear do their thinking for them. They were scared of her, even when they thought they had her in their power (and the weak never had the strong in their power, never truly in their power). If she'd thrown herself in prison, she would have found considerable satisfaction in making herself regret she'd ever been born. But they'd just given her blankets, and worried about her.

Well, she'd be back. There was a big world out there, and she knew how to pull the levers that made people do what she wanted. She wouldn't burden herself with a husband this time, either. Weak! He was the worst of them, no courage in him to be as bad as he knew he was, inside.

She landed heavily on the moss, paused to catch her breath and then, with the knife ready in her hand, slipped away along the castle walls and into the forest.

She'd go all the way down to the far border and swim the river there, or maybe build a raft. By morning she'd be too far away for them ever to find her, and she doubted very much that they'd ever come looking.

Weak!

She moved through the forest with surprising speed. There were tracks, after all, wide enough for carts, and she had a pretty good sense of direction. Besides, all she needed to do was go downhill. If she found the gorge then she just had to follow the flow.

And then there seemed to be too many trees. There was still a track, and it went more or less in the right direction, but the trees on either side of it were planted rather more thickly than one might expect and, when she tried to turn back, there was no track at all behind her. She took to turning suddenly, half expecting to see the trees moving, but they were always standing stoically and firmly rooted in the moss.

She couldn't feel a wind, but there was a sighing in the treetops.

'All right,' she said, under her breath. 'All right. I'm going anyway. I *want* to go. But I will be back.'

It was at this point that the track opened out into a clearing that hadn't been there the day before and wouldn't be there tomorrow, a clearing in which the moonlight glittered off assembled antlers and fangs and serried ranks of glowing eyes.

The weak banded together can be pretty despicable, but it dawned on the duchess that an alliance of the strong can be more of an immediate problem.

There was total silence for a few seconds, broken only by a faint panting, and then the duchess grinned, raised her knife, and charged the lot of them.

The front ranks of the massed creatures opened to let her pass, and then closed in again. Even the rabbits.

The kingdom exhaled.

On the moors under the very shadow of the peaks the mighty nocturnal chorus of nature had fallen silent. The crickets had ceased their chirping, the owls had hooted themselves into silence, and the wolves had other matters to attend to.

There was a song that echoed and boomed from cliff to cliff, and resounded up the high hidden valleys, causing miniature avalanches. It funnelled along the secret tunnels under glaciers, losing all meaning as it rang between the walls of ice.

To find out what was actually being sung you would have to go all the way back down to the dying fire by the standing stone, where the cross-resonances and waves of conflicting echoes focused on a small, elderly woman who was waving an empty bottle.

' – with a snail if you slow to a crawl, but the hedgehog – '

'It tastes better at the bottom of the bottle, doesn't it,' Magrat said, trying to drown out the chorus.

'That's right,' said Granny, draining her cup.

'Is there any more?'

'I think Gytha finished it, by the sound of it.'

They sat on the fragrant heather and stared up at the moon.

'Well, we've got a king,' said Granny. 'And there's an end of it.'

'It's thanks to you and Nanny, really,' said Magrat, and hiccupped.

'Why?'

'None of them would have believed me if you hadn't spoken up.'

'Only because we was asked,' said Granny.

'Yes, but everyone knows witches don't lie, that's the important thing. I mean, everyone could see they *looked* so alike, but that could have been coincidence. You see,' Magrat blushed, 'I looked up *droit de seigneur*. Goodie Whemper had a dictionary.'

Nanny Ogg stopped singing.

'Yes,' said Granny Weatherwax. 'Well.'

Magrat became aware of an uncomfortable atmosphere.

'You did tell the truth, didn't you?' she said. 'They really are brothers, aren't they?'

'Oh yes,' said Gytha Ogg. 'Definitely. I saw to his mother when your – when the new king was born. And to the queen when young Tomjon was born, and she told me who his father was.'

'Gytha!'

'Sorry.'

The wine was going to her head, but the wheels in Magrat's mind still managed to turn.

'Just a minute,' she said.

'I remember the Fool's father,' said Nanny Ogg, speaking slowly and deliberately. 'Very personable young man, he was. He didn't get on with his dad, you know, but he used to visit sometimes. To see old friends.'

'He made friends easily,' said Granny.

'Among the ladies,' agreed Nanny. 'Very athletic, wasn't he? Could climb walls like nobody's business, I remember hearing.'

'He was very popular at court,' said Granny. 'I know that much.'

'Oh, yes. With the queen, at any rate.'

'The king used to go out hunting such a lot,' said Granny.

'It was that droit of his,' said Nanny. 'Always out and about with it, he was. Hardly ever home o'nights.'

'Just a minute,' Magrat repeated.

They looked at her.

'Yes?' said Granny.

'*You* told everyone they were brothers and that Verence was the older!'

'That's right.'

'And you let everyone believe that – '

Granny Weatherwax pulled her shawl around her.

'We're bound to be truthful,' she said. 'But there's no call to be honest.'

'No, no, what you're saying is that the King of Lancre isn't really – '

'What I'm saying *is*,' said Granny firmly, 'that we've got a king who is no worse than most and better than many and who's got his head screwed on right – '

'Even if it is against the thread,' said Nanny.

' – and the old king's ghost has been laid to rest happy, there's been an enjoyable coronation and *some* of us got mugs we weren't entitled to, them being only for the kiddies and, all in all, things are a lot more satisfactory than they might be. That's what I'm saying. Never mind what should be or what might be or what ought to be. It's what things are that's important.'

'But he's not really a king!'

'He might be,' said Nanny.

'But you just said – '

'Who knows? The late queen wasn't very good at counting. Anyway, he doesn't know he isn't royalty.'

'And you're not going to tell him, are you?' said Granny Weatherwax.

Magrat stared at the moon, which had a few clouds across it.

'No,' she said.

'Right, then,' said Granny. 'Anyway, look at it like this. Royalty has to start somewhere. It might as well start with him. It looks as though he means to take it seriously, which is a lot further than most of them take it. He'll do.'

Magrat knew she had lost. You always lost against Granny Weatherwax, the only interest was in seeing exactly how. 'But I'm surprised at the two of you, I really am,' she said. 'You're witches. That means you have to care about things like truth and tradition and destiny, don't you?'

'That's where you've been getting it all wrong,' said Granny. 'Destiny *is* important, see, but people go wrong when they think it controls them. It's the other way around.'

'Bugger destiny,' agreed Nanny.

Granny glared at her.

'After all, you never thought being a witch was going to be easy, did you?'

'I'm learning,' said Magrat. She looked across the moor, where a thin rind of dawn glowed on the horizon.

'I think I'd better be off,' she said. 'It's getting early.'

'Me too,' said Nanny Ogg. 'Our Shirl frets if I'm not home when she comes to get my breakfast.'

Granny carefully scuffed over the remains of the fire.

'When shall we three meet again?' she said. 'Hmm?'

The witches looked at one another sheepishly.

'I'm a bit busy next month,' said Nanny. 'Birthdays and such. Er. And the work has really been piling up with all this hurly-burly. You know. And there's all the ghosts to think about.'

'I thought you sent them back to the castle,' said Granny.

'Well, they didn't want to go,' said Nanny vaguely. 'To be honest, I've got used to them around the place. They're company of an evening. They hardly scream at all, now.'

'That's nice,' said Granny. 'What about you, Magrat?'

'There always seems to be such a lot to do at this time of year, don't you find?' said Magrat.

'Quite,' said Granny Weatherwax, pleasantly. 'It's not good getting yourself tied down to appointments all the time, is it? Let's just leave the whole question open, shall we?'

They nodded. And, as the new day wound across the landscape, each one busy with her own thoughts, each one a witch alone, they went home.*

---

* There is a school of thought that says that witches and wizards can never go home. They went, though, just the same.

WITCHES
ABROAD

Dedicated to all those people – and why not? – who, after the publication of *Wyrd Sisters*, deluged the author with their version of the words of 'The Hedgehog Song'.

Deary deary me . . .

This is the Discworld, which travels through space on the back of four elephants which themselves stand on the shell of Great A'Tuin, the sky turtle.

Once upon a time such a universe was considered unusual and, possibly, impossible.

But then . . . it used to be so simple, once upon a time.

Because the universe was full of ignorance all around and the scientist panned through it like a prospector crouched over a mountain stream, looking for the gold of knowledge among the gravel of unreason, the sand of uncertainty and the little whiskery eight-legged swimming things of superstition.

Occasionally he would straighten up and say things like 'Hurrah, I've discovered Boyle's Third Law.' And everyone knew where they stood. But the trouble was that ignorance became more interesting, especially big fascinating ignorance about huge and important things like matter and creation, and people stopped patiently building their little houses of rational sticks in the chaos of the universe and started getting interested in the chaos itself – partly because it was a lot easier to be an expert on chaos, but mostly because it made really good patterns that you could put on a t-shirt.

And instead of getting on with proper science* scientists suddenly went around saying how impossible it was to know anything, and that there wasn't really anything you could call reality to know anything about, and how all this was tremendously exciting, and incidentally did you know there were possibly all these little universes all over the place but no one can see them because they are all curved in on themselves? Incidentally, don't you think this is a rather good t-shirt?

Compared to all this, a large turtle with a world on its back is practically mundane. At least it doesn't pretend it doesn't exist, and no one on the

---

* Like finding that bloody butterfly whose flapping wings cause all these storms we've been having lately and getting it to stop.

Discworld ever tried to *prove* it didn't exist in case they turned out to be right and found themselves suddenly floating in empty space. This is because the Discworld exists right on the edge of reality. The least little things can break through to the other side. So, on the Discworld, people take things seriously.

Like stories.

Because stories are important.

People think that stories are shaped by people. In fact, it's the other way around.

Stories exist independently of their players. If you know that, the knowledge is power.

Stories, great flapping ribbons of shaped space-time, have been blowing and uncoiling around the universe since the beginning of time. And they have evolved. The weakest have died and the strongest have survived and they have grown fat on the retelling... stories, twisting and blowing through the darkness.

And their very existence overlays a faint but insistent pattern on the chaos that is history. Stories etch grooves deep enough for people to follow in the same way that water follows certain paths down a mountainside. And every time fresh actors tread the path of the story, the groove runs deeper.

This is called the theory of narrative causality and it means that a story, once started, *takes a shape*. It picks up all the vibrations of all the other workings of that story that have ever been.

This is why history keeps on repeating all the time.

So a thousand heroes have stolen fire from the gods. A thousand wolves have eaten grandmother, a thousand princesses have been kissed. A million unknowing actors have moved, unknowing, through the pathways of story.

It is now *impossible* for the third and youngest son of any king, if he should embark on a quest which has so far claimed his older brothers, *not* to succeed.

Stories don't care who takes part in them. All that matters is that the story gets told, that the story repeats. Or, if you prefer to think of it like this: stories are a parasitical life form, warping lives in the service only of the story itself.*

---

* And people are wrong about urban myths. Logic and reason say that these are fictional creations, retold again and again by people who are hungry for evidence of weird coincidence, natural justice and so on. They aren't. *They keep on happening all the time, everywhere,* as the stories bounce back and forth across the universe. At any one time hundreds of dead grandmothers are being whisked away on the roof-racks of stolen cars and loyal Alsatians are choking on the fingers of midnight burglars. And they're not confined to any one world. Hundreds of female Mercurian *jivpts* turn four tiny eyes on their rescuers and say, 'My brood-husband will be livid – it was *his* travel module.' Urban myths are alive.

It takes a special kind of person to fight back, and become the bicarbonate of history.

Once upon a time . . .

Grey hands gripped the hammer and swung it, striking the post so hard that it sank a foot into the soft earth.

Two more blows and it was fixed immovably.

From the trees around the clearing the snakes and birds watched silently. In the swamp the alligators drifted like patches of bad-assed water.

Grey hands took up the crosspiece and fixed it in place, tying it with creepers, pulling them so tight that they creaked.

She watched him. And then she took up a fragment of mirror and tied it to the top of the post.

'The coat,' she said.

He took up the coat and fitted it over the crosspiece. The pole wasn't long enough, so that the last few inches of sleeve draped emptily.

'And the hat,' she said.

It was tall, and round, and black. It glistened.

The piece of mirror gleamed between the darkness of the hat and the coat.

'Will it work?' he said.

'Yes,' she said. 'Even mirrors have their reflection. We got to fight mirrors with mirrors.' She glared up through the trees to a slim white tower in the distance. 'We've got to find *her* reflection.'

'It'll have to reach out a long way, then.'

'Yes. We need all the help we can get.'

She looked around the clearing.

She had called upon Mister Safe Way, Lady Bon Anna, Hotaloga Andrews and Stride Wide Man. They probably weren't very good gods.

But they were the best she'd been able to make.

This is a story about stories.

Or what it really means to be a fairy godmother.

But it's also, particularly, about reflections and mirrors.

All across the multiverse there are backward tribes* who distrust mirrors and images because, they say, they steal a bit of a person's soul and there's only so much of a person to go around. And the people who wear more

* Considered backward, that is, by people who wear more clothes than they do.

clothes say this is just superstition, despite the fact that other people who spend their lives appearing in images of one sort or another seem to develop a *thin* quality. It's put down to over-work and, tellingly, *over-exposure* instead.

Just superstition. But a superstition doesn't have to be wrong.

A mirror can suck up a piece of soul. A mirror can contain the reflection of the whole universe, a whole skyful of stars in a piece of silvered glass no thicker than a breath.

Know about mirrors and you nearly know everything.

Look into the mirror . . .

. . . further . . .

. . . to an orange light on a cold mountaintop, thousands of miles from the vegetable warmth of that swamp . . .

Local people called it the Bear Mountain. This was because it was a *bare* mountain, not because it had a lot of bears on it. This caused a certain amount of profitable confusion, though; people often strode into the nearest village with heavy-duty crossbows, traps and nets and called haughtily for native guides to lead them to the bears. Since everyone locally was making quite a good living out of this, what with the sale of guide books, maps of bear caves, ornamental cuckoo-clocks with bears on them, bear walking-sticks and cakes baked in the shape of a bear, somehow no one had time to go and correct the spelling.*

It was about as bare as a mountain could be.

Most of the trees gave out about halfway to the top, only a few pines hanging on to give an effect very similar to the couple of pathetic strands teased across his scalp by a baldie who won't own up.

It was a place where witches met.

Tonight a fire gleamed on the very crest of the hill. Dark figures moved in the flickering light.

The moon coasted across a lacework of clouds.

Finally, a tall, pointy-hatted figure said, 'You mean *everyone* brought potato salad?'

☆   ☆   ☆

* Bad spelling can be lethal. For example, the greedy Seriph of Al-Ybi was once cursed by a badly educated deity and for some days everything he touched turned to Glod, which happened to be the name of a small dwarf from a mountain community hundreds of miles away who found himself magically dragged to the kingdom and relentlessly duplicated. Some two thousand Glods later the spell wore off. These days, the people of Al-Ybi are renowned for being unusually short and bad-tempered.

There was one Ramtop witch who was not attending the sabbat. Witches like a night out as much as anyone else but, in this case, she had a more pressing appointment. And it wasn't the kind of appointment you can put off easily.

Desiderata Hollow was making her will.

When Desiderata Hollow was a girl, her grandmother had given her four important pieces of advice to guide her young footsteps on the unexpectedly twisting pathway of life.

They were:

Never trust a dog with orange eyebrows,

Always get the young man's name and address,

Never get between two mirrors,

And always wear completely clean underwear every day because you never knew when you were going to be knocked down and killed by a runaway horse and if people found you had unsatisfactory underwear on, you'd die of shame.

And then Desiderata grew up to become a witch. And one of the minor benefits of being a witch is that you know exactly when you're going to die and can wear what underwear you like.*

That had been eighty years earlier, when the idea of knowing exactly when you were going to die had seemed quite attractive because secretly, of course, you knew you were going to live for ever.

That was then.

And this was now.

Forever didn't seem to last as long these days as once it did.

Another log crumbled to ash in the fireplace. Desiderata hadn't bothered to order any fuel for the winter. Not much point, really.

And then, of course, there was this other thing . . .

She'd wrapped it up carefully into a long, slim package. Now she folded up the letter, addressed it, and pushed it under the string. Job done.

She looked up. Desiderata had been blind for thirty years, but this hadn't been a problem. She'd always been blessed, if that was the word, with second sight. So when the ordinary eyes gave out you just trained yourself to see into the present, which anyway was easier than the future. And since the eyeball of the occult didn't depend on light, you saved on candles. There was always a silver lining, if you knew where to look. In a manner of speaking.

There was a mirror on the wall in front of her.

The face in it was not her own, which was round and pink.

* Which explains a lot about witches.

It was the face of a woman who was used to giving orders. Desiderata wasn't the sort to give orders. Quite the reverse, in fact.

The woman said, 'You are dying, Desiderata.'

'I am that, too.'

'You've grown old. Your sort always do. Your power is nearly gone.'

'That's a fact, Lilith,' said Desiderata mildly.

'So your protection is withdrawing from her.'

'' Fraid so,' said Desiderata.

'So now it's just me and the evil swamp woman. And I will win.'

'That's how it seems, I'm afraid.'

'You should have found a successor.'

'Never had the time. I'm not the planning sort, you know.'

The face in the mirror got closer, as if the figure had moved a little nearer to its side of the mirror.

'You've *lost*, Desiderata Hollow.'

'So it goes.' Desiderata got to her feet, a little unsteadily, and picked up a cloth.

The figure seemed to be getting angry. It clearly felt that people who had lost ought to look downcast, and not as if they were enjoying a joke at your expense.

'Don't you understand what losing *means*?'

'Some people are very clear about that,' said Desiderata. 'Goodbye, m'lady.' She hung the cloth over the mirror.

There was an angry intake of breath, and then silence.

Desiderata stood as if lost in thought.

Then she raised her head, and said: 'Kettle boiled just now. Would you like a cup of tea?'

No, THANK YOU, said a voice right behind her.

'How long have you been waiting?'

FOR EVER.

'Not keeping you, am I?'

IT'S A QUIET NIGHT.

'I'm making a cup of tea. I think there's one biscuit left.'

NO, THANK YOU.

'If you feel peckish, it's in the jar on the mantelpiece. That's genuine Klatchian pottery, you know. Made by a genuine Klatchian craftsman. From Klatch,' she added.

INDEED?

'I used to get about a lot in my younger days.'

YES?

'Great times.' Desiderata poked the fire. 'It was the job, you see. Of course, I expect it's very much the same for you.'

YES.

'I never knew when I was going to be called out. Well, of course you'd know about that, wouldn't you. Kitchens, mainly. It always seemed to be kitchens. Balls sometimes, but generally it was kitchens.' She picked up the kettle and poured the boiling water into the teapot on the hearth.

INDEED.

'I used to grant their wishes.'

Death looked puzzled.

WHAT? YOU MEAN LIKE . . . FITTED CUPBOARDS? NEW SINKS? THAT KIND OF THING?

'No, no. The *people*.' Desiderata sighed. 'It's a big responsibility, fairy godmothering. Knowing when to stop, I mean. People whose wishes get granted often don't turn out to be very nice people. So should you give them what they want – or what they *need*?'

Death nodded politely. From his point of view, people got what they were given.

'Like this Genua thing – ' Desiderata began.

Death looked up sharply.

GENUA?

'You know it? Well, of course you would.'

I . . . KNOW EVERYWHERE, OF COURSE.

Desiderata's expression softened. Her inner eyes were looking elsewhere.

'There were two of us. Godmothers go in twos, you know. Me and Lady Lilith? There's a lot of power in godmothering. It's like being part of history. Anyway, the girl was born, out of wedlock but none the worse for that, it wasn't as if they couldn't have married, they just never got round to it . . . and Lilith wished for her to have beauty and power and marry a prince. Hah! And she's been working on that ever since. What could I do? You can't argue with wishes like that. Lilith knows the power of a story. I've done the best I could, but Lilith's got the power. I hear she runs the city now. Changing a whole country just to make a story work! And now it's too late anyway. For me. So I'm handing on the responsibility. That's how it goes, with fairy godmothering. No one ever *wants* to be a fairy godmother. Except Lilith, of course. Got a bee in her bonnet about it. So I'm sending someone else. I may have left things too late.'

Desiderata was a kindly soul. Fairy godmothers develop a very deep understanding about human nature, which makes the good ones kind and the bad ones powerful. She was not someone to use extreme language, but it was possible to be sure that when she deployed a mild term like 'a bee in her bonnet' she was using it to define someone whom she believed to be several miles over the madness horizon and accelerating.

She poured out the tea.

'That's the trouble with second sight,' she said. 'You can *see* what's happenin', but you don't know what it *means*. I've seen the future. There's a coach made out of a pumpkin. And that's impossible. And there's coachmen made out of mice, which is unlikely. And there's a clock striking midnight, and something about a glass slipper. And it's all going to happen. Because that's how stories have to work. And then I thought: I knows some people who make stories work *their* way.'

She sighed again. 'Wish *I* was going to Genua,' she said. 'I could do with the warmth. And it's Fat Tuesday coming up. Always went to Genua for Fat Tuesday in the old days.'

There was an expectant silence.

Then Death said, YOU SURELY ARE NOT ASKING *ME* TO GRANT A WISH?

'Hah! *No one* grants a fairy godmother's wishes.' Desiderata had that inward look again, her voice talking to herself. 'See? I got to get the three of them to Genua. Got to get 'em there because I've *seen* 'em there. Got to be all three. And that ain't easy, with people like them. Got to use headology. Got to make 'em send 'emselves. Tell Esme Weatherwax she's got to go somewhere and she won't go out of contrariness, so tell her she's not to go and she'll run there over broken glass. That's the thing about the Weatherwaxes, see. They don't know how to be beaten.'

Something seemed to strike her as funny.

'But *one* of 'em's going to have to *learn*.'

Death said nothing. From where he sat, Desiderata reflected, losing was something that everyone learned.

She drained her tea. Then she stood up, put on her pointy hat with a certain amount of ceremony, and hobbled out of the back door.

There was a deep trench dug under the trees a little way from the house, down into which someone had thoughtfully put a short ladder. She climbed in and, with some difficulty, heaved the ladder onto the leaves. Then she lay down. She sat up.

'Mr Chert the troll down at the sawmill does a very good deal on coffins, if you don't mind pine.'

I SHALL DEFINITELY BEAR IT IN MIND.

'I got Hurker the poacher to dig the hole out for me,' she said conversationally, 'and he's goin' to come along and fill it in on his way home. I believe in being neat. Take it away, maestro.'

WHAT? OH. A FIGURE OF SPEECH.

He raised his scythe.

Desiderata Hollow went to her rest.

'Well,' she said, 'that was easy. What happens now?'

And this *is* Genua. The magical kingdom. The diamond city. The fortunate country.

In the centre of the city a woman stood between two mirrors, watching herself reflected all the way to infinity.

The mirrors were themselves in the centre of an octagon of mirrors, open to the sky on the highest tower of the palace. There were so many reflections, in fact, that it was only with extreme difficulty that you could tell where the mirrors ended and the real person began.

Her name was Lady Lilith de Tempscire, although she had answered to many others in the course of a long and eventful life. And that was something you learned to do early on, she'd found. If you wanted to get anywhere in this world – and she'd decided, right at the start, that she wanted to get as far as it was possible to go – you wore names lightly, and you took power anywhere you found it. She had buried three husbands, and at least two of them had been already dead.

And you moved around a lot. Because most people *didn't* move around much. Change countries and your name and, if you had the right manner, the world was your mollusc. For example, she'd had to go a mere hundred miles to become a Lady.

She'd go to any lengths now . . .

The two main mirrors were set almost, but not quite, facing one another, so that Lilith could see over her shoulder and watch her images curve away around the universe inside the mirror.

She could feel *herself* pouring into *herself*, multiplying itself via the endless reflections.

When Lilith sighed and strode out from the Space between the mirrors the effect was startling. Images of Lilith hung in the air behind her for a moment, like three-dimensional shadows, before fading.

So . . . Desiderata was dying. Interfering old baggage. She deserved death. She'd never understood the kind of power she'd had. She was one of those people afraid to do good for fear of doing harm, who took it all so seriously that they'd constipate themselves with moral anguish before granting the wish of a single ant.

Lilith looked down and out over the city. Well, there were no barriers now. The stupid voodoo woman in the swamp was a mere distraction, with no understanding.

Nothing stood in the way of what Lilith liked more than anything else.

A happy ending.

Up on the mountain, the sabbat had settled down a bit.

Artists and writers have always had a rather exaggerated idea about what goes on at a witches' sabbat. This comes from spending too much time in small rooms with the curtains drawn, instead of getting out in the healthy fresh air.

For example, there's the dancing around naked. In the average temperate climate there are very few nights when anyone would dance around at midnight with no clothes on, quite apart from the question of stones, thistles, and sudden hedgehogs.

Then there's all that business with goat-headed gods. Most witches don't believe in gods. They know that the gods exist, of course. They even deal with them occasionally. But they don't believe in them. They know them too well. It would be like believing in the postman.

And there's the food and drink – the bits of reptile and so on. In fact, witches don't go for that sort of thing. The worst you can say about the eating habits of the older type of witch is that they tend to like ginger biscuits dipped in tea with so much sugar in it that the spoon won't move *and* will drink it out of the saucer if they think it's too hot. And do so with appreciative noises more generally associated with the cheaper type of plumbing system. Legs of toad and so on might be better than this.

Then there's the mystic ointments. By sheer luck, the artists and writers are on firmer ground here. Most witches are elderly, which is when ointments start to have an attraction, and at least two of those present tonight were wearing Granny Weatherwax's famous goose-grease-and-sage chest liniment. This didn't make you fly and see visions, but it *did* prevent colds, if only because the distressing smell that developed around about the second week kept everyone else so far away you couldn't catch anything from them.

And finally there's sabbats themselves. Your average witch is not, by nature, a social animal as far as other witches are concerned. There's a conflict of dominant personalities. There's a group of ringleaders without a ring. There's the basic unwritten rule of witchcraft, which is 'Don't do what you will, do what I say.' The natural size of a coven is one. Witches only get together when they can't avoid it.

Like now.

The conversation, given Desiderata's absence, had naturally turned to the increasing shortage of witches.*

'What, no one?' said Granny Weatherwax.

'No one,' said Gammer Brevis.

'I call that terrible,' said Granny. 'That's disgustin'.'

'Eh?' said Old Mother Dismass.

'She calls it disgusting!' shouted Gammer Brevis.

'Eh?'

'There's no girl to put forward. To take Desiderata's place!'

'Oh.'

The implications of this sank in.

'If anyone doesn't want their crusts I'll 'ave 'em,' said Nanny Ogg.

'We never had this sort of thing in my young days,' said Granny. 'There was a dozen witches this side of the mountain alone. Of course, that was before all this' – she made a face – 'making your own entertainment. There's far too much of this making your own entertainment these days. We never made our own entertainment when I was a girl. We never had time.'

'Tempers fuggit,' said Nanny Ogg.

'What?'

'Tempers fuggit. Means that was then and this is now,' said Nanny.

'I don't need no one to tell me that, Gytha Ogg. I know when now is.'

'You got to move with the times.'

'I don't see why. Don't see why we – '

'So I reckon we got to shift the boundaries again,' said Gammer Brevis.

'Can't do that,' said Granny Weatherwax promptly. 'I'm doing four villages already. The broomstick hardly has time to cool down.'

'Well, with Mother Hollow passing on, we're definitely short-handed,' said Gammer Brevis. 'I know she didn't do a lot, what with her other work, but she was there. That's what it's all about. Being there. There's got to be a local witch.'

The four witches stared gloomily at the fire. Well, three of them did. Nanny Ogg, who tended to look on the cheerful side, made toast.

'They've got a wizard in, down in Creel Springs,' said Gammer Brevis. 'There wasn't anyone to take over when old Granny Hopliss passed on, so they sent off to Ankh-Morpork for a wizard. An actual wizard. With a staff. He's got a shop there and everything, with a brass sign on the door. It says "Wizard".'

The witches sighed.

* Desiderata had sent a note via Old Mother Dismass asking to be excused on account of being dead. Second sight enables you to keep a very tight rein on your social engagements.

'Mrs Singe passed on,' said Gammer Brevis. 'And Gammer Peavey passed on.'

'Did she? Old Mabel Peavey?' said Nanny Ogg, through a shower of crumbs. 'How old was she?'

'One hundred and nineteen,' said Gammer Brevis. 'I said to her, "You don't want to go climbing mountains at your age" but she wouldn't listen.'

'Some people are like that,' said Granny. 'Stubborn as mules. Tell them they mustn't do something and they won't stop till they've tried it.'

'I actually heard her very last words,' said Gammer.

'What did she say?' said Granny.

'As I recall, "oh bugger",' said Gammer.

'It's the way she would have wanted to go,' said Nanny Ogg. The other witches nodded.

'You know . . . we could be looking at the end of witchcraft in these parts,' said Gammer Brevis.

They stared at the fire again.

'I don't 'spect anyone's brought any marshmallows?' said Nanny Ogg, hopefully.

Granny Weatherwax looked at her sister witches. Gammer Brevis she couldn't stand; the old woman taught school on the other side of the mountain, and had a nasty habit of being reasonable when provoked. And Old Mother Dismass was possibly the most useless sibyl in the history of oracular revelation. And Granny really couldn't be having at all with Nanny Ogg, who was her best friend.

'What about young Magrat?' said Old Mother Dismass innocently. 'Her patch runs right alongside Desiderata's. Maybe she could take on a bit extra?'

Granny Weatherwax and Nanny Ogg exchanged glances.

'She's gone funny in the head,' said Granny.

'Now, come on, Esme,' said Nanny Ogg.

'Well, *I* call it funny,' said Granny. 'You can't tell me that saying all that stuff about relatives isn't going funny in the head.'

'She didn't say that,' said Nanny. 'She said she wanted to relate to herself.'

'That's what I said,' said Granny Weatherwax. 'I told her: Simplicity Garlick was your mother, Araminta Garlick was your granny. Yolande Garlick is your aunt and you're your . . . you're your *me*.'

She sat back with the satisfied look of someone who has solved everything anyone could ever want to know about a personal identity crisis.

'She wouldn't listen,' she added.

Gammer Brevis wrinkled her forehead.

'Magrat?' she said. She tried to get a mental picture of the Ramtops' youngest witch and recalled – well, not a face, just a slightly watery-eyed expression of hopeless goodwill wedged between a body like a maypole and hair like a haystack after a gale. A relentless doer of good works. A worrier. The kind of person who rescued small lost baby birds and cried when they died, which is the function kind old Mother Nature usually reserves for small lost baby birds.

'Doesn't sound like her,' she said.

'And she said she wanted to be more self-assertive,' said Granny.

'Nothing wrong with being self-assertive,' said Nanny. 'Self-asserting's what witching's all about.'

'I never said there was anything wrong with it,' said Granny. 'I told her there was nothing wrong with it. You can be as self-assertive as you like, I said, just so long as you do what you're told.'

'Rub this on and it'll clear up in a week or two,' said Old Mother Dismass.

The other three witches watched her expectantly, in case there was going to be anything else. It became clear that there wasn't.

'And she's running – what's that she's running, Gytha?' said Granny.

'Self-defence classes,' said Nanny.

'But she's a witch,' Gammer Brevis pointed out.

'I told her that,' said Granny Weatherwax, who had walked nightly without fear in the bandit-haunted forests of the mountains all her life in the certain knowledge that the darkness held nothing more terrible than she was. 'She said that wasn't the point. *Wasn't the point.* That's what she said!'

'No one goes to them, anyway,' said Nanny Ogg.

'*I* thought she was going to get married to the king,' said Gammer Brevis.

'Everyone did,' said Nanny. 'But you know Magrat. She tends to be open to Ideas. Now she says she refuses to be a sex object.'

They all thought about this. Finally Gammer Brevis said, slowly, in the manner of one surfacing from the depths of fascinated cogitation, 'But she's never *been* a sex object.'

'I'm pleased to say I don't even know what a sex object *is*,' said Granny Weatherwax firmly.

'I do,' said Nanny Ogg.

They looked at her.

'Our Shane brought one home from foreign parts once.'

They carried on looking at her.

'It was brown and fat and had beads on and a face and two holes for the string.'

This didn't seem to avert their gaze.

'Well, that's what he said it was,' said Nanny.

'I think you're talking about a fertility idol,' said Gammer Brevis helpfully.

Granny shook her head.

'Doesn't sound much like Magrat to me – ' she began.

'You can't tell me that's worth tuppence,' said Old Mother Dismass, from whatever moment of time she was currently occupying.

No one was ever quite sure which it was.

It was an occupational hazard for those gifted with second sight. The human mind isn't really designed to be sent rocketing backwards and forwards along the great freeway of time and can become, as it were, detached from its anchorage, seeing randomly into the past and the future and only occasionally into the present. Old Mother Dismass was temporally unfocused. This meant that if you spoke to her in August she was probably listening to you in March. It was best just to say something now and hope she'd pick it up next time her mind was passing through.

Granny waved her hands experimentally in front of Old Mother Dismass's unseeing eyes.

'She's gone again,' she said.

'Well, if Magrat can't take it on there's Millie Hopgood from over Slice way,' said Gammer Brevis. 'She's a hard-working girl. Mind you, she's got a worse squint than Magrat.'

'Nothing wrong with that. A squint looks good on a witch,' said Granny Weatherwax.

'But you have to know how to use it,' said Nanny Ogg. 'Old Gertie Simmons used to have a squint and she was always putting the evil influence on the end of her own nose. We can't have people thinkin' that if you upsets a witch she curses and mutters and then her own nose drops off.'

They all stared at the fire.

'I suppose Desiderata wouldn't have chosen her own successor?' said Gammer Brevis.

'Can't go doin' that,' said Granny Weatherwax. 'That's not how we do things in these parts.'

'Yes, but Desiderata didn't spend much time in these parts. It was the job. She was always going off to foreign parts.'

'I can't be having with foreign parts,' said Granny Weatherwax.

'You've been to Ankh-Morpork,' said Nanny mildly. 'That's foreign.'

'No it's not. It's just a long way off. That's not the same as foreign. Foreign's where they gabble at you in heathen lingo and eat foreign muck and worship, you know, *objects*,' said Granny Weatherwax, goodwill diplomat. 'Foreign can be quite close too, if you're not careful. Huh,' she added witheringly. 'Yes, she could bring back just about anything from foreign parts.'

'She brought me back a nice blue and white plate once,' said Nanny Ogg.

'That's a point,' said Gammer Brevis. 'Someone'd better go and see to her cottage. She had quite a lot of good stuff there. It'd be dreadful to think of some thief getting in there and having a rummage.'

'Can't imagine any thief'd want to break into a witch's – ' Granny began, and then stopped abruptly.

'Yes,' she said meekly. 'Good idea. I'll see to it directly.'

'No, I'll see to it,' said Nanny Ogg, who'd also had time to work something out. 'It's right on my way home. No problem.'

'No, you'll be wanting to get home early,' said Granny. 'Don't you bother yourself. It'd be no trouble.'

'Oh, it won't be any trouble at all,' said Nanny.

'You don't want to go tiring yourself out at your age,' said Granny Weatherwax.

They glared at one another.

'I really don't see that it matters,' said Gammer Brevis. 'You might as well go together rather than fight about it.'

'I'm a bit busy tomorrow,' said Granny. 'How about after lunch?'

'Right,' said Nanny Ogg. 'We'll meet at her cottage. Right after lunch.'

'We had one once but the bit you unscrew fell off and got lost,' said Old Mother Dismass.

Hurker the poacher shovelled the last of the earth into the hole. He felt he ought to say a few words.

'Well, that's about it, then,' he said.

She'd definitely been one of the better witches, he thought, as he wandered back to the cottage in the pre-dawn gloom. Some of the other ones – while of course being wonderful human beings, he added to himself hurriedly, as fine a bunch of women as you could ever hope to avoid – were just a bit overpowering. Mistress Hollow had been a listening kind of person.

On the kitchen table was a long package, a small pile of coins, and an envelope.

He opened the envelope, although it was not addressed to him.

Inside was a smaller envelope, and a note.

The note said: *I'm watching you, Albert Hurker. Deliver the packige and the envlope and if you dare take a peek inside something dretful will happen to you. As a profesional Good Farey Godmother I aint allowed to curse anyone but I Predict it would probly involve bein bittern by an enraged wolf and your leg going green and runny and dropping off, dont arsk me how I know anyway you carnt because, I am dead. All the best, Desiderata.*

He picked up the package with his eyes shut.

Light travels slowly in the Discworld's vast magical field, which means that time does too. As Nanny Ogg would put it, when it's teatime in Genua it's Tuesday over here . . .

In fact it was dawn in Genua. Lilith sat in her tower, using a mirror, sending her own image out to scan the world. She was searching.

Wherever there was a sparkle on a wave crest, wherever there was a sheet of ice, wherever there was a mirror or a reflecton then Lilith knew she could see out. You didn't need a magic mirror. Any mirror would do, if you knew how to use it. And Lilith, crackling with the power of a million images, knew that very well.

There was just a nagging doubt. Presumably Desiderata would have got rid of *it*. Her sort were like that. Conscientious. And presumably it would be to that stupid girl with the watery eyes who sometimes visited the cottage, the one with all the cheap jewellery and the bad taste in clothes. She looked just the type.

But Lilith wanted to be sure. She hadn't got where she was today without being sure.

In puddles and windows all over Lancre, the face of Lilith appeared momentarily and then moved on . . .

And now it was dawn in Lancre. Autumn mists rolled through the forests.

Granny Weatherwax pushed open the cottage door. It wasn't locked. The only visitor Desiderata had been expecting wasn't the sort to be put off by locks.

'She's had herself buried round the back,' said a voice behind her. It was Nanny Ogg.

Granny considered her next move. To point out that Nanny had deliberately come early, so as to search the cottage by herself, then raised questions about Granny's own presence. She could undoubtedly answer them, given enough time. On the whole, it was probably best just to get on with things.

'Ah,' she said, nodding. 'Always very neat in her ways, was Desiderata.'

'Well, it was the job,' said Nanny Ogg, pushing past her and eyeing the room's contents speculatively. 'You got to be able to keep track of things, in a job like hers. By gor', that's a bloody enormous cat.'

'It's a lion,' said Granny Weatherwax, looking at the stuffed head over the fireplace.

'Must've hit the wall at a hell of a speed, whatever it was,' said Nanny Ogg.

'Someone killed it,' said Granny Weatherwax, surveying the room.

'Should think so,' said Nanny. 'If I'd seen something like that eatin' its way through the wall I'd of hit it myself with the poker.'

There was of course no such thing as a typical witch's cottage, but if there was such a thing as a non-typical witch's cottage, then this was certainly it. Apart from various glassy-eyed animal heads, the walls were covered in bookshelves and water-colour pictures. There was a spear in the umbrella stand. Instead of the more usual earthenware and china on the dresser there were foreign-looking brass pots and fine blue porcelain. There wasn't a dried herb anywhere in the place but there were a great many books, most of them filled with Desiderata's small, neat handwriting. A whole table was covered with what were probably maps, meticulously drawn.

Granny Weatherwax didn't like maps. She felt instinctively that they sold the landscape short.

'She certainly got about a bit,' said Nanny Ogg, picking up a carved ivory fan and flirting coquettishly.*

'Well, it was easy for her,' said Granny, opening a few drawers. She ran her fingers along the top of the mantelpiece and looked at them critically.

'She could have found time to go over the place with a duster,' she said vaguely. 'I wouldn't go and die and leave my place in this state.'

'I wonder where she left . . . you know . . . *it*?' said Nanny, opening the door of the grandfather clock and peering inside.

'Shame on you, Gytha Ogg,' said Granny. 'We're not here to look for *that*.'

'Of course not. I was just wondering . . .' Nanny Ogg tried to stand on tiptoe surreptitiously, in order to see on top of the dresser.

'Gytha! For shame! Go and make us a cup of tea!'

'Oh, all right.'

Nanny Ogg disappeared, muttering, into the scullery. After a few seconds there came the creaking of a pump handle.

Granny Weatherwax sidled towards a chair and felt quickly under the cushion.

There was a clatter from the next room. She straightened up hurriedly.

'I shouldn't think it'd be under the sink, neither,' she shouted.

Nanny Ogg's reply was inaudible.

Granny waited a moment, and then crept rapidly over to the big chimney. She reached up and felt cautiously around.

---

* Nanny Ogg didn't know what a coquette was, although she could probably hazard a guess.

'Looking for something, Esme?' said Nanny Ogg behind her.

'The soot up here is terrible,' said Granny, standing up quickly. 'Terrible soot there is.'

'*It's* not up there, then?' said Nanny Ogg sweetly.

'Don't know what you're talking about.'

'You don't have to pretend. Everyone knows she must have had one,' said Nanny Ogg. 'It goes with the job. It practic'ly *is* the job.'

'Well . . . maybe I just wanted a look at it,' Granny admitted. 'Just hold it a while. Not *use* it. You wouldn't catch me using one of those things. I only ever saw it once or twice. There ain't many of 'em around these days.'

Nanny Ogg nodded. 'You can't get the wood,' she said.

'You don't think she's been buried with it, do you?'

'Shouldn't think so. I wouldn't want to be buried with it. Thing like that, it's a bit of a responsibility. Anyway, it wouldn't stay buried. A thing like that wants to be used. It'd be rattling around your coffin the whole time. You know the trouble they are.'

She relaxed a bit. 'I'll sort the tea things,' she said. 'You light the fire.'

She wandered back into the scullery.

Granny Weatherwax reached along the mantelpiece for the matches, and then realised that there wouldn't be any. Desiderata had always said she was much too busy not to use magic around the house. Even her laundry did itself.

Granny disapproved of magic for domestic purposes, but she was annoyed. She also wanted her tea.

She threw a couple of logs into the fireplace and glared at them until they burst into flame out of sheer embarrassment.

It was then that her eye was caught by the shrouded mirror.

'Coverin' it over?' she murmured. 'I didn't know old Desiderata was frightened of thunderstorms.'

She twitched aside the cloth.

She stared.

Very few people in the world had more self-control than Granny Weatherwax. It was as rigid as a bar of cast iron. And about as flexible.

She smashed the mirror.

Lilith sat bolt upright in her tower of mirrors.

Her?

Her face was different, of course. Older. It had been a long time. But eyes don't change, and witches always look at the eyes.

Her!

☆　☆　☆

Magrat Garlick, witch, was also standing in front of a mirror. In her case it was totally unmagical. It was also still in one piece, but there had been one or two close calls.

She frowned at her reflection, and then consulted the small, cheaply-woodcut leaflet that had arrived the previous day.

She mouthed a few words under her breath, straightened up, extended her hands in front of her, punched the air vigorously and said: 'HAAAAiiiiieeeeeehgh! Um.'

Magrat would be the first to admit that she had an open mind. It was as open as a field, as open as the sky. No mind could be more open without special surgical implements. And she was always waiting for something to fill it up.

What it was currently filling up with was the search for inner peace and cosmic harmony and the true essence of Being.

When people say 'An idea came to me' it isn't just a metaphor. Raw inspirations, tiny particles of self-contained thought, are sleeting through the cosmos all the time. They get drawn to heads like Magrat's in the same way that water runs into a hole in the desert.

It was all due to her mother's lack of attention to spelling, she speculated. A caring parent would have spelled Margaret correctly. And then she could have been a Peggy, or a Maggie – big, robust names, full of reliability. There wasn't much you could do with a Magrat. It sounded like something that lived in a hole in a river bank and was always getting flooded out.

She considered changing it, but knew in her secret heart that this would not work. Even if she became a Chloe or an Isobel on top she'd still be a Magrat underneath. But it would be nice to try. It'd be nice not to be a Magrat, even for a few hours.

It's thoughts like this that start people on the road to Finding Themselves. And one of the earliest things Magrat had learned was that anyone Finding Themselves would be unwise to tell Granny Weatherwax, who thought that female emancipation was a women's complaint that shouldn't be discussed in front of men.

Nanny Ogg was more sympathetic but had a tendency to come out with what Magrat thought of as double-intenders, although in Nanny Ogg's case they were generally single entendres and proud of it.

In short, Magrat had despaired of learning anything at all from her senior witches, and was casting her net further afield. Much further afield. About as far afield as a field could be.

It's a strange thing about determined seekers-after-wisdom that, no matter where they happen to be, they'll always seek that wisdom which is a long way off. Wisdom is one of the few things that looks bigger the further away it is.*

Currently Magrat was finding herself through the Path of The Scorpion, which offered cosmic harmony, inner one-ness and the possibility of knocking an attacker's kidneys out through his ears. She'd sent off for it.

There were problems. The author, Grand Master Lobsang Dibbler, had an address in Ankh-Morpork. This did not seem like a likely seat of cosmic wisdom. Also, although he'd put in lots of stuff about the Way not being used for aggression and only to be used for cosmic wisdom, this was in quite small print between enthusiastic drawings of people hitting one another with rice flails and going 'Hai!' Later on you learned how to cut bricks in half with your hand and walk over red-hot coals and other cosmic things.

Magrat thought that Ninja was a nice name for a girl.

She squared up to herself in the mirror again.

There was a knock at the door. Magrat went and opened it.

'Hai?' she said.

Hurker the poacher took a step backwards. He was already rather shaken. An angry wolf had trailed him part of the way through the forest.

'Um,' he said. He leaned forward, his shock changing to concern. 'Have you hurt your head, Miss?'

She looked at him in incomprehension. Then realisation dawned. She reached up and took off the headband with the chrysanthemum pattern on it, without which it is almost impossible to properly seek cosmic wisdom by twisting an opponent's elbows through 360 degrees.

'No,' she said. 'What do you want?'

'Got a package for you,' said Hurker, presenting it.

It was about two feet long, and very thin.

'There's a note,' said Hurker helpfully. He shuffled around as she unfolded it, and tried to read it over her shoulder.

'It's private,' said Magrat.

* Hence, for example, the Way of Mrs Cosmopolite, very popular among young people who live in the hidden valleys above the snowline in the high Ramtops. Disdaining the utterances of their own saffron-clad, prayer-wheel-spinning elders, they occasionally travel all the way to No. 3 Quirm Street in flat and foggy Ankh-Morpork, to seek wisdom at the feet of Mrs Marietta Cosmopolite, a seamstress. No one knows the reason for this, apart from the aforesaid attractiveness of distant wisdom, since they can't understand a word she says or, more usually, screams at them. Many a bald young monk returns to his high fastness to meditate on the strange mantra vouchsafed to him, such as 'Push off, you!' and 'If I see *one more* of you little orange devils peering in at me he'll feel the edge of my hand, all right?' and 'Why are you buggers all coming round here staring at my feet?' They have even developed a special branch of martial arts based on their experiences, where they shout incomprehensibly at one another and then hit their opponent with a broom.

'Is it?' said Hurker, agreeably.

'Yes!'

'I was tole you'd give me a penny for delivering it,' said the poacher. Magrat found one in her purse.

'Money forges the chains which bind the labouring classes,' she warned, handing it over. Hurker, who had never thought of himself as a labouring class in his life, but who was prepared to listen to almost any amount of gibberish in exchange for a penny, nodded innocently.

'And I hope your head gets better, Miss,' he said.

When Magrat was left alone in her kitchen-cum-dojo she unwrapped the parcel. It contained one slim white rod.

She looked at the note again. It said, *I niver had time to Trane a replaysment so youll have to Do. You must goe to the city of Genua. I would of done thys myself only cannot by reason of bein dead. Ella Saturday muste NOTTE marry the prins. PS This is importent.*

She looked at her reflection in the mirror.

She looked down at the note again.

PSPS Tell those 2 Olde Biddys they are Notte to come with Youe, they will onlie Ruine everythin.

There was more.

PSPSPS It has tendincy to resett to pumpkins but you wil gett the hange of it in noe time.

Magrat looked at the mirror again. And then down at the wand.

One minute life is simple, and then suddenly it stretches away full of complications.

'Oh, my,' she said. 'I'm a fairy godmother!'

Granny Weatherwax was still standing staring at the crazily webbed fragments when Nanny Ogg ran in.

'Esme Weatherwax, what have you done? That's bad luck, that is . . . Esme?'

'Her? *Her?*'

'Are you all right?'

Granny Weatherwax screwed up her eyes for a moment, and then shook her head as if trying to dislodge an unthinkable thought.

'What?'

'You've gone all pale. Never seen you go all pale like that before.'

Granny slowly removed a fragment of glass from her hat.

'Well . . . bit of a turn, the glass breaking like that . . .' she mumbled.

Nanny looked at Granny Weatherwax's hand. It was bleeding. Then she looked at Granny Weatherwax's face, and decided that she'd never admit that she'd looked at Granny Weatherwax's hand.

'Could be a sign,' she said, randomly selecting a safe topic. 'Once someone dies, you get that sort of thing. Pictures fallin' off walls, clocks stopping . . . great big wardrobes falling down the stairs . . . that sort of thing.'

'I've never believed in that stuff, it's . . . what do you mean, *wardrobes* falling down the stairs?' said Granny. She was breathing deeply. If it wasn't well known that Granny Weatherwax was *tough*, anyone might have thought she had just had the shock of her life and was practically desperate to take part in a bit of ordinary everyday bickering.

'That's what happened after my Great-Aunt Sophie died,' said Nanny Ogg. 'Three days and four hours and six minutes *to the very minute* after she died, her wardrobe fell down the stairs. Our Darron and our Jason were trying to get it round the bend and it sort of slipped, just like that. Uncanny. Weeell, I wasn't going to leave it there for her Agatha, was I, only ever visited her mum on Hogswatchday, and it was me that nursed Sophie all the way through to the end – '

Granny let the familiar, soothing litany of Nanny Ogg's family feud wash over her as she groped for the teacups.

The Oggs were what is known as an extended family – in fact not only extended but elongated, protracted and persistent. No normal sheet of paper could possibly trace their family tree, which in any case was more like a mangrove thicket. And every single branch had a low-key, chronic vendetta against every other branch, based on such well-established *causes célèbres* as What Their Keven Said About Our Stan At Cousin Di's Wedding and Who Got The Silver Cutlery That Auntie Em *Promised* Our Doreen Was To Have After She Died, I'd Like To Know, Thank You *Very* Much, *If* You Don't Mind.

Nanny Ogg, as undisputed matriarch, encouraged all sides indiscriminately. It was the nearest thing she had to a hobby.

The Oggs contained, in just one family, enough feuds to keep an entire Ozrak of normal hillbillies going for a century.

And sometimes this encouraged a foolish outsider to join in and perhaps make an uncomplimentary remark about one Ogg to another Ogg. Whereupon *every single Ogg* would turn on him, every part of the family closing up together like the parts of a well-oiled, blue-steeled engine to deal instant merciless destruction to the interloper.

Ramtop people believed that the Ogg feud was a blessing. The thought of them turning their immense energy on the world in general was a terrible one. Fortunately, there was no one an Ogg would rather fight than another Ogg. It was *family*.

Odd things, families, when you came to think of it . . .

'Esme? You all right?'

'What?'

'You've got them cups rattling like nobody's business! *And* tea all over the tray.'

Granny looked down blankly at the mess, and rallied as best she could.

'Not my damn fault if the damn cups are too small,' she muttered.

The door opened.

'Morning, Magrat,' she added, without looking around. 'What're you doing here?'

It was something about the way the hinges creaked. Magrat could even open a door apologetically.

The younger witch sidled speechlessly into the room, face beetroot red, arms held behind her back.

'We'd just popped in to sort out Desiderata's things, as our duty to a sister witch,' said Granny loudly.

'And not to look for her magic wand,' said Nanny.

'Gytha Ogg!'

Nanny Ogg looked momentarily guilty, and then hung her head.

'Sorry, Esme.'

Magrat brought her arms around in front of her.

'Er,' she said, and blushed further.

'You found it!' said Nanny.

'Uh, no,' said Magrat, not daring to look Granny in the eyes. 'Desiderata gave it to . . . me.'

The silence crackled and hummed.

'*She* gave it to *you*?' said Granny Weatherwax.

'Uh. Yes.'

Nanny and Granny looked at one another.

'Well!' said Nanny.

'She does *know* you, doesn't she?' demanded Granny, turning back to Magrat.

'I used to come over here quite often to look at her books,' Magrat confessed. 'And . . . and she liked to cook foreign food and no one else round here would eat it, so I'd come up to keep her company.'

'Ah-*ha*! Curryin' favour!' snapped Granny.

'But I never thought she'd leave me the wand,' said Magrat. 'Really I didn't!'

'There's probably some mistake,' said Nanny Ogg kindly. 'She probably wanted you to give it to one of us.'

'That'll be it, right enough,' said Granny. 'She knew you were good at running errands and so on. Let's have a look at it.'

She held out her hand.

Magrat's knuckles tightened on the wand.

'. . . she gave it me . . .' she said, in a tiny voice.

'Her mind was definitely wandering towards the end,' said Granny.

'. . . she gave it me . . .'

'Fairy godmotherin's a terrible responsibility,' said Nanny. 'You got to be resourceful and flexible and tactful and able to deal with complicated affairs of the heart and stuff. Desiderata would have known that.'

'. . . yes, but she gave it me . . .'

'Magrat Garlick, as senior witch I *command* you to give me the wand,' said Granny. 'They cause nothing but trouble!'

'Hold on, hold on,' said Nanny. 'That's going a bit far – '

'. . . no . . .' said Magrat.

'Anyway, you ain't senior witch,' said Nanny. 'Old Mother Dismass is older'n you.'

'Shut up. Anyway, she's non compost mental,' said Granny.

'. . . you can't order me. Witches are non-hierarchical . . .' said Magrat.

'That is wanton behaviour, Magrat Garlick!'

'No it's not,' said Nanny Ogg, trying to keep the peace. 'Wanton behaviour is where you go around without wearing any – '

She stopped. Both of the older witches watched a small piece of paper fall out of Magrat's sleeve and zigzag down to the floor. Granny darted forward and snatched it up.

'Aha!' she said triumphantly. 'Let's see what Desiderata *really* said . . .'

Her lips moved as she read the note. Magrat tried to wind herself up tighter.

A couple of muscles flickered on Granny's face. Then, calmly, she screwed up the note.

'Just as I thought,' she said, 'Desiderata says we are to give Magrat all the help we can, what with her being young and everything. Didn't she, Magrat?'

Magrat looked up into Granny's face.

You could call her out, she thought. The note was very clear . . . well, the bit about the older witches was, anyway . . . and you could make her read it aloud. It's as plain as day. Do you want to be third witch for ever? And then the flame of rebellion, burning in a very unfamiliar hearth, died.

'Yes,' she muttered hopelessly, 'something like that.'

'It's says it's very important we go to some place somewhere to help someone marry a prince,' said Granny.

'It's Genua,' said Magrat. 'I looked it up in Desiderata's books. And we've got to make sure she *doesn't* marry a prince.'

'A fairy godmother *stopping* a girl from marryin' a prince?' said Nanny. 'Sounds a bit . . . contrary.'

'Should be an easy enough wish to grant, anyway,' said Granny. 'Millions of girls don't marry a prince.'

Magrat made an effort.

'Genua really *is* a long way away,' she said.

'I should 'ope so,' said Granny Weatherwax. 'The last thing we want is foreign parts up close.'

'I mean, there'll be a lot of travelling,' said Magrat wretchedly. 'And you're . . . not as young as you were.'

There was a long, crowded silence.

'We start tomorrow,' said Granny Weatherwax firmly.

'Look,' said Magrat desperately, 'why don't I go by myself?'

''Cos you ain't experienced at fairy godmothering,' said Granny Weatherwax.

This was too much even for Magrat's generous soul.

'Well, nor are you,' she said.

'That's true,' Granny conceded. 'But the point is . . . the point is . . . the point is we've not been experienced for a lot longer than you.'

'We've got a lot of experience of not having any experience,' said Nanny Ogg happily.

'That's what counts every time,' said Granny.

There was only one small, speckled mirror in Granny's house. When she got home, she buried it at the bottom of the garden.

'There,' she said. '*Now* trying spyin' on me.'

It never seemed possible to people that Jason Ogg, master blacksmith and farrier, was Nanny Ogg's son. He didn't look as if he could possibly have been born, but as if he must have been constructed. In a shipyard. To his essentially slow and gentle nature genetics had seen fit to add muscles that should have gone to a couple of bullocks, arms like tree-trunks, and legs like four beer barrels stacked in twos.

To his glowing forge were brought the stud stallions, the red-eyed and foam-flecked kings of the horse nation, the soup-plate-hoofed beasts that had kicked lesser men through walls. But Jason Ogg knew the secret of the mystic Horseman's Word, and he would go alone into the forge, politely shut the door, and lead the creature out again after half an hour, newly shod and strangely docile.*

Behind his huge brooding shape clustered the rest of Nanny Ogg's endless family and a lot of other townsfolk who, seeing some interesting activity involving witches, couldn't resist the opportunity for what was known in the Ramtops as a good oggle.

'We'm off then, our Jason,' said Nanny Ogg. 'They do say the streets in foreign parts are paved with gold. I could prob'ly make my fortune, eh?'

Jason's hairy brow creased in intense thought.

'Us could do with a new anvil down forge,' he volunteered.

'If I come back rich, you won't never have to go down the forge ever again,' said Nanny.

Jason frowned.

'But I *likes* t'forge,' he said, slowly.

Nanny looked momentarily taken aback. 'Well, then – then you shall have an anvil made of solid silver.'

'Wunt be no good, ma. It'd be too soft,' said Jason.

'If I brings you back an anvil made of solid silver you shall have an anvil made of solid silver, my lad, whether you likes it or not!'

Jason hung his huge head. 'Yes, mum,' he said.

'You see to it that someone comes in to keep the house aired every day reg'lar,' said Nanny. 'I want a fire lit in that grate every morning.'

'Yes, mum.'

'And everyone's to go in through the back door, you hear? I've put a curse on the front porch. Where's those girls got to with my luggage?' She scurried off, a small grey bantam scolding a flock of hens.

Magrat listened to all this with interest. Her own preparations had consisted of a large sack containing several changes of clothes to accommodate whatever weather foreign parts might suffer from, and a rather small one containing a number of useful-looking books from Desiderata Hollow's cottage. Desiderata had been a great note-taker, and had filled dozens of little books with neat writing and chapter headings like 'With Wand and Broomstick Across the Great Nef Desert'.

What she had never bothered to do, it seemed, was write down any instructions for the wand. As far as Magrat knew, you waved it and wished.

---

* Granny Weatherwax had once pressed him about this, and since there are no secrets from a witch, he'd shyly replied, 'Well, ma'am, what happens is, I gets hold of 'un and smacks 'un between the eyes with hammer before 'un knows what's 'appening, and then I whispers in his ear, I sez, "Cross me, you bugger, and I'll have thy goolies on t'anvil, thou knows I can."'

Along the track to her cottage, several unanticipated pumpkins bore witness to this as an unreliable strategy. One of them still thought it was a stoat.

Now Magrat was left alone with Jason, who shuffled his feet.

He touched his forelock. He'd been brought up to be respectful to women, and Magrat fell broadly into this category.

'You will look after our mum, won't you, Mistress Garlick?' he said, a hint of worry in his voice. 'She'm acting awful strange.'

Magrat patted him gently on the shoulder.

'This sort of thing happens all the time,' she said. 'You know, after a woman's raised a family and so on, she wants to start living her own life.'

'Whose life she *bin* living, then?'

Magrat gave him a puzzled look. She hadn't questioned the wisdom of the thought when it had first arrived in her head.

'You see, what it is,' she said, making an explanation up as she went along, 'there comes a time in a woman's life when she wants to find herself.'

'Why dint she start looking here?' said Jason plaintively. 'I mean, I ain't wanting to talk out of turn, Miss Garlick, but we was looking to you to persuade her and Mistress Weatherwax not to go.'

'I tried,' said Magrat. 'I really did. I said, you don't want to go, I said. Anno domini, I said. Not as young as you used to be, I said. Silly to go hundreds of miles just for something like this, especially at your age.'

Jason put his head on one side. Jason Ogg wouldn't end up in the finals of the All-Discworld uptake speed trials, but he knew his own mother.

'You said all that to our mum?' he said.

'Look, don't worry,' said Magrat, 'I'm sure no harm can – '

There was a crash somewhere over their heads. A few autumn leaves spiralled gently towards the ground.

'Bloody tree . . . who put that bloody tree there?' came a voice from on high.

'That'll be Granny,' said Magrat.

It was one of the weak spots of Granny Weatherwax's otherwise well-developed character that she'd never bothered to get the hang of steering things. It was alien to her nature. She took the view that it was her job to move and the rest of the world to arrange itself so that she arrived at her destination. This meant that she occasionally had to climb down trees she'd never climbed up. This she did now, dropping the last few feet and daring anyone to comment.

'Well, now we're all here,' said Magrat brightly.

It didn't work. Granny Weatherwax's eyes focused immediately some-where around Magrat's knees.

'And what do you think you're wearing?' she said.

'Ah. Um. I thought . . . I mean, it gets cold up there . . . what with the wind and everything,' Magrat began. She had been dreading this, and hating herself for being so weak. After all, they *were* practical. The idea had come to her one night. Apart from anything else, it was almost impossible to do Mr Lobsang Dibbler's cosmic harmony death kicks when your legs kept getting tangled in a skirt.

'*Trousers?*'

'They're not exactly the same as ordinary – '

'And there's men 'ere lookin',' said Granny. 'I think it's shameful!'

'What is?' said Nanny Ogg, coming up behind her.

'Magrat Garlick, standin' there bifurcated,' said Granny, sticking her nose in the air.

'Just so long as she got the young man's name and address,' said Nanny Ogg amicably.

'Nanny!' said Magrat.

'I think they look quite comfy,' Nanny went on. 'A bit baggy, though.'

'I don't 'old with it,' said Granny. 'Everyone can see her legs.'

'No they can't,' said Nanny. 'The reason being, the material is in the way.'

'Yes, but they can see where her legs *are*,' said Granny Weatherwax.

'That's silly. That's like saying everyone's naked under their clothes,' said Magrat.

'Magrat Garlick, may you be forgiven,' said Granny Weatherwax.

'Well, it's true!'

'*I'm* not,' said Granny flatly. 'I got three vests on.'

She looked Nanny up and down. Gytha Ogg, too, had made sartorial preparations for foreign parts. Granny Weatherwax could find little to disapprove of, although she made an effort.

'And will you look at your hat,' she mumbled. Nanny, who had known Esme Weatherwax for seventy years, merely grinned.

'All the go, ain't it?' she said. 'Made by Mr Vernissage over in Slice. It's got willow reinforcing all the way up to the point and eighteen pockets inside. Can stop a blow with a hammer, this hat. And how about these?'

Nanny raised the hem of her skirt. She was wearing new boots. As boots, Granny Weatherwax could find nothing to complain of in them. They were of proper witch construction, which is to say that a loaded cart could have run over them without causing a dent in the dense leather. As boots, the only thing wrong with them was the colour.

'*Red*?' said Granny. 'That's no colour for a witch's boots!'

'I likes 'em,' said Nanny.

Granny sniffed. 'You can please yourself, I'm sure,' she said. 'I'm sure in foreign parts they goes in for all sorts of outlandish things. But you know what they say about women who wear red boots.'

'Just so long as they also say they've got dry feet,' said Nanny cheerfully. She put her door key into Jason's hand.

'I'll write you letters if you promise to find someone to read them to you,' she said.

'Yes, mum. What about the cat, mum?' said Jason.

'Oh, Greebo's coming with us,' said Nanny Ogg.

'What? But he's a cat!' snapped Granny Weatherwax. 'You can't take cats with you! I'm not going travellin' with no cat! It's bad enough travellin' with trousers and provocative boots!'

'He'll miss his mummy if he's left behind, won't he,' crooned Nanny Ogg, picking up Greebo. He hung limply, like a bag of water gripped around the middle.

To Nanny Ogg Greebo was still the cute little kitten that chased balls of wool around the floor.

To the rest of the world he was an enormous tomcat, a parcel of incredibly indestructible life forces in a skin that looked less like a fur than a piece of bread that had been left in a damp place for a fortnight. Strangers often took pity on him because his ears were non-existent and his face looked as though a bear had camped on it. They could not know that this was because Greebo, as a matter of feline pride, would attempt to fight or rape absolutely anything, up to and including a four-horse logging wagon. Ferocious dogs would whine and hide under the stairs when Greebo sauntered down the street. Foxes kept away from the village. Wolves made a detour.

'He's an old softy really,' said Nanny.

Greebo turned upon Granny Weatherwax a yellow-eyed stare of self-satisfied malevolence, such as cats always reserve for people who don't like them, and purred. Greebo was possibly the only cat who could snigger in purr.

'Anyway,' said Nanny, 'witches are supposed to *like* cats.'

'Not cats like him, they're not.'

'You're just not a cat person, Esme,' said Nanny, cuddling Greebo tightly.

Jason Ogg pulled Magrat aside.

'Our Shawn read to me in the almanac where there's all these fearsome wild beasts in foreign parts,' he whispered. 'Huge hairy things that leap out on travellers, it said. I'd hate to think what'd happen if they leapt out on mum and Granny.'

Magrat looked up into his big red face.

'You will see no harm comes to them, won't you,' said Jason.

'Don't you worry,' she said, hoping that he needn't. 'I'll do my best.'

Jason nodded. 'Only it said in the almanac that some of them were nearly extinct anyway,' he said.

The sun was well up when the three witches spiralled into the sky. They had been delayed for a while because of the intractability of Granny Weatherwax's broomstick, the starting of which always required a great deal of galloping up and down. It never seemed to get the message until it was being shoved through the air at a frantic running speed. Dwarf engineers everywhere had confessed themselves totally mystified by it. They had replaced the stick and the bristles dozens of times.

When it rose, eventually, it was to a chorus of cheers.

The tiny kingdom of Lancre occupied little more than a wide ledge cut into the side of the Ramtop mountains. Behind it, knife-edge peaks and dark winding valleys climbed into the massive backbone of the central ranges.

In front, the land dropped abruptly to the Sto plains, a blue haze of woodlands, a broader expanse of ocean and, somewhere in the middle of it all, a brown smudge known as Ankh-Morpork.

A skylark sang, or at least started to sing. The rising point of Granny Weatherwax's hat right underneath it completely put it off the rhythm.

'I ain't going any higher,' she said.

'If we go high enough we might be able to see where we're going,' said Magrat.

'You said you looked at Desiderata's maps,' said Granny.

'It looks different from up here, though,' said Magrat. 'More . . . sticking up. But I think we go . . . *that* way.'

'You sure?'

Which was the wrong question to ask a witch. Especially if the person doing the asking was Granny Weatherwax.

'Postive,' said Magrat.

Nanny Ogg looked up at the high peaks.

'There's a lot of *big* mountains that way,' she said.

They rose tier on tier, speckled with snow, trailing endless pennants of ice crystals high overhead. No one ski'd in the high Ramtops, at least for more than a few feet and a disappearing scream. No one ran up them wearing dirndls and singing. They were not nice mountains. They were the kind of mountains where winters went for their summer holidays.

'There's passes and things through them,' said Magrat uncertainly.

'Bound to be,' said Nanny.

☆   ☆   ☆

You can use two mirrors like this, if you know the way of it: you set them so that they reflect each other. For if images *can* steal a bit of you, then images of images can amplify you, feeding you back on yourself, giving you power . . .

And your image extends for ever, in reflections of reflections of reflections, and every image is the same, all the way around the curve of light.

Except that it isn't.

Mirrors contain infinity.

Infinity contains more things than you think.

Everything, for a start.

Including hunger.

Because there's a million billion images and only one soul to go around.

Mirrors give plenty, but they take away lots.

Mountains unfolded to reveal more mountains. Clouds gathered, heavy and grey.

'I'm sure we're going the right way,' said Magrat. Freezing rock stretched away. The witches flew along a maze of twisty little canyons, all alike.

'Yeah,' said Granny.

'Well, you won't let me fly high enough,' said Magrat.

'It's going to snow like blazes in a minute,' said Nanny Ogg.

It was early evening. Light was draining out of the high valleys like custard.

'I thought . . . there'd be villages and things,' said Magrat, 'where we could buy interesting native produce and seek shelter in rude huts.'

'You wouldn't even get trolls up here,' said Granny.

The three broomsticks glided down into a bare valley, a mere notch in the mountain side.

'And it's bloody cold,' said Nanny Ogg. She grinned. 'Why're they called rude huts, anyway?'

Granny Weatherwax climbed off her broomstick and looked at the rocks around her. She picked up a stone and sniffed it. She wandered over to a heap of scree that looked like any other heap of scree to Magrat, and prodded it.

'Hmm,' she said.

A few snow crystals landed on her hat.

'Well, well,' she said.

'What're you doing, Granny?' said Magrat.

'Cogitatin'.'

Granny walked to the valley's steep side and strolled along it, peering at the rock. Nanny Ogg joined her.

'Up here,' said Nanny.

'I reckon.'

''S a bit high for 'em, ain't it?'

'Little devils get everywhere. Had one come up in my kitchen once,' said Granny. ' "Following a seam", he said.'

'They're buggers for that,' said Nanny.

'Would you mind telling me,' said Magrat, 'what you're doing? What's so interesting about heaps of stones?'

The snow was falling faster now.

'They ain't stones, they're spoil,' said Granny. She reached a flat wall of ice-covered rock, no different in Magrat's eyes from the rock available in a range of easy-to-die-on sizes everywhere in the mountains, and paused as if listening.

Then she stood back, hit the rock sharply with her broomstick, and spake thusly:

'Open up, you little sods!'

Nanny Ogg kicked the rock. It made a hollow boom.

'There's people catching their death of cold out here!' she added.

Nothing happened for a while. Then a section of rock swung in a few inches. Magrat saw the glint of a suspicious eye.

'Yes?'

'Dwarfs?' said Magrat.

Granny Weatherwax leaned down until her nose was level with the eye.

'My name,' she said, 'is Granny Weatherwax.'

She straightened up again, her face glowing with self-satisfaction.

'Who's that, then?' said a voice from somewhere below the eye. Granny's expression froze.

Nanny Ogg nudged her partner.

'We must be more'n fifty miles away from home,' she said. 'They might not have heard of you in these parts.'

Granny leaned down again. Accumulated snowflakes cascaded off her hat.

'I ain't blaming you,' she said, 'but I know you'll have a King in there, so just you go and tell him Granny Weatherwax is here, will you?'

'He's very busy,' said the voice. 'We've just had a bit of trouble.'

'Then I'm sure he don't want any more,' said Granny.

The invisible speaker appeared to give this some consideration.

'We put writing on the door,' it said sulkily. 'In invisible runes. It's really expensive, getting proper invisible runes done.'

'I don't go around readin' doors,' said Granny.

The speaker hesitated.

'Weatherwax, did you say?'

'Yes. With a W. As in "witch".'

The door slammed. When it was shut, there was barely a visible crack in the rock.

The snow was falling fast now. Granny Weatherwax jiggled up and down a bit to keep warm.

'That's foreigners, for you,' she said, to the frozen world in general.

'I don't think you can call dwarfs foreigners,' said Nanny Ogg.

'Don't see why not,' said Granny. 'A dwarf who lives a long way off has got to be foreign. That's what foreign means.'

'Yeah? Funny to think of it like that,' said Nanny.

They watched the door, their breath forming three little clouds in the darkening air. Magrat peered at the stone door.

'I didn't see any invisible runes,' she said.

'Corse not,' said Nanny. 'That's 'cos they're invisible.'

'Yeah,' said Granny Weatherwax. 'Don't be daft.'

The door swung open again.

'I spoke to the King,' said the voice.

'And what did he say?' said Granny expectantly.

'He said, "Oh, no! Not on top of everything else!"'

Granny beamed. 'I *knew* 'e would have heard of me,' she said.

In the same way that there are a thousand Kings of the Gypsies, so there are a thousand Kings of the dwarfs. The term means something like 'senior engineer'. There aren't any Queens of the Dwarfs. Dwarfs are very reticent about revealing their sex, which most of them don't consider to be very important compared to things like metallurgy and hydraulics.

This king was standing in the middle of a crowd of shouting miners. He* looked up at the witches with the expression of a drowning man looking at a drink of water.

'Are you really any good?' he said.

Nanny Ogg and Granny Weatherwax looked at one another.

'I think 'e's talking to you, Magrat,' said Granny.

'Only we've had a big fall in gallery nine,' said the King. 'It looks bad. A very promising vein of gold-bearing quartz is irretrievably trapped.'

One of the dwarfs beside him muttered something.

'Oh, yeah. And some of the lads,' said the King vaguely. 'And then *you* turn up. So the way I look at it, it's probably fate.'

Granny Weatherwax shook the snow off her hat and looked around.

---

* Many of the more traditional dwarf tribes have no female pronouns, like 'she' or 'her'. It follows that the courtship of dwarfs is an incredibly tactful affair.

She was impressed, despite herself. You didn't often see proper dwarf halls these days. Most dwarfs were off earning big money in the cities down in the lowlands, where it was much easier to be a dwarf – for one thing, you didn't have to spend most of your time underground hitting your thumb with a hammer and worrying about fluctuations in the international metal markets. Lack of respect for tradition, that was the trouble these days. And take trolls. There were more trolls in Ankh-Morpork now than in the whole mountain range. Granny Weatherwax had nothing against trolls but she felt instinctively that if more trolls stopped wearing suits and walking upright, and went back to living under bridges and jumping out and eating people as nature intended, then the world would be a happier place.

'You'd better show us where the problem is,' she said. 'Lots of rocks fallen down, have they?'

'Pardon?' said the King.

It's often said the eskimos have fifty words for snow.*

This is not true.

It's also said that dwarfs have two hundred words for rock.

They don't. They have no words for rock, in the same way that fish have no words for water. They *do* have words for igneous rock, sedimentary rock, metamorphic rock, rock underfoot, rock dropping on your helmet from above, and rock which looked interesting and which they could have sworn they left here yesterday. But what they don't have is a word meaning 'rock'. Show a dwarf a rock and he sees, for example, an inferior piece of crystalline sulphite of barytes.

Or, in this case, about two hundred tons of low-grade shale. When the witches arrived at the disaster site dozens of dwarfs were working feverishly to prop the cracked roof and cart away the debris. Some of them were in tears.

'It's terrible . . . terrible,' muttered one of them. 'A terrible thing.'

Magrat lent him her handkerchief. He blew his nose noisily.

'Could mean a big slippage on the fault line and then we've lost the whole seam,' he said, shaking his head. Another dwarf patted him on the back.

'Look on the bright side,' he said. 'We can always drive a horizontal shaft off gallery fifteen. We're bound to pick it up again, don't you worry.'

'Excuse me,' said Magrat, 'there *are* dwarfs behind all that stuff, are there?'

'Oh, yes,' said the King. His tone suggested that this was merely a

---

* Well, not *often*. Not on a daily basis, anyway. At least, not everywhere. But probably in some cold countries people say, 'Hey, those eskimos! What a people! Fifty words for snow! Can you believe that? Amazing!' quite a lot.

regrettable side-effect of the disaster, because getting fresh dwarfs was only a matter of time whereas decent gold-bearing rock was a finite resource.

Granny Weatherwax inspected the rockfall critically.

'We shall have to have everyone out of here,' she said. 'This is goin' to have to be private.'

'I know how it is,' said the King. 'Craft secrets, I expect?'

'Something like that,' said Granny.

The King shooed the other dwarfs out of the tunnel, leaving the witches alone in the lantern light. A few bits of rock fell out of the ceiling.

'Hmm,' said Granny.

'You've gone and done it now,' said Nanny Ogg.

'Anything's possible if you set your mind to it,' said Granny vaguely.

'Then you'd better set yours good and hard, Esme. If the Creator had meant us to shift rocks by witchcraft, he wouldn't have invented shovels. Knowing when to use a shovel is what being a witch is all about. And put down that wheelbarrow, Magrat. You don't know nothing about machinery.'

'All right, then,' said Magrat. 'Why don't we try the wand?'

Granny Weatherwax snorted. 'Hah! Here? Whoever heard of a fairy godmother in a mine?'

'If I was stuck behind a load of rocks under a mountain *I'd* want to hear of one,' said Magrat hotly.

Nanny Ogg nodded. 'She's got a point there, Esme. There's no rule about where you fairy godmother.'

'I don't trust that wand,' said Granny. 'It looks wizardly to me.'

'Oh, come *on*,' said Magrat, 'generations of fairy godmothers have used it.'

Granny flung her hands in the air.

'All right, all right, all right,' she snapped. 'Go ahead! Make yourself look daft!'

Magrat took the wand out of her bag. She'd been dreading this moment.

It was made of some sort of bone or ivory; Magrat hoped it wasn't ivory. There had been markings on it once, but generations of plump fairy godmotherly hands had worn them almost smooth. Various gold and silver rings were set into the wand. Nowhere were there any instructions. Not so much as a rune or a sigil anywhere on its length indicated what you were supposed to do with it.

'I think you're supposed to wave it,' said Nanny Ogg. 'I'm pretty sure it's something like that.'

Granny Weatherwax folded her arms. 'That's not proper witching,' she said.

Magrat gave the wand an experimental wave. Nothing happened.

'Perhaps you have to say something?' said Nanny.

Magrat looked panicky.

'What do fairy godmothers *say*?' she wailed.

'Er,' said Nanny, 'dunno.'

'Huh!' said Granny.

Nanny Ogg sighed. 'Didn't Desiderata tell you *anything*?'

'Nothing!'

Nanny shrugged.

'Just do your best, then,' she said.

Magrat stared at the pile of rocks. She shut her eyes. She took a deep breath. She tried to make her mind a serene picture of cosmic harmony. It was all very well for monks to go on about cosmic harmony, she reflected, when they were nicely tucked away on snowy mountains with only yetis to worry about. They never tried seeking inner peace with Granny Weatherwax glaring at them.

She waved the wand in a vague way and tried to put pumpkins out of her mind.

She felt the air move. She heard Nanny gasp.

She said, 'Has anything happened?'

After a while Nanny Ogg said, 'Yeah. Sort of. I hope they're hungry, that's all.'

And Granny Weatherwax said, 'That's fairy godmothering, is it?'

Magrat opened her eyes.

There was still a heap, but it wasn't rock any more.

'There's a, wait for it, there's *a bit of a squash* in here,' said Nanny.

Magrat opened her eyes wider.

'*Still* pumpkins?'

'Bit of a squash. *Squash*,' said Nanny, in case anyone hadn't got it.

The top of the heap moved. A couple of small pumpkins rolled down almost to Magrat's feet, and a small dwarfish face appeared in the hole.

It stared down at the witches.

Eventually Nanny Ogg said, 'Everything all right?'

The dwarf nodded. Its attention kept turning to the pile of pumpkins that filled the tunnel from floor to ceiling.

'Er, yes,' it said. 'Is dad there?'

'Dad?'

'The King.'

'Oh.' Nanny Ogg cupped her hands around her mouth and turned to face up the tunnel. 'Hey, King!'

The dwarfs appeared. They looked at the pumpkins, too. The King stepped forward and stared up into the face of his son.

'Everything all right, son?'

'It's all right, dad. No faulting or anything.'

The King sagged with relief. Then, as an afterthought, he added, 'Everyone all right?'

'Fine, dad.'

'I was quite worried for a time there. Thought we might have hit a section of conglomerate or something.'

'Just a patch of loose shale, dad.'

'Good.' The King looked at the heap again. He scratched his beard. 'Can't help noticing you seem to have struck pumpkin.'

'I thought it was an odd kind of sandstone, dad.'

The King walked back to the witches.

'Can you turn anything into anything?' he said hopefully.

Nanny Ogg looked sideways at Magrat, who was still staring at the wand in a sort of shock.

'I think we only do pumpkins at the moment,' she said cautiously.

The King looked a little disappointed.

'Well, then,' he said, 'if there's anything I can do for you ladies . . . a cup of tea or something . . .'

Granny Weatherwax stepped forward. 'I was just thinking something like that myself,' she said.

The King beamed.

'Only more expensive,' said Granny.

The King stopped beaming.

Nanny Ogg sidled up to Magrat, who was shaking the wand and staring at it.

'Very clever,' she whispered. 'Why'd you think of pumpkins?'

'I didn't!'

'Don't you know how to work it?'

'No! I thought you just had to, you know, *want* something to happen!'

'There's probably more to it than just wishing,' said Nanny, as sympathetically as possible. 'There generally is.'

Some time around dawn, in so far as dawn happened in the mines, the witches were led to a river somewhere deep in the mountains, where a couple of barges were moored. A small boat was pulled up to a stone jetty.

'This'll take you right through the mountains,' said the King. 'I think it goes all the way to Genua, to tell the truth.' He took a large basket off an attendant dwarf. 'And we've packed you some lovely food,' he said.

'Are we going to go all the way in a boat?' said Magrat. She gave the wand a few surreptitious flourishes. 'I'm not good at boats.'

'Listen,' said Granny, climbing aboard, 'the river knows its way out of the mountains, which is more than we do. We can use the brooms later on, where the landscape's acting a bit more sensible.'

'And we can have a bit of a rest,' said Nanny, sitting back.

Magrat looked at the two older witches, who were making themselves comfortable in the stern like a couple of hens settling down on a nest.

'Do you know how to row a boat?' she said.

'We don't have to,' said Granny.

Magrat nodded gloomily. Then a tiny bit of self-assertion flashed a fin.

'I don't think I do, too,' she ventured.

'That's all right,' said Nanny. 'If we sees you doing anything wrong, we'll be sure to tell you. Cheerio, your kingship.'

Magrat sighed, and picked up the oars.

'The flat bits go in the water,' said Granny helpfully.

The dwarfs waved. The boat drifted out into mid-stream, moving slowly in a circle of lantern light. Magrat found that all she really had to do was keep it pointing the right way in the current.

She heard Nanny say: 'Beats me why they're always putting invisible runes on their doors. I mean, you pays some wizard to put invisible runes on your door, and how do you know you've got value for money?'

She heard Granny say: 'No problem there. If you can't see 'em, you know you've got proper invisible runes.'

She heard Nanny say: 'Ah, that'd be it. Right, let's see what we've got for lunch.' There was a rustling noise.

'Well, well, well.'

'What is it, Gytha?'

'Pumpkin.'

'Pumpkin what?'

'Pumpkin nothing. Just pumpkin pumpkin.'

'Well, I suppose they've got a lot of pumpkin,' said Magrat. 'You know how it is at the end of the summer, there's always so much in the garden. I'm always at my wits' end to think of new types of chutney and pickles to use it all up – '

In the dim light she could see Granny's face which seemed to be suggesting that if Magrat was at her wits' end, it was a short stroll.

'*I*,' said Granny, 'have never made a pickle in my life.'

'But you *like* pickles,' said Magrat. Witches and pickles went together like

– she hestitated before the stomach-curdling addition of peaches and cream, and mentally substituted 'things that went together very well'. The sight of Nanny Ogg's single remaining tooth at work on a pickled onion could bring tears to the eyes.

'I likes 'em fine,' said Granny. 'I gets 'em *given* to me.'

'You know,' said Nanny, investigating the recesses of the basket, 'whenever I deals with dwarfs, the phrase "Duck's arse" swims across my mind.'

'Mean little devils. You should see the prices they tries to charge me when I takes my broom to be repaired,' said Granny.

'Yes, but you never pay,' said Magrat.

'That's not the point,' said Granny Weatherwax. 'They shouldn't be allowed to charge that sort of money. That's thievin', that is.'

'I don't see how it can be thieving if you don't pay anyway,' Magrat persisted.

'I never pay for anything,' said Granny. 'People never *let* me pay. I can't help if it people gives me things the whole time, can I? When I walks down the street people are always running out with cakes they've just baked, and fresh beer, and old clothes that've hardly been worn at all. "Oh, Mistress Weatherwax, pray take this basket of eggs", they say. People are always very kind. Treat people right an' they'll treat *you* right. That's respect. Not having to pay,' she finished, sternly, 'is what bein' a witch is all about.'

'Here, what's this?' said Nanny, pulling out a small packet. She unwrapped the paper and revealed several hard brown discs.

'My word,' said Granny Weatherwax, 'I take it all back. That's the famous dwarf bread, that is. They don't give that to just anyone.'

Nanny tapped it on the edge of the boat. It made a noise very similar to the kind of noise you get when a wooden ruler is held over the edge of a desk and plucked; a sort of hollow *boioioing* sound.

'They say it never goes stale even if you stores it for years,' said Granny.

'It'd keep you going for days and days,' said Nanny Ogg.

Magrat reached across, took one of the flat loaves, tried to break it, and gave up.

'You're supposed to *eat* it?' she said.

'Oh, I don't think it's for eating,' said Nanny. 'It's more for sort of – '

' – keeping you going,' said Granny. 'They say that – '

She stopped.

Above the noise of the river and the occasional drip of water from the ceiling they could all hear, now, the steady slosh-slosh of another craft heading towards them.

'Someone's following us!' hissed Magrat.

Two pale glows appeared at the edge of the lamplight. Eventually they turned out to be the eyes of a small grey creature, vaguely froglike, paddling towards them on a log.

It reached the boat. Long clammy fingers grabbed the side, and a lugubrious face rose level with Nanny Ogg's.

''ullo,' it said. 'It'sss my birthday.'

All three of them stared at it for a while. Then Granny Weatherwax picked up an oar and hit it firmly over the head. There was a splash, and a distant cursing.

'Horrible little bugger,' said Granny, as they rowed on. 'Looked like a troublemaker to me.'

'Yeah,' said Nanny Ogg. 'It's the slimy ones you have to watch out for.'

'I wonder what he wanted?' said Magrat.

After half an hour the boat drifted out through a cave mouth and into a narrow gorge between cliffs. Ice glistened on the walls, and there were drifts of snow on some of the outcrops.

Nanny Ogg looked around guilelessly, and then fumbled somewhere in the depths of her many skirts and produced a small bottle. There was a glugging noise.

'I bet there's a fine echo here,' she said, after a while.

'Oh no you don't,' said Granny firmly.

'Don't what?'

'Don't sing That Song.'

'Pardon, Esme?'

'I ain't going,' said Granny, 'if you insists on singing That Song.'

'What song would that be?' said Nanny innocently.

'You know the song to whom I am referring,' said Granny icily. 'You always get drunk and let me down and sing it.'

'Can't recall any song like that, Esme,' said Nanny Ogg meekly.

'The one,' said Granny, 'about the rodent that can't – that can't ever be persuaded to care about anything.'

'Oh,' said Nanny, beaming as light dawned, '*you* mean The Hedgehog Can Never Be Bugg– '

'That's the one!'

'But it's *traditional*,' said Nanny. 'Anyway, in foreign parts people won't know what the words mean.'

'They will the way you sings them,' said Granny. 'The way you sings them, creatures what lives on the bottoms of *ponds*'d know what they mean.'

Magrat looked over the side of the boat. Here and there the ripples were edged with white. The current was running a bit faster, and there were lumps of ice in it.

'It's only a folk song, Esme,' said Nanny Ogg.

'Hah!' said Granny Weatherwax. 'I should just say it *is* a folk song! I knows all about folk songs. Hah! You think you're listenin' to a nice song about . . . cuckoos and fiddlers and nightingales and whatnot, and then it turns out to be about . . . about something else entirely,' she added darkly. 'You can't trust folk songs. They always sneak up on you.'

Magrat fended them off a rock. An eddy spun them around slowly.

'I know one about two little bluebirds,' said Nanny Ogg.

'Um,' said Magrat.

'They may start out by being bluebirds, but I bet they ends up some kind of mettyfor,' said Granny.

'Er, Granny,' said Magrat.

'It was bad enough Magrat telling me about maypoles and what's behind 'em,' said Granny. She added, wistfully, 'I used to enjoy looking at a maypole of a spring morning.'

'I think the river's getting a bit sort of rough,' said Magrat.

'I don't see why people can't just let things be,' said Granny.

'I mean really quite rough, really . . .' said Magrat, pushing them away from a jagged rock.

'She's right, you know,' said Nanny Ogg. 'It's a bit on the choppy side.'

Granny looked over Magrat's shoulder at the river ahead. It had a cut-off look, such as might be associated with, for example, an imminent waterfall. The boat was now surging along. There was a muted roar.

'They never said anything about a waterfall,' she said.

'I 'spect they thought we'd find out for ourselves,' said Nanny Ogg, gathering up her possessions and hauling Greebo out of the bottom of the boat by the scruff of his neck. 'Very sparin' with information, your average dwarf. Thank goodness witches float. Anyway, they knew we'd got the brooms.'

'*You've* got brooms,' said Granny Weatherwax. 'How'm I supposed to get mine started in a *boat*? Can't run up and down, can I? And stop movin' about like that, you'll have us all over – '

'Get your foot out of the way, Esme – '

The boat rocked violently.

Magrat rose to the occasion. She pulled out the wand, just as a wavelet washed over the boat.

'Don't worry,' she said, 'I'll use the wand. I think I've got the hang of it now – '

'No!' screamed Granny Weatherwax and Nanny Ogg together.

There was a large, damp noise. The boat changed shape. It also changed colour. It became a cheery sort of orange.

'Pumpkins!' screamed Nanny Ogg, as she was gently tipped into the water. 'More bloody pumpkins!'

Lilith sat back. The ice around the river hadn't been that good as a mirror, but it had been good enough.

Well. A wishy-washy overgrown girl more suitable to the attentions of a fairy godmother than to being one, and a little old washerwoman-type who got drunk and sang songs. And a wand the stupid girl didn't know how to use.

It was annoying. More than that, it was demeaning. Surely Desiderata and Mrs Gogol could have achieved something better than this. You derived status by the strength of your enemies.

Of course, there was *her*. After all this time . . .

Of course. She approved of that. Because there would have to be three of them. Three was an important number for stories. Three wishes, three princes, three billy goats, three guesses . . . three witches. The maiden, the mother and the . . . other one. *That* was one of the oldest stories of all.

Esme Weatherwax had never understood stories. She'd never understood how *real* reflections were. If she had, she'd probably have been ruling the world by now.

'You're always looking in mirrors!' said a petulant voice. 'I hate it when you're always looking in mirrors!'

The Duc sprawled in a chair in one corner, all black silk and well-turned legs. Lilith would not normally allow anyone inside the nest of mirrors but it was, technically, his castle. Besides, he was too vain and stupid to know what was going on. She'd seen to that. At least, she'd thought she had. Lately, he seemed to be picking things up . . .

'I don't know why you have to do that,' he whined. 'I thought magic was just a matter of pointing and going whoosh.'

Lilith picked up her hat, and glanced at a mirror as she adjusted it.

'This way's safer,' she said. 'It's self-contained. When you use mirror magic, you don't have to rely on anyone except yourself. That's why no one's ever conquered the world with magic . . . yet. They try to take it from . . . other places. And there's always a price. But with mirrors, you're beholden to no one but your own soul.'

She lowered the veil from the hat brim. She preferred the privacy of a veil, outside the security of the mirrors.

'I hate mirrors,' muttered the Duc.

'That's because they tell you the truth, my lad.'

'It's cruel magic, then.'

Lilith tweaked the veil into a fetching shape.

'Oh, yes. With mirrors, all the power is your own. There's nowhere else it can come from,' she said.

'The swamp woman gets it from the swamp,' said the Duc.

'Ha! And it'll claim her one day. She doesn't understand what she's doing.'

'And you do?'

She felt a pang of pride. He was actually resenting her! She really had done a good job there.

'I understand stories,' she said. 'That's all I need.'

'But you haven't brought me the girl,' said the Duc. 'You promised me the girl. And then it'll be all over and I can sleep in a real bed and I won't need any more reflecting magic – '

But even a good job can go too far.

'You've had your fill of magic?' said Lilith sweetly. 'You'd like me to stop? It would be the easiest thing in the world. I found you in the gutter. Would you like me to send you back?'

His face became a mask of panic.

'I didn't mean that! I just meant . . . well, then everything will be real. Just one kiss, you said. I can't see why that's so hard to arrange.'

'The right kiss at the right time,' said Lilith. 'It has to be at the right time, otherwise it won't work.' She smiled. He was trembling, partly out of lust, mainly out of terror, and slightly out of heredity.

'Don't worry,' she said. 'It can't *not* happen.'

'And these witches you showed me?'

'They're just . . . part of the story. Don't worry about them. The story will just absorb them. And you'll get *her* because of stories. Won't that be nice? And now . . . shall we go? I expect you've got some ruling to do?'

He picked up the inflexion. It was an order. He stood up, extended an arm to take hers, and together they went down to the palace's audience chamber.

Lilith was proud of the Duc. Of course, there was his embarrassing little nocturnal problem, because his morphic field weakened when he slept, but that wasn't yet a major difficulty. And there was the trouble with mirrors, which showed him as he really was, but that was easily overcome by banning all mirrors save hers. And then there were his eyes. She couldn't do anything about the eyes. There was practically no magic that could do anything about someone's eyes. All she had been able to come up with there were the smoked glasses.

Even so, he was a triumph. And he was so grateful. She'd been good for him.

She'd made a man of him, for a start.

Some way downriver from the waterfall which was the second highest anywhere on the Disc and had been discovered in the Year of the Revolving Crab by the noted explorer Guy de Yoyo,* Granny Weatherwax sat in front of a small fire with a towel around her shoulders and steamed.

'Still, look on the bright side,' said Nanny Ogg. 'At least I was holding my broom and you at the same time. And Magrat had hers. Otherwise we'd all be looking at the waterfall from underneath.'

'Oh, good. A silver lining,' said Granny, her eyes glinting evilly.

'Bit of an adventure, really,' said Nanny, grinning encouragingly. 'One day we'll look back on this and laugh.'

'Oh, good,' said Granny.

Nanny dabbed at the claw marks on her arm. Greebo, with a cat's true instinct for self-preservation, had clawed his way up his mistress and taken a flying leap to safety from the top of her head. Now he was curled up by the fire, dreaming cat dreams.

A shadow passed over them. It was Magrat, who had been combing the riverbanks.

'I think I've got nearly everything,' she said as she landed. 'Here's Granny's broomstick. And . . . oh, yes . . . the wand.' She gave a brave little smile. 'Little pumpkins were bobbing to the surface. That's how I found it.'

'My word, that was lucky,' said Nanny Ogg encouragingly. 'Hear that, Esme? We shan't be wanting food, at any rate.'

'And I've found the basket with the dwarf bread in it,' said Magrat, 'although I'm afraid it might be spoilt.'

'It won't be, take it from me,' said Nanny Ogg. 'You can't spoil dwarf bread. Well, well,' she said, sitting down again. 'We've got quite a little picnic, haven't we . . . and a nice bright fire and . . . and a nice place to sit and . . . I'm sure there's lots of poor people in places like Howondaland and such like who'd give anything to be here right now . . .'

'If you don't stop being so cheerful, Gytha Ogg, I shall give you such a ding around the ear with the flat of my hand,' said Granny Weatherwax.

'You sure you're not catching a chill?' said Nanny Ogg.

'I'm dryin' out,' said Granny Weatherwax, 'from the inside.'

'Look, I'm really sorry,' said Magrat. 'I *said* I was sorry.'

---

* Of course, lots of dwarfs, trolls, native people, trappers, hunters and the merely badly lost had discovered it on an almost daily basis for thousands of years. But they weren't explorers and didn't count.

Not that she was quite certain what for, she told herself. The boat wasn't her idea. She hadn't put the waterfall there. She hadn't even been in a position to see it coming. She'd turned the boat into a pumpkin, but she hadn't meant to. It could have happened to anyone.

'I managed to save Desiderata's notebooks, too,' she said.

'Well, that's a blessing,' said Nanny Ogg. 'Now we know where we're lost.'

She looked around. They were through the worst of the mountains, but there were still peaks around and high meadows stretching to the snowline. From somewhere in the distance came the clonking of goat bells.

Magrat unfolded a map. It was creased, damp, and the pencil had run. She pointed cautiously to a smudged area.

'I think we're here,' she said.

'My word,' said Nanny Ogg, whose grasp of the principles of cartography was even shakier than Granny's. 'Amazing how we can all fit on that little bit of paper.'

'I think perhaps it would be a good idea at the moment if we just followed the river,' said Magrat. 'Without in any way going on it,' she added quickly.

'I suppose you didn't find *my* bag?' said Granny Weatherwax. 'It had pers'nal items in.'

'Probably sank like a stone,' said Nanny Ogg.

Granny Weatherwax stood up like a general who's just had news that his army has come second.

'Come on,' she said. 'Where to next, then?'

What was next was forest – dark and ferociously coniferous. The witches flew over it in silence. There were occasional, isolated cottages half-hidden in the trees. Here and there a crag loomed over the sylvanian gloom, shrouded in mist even in mid-afternoon. Once or twice they flew past castles, if that's what you could call them; they didn't look built, more extruded from the landscape.

It was the kind of landscape that had a particular type of story attached to it, featuring wolves and garlic and frightened women. A dark and thirsty story, a story that flapped wings against the moon . . .

'Der flabberghast,' muttered Nanny.

'What's that?' said Magrat.

'It's foreign for bat.'

'I've always liked bats,' said Magrat. 'In general.'

The witches found that, by unspoken agreement, they were flying closer together.

'I'm getting hungry,' said Granny Weatherwax. 'And don't no one mention pumpkin.'

'There's dwarf bread,' said Nanny.

'There's always the dwarf bread,' said Granny. 'I fancy something cooked *this* year, thank you all the same.'

They flew past another castle, occupying the entire summit of a crag.

'What we need is a nice little town or something,' said Magrat.

'But the one down there will have to do,' said Granny.

They looked down at it. It wasn't so much a town as a huddle of houses, clustering together against the trees. It looked as cheerless as an empty hearth, but the shadows of the mountains were already speeding across the forest and something about the landscape tacitly discouraged night-time flying.

'Can't see many people about,' said Granny.

'Maybe they turn in early in these parts,' said Nanny Ogg.

'It's hardly even sunset,' said Magrat. 'Perhaps we ought to go up to that castle?'

They all looked at the castle.

'No-o-o,' said Granny slowly, speaking for all of them. 'We know our place.'

So they landed, instead, in what was presumably the town square. A dog barked, somewhere behind the buildings. A shutter banged closed.

'*Very* friendly,' said Granny. She walked over to a larger building that had a sign, unreadable under the grime, over the door. She gave the woodwork a couple of thumps.

'Open up!' she said.

'No, no, you don't say that,' said Magrat. She shouldered her way past, and tapped on the door. 'Excuse me! Bona fide travellers!'

'Bona what?' said Nanny.

'That's what you need to say,' said Magrat. 'Any inn has got to open up for Bona Fide travellers and give them succour.'

'Has it?' said Nanny, with interest. 'That sounds like a thing worth knowing.'

The door remained shut.

'Let me 'ave a go,' said Nanny. 'I know some foreign lingo.'

She hammered on the door.

'Openny vous, gunga din, chop-chop, pretty damn quick,' she said.

Granny Weatherwax listened carefully.

'That's speaking foreign, is it?'

'My grandson Shane is a sailor,' said Nanny Ogg. 'You'd be amazed, the words he learns about foreign parts.'

'I expects I would,' said Granny. 'And I 'opes they works better for him.'

She thumped on the door again. And this time it opened, very slowly. A pale face peered around it.

'Excuse me – ' Magrat began.

Granny pushed the door open. The face's owner had been leaning on it; they could hear the scrape of his boots over the floor as he was shoved gently backwards.

'Blessings be on this house,' Granny said, perfunctorily. It was always a good opening remark for a witch. It concentrated people's minds on what *other* things might be on this house, and reminded them about any fresh cakes, newly baked bread or bundles of useful old clothing that might have temporarily escaped their minds.

It looked like one of the other things had been on this house already.

It *was* an inn, of sorts. The three witches had never seen such a cheerless place in their lives. But it was quite crowded. A score or more pale-faced people watched them solemnly from benches around the walls.

Nanny Ogg sniffed.

'Cor,' she said. 'Talk about garlic!' And, indeed, bunches of it hung from every beam. 'You can't have too much garlic, I always say. I can see I'm going to like it here.'

She nodded to a white-faced man behind the bar.

'Gooden day, big-feller mine host! Trois beers pour favour avec us, silver plate.'

'What's a silver plate got to do with it?' demanded Granny.

'It's foreign for please,' said Nanny.

'I bet it isn't really,' said Granny. 'You're just making it up as you goes along.'

The innkeeper, who worked on the fairly simple principle that anyone walking through the door wanted something to drink, drew three beers.

'See?' said Nanny, triumphantly.

'I don't like the way everyone's looking at us,' said Magrat, as Nanny babbled on to the perplexed man in her very own esperanto. 'A man over there *grinned* at me.'

Granny Weatherwax sat down on a bench, endeavouring to position herself so that as small an amount of her body as possible was in contact with the wood, in case being foreign was something you could catch.

'There,' said Nanny, bustling up with a tray, 'nothing to it. I just cussed at him until he understood.'

'It looks horrible,' said Granny.

'Garlic sausage and garlic bread,' said Nanny. 'My favourite.'

'You ought to have got some fresh vegetables,' said Magrat the dietitian.

'I did. There's some garlic,' said Nanny happily, cutting a generous slice of eye-watering sausage. 'And I think I definitely saw something like pickled onions on one of the shelves.'

'Yes? Then we're going to need at least two rooms for tonight,' said Granny sternly.

'Three,' said Magrat, very quickly.

She risked another look around the room. The silent villagers were staring at them intently, with a look she could only describe to herself as a sort of hopeful sadness. Of course, anyone who spent much time in the company of Granny Weatherwax and Nanny Ogg got used to being stared at; they were the kind of people that filled every space from edge to edge. And probably people in these parts didn't often see strangers, what with the thick forests and all. And the sight of Nanny Ogg eating a sausage with extreme gusto would even outrank her pickled onion number as major entertainment anywhere.

Even so . . . the way people were staring . . .

Outside, deep in the trees, a wolf howled.

The assembled villagers shivered in unison, as though they had been practising. The landlord muttered something to them. They got up, reluctantly, and filed out of the door, trying to keep together. An old lady laid her hand on Magrat's shoulder for a moment, shook her head sadly, sighed, and then scuttled away. But Magrat was used to this, too. People often felt sorry for her when they saw her in Granny's company.

Eventually the landlord lurched across to them with a lighted torch, and motioned them to follow him.

'How did you make him understand about the beds?' said Magrat.

'I said, "Hey mister, jigajig toot sweet all same No. 3",' said Nanny Ogg.

Granny Weatherwax tried this under her breath, and nodded.

'Your lad Shane certainly gets around a bit, doesn't he,' she remarked.

'He says it works every time,' said Nanny Ogg.

In fact there *were* only two rooms, up a long, winding and creaky stairway. And Magrat got one to herself. Even the landlord seemed to want it that way. He'd been very attentive.

She wished he hadn't been so keen to bar the shutters, though. Magrat liked to sleep with a window open. As it was, it was too dark and stuffy.

Anyway, she thought, I *am* the fairy godmother. The others are just accompanying me.

She peered hopelessly at herself in the room's tiny cracked mirror and then lay and listened to them on the far side of the paper-thin wall.

'What're you turning the mirror to the wall for, Esme?'

'I just don't like 'em, staring like that.'

'They only stares if you're staring *at* 'em, Esme.'

Silence, and then: 'Eh, what's this round thing for, then?'

'I reckon it's supposed to be a pillow, Esme.'

'Hah! *I* don't call it a pillow. And there's no proper blankets, even. What'd you say this thing's called?'

'I think it's called a duvit, Esme.'

'*We* call them an eiderdown where I come from. Hah!'

There was a respite. Then:

'Have you brushed your tooth?'

And another pause. Then:

'Oo, you haven't half got cold feet, Esme.'

'No, they ain't. They're lovely and snug.'

And another silence. Then:

'Boots! Your boots! You've got your boots on!'

'I should just think I 'ave got my boots on, Gytha Ogg.'

'And your clothes! You haven't even undressed!'

'You can't be too careful in foreign parts. There could be all sorts out there, a-creepin' around.'

Magrat snuggled under the – what was it? – duvit, and turned over. Granny Weatherwax appeared to need one hour's sleep a night, whereas Nanny Ogg would snore on a fence rail.

'Gytha! *Gytha!* GYTHA!'

'Wha'?'

'Are you awake?'

''M now . . .'

'I keep 'earing a noise!'

'. . . so do I . . .'

Magrat dozed for a while.

'Gytha? GYTHA!'

'. . . wha' now? . . .'

'I'm sure someone rattled our shutters!'

'. . . not at our time of life . . . now g'back t' slee' . . .'

The air in the room was getting hotter and stuffier by the minute. Magrat got out of bed, unbolted the shutters and flung them back dramatically.

There was a grunt, and a distant thud of something hitting the ground.

The full moon streamed in. She felt a lot better for that, and got back into bed.

It seemed no time at all before the voice from next door woke her again.

'Gytha Ogg, what are you *doing*?'

'I'm 'aving a snack.'

'Can't you sleep?'

'Just can't seem to be able to get off, Esme,' said Nanny Ogg. 'Can't imagine why.'

'Here, that's garlic sausage you're eating! I'm actually sharing a bed with someone eating garlic sausage.'

'Hey, that's mine. Give it back – '

Magrat was aware of booted footsteps in the pit of the night, and the sound of a shutter being swung back in the next room.

She thought she heard a faint 'oof' and another muted thud.

'I thought you *liked* garlic, Esme,' said Nanny Ogg's resentful voice.

'Sausage is all right in its place, and its place ain't in bed. And don't you say a word. Now move over. You keep taking all the duvit.'

After a while the velvet silence was broken by Granny's deep and resonant snore. Shortly afterwards it was joined by the genteel snoring of Nanny, who had spent far more time sleeping in company than Granny and had evolved a more accommodating nasal orchestra. Granny's snore would have cut logs.

Magrat folded the horrible round hard pillow over her ears and burrowed under the bedclothes.

Somewhere on the chilly ground, a very large bat was trying to get airborne again. It had already been stunned twice, once by a carelessly opened shutter and once by a ballistic garlic sausage, and wasn't feeling very well at all. One more setback, it was thinking, and it's back off to the castle. Besides, it'd be sunrise soon.

Its red eyes glinted as it looked up at Magrat's open window. It tensed –

A paw landed on it.

The bat looked around.

Greebo had not had a very good night. He had investigated the whole place with regard to female cats, and found none. He had prowled among the middens, and drawn a blank. People in this town didn't throw the garbage away. They ate it.

He'd trotted into the woods and found some wolves and had sat and grinned at them until they got uncomfortable and went away.

Yes, it had been a very uneventful night. Until now.

The bat squirmed under his claw. It seemed to Greebo's small cat brain that it was trying to change its shape, and he wasn't having any of that from a mouse with wings on.

Especially now, when he had someone to play with.

☆　☆　☆

Genua was a fairytale city. People smiled and were joyful the livelong day. Especially if they wanted to see *another* livelong day.

Lilith made certain of that. Of course, people had probably thought they were happy in the days before she'd seen to it that the Duc replaced the old Baron, but it was a random, untidy happiness, which was why it was so easy for her to move in.

But it wasn't a way of life. There was no pattern to it.

One day they'd thank her.

Of course, there were always a few difficult ones. Sometimes, people just didn't know how to act. You did your best for them, you ruled their city properly, you ensured that their lives were worthwhile and full of happiness every hour of the day and then, for no reason at all, they turned on you.

Guards lined the audience chamber. And there *was* an audience. Technically, of course, it was the ruler who gave the audience, but Lilith liked to see people watching. One pennyworth of example was worth a pound of punishment.

There wasn't a lot of crime in Genua these days. At least, not what would be considered crime elsewhere. Things like theft were easily dealt with and hardly required any kind of judicial process. Far more important, in Lilith's book, were crimes against narrative expectation. People didn't seem to know how they should behave.

Lilith held a mirror up to Life, and chopped all the bits off Life that didn't fit . . .

The Duc lounged bonelessly on his throne, one leg dangling over the armrest. He'd never got the hang of chairs.

'And what has this one done?' he said, and yawned. Opening his mouth wide was something he *was* good at, at least.

A little old man cowered between two guards.

There's always someone willing to be a guard, even in places like Genua. Besides, you got a really smart uniform, with blue trousers and a red coat and a high black hat with a cockade in it.

'But I . . . I *can't* whistle,' quavered the old man. 'I . . . I didn't know it was compulsory . . . '

'But you are a toymaker,' said the Duc. 'Toymakers whistle and sing the whole day long.' He glanced at Lilith. She nodded.

'I don't know any . . . s-songs,' said the toymaker. 'I never got taught s-songs. Just how to make toys. I was 'prenticed at making toys. Seven years before the little hammer, man and boy . . . '

'It says here,' said the Duc, making a creditable impersonation of someone reading the charge sheet in front of him, 'that you don't tell the children stories.'

'No one ever told me about telling . . . s-stories,' said the toymaker. 'Look, I just make toys. Toys. That's all I'm good at. Toys. I make good t-toys. I'm just a t-toymaker.'

'You can't be a good toymaker if you don't tell stories to the children,' said Lilith, leaning forward.

The toymaker looked up at the veiled face.

'Don't know any,' he said.

'You don't know *any?*'

'I could t-tell 'em how to make toys,' the old man quavered.

Lilith sat back. It was impossible to see her expression under the veil.

'I think it would be a good idea if the People's Guards here took you away,' she said, 'to a place where you will certainly learn to sing. And possibly, after a while, you might even whistle. Won't that be nice?'

The old Baron's dungeons had been disgusting. Lilith had had them repainted and refurnished. With a lot of mirrors.

When the audience was over one member of the crowd slipped through the palace kitchens. The guards on the side gate didn't try to stop her. She was a very important person in the small compass of their lives.

'Hello, Mrs Pleasant.'

She stopped, reached into her basket and produced a couple of roast chicken legs.

'Just tryin' a new peanut coating,' she said. 'Would value your opinions, boys.'

They took them gratefully. Everyone liked to see Mrs Pleasant. She could do things with a chicken that would almost make it glad it had been killed.

'And now I'm just going out to get some herbs,' she said.

They watched her as she went like a fat, determined arrow in the direction of the market place, which was right on the edge of the river. Then they ate the chicken legs.

Mrs Pleasant bustled among the market stalls; and she took great care to bustle. Even in Genua there were always people ready to tell a tale. *Especially* in Genua. She was a cook, so she bustled. And made sure she stayed fat and was, fortunately naturally jolly. She made sure she had floury arms at all times. If she felt under suspicion, she'd say things like 'Lawks!' She seemed to be getting away with it so far.

She looked for the sign. And there it was. Perched up on the roof pole of a stall that was otherwise stacked with cages of hens, gazoots, Wheely cranes and other fowl, was a black cockerel. The voodoo doctor was In.

Even as her eye found it the cockerel's head turned to look at her.

Set a little way back from the rest of the stalls was a small tent, similar to many around the market. A cauldron bubbled in front of it on a charcoal fire. There were bowls beside it, and a ladle, and beside them a plate with coins on it. There were quite a lot of coins; people paid for Mrs Gogol's cooking whatever they thought it was worth, and the plate was hardly big enough.

The thick liquid in the cauldron was an unappetising brown. Mrs Pleasant helped herself to a bowlful, and waited. Mrs Gogol had certain talents.

After a while a voice from the tent said, 'What's new, Mrs Pleasant?'

'She's shut up the toymaker,' said Mrs Pleasant, to the air in general. 'And yesterday it was old Devereaux the innkeeper for not being fat and not having a big red face. That's four times this month.'

'You come in, Mrs Pleasant.'

It was dark and hot inside the tent. There was another fire in there, and another pot. Mrs Gogol was hunched over it, stirring. She motioned the cook to a pair of bellows.

'Blow up the coals a tad, and we'll see what's what,' she said.

Mrs Pleasant obeyed. She didn't use magic herself, other than that necessary to get a roux to turn or bread to rise, but she respected it in others. Especially in the likes of Mrs Gogol.

The charcoal blazed white. The thick liquid in the pot began to churn. Mrs Gogol peered into the steam.

'What're you doing, Mrs Gogol?' said the cook anxiously.

'Trying to see what's goin' to happen,' said the voodoo woman. The voice dropped into the rolling growl of the psychically gifted.

Mrs Pleasant squinted into the roiling mass.

'Someone's going to be eatin' shrimp?' she said helpfully.

'Ye see that bit of okra?' said Mrs Gogol. 'Ye see the way the crab legs keep coming up just there?'

'You never were one to stint the crab meat,' said Mrs Pleasant.

'See the way the bubbles is so thick by the okuh leaves? See the way it all spirals around that purple onion?'

'I see it! I see it!' said Mrs Pleasant.

'And you know what that means?'

'Means it's going to taste real *fine!*'

'Sure,' said Mrs Gogol, kindly. 'And it means some people's coming.'

'Wow! How many?'

Mrs Gogol dipped a spoon into the seething mass and tasted it.

'Three people,' she said. She smacked her lips thoughtfully. 'Women.'

She dipped the spoon again.

'Have a taste,' she said. 'There's a cat, too. Ye can tell by the sassafras.' She smacked her lips. 'Grey. One eye.' She explored the cavity of a tooth with her tongue. 'The . . . left one.'

Mrs Pleasant's jaw dropped.

'They'll find you before they find me,' said Mrs Gogol. 'You lead 'em here.'

Mrs Pleasant stared at Mrs Gogol's grim smile and then back down at the mixture in the pot.

'They coming all this way for a taste?' she said.

'Sure.' Mrs Gogol sat back. 'You been to see the girl in the white house?'

Mrs Pleasant nodded. 'Young Embers,' she said. 'Yeah. When I can. When the Sisters are out at the palace. They got her real scared, Mrs Gogol.'

She looked down at the pot again, and back up to Mrs Gogol.

'Can you really see– ?'

'I expect you've got things to marinate?' said Mrs Gogol.

'Yeah. Yeah.' Mrs Pleasant backed out, but with reluctance. Then she halted. Mrs Pleasant, at rest, was not easily moved again until she wanted to be.

'That Lilith woman says she can see the whole world in mirrors,' she said, in slightly accusing tones.

Mrs Gogol shook her head.

'All anyone gets in a mirror is themselves,' she said. 'But what you gets in a good gumbo is *everything*.'

Mrs Pleasant nodded. This was a well-known fact. She couldn't dispute it.

Mrs Gogol shook her head sadly when the cook had gone. A voodoo woman was reduced to all sorts of stratagems in order to appear knowing, but she felt slightly ashamed of letting an honest woman believe that she could see the future in a pot of gumbo. Because all you could see in a pot of Mrs Gogol's gumbo was that the future certainly contained a very good meal.

She'd really seen it in a bowl of jambalaya she'd prepared earlier.

Magrat lay with the wand under her pillow. She wobbled gently between sleep and wakefulness.

Certainly she was the best person for the wand. There was no doubt about that. Sometimes – and she hardly dared give the thought headroom, when she was under the same roof as Granny Weatherwax – she really wondered about the others' commitment to witchcraft. Half the time they didn't seem to *bother*.

Take medicine, for example. Magrat knew she was much better than them at herbs. She'd inherited several large books on the subject from Goodie Whemper, her predecessor in the cottage, and had essayed a few tentative notes of her own as well. She could tell people things about the uses of Devil's Bit

Scabious that would interest them so much they'd rush off, presumably to look for someone else to tell. She could fractionally distil, and double-distil, and do things that meant sitting up all night watching the colour of the flame under the retort. She *worked* at it.

Whereas Nanny just tended to put a hot poultice on everything and recommend a large glass of whatever the patient liked best on the basis that since you were going to be ill anyway you might as well get some enjoyment out of it. (Magrat forbade her patients alcohol, because of what it did to the liver; if they didn't know what it did to the liver, she spent some time telling them.)

And Granny . . . she just gave people a bottle of coloured water and told them they felt a lot better.

And what was so annoying was that they often did.

Where was the witchcraft in that?

With a wand, though, things could be different. You could help people a lot with a wand. Magic was there to make life better. Magrat knew this in the pink fluttering boudoir of her heart.

She dipped under the surface of sleep again.

And there was an odd dream. She never mentioned it to anyone afterwards because, well, you didn't. Not things like that.

But she thought she'd got up in the night, awakened by the silence, to get some more air. And as she passed the mirror she saw a movement in it.

It wasn't her face. It looked a lot like Granny Weatherwax. It smiled at her – a much nicer and friendlier smile than she'd ever got from Granny, Magrat recalled – and then vanished, the cloudy silver surface closing over it.

She hurried back to bed and awoke to the sound of a brass band, engaged in unrelenting oompah. People were shouting and laughing.

Magrat got dressed quickly, went out into the corridor, and knocked on the door of the older witches. There was no reply. She tried the handle.

After she'd rattled it a couple of times there was a thump as the chair wedged under the handle on the other side, the better to deter ravishers, burglars and other nocturnal intruders, fell over.

Granny Weatherwax's boots protruded from under the covers at one end of the bed. Nanny Ogg's bare feet, Nanny being something of a night-time revolver, were beside them. Faint snores rattled the jug on the washbasin; these were no longer the full-nosed roars of a quick forty-winks catnapper, but the well-paced growls of someone who intends to make a night of it.

Magrat knocked on the sole of Granny's boot.

'Hey, wake up! Something's going on.'

Granny Weatherwax waking up was quite an impressive sight, and one not seen by many people.

Most people, on waking up, accelerate through a quick panicky pre-consciousness check-up: who am I, where am I, who is he/she, good god, why am I cuddling a policeman's helmet, *what happened last night?*

And this is because people are riddled by Doubt. It is the engine that drives them through their lives. It is the elastic band in the little model aeroplane of their soul, and they spend their time winding it up until it knots. Early morning is the worst time – there's that little moment of panic in case You have drifted away in the night and something else has moved in. This never happened to Granny Weatherwax. She went straight from fast asleep to instant operation on all six cylinders. She never needed to find herself because she always knew she was doing the looking.

She sniffed. 'Something's burning,' she said.

'They've got a bonfire, too.' said Magrat.

Granny sniffed again.

'They're roasting *garlic?*' she said.

'I know. I can't imagine why. They're ripping all the shutters off the windows and burning them in the square and dancing around the fire.'

Granny Weatherwax gave Nanny Ogg a vicious jab with her elbow.

'Wake up, you.'

'Wstyph?'

'I didn't get a wink of sleep all night,' said Granny reproachfully, 'what with her snoring.'

Nanny Ogg raised the covers cautiously.

'It's far too early in the morning for it to be early in the morning,' she said.

'Come on,' said Granny. 'We needs your skill with languages.'

The owner of the inn flapped his arms up and down and ran around in circles. Then he pointed at the castle that towered over the forest. Then he sucked vigorously at his wrist. Then he fell over on his back. And then he looked expectantly at Nanny Ogg, while behind him the bonfire of garlic and wooden stakes and heavy window shutters burned merrily.

'No,' said Nanny, after a while. 'Still non conprendy, mine hair.'

The man got up, and brushed some dust off his leather breeches.

'I think he's saying that someone's dead,' said Magrat. 'Someone in the castle.'

'Well, I must say, everyone seems very cheerful about it,' said Granny Weatherwax severely.

In the sunlight of the new day the village looked far more cheerful. Everyone kept nodding happily at the witches.

'That's because it was probably the landlord,' said Nanny Ogg. 'Bit of a bloodsucker, I think he's sayin'.'

'Ah. That'd be it, then.' Granny rubbed her hands together and looked approvingly at the breakfast table, which had been dragged out into the sunshine. 'Anyway, the food has certainly improved. Pass the bread, Magrat.'

'Everyone keeps smiling and waving at us,' said Magrat. 'And look at all this food!'

'That's only to be expected,' said Granny, with her mouth full. 'They've only had us here one night and already they're learnin' it's *lucky* to be kind to witches. Now help me get the lid off this honey.'

Under the table, Greebo sat and washed himself. Occasionally he burped.

Vampires have risen from the dead, the grave and the crypt, but have never managed it from the cat.

Dear Jason and all at No. 21, No. 34, No. 15, No. 87 and No. 61 but not at No. 18 until she gives back the bowl she definitly borrowed whatever she says.

Well here we are, cor what a lark so far, dont arsk ME about pumkins, still, no harm done. Im drawin a picture of where we stayed larst night I have put an X on our room where our room is. The weather—

'What are you doing, Gytha? We're ready to leave.'

Nanny Ogg looked up, her face still creased with the effort of composition.

'I thought it would be nice to send something to our Jason. You know, to stop him worryin'. So I done a drawing of this place on a piece of card and Mine Hair here will give it to someone going our way. You never know, it might get there.'

— continues Fine.

Nanny Ogg sucked at the end of her pencil. Not for the first time in the history of the universe, someone for whom communication normally came as effortlessly as a dream was stuck for inspiration when faced with a few lines on the back of a card.

Well that about wraps it up for now, will ~~right~~ wright again soone MUM. P.S. the Cat is looking very Peeky I think he misses his Home.

'Will you come *on*, Gytha? Magrat's getting my broom started for me.'

P.P.S. Granny sends her Love.

Nanny Ogg sat back, content in the knowledge of a job well done.*

☆　☆　☆

---

* Nanny Ogg sent a number of cards home to her family, not a single one of which got back before she did. This is traditional, and happens everywhere in the universe.

Magrat reached the end of the town square and stopped to rest.

Quite an audience had gathered to see a woman with legs. They were very polite about it. Somehow, that made it worse.

'It doesn't fly unless you run really fast,' she explained, aware even as she spoke how stupid this sounded, especially if you were listening in a foreign language. 'I think it's called hump starting.'

She took a deep breath, scowled in concentration, and ran forward again. This time it started. It jolted in her hands. The bristles rustled.

She managed to slip it into neutral before it could drag her along the ground. One thing about Granny Weatherwax's broomstick – it was one of the very old-fashioned ones, built in the days when broomsticks were built to last and not fall apart with woodworm after ten years – was that while it might take some starting, when it went it didn't hang about.

Magrat had once considered explaining the symbolism of the witches' broomstick to Granny Weatherwax, and decided not to. It would have been worse than the row about the significance of the maypole.

Departure took some time. The villagers insisted on giving them little gifts of food. Nanny Ogg made a speech which no one understood but which was generally cheered. Greebo, hiccuping occasionally, oozed into his accustomed place among the bristles of Nanny's broomstick.

As they rose above the forest a thin plume of smoke also rose from the castle. And then there were flames.

'I see people dancing in front of it,' said Magrat.

'Always a dangerous business, rentin' property,' said Granny Weatherwax. 'I expect he was a bit lax when it came to redecoratin' and repairin' the roof and suchlike. People take against that kind of thing. My landlord hasn't done a hand's turn on my cottage the whole time I've been there,' she added. 'It's shameful. And me an old woman, too.'

'I thought you owned your place,' said Magrat, as the broomsticks set off over the forest.

'She just ain't paid no rent for sixty years,' said Nanny Ogg.

'Is that my fault?' said Granny Weatherwax. 'It's not *my* fault. I'd be quite willin' to pay.' She smiled a slow, self-confident smile. 'All he has to do is *ask*,' she added.

This is the Discworld, seen from above, its cloud formations circling in long curved patterns.

Three dots emerged from the cloud layer.

'I can see why travellin' doesn't catch on. I call this boring. Nothing but forest for hours and hours.'

'Yes, but flying gets you to places quickly, Granny.'

'How long've we been flying, anyway?'

'About ten minutes since you last asked, Esme.'

'You see? *Boring*.'

'It's sitting on the sticks I don't like. I reckon there ought to be a special broomstick for going long distances, right? One you could stretch out on and have a snooze.'

They all considered this.

'And have your meals on,' added Nanny. 'Proper meals, I mean. With gravy. Not just sandwiches and stuff.' An experiment in aerial cookery on a small oil burner had been hastily curtailed after it threatened to set fire to Nanny's broomstick.

'I suppose you could do it if you had a really *big* broomstick,' said Magrat. 'About the size of a tree, perhaps. Then one of us could do the steering and another one could do the cooking.'

'It'd never happen,' said Nanny Ogg. 'The reason being, the dwarfs would make you pay a fortune for a stick that big.'

'Yes, but what you could do,' said Magrat, warming to her subject, 'is get people to pay you to give them rides. There must be lots of people fed up with highwaymen and . . . and being seasick and that sort of thing.'

'How about it, Esme?' said Nanny Ogg. 'I'll do the steering and Magrat'll do the cooking.'

'What shall I do, then?' said Granny Weatherwax suspiciously.

'Oh . . . well . . . there ought to be someone to, you know, welcome people on to the stick and give them their meals,' said Magrat. 'And tell them what to do if the magic fails, for example.'

'If the magic fails everyone'll crash into the ground and die,' Granny pointed out.

'Yes, but someone will have to tell them how to do that,' said Nanny Ogg, winking at Magrat. 'They won't know how to, not being experienced in flying.'

'And we could call ourselves . . . ' she paused. As always on the Discworld, which was right on the very edge of unreality, little bits of realness crept in whenever someone's mind was resonating properly. This happened now.

' . . . Three Witches Airborne,' she said. 'How about that?'

'*Broomsticks* Airborne,' said Magrat. 'Or Pan . . . air . . . '

'There's no need to bring religion into it,' sniffed Granny.

Nanny Ogg looked slyly from Granny to Magrat.

'We *could* call it Vir . . . ' she began.

A gust of wind caught all three sticks and whirled them up. There was a brief panic as the witches brought them under control.

'Load of nonsense,' muttered Granny.

'Well, it passes the time,' said Nanny Ogg.

Granny looked morosely at the greenery below.

'You'd never get people to do it,' she said. 'Load of nonsense.'

Dear Jason en famile,

Overleaf on the other side please find enclosed a sketch of somewhere some king died and was buried, search me why. It's in some village wear we stopped last night. We had some stuff it was chewy you'll never guess it was snails, and not bad and Esme had three helpins before she found out and then had a Row with the cook and Magrat was sick all night just at the thought of it and had the dire rear. Thinking of you your loving MUM. PS the privies here are DESGUSTING, they have them INDORES, so much for HIGEINE.

Several days passed.

In a quiet little inn in a tiny country Granny Weatherwax sat and regarded the food with deep suspicion. The owner hovered with the frantic expression of one who knows, even before he starts, that he's not going to come out of this ahead of the game.

'Good simple home cooking,' said Granny. 'That's all I require. You know me. I'm not the demanding sort. No one could say I'm the demanding sort. I just want simple food. Not all grease and stuff. It comes to something when you complain about something in your lettuce and it turns out to be what you ordered.'

Nanny Ogg tucked her napkin into the top of her dress and said nothing.

'Like that place last night,' said Granny. 'You'd think you'd be all right with sandwiches, wouldn't you? I mean . . . sandwiches? Simplest food there is in the whole world. You'd think even foreigners couldn't get sandwiches wrong. Hah!'

'They didn't call them sandwiches, Granny,' said Magrat, her eyes dwelling on the owner's frying pan. 'They called them . . . I think they called them smorgy's board.'

'They was nice,' said Nanny Ogg. 'I'm very partial to a pickled herring.'

'But they must think we're daft not noticing they'd left off the top slice,' said Granny triumphantly. 'Well, I told them a thing or two! Another time they'll think twice before trying to swindle people out of a slice of bread that's theirs by rights!'

'I expect they will,' said Magrat darkly.

'And I don't hold with all this giving funny names so people don't know what they're eating,' said Granny, determined to explore the drawbacks of international cookery to the full. 'I like stuff that tells you plain what it is, like . . . well . . . Bubble and Squeak, or . . . or . . . '

'Spotted Dick,' said Nanny absently. She was watching the progress of the pancakes with some anticipation.

'That's right. Decent honest food. I mean, take that stuff we had for lunch. I'm not saying it wasn't nice,' said Granny graciously. 'In a foreign sort of way, of course. But they called it Cwuissses dee Grenolly, and who knows what that means?'

'Frogs' legs,' translated Nanny, without thinking.

The silence was filled with Granny Weatherwax taking a deep breath and a pale green colour creeping across Magrat's face. Nanny Ogg now thought quicker than she had done for a very long time.

'Not *actual* frogs' legs,' she said hurriedly. 'It's like Toad-in-the-Hole is really only sausage and batter puddin'. It's just a joke name.'

'It doesn't sound very funny to me,' said Granny. She turned to glare at the pancakes.

'At least they can't muck up a decent pancake,' she said. 'What'd they call them here?'

'Crap suzette, I think,' said Nanny.

Granny forbore to comment. But she watched with grim satisfaction as the owner finished the dish and gave her a hopeful smile.

'Oh, now he expects us to eat them,' she said. 'He only goes and sets fire to them, and then he still expects us to eat them!'

It might later have been possible to chart the progress of the witches across the continent by some sort of demographic survey. Long afterwards, in some quiet, onion-hung kitchens, in sleepy villages nestling among hot hills, you might have found cooks who *wouldn't* twitch and try to hide behind the door when a stranger came into the kitchen.

Dear Jason,

It is defnity more warmer here, Magrat says it is because we are getting further from the Hub and, a funny thing, all the money is different. You have to change it for other money which is all different shapes and is not proper money at all in my opnion. We generally let Esme sort that out, she gets a very good rate of exchange, it is amazing. Magrat says she will write a book called Travelling on One Dollar a Day, and it's always the same dollar.

Esme is getting to act just like a foreigner, yesterday she took her shawl off, next thing it will be dancing on tables. This is a picture of some famous bridge or other. Lots of love, MUM.

The sun beat down on the cobbled street, and particularly on the courtyard of a little inn.

'It's hard to imagine,' said Magrat, 'that it's autumn back home.'

'Garkon? Mucho vino aveck zei, grassy ass.'

The innkeeper, who did not understand one word and was a good-natured man who certainly did not deserve to be called a garkon, smiled at Nanny. He'd smile at anyone with such an unlimited capacity for drink.

'I don't hold with putting all these tables out in the street, though,' said Granny Weatherwax, although without much severity. It was pleasantly warm. It wasn't that she didn't like autumn, it was a season she always looked forward to, but at her time of life it was nice to know that it was happening hundreds of miles away while she wasn't there.

Underneath the table Greebo dozed on his back with his legs in the air. Occasionally he twitched as he fought wolves in his sleep.

'It says in Desiderata's notes,' said Magrat, turning the stiff pages carefully, 'that in the late summer here they have this special traditional ceremony where they let a lot of bulls run through the street.'

'That'd be something worth seeing,' said Granny Weatherwax. 'Why do they do it?'

'So all the young men can chase them to show how brave they are,' said Magrat. 'Apparently they pull their rosettes off.'

A variety of expressions passed across Nanny Ogg's wrinkled face, like weather over a stretch of volcanic badlands.

'Sounds a bit strange,' she said at last. 'What do they do that for?'

'She doesn't explain it very clearly,' said Magrat. She turned another page. Her lips moved as she read on. 'What does cojones mean?'

They shrugged.

'Here, you want to slow down on that drink,' said Granny, as a waiter put down another bottle in front of Nanny Ogg. 'I wouldn't trust any drink that's green.'

'It's not like proper drink,' said Nanny. 'It says on the label it's made from herbs. You can't make a serious drink out of just herbs. Try a drop.'

Granny sniffed the opened bottle.

'Smells like aniseed,' she said.

'It says "Absinthe" on the bottle,' said Nanny.

'Oh, that's just a name for wormwood,' said Magrat, who was good at herbs. 'My herbal says it's good for stomach diforders and prevents sicknefs after meals.'

'There you are, then,' said Nanny. 'Herbs. It's practic'ly medicine.' She poured a generous measure for the other two. 'Give it a go, Magrat. It'll put a cheft on your cheft.'

Granny Weatherwax surreptitiously loosened her boots. She was also debating whether to remove her vest. She probably didn't need all three.

'We ought to be getting on,' she said.

'Oh, I'm fed up with the broomsticks,' said Nanny. 'More than a couple of hours on a stick and I've gone rigid in the dairy air.'

She looked expectantly at the other two. 'That's foreign for bum,' she added. 'Although, it's a funny thing, in some foreign parts "bum" means "tramp" and "tramp" means "hobo". Funny things, words.'

'A laugh a minute,' said Granny.

'The river's quite wide here,' said Magrat. 'There's big boats. I've never been on a proper boat. You know? The kind that doesn't sink easily?'

'Broomsticks is more witchy,' said Granny, but not with much conviction. She did not have Nanny Ogg's international anatomical vocabulary, but bits of her she wouldn't even admit to knowing the names of were definitely complaining.

'I saw them boats,' said Nanny. 'They looked like great big rafts with houses on. You wouldn't hardly know you're *on* a boat, Esme. 'Ere, what's he doing?'

The innkeeper had hurried out and was taking the jolly little tables back inside. He nodded at Nanny and spoke with a certain amount of urgency.

'I think he wants us to go inside,' said Magrat.

'I likes it out here,' said Granny. 'I LIKES IT OUT HERE, THANK YOU,' she repeated. Granny Weatherwax's approach to foreign tongues was to repeat herself loudly and slowly.

''Ere, you stop trying to take our table away!' snapped Nanny, thumping his hands.

The innkeeper spoke hurriedly and pointed up the street.

Granny and Magrat glanced inquiringly at Nanny Ogg. She shrugged.

'Didn't understand any of that,' she admitted.

'WE'RE STOPPIN' WHERE WE ARE, THANK YOU,' said Granny. The innkeeper's eyes met hers. He gave in, waved his hands in the air in exasperation, and went inside.

'They think they can take advantage of you when you're a woman,' said Magrat. She stifled a burp, discreetly, and picked up the green bottle again. Her stomach was feeling a lot better already.

'That's very true. D'you know what?' said Nanny Ogg. 'I barricaded meself in my room last night and a man didn't even *try* to break in.'

'Gytha Ogg, sometimes you—' Granny stopped as she caught sight of something over Nanny's shoulder.

'There's a load of *cows* coming down the street,' she said.

Nanny turned her chair around.

'It must be that bull thing Magrat mentioned,' she said. 'Should be worth seein'.'

Magrat glanced up. All along the street people were craning out of every second-storey window. A jostle of horns and hooves and steaming bodies were approaching rapidly.

'There's people up there *laughing* at us,' she said accusingly.

Under the table Greebo stirred and rolled over. He opened his good eye, focused on the approaching bulls, and sat up. This looked like being fun.

'Laughin'?' said Granny. She looked up. The people aloft did indeed appear to be enjoying a joke.

Her eyes narrowed.

'We're just goin' to carry on as if nothin' is happening,' she declared.

'But they're quite big bulls,' said Magrat nervously.

'They're *nothing* to do with *us*,' said Granny. 'It's nothin' to do with *us* if a lot of foreigners want to get excited about things. Now pass me the herbal wine.'

As far as Lagro te Kabona, innkeeper, could remember the events of that day, they seemed to happen like this:

It was the time of the Thing with the Bulls. And the mad women just sat there, drinking absinthe as if it was water! He tried to get them to come indoors, but the old one, the skinny one, just shouted at him. So he let them bide, but left the door open – people soon got the message when the bulls came down the street with the young men of the village after them. Whoever snatched the big red rosette from between the horns of the biggest bull got the seat of honour at that night's feast plus – Lagro smiled a smile of forty years' remembrance – a certain informal but highly enjoyable relationship with the young women of the town for quite some time after . . .

And the mad women just sat there.

The leading bull had been a bit uncertain about this. Its normal course of action would be to roar and paw the ground a bit to get the targets running in an interesting way and its mind wasn't able to cope with this lack of attention, but that hadn't been its major problem, because its major problem had been twenty other bulls right behind it.

And even that ceased to be its major problem, because the terrible old woman, the one all in black, had stood up, muttered something at it and smacked it between the eyes. Then the horrible dumpy one whose stomach had the resilience and capacity of a galvanised water tank fell backwards off her chair, laughing, and the young one – that is, the one who was younger than the other two – started flapping at the bulls as if they were ducks.

And then the street was full of angry, bewildered bulls, and a lot of shouting, terrified young men. It's one thing to chase a lot of panicking bulls, and quite another to find that they're suddenly trying to run the other way.

The innkeeper, from the safety of his bedroom window, could hear the horrible women shouting things to one another. The dumpy one kept laughing and shouting some sort of battle cry – 'TrytheHorsemanswordEsme!' and then the younger one, who was pushing her way through the animals as if being gored to death was something that only happened to other people, found the lead bull and took *the* rosette off it, with the same air of concern as an old woman may take a thorn out of her cat's paw. She held it as if she didn't know what it was or what she should do with it . . .

The sudden silence affected even the bulls. Their tiny little bloodshot brains sensed something wrong. The bulls were embarrassed.

Fortunately, the horrible women left on a riverboat that afternoon, after one of them rescued her cat which had cornered twenty-five stone of confused bull and was trying to toss it in the air and play with it.

That evening Lagro te Kabona made a point of being very, very kind to his old mother.

And the village held a flower festival next year, and no one ever talked about the Thing with the Bulls ever, ever again.

At least, not in front of the men.

The big paddlewheel sloshed through the thick brown soup of the river. The motive power was several dozen trolls under a sunshade, trudging along an endless belt. Birds sang in the trees on the distant banks. The scent of hibiscus wafted across the water, almost but unfortunately not quite overpowering the scent of the river itself.

'Now *this*,' said Nanny Ogg, 'is more like it.'

She stretched out on the deckchair and turned to look at Granny Weatherwax, whose brows were knitted in the intense concentration of reading.

Nanny's mouth spread in an evil grin.

'You know what this river's called?' she said.

'No.'

''S called the Vieux River.'

'Yes?'

'Know what that means?'

'No.'

'The Old (Masculine) River,' said Nanny.

'Yes?'

'Words have sex in foreign parts,' said Nanny, hopefully.

Granny didn't budge.

'Wouldn't be surprised,' she murmured. Nanny sagged.

'That's one of Desiderata's books, isn't it?'

'Yes,' said Granny. She licked her thumb decorously and turned the page.

'Where's Magrat gone?'

'She's having a lie-down in the cabin,' said Granny, without looking up.

'Tummy upset?'

'It's her head this time. Now be quiet, Gytha. I'm having a read.'

'What about?' said Nanny cheerfully.

Granny Weatherwax sighed, and put her finger on the page to mark her place.

'This place we're going to,' she said. 'Genua. Desiderata says it's decadent.'

Nanny Ogg's smile remained fixed.

'Yes?' she said. 'That's good, is it? I've never been to a city before.'

Granny Weatherwax paused. She'd been pondering for some while. She wasn't at all certain about the meaning of the word 'decadent'. She'd dismissed the possibility that it meant 'having ten teeth' in the same sense that Nanny Ogg, for example, was unident. Whatever it meant, it was something Desiderata had felt necessary to write down. Granny Weatherwax did not generally trust books as a means of information, but now she had no choice.

She had a vague idea that 'decadent' had something to do with not opening the curtains all day.

'She says it's also a city of art, wit and culture,' said Granny.

'We shall be all right there, then,' said Nanny confidently.

'Particularly noted for the beauty of its women, she says here.'

'We shall fade right in, no trouble.'

Granny turned the pages carefully. Desiderata had paid close attention to affairs all over the Disc. On the other hand, she hadn't been writing for readers other than herself, so her notes tended to be cryptic and were *aides mémoire* rather than coherent accounts.

Granny read: 'Now L. rules the citie as the power behint the throne, and Baron S. they say has been killd, drowned in the river. He was a wicked man tho not I think as wicked as L, for she says she wants to make it a Magic

Kingdom, a Happy and Peaseful place, and wen people do that look out for Spies on every corner and no manne dare speak out, for who dare speke out against Evile done in the name of Happyness and Pease? All the Streetes are clean and Axes are sharp. But E. is safe at least, for now. L. has plans for her. And Mrs G who was the Baron's *amour* hides in the swamp and fites back with swamp magic, but you cannot fite mirror magic which is all Reflection.'

Fairy godmothers came in twos, Granny knew. So that was Desiderata and . . . and L . . . but who was this person in the swamp?

'Gytha?' said Granny.

'Wazzat?' said Nanny Ogg, who was dozing off.

'Desiderata says some woman here is someone's armour.'

'Prob'ly a mettyfor,' said Nanny Ogg.

'Oh,' said Granny darkly, 'one of *them* things.'

'But no one can stop Mardi Gras,' she read. 'If anything canne be done it be on Samedi Nuit Morte, the last night of carnivale, the night halfway between the Living and the Dead, when magic flows in the streets. If L. is vooneruble it is then, for carnivale is everythinge she hates . . . '

Granny Weatherwax pulled her hat down over her eyes to shield them from the sun.

'It says here they have a great big carnival every year,' she said. 'Mardi Gras, it's called.'

'That means Fat Lunchtime,' said Nanny Ogg, international linguist. 'Garkon! Etcetra gross Mint Tulip avec petit bowl de peanuts, pour favour!'

Granny Weatherwax shut the book.

She would not of course admit it to a third party, least of all another witch, but as Genua drew nearer Granny was becoming less and less confident.

She was waiting in Genua. After all this time! Staring at her out of the mirror! Smiling!

The sun beat down. She tried defying it. Sooner or later she was going to have to give in, though. It was going to be time to remove another vest.

Nanny Ogg sat and drew cards for her relatives for a while, and then yawned. She was a witch who liked noise and people around her. Nanny Ogg was getting bored. It was a big boat, more like a floating inn, and she felt certain there was some excitement somewhere.

She laid her bag on her seat and wandered away to look for it.

The trolls plodded on.

The sun was red, fat and low when Granny Weatherwax awoke. She looked around guiltily from the shelter of her hatbrim in case anyone had noticed her asleep. Falling asleep during the day was something only old women did, and Granny Weatherwax was an old woman only when it suited her purposes.

The only spectator was Greebo, curled up on Nanny's chair. His one good eye was fixed on her, but it wasn't so terrifying as the milky white stare of his blind one.

'Just considerin' our strategy,' she muttered, just in case.

She closed the book and strode off to their cabin. It wasn't a big one. Some of the staterooms looked huge, but what with the herbal wine and everything Granny hadn't felt up to using any Influence to get one.

Magrat and Nanny Ogg were sitting on a bunk, in gloomy silence.

'I feels a bit peckish,' said Granny. 'I smelled stew on the way here, so let's go and have a look, eh? What about that?'

The other two continued to stare at the floor.

'I suppose there's always pumpkin,' said Magrat. 'And there's always the dwarf bread.'

'There's always dwarf bread,' said Nanny automatically. She looked up, her face a mask of shame.

'Er, Esme . . . er . . . you know the money . . . '

'The money what we all gave you to keep in your knickers for safety?' said Granny. Something about the way the conversation was going suggested the first few pebbles slipping before a major landslide.

'That's the money I'm referrin' to . . . er . . . '

'The money in the big leather bag that we were goin' to be very careful about spendin'?' said Granny.

'You see . . . the money . . . '

'Oh, that money,' said Granny.

' . . . is gone . . . ' said Nanny.

'*Stolen?*'

'She's been *gambling*,' said Magrat, in tones of smug horror. 'With *men*.'

'It wasn't gambling!' snapped Nanny. 'I never gamble! They were no good at cards! I won no end of games!'

'But you *lost* money,' said Granny.

Nanny Ogg looked down again, and muttered something.

'What?' said Granny.

'I said I won nearly all of them,' said Nanny. 'And then I thought, here, we could really have a bit of money to, you know, spend in the city, and I've always been very good at Cripple Mr Onion . . . '

'So you decided to bet heavily,' said Granny.

'How did you know that?'

'Got a feelin' about it,' said Granny wearily. 'And suddenly everyone else was lucky, am I right?'

'It was weird,' said Nanny.

'Hmm.'

'Well, it's not *gambling*,' said Nanny. 'I didn't see it was gambling. They were no good when I started playing. It's not gambling to play against someone who's no good. It's common sense.'

'There was nearly fourteen dollars in that bag,' said Magrat, 'not counting the foreign money.'

'Hmm.'

Granny Weatherwax sat down on the bunk and drummed her fingers on the woodwork. There was a faraway look in her eyes. The phrase 'card sharp' had never reached her side of the Ramtops, where people were friendly and direct and, should they encounter a professional cheat, tended to nail his hand to the table in an easy and outgoing manner without asking him what he called himself. But human nature was the same everywhere.

'You're not upset, are you, Esme?' said Nanny anxiously.

'Hmm.'

'I expect I can soon pick up a new broom when we get home.'

'Hm . . . *what?*'

'After she lost all her money she bet her broom,' said Magrat triumphantly.

'Have we got any money at all?' said Granny.

A trawl of various pockets and knicker legs produced forty-seven pence.

'Right,' said Granny. She scooped it up. 'That ought to be enough. To start with, anyway. Where are these men?'

'What are you going to do?' said Magrat.

'I'm going to play cards,' said Granny.

'You can't do that!' said Magrat, who had recognised the gleam in Granny's eye. 'You're going to use magic to win! You mustn't use magic to win! Not to affect the laws of chance! That's *wicked!*'

The boat was practically a floating town, and in the balmy night air no one bothered much about going indoors. The riverboat's flat deck was dotted with groups of dwarfs, trolls and humans, lounging among the cargo. Granny threaded her way between them and headed for the long saloon that ran almost the entire length of the boat. There was the sound of revelry within.

The riverboats were the quickest and easiest transport for hundreds of miles. On them you got, as Granny would put it, all sorts, and the riverboats going downstream were always crowded with a certain type of opportunist as Fat Lunchtime approached.

She walked into the saloon. An onlooker might have thought it had a magic doorway. Granny Weatherwax, as she walked towards it, strode as she usually strode. As soon as she passed through, though, she was suddenly a bent old woman, hobbling along, and a sight to touch all but the wickedest heart.

She approached the bar, and then stopped. Behind it was the biggest mirror Granny had ever seen. She stared fixedly at it, but it seemed safe enough. Well, she'd have to risk it.

She hunched her back a little more and addressed the barman.

'Excuzee moir, young homme,' she began.*

The barman gave her a disinterested look and went on polishing a glass.

'What can I do for you, old crone?' he said.

There was only the faintest suggestion of a flicker in Granny's expression of elderly imbecility.

'Oh . . . you can understand me?' she said.

'We get all sorts on the river,' said the barman.

'Then I was wondering if you could be so kind as to loan me a deck, I thinks it's called, of cards,' quavered Granny.

'Going to play a game of Old Maid, are you?' said the barman.

There was a chilly flicker across Granny's eyes again as she said, 'No. Just Patience. I'd like to try and get the hang of it.'

He reached under the counter and tossed a greasy pack towards her.

She thanked him effusively and tottered off to a small table in the shadows, where she dealt a few cards randomly on the drink-ringed surface and stared at them.

It was only a few minutes later that a gentle hand was laid on her shoulder. She looked up into a friendly, open face that anyone would lend money to. A gold tooth glittered as the man spoke.

'Excuse me, good mother,' he said, 'but my friends and I' – he gestured to some more welcoming faces at a nearby table – 'would feel much more comfortable in ourselves if you were to join us. It can be very dangerous for a woman travelling by herself.'

Granny Weatherwax smiled nicely at him, and then waved vaguely at her cards.

'I can never remember whether the ones are worth more or less than the pictures,' she said. 'Forget my own head next, I expect!'

They all laughed. Granny hobbled to the other table. She took the vacant seat, which put the mirror right behind her shoulder.

---

* Something about Nanny Ogg rubbed off on people.

She smiled to herself and then leaned forward, all eagerness.

'So tell me,' she said, 'how do you play this game, then?'

All witches are very conscious of stories. They can *feel* stories, in the same way that a bather in a little pool can feel the unexpected trout.

Knowing how stories work is almost all the battle.

For example, when an obvious innocent sits down with three experienced card sharpers and says 'How do you play this game, then?', someone is about to be shaken down until their teeth fall out.

Magrat and Nanny Ogg sat side by side on the narrow bunk. Nanny was distractedly tickling Greebo's stomach, while he purred.

'She'll get into terrible trouble if she uses magic to win,' said Magrat. 'And you know how she hates losing,' she added.

Granny Weatherwax was not a good loser. From her point of view, losing was something that happened to other people.

'It's her eggo,' said Nanny Ogg. 'Everyone's got one o' them. A eggo. And she's got a great big one. Of course, that's all part of bein' a witch, having a big eggo.'

'She's *bound* to use magic,' said Magrat.

'It's tempting Fate, using magic in a game of chance,' said Nanny Ogg. 'Cheatin's all right. That's practic'ly *fair*. I mean, anyone can cheat. But using magic – well, it's tempting Fate.'

'No. Not Fate,' said Magrat darkly.

Nanny Ogg shivered.

'Come on,' said Magrat. 'We can't let her do it.'

'It's her eggo,' said Nanny Ogg weakly. 'Terrible thing, a big eggo.'

'I got,' said Granny, 'three little pictures of kings and suchlike and three of them funny number one cards.'

The three men beamed and winked at one another.

'That's Triple Onion!' said the one who had introduced Granny to the table, and who had turned out to be called Mister Frank.

'And that's good, is it?' said Granny.

'It means you win yet again, dear lady!' He pushed a pile of pennies towards her.

'Gosh,' said Granny. 'That means I've got ... what would it be ... almost five dollars now?'

'Can't understand it,' said Mister Frank. 'It must be the famous beginner's luck, eh?'

'Soon be poor men if it goes on like this,' said one of his companions.

'She'll have the coats off our backs, right enough,' said the third man. 'Haha.'

'Think we should give up right now,' said Mister Frank. 'Haha.'

'Haha.'

'Haha.'

'Oh, I want to go on,' said Granny, grinning anxiously. 'I'm just getting the hang of it.'

'Well, you'd better give us a sporting chance to win a little bit back, haha,' said Mister Frank. 'Haha.'

'Haha.'

'Haha.'

'Haha. What about half a dollar a stake? Haha?'

'Oh, I reckon she'll want a dollar a stake, a sporting lady like her,' said the third man.

'Haha!'

Granny looked down at her pile of pennies. For a moment she looked uncertain and then, they could see, she realised: how much could she lose, the way the cards were going?

'Yes!' she said. 'A dollar a stake!' She blushed. 'This is _exciting_, isn't it!'

'Yeah,' said Mister Frank. He drew the pack towards him.

There was a horrible noise. All three men stared at the bar, where shards of mirror were cascading to the floor.

'What happened?'

Granny gave him a sweet old smile. She hadn't appeared to look around.

'I reckon the glass he was polishing must of slipped out of his hand and smashed right into the mirror,' she said. 'I do hope he don't have to pay for it out of his wages, the poor boy.'

The men exchanged glances.

'Come on,' said Granny, 'I've got my dollar all ready.'

Mister Frank looked nervously at the ravaged frame. Then he shrugged.

The movement dislodged something somewhere. There was a muffled snapping noise, like a mousetrap carrying out the last rites. Mister Frank went white and gripped his sleeve. A small metal contraption, all springs and twisted metal, fell out. A crumpled-up Ace of Cups was tangled up in it.

'Whoops,' said Granny.

☆ ☆ ☆

Magrat peered through the window into the saloon.

'What's she doin' now?' hissed Nanny Ogg.

'She's grinning again,' said Magrat.

Nanny Ogg shook her head. 'Eggo,' she said.

Granny Weatherwax had that method of play that has reduced professional gamblers to incoherent rage throughout the multiverse.

She held her cards tightly cupped in her hands a few inches from her face, allowing the merest fraction of each one to protrude. She glared at them as if daring them to offend her. And she never seemed to take her eyes off them, except to watch the dealing.

And she took far too long. And she never, ever, took risks.

After twenty-five minutes she was down one dollar and Mister Frank was sweating. Granny had already helpfully pointed out three times that he'd accidentally dealt cards off the bottom of the deck, and she'd asked for another pack 'because, look, this one's got all little marks on the back.'

It was her eyes, that was what it was. Twice he'd folded on a perfectly good three-card Onion only to find that she'd been holding a lousy double Bagel. Then the third time, thinking he'd worked out her play, he'd called her out and run a decent flush right into the maw of a five-card Onion that the old bag must have been patiently constructing for ages. And then – his knuckles went white – and then the dreadful, terrible hag had said, 'Have I won? With all these little cards? Gosh – aren't I the lucky one!'

And then she started humming when she looked at her cards. Normally, the three of them would have welcomed this sort of thing. The teeth tappers, the eyebrow raisers, the ear rubbers – they were as good as money in the sock under the mattress, to a man who knew how to read such things. But the appalling old crone was as transparent as a lump of coal. And the humming was . . . insistent. You found yourself trying to follow the tune. It made your teeth tingle. Next thing you were glumly watching while she laid down a measly Broken Flush in front of your even more measly two-card Onion and said, 'What, is it me again?'

Mister Frank was desperately trying to remember how to play cards without his sleeve device, a handy mirror and a marked deck. In the teeth of a hum like a fingernail down a blackboard.

It wasn't as if the ghastly old creature even knew how to play properly.

After an hour she was four dollars ahead and when she said, 'I *am* a lucky girl!' Mister Frank bit through his tongue.

And then he got a natural Great Onion. There was no realistic way to beat a Great Onion. It was something that happened to you once or twice in a lifetime.

She folded! The old bitch folded! She abandoned one blasted dollar and she folded!

Magrat peered through the window again.

'What's happening?' said Nanny.

'They all look very angry.'

Nanny took off her hat and removed her pipe. She lit it and tossed the match overboard. 'Ah. She'll be humming, you mark my words. She's got a very annoying hum, has Esme.' Nanny looked satisfied. 'Has she started cleaning out her ear yet?'

'Don't think so.'

'No one cleans out her ear like Esme.'

She was cleaning out her ear!

It was done in a very ladylike way, and the daft old baggage probably wasn't even aware she was doing it. She just kept inserting her little finger in her ear and swivelling it around. It made a noise like a small pool cue being chalked.

It was displacement activity, that's what it was. They all cracked in the end . . .

She folded again! And it had taken him bloody five bloody minutes to put together a bloody double Onion!

'I remember,' said Nanny Ogg, 'when she come over our house for the party when King Verence got crowned and we played Chase My Neighbour Up the Passage with the kiddies for ha'pennies. She accused Jason's youngest of cheating and sulked for a week afterwards.'

'Was he cheating?'

'I expect so,' said Nanny proudly. 'The trouble with Esme is that she don't know how to lose. She's never had much practice.'

'Lobsang Dibbler says sometimes you have to lose in order to win,' said Magrat.

'Sounds daft to me,' said Nanny. 'That's Yen Buddhism, is it?'

'No. They're the ones who say you have to have lots of money to win,' said Magrat.* 'In the Path of the Scorpion, the way to win is to lose every fight except the last one. You use the enemy's strength against himself.'

'What, you get him to hit himself, sort of thing?' said Nanny. 'Sounds daft.'

Magrat glowered.

'What do you know about it?' she said, with uncharacteristic sharpness.

'What?'

'Well, I'm fed up!' said Magrat. 'At least I'm making an effort to learn things! I don't go around just bullying people and acting bad-tempered all the time!'

Nanny took her pipe out of her mouth.

'I'm not bad-tempered,' she said mildly.

'I wasn't talking about you!'

'Well, Esme's always been bad-tempered,' said Nanny. 'It comes natural to her.'

'And she hardly ever does real magic. What good is being a witch if you don't do magic? Why doesn't she use it to help people?'

Nanny peered at her through the pipe smoke.

''Cos she knows how good she'd be at it, I suppose,' she said. 'Anyway, I've known her a long time. Known the whole family. All the Weatherwaxes is good at magic, even the men. They've got this magical streak in 'em. Kind of a curse. Anyway . . . she thinks you can't help people with magic. Not *properly*. It's true, too.'

'Then what good – ?'

Nanny prodded at the pipe with a match.

'I seem to recall she come over and helped you out when you had that spot of plague in your village,' she said. 'Worked the clock around, I recall. Never known her not treat someone ill who needed it, even when they, you know, were pretty oozy. And when the big ole troll that lives under Broken Mountain came down for help because his wife was sick and everyone threw rocks at him, I remember it was Esme that went back with him and delivered the baby. Hah . . . then when old Chickenwire Hopkins threw a rock at *Esme* a little while afterwards all his barns was mysteriously trampled flat in the night. She always said you can't help people with magic, but you can help them with skin. By doin' real things, she meant.'

'I'm not saying she's not basically a nice person – ' Magrat began.

'Hah! I am. You'd have to go a long day's journey to find someone basically nastier than Esme,' said Nanny Ogg, 'and this is *me* sayin' it.

* The Yen Buddhists are the richest religious sect in the universe. They hold that the accumulation of money is a great evil and burden to the soul. They therefore, regardless of personal hazard, see it as their unpleasant duty to acquire as much as possible in order to reduce the risk to innocent people.

She knows exactly what she is. She was born to be good and she don't like it.'

Nanny tapped her pipe out on the rail and turned back to the saloon.

'What you got to understand about Esme, my girl,' she said, 'is that she's got a psycholology as well as a big eggo. I'm damn glad I ain't.'

Granny was twelve dollars ahead. Everything else in the saloon had stopped. You could hear the distant splash of the paddles and the cry of the leadman.

Granny won another five dollars with a three-card Onion.

'What do you mean, a psycholology?' said Magrat. 'Have you been reading books?'

Nanny ignored her.

'The thing to watch out for now,' she said, 'is when she goes "tch, tch, tch" under her breath. That comes after the ear-cleanin'. It gen'rally means she's plannin' somethin'.'

Mister Frank drummed his fingers on the table, realised to his horror that he was doing it, and bought three new cards to cover his confusion. The old baggage didn't appear to notice.

He stared at the new hand.

He ventured two dollars and bought one more card.

He stared again.

What were the odds, he thought, against getting a Great Onion twice in one day?

The important thing was not to panic.

'I think,' he heard himself say, 'that I may hazard another two dollars.'

He glanced at his companions. They obediently folded, one after another.

'Well, I don't know,' said Granny, apparently talking to her cards. She cleaned her ear again. 'Tch, tch, tch. What d'you call it when, you know, you want to put more money in, sort of thing?'

'It's calling raising,' said Mister Frank, his knuckles going white.

'I'll do one of them raisins, then. Five dollars, I think.'

Mister Frank's knees ground together.

'I'll see you and raise you ten dollars,' he snapped.

'I'll do that too,' said Granny.

'I can go another twenty dollars.'

'I—' Granny looked down, suddenly crestfallen. 'I've ... got a broomstick.'

A tiny alarm bell rang somewhere at the back of Mister Frank's mind, but now he was galloping headlong to victory.

'Right!'

He spread the cards on the table.

The crowd sighed.

He began to pull the pot towards him.

Granny's hand closed over his wrist.

'I ain't put *my* cards down yet,' she said archly.

'You don't need to,' snapped Mister Frank. 'There's no chance you could beat that, madam.'

'I can if I can Cripple it,' said Granny. 'That's why it's called Cripple Mister Onion, ain't it?'

He hesitated.

'But – but – you could only do that if you had a perfect nine-card run,' he burbled, staring into the depths of her eyes.

Granny sat back.

'You know,' she said calmly, 'I *thought* I had rather a lot of these black pointy ones. That's good, is it?'

She spread the hand. The collective audience made a sort of little gasping noise, in unison.

Mister Frank looked around wildly.

'Oh, very well done, madam,' said an elderly gentleman. There was a round of polite applause from the crowd. The big, inconvenient crowd.

'Er ... yes,' said Mister Frank. 'Yes. Well done. You're a very quick learner, aren't you.'

'Quicker'n you. You owe me fifty-five dollars and a broomstick,' said Granny.

Magrat and Nanny Ogg were waiting for her as she swept out.

'Here's your broom, she snapped. 'And I hopes you've got all your stuff together, 'cos we're leaving.'

'Why?' said Magrat.

'Because as soon as it gets quiet, some men are going to come looking for us.'

They scurried after her towards their tiny cabin.

'You weren't using magic?' said Magrat.

'No.'

'And not cheating?' said Nanny Ogg.

'No. Just headology,' said Granny.

'Where did you learn to play like that?' Nanny demanded.

Granny stopped. They cannoned into her.

'Remember last winter, when Old Mother Dismass was taken really bad and I went and sat up with her every night for almost a month?'

'Yes?'

'You sit up every night dealing Cripple Mister Onion with someone who's got a detached retina in her second sight and you soon learn how to play,' said Granny.

Dear Jason and everyone,

What you get more of in foreign parts is smells, I am getting good at them. Esme is shouting at everyone, I think she thinks they're bein forein just to Spite her, don't know when I last saw her enjoi herselfe so much. Mind you they need a good Shakin up if you ask me, for lunch we stopped somewhere and they did Steak Tartere and they acted VERY snooty just becos I wanted myne well done. All the best, MUM

The moon was closer here.

The orbit of the Discworld's moon meant that it was quite high when it passed over the high Ramtops. Here, nearer to the Rim, it was bigger. And more orange.

'Like a pumpkin,' said Nanny Ogg.

'I thought we said we weren't going to mention pumpkins,' said Magrat.

'Well, we didn't have any supper,' said Nanny.

And there was another thing. Except during the height of summer the witches weren't used to warm nights. It didn't seem right, gliding along under a big orange moon over dark foliage that clicked and buzzed and whirred with insects.

'We must be far enough from the river now,' said Magrat. 'Can't we land, Granny? No one could have followed us!'

Granny Weatherwax looked down. The river in this countryside meandered in huge glistening curves, taking twenty miles to cover five. The land between the snaking water was a patchwork of hillsides and woodlands. A distant glow might have been Genua itself.

'Riding a broomstick all night is a right pain in the itinerant,' said Nanny.

'Oh, all *right*.'

'There's a town over there,' said Magrat. 'And a castle.'

'Oh, not another one . . . '

'It's a nice little castle,' said Magrat. 'Can't we just call in? I'm fed up with inns.'

Granny looked down. She had very good night vision.

'Are you sure that's a castle?' she said.

'I can see the turrets and everything,' said Magrat. 'Of course it's a castle.'

'Hmm. I can see more than turrets,' said Granny. 'I think we'd better have a look at this, Gytha.'

There was never any noise in the sleeping castle, except in the late summer when ripe berries fell off the bramble vines and burst softly on the floor. And sometimes birds would try to nest in the thorn thickets that now filled the throne room from floor to ceiling, but they never got very far before they, too, fell asleep. Apart from that, you'd need very keen hearing indeed to hear the growth of shoots and the opening of buds.

It had been like this for ten years. There was no sound in the –

'Open up there!'

'Bony fidy travellers seeking sucker!'

– no sound in the –

'Here, give us a leg up, Magrat. Right. Now . . . '

There was a tinkle of broken glass.

'You've broken their window!'

– *not a sound* in the –

'You'll have to offer to pay for it, you know.'

The castle gate swung open slowly. Nanny Ogg peered around it at the other two witches, while pulling thorns and burrs from her hair.

'It's bloody disgusting in here,' she said. 'There's people asleep all over the place with spiders' webs all over 'em. You were right, Esme. There's been magic going on.'

The witches pushed their way through the overgrown castle. Dust and leaves had covered the carpets. Young sycamores were making a spirited attempt to take over the courtyard. Vines festooned every wall.

Granny Weatherwax pulled a slumbering soldier to his feet. Dust billowed off his clothes.

'Wake up,' she demanded.

'Fzhtft,' said the soldier, and slumped back.

'It's like that everywhere,' said Magrat, fighting her way through a thicket of bracken that was growing up from the kitchen regions. 'There's the cooks all snoring and nothing but mould in the pots! There's even mice asleep in the pantry!'

'Hmm,' said Granny. 'There'll be a spinning wheel at the bottom of all this, you mark my words.'

'A Black Aliss job?' said Nanny Ogg.

'Looks like it,' said Granny. Then she added, quietly, 'Or someone like her.'

'Now *there* was a witch who knew how stories worked,' said Nanny. 'She used to be in as many as three of 'em at once.'

Even Magrat knew about Black Aliss. She was said to have been the greatest witch who ever lived – not exactly *bad*, but so powerful it was sometimes hard to tell the difference. When it came to sending palaces to sleep for a hundred years or getting princesses to spin straw into Glod,* no one did it better than Black Aliss.

'I met her once,' said Nanny, as they climbed the castle's main staircase, which was a cascade of Old Man's Trousers. 'Old Deliria Skibbly took me to see her once, when I was a girl. Of course, she was getting pretty . . . eccentric by then. Gingerbread houses, that kind of thing.' She spoke sadly, as one might talk about an elderly relative who'd taken to wearing her underwear outside her clothes.

'That must have been before those two children shut her up in her own oven?' said Magrat, untangling her sleeve from a briar.

'Yeah. Sad, that. I mean, she didn't really ever *eat* anyone,' said Nanny. 'Well. Not often. I mean, there was talk, but . . . '

'That's what happens,' said Granny. 'You get too involved with stories, you get confused. You don't know what's really real and what isn't. And they get you in the end. They send you weird in the head. I don't like stories. They're not real. I don't like things that ain't real.'

She pushed open a door.

'Ah. A chamber,' she said sourly. 'Could even be a bower.'

'Doesn't the stuff grow quickly!' said Magrat.

'Part of the time spell,' said Granny. 'Ah. There she is. Knew there'd be someone somewhere.'

There was a figure lying on a bed, in a thicket of rose bushes.

'And there's the spinning wheel,' said Nanny, pointing to a shape just visible in a clump of ivy.

'Don't touch it!' said Granny.

'Don't worry, I'll pick it up by the treadle and pitch it out of the window.'

'How do you know all this?' said Magrat.

''Cos it's a rural myth,' said Nanny. 'It's happened lots of times.'

---

* Black Aliss wasn't very good with words either. They had to give him quite a lot of money to go away and not make a scene.

Granny Weatherwax and Magrat looked down at the sleeping figure of a girl of about thirteen, almost silvery under the dust and pollen.

'Isn't she pretty,' sighed Magrat, the generous-hearted.

From behind them came the crash of a spinning wheel on some distant cobbles, and then Nanny Ogg appeared, brushing her hands.

'Seen it happen a dozen times,' she said.

'No you ain't,' said Granny.

'Once, anyway,' said Nanny, unabashed. 'And I *heard* about it dozens of times. Everyone has. Rural myth, like I said. Everyone's heard about it happening in their cousin's friend's neighbour's village – '

'That's because it does,' said Granny.

Granny picked up the girl's wrist.

'She's asleep because she'll have got a – ' Nanny said.

Granny turned.

'I know, I know. I know, right? I know as well as you. You think I don't know?' She bent over the limp hand. 'That's fairy godmothering, this is,' she added, half to herself. 'Always do it *impressively*. Always meddling, always trying to be in control! Hah! Someone got a bit of poison? Send everyone to sleep for a hundred years! Do it the *easy* way. All this for one prick. As if that was the end of the world.' She paused. Nanny Ogg was standing behind her. There was no possible way she could have detected her expression. 'Gytha?'

'Yes, Esme?' said Nanny Ogg innocently.

'I can *feel* you grinnin'. You can save the tu'penny-ha'penny psycholo-logy for them as wants it.'

Granny shut her eyes and muttered a few words.

'Shall I use my wand?' said Magrat hesitantly.

'Don't you dare,' said Granny, and went back to her muttering.

Nanny nodded. 'She's definitely getting a bit of colour back,' she said.

A few minutes later the girl opened her eyes and stared up blearily at Granny Weatherwax.

'Time to get up,' said Granny, in an unusually cheerful voice, 'you're missing the best part of the decade.'

The girl tried to focus on Nanny, then on Magrat, and then looked back at Granny Weatherwax.

'You?' she said.

Granny raised her eyebrows and looked at the other two.

'Me?'

'You are – still here?'

'Still?' said Granny. 'Never been here before in my life, Miss.'

'But – ' the girl looked bewildered. And frightened, Magrat noticed.

'I'm like that myself in the mornings, dear,' said Nanny Ogg, taking the girl's other hand and patting it. 'Never at my best till I've had a cup of tea. I expect everyone else'll be waking up any minute. Of course, it'll take 'em a while to clean the rats' nests out of the kettles – Esme?'

Granny was staring at a dust-covered shape on the wall.

'Meddling . . . ' she whispered.

'What's up, Esme?'

Granny Weatherwax strode across the room and wiped the dust off a huge ornate mirror.

'Hah!' she said, and spun around. 'We'll be going now,' she said.

'But I thought we were going to have a rest. I mean, it's nearly dawn,' said Magrat.

'No sense in outstaying our welcome,' said Granny, as she left the room.

'But we haven't even *had* a . . . ' Magrat began. She glanced at the mirror. It was a big oval one, in a gilt frame. It looked perfectly normal. It wasn't like Granny Weatherwax to be frightened of her own reflection.

'She's in one of her moods again,' said Nanny Ogg. 'Come on. No sense in staying here.' She patted the bewildered princess on the head. 'Cheerio, Miss. A couple of weeks with a broom and an axe and you'll soon have the old place looking like new.'

'She looked as if she recognised Granny,' said Magrat, as they followed the stiff hurrying figure of Esme Weatherwax down the stairs.

'Well, we know she doesn't, don't we,' said Nanny Ogg. 'Esme has never been in these parts in her life.'

'But I still don't see why we have to rush off,' Magrat persisted. 'I expect people will be jolly grateful that we've broken the spell and everything.'

The rest of the palace was waking up. They jogged past guards staring in amazement at their cobwebbed uniforms and the bushes that were growing everywhere. As they crossed the forested courtyard an older man in faded robes staggered out of a doorway and leaned against the wall, trying to get his bearings. Then he saw the accelerating figure of Granny Weatherwax.

'You?' he shouted, and 'Guards!'

Nanny Ogg didn't hesitate. She snatched Magrat's elbow and broke into a run, catching up with Granny Weatherwax at the castle gates. A guard who was better at mornings than his colleague staggered forward and made an attempt to bar their way with his pike, but Granny just pushed at it and swivelled him around gently.

Then they were outside and running for the broomsticks leaning against a convenient tree. Granny snatched at hers without stopping and, for once, it fired up on almost the first attempt.

An arrow whiffled past her hat and stuck in a branch.

'I don't call *that* gratitude,' said Magrat, as the brooms glided up and over the trees.

'A lot of people are never at their best just after waking up,' said Nanny.

'Everyone seemed to think they knew you, Granny,' said Magrat.

Granny's broomstick jerked in the wind.

'They didn't!' she shouted. 'They never saw me before, all right?'

They flew on in troubled silence for a while.

Then Magrat, who in Nanny Ogg's opinion had an innocent talent for treading on dangerous ground, said: 'I wonder if we did the right thing? I'm sure it was a job for a handsome prince.'

'Hah!' said Granny, who was riding ahead. 'And what good would that be? Cutting your way through a bit of bramble is how you can tell he's going to be a good husband, is it? That's fairy godmotherly thinking, that is! Goin' around inflicting happy endings on people whether they wants them or not, eh?'

'There's nothing wrong with happy endings,' said Magrat hotly.

'Listen, happy endings is fine if they *turn out* happy,' said Granny, glaring at the sky. 'But you can't make 'em for other people. Like the only way you could make a happy marriage is by cuttin' their heads off as soon as they say "I do", yes? You can't make happiness . . . '

Granny Weatherwax stared at the distant city.

'All you can do,' she said, 'is make an ending.'

They had breakfast in a forest clearing. It was grilled pumpkin. The dwarf bread was brought out for inspection. But it was miraculous, the dwarf bread. No one ever went hungry when they had some dwarf bread to avoid. You only had to look at it for a moment, and instantly you could think of dozens of things you'd rather eat. Your boots, for example. Mountains. Raw sheep. Your own foot.

Then they tried to get some sleep. At least, Nanny and Magrat did. But all it meant was that they lay awake and listened to Granny Weatherwax muttering under her breath. They'd never seen her so upset.

Afterwards, Nanny suggested that they walk for a while. It was a nice day, she said. This was an interesting kind of forest, she said, with lots of new herbs which could do with bein' looked at. Everyone'd feel better for a stroll in the sunshine, she said. It'd improve their tempers.

And it was, indeed, a nice forest. After half an hour or so, even Granny Weatherwax was prepared to admit that in certain respects it wasn't totally foreign and shoddy. Magrat wandered off the path occasionally, picking flowers. Nanny even sang a few verses of A Wizard's Staff Has A Knob

On The End with no more than a couple of token protests from the other two.

But there was still something wrong. Nanny Ogg and Magrat could feel something between them and Granny Weatherwax, some sort of mental wall, something important deliberately hidden and unsaid. Witches usually had few secrets from one another, if only because they were all so nosy that there was never any chance to *have* secrets. It was worrying.

And then they turned a corner by a stand of huge oak trees and met the little girl in the red cloak.

She was skipping along in the middle of the path, singing a song that was simpler and a good deal cleaner than any in Nanny Ogg's repertoire. She didn't see the witches until she was almost on top of them. She stopped, and then smiled innocently.

'Hello, old women,' she said.

'Ahem,' said Magrat.

Granny Weatherwax bent down.

'What're you doing out in the forest all by yourself, young lady?'

'I'm taking this basket of goodies to my granny,' said the girl.

Granny straightened up, a faraway look in her eyes.

'Esme,' said Nanny Ogg urgently.

'I know. I know,' said Granny.

Magrat leaned down and set her face in the idiot grimace generally used by adults who'd love to be good with children and don't stand a dog's chance of ever achieving it. 'Er. Tell me, Miss . . . did your mother tell you to watch out for any bad wolves that might happen to be in the vicinity?'

'That's right.'

'And your granny . . . ' said Nanny Ogg. 'I guess she's a bit bed-bound at the moment, right?'

'That's why I'm taking her this basket of goodies – ' the child began.

'Thought so.'

'Do you know my granny?' said the child.

'Ye-ess,' said Granny Weatherwax. 'In a way.'

'It happened over Skund way when I was a girl,' said Nanny Ogg quietly. 'They never even found the gran– '

'And where is your granny's cottage, little girl?' said Granny Weatherwax loudly, nudging Nanny sharply in the ribs.

The girl pointed up a side track.

'You're not the wicked witch, are you?' she said.

Nanny Ogg coughed.

'Me? No. We're – we're – ' Granny began.

'Fairies,' said Magrat.

Granny Weatherwax's mouth dropped open. Such an explanation would never have occurred to her.

'Only my mummy warned me about the wicked witch too,' said the girl. She gave Magrat a sharp look. 'What kind of fairies?'

'Er. Flower fairies?' said Magrat. 'Look, I've got a wand – '

'Which ones?'

'What?'

'Which flowers?'

'Er,' said Magrat. 'Well. I'm . . . Fairy Tulip and that's . . . ' she avoided looking directly at Granny, ' . . . Fairy . . . Daisy . . . and this is . . . '

'Fairy Hedgehog,' said Nanny Ogg.

This addition to the supernatural pantheon was given due consideration.

'You can't be Fairy Hedgehog,' said the child, after some thought. 'A hedgehog's not a flower.'

'How do you know?'

' 'Cos it's got spikes.'

'So's holly. *And* thistles.'

'Oh.'

'And I've got a wand,' said Magrat. Only now did she risk a look at Fairy Daisy.

'We ought to be getting along,' said Granny Weatherwax. 'You just stay here with Fairy Tulip, I think it was, and we'll just go and make sure your granny's all right. All right?'

'I bet it's not a real wand,' said the child, ignoring her and facing Magrat with a child's unerring ability to find a weak link in any chain. 'I bet it can't turn things into things.'

'Well – ' Magrat began.

'I *bet*,' said the girl, 'I bet you can't turn that tree stump over there into . . . into . . . into a *pumpkin*. Haha, bet you anything you can't. Bet you a trillion dollars you can't turn that stump into a pumpkin.'

'I can see the two of you are going to get along fine,' said Fairy Hedgehog. 'We won't be long.'

Two broomsticks skimmed low above the forest path.

'Could just be coincidence,' said Nanny Ogg.

'T'aint,' said Granny. 'The child even has a red cloak on!'

'I had a red cloak when I was fifteen,' said Nanny.

'Yes, but your granny lived next door. You didn't have to worry about wolves when you visited her,' said Granny.

'Except old Sumpkins the lodger.'

'Yes, but that was just coincidence.'

A trail of blue smoke drifted among the trees ahead of them. Somewhere away to one side there was the sound of a falling tree.

'Woodcutters!' said Nanny. 'It's all right if there's woodcutters! One of them rushes in – '

'That's only what children get told,' said Granny, as they sped onwards. 'Anyway, that's no good to the grandmother, is it? She's already *been* et!'

'I always hated that story,' said Nanny. 'No one ever cares what happens to poor defenceless women.'

The path vanished abruptly on the edge of a glade. Hemmed in by the trees was a straggly kitchen garden, in which a few pathetic stalks fought for what little sun there was. In the middle of the garden was what had to be a thatched cottage because no one would build a haystack that badly.

They leapt off the broomsticks, leaving them to drift to a halt in the bushes, and hammered on the cottage door.

'We could be too late,' said Nanny. 'The wolf might – '

After a while there was the muffled sound of someone shuffling across the floor within, and then the door opened a crack. A suspicious eye was visible in the gloom.

'Yes?' said a small and quavering voice from somewhere beneath the eye.

'Are you grandmother?' Granny Weatherwax demanded.

'Are you the taxgatherers, dear?'

'No, ma'am, we're – '

' – fairies,' said Fairy Hedgehog quickly.

'I don't open the door to people I don't know, dear,' said the voice, and then it took on a slightly petulant tone. ' 'Specially people who never does the washing up even after I leaves out a bowl of nearly fresh milk for 'em.'

'We'd like to talk to you for a few minutes,' said Fairy Daisy.

'Yes? Have you got any identification, dear?'

'I *know* we've got the right grandmother,' said Fairy Hedgehog. 'There's a family likeness. She's got big ears.'

'Look, it's not *her* that's got the big ears,' snapped Fairy Daisy. 'It'll be the wolf that's got big ears. That's the whole point. Don't you ever pay attention?'

The grandmother watched them with interest. After a lifetime of believing in them she was seeing fairies for the first time, and it was an experience. Granny Weatherwax caught her perplexed expression.

'Put it like this, ma'am,' she said, in a despotically reasonable tone of voice, 'how would you like to be eaten alive by a wolf?'

'I don't think I would like that, dear, no,' said the hidden grandmother.

'The alternative's us,' said Granny.

'Lawks. Are you sure?'

'On our word as fairies,' said Fairy Hedgehog.

'Well. Really? All right. You can come in. But none of your tricks. And mind you do the washing up. You haven't got a pot of gold about you, have you?'

'That's pixies, isn't it?'

'No, they're the ones in wells. It's goblins she means.'

'Don't be daft. They're the ones you get under bridges.'

'That's trolls. Everyone knows that's trolls.'

'Not us, anyway.'

'Oh,' said the grandmother. 'I might have known.'

Magrat liked to think she was good with children, and worried that she wasn't. She didn't like them very much, and worried about this too. Nanny Ogg seemed to be effortlessly good with children by alternately and randomly giving them either a sweet or a thick ear, while Granny Weatherwax ignored them for most of the time and that seemed to work just as well. Whereas Magrat *cared*. It didn't seem fair.

'Bet you a million trillion zillion dollars you can't turn *that* bush into a pumpkin,' said the child.

'But, look, all the others got turned into pumpkins,' Magrat pointed out.

'It's bound not to work sooner or later,' said the child placidly.

Magrat looked helplessly at the wand. She'd tried everything – wishing, sub-vocalising and even, when she'd thought the other witches were out of earshot, banging it against things and shouting. 'Anything but pumpkins!'

'You don't know how to do it really, do you,' stated the child.

'Tell me,' said Magrat, 'you said your mummy knows about the big bad wolf in the woods, didn't you?'

'That's right.'

'But *nevertheless* she sent you out by yourself to take those goodies to your granny?'

'That's right. Why?'

'Nothing. Just thinking. And you owe me a million trillion zillion squillion dollars.'

There's a certain freemasonry about grandmothers, with the added benefit that no one has to stand on one leg or recite any oaths in order to join. Once inside the cottage, and with a kettle on the boil, Nanny Ogg was quite at home. Greebo stretched out in front of the meagre fire and dozed off as the witches tried to explain.

'I don't see how a wolf can get in here, dear,' said the grandmother kindly. 'I mean, they're *wolves*. They can't open doors.'

Granny Weatherwax twitched aside a rag of curtain and glared out at the clearing.

'We know,' she said.

Nanny Ogg nodded towards the little bed in an alcove by the fireplace.

'Is that where you always sleep?' she said.

'When I'm feeling poorly, dear. Other times I sleeps in the attic.'

'I should get along up there now, if I was you. And take my cat up with you, will you? We don't want him getting in the way.'

'Is this the bit where you clean the house and do all the washing for a saucer of milk?' said the grandmother hopefully.

'Could be. You never know.'

'Funny, dear. I was expecting you to be shorter – '

'We get out in the fresh air a lot,' said Nanny. 'Off you go now.'

That left the two of them. Granny Weatherwax looked around the cave-like room. The rushes on the floor were well on the way to composthood. Soot encrusted the cobwebs on the ceiling.

The only way housework could be done in this place was with a shovel or, for preference, a match.

'Funny, really,' said Nanny, when the old woman had climbed the rickety stairs. 'She's younger'n me. Mind you, I take exercise.'

'You never took exercise in your life,' said Granny Weatherwax, still watching the bushes. 'You never did anything you didn't want to do.'

'That's what I mean,' said Nanny happily. 'Look, Esme, I still say this could all be just – '

'It ain't! I can *feel* the story. Someone's been making stories happen in these parts, I know it.'

'And you know who, too. Don't you Esme?' said Nanny slyly.

She saw Granny look around wildly at the grubby walls.

'I reckon she's too poor to afford a mirror,' said Nanny. 'I ain't blind, Esme. And I know mirrors and fairy godmothers go together. So what's going on?'

'I ain't saying. I don't want to look a fool if I'm wrong. I'm not going to – there's something coming!'

Nanny Ogg pressed her nose against the dirty window.

'Can't see anything.'

'The bushes moved. Get into the bed!'

'Me? I thought it was you who was going into the bed!'

'Can't imagine why you'd think that.'

'No. Come to think of it, neither can I,' said Nanny wearily. She picked up the floppy mob-cap from the bedpost, put it on, and slid under the patchwork quilt.

''Ere, this mattress is stuffed with straw!'

'You won't have to lie on it for long.'

'It prickles! And I think there's *things* in it.'

Something bumped against the wall of the house. The witches fell silent.

There was a snuffling noise under the back door.

'You know,' whispered Nanny, as they waited, 'the scullery's terrible. There's no firewood. And there's hardly any food. And there's a jug of milk that's practically on the march – '

Granny sidled quickly across the room to the fireplace, and then back to her station by the front door.

After a moment there was a scrabbling at the latch, as if it was being operated by someone who was unfamiliar either with doors or with fingers.

The door creaked open slowly.

There was an overwhelming smell of musk and wet fur.

Uncertain footsteps tottered across the floor and towards the figure huddling under the bedclothes.

Nanny raised the mob-cap's floppy frill just enough to see out.

'Wotcha,' she said, and then, 'Oh, blimey, I never realised you had teeth *that* big – '

Granny Weatherwax pushed the door shut and stepped forward briskly. The wolf spun around, a paw raised protectively.

'Nooaaaaaw!'

Granny hesitated for a second, and then hit it very hard on the head with a cast-iron frying pan.

The wolf crumpled.

Nanny Ogg swung her legs out of the bed.

'When it happened over Skund way they said it was a werewolf or something, and I thought, no, werewolves aren't like that,' she said. 'I never thought it was a *real* wolf. Gave me quite a turn, that.'

'Real wolves don't walk on their hind legs and open doors,' said Granny Weatherwax. 'Come on, help me get it outside.'

'Took me right back, seeing a great big hairy slathering thing heading towards me,' said Nanny, picking up one end of the stunned creature. 'Did you ever meet old Sumpkins?'

It was, indeed, a normal-looking wolf, except that it was a lot thinner than most. Ribs showed plainly under the skin and the fur was matted. Granny hauled a bucket of cloudy water from the well next to the privy and poured it over its head.

Then she sat down on a tree stump and watched it carefully. A few birds sang, high in the branches.

'It spoke,' she said. 'It tried to say "no".'

'I wondered about that,' said Nanny. 'Then I thought maybe I was imagining things.'

'No point in imagining anything,' said Granny. 'Things are bad enough as they are.'

The wolf groaned. Granny handed the frying pan to Nanny Ogg.

After a while she said, 'I think I'm going to have a look inside its head.'

Nanny Ogg shook her head. 'I wouldn't do that, if I was you.'

'I'm the one who's me, and I've got to know. Just you stand by with the frying pan.'

Nanny shrugged.

Granny concentrated.

It is very difficult to read a human mind. Most humans are thinking about so many things at any given moment that it is almost impossible to pick out one stream in the flood.

Animal minds are different. Far less cluttered. Carnivore minds are easiest of all, especially before meals. Colours don't exist in the mental world, but, if they did, a hungry carnivore mind would be hot and purple and sharp as an arrow. And herbivore minds are simple, too – coiled silver springs, poised for flight.

But this wasn't any kind of normal mind. It was two minds.

Granny had sometimes picked up the mind of hunters in the forest, when she was sitting quietly of an evening and letting her mind wander. Just occasionally they felt like this, or at least like a faint shadow of this. Just occasionally, when the hunter was about to make a kill, the random streams of thought came together. But this was different. This was the opposite – this was cracked and crippled attempts at cogitation peeling away from the sleek arrowhead of predatory intent. This was a predatory mind trying to *think*.

No wonder it was going mad.

She opened her eyes.

Nanny Ogg held the frying pan over her head. Her arm trembled.

'Well,' she said, 'who's there?'

'I could do with a glass of water,' said Granny. Natural caution surfaced through the turmoil of her mind. 'Only not out of that well, mind you.'

Nanny relaxed a little. When a witch started rummaging in someone else's mind, you could never be sure who was coming back. But Granny Weatherwax was the best. Magrat might always be trying to find herself, but Granny didn't even understand the idea of the search. If she couldn't find the way back to her own head, there wasn't a path.

'There's that milk in the cottage,' Nanny volunteered.

'What colour was it again?'

'Well . . . still fairly white.'

'Okay.'

When Nanny Ogg's back was safely turned Granny permitted herself a small shudder.

She stared at the wolf, wondering what she could do for it. A normal wolf wouldn't enter a cottage, even if it could open the door. Wolves didn't come near humans at all, except if there were a lot of them and it was the end of a very hard winter. And they didn't do that because they were big and bad and wicked, but because they were wolves.

This wolf was trying to be human.

There was probably no cure.

'Here's your milk,' said Nanny Ogg.

Granny reached up and took it without looking.

'Someone made this wolf think it was a person,' she said. 'They made it think it was a person and then they didn't think any more about it. It happened a few years ago.'

'How do you know?'

'I've . . . got its memories,' said Granny. And instincts, too, she thought. She knew it'd be some days before she'd stop wanting to chase sledges over the snow.

'Oh.'

'It's stuck between species. In its head.'

'Can we help it?' said Nanny.

Granny shook her head.

'It's gone on for too long. It's habit now. And it's starving. It can't go one way, it can't go t'other. It can't act like a wolf, and it can't manage being a human. And it can't go on like it is.'

She turned to face Nanny for the first time. Nanny took a step back.

'You can't imagine how it feels,' she said. 'Wandering around for years. Not capable of acting human, and not able to be a wolf. You can't imagine how that feels.'

'I reckon maybe I can,' said Nanny. 'In your face. Maybe I can. Who'd do that to a creature?'

'I've got my suspicions.'

They looked around.

Magrat was approaching, with the child. Beside them walked one of the woodcutters.

'Hah,' said Granny. 'Yes. Of course. There's always got to be' – she spat the words – '*a happy ending.*'

A paw tried to grip her ankle.

Granny Weatherwax looked down into the wolf's face.

'Preeees, Annn enndinggg? Noaaaow?'

She knelt down, and took the paw.

'Yes?' she said.

'Yessss!'

She stood up again, all authority, and beckoned to the approaching trio.

'Mr Woodcutter?' she said. 'A job for you . . . '

The woodcutter never understood why the wolf laid its head on the stump so readily.

Or why the old woman, the one in whom anger roiled like pearl barley in a bubbling stew, insisted afterwards that it be buried properly instead of skinned and thrown in the bushes. She had been very insistent about that.

And that was the end of the big bad wolf.

It was an hour later. Quite a few of the woodcutters had wandered up to the cottage, where there seemed to be a lot of interesting activity going on. Woodcutting is not a job that normally offers much in the way of diversion.

Magrat was washing the floor with as much magical assistance as could be afforded by a bucket of soapy water and a scrubbing brush. Even Nanny Ogg, whose desultory interest in the proud role of housewife had faded completely just as soon as her eldest daughter was old enough to hold a duster, was cleaning the walls. The old grandmother, who wasn't entirely in touch with events, was anxiously following both of them around with a saucer of milk. Spiders who had inherited the ceiling for generations were urged gently but firmly out of the door.

And Granny Weatherwax was walking around the clearing with the head woodcutter, a barrel-chested young man who clearly thought he looked better in his studded leather wristlets than was, in fact, the case.

'It's been around for years, right?' he said. 'Always lurking around the edges of villages and that.'

'And you never tried to talk to it?' said Granny.

'Talk to it? It's a *wolf*, right? You don't talk to *wolves*. Animals can't talk.'

'Hmm. I see. And what about the old woman? There's a lot of you woodcutters. Did you ever, you know, drop in to see her?'

'Huh? No fear!'

'Why?'

The head woodcutter leaned forward conspiratorially.

'Well, they say she's a witch, right?'

'Really?' said Granny. 'How do you know?'

'She's got all the signs, right?'

'What signs are those?'

The woodcutter was pricked by a slight uneasiness.

'Well . . . she's . . . she lives all by herself in the wood, right?'

'Yes . . ?'

'And . . . and . . . she's got a hook nose and she's always muttering to herself . . . '

'Yes . . ?'

'And she's got no teeth, right?'

'Lawks,' said Granny. 'I can see where you wouldn't want to be having with the likes of her, right?'

'Right!' said the woodcutter, relieved.

'Quite likely turn you into just about anything as soon as look at you, right?' Granny stuck her finger in her ear and twiddled it reflectively. 'They can do that, you know.'

'I bet they can. I bet they can,' said Granny. 'Makes me glad there's all you big strong lads around. Tch, tch. Hmm. Can I have a look at your chopper, young man?'

He handed over his axe. Granny sagged dramatically as she grasped it. There were still traces of wolf blood on the blade.

'Deary me, it's a big one,' she said. 'And you're good with this, I expect.'

'Won the silver belt two years running at the forest revels,' said the woodcutter proudly.

'Two years running? Two years running? Lawks. That *is* good. That's *very* good. And here's me hardly able to lift it.' Granny grasped the axe in one hand and swung it inexpertly. The woodcutter jumped backwards as the blade whirred past his face and then buried itself a quarter of an inch deep in a tree.

'Sorry about that,' said Granny Weatherwax. 'Aren't I a daft old woman! Never was any good with anything technical!'

He grinned at her, and tried to pull the axe free.

He sank to his knees, his face suddenly white.

Granny leaned down until she was level with his ear.

'You could have seen to the old woman,' she said quietly. 'You could have talked to the wolf. But you didn't, right?'

He tried to speak, but his teeth didn't seem to want to part.

'I can see you're very sorry about all that,' she said. 'I can see you're seein' the error of your ways. I bet you can't wait to be up and repairing her cottage for her, and getting the garden back in good order, and seeing she has fresh milk every day and a good supply of wood, right? In fact I wouldn't be surprised if you wasn't generous enough to build her a *new* cottage, with a proper well an' all. Somewhere near the village so she don't have to live alone, right? You know, I can see the future sometimes and I just *know* that's what's goin' to happen, *right*?'

Sweat ran off his face. Now his lungs didn't seem to be operating, either.

'An' I knows you're goin' to keep your word, and I'm so pleased about it that I'm going to make sure you're especially lucky,' said Granny, her voice still in the same pleasant monotone. 'I knows it can be a dangerous job, woodchoppin'. People can get hurt. Trees can accidentally fall on 'em, or the top of their chopper can suddenly come off and cut their head open.' The woodcutter shuddered as Granny went on: 'So what I'm goin' to do is a little spell to make sure that none of this 'appens to you. On account of me bein' so grateful. Because of you helpin' the old lady. Right? Just nod.'

He managed to move his head a fraction. Granny Weatherwax smiled.

'There!' she said, standing up and brushing a speck of leafmould off her dress. 'You see how sweet life can be, if we all helps one another?'

The witches left around lunchtime. By then the old woman's garden was full of people, and the air with the sound of sawing and hammering. News like Granny Weatherwax travels fast. Three woodcutters were digging over the vegetable plot, two more were fighting to clean the chimney, and four of them were halfway down a new well that was being dug with impressive speed.

The old grandmother, who was still the kind of person who hangs on to one idea until another one dislodges it by force, was running out of saucers to put the milk in.

The witches sneaked away in all the busyness.

'There,' said Magrat, as they strolled down the path, 'it just goes to show how people will pitch in and help, if only someone sets an example. You don't have to bully people all the time, you know.'

Nanny Ogg glanced at Granny.

'I saw you talking to the head woodcutter,' she said. 'What was you talking about?'

'Sawdust,' said Granny.

'Oh, yes?'

'One of the woodcutters told *me*,' said Magrat, 'that there's been other odd things happening in this forest. Animals acting human, he said. There used to be a family of bears living not far away.'

'Nothing unusual about a family of bears living together,' said Nanny. 'they're very convivial animals.'

'In a cottage?'

'*That's* unusual.'

'That's what I mean,' said Magrat.

'You'd definitely feel a bit awkward about going round to borrow a cup of sugar,' said Nanny. 'I expect the neighbours had something to say about it.'

'Yes,' said Magrat. 'They said "oink".'

'What'd they say "oink" for?'

'Because they couldn't say anything else. They were pigs.'

'We had people like that next door when we lived at – ' Nanny began.

'I mean *pigs*. You know. Four legs? Curly tail? What pork is before it's pork? Pigs.'

'Can't see anyone letting pigs live in a cottage,' said Granny.

'He said they didn't. The pigs built their own. There were three of them. Little pigs.'

'What happened to them?' said Nanny.

'The wolf ate them. They were the only animals stupid enough to let him get near them, apparently. Nothing was found of them except their spirit level.'

'That's a shame.'

'The woodcutter says they didn't build very good houses, mind you.'

'Well, it's only to be expected. What with the trotters and all,' said Nanny.

'He says the roof leaks something dreadful, right over his bed.'

The witches walked on in silence.

'I remember hearing once,' said Nanny, with the occasional glance at Granny Weatherwax, 'about some ole enchantress in history who lived on an island and turned shipwrecked sailors into pigs.'

'That's a terrible thing to do,' said Magrat, on cue.

'I suppose it's all according to what you really *are*, inside,' said Nanny.'I mean, look at Greebo here.' Greebo, curled around her shoulders like a smelly fur, purred. 'He's practically a human.'

'You do talk a lot of tosh, Gytha,' said Granny Weatherwax.

'That's 'cos people won't tell me what they *really* think is going on,' said Nanny Ogg, grimly.

'I said I'm not sure,' said Granny.

'You looked into the wolf's mind.'

'Yes. I did.'

'Well, then . . . '

Granny sighed. 'Someone's been here before us. Passing through. Someone who knows about the power of stories, and uses 'em. And the stories have . . . kind of hung around. They do that, when they get fed . . . '

'What'd anyone want to do that for?' said Nanny.

'*Practice*,' said Granny.

'Practice? What for?' said Magrat.

'I expect we'll find out presently,' said Granny gnomically.

'You ought to tell me what you think,' said Magrat. 'I *am* the official godmother around here, you know. I ought to be told things. You've got to tell me things.'

Nanny Ogg went chilly. This was the kind of emotional countryside with which she was, as head Ogg, extremely familiar. That sort of comment at this sort of time was like the tiny sliding of snow off the top branch of a tall tree high in the mountains during the thaw season. It was one end of a process that, without a doubt, would end with a dozen villages being engulfed. Whole branches of the Ogg family had stopped talking to other branches of the Ogg family because of a 'Thank you very much' in the wrong tones and the wrong place, and this was far worse.

'Now,' she said hurriedly, 'why don't we – '

'I don't have to explain anything,' said Granny Weatherwax.

'But we're supposed to be *three* witches,' said Magrat. 'If you can call us witches,' she added.

'What do you mean by that, pray?' said Granny.

'Pray?' thought Nanny. Someone has ended a sentence with 'pray?' That's like that bit when someone hits someone else with a glove and then throws it on the floor. There's no going back when someone's ended a sentence with 'pray?' But she tried, anyway.

'How about a nice – '

Magrat plunged on with the brave desperation of someone dancing in the light of their burning bridges.

'Well,' she said, 'it seems to *me* – '

'Yes?' said Granny.

'It seems to *me*,' Magrat tried again, 'that the only *magic* we do is all – well, headology. Not what anyone else would call magic. It's just glaring at

people and tricking them. Taking advantage of their gullibility. It wasn't what
I expected when *I* set out to become a witch – '

'And who says,' said Granny Weatherwax, slowly and deliberately 'that
you've become a witch now?'

'My word, the wind is getting up, perhaps we should – ' said Nanny Ogg.

'*What* did you say?' said Magrat.

Nanny Ogg put her hand over her eyes. Asking someone to repeat a phrase
you'd not only heard very clearly but were also exceedingly angry about was
around Defcon II in the lexicon of squabble.

'I should have thought my voice was clear enough,' said Granny. 'I'm very
amazed my voice wasn't clear enough. It sounded clear enough to *me*.'

'Looks a bit gusty, why don't we – ?'

'Well, I should just think I can be smug and bad-tempered and ill-
considerate enough to be a witch,' said Magrat. 'That's all that's required isn't
it?'

'Ill-considerate? *Me*?'

'You like people who need help, because when they need help they're weak,
and helping them makes you feel *strong!* What harm would a bit of magic do?'

'Because it'd never stop at just a bit, you stupid girl!'

Magrat backed off, her face flushed. She reached into her bag and pulled out
a slim volume, which she flourished like a weapon.

'Stupid I may be,' she panted, 'but at least I'm trying to learn things! Do you
know the kind of things people can use magic for? Not just illusion and
bullying! There's people in this book that can . . . can . . . walk on hot coals,
and stick their hands in a fire and not get hurt!'

'Cheap trickery!' said Granny.

'They really can!'

'Impossible. No one can do that!'

'It shows they can control things! Magic's got to be more than just knowing
things and manipulating people!'

'Oh? It's all wishing on stars and fairy dust, is it? *Making* people happier?'

'There's got to be some of that! Otherwise what's the good of *anything*?
Anyway . . . when I went to Desiderata's cottage you were looking for the
wand, weren't you?'

'I just didn't want it falling into the wrong hands!'

'Like any hands but yours, I expect!'

They glared at each other.

'Haven't you got any romance in your soul?' said Magrat plaintively.

'No,' said Granny. 'I ain't. And stars don't care what you wish, and magic
don't make things better, and no one doesn't get burned who sticks their hand
in a fire. If you want to amount to anything as a witch, Magrat Garlick, you

got to learn three things. What's real, what's not real, and what's the difference – '

'And always get the young man's name and address,' said Nanny. 'It worked for me every time. Only joking,' she said, as they both glared at her.

The wind was rising, here on the edge of the forest. Bits of grass and leaves whirled through the air.

'We're going the right way, anyway,' said Nanny madly, seeking anything that would be a distraction. 'Look. It says "Genua" on the signpost.'

It did indeed. It was an old, worm-eaten signpost right on the edge of the forest. The end of the arm had been carved into the likeness of a pointing finger.

'A proper road, too,' Nanny burbled on. The row cooled a bit, simply because both sides were not talking to each other. Not simply not exchanging vocal communication – that's just an absence of speaking. This went right through that and out the other side, into the horrible glowering worlds of Not Talking to One Another.

'Yellow bricks,' said Nanny. 'Whoever heard of anyone making a road out of yellow bricks?'

Magrat and Granny Weatherwax stood looking in opposite directions with their arms folded.

'Brightens the place up, I suppose,' said Nanny. On the horizon, Genua sparkled in the middle of some more greenery. In between, the road dipped into a wide valley dotted with little villages. A river snaked through them on the way to the city.

The wind whipped at their skirts.

'We'll never fly in this,' said Nanny, still womanfully trying to make enough conversation for three people.

'So we'll walk, then, eh?' she said, and added, because there's a spark of spitefulness even in innocent souls like Nanny Ogg's, 'Singing as we go, how about it?'

'I'm sure it's not my place to mind what anyone chooses to do,' said Granny. 'It's nothing to do with me. I expect *some* people with wands and big ideas might have something to say.'

'Huh!' said Magrat.

They set off along the brick road towards the distant city, in single file with Nanny Ogg as a kind of mobile buffer state in the middle.

'What some people need,' said Magrat, to the world in general, 'is a bit more heart.'

'What some people need,' said Granny Weatherwax, to the stormy sky, 'is a lot more brain.'

Then she clutched at her hat to stop the wind from blowing it off.

What *I* need, thought Nanny Ogg fervently, is a drink.

Three minutes later a farmhouse dropped on her head.

By this time the witches were well spaced out. Granny Weatherwax was striding along in front, Magrat was sulking along at the rear, and Nanny was in the middle.

As she said afterwards, it wasn't even as if she was singing. It was just that one moment there was a small, plump witch, and the next there was the collapsing remains of a wooden farmhouse.

Granny Weatherwax turned and found herself looking at a crumbling, unpainted front door. Magrat nearly walked into a back door of the same grey, bleached wood.

There was no sound but the crackle of settling timber.

'Gytha?' said Granny.

'Nanny?' said Magrat.

They both opened their doors.

It was a very simple design of house, with two downstairs rooms separated by a front-to-back passageway. In the middle of the passageway, surrounded by shattered and termite-ridden floorboards, under the pointy hat that had been rammed down to her chin, was Nanny Ogg. There was no sign of Greebo.

'Wha' happened?' she said. 'Wha' happend?'

'A farmhouse dropped on your head,' said Magrat.

'Oh. One o' them things,' said Nanny vaguely.

Granny gripped her by the shoulders.

'Gytha? How many fingers am I holding up?' she said urgently.

'Wha' fingers? 'S all gone dark.'

Magrat and Granny gripped the brim of Nanny's hat and half lifted, half unscrewed it from her head. She blinked at them.

'That's the willow reinforcement,' she said, as the pointy hat creaked back into shape like a resurrecting umbrella. She was swaying gently. 'Stop a hammer blow, a hat with willow reinforcement. All them struts, see. Distributes the force. I shall write to Mr Vernissage.'

Magrat, bemused, looked around the little house.

'It just dropped out of the sky!' she said.

'Could have been a big tornado or something somewhere,' said Nanny Ogg. 'Picked it up, see, then the wind drops and down it comes. You get funny things happening in high winds. Remember that big gale we had last year? One of my hens laid the same egg four times.'

'She's rambling,' said Magrat.

'No, I ain't, that's just my normal talking,' said Nanny.

Granny Weatherwax peered into one of the rooms. 'I suppose there wouldn't be any food and drink about the place?' she said.

'I think I could force myself to drink some brandy,' said Nanny quickly.

Magrat peered up the stairs.

'Coo-ee,' she called, in the strangled voice of someone who wants to be heard without doing anything so bad-mannered as raise their voice. 'Is there anyone here?'

Nanny, on the other hand, looked under the stairs. Greebo was a cowering ball of fur in a corner. She hauled him out by the scruff of his neck and gave him a slightly bewildered pat. Despite Mr Vernissage's millinery masterpiece, despite the worm-eaten floor, and despite even the legendary thick skull of the Oggs, she was definitely feeling several twinkles short of a glitter and suffering a slight homesick-tinged dip in her usual sunny nature. People didn't hit you over the head with farmhouses back home.

'You know, Greebo,' she said. 'I don't think we're in Lancre.'

'I've found some jam,' said Granny Weatherwax, from the kitchen.

It didn't take a lot to cheer up Nanny Ogg. 'That's fine,' she called out. 'It'll go nicely on the dwarf bread.'

Magrat came into the room.

'I'm not sure we should be taking other people's provisions,' she said. 'I mean, this place must belong to someone.'

'Oh. Did someone speak, Gytha?' said Granny Weatherwax archly.

Nanny rolled her eyes.

'I was merely saying, Nanny,' said Magrat, 'that this isn't our property.'

'She says it don't belong to us, Esme,' said Nanny.

'Tell anyone who wants to know, Gytha, that it's like salvage from a shipwreck,' said Granny.

'She says finders keepers, Magrat,' said Nanny.

Something flickered past the window. Magrat went and peered out through the grimy pane.

'That's funny. There's a lot of dwarfs dancing round the house,' she said.

'Oh, yes?' said Nanny, opening a cupboard.

Granny stiffened. 'Are they – I means, ask her if they're singing,' she said. 'They singing, Magrat?'

'I can hear something,' said Magrat. 'Sounds like "Dingdong, dingdong".'

'That's a dwarf song all right,' said Nanny. 'They're the only people who can make a hiho last all day.'

'They seem very happy about it,' said Magrat doubtfully.

'Probably it was their farmhouse and they're glad to get it back.'

There was a hammering on the back door. Magrat opened it. A crowd of brightly dressed and embarrassed dwarfs stepped back hurriedly and then peered up at her.

'Er,' said the one who was apparently the leader, 'is . . . is the old witch dead?'

'Which old witch?' said Magrat.

The dwarf looked at her for a while with his mouth open. He turned and had a whispered consultation with his colleagues. Then he turned back.

'How many have you got?'

'There's a choice of two,' said Magrat. She wasn't feeling in a very good mood and wasn't prompted to aid the conversation more than necessary. Uncharacteristic nastiness made her add, 'Free for the asking.'

'Oh.' The dwarf considered this. 'Well, which old witch did the house land on?'

'Nanny? No, she's not dead. She's just a bit stunned. But thanks all the same for asking,' said Magrat. 'That's very kind of you.'

This seemed to puzzle the dwarfs. They went into a huddle. There was a lot of *sotto voce* arguing.

Then the head dwarf turned back to Magrat. He removed his helmet and turned it around and around nervously in his hands.

'Er,' he said, 'can we have her boots?'

'What?'

'Her boots?' said the dwarf, blushing. 'Can we have them, please?'

'What do you want her boots for?'

The dwarf looked at her. Then he turned and went into a huddle with his colleagues again. He turned back to Magrat.

'We've just got this . . . feeling . . . that we ought to have her boots,' he said.

He stood there blinking.

'Well, I'll go and ask,' said Magrat. 'But I don't think she'll say yes.'

As she went to close the door the dwarf twiddled his hat some more.

'They *are* ruby-coloured, aren't they?' he said.

'Well, they're red,' said Magrat. 'Is red all right?'

'They've got to be red.' All the other dwarfs nodded. 'It's no good if they're not red.'

Magrat gave him a blank look and shut the door.

'Nanny,' she said slowly, when she was back in the kitchen, 'there's some dwarfs outside who want your boots.'

Nanny looked up. She'd found a stale loaf in a cupboard and was industriously chewing. It was amazing what you'd eat if the alternative was dwarf bread.

'What d'they want 'em for?' she said.

'Didn't say. They just said they had a feeling they want your boots.'

'That sounds highly suspicious to me,' said Granny.

'Old Shaker Wistley over Creel Springs way was a devil for boots,' said Nanny, putting down the breadknife. 'Especially black button boots. He used to collect 'em. If he saw you going past in a new pair he had to go and have a lie-down.'

'I reckon that's a bit *sophisticated* for dwarfs,' said Granny.

'Maybe they want to drink out of 'em,' said Nanny.

'What do you mean, drink out of them?' said Magrat.

'Ah, well, that's what they do in foreign parts,' said Nanny. 'They drink fizzy wine out of ladies' boots.'

They all looked down at Nanny's boots.

Not even Nanny could imagine what anyone would want to drink out of them, or what they would do afterwards.

'My word. That's even more sophisticated than old Shaker Wistley,' said Nanny reflectively.

'They seemed a bit puzzled about it,' said Magrat.

'I expect they would be. It ain't often people get a feeling they ought to go around pulling a decent witch's boots off. This sounds like another story flapping around. I think,' said Granny Weatherwax, 'that we ought to go and talk to these dwarfs.'

She strode out into the passageway and opened the door.

'Yes?' she demanded.

The dwarfs backed away at the sight of her. There was a lot of whispering and elbowing and muttered comments in the nature of 'No, *you*', and 'I asked *last* time.' Finally a dwarf was pushed forward. It might have been the original dwarf. It was hard to tell, with dwarfs.

'Er,' he said. 'Er. Boots?'

'What *for*?' said Granny.

The dwarf scratched its head. 'Damned if I know,' he said. 'We were just wondering about it ourselves, 'smatterofact. We were just coming off shift in the coal mine half an hour ago, we saw the farmouse land on . . . on the witch, and . . . well . . . '

'You just *knew* you had to run up and steal her boots?' said Granny.

The dwarf's face widened into a relieved grin.

'That's right!' he said. 'And sing the Ding-dong song. Only she was supposed to be squashed. No offence meant,' he added quickly.

'It's the willow reinforcement,' said a voice behind Granny. 'Worth its weight in glod.'

Granny stared for a while, and then smiled.

'I think you lads ought to come inside,' she said. 'I've got some questions to ask you.'

The dwarfs looked very uncertain.

'Um,' said the spokesdwarf.

'Nervous of going into a house with witches in it?' said Granny Weatherwax.

The spokesdwarf nodded, and then went red. Magrat and Nanny Ogg exchanged glances behind Granny's back. Something had definitely gone wrong somewhere. In the mountains dwarfs certainly weren't afraid of witches. The problem was to stop them digging up your floor.

'You've been down from the mountains for some time, I expect,' said Granny.

'Very promising seam of coal down here,' mumbled the spokesdwarf, twiddling his hat.

'Bet it's a long time since you've had proper dwarf bread, then,' said Granny. The spokesdwarf's eyes misted over.

'Baked from the finest stone-ground grit, just like mother used to jump up and down on it,' Granny went on.

A sort of collective sigh went up from the dwarfs.

'You just can't get it down here,' said the spokesdwarf, to the ground. 'It's the water, or something. It falls to bits after hardly any years at all.'

'They puts *flour* in it,' said someone behind him, sourly.

'It's worse'n that. The baker over in Genua puts dried fruit in it,' said another dwarf.

'Well, now,' said Granny, rubbing her hands together, 'I may be able to help you here. Could be I've got some dwarf bread to spare.'

'Nah. Not proper dwarf bread,' said the spokesdwarf moodily. 'Proper dwarf bread's got to be dropped in rivers and dried out and sat on and left and looked at every day and put away again. You just can't get it down here.'

'This could be,' said Granny Weatherwax, 'your lucky day.'

'To be frank,' said Nanny Ogg, 'I think the cat pissed on some of it.'

The spokesdwarf looked up, his eyes aglow.

'Hot damn!'

Dear Jason et everybody,

What a life, all kinds of thing goin on, what with talkin wolves and women asleep in castles, I shall have a story or two to tell you when I gets back and no mistake. Also, dont tawk to me about farmhouses, which reminds me, please send someone to Mr Vernissage over in Slice and present Mrs Ogg's compliments and what a good hat he makes, he can say 'As Approved by

Nanny Ogg', it stops 100% of all known farmhouses, also, if you writes to people saying how good their stuff is sometimes you get free stuff, there could be a new hat in this for me so see to it.

Lilith stepped out from her room of mirrors. Shadowy images of herself trailed after her, fading.

Witches ought to be squashed when a farmhouse lands on them. Lilith knew that. All squashed, except for their boots sticking out.

Sometimes she despaired. People just didn't seem able to play their parts properly.

She wondered whether there was such a thing as the *opposite* of a fairy godmother. Most things had their opposite, after all. If so, she wouldn't be a *bad* fairy godmother, because that's just a good fairy godmother seen from a different viewpoint.

The opposite would be someone who was poison to stories and, thought Lilith, quite the most evil creature in the world.

Well, here in Genua was one story no one could stop. It had momentum, this one. Try to stop it and it'd absorb you, make you part of its plot. She didn't have to do a thing. The story would do it for her. And she had the comfort of knowing that she couldn't lose. After all, she was the good one.

She strolled along the battlements and down the stairs to her own room, where the two sisters were waiting. They were good at waiting. They could sit for hours without blinking.

The Duc refused even to be in the same room as them.

Their heads turned as she came in.

She'd never given them voices. It wasn't necessary. It was enough that they were beautiful and could be made to understand.

'Now you must go to the house,' she said. 'And this is very important. Listen to me. Some people will be coming to see Ella tomorrow. You must let them do so, do you understand?'

They were watching her lips. They watched anything that moved.

'We shall need them for the story. It won't work properly unless they try to stop it. And afterwards . . . perhaps I will give you voices. You'll like that, won't you?'

They looked at one another, and then at her. And then at the cage in the corner of the room.

Lilith smiled, and reached in, and took out two white mice.

'The youngest witch might be just your type,' she said. 'I shall have to see what I can do with her. And now . . . open . . . '

☆   ☆   ☆

The broomsticks drifted through the afternoon air.

For once, the witches weren't arguing.

The dwarfs had been a taste of home. It would have done anyone's heart good to see the way they just sat and stared at the dwarf bread, as if consuming it with their eyes, which was the best way to consume dwarf bread. Whatever it was that had driven them to seek ruby-coloured boots seemed to wear off under its down-to-earth influence. As Granny said, you could look a long way before you found anything realer than dwarf bread.

Then she'd gone off alone to talk to the head dwarf.

She wouldn't tell the others what he'd told her, and they didn't feel bold enough to ask. Now she flew a little ahead of them.

Occasionally she'd mutter something like 'Godmothers!' or 'Practising!'

But even Magrat, who hadn't had as much experience, could *feel* Genua now, as a barometer feels the air pressure. In Genua, stories came to life. In Genua, someone set out to make dreams come true.

Remember some of your dreams?

Genua nestled on the delta of the Vieux river, which was the source of its wealth. And Genua was wealthy. Genua had once controlled the river mouth and taxed its traffic in a way that couldn't be called piracy because it was done by the city government, and therefore sound economics and perfectly all right. And the swamps and lakes back in the delta provided the crawling, swimming and flying ingredients of a cuisine that would have been world famous if, as has already been indicated, people travelled very much.

Genua was rich, lazy and unthreatened, and had once spent quite a lot of time involved in that special kind of civic politics that comes naturally to some city states. For example, once it had been able to afford the largest branch of the Assassins' Guild outside Ankh-Morpork, and its members were so busy that you sometimes had to wait for months.*

But the Assassins had all left years ago. Some things sicken even jackals.

The city came as a shock. From a distance, it looked like a complicated white crystal growing out of the greens and browns of the swamp.

Closer to, it resolved into, firstly, an outer ring of smaller buildings, then an inner ring of large, impressive white houses and, finally, at the very centre, a palace. It was tall and pretty and multi-turreted, like a toy castle or some kind of confectionery extravaganza. Every slim tower looked designed to hold a captive princess.

---

* Whereas in Ankh-Morpork, business was often so slow that some of the more go-ahead Guild members put adverts in shop windows offering deals like 'Stab two, poison one free'.

Magrat shivered. But then she thought of the wand. A godmother had responsibilities.

'Reminds me of another one of them Black Aliss stories,' said Granny Weatherwax. 'I remember when she locked up that girl with the long pigtails in a tower just like one of them. Rumplestiltzel or someone.'

'But she got out,' said Magrat.

'Yes, it does you good to let your hair down,' said Nanny.

'Huh. Rural myths,' said Granny.

They drew nearer to the city walls. Then Magrat said, 'There's guards on the gate. Are we going to fly over?'

Granny stared at the highest tower through narrowed eyes. 'No,' she said. 'We'll land and walk in. So's not to worry people.'

'There's a nice flat green bit just behind those trees,' said Magrat.

Granny walked up and down experimentally. Her boots squeaked and gurgled in watery accusation.

'Look, I *said* I'm sorry,' said Magrat. 'It just looked so flat!'

'Water gen'rally does,' said Nanny, sitting on a tree stump and wringing out her dress.

'But even you couldn't tell it was water,' said Magrat. 'It looks so . . . so *grassy* with all that weed and stuff floating on it.'

'Seems to me the land and the water round here can't decide who is which,' said Nanny. She looked around at the miasmic landscape.

Trees grew out of the swamp. They had a jagged, foreign look and seemed to be rotting as they grew. Where the water was visible, it was black like ink. Occasionally a few bubbles would eructate to the surface like the ghosts of beans on bath night. And somewhere over in the distance was the river, if it was possible to be that sure in this land of thick water and ground that wobbled when you set foot on it.

She blinked.

'That's odd,' she said.

'What?' said Granny.

'Thought I saw . . . something running . . . ' muttered Nanny. 'Over there. Between the trees.'

'Must be a duck then, in this place.'

'It was bigger'n a duck,' said Nanny. 'Funny thing is, it looked a bit like a little house.'

'Oh yes, running along with smoke coming out of the chimney, I expect,' said Granny witheringly.

Nanny brightened. 'You saw it too?'

Granny rolled her eyes.

'Come on,' she said, 'let's get to the road.'

'Er,' said Magrat, 'how?'

They looked at the nominal ground between their reasonably dry refuge and the road. It had a yellowish appearance. There were floating branches and tufts of suspiciously green grass. Nanny pulled a branch off the fallen tree she was sitting on and tossed it a few yards. It struck damply, and sank with the noise of someone trying to get the last bit out of the milkshake.

'We fly over to it, of course,' Nanny said.

'You two can,' said Granny. 'There's nowhere for me to run and get mine started.'

In the end Magrat ferried her across on her broom, Nanny bringing up the rear with Granny's erratic stick in tow.

'I just 'ope no one saw us, that's all,' said Granny, when they'd reached the comparative safety of the road.

Other roads joined the swamp causeway as they got nearer to the city. They were crowded, and there was a long line at the gate.

From ground level, the city was even more impressive. Against the steam of the swamps it shone like a polished stone. Coloured flags flew over the walls.

'Looks very jolly,' said Nanny.

'Very *clean*,' said Magrat.

'It just looks like that from outside,' said Granny, who had seen a city before. 'When you get inside it'll be all beggars and noise and gutters full of I don't know what, you mark my words.'

'They're turning quite a lot of people away,' said Nanny.

'They said on the boat that lots of people come here for Fat Lunchtime,' said Granny. 'Probably you get lots of people who ain't the right sort.'

Half a dozen guards watched them approach.

'Very smartly turned out,' said Granny. 'That's what I like to see. Not like at home.'

There were only six suits of chain mail in the whole of Lancre, made on the basis of one-size-doesn't-quite-fit-all. Bits of string and wire had to be employed to take in the slack, since in Lancre the role of palace guard was generally taken by any citizen who hadn't got much to do at the moment.

These guards were all six-footers and, even Granny had to admit, quite impressive in their jolly red-and-blue uniforms. The only other *real* city guards she'd ever seen were those in Ankh-Morpork. The sight of Ankh-Morpork's city guard made thoughtful people wonder who could possibly attack that was worse. They certainly weren't anything to look at.

To her amazement, two pikes barred her way as she stepped under the arched gateway.

'We're not attacking, you know,' she said.

A corporal gave her a salute.

'No ma'am,' he said. 'But we have orders to stop borderline cases.'

'Borderline?' said Nanny. 'What's borderline about us?'

The corporal swallowed. Granny Weatherwax's gaze was a hard one to meet.

'Well,' he said, 'you're a bit . . . grubby.'

There was a ringing silence. Granny took a deep breath.

'We had a bit of an accident in the swamp,' said Magrat quickly.

'I'm sure it'll be all right,' said the corporal wretchedly. 'The captain'll be here directly. Only there's all kinds of trouble if we let the wrong sort in. You'd be amazed at some of the people we get here.'

'Can't go letting the wrong sort in,' said Nanny Ogg. 'We wouldn't want you to let the wrong sort in. I daresay we wouldn't want to come into the kind of city that'd let the wrong sort in, would we, Esme?'

Magrat kicked her on the ankle.

'Good thing we're the right sort,' said Nanny.

'What's happening, corporal?'

The captain of the guard strolled out of a door in the archway and walked over to the witches.

'These . . . ladies want to come in, sir,' said the corporal.

'Well?'

'They're a bit . . . you know, not one hundred per cent clean,' said the corporal, wilting under Granny's stare. 'And one of them's got messy hair – '

'Well!' snapped Magrat.

' – and one of them looks like she uses bad language.'

'What?' said Nanny, her grin evaporating. 'I'll tan your hide, you little bugger!'

'But, corporal, they have got brooms,' said the captain. 'It's very hard for cleaning staff to look tidy all the time.'

'Cleaning staff?' said Granny.

'I'm sure they're as anxious as you are to get tidied up,' said the captain.

'Excuse me,' said Granny, empowering the words with much the same undertones as are carried by words like 'Charge!' and 'Kill!', 'Excuse me, but does this pointy hat I'm wearing mean anything to you?'

The soldiers looked at it politely.

'Can you give me a clue?' said the captain, eventually.

'It means – '

'We'll just trot along in, if it's all the same to you,' said Nanny Ogg. 'Got a lot of cleaning up to do.' She flourished her broomstick. 'Come, ladies.'

She and Magrat grasped Granny's elbows firmly and propelled her under the archway before her fuse burned out. Granny Weatherwax always held that you ought to count up to ten before losing your temper. No one knew why, because the only effect of this was to build up the pressure and make the ensuing explosion a whole lot worse.

The witches didn't stop until they were out of sight of the gate.

'Now, Esme,' said Nanny soothingly, 'you shouldn't take it personal. And we are a bit mucky, you must admit. They were just doing their job, all right? How about that?'

'They treated us as if we was *ordinary people*,' said Granny, in a shocked voice.

'This *is* foreign parts, Granny,' said Magrat. 'Anyway, you said the men on the boat didn't recognise the hat, either.'

'But then I didn't want 'em to,' said Granny. 'That's different.'

'It's just an . . . an incident, Granny,' said Magrat. 'They were just stupid soldiers. They don't even know a proper free-form hairstyle when they see it.'

Nanny looked around. Crowds milled past them, almost in silence.

'And you must admit it's a nice clean city,' she said.

They took stock of their surroundings.

It was certainly the cleanest place they'd ever seen. Even the cobblestones had a polished look.

'You could eat your tea off the street,' said Nanny, as they strolled along.

'Yes, but you'd eat your tea off the street anyway,' said Granny.

'I wouldn't eat all of it. Even the gutters are scrubbed. Not a Ronald* in sight, look.'

'Gytha!'

Well, you *said* that in Ankh-Morpork – '

'This is somewhere else!'

'It's so spotless,' said Magrat. 'Makes you wish you'd cleaned your sandals.'

'Yeah.' Nanny Ogg squinted along the street. 'Makes you wish you were a better person, really.'

'Why are you two whispering?' said Granny.

She followed their gaze. There was a guard standing on the street corner. When he saw them looking at him he touched his helmet and gave them a brief smile.

'Even the guards are polite,' said Magrat.

'And there's so many of them, too,' said Granny.

* Ronald the Third of Lancre, believed to be an extremely unpleasant monarch, was remembered by posterity only in this obscure bit of rhyming slang.

'Amazing, really, needing all these guards in a city where people are so clean and quiet,' said Magrat.

'Perhaps there's so much niceness to be spread around they need a lot of people to do it,' said Nanny Ogg.

The witches wandered through the packed streets.

'Nice houses, though,' said Magrat. 'Very decorative and olde-worlde.'

Granny Weatherwax, who lived in a cottage that was as olde-worlde as it was possible to be without being a lump of metamorphic rock, made no comment.

Nanny Ogg's feet started to complain.

'We ought to find somewhere to stop the night,' she said. 'We can look for this girl in the morning. We'll all do a lot better for a good night's sleep.'

'And a bath,' said Magrat. 'With soothing herbs.'

'Good idea. I could just go a bath too,' said Nanny.

'My word, doesn't autumn roll around quickly,' said Granny sourly.

'Yeah? When did *you* last have a bath, Esme?'

'What do you mean, *last*?'

'See? Then there's no call to make comments about my ablutions.'

'Baths is unhygienic,' Granny declard. 'You know I've never agreed with baths. Sittin' around in your own dirt like that.'

'What do *you* do, then?' said Magrat.

'I just washes,' said Granny. 'All the bits. You know. As and when they becomes available.'

However available they were, and no further information was vouchsafed on this point, they were certainly more available than accommodation in Genua in Fat Lunchtime.

All the taverns and inns were more than full. Gradually the press of crowds pushed them out of the main streets and into the less fashionable quarters of the city, but still there was no room for the three of them.

Granny Weatherwax had had enough.

'The very next place we see,' she said, setting her jaw firmly, 'we're goin' in. What's that inn over there?'

Nanny Ogg peered at the sign.

'Hotel . . . No . . . Va . . . cancies,' she muttered, and then brightened up. 'Hotel Nova Cancies,' she repeated. 'That means "new, er, Cancies" in foreign,' she added helpfully.

'It'll do,' said Granny.

She pushed open the door. A round, red-faced man looked up from the desk. He was new to the job and very nervous; the last incumbent had disappeared for not being round and red-faced enough.

Granny didn't waste time.

'You see this hat?' she demanded. 'You see this broom?'

The man looked from her to the broom, and back again.

'Yes?' he said. 'What's that mean?'

'Means we want three rooms for the night,' said Granny, looking smugly at the other two.

'With sausage,' said Nanny.

'And one vegetarian meal,' said Magrat.

The man looked at all three of them. Then he went over to the door.

'You see this door? You see this sign?' he said.

'We don't bother about signs,' said Granny.

'Well, then,' said the man, 'I give up. What's a pointy hat and a broom really mean?'

'That means I'm a witch,' said Granny.

The man put his head on one side.

'Yeah?' he said. 'Is that another word for daft old woman?'

Dear Jason and everyone, wrote Nanny Ogg, Dyou know, they dont know about witches here, thats how bakcward they are in foreign parts. A man gave Esme some Cheek and she would of lost her Temper so me and Magrat and I got hold of her and rushed her out because if you make someone think they've been turned into something there's always trouble, you remember what happened larst time when afterwards you had to go and dig a pond for Mr Wilkins to live in . . .

They had managed to find a table to themselves in a tavern. It was packed with people of all species. The noise was at shouting level and smoke wreathed the air.

'Will you stop that scribbling, Gytha Ogg. It gets on my nerves,' snapped Granny.

'They *must* have witches here,' said Magrat. 'Everywhere has witches. You've got to have witches abroad. You find witches everywhere.'

'Like cockroaches,' said Nanny Ogg cheerfully.

'You should've let me make him believe he was a frog,' muttered Granny.

'You can't do that, Esme. You can't go around making people believe they're things just because they've been cheeky and don't know who you are,' said Gytha. 'Otherwise we'd be up to here in people hopping about.'

Despite many threats, Granny Weatherwax had never turned anyone into a frog. The way she saw it, there was a technically less cruel but cheaper and much more satisfying thing you could do. You could leave them human and make them *think* they were a frog, which also provided much innocent entertainment for passers-by.

'I always felt sorry for Mr Wilkins,' said Magrat, staring moodily at the table top. 'It was so sad watching him try to catch flies on his tongue.'

'He shouldn't have said what he said,' said Granny.

'What, that you were a domineering old busybody?' said Nanny innocently.

'I don't mind criticism,' said Granny. 'You know me. I've never been one to take offence at criticism. No one could say I'm the sort to take offence at criticism – '

'Not twice, anyway,' said Nanny. 'Not without blowing bubbles.'

'It's just that I can't stand unfairness,' said Granny. 'And you stop that grinning! Anyway, I don't see why you're making a fuss about it. It wore off after a couple of days.'

'Mrs Wilkins says he still goes out swimming a lot,' said Magrat. 'It's given him a whole new interest, she said.'

'Perhaps they have a different kind of witch in the city,' said Magrat hopelessly. 'Perhaps they wear different sort of clothes.'

'There's only one kind of witch,' said Granny. 'And we're it.'

She looked around the room. Of course, she thought, if someone was keeping witches out, people *wouldn't* know about them. Someone who didn't want anyone else meddling here. But she let us in . . .

'Oh, well, at least we're in the dry,' said Nanny. A drinker standing in a crowd behind her threw back his head to laugh and spilled beer down her back.

She muttered something under her breath.

Magrat saw the man look down to take another swig and stare, wide-eyed, into the mug. Then he dropped it and fought his way out of the room, clutching at his throat.

'What did you do to his drink?' she said.

'You ain't old enough to be tole,' said Nanny.

At home, if a witch wanted a table to herself it . . . just happened. The sight of the pointy hat was enough. People kept a polite distance, occasionally sending free drinks to her. Even Magrat got respect, not particularly because anyone was in awe of her, but because a slight to one witch was a slight to all witches and no one wanted Granny Weatherwax coming around to explain this to them. Here they were being *jostled*, as if they were *ordinary*. Only Nanny Ogg's warning hand on Granny Weatherwax's arm was keeping a dozen jovial drinkers from unnatural amphibianhood, and even Nanny's usually very elastic temper was beginning to twang. She

always prided herself on being as ordinary as muck, but there was ordinary
and there was ordinary. It was like being that Prince Whatsisname, in the
nursery story, who liked to wander around his kingdom dressed up as a
commoner, she'd always had a shrewd suspicion that the little pervert
made sure people knew who he was beforehand, just in case anyone tried
to get too common. It was like getting muddy. Getting muddy when you
had a nice hot tub to look forward to was fun; getting muddy when all you
had to look forward to was more mud was no fun at all. She reached a
conclusion.

'Hey, why don't we have a drink?' said Nanny Ogg brightly. 'We'd all
feel better for a drink.'

'Oh no,' said Granny. 'You caught me with that herbal drink last time.
I'm sure there was alcohol in that. I def'nitely felt a bit woozy after the sixth
glass. I ain't drinking any more foreign muck.'

'You've got to drink something,' said Magrat soothingly. 'I'm thirsty,
anyway.' She looked vaguely at the crowded bar. 'Perhaps they do some
kind of fruit cup, or something.'

'Bound to,' said Nanny Ogg. She stood up, glanced at the bar, and
surreptitiously removed a hatpin from her hat. 'Shan't be a moment.'

The two of them were left in their own private gloom. Granny sat staring
fixedly in front of her.

'You really shouldn't take it so bad, just because people aren't showing
you any respect,' said Magrat, pouring soothing oil on the internal fires.
'They've hardly ever shown me any respect at all. It's not a problem.'

'If you ain't got respect, you ain't got a thing,' said Granny distantly.

'Oh, I don't know. I've always managed to get along,' said Magrat.

'That's 'cos you're a wet hen, Magrat Garlick,' said Granny.

There was a short, hot silence, ringing with the words that shouldn't have
escaped and a few grunts of pained surprise from the direction of the bar.

I know she's always thought that, Magrat told herself within the glowing
walls of her embarrassment. I just never thought she'd ever say it. And she'll
never say sorry, because that's not the kind of thing she does. She just
expects people to forget things like that. I was just trying to be friends again.
If she ever really has any friends.

'Here we are then,' said Nanny Ogg, emerging from the crush with a tray.
'Fruit drinks.'

She sat down and looked from one to the other.

'Made from bananas,' she said, in the hope of striking a spark of interest
from either woman. 'I remember our Shane brought a banana home once.
My, we had a good laugh about that. I said to the man, "What kind of fruit
drinks do people drink around here?" and this is what he gave me. Made

from bananas. A banana drink. You'll like it. It's what everyone drinks here. It's got bananas in it.'

'It's certainly very . . . strongly flavoured,' said Magrat, sipping hers cautiously. 'Has it got sugar in it too?'

'Very likely,' said Nanny. She looked at Granny's middle-distance frown for a moment, and then picked up her pencil and licked the end profession-ally.

Anywey one good thing is the drink here is v. cheap theres this one called a Bananana dakry which is basicly Rum with a banananana* in it. I can feel it doin me good. It is v. damp here. I hope we find somewhere to stay tonigt I expect we shal becaus Esme alweys falls on her feet or at any rate on someones feet. I have drawern a picture of a banananana dakry you can see it is empty right down to the bottom. Love, MUM XXXX

In the end they found a stable. It was, as Nanny Ogg cheerfully commented, probably warmer and more hygienic than any of the inns and there were millions of people in foreign parts who'd give their right arms for such a comfy, dry place to sleep.

This cut about as much ice as a soap hacksaw.

It doesn't take much to make witches fall out.

Magrat lay awake, using her sack of clothes as a pillow and listening to the warm soft rain on the roof.

It's all gone wrong before we've even started, she thought. I don't know why I let them come with me. I'm perfectly capable of doing something by myself for once, but they always treat me as if I was a . . . a wet hen. I don't see why I should have to put up with *her* sulking and snapping at me the whole time. What's so special about her, anyway? She hardly ever does anything really magical, whatever Nanny says. She really *does* just shout a lot and bully people. And as for Nanny, she means well but she has no sense of responsibility, I thought I'd *die* when she started singing the Hedgehog Song in the inn, I just hope to goodness the people didn't know what the words meant.

I'm the fairy godmother around here. We're not at home now. There's got to be different ways of doing things, in foreign parts.

She got up at first light. The other two were asleep, although 'asleep' was too moderate a word for the sounds Granny Weatherwax was making.

---

* Nanny Ogg knew how to start spelling 'banana', but didn't know how you stopped.

Magrat put on her best dress, the green silk one that was unfortunately now a mass of creases. She took out a bundle of tissue paper and slowly unwrapped her occult jewellery; Magrat bought occult jewellery as a sort of distraction from being Magrat. She had three large boxes of the stuff and was still exactly the same person.

She did her best to remove the straw from her hair. Then she unpacked the magic wand.

She wished she had a mirror to inspect herself in.

'I've got the wand,' she said quietly. 'I don't see why I need any help. Desiderata *said* I was to tell them not to help.'

It crossed her mind to reflect that Desiderata had been very lax on that point. The one thing you could be sure of if you told Granny Weatherwax and Nanny Ogg not to help, was that they would rush to help if only out of spite. It was quite surprising to Magrat that anyone as clever as Desiderata should have slipped up on that minor point. She'd probably got a psychology too – whatever *that* was.

Moving quietly, so as not to wake the other two, she opened the door and stepped lightly into the damp air. Wand at the ready, she was prepared to give the world whatever it wished for.

It would help if this included pumpkins.

Nanny Ogg opened one eye as the door creaked shut.

She sat up and yawned and scratched herself. She fumbled in her hat and retrieved her pipe. She nudged Granny Weatherwax in the ribs.

'I ain't asleep,' said Granny.

'Magrat's gone off somewhere.'

'Hah!'

'And I'm going out to get something to eat,' muttered Nanny. There was no talking to Esme when she was in that kind of mood.

As she stepped out Greebo dropped lightly off a beam and landed on her shoulder.

Nanny Ogg, one of life's great optimists, stepped out to take whatever the future had to offer.

Preferably with rum and bananas in it.

The house wasn't hard to find. Desiderata had made very exact notes.

Magrat's gaze took in the high white walls and ornate metal balconies. She tried to straighten a few wrinkles in her dress, tugged some recalcitrant bits of hay from her hair, and then marched up the driveway and knocked on the door.

The knocker broke off in her hand.

Looking around anxiously lest someone should have noted this vandalism, Magrat tried to wedge it back. It fell off, knocking a lump out of the marble step.

Finally she knocked gently with her knuckle. A fine cloud of paint dust lifted off the door and floated down to the ground. That was the only effect.

Magrat considered her next move. She was pretty sure that fairy godmothers weren't supposed to leave a little card pushed under the door saying something like 'Called today but you were out, please contact the depot for a further appointment.' Anyway, this wasn't the kind of house that got left empty; there would be a score of servants infesting a place like this.

She crunched over the gravel and peered around the side of the house. Maybe the back door . . . witches were generally more at home around back doors . . .

Nanny Ogg always was. She was heading for the one belonging to the palace. It was easy enough to get into; this wasn't a castle like the ones back home, which expressed very clear ideas about inside and outside and were built to keep the two separate. This was, well, a fairy-tale castle, all icing-sugar battlements and tiny, towering turrets. Anyway, no one took much notice of little old ladies. Little old ladies were by definition harmless, although in a string of villages across several thousand miles of continent this definition was currently being updated.

Castles, in Nanny Ogg's experience, were like swans. They looked as if they were drifting regally through the waters of Time, but in fact there was a hell of a lot of activity going on underneath. There'd be a maze of pantries and kitchens and laundries and stables and breweries – she liked the idea of breweries – and people never noticed another old biddy around the place, eating any spare grub that was lying around.

Besides, you got gossip. Nanny Ogg liked gossip, too.

Granny Weatherwax wandered disconsolately along the clean streets. She wasn't looking for the other two. She was quite certain of that. Of course, she might just happen to bump into them, sort of accidentally, and give them a meaningful look. But she certainly wasn't looking for them.

There was a crowd at the end of the street. Working on the reasonable assumption that Nanny Ogg might be in the middle of it, Granny Weatherwax drifted over.

Nanny wasn't there. But there was a raised platform. And a small man in chains. And some bright-uniformed guards. One of them was holding an axe.

You did not have to be a great world traveller to understand that the purpose of this tableau was not to give the chained man a signed testimonial and a collection from everyone at the office.

Granny nudged a bystander.

'What's happening?'

The man looked sideways at her.

'The guards caught him thieving,' he said.

'Ah. Well, he looks guilty enough,' said Granny. People in chains had a tendency to look guilty. 'So what're they going to do to him?'

'Teach him a lesson.'

'How d'they do that, then?'

'See the axe?'

Granny's eyes hadn't left it the whole time. But now she let her attention rove over the crowd, picking up scraps of thought.

An ant has an easy mind to read. There's just one stream of big simple thoughts: Carry, Carry, Bite, Get Into The Sandwiches, Carry, Eat. Something like a dog is more complicated – a dog can be thinking several thoughts at the same time. But a human mind is a great sullen lightning-filled cloud of thoughts, all of them occupying a finite amount of brain processing time. Finding whatever the owner *thinks* they're thinking in the middle of the smog of prejudices, memories, worries, hopes and fears is almost impossible.

But enough people thinking much the same thing can be heard, and Granny Weatherwax was aware of the fear.

'Looks like it'll be a lesson he won't forget in a hurry,' she murmured.

'I reckon he'll forget it quite quickly,' said the watcher, and then shuffled away from Granny, in the same way that people move away from lightning rods during a thunderstorm.

And at this point Granny picked up the discordant note in the orchestra of thought. In the middle of it were two minds that were not human.

Their shape was as simple, clean and purposeful as a naked blade. She'd felt minds like that before, and had never cherished the experience.

She scanned the crowd and found the minds' owners. They were staring unblinkingly at the figures on the platform.

The watchers were women, or at least currently the same shape as women; taller than she was, slender as sticks, and wearing broad hats with veils that covered their faces. Their dresses shimmered in the sunlight – possibly blue, possibly yellow, possibly green. Possibly patterned. It was impossible to tell. The merest movement changed the colours.

She couldn't make out their faces.

There were witches in Genua all right. One witch, anyway.

A sound from the platform made her turn.

And she knew why people in Genua were quiet and nice.

There were countries in foreign parts, Granny had heard, where they chopped off the hands of thieves so that they wouldn't steal again. And she'd never been happy with that idea.

They didn't do that in Genua. They cut their heads off so they wouldn't *think* of stealing again.

Granny knew exactly where the witches were in Genua now.

They were in charge.

Magrat reached the house's back door. It was ajar.

She pulled herself together again.

She knocked, in a polite, diffident sort of way.

Er – ' she said.

A bowlful of dirty water hit her full in the face. Through the tidal roaring of a pair of ears full of suds, she heard a voice say, 'Gosh, I'm sorry. I didn't know anyone was standing there.'

Magrat wiped the water out of her eyes, and tried to focus on the dim figure in front of her. A kind of narrative certainty rose in her mind.

'Is your name Ella?' she said.

'That's right. Who're you?'

Magrat looked her new-found god-daughter up and down. She was the most attractive young woman Magrat had ever seen – skin as brown as a nut, hair so blonde as to be almost white, a combination not totally unusual in such an easy going city as Genua had once been.

What were you supposed to say at a time like this?

She removed a piece of potato peel from her nose.

'I'm your fairy godmother,' she said. 'Funny thing, it sounds silly now I come to tell someone – '

Ella peered at her.

'*You?*'

'Um. Yes. I've got the wand, and everything.' Magrat waggled the wand, in case this helped. It didn't.

Ella put her head on one side.

'I thought you people were supposed to appear in a shower of glittering little lights and a twinkly noise,' she said suspiciously.

'Look, you just get the wand,' said Magrat desperately. 'You don't get a whole book of instructions.'

Ella gave her another searching look. Then she said, 'I suppose you'd better come in, then. You're just in time. I was making a cup of tea, anyway.'

The iridescent women got into an open-topped carriage. Beautiful as they were, Granny noted, they walked awkwardly.

Well, they would. They wouldn't be used to legs.

She also noticed the way people didn't look at the carriage. It wasn't that they didn't see it. It was simply that they wouldn't let their gaze dwell on it, as if merely recognising it would lead them into trouble.

And she noticed the coach horses. They had better senses than the humans did. They knew what was behind them, and they didn't like it at all.

She followed them as they trotted, flat-eared and wild-eyed, through the streets. Eventually they were driven into the driveway of a big and dilapidated house near the palace.

Granny lurked by the wall and noted the details. Plaster was dropping off the house walls, and even the knocker had fallen off the door.

Granny Weatherwax did not believe in atmospheres. She did not believe in psychic auras. Being a witch, she'd always thought, depended more on what you *didn't* believe. But she was prepared to believe that there was something very unpleasant in that house. Not *evil*. The two not-exactly-women weren't evil, in the same way that a dagger or a sheer cliff isn't evil. Being evil means being able to make choices. But the hand wielding a dagger or pushing a body over a cliff could be evil, and something like that was going on.

She really wished that she didn't know who was behind it.

People like Nanny Ogg turn up everywhere. It's as if there's some special morphic generator dedicated to the production of old women who like a laugh and aren't averse to the odd pint, especially of some drink normally sold in very small glasses. You find them all over the place, often in pairs.*

They tend to attract one another. Possibly they broadcast inaudible signals indicating that here is someone who could be persuaded to go 'Ooo' at pictures of other people's grandchildren.

Nanny Ogg had found a friend. Her name was Mrs Pleasant, she was a

---

* Always in front of you in any queue for a start.

cook, and she was the first black person Nanny had ever spoken to.* She was also a cook of that very superior type who spends most of the time holding court in a chair in the centre of the kitchen, apparently taking very little heed of the activity going on around her.

Occasionally she'd give an order. And they'd only need to be occasionally, because she'd seen to it over the years that people either did things her way or not at all. Once or twice, with some ceremony, she'd get up, taste something, and maybe add a pinch of salt.

Such people are always ready to chat to any wandering pedlars, herbalists, or little old women with cats on their shoulders. Greebo rode on Nanny's shoulder as though he'd just eaten the parrot.

'You be a-comin' here for Fat Lunchtime, then?' said Mrs Pleasant.

'Helping a friend with a bit of business,' said Nanny. 'My, these biscuits are tasty.'

'I means, I see by your eye,' said Mrs Pleasant, pushing the plate nearer to her, 'that you are of a magical persuasion.'

'Then you sees a lot further than most people in these parts,' said Nanny. 'Y'know, what'd improve these biscuits no end'd be something to dip 'em in, what d'you think?'

'How 'bout something with bananas in it?'

'Bananas would be just the thing,' said Nanny happily. Mrs Pleasant waved imperiously at one of the maids, who set to work.

Nanny sat on her chair, swinging her stumpy legs and looking around the kitchen with interest. A score of cooks were working with the single-mindedness of an artillery platoon laying down a barrage. Huge cakes were being constructed. In the fireplaces whole carcasses of animals were being roasted; turnspit dogs galloped in their treadmills. A huge man with a bald head and a scar right across his face was patiently inserting little sticks into sausages.

Nanny hadn't had any breakfast. Greebo *had* had some breakfast, but this didn't make any difference. They were both undergoing a sort of exquisite culinary torture.

They both turned, as if hypnotised, to watch two maids stagger by under a tray of canapés.

'I can see you is a very observant woman, Mrs Ogg,' said Mrs Pleasant.

'Just a slice,' said Nanny, without thinking.

'I also determines,' Mrs Pleasant said, after a while, 'that you have a cat of no usual breed upon your shoulder there.'

---

* Racism was not a problem on the Discworld, because – what with trolls and dwarfs and so on – speciesism was more interesting. Black and white lived in perfect harmony and ganged up on green.

'You're right there.'

'I knows I'm right.'

A brimming glass of yellow foam was slid in front of Nanny. She looked at it reflectively and tried to get back to the matter in hand.

'So,' she said, 'where would I go, do you think, to find out about how you do magic in – '

'Would you like somethin' to eat?' said Mrs Pleasant.

'What? My word!'

Mrs Pleasant rolled her eyes.

'Not this stuff. I wouldn't eat this stuff,' she said bitterly.

Nanny's face fell.

'But you cook it,' she pointed out.

'Only 'cos I'm *told* to. The old baron knew what good food was. This stuff? It's nothing but pork and beef and lamb and rubbish for them that never tasted anything better. The only thing on four legs that's worth eating is alligator. I mean *real* food.'

Mrs Pleasant looked around at the kitchen.

'Sara!' she shouted.

One of the sub-cooks turned around.

'Yes, 'm?'

'Me and this lady is just going out. Just you see to everything, okay?'

'Yes, 'm.'

Mrs Pleasant stood up and nodded meaningfully at Nanny Ogg.

'Walls have ears,' she said.

'Coo! Do they?'

'We goin' to go for a little stroll.'

There were, it now seemed to Nanny Ogg, two cities in Genua. There was the white one, all new houses and blue-roofed palaces, and around it and even under it was the old one. The new one might not like the presence of the old one, but it couldn't quite ever do without it. Someone, somewhere, has to do the cooking.

Nanny Ogg quite liked cooking, provided there were other people around to do things like chop up the vegetables and wash the dishes afterwards. She'd always reckoned that she could do things to a bit of beef that the bullock had never thought of. But now she realised that wasn't cooking. Not compared to cooking in Genua. It was just staying alive as pleasantly as possible. Cooking anywhere outside Genua was just heating up things like bits of animals and birds and fish and vegetables until they went brown.

And yet the weird thing was that the cooks in Genua had nothing edible to cook; at least, not what Nanny would have thought of as food. To her mind, food went around on four legs, or possibly one pair of legs and one pair of wings. Or at least it had fins on. The idea of food with more than four legs was an entirely new kettle of fi– of miscellaneous swimming things.

They didn't have much to cook in Genua. So they cooked *everything*. Nanny had never heard of prawns or crawfish or lobsters; it just looked to her as though the citizens of Genua dredged the river bottom and boiled whatever came up.

The point was that a good Genuan cook could more or less take the squeezings of a handful of mud, a few dead leaves and a pinch or two of some unpronounceable herbs and produce a meal to make a gourmet burst into tears of gratitude and swear to be a better person for the rest of their entire life if they could just have one more plateful.

Nanny Ogg ambled along as Mrs Pleasant led her through the market. She peered at cages of snakes, and racks of mysteriously tendrilled herbs. She prodded trays of bivalves. She stopped for a chat to the Nanny Ogg-shaped ladies who ran the little stalls that, for a couple of pennies, dispensed strange chowders and shellfish in a bun. She sampled everything. She was enjoying herself immensely. Genua, city of cooks, had found the appetite it deserved.

She finished a plate of fish and exchanged a nod and a grin with the little old woman who ran the fish stall.

'Well, all this is – ' she began, turning to Mrs Pleasant.

Mrs Pleasant had gone.

Some people would have bustled off to look for her in the crowds, but Nanny Ogg just stood and thought.

I asked about magic, she thought, and she brought me here and left me. Because of them walls with ears in, I expect. So maybe I got to do the rest myself.

She looked around her. There was a very rough tent a little way from the stalls, right by the river. There was no sign outside it, but there was a pot bubbling gently over a fire. Rough clay bowls were stacked beside the pot. Occasionally someone would step out of the crowd, help themselves to a bowlful of whatever was in the pot, and then throw a handful of coins into the plate in front of the tent.

Nanny wandered over and looked into the pot. Things came to the surface and sank again. The general colour was brown. Bubbles formed, grew, and burst stickily with an organic 'blop'. Anything could be happening in that pot. Life could be spontaneously creating.

Nanny Ogg would try anything once. Some things she'd try several thousand times.

She unhooked the ladle, picked up a bowl, and helped herself.

A moment later she pushed aside the tent flap and looked into the blackness of the interior.

A figure was seated cross-legged in the gloom, smoking a pipe.

'Mind if I step inside?' said Nanny.

The figure nodded.

Nanny sat down. After a decent interval she pulled out her own pipe.

'Mrs Pleasant's a friend of yours, I expect.'

'She knows me.'

'Ah.'

From outside, there was the occasional clink as customers helped themselves.

Blue smoke coiled from Nanny Ogg's pipe.

'I don't reckon,' she said, 'that many people goes away without paying.'

'No.'

After another pause Nanny Ogg said: 'I 'spects some of 'em tries to pay with gold and jewels and scented ungulants and stuff like that?'

'No.'

'Amazin'.'

Nanny Ogg sat in silence for a while, listening to the distant noises of the market and summoning her powers.

'What's it called?'

'Gumbo.'

'It's good.'

'I know.'

'I reckon anyone who could cook like that could do anything' – Nanny Ogg concentrated – 'Mrs . . . Gogol.'

She waited.

'Pretty near, Mrs Ogg.'

The two women stared at one another's shadowy outline, like plotters who had given the sign and countersign and were waiting to see what would happen next.

'Where I come from, we call it witchcraft,' said Nanny, under her breath.

'Where I come from, we call it voodoo,' said Mrs Gogol.

Nanny's wrinkled forehead wrinkled still further.

'Ain't that all messin' with dolls and dead people and stuff?' she said.

'Ain't witchcraft all runnin' around with no clothes on and stickin' pins in people?' said Mrs Gogol levelly.

'Ah,' said Nanny. 'I sees what you mean.'

She shifted uneasily. She was a fundamentally honest woman.

'I got to admit, though . . . ' she added, 'sometimes . . . maybe just one pin . . . '

Mrs Gogol nodded gravely. 'Okay. Sometimes . . . maybe just one zombie,' she said.

'But only when there ain't no alternative.'

'Sure. When there ain't no alternative.'

'When . . . you know . . . people ain't showing respect, like.'

'When the house needs paintin'.'

Nanny grinned, toothily. Mrs Gogol grinned, outnumbering her in teeth by a factor of thirty.

'My full name's Gytha Ogg,' she said. 'People calls me Nanny.'

'My full name's Erzulie Gogol,' said Mrs Gogol. 'People call me Mrs Gogol.'

'The way I saw it,' said Nanny, 'this is foreign parts, so maybe there's a *different* kind of magic. Stands to reason. The trees is different, the people is different, the drinks is different and has got banana in 'em, so the magic'd be different too. Then I thought . . . Gytha, my girl, you're never too old to learn.'

'Sure thing.'

'There's something wrong with this city. Felt it as soon as we set foot here.'

Mrs Gogol nodded.

There was no sound for a while but the occasional puffing of a pipe.

Then there was a clink from outside, followed by a thoughtful pause.

A voice said, 'Gytha Ogg? I know you're in there.'

The outline of Mrs Gogol took its pipe out of its mouth.

'That's good,' she said. 'Good sense of taste there.'

The tent flap opened.

'Hallo, Esme,' said Nanny Ogg.

'Blessings be on this . . . tent,' said Granny Weatherwax, peering into the gloom.

'This here's Mrs Gogol,' said Nanny. 'She's by way of bein' a voodoo lady. That's what witches are in these parts.'

'They ain't the only witches in *these* parts,' said Granny.

'Mrs Gogol was very impressed at you detecting me in here,' said Nanny.

'It wasn't hard,' said Granny. 'Once I'd spotted that Greebo washing himself outside, the rest was all deduction.'

In the gloom of the tent Nanny had formed a mental picture of Mrs Gogol as being old. What she hadn't expected, when the voodoo lady stepped out into the open air, was a handsome middle-aged woman taller than Granny. Mrs Gogol wore heavy gold earrings, a white blouse and a full red skirt with flounces. Nanny could feel Granny Weatherwax's disapproval. What they said about women with red skirts was even worse than whatever they said about women with red shoes, whatever *that* was.

Mrs Gogol stopped and raised an arm. There was a flurry of wings.

Greebo, who had been rubbing obsequiously against Nanny's leg, looked up and hissed. The largest and blackest cockerel Nanny had ever seen had settled on Mrs Gogol's shoulder. It turned on her the most intelligent stare she had ever seen on a bird.

'My word,' she said, taken aback. 'That's the biggest cock I've ever seen, and I've seen a few in my time.'

Mrs Gogol raised one disapproving eyebrow.

'She never had no proper upbringing,' said Granny.

'What with living next to a chicken farm and all, *is what I was going to say next*,' said Nanny.

'This is Legba, a dark and dangerous spirit,' said Mrs Gogol. She leaned closer and spoke out of the corner of her mouth. 'Between you and me, he just a big black cockerel. But you know how it is.'

'It pays to advertise,' Nanny agreed. 'This is Greebo. Between you and me, he's a fiend from hell.'

'Well, he's a cat,' said Mrs Gogol, generously. 'It's only to be expected.'

Dear Jason and everyone,
Isn't it amazing the things what happen when you dont expect it, for example we met Mrs Gogol who works as a coke by day but is a Voodoo witch, you mustnt beleive all the stuff about black magic, exetra, this is a Blind, shes just like us only different. Its true about the zombies though but its not what you think . . .

Genua was a strange city, Nanny decided. You got off the main streets, walked along a side road, went through a little gate and suddenly there were trees everywhere, with moss and them llamas hanging from them, and the ground began to wobble underfoot and become swamp. On either side of the track there were dark pools in which, here and there, among the lilies, were the kind of logs the witches had never seen before.

'Them's bloody big newts,' she said.

'They're alligators.'

'By gods. They must get good grub.'

'Yeah!'

Mrs Gogol's house itself looked a simple affair of driftwood from the river, roofed with moss and built out over the swamp itself on four stout poles. It was close enough to the centre of the city that Nanny could hear street cries and the clip-clop of hooves, but the shack in its little swamp was wreathed in silence.

'Don't people bother you here?' said Nanny.

'Not them as I don't want to meet.' The lily pads moved. A v-shaped ripple drifted across the nearest pool.

'Self-reliance,' said Granny approvingly. 'That's always very important.'

Nanny regarded the reptiles with a calculating stare. They tried to match it, and gave up when their eyes started watering.

'I reckon I could just do with a couple of them at home,' she said thoughtfully as they slid away again. 'Our Jason could dig another pond, no problem. What was it you said they et?'

'Anything they want to.'

'I knows a joke about alligators,' said Granny, in the tones of one announcing a great and solemn truth.

'You never!' said Nanny Ogg. 'I never heard you tell a joke in your whole life!'

'Just because I don't *tell* 'em don't mean I don't *know* 'em,' said Granny haughtily. 'It's about this man – '

'What man?' said Nanny.

'*This man* went into an inn. Yes. It was an inn. And he saw a sign. The sign said "We serve every kind of sandwich." So he said "Get me an alligator sandwich – and make it quick!" '

They looked at her.

Nanny Ogg turned to Mrs Gogol.

'So . . . you live alone here, then?' she said brightly. 'Not a living soul around?'

'In a manner of speakin',' said Mrs Gogol.

'You see, the point is, alligators are – ' Granny began, in a loud voice, and then stopped.

The shack's door had opened.

This was another big kitchen.* Once upon a time it had provided employment for half a dozen cooks. Now it was a cave, its far corners shadowy, its hanging saucepans and tureens dulled by dust. The big tables had been pushed to one side and stacked almost ceiling high with ancient crockery; the stoves, which looked big enough to take whole cows and cook for an army, stood cold.

In the middle of the grey desolation someone had set up a small table by

---

* As Desiderata said, fairy godmothers tend to get heavily involved with kitchens.

the fireplace. It was on a square of bright carpet. A jam-jar contained flowers that had been arranged by the simple method of grabbing a handful of them and ramming them in. The effect was a little area of slightly soppy brightness in the general gloom.

Ella shuffled a few things around desperately and then stood looking at Magrat with a sort of defensively shy smile.

'Silly of me, really. I expect you're used to this sort of thing,' she said.

'Um. Yes. Oh, yes. All the time,' said Magrat.

'It was just that I expected you to be a bit . . . older? Apparently you were at my christening?'

'Ah. Yes?' said Magrat. 'Well, you see, the thing is – '

'Still, I expect you can look like whatever you want,' said Ella helpfully.

'Ah. Yes. Er.'

Ella looked slightly puzzled for a moment, as if trying to work out why – if Magrat could look like whatever she wanted – she'd chosen to look like Magrat.

'Well, now,' she said. 'What do we do next?'

'You mentioned tea,' said Magrat, buying time.

'Oh, sure.' Ella turned to the fireplace, where a blackened kettle hung over what Granny Weatherwax always called an optimist's fire.*

'What's your name?' she said over her shoulder.

'Magrat,' said Magrat, sitting.

'That's a . . . nice name,' said Ella, politely. 'Of course, you know mine. Mind you, I spend so much time cooking over this wretched thing now that Mrs Pleasant calls me Embers. Silly, isn't it.'

Emberella, thought Magrat. I'm fairy godmothering a girl who sounds like something you put up in the rain.

'It could use a little work,' she conceded.

'I haven't the heart to tell her off, she thinks it sounds jolly,' she said. 'I think it sounds like something you put up in the rain.'

'Oh, I wouldn't say that,' said Magrat. 'Uh. Who's Mrs Pleasant?'

'She's the cook at the palace. She comes around to cheer me up when they're out . . . '

Ella spun around, holding the blackened kettle like a weapon.

'I'm *not* going to that ball!' she snapped. 'I'm *not* going to marry the prince! Do you understand?'

The words came out like steel ingots.

'Right! Right!' said Magrat, taken aback by their force.

* Two logs and hope.

'He looks slimy. He makes my flesh crawl,' said Embers darkly. 'They say he's got funny eyes. And everyone knows what he does at night!'

Everyone bar one, Magrat thought. No one ever tells me things like that.

Aloud, she said: 'Well, it shouldn't be too much to arrange. I mean, normally it's *marrying* princes that's the hard bit.'

'Not for me it isn't,' said Embers. 'It's all *been* arranged. My other godmother says I've got to do it. She says it's my destiny.'

'Other godmother?' said Magrat.

'Everyone gets two,' said Ella. 'The good one and the bad one. You *know* that. Which one are you?'

Magrat's mind raced.

'Oh, the good one,' she said. 'Definitely.'

'Funny thing,' said Ella. 'That's just what the other one said, too.'

Granny Weatherwax sat in her special knees-clenched, elbow-in way that put as little as possible of herself in contact with the outside world.

'By gor', this is good stuff,' said Nanny Ogg, polishing her plate with what Granny could only hope was bread. 'You ought to try a drop, Esme.'

'Another helping, Mrs Ogg?' said Mrs Gogol.

'Don't mind if I do, Mrs Gogol.' Nanny nudged Granny in the ribs. 'It's really good, Esme. Just like stew.'

Mrs Gogol looked at Granny with her head on one side.

'I think perhaps Mistress Weatherwax isn't worried about the food,' she said. 'I think Mistress Weatherwax is worried about the service.'

A shadow loomed over Nanny Ogg. A grey hand took her plate away.

Granny Weatherwax gave a little cough.

'I've got nothing *against* dead people,' she said. 'Some of my best friends are dead. It just don't seem right, though, dead people walking about.'

Nanny Ogg looked up at the figure even now ladling a third helping of mysterious liquid on to her plate.

'What d'*you* think about it, Mr Zombie?'

'It's a great life, Mrs Ogg,' said the zombie.

'There. See, Esme? He don't mind. Better than being shut up in a stuffy coffin all day, I'll be bound.'

Granny looked up at the zombie. He was – or, technically, had *been* – a tall, handsome man. He still was, only now he looked like someone who had walked through a room full of cobwebs.

'What's your name, dead man?' she said.

'I am called Saturday.'

'Man Saturday, eh?' said Nanny Ogg.

'No. Just Saturday, Mrs Ogg. Just Saturday.'

Granny Weatherwax looked into his eyes. They were more sentient than most eyes she had seen that belonged to people who were, technically, alive.

She was vaguely aware that there were things you had to do to a dead person to turn them into a zombie, although it was a branch of magic she'd never wanted to investigate. Yet you needed more than just a lot of weird fish innards and foreign roots – the person had to *want* to come back. They had to have some terrible dream or desire or purpose that would enable them to overcome the grave itself . . .

Saturday's eyes *burned*.

She reached a decision. She held out a hand.

'Very pleased to meet you, Mister Saturday,' she said. 'And I'm sure I'd enjoy your lovely stew.'

'It's called gumbo,' said Nanny. 'It's got lady's fingers in it.'

'I know well enough that lady's fingers is a kind of plant, thank you very much,' said Granny. 'I'm not entirely ignorant.'

'All right, but make sure you get a helping with snakes' heads in it as well,' said Nanny Ogg. 'They're the best part.'

'What kind of plant is snakes' heads?'

'Best if you just eat up, I reckon,' said Nanny.

They were sitting on the warped wood veranda round the back of Mrs Gogol's shack, overlooking the swamp. Mossy beards hung from every branch. Unseen creatures buzzed in the greenery. And everywhere there were v-shaped ripples cutting gently through the water.

'I expect it's really nice here when the sun's out,' said Nanny.

Saturday trudged into the shack and returned with a makeshift fishing pole, which he baited and cast over the rail. Then he sort of switched off; no one has more patience than a zombie.

Mrs Gogol leaned back in her rocking-chair and lit her pipe.

'This used to be a great ole city,' she said.

'What happened to it?' said Nanny.

Greebo was having a lot of trouble with Legba the cockerel.

For one thing, the bird refused to be terrorised. Greebo could terrorise most things that moved upon the face of the Discworld, even creatures nominally much bigger and tougher than he was. Yet somehow none of his well-tried tactics – the yawn, the stare and above all the slow grin – seemed to work. Legba merely looked down his beak at him, and pretended to scratch at the ground in a way that brought his two-inch spurs into even greater prominence.

That only left the flying leap. This worked on nearly every creature. Very few animals remained calm in the face of an enraged ball of whirring claws in the face. In the case of this bird, Greebo suspected, it might well result in his becoming a furry kebab.

But this had to be resolved. Otherwise generations of cats would laugh at him.

Cat and bird circled through the swamp, each apparently paying the other no attention whatsoever.

Things gibbered in the trees. Small iridescent birds barrelled through the air. Greebo glared up at them. He would sort them out later.

And the cockerel had vanished.

Greebo's ears flattened against his head.

There was still the birdsong and the whine of insects, but they were elsewhere. Here there was silence – hot, dark and oppressive – and trees that were somehow much closer together than he remembered.

Greebo looked around.

He was in a clearing. Around its sides, hanging from bushes or tied to trees, were things. Bits of ribbon. White bones. Tin pots. Perfectly ordinary things, anywhere else.

And in the centre of the clearing, something like a scarecrow. An upright pole with a crosspiece, on which someone had put an old black coat. Above the coat, on the tip of the pole, was a top hat. On top of the hat, watching him thoughtfully, was Legba.

A breeze blew through the stifling air, causing the coat to flap gently.

Greebo remembered a day when he'd chased a rat into the village windmill and had suddenly found that what had seemed merely a room with odd furniture in it was a great big machine which would, if he put a paw wrong, crush him utterly.

The air sizzled gently. He could feel his fur standing on end.

Greebo turned and stalked away haughtily, until he judged himself out of sight, whereupon his legs spun so fast that his paws skidded.

Then he went and grinned at some alligators, but his heart wasn't in it.

In the clearing, the coat moved gently again and then was still. Somehow, that was worse.

Legba watched. The air grew heavier, just as it does before a storm.

'This used to be a great old city. A happy place. No one *tried* to make it happy. It just happened, all by itself,' said Mrs Gogol. 'That was when the old baron was alive. But he was murdered.'

'Who done it?' said Nanny Ogg.

'Everyone knows it was the Duc,' said Mrs Gogol.

The witches looked at one another. Royal intrigues were obviously a bit different in foreign parts.

'Pecked to death, was he?' said Nanny.

'A foul deed?' said Granny.

'The Duc is a title, not a bird,' said Mrs Gogol patiently. 'The Baron was poisoned. It was a terrible night. And, in the morning, the Duc was in the palace. Then there was the matter of the will.'

'Don't tell me,' said Granny. 'I bet there was a will leaving everything to this Duc. I bet the ink was still wet.'

'How did you know that?' said Mrs Gogol.

'Stands to reason,' said Granny loftily.

'The baron had a young daughter,' said Mrs Gogol.

'She'd be still alive, I reckon,' said Granny.

'You surely know a lot of things, lady,' said Mrs Gogol. 'Why'd you think that, then?'

'Well . . . ' said Granny. She was about to say: because I know how the stories work. But Nanny Ogg interrupted.

'If this baron was as great as you say, he must have had a lot of friends in the city, right?' she said.

'This is so. The people liked him.'

'Well, if I was a Duc with no more claim on things than a smudgy will and a little bottle of ink with the cork still out, I'd be lookin' for any chance to make things a bit more official,' said Nanny. 'Marryin' the real heir'd be favourite. He could thumb his nose at everyone, then. I bet she don't know who she really is, eh?'

'That's right,' said Mrs Gogol. 'The Duc's got friends, too. Or keepers, maybe. Not people you'd want to cross. They've brought her up, and they don't let her out much.'

The witches sat in silence for a while.

Granny thought: no. That's not quite right. That's how it'd appear in a history book. But that's not the *story*.

Then Granny said, ' 'Scuse me, Mrs Gogol, but where do you come in all this? No offence, but I reckon that out here in the swamp it'd be all the same whoever was doing the rulin'.'

For the first time since they'd met her, Mrs Gogol looked momentarily uneasy.

'The baron was . . . a friend of mine,' she said.

'Aha,' said Granny understandingly.

'He wasn't keen on zombies, mark you. He said he thought the dead should be allowed their rest. But he never insisted. Whereas this new one . . . '

'Not keen on the Interestin' Arts?' said Nanny.

'Oh, I reckon he is,' said Granny. 'He'd have to be. Not *your* magic, maybe, but I bet he's got a lot of magic around him.'

'Why d'you say that, lady?' said Mrs Gogol.

'Well,' said Nanny, 'I can see that you, being a lady o' spirit, wouldn't put up with this if you didn't have to. There's lots of ways to sort matters out, I 'spect. I 'spect, if you dint like someone, their legs might unexpectedly drop off, or they might find mysterious snakes in their boots . . .'

'Alleygators under their bed,' suggested Granny.

'Yes. He's got protection,' said Mrs Gogol.

'Ah.'

'Powerful magic.'

'More powerful'n you?' said Granny.

There was a long and difficult pause.

'Yes.'

'Ah.'

'For now,' Mrs Gogol added.

There was another pause. No witch ever liked admitting to less than near-absolute power, or even hearing another witch doing so.

'You're biding your time, I expect,' said Granny kindly.

'Wifing your strength,' said Nanny.

'It's powerful protection,' said Mrs Gogol.

Granny sat back in her chair. When she spoke next, it was as a person who has certain ideas in their mind and wants to find out what someone else knows.

'What sort?' she said. 'Exactly?'

Mrs Gogol reached into the cushions of her rocking-chair and, after some rummaging, produced a leather bag and a pipe. She lit the pipe and puffed a cloud of bluish smoke into the morning air.

'You look in mirrors a lot these days, Mistress Weatherwax?' she said.

Granny's chair tipped backwards, almost throwing her off the veranda and into the inky waters. Her hat flew away into the lily pads.

She had time to see it settle gently on the water. It floated for a moment and then –

– was eaten. A very large alligator snapped its jaws shut and gazed smugly at Granny.

It was a relief to have something to shout about.

'My hat! It *ate* my hat! One of your alleygators *ate* my *hat*! It was my *hat*! Make it give it back!'

She snatched a length of creeper off the nearest tree and flailed at the water.

Nanny Ogg backed away.

'You shouldn't do that, Esme! You shouldn't do that!' she quavered. The alligator backed water.

'I can hit cheeky lizards if I want!'

'Yes, you can, you can,' said Nanny soothingly, 'but not . . . with a . . . snake . . .'

Granny held up the creeper for inspection. A medium-sized Three-Banded Coit gave her a frightened look, considered biting her nose for a moment, thought better of it, and then shut its mouth very tightly in the hope she'd get the message. She opened her hand. The snake dropped to the boards and slithered away quickly.

Mrs Gogol hadn't stirred in her chair. Now she half turned. Saturday was still patiently watching his fishing line.

'Saturday, go and fetch the lady's hat,' she said.

'Yes, m'm.'

Even Granny hesitated at that.

'You can't make him do that!' she said.

'But he's dead,' said Mrs Gogol.

'Yes, but it's bad enough being dead without bein' in bits too,' said Granny. 'Don't you go in there, Mr Saturday!'

'But it was your *hat*, lady,' said Mrs Gogol.

'Yes, but . . .' said Granny, '. . . a . . . hat was all it was. I wouldn't send anyone into any alligators for any hat.'

Nanny Ogg looked horrified.

No one knew better than Granny Weatherwax that hats were important. They weren't just clothing. Hats defined the head. They defined who you *were*. No one had ever heard of a wizard without a pointy hat – at least, no wizard worth speaking of. And you certainly never heard of a witch without one. Even Magrat had one, although she hardly ever wore it on account of being a wet hen. That didn't matter too much, it wasn't the wearing of the hats that counted so much as having one to wear. Every trade, every craft had its hat. That's why kings had hats. Take the crown off a king and all you had was someone good at having a weak chin and waving to people. Hats had power. Hats were important. But so were people.

Mrs Gogol took another puff at her pipe.

'Saturday, go and get my best hat for holidays,' she said.

'Yes, Mrs Gogol.'

Saturday disappeared into the hut for a moment, and came out with a large and battered box securely wrapped with twine.

'I can't take that,' said Granny. 'I can't take your best hat.'

'Yes you can,' said Mrs Gogol. 'I've got another hat. Oh, yes. I've got another hat all right.'

Granny put the box down carefully.

'It occurs to me, Mrs Gogol,' she said, 'that you ain't everything you seem.'

'Oh yes I is, Mistress Weatherwax. I never bin nothing else, just like you.'

'You brought us here?'

'No. You brought yourselves here. Of your own free will. To help someone, ain't that right? You decided to do it, ain't that right? No one forced you, ain't that right? 'Cept yourselves.'

'She's right about all that,' said Nanny. 'We'd have felt it, if it was magic.'

'That's right,' said Granny. 'No one forced us, except ourselves. What's your game, Mrs Gogol?'

'I ain't playing no game, Mistress Weatherwax. I just want back what's mine. I want justice. And I wants *her* stopped.'

'Her who?' said Nanny Ogg.

Granny's face had frozen into a mask.

'Her who's behind all this,' said Mrs Gogol. 'The Duc hasn't got the brains of a prawn, Mrs Ogg. I mean *her*. Her with her mirror magic. Her who likes to control. Her who's in charge. Her who's tinkering with destiny. Her that Mistress Weatherwax knows all about.'

Nanny Ogg was lost.

'What's she talking about, Esme?' she said.

Granny muttered something.

'What? Didn't hear you,' Nanny said.

Granny Weatherwax looked up, her face red with anger.

'She means my *sister*, Gytha! Right? Got that? Do you understand? Did you hear? My sister! Want me to repeat it again? Want to know who she's talking about? You want me to write it down? My sister! That's who! My *sister*!'

'They're sisters?' said Magrat.

Her tea had gone cold.

'I don't know,' said Ella. 'They look . . . alike. They keep themselves to themselves most of the time. But I can feel them watching. They're very good at watching.'

'And they make you do *all* the work?' she said.

'Well, I only have to cook for myself and the outside staff,' said Ella. 'And I don't mind the cleaning and the laundry all that much.'

'Do they do their own cooking, then?'

'I don't think so. They walk around the house at night, after I've gone to bed. Godmother Lilith says I must be kind to them and pity them because they can't talk, and always see that we've got plenty of cheese in the larder.'

'They eat nothing but cheese?' said Magrat.

'I don't think so,' said Ella.

'I should think the rats and mice get it, then, in an old place like this.'

'You know, it's a funny thing,' said Ella, 'but I've never seen a mouse anywhere in this house.'

Magrat shivered. She felt *watched*.

'Why don't you just walk away? *I* would.'

'Where to? Anyway, they always find me. Or they send the coachmen and grooms after me.'

'That's horrible!'

'I'm sure they think that sooner or later I'll marry anyone to get away from laundry,' said Ella. 'Not that the Prince's clothes get washed, I expect,' she added bitterly. 'I expect they get burned after he's worn them.'

'What *you* want to do is make a career of your own,' said Magrat encouragingly, to keep her spirits up. 'You want to be your own woman. You want to emancipate yourself.'

'I don't think I want to do that,' said Ella, speaking with caution in case it was a sin to offend a fairy godmother.

'You do really,' said Magrat.

'Do I?'

'Yes.'

'Oh.'

'You don't have to marry anyone you don't want to.'

Ella sat back.

'How good are you?' she said.

'Er . . . well . . . I suppose I –'

'The dress arrived yesterday,' said Ella. 'It's up in the big front room, on a stand so it doesn't get creased. So that it stays *perfect*. And they've polished up the coach specially. They've hired extra footmen, too.'

'Yes, but perhaps –'

'I think I'm going to have to marry someone I don't want to,' said Ella.

Granny Weatherwax strode up and down the driftwood balcony. The whole shack trembled to her stamping. Ripples spread out as it bounced on the water.

'Of course you don't remember her!' she shouted. 'Our mam kicked her out when she was thirteen! We was both tiny then! But *I* remember the rows! I used to hear them when I was in bed! She was *wanton*!'

'You always used to say *I* was wanton, when we was younger,' said Nanny.

Granny hesitated, caught momentarily off balance. Then she waved a hand irritably.

'You was, of course,' she said dismissively. 'But you never used magic for it, did you?'

'Din't have to,' said Nanny happily. 'An off-the-shoulder dress did the trick most of the time.'

'Right off the shoulder and on to the grass, as I recall,' said Granny. 'No, *she* used magic. Not just ordinary magic, neither. Oh, she was *wilful*!'

Nanny Ogg was about to say: What? You mean not compliant and self-effacing like what you is, Esme? But she stopped herself. You didn't juggle matches in a fireworks factory.

'Young men's fathers used to come round to complain,' said Granny darkly.

'They never came round to complain about *me*,' said Nanny happily.

'And always looking at herself in mirrors,' said Granny. 'Prideful as a cat, she was. Prefer to look in a mirror than out of a window, she would.'

'What's her name?'

'Lily.'

'That's a nice name,' said Nanny.

'It isn't what she calls herself now,' said Mrs Gogol.

'I bet it isn't!'

'And she's, like, in charge of the city?' said Nanny.

'She was *bossy*, too!'

'What'd she want to be in charge of a city for?' said Nanny.

'She's got plans,' said Mrs Gogol.

'And vain? Really *vain*!' said Granny, apparently to the world in general.

'Did you know she was here?' said Nanny.

'I had a feelin'! Mirrors!'

'Mirror magic isn't bad,' protested Nanny. 'I've done all kinds of stuff with mirrors. You can have a lot of fun with a mirror.'

'She doesn't just use one mirror,' said Mrs Gogol.

'Oh.'

'She uses two.'

'Oh. That's different.'

Granny stared at the surface of the water. Her own face stared back at her from the darkness.

She hoped it was her own face, anyway.

'I've felt her watchin' us, the whole way here,' she said. 'That's where she's happiest, inside mirrors. Inside mirrors, making people into stories.'

She prodded the image with a stick. 'She even got a look at me in Desiderata's house, just before Magrat came in. It ain't nice, seeing someone else in your reflection –'

She paused. 'Where is Magrat, anyway?'

'Out fairy godmothering, I think,' said Nanny. 'She said she didn't need any help.'

Magrat was annoyed. She was also frightened, which made her even more annoyed. It was hard for people when Magrat was annoyed. It was like being attacked by damp tissue.

'You have my personal word on it,' she said. 'You don't have to go to the ball if you don't want to.'

'You won't be able to stop them,' said Ella darkly. 'I know how things work in this city.'

'Look, I said you won't have to go!' said Magrat.

She looked thoughtful.

'There isn't someone else you'd rather marry, is there?' she said.

'No. I don't know many people. I don't get much chance.'

'Good,' said Magrat. 'That makes it easier. I suggest we get you out of here and – and take you somewhere else.'

'There isn't anywhere else. I told you. There's just swamp. I tried once or twice, and they sent the coachmen after me. They weren't unkind. The coachmen, I mean. They're just afraid. Everyone's afraid. Even the Sisters are afraid, I think.'

Magrat looked around at the shadows.

'What of?' she said.

'They say that people disappear. If they upset the Duc. Something happens to them. Everyone's very *polite* in Genua,' said Ella sourly. 'And no one steals and no one raises their voice and everyone stays indoors at night, except when it's Fat Tuesday.' She sighed. 'Now *that's* something I'd like to go to. To the carnival. They always make me stay in, though. But I hear it passing through the city and I think: that's what Genua ought to be. Not a few people dancing in palaces, but everyone dancing in the streets.'

Magrat shook herself. She felt a long way from home.

'I think perhaps I might need a bit of help with this one,' she said.

'You've got a wand,' said Ella.

'I think there's times when you need more than a wand,' said Magrat. She stood up.

'But I'll tell you this,' she said. 'I don't like this house. I don't like this city. Emberella?'

'Yes?'

'You *won't* go to the ball. I'll make sure of that –'

She turned around.

'I told you,' murmured Ella, looking down. 'You can't even hear them.'

One of the sisters was at the top of the steps leading into the kitchen. Her gaze was fixed immovably on Magrat.

They say that everyone has the attributes of some kind of animal. Magrat possibly had a direct mental link to some small furry creature. She felt the terror of all small rodents in the face of unblinking death. Modulated over the menace of the gaze were all sorts of messages: the uselessness of flight, the stupidity of resistance, the inevitability of oblivion.

She knew she could do nothing. Her legs weren't under her control. It was as if commands were coming straight down that stare and into her spinal cord. The sense of helplessness was almost peaceful . . .

'Blessings be upon this house.'

The sister spun around much faster than any human should be able to move.

Granny Weatherwax pushed open the door. 'Oh deary me,' she thundered, 'and lawks.'

'Yeah,' said Nanny Ogg, crowding through the doorway behind her. 'Lawks too.'

'We're just a couple of old beggar women,' said Granny, striding across the floor.

'Begging from house to house,' said Nanny Ogg. 'Not coming directly here by any manner o' means.'

They each caught one of Magrat's elbows and lifted her off her feet.

Granny turned her head.

'What about you, Miss?'

Ella shook her head without looking up.

'No,' she said, 'I mustn't come.'

Granny's eyes narrowed. 'I suppose not,' she said. 'We all have our path to walk, or so it is said, although not by me. Come, Gytha.'

'We're just off,' said Nanny Ogg, brightly.

They turned.

Another sister appeared in the doorway.

'Ye gods,' said Nanny Ogg. 'I never saw her move!'

'We was just going out,' said Granny Weatherwax loudly. 'If it's all the same with you, m'lady?'

She met the stare head-on.

The air tingled.

Then Granny Weatherwax said, between gritted teeth, 'When I say run, Gytha –'

'I hear you,' said Nanny.

Granny groped behind her and found the teapot Magrat had just used. She weighed it in her hands, keeping the movements slow and gentle.

'Ready, Gytha?'

'Waitin', Esme.'

'Run!'

Granny hurled the teapot high into the air. The heads of both sisters snapped around.

Nanny Ogg helped the stumbling Magrat out of the door. Granny slammed it shut as the nearer sister darted forward, mouth open, too late.

'We're leaving the girl in there!' shouted Nanny, as they ran down the drive.

'They're guarding her,' said Granny. 'They're not going to harm her!'

'I ain't seen teeth like those on anyone before!' said Nanny.

'That's 'cos they ain't anyone! They're snakes!'

They reached the comparative security of the roadway and leaned against the wall.

'Snakes?' Nanny wheezed. Magrat opened her eyes.

'It's Lily's doing,' said Granny. 'She was good at that kind of thing, I remember.'

'*Really* snakes?'

'Yeah,' said Granny darkly. 'She made friends easily.'

'Blimey! *I* couldn't do that.'

'She didn't used to be able to either, for more'n a few seconds. That's what using mirrors does for you.'

'I – I –' Magrat stuttered.

'You're all *right*,' said Nanny. She looked up at Esme Weatherwax.

'We shouldn't leave the girl, whatever you say. In a house with snakes walking around thinking they're human,' she said.

'It's worse than that. They're walking around thinking they're snakes,' said Granny.

'Well, whatever. *You* never do that sort of thing. The worst you ever did was make people a bit confused about what they was.'

'That's because I'm the good one,' said Granny bitterly.

Magrat shuddered.

'So are we going to get her out?' said Nanny.

'Not yet. There's going to be a proper time,' said Granny. 'Can you hear me, Magrat Garlick?'

'Yes, Granny,' said Magrat.

'We've got to go somewhere and talk,' said Granny. 'About stories.'

'What about stories?' said Magrat.

'Lily is using them,' said Granny. 'Don't you see that? You can feel it in this whole country. The stories collect round here because here's where they find a way out. She *feeds* 'em. Look, she don't want your Ella to marry that Duc man just because of politics or something. That's just an . . . explanation. 'S not a *reason*. She wants the girl to marry the prince because that's what the story demands.'

'What's in it for her?' said Nanny.

'In the middle of 'em all, the fairy godmother or the wicked witch . . . you remember? That's where Lily is putting herself, like . . . like . . .' she paused, trying to find the right word. 'Remember that time last year when the circus thing came to Lancre?'

'I remember,' said Nanny. 'Them girls in the spangly tights and the fellows pourin' whitewash down their trousers. Never saw a elephant, though. They said there'd be elephants and there wasn't any. It had elephants on the posters. I spent a whole tuppence and there wasn't a single ele–'

'Yes, but what I'm *sayin'*,' said Granny, as they hurried along the street, 'is there was that man in the middle, you remember. With the moustache and the big hat?'

'Him? But he didn't do anything much,' said Nanny. 'He just stood in the middle of the tent and sometimes he cracked his whip and all the acts just went on round him.'

'That's why he was the most important one there,' said Granny. 'It was the things going on around him that made him important.'

'What's Lily feeding the stories?' said Magrat.

'People,' said Granny. She frowned.

'Stories!' she said. 'Well, we'll have to see about that . . .'

Green twilight covered Genua. The mists curled up from the swamp.

Torches flared in the streets. In dozens of yards shadowy figures moved, pulling the covers off floats. In the darkness there was a flash of sequins and a jingle of bells.

All year the people of Genua were nice and quiet. But history has always allowed the downtrodden one night somewhere in any calendar to restore temporarily the balance of the world. It might be called the Feast of Fools, or the King of the Bean. Or even Samedi Nuit Mort, when even those with the most taxing and responsible of duties can kick back and have fun.

Most of them, anyway . . .

The coachmen and the footmen were sitting in their shed at one side of the stable yard, eating their dinner and complaining about having to work on Dead Night. They were also engaging in the time-honoured rituals that go therewith, which largely consist of finding out what their wives have packed for them today and envying the other men whose wives obviously cared more.

The head footman raised a crust cautiously.

'I've got chicken neck and pickle,' he said. 'Anyone got any cheese?'

The second coachman inspected his box. 'It's boiled bacon again,' he complained. 'She always gives me boiled bacon. She knows I don't like it. She don't even cut the fat off.'

'Is it thick white fat?' said the first coachman.

'Yeah. Horrible. Is this right for a holiday feast or what?'

'I'll swap you a lettuce and tomato.'

'Right. What *you* got, Jimmy?'

The underfootman shyly opened his perfect package. There were four sandwiches, crusts cut off. There was a sprig of parsley. There was even a napkin.

'Smoked salmon and cream cheese,' he said.

'*And* still a bit of the wedding cake,' said the first coachman. 'Ain't you et that all up yet?'

'We have it every night,' said the underfootman.

The shed shook with the ensuing laughter. It is a universal fact that any innocent comment made by any recently married young member of any workforce is an instant trigger for coarse merriment among his or her older and more cynical colleagues. This happens even if everyone concerned has nine legs and lives at the bottom of an ocean of ammonia on a huge cold planet. It's just one of those things.

'You make the most of it,' said the second coachman gloomily, when they'd settled down again. 'It starts off kisses and cake and them cutting the crusts off, and next thing you know it's down to tongue pie, cold bum and the copper stick.'

'The way I see it,' the first coachman began, 'it's all about the way you –'

There was a knocking at the door.

The underfootman, being the junior member, got up and opened it.

'It's an old crone,' he said. 'What do you want, old crone?'

'Fancy a drink?' said Nanny Ogg. She held up a jug over which hung a perceptible haze of evaporating alcohol, and blew a paper squeaker.

'What?' said the footman.

'Shame for you lads to be working. It's a holiday! Whoopee!'

'What's going on?' the senior coachman began, and then he entered the cloud of alcohol. 'Gods! What is that *stuff*?'

'Smells like rum, Mr Travis.'

The senior coachman hesitated. From the streets came music and laughter as the first of the processions got under way. Fireworks popped across the sky. It wasn't a night to be without just a sip of alcohol.

'What a nice old lady,' he said.

Nanny Ogg waved the jug again. 'Up your eye!' she said. 'Mud in your bottom!'

What might be called the *classical* witch comes in two basic varieties, the complicated and the simple, or, to put it another way, the ones that have a room full of regalia and the ones that don't. Magrat was by inclination one of the former sort. For example, take magical knives. She had a complete collection of magical knives, all with the appropriate coloured handles and complicated runes all over them.

It had taken many years under the tutelage of Granny Weatherwax for Magrat to learn that the common kitchen breadknife was better than the most ornate of magic knives. It could do all that the magical knife could do, plus you could also use it to cut bread.

Every established kitchen has one ancient knife, its handle worn thin, its blade curved like a banana, and so inexplicably sharp that reaching into the drawer at night is like bobbing for apples in a piranha tank.

Magrat had hers stuck in her belt. Currently she was thirty feet above the ground, one hand holding on to her broomstick, the other on to a drainpipe, both legs dangling. Housebreaking ought to be easy, when you had a broomstick. But this did not appear to be the case.

Finally she got both legs around the pipe and a firm grip on a timely gargoyle. She waggled the knife in between the two halves of the window and lifted the latch. After a certain amount of grunting, she was inside, leaning against the wall and panting. Blue lights flashed in front of her eyes, echoing the fireworks that laced the night outside.

Granny had kept on asking her if she was sure she wanted to do this. And she was amazed to find that she *was* sure. Even if the snake women were already wandering around the house. Being a witch meant going into places you didn't want to go.

She opened her eyes.

There was the dress, in the middle of the floor, on a dressmaker's dummy.

A Klatchian Candle burst over Genua. Green and red stars exploded in the velvet darkness, and lit up the gems and silks in front of Magrat.

It was the most beautiful thing she had ever seen.
She crept forward, her mouth dry.

Warm mists rolled through the swamp.
Mrs Gogol stirred the cauldron.
'What are they doing?' said Saturday.
'Stopping the story,' she said. 'Or . . . maybe not . . .'
She stood up.
'One way or another, it's our time now. Let's go to the clearing.'
She looked at Saturday's face.
'Are you frightened?'
'I . . . know what will happen afterwards,' said the zombie. 'Even if we win.'
'We both do. But we've had twelve years.'
'Yes. We've had twelve years.'
'And Ella will rule the city.'
'Yes.'

In the coachmen's shed Nanny Ogg and the coachmen were getting along, as she put it, like a maison en flambé.
The underfootman smiled vaguely at the wall, and slumped forward.
'That's youngpipple today,' said the head coachman, trying to fish his wig out of his mug. 'Can't hold their drin . . . their drine . . . stuff . . .'
'Have a hair of the dog, Mr Travis?' said Nanny, filling the mug. 'Or scale of the alligator or whatever you call it in these parts.'
'Reckon,' said the senior footman, 'we should be gettin' the coesshe ready, what say?'
'Reckon you've got time for one more yet,' said Nanny Ogg.
'Ver' generous,' said the coachman. 'Ver' generous. Here's lookin' at you, Mrsrsrs Goo . . .'

Magrat had dreamed of dresses like this. In the pit of her soul, in the small hours of the night, she'd danced with princes. Not shy, hardworking princes like Verence back home, but real ones, with crystal blue eyes and white teeth. And she'd *worn* dresses like this. And they had *fitted*.
She stared at the ruched sleeves, the embroidered bodice, the fine white lace. It was all a world away from her . . . well . . . Nanny Ogg kept calling them 'Magrats', but they were trousers, and very practical.

As if being practical mattered at all.

She stared for a long time.

Then, with tears streaking her face and changing colour as they caught the light of the fireworks, she took the knife and began to cut the dress into very small pieces.

The senior coachman's head bounced gently off his sandwiches.

Nanny Ogg stood up, a little unsteadily. She placed the junior footman's wig under his slumbering head, because she was not an unkind woman. Then she stepped out into the night.

A figure moved near the wall.

'Magrat?' hissed Nanny.

'Nanny?'

'Did you see to the dress?'

'Have you seen to the footmen?'

'Right, then,' said Granny Weatherwax, stepping out of the shadows. 'Then there's just the coach.'

She tiptoed theatrically to the coachhouse and opened the door. It grated loudly on the cobbles.

'Shsss!' said Nanny.

There was a stub of candle and some matches on a ledge. Magrat fumbled the candle alight.

The coach lit up like a glitter ball.

It was excessively ornate, as if someone had taken a perfectly ordinary coach and then gone insane with fretwork and gold paint.

Granny Weatherwax walked around it.

'A bit showy,' she said.

'Seems a real shame to smash it up,' said Nanny sadly. She rolled up her sleeves and then, as an afterthought, tucked the hem of her skirt into her drawers.

'Bound to be a hammer somewhere around here,' she said, turning to the benches along the walls.

'Don't! That'd make too much noise!' hissed Magrat. 'Hang on a moment . . .'

She pulled the despised wand out of her belt, gripped it tightly, and waved it towards the coach.

There was a brief inrush of air.

'Blow me down,' said Nanny Ogg. 'I never would have thought of that.'

On the floor was a large orange pumpkin.

'It was nothing,' said Magrat, risking a touch of pride.

'Hah! That's one coach that'll never roll again,' said Nanny.

'Hey . . . can you do that to the horses too?' said Granny.

Magrat shook her head. 'Um, I think that would be very cruel.'

'You're right. You're right,' said Granny. 'No excuse for cruelty to dumb animals.'

The two stallions watched her with equine curiosity as she undid the loose-box gates.

'Off you go,' she said. 'Big green fields out there somewhere.' She glanced momentarily at Magrat. 'You have been em-horsesipated.'

This didn't seem to have much effect.

Granny sighed. She climbed up onto the wooden wall that separated the boxes, reached up, grabbed a horse ear in either hand, and gently dragged their heads down level with her mouth.

She whispered something. The stallions turned and looked one another in the eye.

Then they looked down at Granny.

She grinned at them, and nodded.

Then . . .

It is impossible for a horse to go instantly from a standing start to a gallop, but they almost managed it.

'What on earth did you say to them?' said Magrat.

'Mystic horseman's word,' said Granny. 'Passed down to Gytha's Jason, who passed it up to me. Works every time.'

'He told you it?' said Nanny.

'Yes.'

'What, all of it?'

'Yes,' said Granny, smugly.

Magrat tucked the wand back into her belt. As she did so, a square of white material fell on to the floor.

White gems and silk glimmered in the candlelight as she reached down hurriedly to pick it up, but there wasn't a lot that escaped Granny Weatherwax.

She sighed.

'Magrat Garlick . . .' she began.

'Yes,' said Magrat meekly. 'Yes. I know. I'm a wet hen.'

Nanny patted her gently on the shoulder.

'Never mind,' she said. 'We've done a good night's work here. That Ella has about as much chance of being sent to the ball tonight as I have of . . . of becoming queen.'

'No dress, no footmen, no horses and no coach,' said Granny. 'I'd like to see *her* get out of *that* one. Stories? Hah!'

'So what're we going to do now?' said Magrat, as they crept out of the yard.

'It's Fat Lunchtime!' said Nanny. 'Hot diggety pig!' Greebo wandered out of the darkness and rubbed against her legs.

'I thought Lily was trying to stamp it out,' said Magrat.

'May as well try to stamp out a flood.' said Nanny. 'Kick out a jam!'

'I don't agree with dancing in the streets,' said Granny. 'How much of that rum did you drink?'

'Oh, come *on*, Esme,' said Nanny. 'They say if you can't have a good time in Genua you're probably dead.' She thought about Saturday. 'You can probably have a bit of quiet fun even if you *are* dead, in Genua.'

'Hadn't we better stay here, though?' said Magrat. 'Just to make sure?'

Granny Weatherwax hesitated.

'What do you think, Esme?' said Nanny Ogg. 'You think she's going to be sent to the ball in a *pumpkin*, eh? Get a few mice to pull it, eh? Heheh!'

A vision of the snake women floated across Granny Weatherwax's mind, and she hesitated. But, after all, it had been a long day. And it was ridiculous, when you came to think about it . . .

'Well, all right,' she said. 'But I'm not going to kick any jam, you understand.'

'There's dancing and all sorts,' said Nanny.

'And banana drinks, I expect,' said Magrat.

'It's a million to one chance, yes,' said Nanny Ogg happily.

Lilith de Tempscire smiled at herself in the double mirror.

'Oh deary me,' she said. 'No coach, no dress, no horses. What *is* a poor old godmother to do? Deary me. And probably lawks.'

She opened a small leather case, such as a musician might use to carry his very best piccolo.

There was a wand in there, the twin of the one carried by Magrat. She took it out and gave it a couple of twists, moving the gold and silver rings into a new position.

The clicking sounded like the nastiest pump-action mechanism.

'And me with nothing but a pumpkin, too,' said Lilith.

And of course the difference between sapient and non-sapient things was that while it was hard to change the shape of the former it was not actually impossible. It was just a matter of changing a mental channel. Whereas a non-sapient thing like a pumpkin, and it was hard to imagine anything less sapient than a pumpkin, could not be changed by any magic short of sourcery.

Unless its molecules remembered a time when they weren't a pumpkin . . .

She laughed, and a billion reflected Liliths laughed with her, all around the curve of the mirror universe.

Fat Lunchtime was no longer celebrated in the centre of Genua. But in the shanty town around the high white buildings it strutted its dark and torchlit stuff. There were fireworks. There were dancers, and fire-eaters, and feathers, and sequins. The witches, whose idea of homely entertainment was a Morris dance, watched open-mouthed from the crowded sidewalk as the parades strutted by.

'There's dancing skeletons!' said Nanny, as a score of bony figures whirred down the street.

'They're not,' said Magrat. 'They're just men in black tights with bones painted on.'

Someone nudged Granny Weatherwax. She looked up into the large, grinning face of a black man. He passed her a stone jug.

'There you go, honey.'

Granny took it, hesitated for a moment, and then took a swig. She nudged Magrat and passed on the bottle.

'Frgtht!! Gizeer!' she said.

'What?' shouted Magrat, above the noise of a marching band.

'The man wants us to pass it on,' said Granny.

Magrat looked at the bottle neck. She tried surreptitiously to wipe it on her dress, despite the self-evident fact that germs on it would have burned off long ago. She ventured a brief nip, and then nudged Nanny Ogg.

'Kwizathugner!' she said, and dabbed at her eyes.

Nanny up-ended the bottle. After a while Magrat nudged her again.

'I think we're meant to pass it on?' she ventured.

Nanny wiped her mouth and passed the now rather lighter jug randomly to a tall figure on her left.

'Here you go, mister,' she said.

THANK YOU.

'Nice costume you got there. Them bones are painted on really good.'

Nanny turned back to watch a procession of juggling fire-eaters. Then a connection appeared to be made somewhere in the back of her mind. She looked up. The stranger had wandered off.

She shrugged.

'What shall we do next?' she said.

Granny Weatherwax was staring fixedly at a group of ground-zero limbo dancers. A lot of the dances in the parades had this in common: they expressed explicitly what things like maypoles only hinted at. They covered it with sequins, too.

'You'll never feel safe in the privy again, eh?' said Nanny Ogg. At her feet Greebo sat primly watching some dancing women wearing nothing but feathers, trying to work out what to do about them.

'No. I was thinkin' of something else. I was thinkin' about . . . how stories work. And now . . . I think I'd like something to eat,' said Granny weakly. She rallied a bit. 'And I mean some proper food, not somethin' scraped off the bottom of a pond. And I don't want any of this *cuisine* stuff, neither.'

'You ought to be more adventurous, Granny,' said Magrat.

'I ain't against adventure, in moderation,' said Granny, 'but not when I'm eatin'.'

'There's a place back there that does alligator sandwiches,' said Nanny, turning away from the parade. 'Can you believe that? Alligators in a sandwich?'

'That reminds me of a joke,' said Granny Weatherwax. Something was nagging at her consciousness.

Nanny Ogg started to cough, but it didn't work.

'This man went into an inn,' said Granny Weatherwax, trying to ignore the rising uneasiness. 'And he saw this sign. And it said "We serve all kinds of sandwiches." And he said, "Get me an alligator sandwich – and I want it right away!"'

'I don't think alligator sandwiches is very kind to alligators,' said Magrat, dropping the observation into the leaden pause.

'I always say a laugh does you good,' said Nanny.

Lilith smiled at the figure of Ella, standing forlornly between the snake woman.

'And such a raggedy dress, too,' she said. 'And the door to the room was locked. Tut-tut. However can it have happened?'

Ella stared at her feet.

Lilith smiled at the sisters. 'Well,' she said, 'we'll just have to do the best we can with what we've got. Hmm? Fetch me . . . fetch me two rats and two mice. I *know* you can always find rats and mice. And bring in the big pumpkin.'

She laughed. Not the mad, shrill laughter of the bad fairy who's been defeated, but the rather pleasant laughter of someone who's just seen the joke.

She looked reflectively at the wand.

'But first,' she said, transferring her gaze to Ella's pale face, 'you'd better bring in those *naughty* men who let themselves get so drunk. That's not respectful. And if you haven't got respect, you haven't got anything.'

The clicking of the wand was the only sound in the kitchen.

Nanny Ogg poked at the tall drink in front of her.

'Beats me why they puts an umbrella in it,' she said, sucking the cocktail cherry off the stick. 'I mean, do they want to stop it getting wet or something?'

She grinned at Magrat and Granny, who were both staring gloomily at the passing celebrations.

'Cheer up,' she said. 'Never seen such a pair of long faces in all my puff.'

'That's neat rum you're drinking,' said Magrat.

'You're telling me,' said Nanny, taking a swig. 'Cheers!'

'It was too easy,' said Granny Weatherwax.

'It was only easy 'cos *we* done it,' said Nanny. 'You want something done, we're the girls to do it, eh? You show me anyone else who could have nipped in there and done all that in the nick of time, eh? Especially the coach bit.'

'It doesn't make a good story,' said Granny.

'Oh, bugger stories,' said Nanny loftily. 'You can always change a story.'

'Only at the right places,' said Granny. 'Anyway, maybe they could get her a new dress and horses and a coach and everything.'

'Where? When?' said Nanny. 'It's a holiday. And there's no *time*, anyway. They'll be starting the ball at any moment.'

Granny Weatherwax's fingers drummed on the edge of the café table.

Nanny sighed.

'Now what?' she said.

'It doesn't happen like this,' said Granny.

'Listen, Esme, the only kind of magic that'd work right now is wand magic. And Magrat's got the wand.' Nanny nodded at Magrat. 'Ain't that so, Magrat?'

'Um,' said Magrat.

'Not lost it, have you?'

'No, but –'

'There you are, then.'

'Only . . . um . . . Ella said she'd got *two* godmothers . . .'

Granny Weatherwax's hand thumped down on the table. Nanny's drink flew into the air and overturned.

'That's *right*!' roared Granny.

'That was nearly full. That was a nearly full drink,' said Nanny reproachfully.

'Come on!'

'Best part of a whole glass of –'

'Gytha!'

'Did I say I wasn't coming? I was just pointing out –'

'*Now!*'

'Can I just ask the man to get me ano–'

'*Gytha!*'

The witches were halfway up the street when a coach rattled out of the
driveway and trundled away.

'That can't be it!' said Magrat. 'We got rid of it!'

'We ort to have chopped it up,' said Nanny. 'There's good eating on a
pumpk–'

'They've got us,' said Granny, slowing down to a stop.

'Can't you get into the minds of the horses?' said Magrat.

The witches concentrated.

'They ain't horses,' said Nanny. 'They feel like . . .'

'Rats turned into horses,' said Granny, who was even better at getting into
people's minds than she was at getting under their skins. 'They feel like that
poor old wolf. Minds like a firework display.' She winced at the taste of
them in her own head.

'I bet,' said Granny, thoughtfully, as the coach skidded around the corner,
'I bet I could make the wheels fall right off.'

'That's not the way,' said Magrat. 'Anyway, Ella's in there!'

'There may be another way,' said Nanny. 'I know someone who could get
inside them minds right enough.'

'Who?' said Magrat.

'Well, we've still got our brooms,' said Nanny. 'It should be easy to
overtake it, right?'

The witches landed in an alley-way a few minutes ahead of the coach.

'I don't hold with this,' said Granny. 'It's the sort of thing Lily does. You
can't expect me to like this. Think of that wolf!'

Nanny lifted Greebo out of his nest among the bristles.

'But Greebo's nearly human anyway,' she said.

'Hah!'

'And it'll only be temp'ry, even with the three of us doing it,' she said. 'Anyway, it'll be int'resting to see if it works.'

'Yes, but it's *wrong*,' said Granny.

'Not for these parts, it seems,' said Nanny.

'Besides,' said Magrat virtuously, 'it can't be bad if *we're* doing it. We're the good ones.'

'Oh yes, so we is,' said Granny, 'and there was me forgetting it for a minute there.'

Nanny stood back. Greebo, aware that something was expected of him, sat up.

'You must admit we can't think of anything better, Granny,' said Magrat.

Granny hesitated. But under all the revulsion was the little treacherous flame of fascination with the idea. Besides, she and Greebo had hated one another cordially for years. Almost human, eh? Give him a taste of it, then, and see how he likes it . . . She felt a bit ashamed of the thought. But not much.

'Oh, *all* right.'

They concentrated.

As Lily knew, changing the shape of an object is one of the hardest magics there is. But it's easier if the object is alive. After all, a living thing already knows what shape it is. All you have to do is change its mind.

Greebo yawned and stretched. To his amazement he went on stretching.

Through the pathways of his feline brain surged a tide of belief. He suddenly believed he was human. He wasn't simply under the *impression* that he was human; he believed it implicitly. The sheer force of the unshakable belief flowed out into his morphic field, overriding its objections, rewriting the very blueprint of his self.

Fresh instructions surged back.

If he was human, he didn't need all this fur. And he ought to be bigger . . .

The witches watched, fascinated.

'I *never* thought we'd do it,' said Granny.

. . . no points on the ears, the whiskers were too long . . .

. . . he needed more muscle, all these bones were the wrong shape, these legs ought to be longer . . .

And then it was finished.

Greebo unfolded himself and stood up, a little unsteadily.

Nanny stared, her mouth open.

Then her eyes moved downwards.

'Cor,' she said.

'I think,' said Granny Weatherwax, 'that we'd better imagine some clothes on him *right now*.'

That was easy enough. When Greebo had been clothed to her satisfaction Granny nodded and stood back.

'Magrat, you can open your eyes,' she said.

'I hadn't got them closed.'

'Well, you should have had.'

Greebo turned slowly, a faint, lazy smile on his scarred face. As a human, his nose was broken and a black patch covered his bad eye. But the other one glittered like the sins of angels, and his smile was the downfall of saints. Female ones, anyway.

Perhaps it was pheromones, or the way his muscles rippled under his black leather shirt. Greebo broadcast a kind of greasy diabolic sexuality in the megawatt range. Just looking at him was enough to set dark wings fluttering in the crimson night.

'Uh, Greebo,' said Nanny.

He opened his mouth. Incisors glittered.

'Wrowwwwl,' he said.

'Can you understand me?'

'Yessss, Nannyyy.'

Nanny Ogg leaned against the wall for support.

There was the sound of hooves. The coach had turned into the street.

'Get out there and stop that coach!'

Greebo grinned again, and darted out of the alley.

Nanny fanned herself with her hat.

'Whoo-eee,' she said. 'And to think I used to tickle his tummy . . . No wonder all the lady cats scream at night.'

'Gytha!'

'Well, *you've* gone very red, Esme.'

'I'm just out of breath,' said Granny.

'Funny, that. It's not as if you've been running.'

The coach rattled down the street.

The coachmen and footmen were not at all sure what they were. Their minds oscillated wildly. One moment they were men thinking about cheese and bacon rinds. And the next they were mice wondering why they had trousers on.

As for the horses . . . horses are a little insane anyway, and being a rat as well wasn't any help.

So none of them were in a very stable frame of mind when Greebo stepped out of the shadows and *grinned* at them.

He said, 'Wrowwwl.'

The horses tried to stop, which is practically impossible with a coach still piling along behind you. The coachmen froze in terror.

'Wrowwwl?'

The coach skidded around and came up broadside against a wall, knocking the coachmen off. Greebo picked one of them up by his collar and bounced him up and down while the maddened horses fought to get out of the shafts.

'Run awayy, furry toy?' he suggested.

Behind the frightened eyes man and mouse fought for supremacy. But they needn't have bothered. They would lose either way. As consciousness flickered between the states it saw either a grinning cat or a six-foot, well-muscled, one-eyed grinning bully.

The coachmouse fainted. Greebo patted him a few times, in case he was going to move . . .

'Wake up, little mousey . . .'

. . . and then lost interest.

The coach door rattled, jammed, and then opened.

'What's happening?' said Ella.

'Wrow*wwwl*!'

Nanny Ogg's boot hit Greebo on the back of his head.

'Oh no you don't, my lad,' she said.

'Want to,' said Greebo sulkily.

'You always do, that's your trouble,' said Nanny, and smiled at Ella. 'Out you come, dear.'

Greebo shrugged, and then slunk off, dragging the stunned coachman after him.

'What's *happening*?' complained Ella. 'Oh. Magrat. Did you do this?'

Magrat allowed herself a moment's shy pride.

'I *said* you wouldn't have to go to the ball, didn't I?'

Ella looked around at the disabled coach, and then back to the witches.

'You ain't got any snake women in there with you, have you?' said Granny. Magrat gripped the wand.

'They went on ahead,' said Ella. Her face clouded as she recalled something.

'Lilith turned the real coachmen into beetles,' she whispered. 'I mean, they weren't that bad! She made them get some mice and she made them human and then she said, there's got to be balance, and the sisters dragged in the coachmen and she turned them into beetles and then . . . she *trod* on them . . .'

She stopped, horrified.

A firework burst in the sky, but in the street below a bubble of terrible silence hung in the air.

'Witches don't kill people,' said Magrat.

'This is foreign parts,' muttered Nanny, looking away.

'I think,' said Granny Weatherwax, 'that you ought to get right away from here, young lady.'

'They just went crack –'

'We've got the brooms,' said Magrat. 'We could *all* get away.'

'She'd send something after you,' said Ella darkly. 'I know her. Something from out of a mirror.'

'So we'd fight it,' said Magrat.

'No,' said Granny. 'Whatever's going to happen's going to happen here. We'll send the young lady off somewhere safe and then . . . we shall see.'

'But if I go away *she'll* know,' said Ella. 'She's expecting to see me at the ball right now! And she'll come looking!'

'That sounds right, Esme,' said Nanny Ogg. 'You want to face her somewhere you choose. I don't want her lookin' for us on a night like this. I want to see her coming.'

There was a fluttering in the darkness above them. A small dark shape glided down and landed on the cobbles. Even in the darkness its eyes gleamed. It stared expectantly at the witches with far too much intelligence for a mere fowl.

'That's Mrs Gogol's cockerel,' said Nanny, 'ain't it?'

'Exactly what it is I might never exactly decide,' said Granny. 'I wish I knew where she stood.'

'Good or bad, you mean?' said Magrat.

'She's a good cook,' said Nanny. 'I don't think anyone can cook like she do and be *that* bad.'

'Is she the woman who lives out in the swamp?' said Ella. 'I've heard all kinds of stories about her.'

'She's a bit too ready to turn dead people into zombies,' said Granny. 'And that's not right.'

'Well, we just turned a cat into a person – I mean, a *human* person' – Nanny, inveterate cat lover, corrected herself – 'and that's not strictly right either. It's probably a long way from strictly right.'

'Yes, but we did it for the right reasons,' said Granny.

'We don't know what Mrs Gogol's reasons are –'

There was a growl from the alley-way. Nanny scuttled towards it, and they heard her scolding voice.

'No! Put him down this minute!'

'Mine! Mine!'

Legba strutted a little way along the street, and then turned and looked expectantly at them.

Granny scratched her chin, and walked a little way away from Magrat and Ella, sizing them up. Then she turned and looked around.

'Hmm,' she said. 'Lily is expecting to see you, ain't she?'

'She can look out of reflections,' said Ella nervously.

'Hmmm,' said Granny again. She stuck her finger in her ear and twiddled it for a moment. 'Well, Magrat, you're the godmother around here. What's the most important thing we have to do?'

Magrat had never played a card game in her life.

'Keep Ella safe,' she said promptly, amazed at Granny suddenly admitting that she was, after all, the one who had been given the wand. 'That's what fairy godmothering is all about.'

'Yes?'

Granny Weatherwax frowned.

'You know,' she said, 'you two are just about the same size . . .'

Magrat's expression of puzzlement lasted for half a second before it was replaced by one of sudden horror.

She backed away.

'Someone's got to do it,' said Granny.

'Oh, no! No! It wouldn't work! It really wouldn't work! No!'

'Magrat Garlick,' said Granny Weatherwax, triumphantly, 'you *shall* go to the ball!'

The coach cornered on two wheels. Greebo stood on the coachman's box, swaying and grinning madly and cracking the whip. This was even better than his fluffy ball with a bell in it . . .

Inside the coach Magrat was wedged between the two older witches, her head in her hands.

'But Ella might get lost in the swamp!'

'Not with that cockerel leading the way. She'll be safer in Mrs Gogol's swamp than at the ball, I know that,' said Nanny.

'Thank *you*!'

'You're welcome,' said Granny.

'Everyone'll know I'm not her!'

'Not with the mask on they won't,' said Granny.

'But my hair's the wrong *colour*!'

'I can tint that up a treat, no problem,' said Nanny.

'I'm the wrong *shape*!'

'We can –' Granny hesitated. 'Can you, you know, puff yourself out a bit more?'

'No!'

'Have you got a spare handkerchief, Gytha?'

'I reckon I could tear a bit off my petticoat, Esme.'

'Ouch!'

'There!'

'And these glass shoes don't *fit*!'

'They fit me fine,' said Nanny. 'I gave 'em a try.'

'Yes, but I've got smaller feet than you!'

'That's all right,' said Granny. 'You put on a couple of pairs of my socks and they'll fit real snug.'

Bereft of all further excuses, Magrat struck out in sheer desperation.

'But I don't know how to *behave* at balls!'

Granny Weatherwax had to admit that she didn't, either. She raised her eyebrows at Nanny.

'You used to go dancin' when you were young,' she said.

'Well,' said Nanny Ogg, social tutor, 'what you do is, you tap men with your fan – got your fan? – and say things like "La, sir!" It helps to giggle, too. And flutter your eyelashes a bit. And pout.'

'How am I supposed to *pout*?'

Nanny Ogg demonstrated.

'Yuk!'

'Don't worry,' said Granny. 'We'll be there too.'

'And that's supposed to make me feel *better*, is it?'

Nanny reached behind Magrat and grabbed Granny's shoulder. Her lips formed the words: Won't work. She's all to pieces. No *confidence*.

Granny nodded.

'Perhaps I ought to do it,' said Nanny, in a loud voice. 'I'm experienced at balls. I bet if I wore my hair long and wore the mask and them shiny shoes and we hemmed up the dress a foot no one'd know the difference, what do you say?'

Magrat was so overawed by the sheer fascinating picture of this that she obeyed unthinkingly when Granny Weatherwax said, '*Look at me, Magrat Garlick.*'

The pumpkin coach entered the palace drive at high speed, scattering horses and pedestrians, and braked by the steps in a shower of gravel.

'That was *fun*,' said Greebo. And then lost interest.

A couple of flunkies bustled forward to open the door, and were nearly thrown back by the sheer force of the arrogance that emanated from within.

'Hurry up, peasants!'

Magrat swept out, pushing the major-domo away. She gathered up her skirts and ran up the red carpet. At the top, a footman was unwise enough to ask her for her ticket.

'You impertinent *lackey*!'

The footman, recognising instantly the boundless bad manners of the well-bred, backed away quickly.

Down by the coach, Nanny Ogg said, 'You don't think you might have overdone it a little bit?'

'I had to,' said Granny. 'You know what she's like.'

'How are we going to get in? We ain't got tickets. And we ain't dressed properly, either.'

'Get the broomsticks down off the rack,' said Granny. 'We're going straight to the top.'

They touched down on the battlements of a tower overlooking the palace grounds. The strains of courtly music drifted up from below, and there was the occasional pop and flare of fireworks from the river.

Granny opened a likely-looking door in the tower and descended the circular stairs, which led to a landing.

'Posh carpet on the floor,' said Nanny. 'Why's it on the walls too?'

'Them's *tapestries*,' said Granny.

'Cor,' said Nanny. 'You live and learn. Well, I do anyway.'

Granny stopped with her hand on a doorknob.

'What do you mean by that?' she said.

'Well, I never knew you had a sister.'

'We never talked about her.'

'It's a shame when families break up like that,' said Nanny.

'Huh! *You* said *your* sister Beryl was a greedy ingrate with the conscience of an oyster.'

'Well, yes, but she *is* my sister.'

Granny opened the door.

'Well, well,' she said.

'What's up? What's up? Don't just stand there.' Nanny peered around her and into the room.

'Coo,' she said.

Magrat paused in the big, red-velvet ante-room. Strange thoughts fire-worked around her head; she hadn't felt like this since the herbal wine. But struggling among them like a tiny prosaic potato in a spray of psychedelic chrysanthemums was an inner voice screaming that she didn't even know how to dance. Apart from in circles.

But it couldn't be difficult if ordinary people managed it.

The tiny inner Magrat struggling to keep its balance on the surge of arrogant self-confidence wondered if this was how Granny Weatherwax felt *all the time*.

She raised the hem of her dress slightly and looked down at her shoes.

They couldn't be real glass, or else she'd be hobbling towards some emergency first aid by now. Nor were they transparent. The human foot is a useful organ but is not, except to some people with highly specialised interests, particularly attractive to look at.

The shoes were mirrors. Dozens of facets caught the light.

Two mirrors on her feet. Magrat vaguely recalled something about . . . about a witch never getting caught between two mirrors, wasn't it? Or was it never trust a man with orange eyebrows? Something she'd been taught, back when she'd been an ordinary person. Something . . . like . . . a witch should never stand between two mirrors because, because, because the person that walked away might not be the same person. Or something. Like . . . you were spread out among the images, your whole soul was pulled out thin, and somewhere in the distant images a dark part of you would get out and come looking for you, if you weren't very careful. Or something.

She overruled the thought. It didn't matter.

She stepped forward, to where a little knot of other guests were waiting to make their entrance.

'Lord Henry Gleet and Lady Gleet!'

The ballroom wasn't a room at all, but a courtyard open to the soft night airs. Steps led down into it. At the far end, another much wider staircase, lined with flickering torches, led up into the palace itself. On the far wall, huge and easily visible, was a clock.

'The Honourable Douglas Incessant!'

The time was a quarter to eight. Magrat had a vague recollection of some old woman shouting something about the time, but . . . that didn't matter either . . .

'Lady Volentia D'Arrangement!'

She reached the top of the stairs. The butler who was announcing the arrivals looked her up and down and then, in the manner of one who had been coached carefully all afternoon for this very moment, bellowed:

'Er . . . Mysterious and beautiful stranger!'

Silence spread out from the bottom of the steps like spilled paint. Five hundred heads turned to look at Magrat.

A day before, even the mere thought of having five hundred people staring at her would have melted Magrat like butter in a furnace. But now she stared back, smiled, and raised her chin haughtily.

Her fan snapped open like a gunshot.

The mysterious and beautiful stranger, daughter of Simplicity Garlick, granddaughter of Araminta Garlick, her self-possession churning so strongly that it was crystallising out on the sides of her personality . . .

. . . stepped out.

A moment later another guest stalked past the butler.

The butler hesitated. Something about the figure worried him. It kept going in and out of focus. He wasn't entirely certain if there was anyone else there at all.

Then his common sense, which had temporarily gone and hidden behind something, took over. After all, it was Samedi Nuit Mort – people were *supposed* to dress up and look weird. You were *allowed* to see people like that.

'Excuse me, er, sir,' he said. 'Who shall I say it is?'

I'M HERE INCOGNITO.

The butler was sure nothing had been said, but he was also certain that he had heard the words.

'Um . . . fine . . .' he mumbled. 'Go on in, then . . . um.' He brightened. 'Damn good mask, sir.'

He watched the dark figure walk down the steps, and leaned against a pillar.

Well, that was about it. He pulled a handkerchief out from his pocket, removed his powdered wig, and wiped his brow. He felt as though he'd just had a narrow escape, and what was even worse was that he didn't know from *what*.

He looked cautiously around, and then sidled into the ante-room and took up a position behind a velvet curtain, where he could enjoy a quiet roll-up.

He nearly swallowed it when another figure loped silently up the red carpet. It was dressed like a pirate that had just raided a ship carrying black leather goods for the discerning customer. One eye had a patch over it. The other gleamed like a malevolent emerald. And no one that big ought to be able to walk that quietly.

The butler stuck the dog-end behind his ear.

'Excuse me, milord,' he said, running after the man and touching him firmly yet respectfully on the arm. 'I shall need to see your tic . . . your . . . tic . . .'

The man transferred his gaze to the hand on his arm. The butler let go hurriedly.

'Wrowwwl?'

'Your . . . ticket . . .'

The man opened his mouth and hissed.

'Of course,' said the butler, backing away with the efficient speed of someone who certainly isn't being paid enough to face a needle-toothed maniac in black leather, 'I expect you're one of the Duc's friends, yes?'

'Wrowwl.'

'No problem . . . no problem . . . but Sir has forgotten Sir's mask . . .'

'Wrowwl?'

The butler waved frantically to a side-table piled high with masks.

'The Duc requested that everyone here is masked,' said the butler. 'Er. I wonder if Sir would find something here to his liking?'

There's always a few of them, he thought to himself. It says 'Masque' in big curly letters on the invite, in gold yet, but there's always a few buggers who thinks it means it's from someone called Maskew. This one was quite likely looting towns when he should have been learning to read.

The greasy man stared at the masks. All the good ones had been taken by earlier arrivals, but that didn't seem to dismay him.

He pointed.

'Want that one,' he said.

'Er . . . a . . . very good choice, my lord. Allow me to help you on –'

'Wrowwl!'

The butler backed away, clutching at his own arm.

The man glared at him, then dropped the mask over his head and squinted out through an eyehole at a mirror.

Damn odd, the butler thought. I mean, it's not the kind of mask the men choose. They go for skulls and birds and bulls and stuff like that. Not *cats*.

The odd thing was that the mask had just been a pretty ginger cat head when it was on the table. On its wearer it was . . . still a cat head, only a lot more so, and somehow slightly more feline and a lot nastier than it should have been.

'Aaalwaaays waanted to bee ginger,' said the man.

'On you it looks good, sir,' trilled the butler.

The cat-headed man turned his head this way and that, clearly in love with what he was seeing.

Greebo yowled softly and happily to himself and ambled into the ball. He wanted something to eat, someone to fight, and then . . . well, he'd have to see.

For wolves and pigs and bears, thinking that they're human is a tragedy. For a cat, it's an experience.

Besides, this new shape was a lot more fun. No one had thrown an old boot at him for over ten minutes.

The two witches looked around the room.

'Odd,' said Nanny Ogg. 'Not what I'd expect in, you know, a royal bedroom.'

'Is it a royal bedroom?'

'There's a crown on the door.'

'Oh.'

Granny looked around at the decor.

'What do you know about royal bedrooms?' she said, more or less for something to say. 'You've never been in a royal bedroom.'

'I might have been,' said Nanny.

'You never have!'

'Remember young Verence's coronation? We all got invited to the palace?' said Nanny. 'When I went to have a – to powder my nose I saw the door open, so I went in and had a bit of a bounce up and down.'

'That's treason. You can get put in prison for that,' said Granny severely, and added, 'What was it like?'

'Very comfy. Young Magrat doesn't know what she's missing. And it was a lot better than this, I don't mind saying,' said Nanny.

The basic colour was green. Green walls, green floor. There was a wardrobe and a bedside table. Even a bedside rug, which was green. The light filtered in through a window filled with greenish glass.

'Like being at the bottom of a pond,' said Granny. She swatted something. 'And there's flies everywhere!' She paused, as if thinking very hard, and said, 'Hmm . . .'

'A Duc pond,' said Nanny.

There *were* flies everywhere. They buzzed on the window and zigzagged aimlessly back and forth across the ceiling.

'Duc pond,' Nanny repeated, because people who make that kind of joke never let well alone, 'like duck –'

'I heard,' said Granny. She flailed at a fat bluebottle.

'Anyway, you'd think there wouldn't be flies in a royal bedroom,' muttered Nanny.

'You'd think there'd be a bed, in fact,' said Granny.

Which there wasn't. What there was instead, and what was preying somewhat on their minds, was a big round wooden cover on the floor. It was about six feet across. There were convenient handles.

They walked around it. Flies rose up and hummed away.

'I'm thinking of a story,' said Granny.

'Me too,' said Nanny Ogg, her tone slightly shriller than usual. 'There was this girl who married this man and he said you can go anywhere you like in the palace but you mustn't open *that* door and she did and she found he'd murdered all his other . . .'

Her voice trailed off.

Granny was staring hard at the cover, and scratching her chin.

'Put it like this,' said Nanny, trying to be reasonable against all odds. 'What could we possibly find under there that's worse than we could imagine?'

They each took a handle.

Five minutes later Granny Weatherwax and Nanny Ogg stepped outside the Duc's bedroom. Granny closed the door very quietly.

They stared at one another.

'Cor,' said Nanny, her face still pale.

'Yes,' said Granny. 'Stories!'

'I'd heard about . . . you know, people like him, but I never believed it. Yuk. I wonder what he looks like.'

'You can't tell just by lookin',' said Granny.

'It explains the flies, at any rate,' said Nanny Ogg.

She raised a hand to her mouth in horror.

'And our Magrat's down there with him!' she said. 'And you know what's going to happen. They're going to meet one another and –'

'But there's hundreds of other people,' said Granny. 'It's hardly what you'd call *intimate*.'

'Yes . . . but even the thought of him, you know, even *touching* her . . . I mean, it'd be like holding a –'

'Does Ella count as a princess, d'you think?' said Granny.

'What? Oh. Yeah. Probably. For foreign parts. Why?'

'Then that means there's more than one story here. Lily's letting several happen all at the same time,' said Granny. 'Think about it. It's not touching that's the trick. It's *kissing*.'

'We've got to get down there!' said Nanny. 'We've got to stop it! I mean, you know me, I'm no prude, but . . . yuk . . .'

'I say! Old woman!'

They turned. A small fat woman in a red dress and a towering white wig was peering haughtily at them from behind a fox mask.

'Yes?' snapped Granny.

'Yes, *my lady*,' said the fat woman. 'Where are your manners? I demand that you direct me to the powder room this instant! *And what do you think you're doing?*'

This was to Nanny Ogg, who was walking around her and staring critically at her dress.

'You're a 20, maybe a 22?' said Nanny.

'What? What is this *impertinence*?'

Nanny Ogg rubbed her chin thoughtfully. 'Well, I dunno,' she said, 'red in a dress has never been *me*. You haven't got anything in blue, have you?'

The choleric woman turned to strike Nanny with her fan, but a skinny hand tapped her on the shoulder.

She looked up into Granny Weatherwax's face.

As she passed out dreamily she was aware of a voice, a long way off, saying, 'Well, that's me fitted. But she's never a size 20. And if I had a face like that *I'd* never wear red . . .'

Lady Volentia D'Arrangement relaxed in the inner sanctum of the ladies' rest room. She removed her mask and fished an errant beauty spot from the depths of her décolletage. Then she reached around and down to try and adjust her bustle, an exercise guaranteed to produce the most ridiculous female gymnastics on every world except those where the panty girdle had been invented.

Apart from being as well-adapted a parasite as the oak bracket fungus Lady Volentia D'Arrangement was, by and large, a blameless sort of person. She always attended events for the better class of charity, and made a point of knowing the first names of nearly all her servants – the cleaner ones, at least. And she was, on the whole, kind to animals and even to children if they had been washed and didn't make too much noise. All in all, she didn't deserve what was about to happen to her, which was the fate Mother Nature had in store for any woman in this room on this night who happened to have approximately the same measurements as Granny Weatherwax.

She was aware of someone coming up beside her.

'S'cuse me, missus.'

It turned out to be a small, repulsive lower-class woman with a big ingratiating smile.

'What do you want, old woman?' said Lady Volentia.

'S'cuse me,' said Nanny Ogg. 'My friend over there would like a word with you.'

Lady Volentia looked around haughtily into . . .

. . . icy, blue-eyed, hypnotic oblivion.

✫   ✫   ✫

'What's this thing like an extra bu . . . hobo?'

'It's a bustle, Esme.'

'It's damn uncomfortable is what it is. I keep on feeling someone's following me around.'

'The white suits you, anyway.'

'No it don't. Black's the only colour for a proper witch. And this wig is too hot. Who wants a foot of hair on their heads?'

Granny donned her mask. It was an eagle's face in white feathers stuck with sequins.

Nanny adjusted some unmentionable underpinning somewhere beneath her crinoline and straightened up.

'Cor, look at us,' she said. 'Them feathers in your hair really look good.'

'I've never been vain,' said Granny Weatherwax. 'You know that, Gytha. No one could ever call *me* vain.'

'No, Esme,' said Nanny Ogg.

Granny twirled a bit.

'Are you ready then, Dame Ogg?' she said.

'Yes. Let's *do* it, Lady Weatherwax.'

The dance floor was thronged. Decorations hung from every pillar, but they were black and silver, the colours of the festival of Samedi Nuit Mort. An orchestra was playing on a balcony. Dancers whirled. The din was immense.

A waiter with a tray of drinks suddenly found that he was a waiter without a tray of drinks. He looked around, and then down to a small fox under a huge white wig.

'Bugger off and get us some more,' said Nanny pleasantly. 'Can you see her, your ladyship?'

'There's too many people.'

'Well, can you see the Duc?'

'How do I know? Everyone's got masks on!'

'Hey, is that food over there?'

Many of the less energetic or more hungry of the Genua nobility were clustered around the long buffet. All they were aware of, apart from sharp digs with a pair of industrious elbows, was an amiable monotone at chest height, on the lines of '. . . mind your backs . . . stand aside there . . . comin' through.'

Nanny fought her way to the table and nudged a space for Granny Weatherwax.

'Cor, what a spread, eh?' she said. 'Mind you, they have tiny chickens in these parts.' She grabbed a plate.

'Them's quails.'

'I'll 'ave three. 'Ere, charlie chan!'

A flunkey stared at her.

'Got any pickles?'

'I'm afraid not, ma'am.'

Nanny Ogg looked along a table which included roast swans, a roasted peacock that probably wouldn't have felt any better about it even if it *had* known that its tail feathers were going to be stuck back in afterwards, and more fruits, boiled lobsters, nuts, cakes, creams and trifles than a hermit's dream.

'Well, got any relish?'

'No, ma'am.'

'Tomato ketchup?'

'*No*, ma'am.'

'And they call this a gormay paradise,' muttered Nanny, as the band struck up the next dance. She nudged a tall figure helping himself to the lobster. 'Some place, eh?'

VERY NICE.

'Good mask you've got there.'

THANK YOU.

Nanny was spun around by Granny Weatherwax's hand on her shoulder.

'There's Magrat!'

'Where? Where?' said Nanny.

'Over there . . . sitting by the potted plants.'

'Oh, yes. On the chassy longyew,' said Nanny. 'That's "sofa" in foreign, you know,' she added.

'What's she doing?'

'Being attractive to men, I think.'

'What, *Magrat*?'

'Yeah. You're really getting good at that hypnotism, ain't you.'

Magrat fluttered her fan and looked up at the Compte de Yoyo.

'La, sir,' she said. 'You may get me another plate of lark's eggs, if you *really* must.'

'Like a shot, dear lady!' The old man bustled off in the direction of the buffet.

Magrat surveyed her empire of admirers, and then extended a languorous hand towards Captain de Vere of the Palace Guard. He stood to attention.

'*Dear* captain,' she said, 'you may have the pleasure of the next dance.'

☆   ☆   ☆

'Acting like a hussy,' said Granny disapprovingly.

Nanny gave her an odd look.

'Not really,' she said. 'Anyway, a bit of hussing never did anyone any harm. At least none of those men look like the Duc. 'Ere, what you doing?'

This was to a small bald-headed man who was trying surreptitiously to set up a small easel in front of them.

'Uh . . . if you ladies could just hold still for a few minutes,' he said shyly. 'For the woodcut.'

'What woodcut?' said Granny Weatherwax.

'You *know*,' said the man, opening a small penknife. 'Everyone likes to see their woodcut in the broadsheets after a ball like this? "Lady Thing enjoying a joke with Lord Whatsit", that sort of thing?'

Granny Weatherwax opened her mouth to reply, but Nanny Ogg laid a gentle hand on her arm. She relaxed a little and sought for something more suitable to say.

'I knows a joke about alligator sandwiches,' she volunteered, and shook Nanny's hand away. 'There was a man, and he went into an inn and he said "Do you sell alligator sandwiches?" and the other man said "Yes" and he said, "Then give me an alligator sandwich – and don't be a long time about it!"'

She gave him a triumphant look.

'Yes?' said the woodcutter, chipping away quickly, 'and then what happened?'

Nanny Ogg dragged Granny away quickly, searching for a distraction.

'Some people don't know a joke when they hear it,' said Granny.

As the band launched into another number Nanny Ogg fumbled in a pocket and found the dance card that belonged to an owner now slumbering peacefully in a distant room.

'This is,' she turned the card round, her lips moving wonderingly, 'Sir, Roger the Coverley?'

'Ma'am?'

Granny Weatherwax looked around. A plump military man with big whiskers was bowing to her. He looked as though he'd enjoyed quite a few jokes in his time.

'Yes?'

'You promised me the honour of this dance, m'lady?'

'No I didn't.'

The man looked puzzled. 'But I assure you, Lady D'Arrangement . . . your card . . . my name is Colonel Moutarde . . .'

Granny gave him a look of deep suspicion, and then read the dance card attached to her fan.

'Oh.'

'Do *you* know how to dance?' hissed Nanny.

'Of course.'

'Never *seen* you dance,' said Nanny.

Granny Weatherwax had been on the point of giving the colonel as polite a refusal as she could manage. Now she threw back her shoulders defiantly.

'A witch can do anything she puts her mind to, Gytha Ogg. Come, Mr Colonel.'

Nanny watched as the pair disappeared into the throng.

''Allo, foxy lady,' said a voice behind her. She looked around. There was no one there.

'Down here.'

She looked down.

A very small body wearing the uniform of a captain in the palace guard, a powdered wig and an ingratiating smile beamed up at her.

'My name's Casanunda,' he said. 'I'm reputed to be the world's greatest lover. What do you think?'

Nanny Ogg looked him up and down or, at least, down and further down.

'You're a dwarf,' she said.

'Size isn't important.'

Nanny Ogg considered her position. One colleague known for her shy and retiring nature was currently acting like that whatshername, the heathen queen who was always playing up to men and bathing in asses' milk and stuff, and the *other* one was acting very odd and dancing with a *man* even though she didn't know one foot from the other. Nanny Ogg felt she was at least owed a bit of time in which to be her own woman.

'Can you dance as well?' she said wearily.

'Oh yes. How about a date?'

'How old do you think I am?' said Nanny.

Casanunda considered. 'All right, then. How about a prune?'

Nanny sighed, and reached down for his hand. 'Come on.'

Lady Volentia D'Arrangement staggered limply along a passageway, a forlorn thin shape in complicated corsetry and ankle-length underwear.

She wasn't at all sure what had happened. There had been that *frightful* woman, and then this feeling of absolute *bliss* and then . . . she'd been sitting on the carpet with her *dress* off. Lady Volentia had been to enough balls in her dull life to know that there were occasions when you woke up in strange rooms with your dress off, but that tended to be later in the evening and at least you had some idea of why you were there . . .

She eased her way along, holding on to the wall. Someone was definitely going to get told off about this.

A figure came around a bend in the corridor, idly tossing a turkey leg into the air with one hand and catching it with the other.

'I say,' said Lady Volentia, 'I wonder if you would be so good as to – oh . . .'

She looked up at a leather-clad figure with an eyepatch and a grin like a corsair raider.

'Wroowwwwl!'

'Oh. I say!'

Nothing to this dancing, Granny Weatherwax told herself. It's just moving around to music.

It helped to be able to read her partner's mind. Dancing is instinctive, after you've got past that stage of looking down to see what your feet are doing, and witches are good at reading resonating instincts. There was a slight struggle as the colonel tried to lead, but he soon gave in, partly in the face of Granny Weatherwax's sheer refusal to compromise but mainly because of her boots.

Lady D'Arrangement's shoes hadn't fitted. Besides, Granny was attached to her boots. They had complicated iron fixtures, and toecaps like battering rams. When it came to dancing, Granny's boots went exactly wherever they wanted to go.

She steered her helpless and slightly crippled partner towards Nanny Ogg, who had already cleared quite a space around her. What Granny could achieve with two pounds of hobnailed syncopation Nanny Ogg could achieve merely with her bosom.

It was a large and experienced bosom, and not one that was subject to restraint. As Nanny Ogg bounced down, it went up; when she gyrated right, it hadn't finished twirling left. In addition, Nanny's feet moved in a complicated jig step regardless of the actual tempo, so that while her body actually progressed at the speed of a waltz her feet were doing something a bit nearer to a hornpipe. The total effect obliged her partner to dance several feet away, and many surrounding couples to stop dancing just to watch in fascination, in case the build-up of harmonic vibrations dropped her into the chandeliers.

Granny and her helpless partner whirled past.

'Stop showin' off,' Granny hissed, and disappeared into the throng again.

'Who's your friend?' said Casanunda.

'She's –' Nanny began.

There was a blast of trumpets.

'That was a bit off the beat,' she said.

'No, that means the Duc is arriving,' said Casanunda.

The band stopped playing. The couples, as one, turned and faced the main staircase.

There were two figures descending in stately fashion.

My word, he's a sleek and handsome devil, Nanny told herself. It just goes to show. Esme's right. You can never tell by lookin'.

And her . . .

. . . that's Lily Weatherwax?

The woman wasn't masked.

Give or take the odd laughter line and wrinkle, it was Granny Weatherwax to the life.

Almost . . .

Nanny found she was turning to find the white eagle head in the crowd. All heads were turned to the staircase, but there was one staring as if her gaze was a steel rod.

Lily Weatherwax wore white. Until that point it had never occurred to Nanny Ogg that there could be different colours of white. Now she knew better. The white of Lily Weatherwax's dress seemed to radiate; if all the lights went out, she felt, Lily's dress would glow. It had style. It gleamed, and had puffed sleeves and was edged with lace.

And Lily Weatherwax looked – Nanny Ogg had to admit it – younger. There was the same bone structure and fine Weatherwax complexion, but it looked . . . less worn.

If that's what bein' bad does to you, Nanny thought, I could of done with some of that years ago. The wages of sin is death but so is the salary of virtue, and at least the evil get to go home early on Fridays.

The eyes were the same, though. Somewhere in the genetics of the Weatherwaxes was a piece of sapphire. Maybe generations of them.

The Duc was unbelievably handsome. But that was understandable. He was wearing black. Even his eyes wore black.

Nanny surfaced, and pushed her way through the throng to Granny Weatherwax.

'Esme?'

She grabbed Granny's arm.

'Esme?'

'Hmm?'

Nanny was aware that the crowd was moving, parting like a sea, between the staircase and the chaise-longue at the far end of the hall.

Granny Weatherwax's knuckles were as white as her dress.

'Esme? What's happening? What are you *doing*?' said Nanny.

'Trying . . . to . . . stop . . . the story,' said Granny.

'What's *she* doing, then?'

'Letting . . . things . . . happen!'

The crowd were pulling back past them. It didn't seem to be a conscious thing. It was just happening that a sort of corridor was forming.

The Prince walked slowly along it. Behind Lily, faint images hung in the air so that she appeared to be followed by a succession of fading ghosts.

Magrat stood up.

Nanny was aware of a rainbow hue in the air. Possibly there was the tweeting of bluebirds.

The Prince took Magrat by the hand.

Nanny glanced up at Lily Weatherwax, who had remained a few steps up from the foot of the stairs and was smiling beneficently.

Then she tried to put a focus on the future.

It was horribly easy.

Normally the future is branching off at every turn and it's only possible to have the haziest idea of what is likely to happen, even when you're as temporally sensitive as a witch. But here there were stories coiled around the tree of events, bending it into a new shape.

Granny Weatherwax wouldn't know what a pattern of quantum inevitability was if she found it eating her dinner. If you mentioned the words 'paradigms of space-time' to her she'd just say 'What?'. But that didn't mean she was ignorant. It just meant that she didn't have any truck with words, especially gibberish. She just knew that there were certain things that happened continually in human history, like three-dimensional clichés. Stories.

'And now we're part of it! And I can't stop it,' said Granny. 'There's got to be a place where I can stop it, and I can't find it!'

The band struck up. It was playing a waltz.

Magrat and the Prince whirled around the dance floor once, never taking their eyes off each other. Then a few couples dared to join them. And then, as if the whole ball was a machine whose spring had been wound up again, the floor was full of dancing couples and the sounds of conversation flowed back into the void.

'Are you going to introduce me to your friend?' said Casanunda, from somewhere near Nanny's elbow. People swept past them.

'It's all got to happen,' said Granny, ignoring the low-level interruption. 'Everything. The kiss, the clock striking midnight, her running out and losing the glass slipper, everything.'

'Ur, yuk,' said Nanny, leaning on her partner's head. 'I'd rather lick toads.'

'She looks just my type,' said Casanunda, his voice slightly muffled. 'I've always been very attracted to dominant women.'

The witches looked at the whirling couple, who were staring into one another's eyes.

'I could trip them up, no trouble,' said Nanny.

'You can't. That's not something that can happen.'

'Well, Magrat's sensible . . . more or less sensible,' said Nanny. 'Maybe she'll notice something's wrong.'

'I'm good at what I do, Gytha Ogg,' said Granny. 'She won't notice nothing until the clock strikes midnight.'

They both turned to look up. It was barely nine.

'Y'know,' said Nanny Ogg. 'Clocks don't strike midnight. Seems to me they just strike twelve. I mean, it's just a matter of bongs.'

They both looked up at the clock again.

In the swamp, Legba the black cockerel crowed. He always crowed at sunset.

Nanny Ogg pounded up another flight of stairs and leaned against the wall to catch her breath.

It had to be somewhere round here.

'Another time you'll learn to keep your mouth shut, Gytha Ogg,' she muttered.

'I expect we're leaving the hurly-burly of the ball for an intimate tête-à-tête somewhere?' said Casanunda hopefully, trotting along behind her.

Nanny tried to ignore him and ran along a dusty passage. There was a balcony rail on one side, looking down into the ballroom. And there . . .

. . . a small wooden door.

She rammed it open with her elbow. Within, mechanisms whirred in counterpoint to the dancing figures below as if the clock was propelling them, which, in a metaphorical sense, it was.

Clockwork, Nanny thought. Once you know about clockwork, you know about *everything*.

I wish I bloody well knew about clockwork.

'Very cosy,' said Casanunda.

She squeezed through the gap and into the clock space. Cog-wheels clicked past her nose.

She stared at them for a moment.

Lawks. All this just to chop Time up into little bits.

'It might be just the teensiest bit cramped,' said Casanunda, from somewhere near her armpit. 'But needs must, ma'am. I remember once in Quirm, there was this sedan chair and . . .'

Let's see, thought Nanny. This bit is connected to that bit, this one turns, that one turns *faster*, this spiky bit wobbles backwards and forwards . . .

Oh, well. Just twist the first thing you can grab, as the High Priest said to the vestal virgin.*

Nanny Ogg spat on her hands, gripped the largest cog-wheel, and twisted. It carried on turning, pulling her with it.

Blimey. Oh, well . . .

Then she did what neither Granny Weatherwax nor Magrat would have dreamed of doing in the circumstances. But Nanny Ogg's voyages on the sea of intersexual dalliance had gone rather further than twice around the lighthouse, and she saw nothing demeaning in getting a man to help her.

She simpered at Casanunda.

'Things would be a lot more comfortable in our little *pie-de-terre* if you could just push this little wheel around a bit,' she said. 'I'm sure *you* could manage it,' she added.

'Oh, no problem, good lady,' said Casanunda. He reached up with one hand. Dwarfs are immensely strong for their size. The wheel seemed to offer him no resistance at all.

Somewhere in the mechanism something resisted for a moment and then went *clonk*. Big wheels turned reluctantly. Little wheels screamed on their axles. A small important piece flew out and pinged off Casanunda's small bullet head.

And, much faster than nature had ever intended, the hands sped round the face.

A new noise right overhead made Nanny Ogg look up.

Her self-satisfied expression faded. The hammer that struck the hours was swinging slowly backwards. It struck Nanny that she was standing right under the bell at the same time as the bell, too, was struck.

Bong . . .

'Oh, bugger!'

. . . *bong* . . .

. . . *bong* . . .

. . . *bong* . . .

Mist rolled through the swamp. And shadows moved with it, their shapes

---

* This is the last line of a Discworld joke lost, alas, to posterity.

indistinct on this night when the difference between the living and the dead was only a matter of time.

Mrs Gogol could feel them among the trees. The homeless. The hungry. The silent people. Those forsaken by men and gods. The people of the mists and the mud, whose only strength was somewhere on the other side of weakness, whose beliefs were as rickety and home-made as their homes. And the people from the city – not the ones who lived in the big white houses and went to balls in fine coaches, but the other ones. They were the ones that stories are never about. Stories are not, on the whole, interested in swineherds who remain swineherds and poor and humble shoemakers whose destiny is to die slightly poorer and much humbler.

These people were the ones who made the magical kingdom work, who cooked its meals and swept its floors and carted its night soil and were its faces in the crowd and whose wishes and dreams, undemanding as they were, were of no consequence. The *invisibles*.

And me out here, she thought. Building traps for gods.

There are various forms of voodoo in the multiverse, because it's a religion that can be put together from any ingredients that happen to be lying around. And all of them try, in some way, to call down a god into the body of a human being.

That was stupid, Mrs Gogol thought. That was dangerous.

Mrs Gogol's voodoo worked the other way about. What was a god? A focus of belief. If people believed, a god began to grow. Feebly at first, but if the swamp taught anything, it taught patience. Anything could be the focus of a god. A handful of feathers with a red ribbon around them, a hat and coat on a couple of sticks . . . anything. Because when all people had was practically nothing, then anything could be almost everything. And then you fed it, and lulled it, like a goose heading for pâté, and let the power grow very slowly, and when the time was ripe you opened the path . . . backwards. A human could ride the god, rather than the other way around. There would be a price to pay later, but there always was. In Mrs Gogol's experience, everyone ended up dying.

She took a pull of rum and handed the jug to Saturday.

Saturday took a mouthful, and passed the jug up to something that might have been a hand.

'Let it begin,' said Mrs Gogol.

The dead man picked up three small drums and began to beat out a rhythm, heartbeat fast.

After a while something tapped Mrs Gogol on the shoulder and handed her the jug. It was empty.

Might as well begin . . .

'Lady Bon Anna smile on me. Mister Safe Way protect me. Stride Wide Man guide me. Hotaloga Andrews catch me.

'I stand between the light and the dark, but that no matter, because I *am* between.

'Here is rum for you. Tobacco for you. Food for you. A home for you.

'Now you listen to me good . . .'

. . . *bong*.

For Magrat it was like waking from a dream into a dream. She'd been idly dreaming that she was dancing with the most handsome man in the room, and . . . she was dancing with the most handsome man in the room.

Except that he wore two circles of smoked glass over his eyes.

Although Magrat was soft-hearted, a compulsive daydreamer and, as Granny Weatherwax put it, a wet hen, she wouldn't be a witch if she didn't have certain instincts and the sense to trust them. She reached up and, before his hands could move, tweaked the things away.

Magrat had seen eyes like that before, but never on something walking upright.

Her feet, which a moment before had been moving gracefully across the floor, tripped over themselves.

'Er . . .' she began.

And she was aware that his hands, pink and well-manicured, were also cold and damp.

Magrat turned and ran, knocking the couples aside in her madness to get away. Her legs tangled in the dress. The stupid shoes skittered on the floor.

A couple of footmen blocked the stairs to the hall.

Magrat's eyes narrowed. Getting out was what mattered.

'Hai!'

'Ouch!'

And then she ran on, slipping at the top of the stairs. A glass slipper slithered across the marble.

'How the hell's anyone supposed to *move* in these things?' she screamed at the world in general. Hopping frantically on one foot, she wrenched the other shoe off and ran into the night.

The Prince walked slowly to the top of the steps and picked up the discarded slipper.

He held it. The light glittered off its facets.

Granny Weatherwax leaned against the wall in the shadows. All stories had a turning point, and it had to be close.

She was good at getting into other people's minds, but now she had to get into hers. She concentrated. Down deeper . . . past everyday thoughts and minor concerns, *faster, faster* . . . through layers of deep cogitation . . . deeper . . . past things sealed off and crusted over, old guilts and congealed regrets, but there was no time for them now . . . down . . . and there . . . the silver thread of the story. She'd been part of it, *was* part of it, so it had to be a part of her.

It poured past. She reached out.

She hated everything that predestined people, that fooled them, that made them slightly less than human.

The story whipped along like a steel hawser. She gripped it.

Her eyes opened in shock. Then she stepped forward.

'Excuse me, Your Highness.'

She snatched the shoe from the Duc's hands, and raised it over her head.

Her expression of evil satisfaction was terrible to behold.

Then she dropped the shoe.

It smashed on the stairs.

A thousand glittering fragments scattered across the marble.

Coiled as it was around the length of turtle-shaped space-time known as the Discworld, the story shook. One broken end flapped loose and flailed through the night, trying to find any sequence to feed on . . .

In the clearing the trees moved. So did the shadows. Shadows shouldn't be able to move unless the light moves. These did.

The drumming stopped.

In the silence there was the occasional sizzle as power crackled across the hanging coat.

Saturday stepped forward. Green sparks flew out to his hands as he gripped the jacket and put it on.

His body jerked.

Erzulie Gogol breathed out.

'You are here,' she said. 'You are still yourself. You are exactly yourself.'

Saturday raised his hands, with his fists clenched. Occasionally an arm or leg would jerk as the power inside him squirrel-caged around in its search for freedom, but she could see that he was riding it.

'It will become easier,' she said, more gently now.

Saturday nodded.

With the power flowing inside him he had, she thought, the fire he'd had when he was alive. He had not been a particularly good man, she knew.

Genua had not been a model of civic virtue. But at least he'd never told people that they wanted him to oppress them, and that everything he did was for their own good.

Around the circle, the people of New Genua – the *old* New Genua – knelt or bowed.

He hadn't been a kind ruler. But he'd fitted. And when he'd been arbitrary or arrogant or just plain wrong, he'd never suggested that this was justified by anything other than the fact that he was bigger and stronger and occasionally nastier than other people. He'd never suggested that it was because he was *better*. And he'd never told people they ought to be happy, and imposed a kind of happiness on them. The invisible people knew that happiness is not the natural state of mankind, and is never achieved from the outside in.

Saturday nodded again, this time in satisfaction. When he opened his mouth, sparks flashed between his teeth. And when he waded through the swamp, the alligators fought to get out of his way.

It was quiet in the palace kitchens now. The huge trays of roast meat, the pigs' heads with apples in their mouths, the multi-layered trifles had long ago been carried upstairs. There was a clattering from the giant sinks at the far end, where some of the maids were making a start on the washing up.

Mrs Pleasant the cook had made herself a plate of red stripefish in crawfish sauce. She wasn't the finest cook in Genua – no one got near Mrs Gogol's gumbo, people would almost come back from the dead for a taste of Mrs Gogol's gumbo – but the comparison was as narrow as that between, say, diamonds and sapphires. She'd done her best to cook up a good banquet, because she had her professional pride, but there wasn't much she felt she was able to do with lumps of meat.

Genuan cooking, like the best cooking everywhere in the multiverse, had been evolved by people who had to make desperate use of ingredients their masters didn't want. No one would even *try* a bird's nest unless they had to. Only hunger would make a man taste his first alligator. No one would eat a shark's fin if they were allowed to eat the rest of the shark.

She poured herself a rum and was just picking up the spoon when she felt herself being watched.

A large man in a black leather doublet was staring at her from the doorway, dangling a ginger cat mask from one hand.

It was a very direct stare. Mrs Pleasant found herself wishing she'd done something about her hair and was wearing a better dress.

'Yes?' she said. 'What d'you want?'

'Waaant foood, Miss-uss Pleassunt,' said Greebo.

She looked him up and down. There were some odd types in Genua these days. This one must have been a guest at the ball, but there was something very . . . *familiar* about him.

Greebo wasn't a happy cat. People had made a fuss just because he'd dragged a roast turkey off the table. Then the skinny female with the teeth had kept simpering at him and saying she'd see him later in the rose garden, which wasn't at all the cat way of doing things, and that'd got him confused, because this wasn't the right kind of body and nor was hers. And there were too many other males around.

Then he'd smelled the kitchen. Cats gravitate to kitchens like rocks gravitate to gravity.

'I seen you somewhere before?' said Mrs Pleasant.

Greebo said nothing. He'd followed his nose to a bowl on one of the big tables.

'Waaant,' he demanded.

'Fish heads?' said Mrs Pleasant. They were technically garbage, although what she was planning with some rice and a few special sauces would turn them into the sort of dish kings fight for.

'Waant,' Greebo repeated.

Mrs Pleasant shrugged.

'You want raw fish heads, man, you take 'em,' she said.

Greebo lifted the bowl uncertainly. He wasn't too good with fingers. Then he looked around conspiratorially and ducked under the table.

There were the sounds of keen gurgitation and the bowl being scraped around on the floor.

Greebo emerged.

'Millluk?' he suggested.

Fascinated, Mrs Pleasant reached for the milk jug and a cup –

'Saaaaucerrr,' Greebo said.

– and a saucer.

Greebo took the saucer, gave it a long hard look, and put it on the floor. Mrs Pleasant stared.

Greebo finished the milk, licking the remnant off his beard. He felt a lot better now. And there was a big fire over there. He padded over to it, sat down, spat on his paw and made an attempt to clean his ears, which didn't work because inexplicably neither ears nor paw were the right shape, and then curled up as best he could. Which wasn't very well, given that he seemed to have the wrong sort of backbone, too.

After a while Mrs Pleasant heard a low, asthmatic rumble.

Greebo was trying to purr.

He had the wrong kind of throat.

In a minute he was going to wake up in a bad temper and want to fight something.

Mrs Pleasant got on with her own supper. Despite the fact that a hulking great man had just eaten a bowl of fish heads and lapped a saucer of milk in front of her, and was now stretched out uncomfortably in front of the fire, she found she didn't feel the least bit afraid. In fact she was fighting down an impulse to scratch his tummy.

Magrat wrenched off the other slipper as she ran down the long red carpet towards the palace gateway and freedom. Just getting away, that was the important thing. *From* was more urgent than *to*.

And then two figures drifted out of the shadows and faced her. She raised the slipper pathetically as they approached in absolute silence, but even in the twilight she could feel their gaze.

The crowds parted. Lily Weatherwax glided through, in a rustle of silk.

She looked Granny up and down, without any expression of surprise.

'All in white, too,' she said, dryly. 'My word, aren't you the *nice* one.'

'But I've stopped you,' said Granny, still panting with the effort. 'I've *broken* it.'

Lily Weatherwax looked past her. The snake sisters were coming up the steps, holding a limp Magrat between them.

'Save us all from people who think literally,' said Lily. 'The damn things come in pairs, you know.'

She crossed to Magrat and snatched the second slipper out of her hand.

'The clock was interesting,' she said, turning back to Granny. 'I was impressed with the clock. But it's no good, you know. You can't stop this sort of thing. It has the momentum of inevitability. You can't spoil a good story. I should know.'

She handed the slipper to the Prince, but without taking her eyes off Granny.

'It'll fit her,' she said.

Two of the courtiers held Magrat's leg as the Prince wrestled the slipper past her protesting toes.

'There,' said Lily, still without looking down. 'And do stop trying that hedge-witch hypnotism on me, Esme.'

'It fits,' said the Prince, but in a doubtful tone of voice.

'Yes, anything would fit,' said a cheerful voice from somewhere towards the back of the crowd, 'if you were allowed to put two pairs of hairy socks on first.'

Lily looked down. Then she looked at Magrat's mask. She reached out and pulled it off.

'Ow!'

'Wrong girl,' said Lily. 'But it still doesn't matter, Esme, because it *is* the right slipper. So all we have to do is find the girl whose foot it fits –'

There was a commotion at the back of the crowd. Courtiers parted, revealing Nanny Ogg, oil-covered and hung with spider webs.

'If it's a five-and-a-half narrow fit, I'm your man,' she said. 'Just let me get these boots off . . .'

'I wasn't referring to you, old woman,' said Lily coldly.

'Oh, yes you was,' said Nanny. 'We know how this bit goes, see. The Prince goes all round the city with the slipper, trying to find the girl whose foot fits. That's what you was plannin'. So I can save you a bit of trouble, how about it?'

There was a flicker of uncertainty in Lily's expression.

'A *girl*,' she said, 'of *marriageable* age.'

'No problem there,' said Nanny cheerfully.

The dwarf Casanunda nudged a courtier proudly in the knees.

'She's a very close personal friend of mine,' he said proudly.

Lily looked at her sister.

'*You're* doing this. Don't think I don't know,' she said.

'I ain't doing a thing,' said Granny. 'It's real life happening all by itself.'

Nanny grabbed the slipper out of the Prince's hands and, before anyone else could move, slid it on to her foot.

Then she waggled the foot in the air.

It was a perfect fit.

'There!' she said. 'See? You could have wasted the whole day.'

'Especially because there must be hundreds of five-and-a-half –'

'– narrow fit –'

'– narrow fit wearers in a city this size,' Granny went on. 'Unless, of course, you happened to sort of go to the right house right at the start. If you had, you know, a lucky guess?'

'But that'd be *cheatin'*,' said Nanny.

She nudged the Prince.

'I'd just like to add,' she said, 'that I don't mind doin' all the waving and opening things and other royal stuff, but I draw the line at sleepin' in the same bed as sunny jim here.'

'Because he doesn't sleep in a bed,' said Granny.

'No, he sleeps in a pond,' said Nanny. 'We had a look. Just a great big indoor pond.'

'Because he's a frog,' said Granny.

'With flies all over the place in case he wakes up in the night and fancies a snack,' said Nanny.

'I thought so!' said Magrat, pulling herself out of the grip of the guards. 'He had clammy hands!'

'Lots of men have clammy hands,' said Nanny. 'But this one's got 'em because he's a frog.'

'I'm a prince of blood royal!' said the Prince.

'And a frog,' said Granny.

'I don't mind,' said Casanunda, from somewhere down below. 'I enjoy open relationships. If you want to go out with a frog, that's fine by me . . .'

Lily looked around at the crowd. Then she snapped her fingers.

Granny Weatherwax was aware of a sudden silence.

Nanny Ogg looked up at the people on either side of her. She waved a hand in front of a guard's face.

'Coo,' she said.

'You can't do that for long,' said Granny. 'You can't stop a thousand people for long.'

Lily shrugged. 'They're not important. Whoever will remember who was at the ball? They'll just remember the flight and the slipper and the happy ending.'

'I've told you. You can't start it again. And he's a frog. Even you can't keep him in shape the whole day long. He turns back into his old shape at night. He's got a bedroom with a *pond* in it. He's a frog,' said Granny flatly.

'But only inside,' said Lily.

'Inside's where it counts,' said Granny.

'Outside's quite important, mind,' said Nanny.

'Lots of people are animals inside. Lots of animals are people inside,' said Lily. 'Where's the harm?'

'He's a frog.'

'Especially at night,' said Nanny. It had occurred to her that a husband who was a man all night and a frog all *day* might be almost acceptable; you wouldn't get the wage packet, but there'd be less wear and tear on the furniture. She also couldn't put out of her mind certain private speculations about the length of his tongue.

'And you killed the Baron,' said Magrat.

'You think he was a particularly nice man?' said Lily. 'Besides, he didn't show me any respect. If you've got no respect, you've got nothing.'

Nanny and Magrat found themselves looking at Granny.

'He's a frog.'

'I found him in the swamp,' said Lily. 'I could tell he was pretty bright. I needed someone . . . amenable to persuasion. Shouldn't frogs have a chance? He'll be no worse a husband than many. Just one kiss from a princess seals the spell.'

'A lot of men are animals,' said Magrat, who'd picked up the idea from somewhere.

'Yes. But he's a frog,' said Granny.

'Look at it my way,' said Lily. 'You see this country? It's all swamps and fogs. There's no *direction*. But I can make this a great city. Not a sprawling place like Ankh-Morpork, but a place that works.'

'The girl doesn't want to marry a frog.'

'What will that matter in a hundred years' time?'

'It matters now.'

Lily threw up her hands. 'What do you want, then? It's your choice. There's me . . . or there's that woman in the swamp. Light or dark. Fog or sunshine. Dark chaos or happy endings.'

'He's a frog, and you killed the old Baron,' said Granny.

'You'd have done the same,' said Lily.

'No,' said Granny. 'I'd have *thought* the same, but I wouldn't have done it.'

'What difference does that make, deep down?'

'You mean you don't *know*?' said Nanny Ogg.

Lily laughed.

'Look at the three of you,' she said. 'Bursting with inefficient good intentions. The maiden, the mother and the crone.'

'Who are you calling a maiden?' said Nanny Ogg.

'Who are you calling a mother?' said Magrat.

Granny Weatherwax glowered briefly like the person who has discovered that there is only one straw left and everyone else has drawn a long one.

'Now, what shall I do with you?' said Lily. 'I really am against killing people unless it's necessary, but I can't have you running around acting stupidly . . .'

She looked at her fingernails.

'So I think I shall have you put away somewhere until this has run its course. And then . . . can you guess what I'm going to do next?

'I'm going to expect you to escape. Because, after all, I am the good one.'

Ella walked cautiously through the moonlit swamp, following the strutting shape of Legba. She was aware of movement in the water, but nothing emerged – bad news like Legba gets around, even among alligators.

An orange light appeared in the distance. It turned out to be Mrs Gogol's shack, or boat, or whatever it was. In the swamp, the difference between the water and the land was practically a matter of choice.

'Hallo? Is there anyone there?'

'Come along in, child. Take a seat. Rest up a little.'

Ella stepped cautiously on to the rocking veranda. Mrs Gogol was sitting in her chair, a white-clad raggedy doll in her lap.

'Magrat said –'

'I know all about it. Come to Erzulie.'

'Who are you?'

'I am your – friend, girl.'

Ella moved so as to be ready to run.

'You're not a godmother of any kind, are you?'

'No. No gods. Just a friend. Did anyone follow you?'

'I . . . don't think so.'

'It's no matter if they did, girl. No matter if they did. Maybe we ought to move out into the river for a spell, even so. We'll be a lot safer with water all round.'

The shack lurched.

'You better sit down. The feets make it shaky until we get into deep water.'

Ella risked a look, nevertheless.

Mrs Gogol's hut travelled on four large duck feet, which were now rising out of the swamp. They splashed their way through the shallows and, gently, sculled out into the river.

Greebo woke up and stretched.

And the wrong sort of arms and legs!

Mrs Pleasant, who had been sitting watching him, put down her glass.

'What do you want to do now, Mr Cat?' she said.

Greebo padded over to the door into the outside world and scratched at it.

'Waant to go *owwwt*, Miss-uss Pleas-unt,' he said.

'You just have to turn the handle there,' she said.

Greebo stared at the door handle like someone trying to come to terms with a piece of very advanced technology, and then gave her a pleading look.

She opened the door for him, stood aside as he slunk out, and then shut it, locked it and leaned against it.

'Ember's bound to be safe with Mrs Gogol,' said Magrat.

'Hah!' said Granny.

'I quite liked her,' said Nanny Ogg.

'I don't trust anyone who drinks rum and smokes a pipe,' said Granny.

'Nanny Ogg smokes a pipe and drinks *anything*,' Magrat pointed out.

'Yes, but that's because she's a disgustin' old baggage,' said Granny, without looking up.

Nanny Ogg took her pipe out of her mouth.

'That's right,' she said amiably. 'You ain't nothing if you don't maintain an image.'

Granny looked up from the lock.

'Can't shift it,' she said. 'It's octiron, too. Can't magic it open.'

'It's daft, locking us up,' said Nanny. 'I'd have had us killed.'

'That's because you're basically good,' said Magrat. 'The good are innocent and create justice. The bad are guilty, which is why they invent mercy.'

'No, I know why she's done this,' said Granny, darkly. 'It's so's we'll know we've lost.'

'But she said we'd escape,' said Magrat. 'I don't understand. She must know the good ones always win in the end!'

'Only in stories,' said Granny, examining the door hinges. 'And she thinks she's in charge of the stories. She bends them round herself. She thinks she's the good one.'

'Mind you,' said Magrat, 'I don't like swamps. If it wasn't for the frog and everything, I'd see Lily's point –'

'Then you're nothing but a daft godmother,' snapped Granny, still fiddling with the lock. 'You can't go around building a better world for people. Only people can build a better world for people. Otherwise it's just a cage. Besides, you don't build a better world by choppin' heads off and giving decent girls away to frogs.'

'But progress –' Magrat began.

'Don't you talk to me about progress. Progress just means bad things happen faster. Anyone got another hatpin? This one's useless.'

Nanny, who had Greebo's ability to make herself instantly at home wherever she happened to be, sat down in the corner of the cell.

'I heard this story once,' she said, 'Where this bloke got locked up for years and years and he learned amazin' stuff about the universe and everythin' from another prisoner who was incredibly clever, and then he escaped and got his revenge.'

'What incredibly clever stuff do *you* know about the universe, Gytha Ogg?' said Granny.

'Bugger all,' said Nanny cheerfully.

'Then we'd better bloody well escape right now.'

Nanny pulled a scrap of pasteboard out of her hat, found a scrap of pencil up there too, licked the end and thought for a while. Then she wrote:

Dear Jason unt so witer (as they say in foreign parts),

Well here's a thing yore old Mum doin Time in prison again, Im a old lag, youll have to send me a cake with a phial in it and I shall have little arrows on my close just my joke. This is a Sketch of the dunjon. Im putting a X where we are, which is Inside. Magrat is shown wering a posh dress, she has been acting like a Courgette. Also inc. Esme getting fed up becaus she can't get the lock to work but I expect it will all be OK because the good ones win in the end and that's US. And all because some girl don't want to marry a Prince who is a Duck who is really a Frog and I cant say I blame her, you don't want descendants who have got Jenes and start off living in a jamjar and then hop about and get squashed . . .

She was interrupted by the sound of a mandolin being played quite well, right on the other side of the wall, and a small but determined voice raised in song.

'*– si consuenti d'amoure, ventre dimo tondreturo-ooo –*'

'How I hunger my love for the dining-room of your warm maceration,' said Nanny, without looking up.

'*– della della t'ozentro, audri t'dren vontarieeeeee –*'

'The shop, the shop, I have a lozenge, the sky is pink,' said Nanny.

Granny and Magrat looked at one another.

'*– guarunto del tari, bella pore di larientos –*'

'Rejoice, candlemaker, you have a great big –'

'I don't believe any of this,' said Granny. 'You're making it up.'

'Word for word translation,' said Nanny. 'I can speak foreign like a native, you know that.'

'Mrs Ogg? Is that you, my love?'

They all looked up towards the barred window. There was a small face peering in.

'Casanunda?' said Nanny.

'That's me, Mrs Ogg.'

'My love,' muttered Granny.

'How did you get up to the window?' said Nanny, ignoring this.

'I always know where I can get my hands on a step-ladder, Mrs Ogg.'

'I suppose you don't know where you can get your hands on a key?'

'Wouldn't do any good. There's too many guards outside your door, Mrs Ogg. Even for a famous swordsman like me. Her ladyship gave strict orders. No one's to listen to you or look at you, even.'

'How come you're in the palace guard, Casanunda?'

'Soldier of fortune takes whatever jobs are going, Mrs Ogg,' said Casanunda earnestly.

'But all the rest of 'em are six foot tall and you're – of the shorter persuasion.'

'I lied about my height, Mrs Ogg. I'm a world-famous liar.'

'Is that true?'

'No.'

'What about you being the world's greatest lover?'

There was silence for a while.

'Well, maybe I'm only No.2,' said Casanunda. 'But I try harder.'

'Can't you go and find us a file or something, Mr Casanunda?' said Magrat.

'I'll see what I can do, Miss.'

The face disappeared.

'Maybe we could get people to visit us and then we could escape in their clothes?' said Nanny Ogg.

'Now I've gone and stuck the pin in my finger,' muttered Granny Weatherwax.

'Or maybe we could get Magrat to seduce one of the guards,' said Nanny.

'Why don't *you*?' said Magrat, as nastily as she could manage.

'All right. I'm game.'

'Shut up, the pair of you,' said Granny. 'I'm trying to think –'

There was another sound at the window.

It was Legba.

The black cockerel peered in between the bars for a moment, and then fluttered away.

'Gives me the creeps, that one,' said Nanny. 'Can't look at him without thinking wistfully of sage-and-onion and mashed potatoes.'

Her crinkled face crinkled further.

'Greebo!' she said. 'Where'd we leave him?'

'Oh, he's only a cat,' said Granny Weatherwax. 'Cats know how to look after themselves.'

'He's really just a big softy –' Nanny began, before someone started pulling down the wall.

A hole appeared. A grey hand appeared and grasped another stone. There was a strong smell of river mud.

Rock crumbled under heavy fingers.

'Ladies?' said a resonant voice.

'Well, Mister Saturday,' said Nanny, 'as I live and breathe – saving your presence, o'course.'

Saturday grunted something and walked away.

There was a hammering on the door and someone started fumbling with keys.

'We don't want to hang around here,' said Granny. 'Come on.'

They helped one another out through the hole.

Saturday was on the other side of a small courtyard, striding towards the sound of the ball.

And there was something behind him, trailing out like the tail of a comet.

'What's that?'

'Mrs Gogol's doing,' said Granny Weatherwax grimly.

Behind Saturday, widening as it snaked through the palace grounds to the gate, was a stream of deeper darkness in the air. At first sight it seemed to contain shapes, but closer inspection indicated that they weren't shapes at all but a mere suggestion of shapes, forming and reforming. Eyes gleamed momentarily in the swirl. There was the chittering of crickets and the whine of mosquitoes, the smell of moss and the stink of river mud.

'It's the swamp,' said Magrat.

'It's the *idea* of the swamp,' said Granny. 'It's what you have to have first, before you have the swamp.'

'Oh, dear,' said Nanny. She shrugged. 'Well, Ella's got away and so have we, so this is the part where we escape, yes? That's what we're supposed to do.'

None of them moved.

'They aren't very nice people in there,' said Magrat, after a while, 'but they don't deserve alligators.'

'You witches stand right there,' said a voice behind them. Half a dozen guards were crowded around the hole in the wall.

'Life's certainly busier in the city,' said Nanny, pulling another hatpin from her hat.

'They've got crossbows,' warned Magrat. 'There's not much you can do against crossbows. Projectile weapons is Lesson Seven and I haven't had that yet.'

'They can't pull triggers if they think they've got flippers,' said Granny menacingly.

'Now,' said Nanny, 'let's not have any of that, eh? Everyone knows the good ones always win *specially* when they're out-numbered.'

The guards emerged.

As they did so a tall black shape dropped noiselessly from the wall behind them.

'There,' said Nanny, 'I said he wouldn't go far from his mummy, didn't I?'

One or two of the guards realised that she was staring proudly past them, and turned.

As far as they were concerned, they confronted a tall, broad-shouldered man with a mane of black hair, an eyepatch and a very wide grin.

He stood with his arms casually folded.

He waited until he had their full attention, and then Greebo let his lips part slowly.

Several of the men took a step backwards then.

One of them said, 'Why worry? It's not as if he's got a weap–'

Greebo raised one hand.

Claws make no noise as they slide out, but they *ought* to. They ought to make a noise like 'tzing'.

Greebo's grin widened.

Ah! *These* still worked . . .

One of the men was bright enough to raise his crossbow but stupid enough to do it with Nanny Ogg standing behind him with a hatpin. Her hand moved so swiftly that any wisdom-seeking saffron-clad youth would have started the Way of Mrs Ogg there and then. The man screamed and dropped the bow.

'Wrowwwl . . .'

Greebo leapt.

Cats are like witches. They don't fight to kill, but to win. There is a difference. There's no point in killing an opponent. That way, they won't know they've lost, and to be a real winner you have to have an opponent who is beaten and knows it. There's no triumph over a corpse, but a beaten opponent, who will remain beaten every day of the remainder of their sad and wretched life, is something to treasure.

Cats do not, of course, rationalise this far. They just like to send someone limping off minus a tail and a few square inches of fur.

Greebo's technique was unscientific and wouldn't have stood a chance against any decent swordsmanship, but on his side was the fact that it is almost impossible to develop decent swordsmanship when you seem to have run into a food mixer that is biting your ear off.

The witches watched with interest.

'I think we can leave him now,' said Nanny. 'I think he's having fun.'

They hurried towards the hall.

The orchestra was in the middle of a complicated number when the lead violinist happened to glance towards the door, and then dropped his bow. The cellist turned to see what had caused this, followed his colleague's fixed stare, and in a moment of confusion tried to play his instrument backwards.

In a succession of squeaks and flats, the orchestra stopped playing. The dancers continued for a while out of sheer momentum, and then stopped and milled about in confusion. And then, one by one, they too looked up.

Saturday stood at the top of the steps.

In the silence came the drumming, making the music that had gone before seem as insignificant as the chittering of crickets. This was the real blood music; every other music that had ever been written was merely a pitiful attempt to sing along.

It poured into the room, and with it came the heat and the warm, vegetable smell of the swamp. There was a suggestion of alligator in the air – not the presence of them, but the promise.

The drumming grew louder. There were complex counter-rhythms, much more felt than heard.

Saturday brushed a speck of dust off the shoulder of his ancient coat, and reached out an arm.

The tall hat appeared in his hand.

He reached out his other hand.

The black cane with the silver top whirred out of the empty air and was snatched up triumphantly.

He put the hat on his head. He twirled the cane.

The drums rolled. Except that . . . maybe it wasn't drums now, maybe it was a beat in the floor itself, or in the walls, or in the air. It was fast and hot and people in the hall found their feet moving of their own accord, because the drumming seemed to reach the toes via the hindbrain without ever passing near the ears.

Saturday's feet moved too. They beat out their own staccato rhythms on the marble floor.

He danced down the steps.

He whirled. He leapt. The tails of his coat whipped through the air. And then he landed at the foot of the step, his feet striking the ground like the thud of doom.

And only now was there a stirring.

There was a croak from the Prince.

'It can't be him! He's *dead*! Guards, *Kill* him!'

He looked around madly at the guards by the stairs.

The guard captain went pale.

'I, uh, *again*? I mean, I don't think . . .' he began.

'Do it now!'

The captain raised his crossbow nervously. The point of the bolt wove figures-of-eight in front of his eyes.

'I said *do* it!'

The bow twanged.

There was a thud.

Saturday looked down at the feathers buried in his chest, and then grinned and raised his cane.

The captain looked up with the certain terror of death in his face. He dropped his bow and turned to run, and managed two steps before he toppled forward.

'No,' said a voice behind the Prince. '*This* is how you kill a dead man.'

Lily Weatherwax stepped forward, her face white with fury.

'You don't belong here any more,' she hissed. 'You're not part of the story.'

She raised a hand.

Behind her, the ghost images suddenly focused on her, so that she became more iridescent. Silver fire leapt across the room.

Baron Saturday thrust out his cane. The magic struck, and coursed down him to earth, leaving little silver trails that crackled for a while and then winked out.

'No, ma'am,' he said, 'there ain't *no* way to kill a dead man.'

The three witches watched from the doorway.

'*I* felt that,' said Nanny. 'It should have blown him to bits!'

'Blown what to bits?' said Granny. 'The swamp? The river? The world? He's all of them! Ooh, she's a clever one, that Mrs Gogol!'

'What?' said Magrat. 'What do you mean, all of them?'

Lily backed away. She raised her hand again and sent another fireball towards the Baron. It hit his hat and burst off it like a firework.

'Stupid, stupid!' muttered Granny. 'She's seen it doesn't work and she's still trying it!'

'I thought you weren't on her side,' said Magrat.

'I ain't! But I don't like to see people being stupid. That kind of stuff's no use, Magrat Garlick, even you can . . . oh, no, surely not again . . .'

The Baron laughed as a third attempt earthed itself harmlessly. Then he raised his cane. Two courtiers tumbled forward.

Lily Weatherwax, still backing away, came up against the foot of the main staircase.

The Baron strolled forward.

'You want to try anything else, lady?' he said.

Lily raised both hands.

All three witches felt it – the terrible suction as she tried to concentrate all the power in the vicinity.

Outside, the one guard remaining upright found that he was no longer fighting a man but merely an enraged tomcat, although this was no consolation. It just meant that Greebo had an extra pair of claws.

The Prince screamed.

It was a long, descending scream, and ended in a croak, somewhere around ground level.

Baron Saturday took one heavy, deliberate step forward, and there was no more croak.

The drums stopped abruptly.

And then there was a real silence, broken only by the swish of Lily's dress as she fled up the stairs.

A voice behind the witches said, 'Thank you, ladies. Could you step aside, please?'

They looked around. Mrs Gogol was there, holding Embers by the hand. She had a fat, gaily embroidered bag over her shoulder.

All three watched as the voodoo woman led the girl down into the hall and through the silent crowds.

'That's not right either,' said Granny under her breath.

'What?' said Magrat. 'What?'

Baron Saturday thumped his stick on the floor.

'You know me,' he said. 'You *all* know *me*. You know I was killed. And now here I am. I was murdered and what did you do –?'

'How much did *you* do, Mrs Gogol?' muttered Granny. 'No, we ain't having this.'

'Ssh, I can't hear what he's saying,' said Nanny.

'He's telling them they can have him ruling them again, or Embers,' said Magrat.

'They'll have Mrs Gogol,' muttered Granny. 'She'll be one o' them *eminences greases.*'

'Well, she's not too bad,' said Nanny.

'In the swamp she's not too bad,' said Granny. 'With someone to balance her up she's not too bad. But Mrs Gogol tellin' a whole city what to do . . . that's not right. Magic's far too important to be used for rulin' people. Anyway, Lily only had people killed – Mrs Gogol'd set 'em to choppin' wood and doin' chores afterwards. I reckon, after you've had a busy life, you ort to be able to relax a bit when you're dead.'

'Lie back and enjoy it, sort of thing,' said Nanny.

Granny looked down at the white dress.

'I wish I had my old clothes on,' she said. 'Black's the proper colour for a witch.'

She strode down the steps, and then cupped her hands around her mouth.

'Coo-ee! Mrs Gogol!'

Baron Saturday stopped speaking. Mrs Gogol nodded at Granny.

'Yes, Miss Weatherwax?'

'*Mistress*,' snapped Granny, and then softened her voice again.

'This ain't right, you know. She's the one who ought to rule, fair enough. And you used magic to help her this far, and that's all right. But it stops right here. It's up to her what happens next. You can't make things right by magic. You can only stop making them wrong.'

Mrs Gogol pulled herself up to her full, impressive height. 'Who's you to say what I can and can't do here?'

'We're her godmothers,' said Granny.

'That's right,' said Nanny Ogg.

'We've got a wand, too,' said Magrat.

'But you *hate* godmothers, Mistress Weatherwax,' said Mrs Gogol.

'We're the other kind,' said Granny. 'We're the kind that gives people what they know they really need, not what we think they ought to want.'

Among the fascinated crowd several pairs of lips moved as people worked this out.

'Then you've done your godmothering,' said Mrs Gogol, who thought faster than most. 'You did it very well.'

'You didn't listen,' said Granny. 'There's all sorts of things to godmotherin'. She might be quite good at ruling. She might be bad at it. But she's got to find out for herself. With no interference from anyone.'

'What if I say no?'

'Then I expect we'll just have to go on godmotherin',' said Granny.

'Do you know how long I worked to win?' said Mrs Gogol, haughtily. 'Do you know what I *lost*?'

'And now you've won, and there's the end of it,' said Granny.

'Are you looking to challenge me, Mistress Weatherwax?'

Granny hesitated, and then straightened her shoulders. Her arms moved away from her sides, almost imperceptibly. Nanny and Magrat moved away slightly.

'If that's what you want.'

'My voodoo against your . . . headology?'

'If you like.'

'And what's the stake?'

'No more magic in the affairs of Genua,' said Granny. 'No more stories. No more godmothers. Just people, deciding for themselves. For good or bad. Right or wrong.'

'Okay.'

'And you leave Lily Weatherwax to me.'

Mrs Gogol's intake of breath was heard around the hall.

'Never!'

'Hmm?' said Granny. 'You don't think you're going to lose, do you?'

'I don't want to hurt you, Mistress Weatherwax,' said Mrs Gogol.

'That's good,' said Granny. 'I don't want you to hurt me either.'

'I don't want there to be any fighting,' said Ella.

They all looked at her.

'She's the ruler now, ain't she?' said Granny. 'We've got to listen to what she says.'

'I'll keep out of the city,' said Mrs Gogol, ignoring her, 'but Lilith is mine.'

'No.'

Mrs Gogol reached into her bag, and flourished the raggedy doll.

'See this?'

'Yes. I do,' said Granny.

'It was going to be her. Don't let it be you.'

'Sorry, Mrs Gogol,' said Granny firmly, 'but I see my duty plain.'

'You're a clever woman, Mistress Weatherwax. But you're a long way from home.'

Granny shrugged. Mrs Gogol held up the doll by its waist. It had sapphire blue eyes.

'You know about magic with mirrors? This is *my* kind of mirror, Mistress Weatherwax. I can make it be *you*. And then I can make it *suffer*. Don't make me do that. Please.'

'Please yourself, Mrs Gogol. But I'll deal with Lily.'

'I should box a bit clever if I was you, Esme,' muttered Nanny Ogg. 'She's good at this sort of thing.'

'I think she could be very ruthless,' said Magrat.

'I've got nothing but the greatest respect for Mrs Gogol,' said Granny. 'A fine woman. But talks a bit too much. If I was her, I'd have a couple of big nails right through that thing by now.'

'You would, too,' said Nanny. 'It's a good thing you're good, ain't it.'

'Right,' said Granny, raising her voice again. 'I'm going to find my sister, Mrs Gogol. This is *family*.'

She walked steadfastly towards the stairs.

Magrat took out the wand.

'If she does anything bad to Granny, she's going to go through the rest of her life bright orange and round, with seeds in,' she said.

'I don't think Esme would like it if you did something like that,' said Nanny. 'Don't worry. She doesn't believe all that stuff about pins and dolls.'

'She doesn't believe *anything*. But that doesn't matter!' said Magrat. 'Mrs Gogol does! It's *her* power! It's what *she* thinks that matters.'

'Don't you reckon Esme knows that too?'

Granny Weatherwax reached the foot of the stairs.

'Mistress Weatherwax!'

Granny turned.

Mrs Gogol had a long sliver of wood in her hand. Shaking her head desperately, she jabbed it into the doll's foot.

Everyone saw Esme Weatherwax wince.

Another sliver was thrust into a raggedy arm.

Slowly, Granny raised her other hand and shuddered when she touched her sleeve. Then, limping slightly, she continued to climb the stairs.

'I can do the heart next, Mistress Weatherwax!' shouted Mrs Gogol.

'I'm sure you can. You're good at it. You know you're good at it,' said Granny, without looking around.

Mrs Gogol stuck another sliver into a leg. Granny sagged, and clutched at the banister. Beside her, one of the big torches flamed.

'Next time!' said Mrs Gogol. 'Right? Next time. I can do it!'

Granny turned around.

She looked at the hundreds of upturned faces.

When she spoke, her voice was so quiet that they had to strain to hear.

'I know you can too, Mrs Gogol. You really believe. Just remind me again – we're playin' for Lily, right? And for the city?'

'What does that matter now?' said Mrs Gogol. 'Ain't you going to give in?'

Granny Weatherwax thrust a little finger into her ear and wiggled it thoughtfully.

'No,' she said. 'No, I don't reckon that's what I do now. Are you watchin', Mrs Gogol? Are you watchin' real close?'

Her gaze travelled the room and rested for just a fraction of a second on Magrat.

Then she reached over, carefully, and thrust her arm up to the elbow into the burning torch.

And the doll in Erzulie Gogol's hands burst into flame.

It went on blazing even after the witch had screamed and dropped it on to the floor. It went on burning until Nanny Ogg ambled over with a jug of fruit juice from the buffet, whistling between her teeth, and put it out.

Granny withdrew her hand. It was unscathed.

'*That's* headology,' she said. 'It's the only thing that matters. Everything else is just messin' about. Hope I didn't hurt you, Mrs Gogol.'

She went on up the stairs.

Mrs Gogol kept on staring at the damp ashes. Nanny Ogg patted her companionably on the shoulder.

'How did she do that?' said Mrs Gogol.

'She didn't. She let *you* do it,' said Nanny. 'You got to watch yourself around Esme Weatherwax. I'd like to see one of them Zen buggers come up against *her* one day.'

'And she's the *good* one?' said Baron Saturday.

'Yeah,' said Nanny. 'Funny how things work out, really.'

She looked thoughtfully at the empty fruit-juice jug in her hand.

'What this needs,' she said, in the manner of one reaching a conclusion after much careful consideration, 'is some bananas and rum and stuff in it –'

Magrat grabbed her dress as Nanny strode determinedly dak'rywards.

'Not now,' she said. 'We'd better get after Granny! She might need us!'

'Shouldn't think so for one minute,' said Nanny. 'I wouldn't like to be in Lily's shoes when Esme catches up with her.'

'But I've never seen Granny so agitated,' said Magrat. 'Anything could happen.'

'Good job if it does,' said Nanny. She nodded meaningfully at a flunkey who, being quick on the uptake, leapt to attention.

'But she might do something – dreadful.'

'Good. She's always wanted to,' said Nanny. 'Another banana dak'ry, mahatma coat, chopchop.'

'No. It wouldn't be a good idea,' Magrat persisted.

'Oh, *all* right,' said Nanny. She handed the empty jug to Baron Saturday, who took it in a kind of hypnotic daze.

'We're just going to sort things out,' she said. 'Sorry about this. On with the motley . . . if anyone's got any left.'

When the witches had gone Mrs Gogol reached down and picked up the damp remains of the doll.

One or two people coughed.

'Is that it?' said the Baron. 'After twelve years?'

'The Prince is dead,' said Mrs Gogol. 'Such as he was.'

'But you promised that I would be revenged on *her*,' the Baron said.

'I think there will be revenge,' said Mrs Gogol. She tossed the doll on to the floor. 'Lilith has been fighting me for twelve years and she never got through. This one didn't even have to sweat. So I think there will be revenge.'

'You don't have to keep your word!'

'I do. I've got to keep something.' Mrs Gogol put her arm around Ella's shoulder.

'This is it, girl,' she said. 'Your palace. Your city. There isn't a person here who will deny it.'

She glared at the guests. One or two of them stepped backwards.

Ella looked up at Saturday.

'I feel I should know you,' she said. She turned to Mrs Gogol. 'And you,' she added. 'I've seen you both . . . before. A long time ago?'

Baron Saturday opened his mouth to speak. Mrs Gogol held up her hand.

'We promised,' she said. 'No interference.'

'Not from *us*?'

'Not even from us.' She turned back to Ella. 'We're just people.'

'You mean . . .' said Ella, 'I've slaved in a kitchen for years . . . and now . . . I'm supposed to rule the city? Just like that?'

'That's how it goes.'

Ella looked down, deep in thought.

'And anything I say people have to do?' she said innocently.

There were a few nervous coughs from the crowd.

'Yes,' said Mrs Gogol.

Ella stood looking down at the floor, idly biting a thumbnail. Then she looked up.

'Then the first thing that's going to happen is the end of the ball. Right now! I'm going to find the carnival. I've always wanted to dance in the carnival.' She looked around at the worried faces. 'It's not compulsory for anyone else to come,' she added.

The nobles of Genua had enough experience to know what it means when a ruler says something is not compulsory.

Within minutes the hall was empty, except for three figures.

'But . . . but . . . I wanted *revenge*,' said the Baron. 'I wanted *death*. I wanted our daughter in power.'

TWO OUT OF THREE ISN'T BAD.

Mrs Gogol and the Baron turned around. Death put down his drink and stepped forward.

Baron Saturday straightened up.

'I am ready to go with you,' he said.

Death shrugged. Ready or not, he seemed to indicate, was all the same to him.

'But I held you off,' the Baron added. 'For twelve years!' He put his arm around Erzulie's shoulders. 'When they killed me and threw me in the river, we stole life from you!'

YOU STOPPED LIVING. YOU NEVER DIED. I DID NOT COME FOR YOU THEN.

'You didn't?'

I HAD AN APPOINTMENT WITH YOU TONIGHT.

The Baron handed his cane to Mrs Gogol. He removed the tall black hat. He shrugged off the coat.

Power crackled in its folds.

'No more Baron Saturday,' he said.

PERHAPS. IT'S A NICE HAT.

The Baron turned to Erzulie.

'I think I have to go.'

'Yes.'

'What will you do?'

The voodoo woman looked down at the hat in her hands.

'I will go back to the swamp,' she said.

'You could stay here. I don't trust that foreign witch.'

'I do. So I will go back to the swamp. Because some stories have to end. Whatever Ella becomes, she'll have to make it herself.'

It was a short walk to the brown, heavy waters of the river.

The Baron paused at the edge.

'Will she live happily ever after?' he said.

NOT FOR EVER. BUT PERHAPS FOR LONG ENOUGH.

And so stories end.

The wicked witch is defeated, the ragged princess comes into her own, the kingdom is restored. Happy days are here again. Happy ever after. Which means that life stops here.

Stories *want* to end. They don't care what happens next . . .

Nanny Ogg panted along a corridor.

'Never seen Esme like that before,' she said. 'She's in a very funny mood. She could be a danger to herself.'

'She's a danger to everyone else,' said Magrat. 'She –'

The snake women stepped out into the passageway ahead of them.

'Look at it like this,' said Nanny, under her breath, 'what can they do to us?'

'I can't stand snakes,' said Magrat quietly.

'They've got those teeth, of course,' said Nanny, as if conducting a seminar. 'More like fangs, really. Come on, girl. Let's see if we can find another way.'

'I hate them.'

Nanny tugged at Magrat, who did not move.

'Come *on!*'

'I really hate them.'

'You'll be able to hate them even better from a long way off!'

The sisters were nearly on them. They didn't walk, they glided. Perhaps Lily wasn't concentrating now, because they were more snake-like than ever. Nanny thought she could see scale patterns under the skin. The jawline was all wrong.

'Magrat!'

One of the sisters reached out. Magrat shuddered.

The snake sister opened its mouth.

Then Magrat looked up and, almost dreamily, punched it so hard that it was carried several feet along the passage.

It wasn't a blow that featured in any Way or Path. No one ever drew this one as a diagram or practised it in front of a mirror with a bandage tied round their head. It was straight out of the lexicon of inherited, terrified survival reflexes.

'Use the wand!' shouted Nanny, darting forward. 'Don't ninj at them! Use the wand! That's what it's for!'

The other snake instinctively turned to follow the movement, which is why instinct is not always the keynote to survival, because Magrat clubbed it on the back of the head. With the wand. It sagged, losing shape as it fell.

The trouble with witches is that they'll never run away from things they really hate.

And the trouble with small furry animals in a corner is that, just occasionally, one of them's a mongoose.

Granny Weatherwax had always wondered: what was supposed to be so special about a full moon? It was only a big circle of light. And the dark of the moon was only darkness.

But halfway between the two, when the moon was between the worlds of light and dark, when even the moon lived on the edge . . . maybe *then* a witch could believe in the moon.

Now a half-moon sailed above the mists of the swamp.

Lily's nest of mirrors reflected the cold light, as they reflected everything else. Leaning against the wall were the three broomsticks.

Granny picked up hers. She wasn't wearing the right colour and she wasn't wearing a hat; she needed *something* she was at home with.

Nothing moved.

'Lily?' said Granny softly.

Her own image looked out at her from the mirrors.

'It can all stop now,' said Granny. 'You could take my stick and I'll take Magrat's. She can always share with Gytha. And Mrs Gogol won't come after you. I've fixed that. And we could do with more witches back home. And no more godmothering. No more getting people killed so their daughters are ready to be in a story. I know that's why you did it. Come on home. It's an offer you can't refuse.'

The mirror slid back noiselessly.

'You're trying to be *kind* to me?' said Lily.

'Don't think it don't take a lot of effort,' said Granny in a more normal voice.

Lily's dress rustled in the darkness as she stepped out.

'So,' she said, 'you beat the swamp woman.'

'No.'

'But you're here instead of her.'

'Yes.'

Lily took the stick out of Granny's hands, and inspected it.

'Never used one of these things,' she said. 'You just sit on it and away you go?'

'With *this* one you have to be running quite fast before it takes off,' said Granny, 'but that's the general idea, yes.'

'Hmm. Do you know the symbology of the broomstick?' said Lily.

'Is it anything to do with maypoles and folksongs and suchlike?' said Granny.

'Oh, yes.'

'Then I don't want to hear about it.'

'No,' said Lily. 'I imagine you don't.'

She handed the stick back.

'I'm staying here,' she said. 'Mrs Gogol may have come up with a new trick, but that doesn't mean she has won.'

'No. Things have come to an end, see,' said Granny. 'That's how it works when you turn the world into stories. You should never have done that. You shouldn't turn the world into stories. You shouldn't treat people like they was *characters*, like they was *things*. But if you *do*, then you've got to know when the story ends.'

'You've got to put on your red-hot shoes and dance the night away?' said Lily.

'Somethin' like that, yes.'

'While everyone else lives happily ever after?'

'I don't know about that,' said Granny. 'That's up to them. What *I'm* sayin' is, you're not allowed to go round one more time. You've *lost*.'

'You know a Weatherwax never loses,' said Lily.

'One of 'em learns tonight,' said Granny.

'But *we're* outside the stories,' said Lily. 'Me because I . . . am the medium through which they happen, and you because you fight them. We're the ones in the middle. The free ones —'

There was a sound behind them. The faces of Magrat and Nanny Ogg appeared over the top of the stairwell.

'You need any help, Esme?' said Nanny cautiously.

Lily laughed.

'Here's *your* little snakes, Esme.'

'You know,' she added, 'you're really just like me. Don't you know that? There isn't a thought that's gone through my head that you haven't thought, too. There isn't a deed I've done that you haven't contemplated. But you never found the courage. That's the difference between people like me and people like you. *We* have the courage to *do* what you only dream of.'

'Yes?' said Granny. 'Is that what you think? You think I dream?'

Lily moved a finger. Magrat floated up out of the stairwell, struggling. She waved her wand frantically.

'That's what I like to see,' said Lily. 'People wishing. I never wished for anything in my life. I always *made* things happen. So much more rewarding.'

Magrat gritted her teeth.

'I'm sure I wouldn't look good as a pumpkin, dear,' said Lily. She waved a hand airily. Magrat rose.

'You'd be surprised at the things I can do,' said Lily dreamily, as the younger witch drifted smoothly over the flagstones. 'You should have tried mirrors yourself, Esme. It does wonders for a soul. I only let the swamp woman survive because her hate was invigorating. I do like being hated, you know. And you *do* know. It's a kind of respect. It shows you're having an effect. It's like a cold bath on a hot day. When stupid people find themselves powerless, when they fume in their futility, when they're beaten and they've got nothing but that yawning in the acid pit of their stomachs – well, to be honest, it's like a prayer. And the *stories* . . . to *ride* on stories . . . to borrow the strength of them . . . the *comfort* of them . . . to be in the hidden centre of them . . . Can you understand that? The sheer pleasure of seeing the patterns repeat themselves? I've always loved a pattern. Incidentally, if the Ogg woman continues to try to sneak up behind me I shall really let your young friend drift out over the courtyard and then, Esme, I might just lose interest.'

'I was just walkin' about,' said Nanny. 'No law against it.'

'You changed the story your way, and now I'm going to do it mine,' said Lily. 'And once again . . . all you have to do is go. Just go away. What happens here doesn't matter. It's a city far away of which you know little. I'm not totally certain I could out-trick you,' she added, 'but these two . . . they haven't got the right stuff in them. I could make jam of them. I hope you know that. So tonight, I suggest, a Weatherwax learns to lose?'

Granny stood silent for a while, leaning on her useless broom.

'All right. Put her down,' she said. 'And then I'll say you've won.'

'I wish I could believe that,' said Lily. 'Oh . . . but you're the nice one, aren't you? You have to keep your word.'

'Watch me,' said Granny. She walked to the parapet and looked down. The two-faced moon was still bright enough to illuminate the billowing fogs that surrounded the palace like a sea.

'Magrat? Gytha?' she said. 'Sorry about this. You've won, Lily. There ain't nothing I can do.'

She jumped.

Nanny Ogg rushed forward and stared over the edge, just in time to see a dim figure vanish in the mists.

All three figures left on the tower took a deep breath.

'It's a trick,' said Lily, 'to get me off guard.'

'It isn't!' screamed Magrat, dropping to the stones.

'She had her broomstick,' said Lily.

'It don't work! It won't start!' shouted Nanny. '*Right*,' she said, menacingly, striding towards the slim shape of Lily. 'We'll soon wipe that smug look off your face –'

She halted as silver pain shot through her body.

Lily laughed.

'It's true, then?' she said. 'Yes. I can see it in your faces. Esme was bright enough to know she couldn't win. Don't be stupid. And don't point that silly wand at me, Miss Garlick. Old Desiderata would have defeated me long ago if she could. People have no understanding.'

'We ought to go down there,' said Magrat. 'She might be lying there –'

'That's it. Be good. It's what you're good at,' said Lily, as they ran to the stairwell.

'But we'll be back,' snarled Nanny Ogg. 'Even if we have to live in the swamp with Mrs Gogol and eat snakes' heads!'

'Of course,' said Lily, arching an eyebrow. 'That's what I said. One needs people like you around. Otherwise one is never quite sure one is still working. It's a way of keeping score.'

She watched them disappear down the steps.

A wind blew over the tower. Lily gathered up her skirts and walked to the end, where she could see the shreds of mist streaming over the rooftops far below. There were the faint strains of music from the distant carnival dance as it wound its way through the streets.

It would soon be midnight. Proper midnight, not some cut-price version caused by an old woman crawling around in a clock.

Lily tried to see through the murk to the bottom of the tower.

'Really, Esme,' she murmured, 'you did take losing hard.'

☆   ☆   ☆

Nanny reached out and restrained Magrat as they ran down the spiral stairs.

'Slow down a bit, I should,' she said.

'But she could be hurt –!'

'So could you, if you trip. Anyway,' said Nanny, 'I don't reckon Esme is lyin' in a crumpled heap somewhere. That's not the way she'd go. I reckon she did it just to make sure Lily forgot about us and wouldn't try anything on us. I reckon she thought we were – what was that Tsortean bloke who could only be wounded if you hit 'im in the right place? No one ever beat 'im until they found out about it. His knee, I think it was. We're her Tsortean knee, right?'

'But we know you have to run really fast to get her broomstick going!' shouted Magrat.

'Yeah, I know,' said Nanny. 'That's what I thought. And now I'm thinking . . . how fast do you go when you're dropping? I mean, straight down?'

'I . . . don't know,' said Magrat.

'I reckon Esme thought it was worth findin' out,' said Nanny. 'That's what I reckon.'

A figure appeared around the bend in the stairs, plodding upwards. They stood aside politely to let it pass.

'Wish I could remember what bit of him you had to hit,' Nanny said. 'That's going to be nagging at me all night, now.'

THE HEEL.

'Right? Oh, thanks.'

ANY TIME.

The figure continued onwards and upwards.

'He had a good mask on, didn't he,' said Magrat, eventually.

She and Nanny sought confirmation in each other's face.

Magrat went pale. She looked up the stairs.

'I think we should run back up and –' she began.

Nanny Ogg was much older. 'I think we should walk,' she said.

Lady Volentia D'Arrangement sat in the rose garden under the big tower and blew her nose.

She'd been waiting for half an hour and she'd had enough.

She'd hoped for a romantic tête-à-tête: he'd seemed such a nice man, sort of eager and shy at the same time. Instead, she'd nearly been hit on the head when an old woman on a broom and wearing what looked, as far as she could see through the blur of speed, like Lady Volentia's own dress, had screamed down out of the mist. Her boots had ploughed through the roses before the curve of her flight took her up again.

And some filthy smelly tomcat kept brushing up against her legs.

And it had started off as such a nice evening . . .

''ullo, your Ladyship?'

She looked around at the bushes.

'My name's Casanunda,' said a hopeful voice.

Lily Weatherwax turned when she heard the tinkle of glass from within the maze of mirrors.

Her brow wrinkled. She ran across the flagstones and opened the door into the mirror world.

There was no sound but the rustle of her dress and the soft hiss of her own breathing. She glided into the place between the mirrors.

Her myriad selves looked back at her approvingly. She relaxed.

Then her foot struck something. She looked down and saw on the flagstones, black in the moonlight, a broomstick lying in shards of broken glass.

Her horrified gaze rose to meet a reflection.

It glared back at her.

'Where's the pleasure in bein' the winner if the loser ain't alive to know they've lost?'

Lilith backed away, her mouth opening and shutting.

Granny Weatherwax stepped through the empty frame. Lily looked down, beyond her avenging sister.

'*You broke my mirror!*'

'Was this what it was all for, then?' said Granny. 'Playin' little queens in some damp city? Serving stories? What sort of power is that?'

'You don't understand . . . you've broken the *mirror* . . .'

'They say you shouldn't do it,' said Granny. 'But I reckoned: what's another seven years' bad luck?'

Image after image shatters, all the way around the great curve of the mirror world, the crack flying out faster than light . . .

'You have to break *both* to be safe . . . you've upset the *balance* . . .'

'Hah! *I* did?' Granny stepped forward, her eyes two sapphires of bitterness. 'I'm goin' to give you the hidin' our Mam never gave you, Lily Weatherwax. Not with magic, not with headology, not with a stick like our Dad had, aye, and used a fair bit as I recall – but with skin. And not because you was the bad one. Not because you meddled with stories. Everyone has a path they got to tread. But because, and I wants you to understand this prop'ly, after you went *I had to be the good one*. You had all the fun. An' there's no way I can make you pay for that, Lily, but I'm surely goin' to give it a try . . .'

'But . . . I . . . I . . . *I'm* the good one,' Lily murmured, her face pale with shock. 'I'm the good one. I can't lose. I'm the godmother. You're the wicked witch . . . and you've broken the mirror . . .'

. . . moving like a comet, the crack in the mirrors reaches its furthest point and curves back, speeding down the countless worlds . . .

'You've got to help me put . . . the images must be balanced . . .' Lily murmured faintly, backing up against the remaining glass.

'Good? Good? Feeding people to stories? Twisting people's lives? That's *good*, is it?' said Granny. 'You mean you didn't even have *fun*? If I'd been as bad as you, I'd have been a whole lot worse. Better at it than you've ever dreamed of.'

She drew back her hand.

. . . the crack returned towards its point of origin, carrying with it the fleeing reflections of all the mirrors . . .

Her eyes widened.

The glass smashed and crazed behind Lily Weatherwax.

And in the mirror, the image of Lily Weatherwax turned around, smiled beatifically, and reached out of the frame to take Lily Weatherwax into its arms.

'Lily!'

All the mirrors shattered, exploding outwards in a thousand pieces from the top of the tower so that, just for a moment, it was wreathed in twinkling fairy dust.

Nanny Ogg and Magrat came up on to the roof like avenging angels after a period of lax celestial quality control.

They stopped.

Where the maze of mirrors had been were empty frames. Glass shards covered the floor and, lying on them, was a figure in a white dress.

Nanny pushed Magrat behind her and crunched forward cautiously. She prodded the figure with the toe of her boot.

'Let's throw her off the tower,' said Magrat.

'All right,' said Nanny. 'Do it, then.'

Magrat hesitated. 'Well,' she said, 'when I said let's throw her off the tower, I didn't mean me personally throwing her off, I meant that if there was any justice she ought to be thrown off –'

'Then I shouldn't say any more on that score, if I was you,' said Nanny, kneeling carefully on the crunching shards. 'Besides, I was right. *This* is Esme. I'd know that face anywhere. Take off your petticoat.'

'Why?'

'Look at her arms, girl!'

Magrat stared. Then she raised her hands to her mouth.

'What has she been *doing*?'

'Trying to reach straight through glass, by the looks of it,' said Nanny. 'Now get it off and help me tear it into strips and then go and find Mrs Gogol and see if she's got any ointments and can help us, and tell her if she can't she'd better be a long way away by morning.' Nanny felt Granny Weatherwax's wrist. 'Maybe Lily Weatherwax could make jam of us but I'm damn sure I could knock Mrs Gogol's eye out with the fender if it came to it.'

Nanny removed her patent indestructible hat and fished around inside the point. She pulled out a velvet cloth and unwrapped it, revealing a little cache of needles and a spool of thread.

She licked a thread and held a needle against the moon, squinting.

'Oh, Esme, Esme,' she said, as she bent to her sewing, 'you do take winning hard.'

Lily Weatherwax looked out at the multi-layered, silvery world.

'Where am I?'

INSIDE THE MIRROR.

'Am I dead?'

THE ANSWER TO THAT, said Death, IS SOMEWHERE BETWEEN NO AND YES.

Lily turned, and a billion figures turned with her.

'When can I get out?'

WHEN YOU FIND THE ONE THAT'S REAL.

Lily Weatherwax ran on through the endless reflections.

A good cook is always the first one into the kitchen every morning and the last one to go home at night.

Mrs Pleasant damped down the fires. She did a quick inventory of the silverware and counted the tureens. She –

She was aware of being stared at.

There was a cat in the doorway. It was big and grey. One eye was an evil yellow-green, the other one pearly white. What remained of its ears looked like the edge of a stamp. Nevertheless, it had a certain swagger, and generated an I-can-beat-you-with-one-paw feel that was strangely familiar.

Mrs Pleasant stared at it for a while. She was a close personal friend of Mrs Gogol and knew that shape is merely a matter of deeply ingrained personal habit, and if you're a resident of Genua around Samedi Nuit Mort you learn to trust your judgement rather more than you trust your senses.

'Well now,' she said, with barely a trace of a tremor in her voice, 'I expect you'd like some more fish legs, I mean heads, how about that?'

Greebo stretched and arched his back.

'And there's some milk in the coolroom,' said Mrs Pleasant.

Greebo yawned happily.

Then he scratched his ear with his back leg. Humanity's a nice place to visit, but you wouldn't want to live there.

It was a day later.

'Mrs Gogol's healing ointment really seems to work,' said Magrat. She held up a jar that was half-full of something pale green and strangely gritty and had a subtle smell which, you could quite possibly believe, occupied the whole world.

'It's got snakes' heads in it,' said Nanny Ogg.

'Don't you try to upset me,' said Magrat. 'I know the Snake's Head is a kind of flower. A fritillary, I think. It's amazing what you can do with flowers, you know.'

Nanny Ogg, who had in fact spent an instructive if gruesome half-hour watching Mrs Gogol make the stuff, hadn't the heart to say so.

'That's right,' she said. 'Flowers. No getting anything past you, I can see that.'

Magrat yawned.

They had been given the run of the palace, although no one felt like running anywhere. Granny had been installed in the next room.

'Go and get some sleep,' said Nanny. 'I'll go and take over from Mrs Gogol in a moment.'

'But Nanny . . . Gytha . . .' said Magrat.

'Hmm?'

'All that . . . stuff . . . she was saying, when we were travelling. It was so . . . so *cold*. Wasn't it? Not wishing for things, not using magic to help people, not being able to do that fire thing – and then she went and did all those things! What am I supposed to make of that?'

'Ah, well,' said Nanny. 'It's all according to the general and the specific, right?'

'What does that mean?' Magrat lay down on the bed.

'Means when Esme uses words like "Everyone" and "No one" she doesn't include herself.'

'You know . . . when you think about it . . . that's terrible.'

'That's witchcraft. Up at the sharp end. And now . . . get some sleep.'

Magrat was too tired to object. She stretched out and was soon snoring in a genteel sort of way.

Nanny sat and smoked her pipe for a while, staring at the wall.

Then she got up and pushed open the door.

Mrs Gogol looked up from her stool by the bed.

'You go and get some sleep too,' said Nanny. 'I'll take over for a spell.'

'There's something not right,' said Mrs Gogol. 'Her hands are fine. She just won't wake up.'

'It's all in the mind, with Esme,' said Nanny.

'I could make some new gods and get everyone to believe in 'em real good. How about that?' said Mrs Gogol. Nanny shook her head.

'I shouldn't think Esme'd want that. She's not keen on gods. She thinks they're a waste of space.'

'I could cook up some gumbo, then. People'll come a long way to taste that.'

'It might be worth a try,' Nanny conceded. 'Every little helps, I always say. Why not see to it? Leave the rum here.'

After the voodoo lady had gone Nanny smoked her pipe some more and drank a little rum in a thoughtful sort of way, looking at the figure on the bed.

Then she bent down close to Granny Weatherwax's ear, and whispered:

'You ain't going to *lose*, are you?'

Granny Weatherwax looked out at the multi-layered, silvery world.

'Where am I?'

INSIDE THE MIRROR.

'Am I dead?'

THE ANSWER TO THAT, said Death, IS SOMEWHERE BETWEEN NO AND YES.

Esme turned, and a billion figures turned with her.

'When can I get out?'

WHEN YOU FIND THE ONE THAT'S REAL.

'Is this a trick question?'

No.

Granny looked down at herself.

'This one,' she said.

☆   ☆   ☆

And stories just want *happy* endings. They don't give a damn who they're for.

Dear Jason eksetra,

Well so much for Genua but I leanred about Mrs Gogol's zombie medicin and she gave me the ~~reltpt resarpy~~ told me how to make banananana dakry and gave me a thing call a banjo youll be amazed and all in all is a decent soul I reckon if you keeps her where you can see her. It looks like we got Esme back but I don't know shes actin funny and quiet not like herself normally so Im keepin an Eye on her just in case Lily puled a farst one in the mirror. But I think shes getting better because when she woke up she arsked Magrat for a look at the wand and then she kind of twidled and twisted them rings on it and turned the po into a bunch of flowers and Magrat said she could never make the wand do that and Esme said no because, she wasted time wishing for thinges instead of working out how to make them happen. What I say is, what a good job Esme never got a wand when she was young, Lily would have bin a Picnic by comparisen. Enclosed is a picture of the cemtry here you can see folks are buried in boxes above ground the soil being so wet because you dont want to be dead and drownded at the same time, they say travelin brordens the mind, I reckon I could pull mine out my ears now and knot it under my chin, all the best, MUM.

In the swamp Mrs Gogol the voodoo witch draped the tail coat over its crude stand, stuck the hat on the top of the pole and fastened the cane to one end of the crosspiece with a bit of twine.

She stood back.

There was a fluttering of wings. Legba dropped out of the sky and perched on the hat. Then he crowed. Usually he only crowed at nightfall, because he was a bird of power, but for once he was inclined to acknowledge the new day.

It was said afterwards that, every year on Samedi Nuit Mort, when the carnival was at its height and the drums were loudest and the rum was nearly all gone, a man in a tail coat and a top hat and with the energy of a demon would appear out of nowhere and lead the dance.

After all, even stories have to start somewhere.

There was a splash, and then the waters of the river closed again.

Magrat walked away.

The wand settled into the rich mud, where it was touched only by the feet of the occasional passing crawfish, who don't have fairy godmothers and aren't allowed to wish for anything. It sank down over the months and passed, as most things do, out of history. Which was all anyone could wish for.

The three broomsticks rose over Genua, with the mists that curled towards the dawn.

The witches looked down at the green swamps around the city. Genua dozed. The days after Fat Lunchtime were always quiet, as people slept it off. Currently they included Greebo, curled up in his place among the bristles. Leaving Mrs Pleasant had been a real wrench.

'Well, so much for *la douche vita*,' said Nanny philosophically.

'We never said goodbye to Mrs Gogol,' said Magrat.

'I reckon she knows we're going right enough,' said Nanny. 'Very knowin' woman, Mrs Gogol.'

'But can we trust her to keep her word?' said Magrat.

'Yes,' said Granny Weatherwax.

'She's very honest, in her way,' said Nanny Ogg.

'Well, there's that,' Granny conceded. 'Also, I said I might come back.'

Magrat looked across at Granny's broomstick. A large round box was among the baggage strapped to the bristles.

'You never tried on that hat she gave you,' she said.

'I had a look at it,' said Granny coldly. 'It don't fit.'

'I reckon Mrs Gogol wouldn't give anyone a hat that didn't fit,' said Nanny. 'Let's have a look, eh?'

Granny sniffed, and undid the lid of the box. Balls of tissue paper tumbled down towards the mists as she lifted the hat out.

Magrat and Nanny Ogg stared at it.

They were of course used to the concept of fruit on a hat – Nanny Ogg herself had a black straw hat with wax cherries on for special family feuding occasions. But this one had rather more than just cherries. About the only fruit not on it somewhere was a melon.

'It's definitely very . . . *foreign*,' said Magrat.

'Go on,' said Nanny. 'Try it on.'

Granny did so, a bit sheepishly, increasing her apparent height by two feet, most of which was pineapple.

'Very colourful. Very . . . stylish,' said Nanny. 'Not everyone could wear a hat like that.'

'The pomegranates suit you,' said Magrat.

'And the lemons,' said Nanny Ogg.

'Eh? You two ain't laughing at me, are you?' said Granny Weatherwax suspiciously.

'Would you like to have a look?' said Magrat. 'I have a mirror somewhere . . .'

The silence descended like an axe. Magrat went red. Nanny Ogg glared at her.

They watched Granny carefully.

'Ye-ess,' she said, after what seemed a long time, 'I think I should look in a mirror.'

Magrat unfroze, fumbled in her pockets and produced a small, wooden-framed hand-mirror. She passed it across.

Granny Weatherwax looked at her reflection. Nanny Ogg surreptitiously manœuvred her broomstick a bit closer.

'Hmm,' said Granny, after a while.

'It's the way the grapes hang over your ear,' said Nanny, encouragingly. 'You know, that's a hat of authority if ever I saw one.'

'Hmm.'

'Don't you think?' said Magrat.

'Well,' said Granny, grudgingly, 'maybe it's fine for foreign parts. Where I ain't going to be seen by anyone as knows me. No one important, anyway.'

'And when we get home you can always eat it,' said Nanny Ogg.

They relaxed. There was a feeling of a hill climbed, a dangerous valley negotiated.

Magrat looked down at the brown river and the suspicious logs on its sandbanks.

'What I want to know is,' she said, 'was Mrs Gogol really good or bad? I mean, dead people and alligators and everything . . .'

Granny looked at the rising sun, poking through the mists.

'Good and bad is tricky,' she said. 'I ain't too certain about where people stand. P'raps what matters is which way you face.

'You know,' she added, 'I truly believe I can see the edge from here.'

'Funny thing,' said Nanny, 'they say that in some foreign parts you get elephants. You know, I've always wanted to see an elephant. And there's a place in Klatch or somewhere where people climb up ropes and disappear.'

'What for?' said Magrat.

'Search me. There's prob'ly some cunnin' foreign reason.'

'In one of Desiderata's books,' said Magrat, 'she says that there's a very interesting thing about seeing elephants. She says that on the Sto plains, when people say they're going to see the elephant, it means they're simply going on a journey because they're fed up with staying in the same place.'

'It's not staying in the same place that's the problem,' said Nanny, 'it's not letting your mind wander.'

'*I'd* like to go up towards the Hub,' said Magrat. 'To see the ancient temples such as are described in Chapter One of *The Way of the Scorpion*.'

'And they'd teach you anything you don't know already, would they?' said Nanny, with unusual sharpness.

Magrat glanced at Granny.

'Probably not,' she said meekly.

'Well,' said Nanny. 'What's it to be, Esme? Are we going home? Or are we off to see the elephant?'

Granny's broomstick turned gently in the breeze.

'You're a disgustin' old baggage, Gytha Ogg,' said Granny.

'That's me,' said Nanny cheerfully.

'And, Magrat Garlick –'

'I know,' said Magrat, overwhelmed with relief, 'I'm a wet hen.'

Granny looked back towards the Hub, and the high mountains. Somewhere back there was an old cottage with the key hanging in the privy. All sorts of things were probably going on. The whole kingdom was probably going to rack and ruin without her around to keep people on the right track. It was her job. There was no telling what stupidities people would get up to if she wasn't there . . .

Nanny kicked her red boots together idly.

'Well, I suppose there's no place like home,' she said.

'No,' said Granny Weatherwax, still looking thoughtful. 'No. There's a billion places like home. But only one of 'em's where you live.'

'So we're going back?' said Magrat.

'Yes.'

But they went the long way, and saw the elephant.